The
Ghost Goes
TO THE
Dogs

CLEO COYLE

BERKLEY PRIME CRIME
New York

BERKLEY PRIME CRIME
Published by Berkley
An imprint of Penguin Random House LLC
penguinrandomhouse.com

Copyright © 2023 by Alice Alfonsi and Marc Cerasini
Penguin Random House supports copyright. Copyright fuels creativity, encourages
diverse voices, promotes free speech, and creates a vibrant culture. Thank you for
buying an authorized edition of this book and for complying with copyright laws by not
reproducing, scanning, or distributing any part of it in any form without permission.
You are supporting writers and allowing Penguin Random House to continue to
publish books for every reader.

BERKLEY is a registered trademark and BERKLEY PRIME CRIME and
the B colophon are trademarks of Penguin Random House LLC.
A HAUNTED BOOKSHOP MYSTERY is a registered trademark of
Penguin Random House LLC.

ISBN: 9780425255490

First Edition: May 2023

Printed in the United States of America
1   3   5   7   9   10   8   6   4   2

Once upon a time, a boy loved a dog.
Half a century gone, and he's still missed.
To Eric . . .

FOREWORD

Animals have been a staple of the mystery genre since Edgar Allan Poe penned the first modern detective story featuring literature's first amateur sleuth. While the genesis of *The Murders of the Rue Morgue* remains a mystery, *The Ghost Goes to the Dogs* had a definite origin. It sprang from the fact that we've written dozens of mysteries in which cats appear (no surprise, since we care for many rescued felines), but we never gave dogs their day. Consequently, this book is dedicated to Marc's cherished childhood friend, Eric, who helped inspire this story. Likewise, Alice's fond memories of dog-sitting duties for her sister's sweet canines, Sparky and Fred, as well as her admiration for Dorothy's best friend, Toto (created by author L. Frank Baum), served as inspirations, too.

Although *The Ghost Goes to the Dogs* marks the ninth entry in our Haunted Bookshop Mysteries, our hard-boiled ghost has been haunting the cozy streets of Quindicott, Rhode Island, since 2004. A grateful tip of the fedora goes to our publisher for their faith in this series, not only with the release of this title, but also *The Ghost and the Bogus Bestseller*, *The Ghost and the Haunted Portrait*, and *The Ghost and the Stolen Tears*, all of which we wrote following a decade-long hiatus (after penning the first five entries).

We especially wish to thank our brilliant and insightful editor, Tracy Bernstein, along with everyone on the Berkley team who worked to transform our words into this beautiful publication. Spirited thanks also goes to our longtime agent, John Talbot, and the many loyal readers of our Haunted Bookshop series for your belief in us and our characters. Your love of Jack and Pen continues to keep both alive, and we look forward to sharing many more of their adventures with you.

As for our other works and worlds, you can learn more about them (and us) by visiting coffeehousemystery .com and cleocoyle.com.

—*Alice Alfonsi and Marc Cerasini*
aka Cleo Coyle, New York City

CONTENTS

This little creature . . . was just a dog . . . altogether amusing and companionable . . . With Tags, as she called him, she went farther and farther afield after the housework was done, coming home with glowing cheeks . . . And almost every evening Captain Gregg visited her and told her tales of the sea . . .

—*The Ghost and Mrs. Muir* by R.A. Dick
(aka Josephine Aimee Campbell Leslie)

PROLOGUE

I'm a lone wolf, unmarried . . . and not rich . . . I like liquor and women . . . The cops don't like me too well . . . and when I get knocked off in a dark alley . . . nobody will feel that the bottom has dropped out of his or her life.

—Raymond Chandler, *The Long Goodbye*

New York City
Friday, April 18, 1947
5:45 P.M.

"HIYA, MR. SHEPARD. Want your messages?"

"Sure, Doris. Lemme get a load off first."

As Jack hung up his trench coat, he heard Doris snap her gum.

"Suit yourself, Mr. Shepard. But I gotta leave real soon!"

"Hot date, huh?"

"You bet! Me and the girls got tickets to see Frank's new

movie, *It Happened in Brooklyn*. He's so dreamy. You seen it yet?"

"No, honey."

"Well, I *cannot* miss it!"

Doris was the younger cousin of Jack's regular secretary, who'd been out for most of the week (on a date with a dentist). He didn't mind since he'd been tied up giving trial testimony in three different cases: two Cheating Charlies in divorce proceedings that made the Battle of the Bulge look like the Ice Capades and one case of a young woman who'd gone missing and then caught the big chill. He'd been hired to track her down, and he had—too late.

Jack still felt the gut punch of defeat over that one.

At least his work had helped the city dicks find her killer and secure evidence to convict, but it was a grim business. Nothing he planned on sharing with young Doris here.

All of nineteen, she'd flown fresh as a newly hatched bird out of some midtown secretarial school and landed in his office with bubble-gum cheeks, a bouncy yellow ponytail, and the kind of blindingly sunny disposition that made Jack want to shove on dark glasses and head for the nearest gin mill.

The past decade alone, Jack had seen the rise and fall of a madman named Hitler, devastation in European and Pacific theaters, and history's first god-awful atomic bomb.

The defining moment of Doris's young life (as she'd informed Jack with breathless detail over morning coffee) wasn't D-Day or V-E Day, but Columbus Day 1944—the day she'd been lucky enough to wedge herself into the Paramount Theater with thirty-six hundred other squealing, swooning bobby-sox girls to witness the crooning of a skinny kid from Hoboken named Sinatra.

The *unlucky* ladies (twenty-five thousand of them) became a crushing pink wave that washed over Times Square, leaving traffic rerouted, shopwindows smashed, and some of New York's Finest with their most bemused riot duty in recent memory.

According to one of Jack's old partners in the PD, the bobby-sox blitzkrieg required twenty radio cars, seventy patrolmen, sixty-two traffic cops (twelve of them mounted), six sergeants, and forty temporary badges who'd been pulled from parade duty on Fifth.

"Ain't life grand?" Doris chirped, filing her nails.

Jack blew out air.

Leaving the postage-stamp reception area, he moved into his office proper, shrugged off his best navy blue suit coat from his acre of shoulders, rolled up his shirtsleeves, loosened his tie, and settled into the creaky chair behind his desk.

As he considered his day—and the whole lousy world at large—he rubbed the dagger-shaped scar on his jaw, reached for the bottle in his drawer, and knocked back a satisfying shot of single-malt therapy.

"Okay, Doris. What have you got for me?"

"First message," she announced before snapping her gum. "From Assistant District Attorney Donovan's assistant. Ain't that comical? An assistant has an assistant?"

"Barrel of laughs," Jack said. "What's the message?"

"'Judge Hoffman moved Monday's proceedings to Wednesday. Kindly remember to be on time and wear proper *tires* for your courtroom appearance.'"

"Uh, Doris, I think you meant to write *attire*. What do you think?

"Oh, Mr. Shepard, you're right! I guess I heard it wrong, but I figured maybe it was a park-in deal. You know, like that theater in New Jersey?"

"There are no *park-in* courtrooms in the tristate area. Not yet, anyway. Go on . . ."

"Sure thing! Message two was from a lady who wouldn't leave her name." Doris squinted at the note card. "'I would like to hire you, but I need to know your rates, your address, and could you be the street?'"

"I think she meant *discreet*. She leave a number?"

Doris nodded. "Gramercy 5-3—"

"I'll ring her back next week. Anything else?"

"A Mr. Larsen called. Says he has two Great Danes and would like to schedule your walking services."

"You pulling my leg?"

"No, sir! You wanna see the note?"

"Must have been a wrong number. That it?"

Doris shook her head. "I got four more calls asking about your dog-walking services—"

"Hey, what's the idea? You trying out for vaudeville?"

"No, Mr. Shepard. I swear the messages are on the up-and-up! Plus I got three more asking about your canine-kenneling rates for summer weekends."

"Your cousin's coming back Monday, right?"

"She sure is. Her bad tooth got pulled without a hitch."

"Send her some flowers for me—and leave her a message on your desk. Tell her to straighten out Ma Bell ASAP."

"I will, Mr. Shepard, but I don't think it's a phone company mix-up. Didn't you see that dog story in the afternoon paper?"

"Which paper?"

"This one." Doris ricocheted to her desk and back, then handed him one of the many daily rags. "You're in it!"

Doris pointed to the picture of a well-heeled society matron posing with her Pekingese. "DOGNAPPED!" screamed the headline. "PRIZEWINNING POOCH IN PERIL!"

The story revealed how the little lapdog with the long pedigree was kidnapped from her loving mistress by an "insensitive brute," but reunited with her grateful grande dame due entirely to the heroic efforts of one Mr. Jack Shepard, "lover of creatures great and small."

The overwrought feature included exaggerated details of

Jack's recently closed case, along with his address and phone number and a fake quote from Jack himself: "In this dog-eat-dog world, I'll do anything to help my four-legged friends."

The dognapping story was mostly true, though some of it was complete fiction, including the line extolling the virtues of Jack Shepard's "reliable dog-walking services."

Smelling a rat, Jack searched for the byline, which explained everything—

"Timothy Brennan," he spat.

"You know him?" Doris asked.

"Yeah, I know him . . ."

A yellow journalist and a degenerate gambler, Brennan had a penchant for making up quotes, double-crossing sources, drinking his lunch, and pretzeling facts when it suited—or amused—him.

Identifying Jack not as a licensed private investigator, but as an expert in "doggy business," was obviously a case of the latter. Jack could have run it all down for Doris, but he didn't want to burn her little pink ears off with the curses he'd surely utter in the process. Instead, he checked his watch.

"Quitting time. You run along now, Doris."

"Thanks, Mr. Shepard. Oh, hold the phone. I got one more!" she cried, waving the message like a winning bingo card.

"Just hand it to me, honey, and you can go."

"Okey-doke!"

As the young woman made her earsplitting exit, Jack held his breath. After the screeching of a desk chair, slamming of a file drawer, and bang of the front door, Doris was finally off, headed for that date with her celluloid boyfriend.

At the blessed sound of silence, Jack sat back, put his feet up, and sighed. *Peace in our time.* Sipping another shot of Scotch, he glanced at Doris's last message card, expecting another load of doggy business.

It wasn't.

A man named "Muggsy" had called. At the sight of that moniker, Jack felt his muscles stiffen.

Myles "Muggsy" Malone was a Hell's Kitchen hothead famous for his short temper and long switchblade. A few years back, he gutted some poor sixteen-year-old kid during an argument over a dice game. Nothing new for the locals who lived in the tenements and worked on the docks. Only this time, there was a hitch.

The victim's older sister, Irene, was a real looker, and she'd married well. Outraged at the police's lack of enthusiasm for tracking down the man who tried to fillet her little brother, Irene hired Jack to find Muggsy Malone, drag him into the nearest precinct, and make sure he did time.

Jack complied.

Little brother recovered and testified, putting Muggsy behind the eight ball, with a hefty fine and sentence to two years of hard labor, less on good behavior.

Well, Malone obviously made parole, and he wanted Jack to know it.

I'm out of the joint where you put me and back in town.
I'll be seeing you, Shepard. I owe you payback.
Expect me soon.

"So much for peace," Jack muttered, and knocked back the rest of his drink.

HOURS LATER, LOADED gun by his bedside, Jack was back at his apartment alone, a rarity for a Friday night.

Stretched out in pajama bottoms, twiddling his thumbs over his bare chest, he'd been staring at the bedroom ceiling. The pounding rain and cracking thunder were loud enough to split Zeus's eardrums, but nature's racket wasn't the reason he couldn't get any shut-eye.

Jack couldn't stop thinking about Muggsy Malone's message.

By now, Irene was long gone, somewhere out West with her well-off hubby. She'd taken her little brother with her, which left Jack as the only fish left to catch the ex-con's fillet knife.

Would Malone come for him at home or jump him at the office? How many days would it take for the ugly Muggs to show?

Jack considered reporting the message to the ex-con's parole officer, but that was weak coffee. Malone could easily dodge the flack by claiming his *innocent* phone message had been *misunderstood*.

No, if Jack wanted charges to stick, he would have to catch Muggsy in the act of coming for him, weapon in hand . . .

As the spring storm finally subsided and the thunder rolled away, Jack could swear he heard a noise in the front room—a kind of scratching.

Jack was a big guy, but after years Over There, he knew how to move quick and quiet. Picking up his gun from the nightstand, he slipped barefoot from his bedroom to the front room.

Someone was scratching at the door, all right. He could even hear breathing.

Geez, Louise. That was more than breathing. It was *panting*.

Now Jack had a clue why Muggsy was so steamed. He must have picked up TB in prison!

"All right, Muggsy, I hear you out there!" Jack shouted at the closed door. "If I see that switchblade in your hand, I swear I'll end your days!"

In one swift motion, Jack jerked open the door and leveled his gun at—

Empty air.

Ruff! Ruff! Ruff!

Jack looked down. A leather leash had been wrapped around the doorknob. At the other end stood a little dog. The fur ball with legs was the spitting image of Toto, that cute little canine who caused all the trouble in that kiddie film with the yellow brick road.

Weapon raised again, Jack stepped into the hallway. He searched it up and down, even checked the stairwell. But there was nobody. Nothing. Just the little—

Ruff-ruff-ruff!

"Where did you come from? Who are you, girl?"

He assumed it was a girl because of the little pink bow clipped to a tuft of fur at the top of its head. Something was around its neck, too, slipped under its collar—

An envelope.

Inside, Jack found a C-note and a typewritten letter.

Dear Jack Shepard, I want you to find me some answers . . .

What in the Sam Hill is this? Jack wondered, frowning down at the pup.

"Are you hiring me?"

Ruff-ruff-ruff!

Jack brought the dog inside, closed the door, and bolted it. While the little fur hat ran in circles, sniffing up the rug and every stick of Jack's furniture, the PI sank to the sofa in disbelief.

The C-note was good. He couldn't dispute it. One hundred clams made it official.

Jack Shepard had gone to the dogs.

CHAPTER 1

The Language of Canines

People love dogs. You can never go wrong adding a dog
to a story.

—Jim Butcher, *White Night*

Buy the Book
Quindicott, Rhode Island
Present day

"YOU HAVE MANY fans here at my shop, Ms. Breen," I
said into the phone. "They'll be thrilled to meet you. I
booked a room for you at the Finch Inn, and you're scheduled to arrive tomorrow night."

"Tomorrow's flight?" Amber Breen shouted back.

"What did you say?" I replied so loudly that several customers who'd been browsing our stacks were now staring
my way.

"I'm sorry, Mrs. McClure, but you'll have to speak up,"
Amber yelled over the sound of barking dogs—very loud

and excited dogs. "You see, I'm in the shelter with my babies . . ."

(I'd already deduced that.) "Hold the line—"

After whispering my dilemma to my aunt Sadie behind the counter, I moved with all speed to the back of the book-shop and closed the stockroom door.

Now, Amber Breen was as delightful a human being as you could find on God's green earth. The prolific author of the Kennel Club Mysteries even ran her own animal shelter with a portion of profits from her book sales and the smash hit stream-ing series adapted from her works. But attempting to converse with the bestselling novelist by phone was clearly a challenge. The canine interference was worse than cellular static!

"Can you hear me now?" I asked forcefully.

WOOF-WOOF!

The loudest dog in the pack suddenly took over Amber's device. Even as I yanked the phone away from my ear, I heard the author scolding—

"Down, Biscuit! Down, girl!"

When the yapping of a smaller, more belligerent canine replaced the howls of the dog called Biscuit, Amber Breen shouted—

"Mrs. McClure, I don't like airplanes! I'll be driving a rental car to your charming little town in the wee hours. I prefer night driving, far less traffic. So, you see? No need to arrange a flight for me—"

"I didn't arrange a flight! I booked you a room at our lo-cal B and B. Check your email box for the details, and—"

"I'm sorry, dear. I simply cannot hear you. My babies are too excited about lunch. Yes, Toto Seven, I know you're hun-gry! When I see you tomorrow, Mrs. McClure, I shall re-spond to any questions face-to-face."

I replied with a renewed suggestion that she check her email and text messages—though I doubted Ms. Breen heard that, either—and (with great relief) I ended the call.

Mother Machree! I haven't heard that much yapping since Lassie came home.

Hello, Jack . . .

I began the afternoon with dogs barking in my ear. Now I was hearing the bark of a disgruntled man in my head—a dead one.

CHAPTER 2

A Loyal Companion

Never tease an old dog; he might have one bite left.

—Robert Heinlein, *Time Enough for Love*

I KNOW, I know. The very idea of conversing with a ghost defies rational thinking, and I sometimes did question my sanity, but I seldom questioned Jack, who had become a loyal companion to me—and almost always turned out to be right. The key word being *almost* . . .

Decades before I was even born, private detective Jack Shepard had trekked up to our little Rhode Island town from New York City. He'd been following a lead in a case, and he must have made a tragic misstep because he'd been gunned down on these premises.

Such was the end of his life, though clearly not his afterlife.

While our family's shop was long rumored to be haunted, no one had ever reported hearing the dead detective's voice. Not until I began working here and (in a moment of startled awareness) Jack and I discovered we had some kind of cosmic connection.

Was Jack *really* a ghost? Or was he simply (as any therapist would likely conclude) a figment of my overactive reader's mind? It seemed a logical conclusion. After all, I'd grown up devouring the big, bold tales of hard-boiled detectives in my late father's library. Those trench-coated knights of the noir streets always seemed larger than life to me. And so did Jack Shepard, whose actual PI files fell into the hands of an old newshound—a New York reporter from Jack's time who used the files as the basis for an internationally bestselling series of Jack Shield novels.

I read those, too.

Whatever Jack was—the spirit of a dead PI or some elaborate alter ego—he helped me cope with many of the challenges in my life. Being a widow, a single mom, and a busy bookshop owner, I had plenty.

The thing is . . . if my ghost was merely a *coping mechanism*, he didn't always behave like one, especially when it came to voicing strong opinions or reacting to troubling situations in our small town. While my more practical side counseled me to stay on dry land—or at least out of hot water—my PI spirit continuously pushed me to dive into the deep end. In fact, the ghost seemed to *enjoy* egging me on.

But that was Jack, a man who once viewed trouble as his business. Even though his spirit was confined to our quiet, little bookshop, resting in peace wasn't on his agenda. And neither was keeping his opinions to himself. Take my phone conversation with Amber Breen—

Who were you talkin' to with all that barkin' in the background? The dog pound?

No, Jack, an author with a bestselling book series about man's best friend.

Sounds to me like man's best friend needs a muzzle.

I don't believe you mean that! I told the ghost as I returned to work behind the bookshop counter. *You're the one who mentioned* Lassie Come Home. *You have to love dogs*

*after screening that film. Hey, would you like to see it
again? I'll bet Brainert has it on his Movie Town Theater
schedule this week. I haven't seen his final list, but I know
he'll be programming animal-themed films.*

Why? Was he brought up in a barn?

*You know very well Professor Parker was brought up in
an old Victorian, which he meticulously restored, along
with our vintage town theater—with the help of his partners
and the university, of course—*

*You haven't answered my question. Why all this jabber-
ing about four-legged friends?*

*It's the upcoming theme week for our bookshop. Seven
days and nights celebrating stories that feature animals as
sleuths, partners in crime fighting, or comedy relief . . .*

Considering the long, staid history of our family bookshop, the very idea of a *theme week* to spur sales was practically a revolutionary concept, one that I'd introduced to my
aunt Sadie after joining her as a co-owner of Buy the Book.

Of course, ever since I'd relocated myself and young son
to Quindicott (and used my late husband's life insurance
money to help Sadie remodel and relaunch the place), we'd
tried all sorts of new things to encourage reading (and book
buying). Our shop had hosted reading groups, author signings, and community events. As for our theme weeks, so far
we'd celebrated Edgar Allan Poe, film noir, culinary mysteries, hard-boiled pulps, and vintage cover art.

Our upcoming Pet Mystery Week wasn't my idea, but the
brainchild of the Paw-some Pals, one of Buy the Book's
largest and most enthusiastic reading groups.

St. Francis Day was coming up at the local university—
which was named in honor of that devout lover of creatures
great and small—and Jane Cunningham, the leader of the
Pals, had hatched the bright idea to expand events beyond
their campus to our small town.

Unfortunately, the Paw-some group members didn't always get along. Squabbles broke out about *who* the guest author should be. (The dog lovers ended up winning over the cat fans.) Suffice it to say, after sitting in on the first Pet Week planning meeting, Aunt Sadie dryly declared, "People who fight like cats and dogs, over dogs and cats, might consider a group name that doesn't include the word *Pals*."

Despite the ongoing feuds and petty spats, Jane Cunningham—an accomplished businesswoman and respected member of the community—was able to marshal a core group of the Pals into helping her arrange all sorts of events, including a shelter-pet-adoption day in the town square; complimentary dog biscuits at Coopers Family Bakery; a mobile veterinarian van offering discounted pet care; a blessing-of-the-animals service by Reverend Waterman; and a Pet Parade ending in an amateur dog-and-cat show with a big raffle and grand prizes, all of which were sure to bring (two- and four-legged) foot traffic to Cranberry, the main street of Quindicott's business district.

Everyone was excited about the upcoming week's events, including and especially the appearance of the Paw-some Pals' selected guest author, Amber Breen, whose books Sadie and I had stocked for her talk and signing.

Given the ghost's annoyed reaction to all that background barking, however, I was starting to worry less about keeping our sidewalk clean of doggy doo and more about keeping our bookshop free of hard-boiled hauntings.

While the ghost behaved most of the time, he'd been known to—shall we say, interfere with business as usual? Cold spots in the store were an ongoing problem. Sometimes shopping baskets were suddenly filled with twice as many books as customers remembered picking out—though remarkably every customer ended up liking the extra selections and buying the whole basket, anyway.

I didn't mind that particular trick since it benefited our bottom line. On the other hand, if Jack took offense at someone's rudeness to me or Sadie, his goosing them out of the shop with an icy draft wasn't out of the question.

"Unexplained" knocking, rearranged furniture, slamming doors, and the front bell ringing, without the door actually opening, had contributed to the shop's "haunted" reputation, which was also good for business (I had to admit) since amateur ghost hunters and tourists found us a curiosity—and never departed without a "souvenir" book purchase or two.

So, what do you think, Jack? I challenged, determined to get any objections to our theme week out in the open. *You're an animal lover, aren't you?*

Me? Sure. I bet on the ponies at least twice a week. Sometimes I even made it out to the track.

That's not what I meant.

Oh, you're wondering if I ever took care of a—

Arf-arf . . . arf-arf!

I blinked. The raucous call to Amber Breen was long over, yet I was still hearing the barking of an agitated—

Arf-arf . . . arf-arf!

Arf-arf . . . arf-arf!

"Am I crazy, or is that—"

My aunt Sadie, who'd witnessed my beeline to the backroom, replied with an amused twinkle in her eye, "You're not crazy, Pen. The barking is coming from outside. Right in front of our shop."

CHAPTER 3

Sparky Always Barks Twice

The collie heard the word "lass," and barked at it. The pedlar shook his head. "Nay, that's the pity of it. Ye can understand some o' man's language, but man isn't bright enough to understand thine. And yet it's us that's supposed to be most intelligent!"

—Eric Knight, *Lassie Come-Home*

SADIE PULLED HER glasses out of her pageboy haircut and balanced them precariously on her nose. I joined her and we spied the problem immediately.

Strutting among the hardcovers and paperbacks on display inside the store window, Bookmark, our marmalade tabby, was lazily taunting an adorable, floppy-eared dog that was staring at her through the plate-glass window. Medium-sized with chocolate brown fur and big black eyes, the canine barked in mad, helpless frustration as a nonchalant Bookmark yawned and stretched, her striped tail held high.

Indifferent to the raucous dog, she cleaned her ears with a paw, then vigorously groomed her back leg. The final insult came when she brushed against the glass, setting off an intense new round of boisterous barking.

"Our little cat knows exactly what she's doing to tease that poor dog," I declared.

Sadie nodded. "I swear Bookmark has a self-satisfied smirk on her face!"

Meanwhile the dog was so agitated that it repeatedly bumped the window, leaving nose smears on the glass.

Arf-arf . . . arf-arf!

Arf-arf . . . arf-arf!

Sadie adjusted her spectacles. "That dog looks familiar."

"It does," I agreed. "Wait! Isn't that—"

"It's Sparky, Mom!"

My copper-topped young son, Spencer, appeared at my side.

Sadie blinked. "Sparky?"

"Mrs. Cunningham's dog, Aunt Sadie!"

Spencer was in a position to know. He loved dogs and was familiar with every canine that came by the store, from Mrs. Tanner's Pekingese and Harry Thorndike's beagle to Mary Lidford's Labrador service dog.

I should have recognized Sparky, because Jane Cunningham had been visiting our shop a lot lately, given her leadership role in the Paw-some Pals, and her hard work as chair of the committee of Pet Week organizers.

But the Sparky I knew was calm and well-behaved. The dog on the sidewalk seemed touched in the head. Sadie was not convinced, either.

"Are you sure that's Mrs. Cunningham's dog, Spencer? Jane didn't mention that she'd be dropping by today."

"Sure, I'm sure. Sparky always barks twice. Just listen."

Arf-arf!

Arf-arf!

"Well, if that's Sparky, then where is Jane Cunningham?" Sadie said, suddenly concerned.

"I bet the dog got loose, and Mrs. Cunningham was too slow to catch him," Spencer said. "I'd better get out there and grab him before he gets lost for good."

Spencer was out the front door in a flash. Sadie and I followed. But on the sidewalk, Sadie stopped short.

"Goodness, Pen. There's a leash attached to that dog's collar!"

"Spencer's right. Sparky must have slipped away from Jane's grip. But why did the dog come here?"

"Sparky!" Spencer called, slapping his thighs. "Come to me, boy."

The dog clearly recognized Spencer. He immediately stopped barking at the cat and whirled to focus on my son. Though Sparky's tail was slowly wagging, his head hung low, and his gaze appeared uncertain. As Spencer tried to approach, the dog backed away.

"What's the matter, Sparky?" Spencer said in a calm voice. "Don't you want to go home to Mrs. Cunningham?"

Upon hearing his owner's name, Sparky barked twice, then turned tail and bolted down the sidewalk.

"He's trying to lead us somewhere!" Spencer cried.

Though traffic was light on Cranberry Street, Sadie and I were horrified watching the dog, seemingly oblivious to the cars on the road, scamper on and off the sidewalk to dodge pedestrians.

"I'm going after him, Mom!"

Spencer had already unlocked his bicycle from the faux-Victorian lamp in front of our shop. Before I could stop him, he'd mounted the bike and shot down the sidewalk, his pedaling feet spinning faster than windmills in a storm.

"Wait!" I cried. "I'll get the car."

"No time!" Spencer called over his shoulder. "We'll lose Sparky."

As Spencer receded into the distance, a voice in my head jolted me like a crack of thunder—

What are you waiting for, doll? The bus? Shake a leg and follow that mutt!

That's exactly what I did.

CHAPTER 4

Car Chases Dog

The poor dog, in life the firmest friend.
The first to welcome, foremost to defend.

—Lord Byron

INSIDE A MINUTE, I was behind the wheel of my car and close to breaking the speed limit—not the smartest decision, given the wet pavement from the drizzly weather.

As I passed through every intersection, I hit the brakes and scanned the streets on either side. Traffic was (thankfully) light, but despite the empty roads, I saw no sign of my son or Mrs. Cunningham's dog.

"Jack, is it possible Sparky made a turn we missed?"

Naw, that mutt ran like a jackrabbit on the lam, and rabbits only go in one direction—straight ahead.

"But we've followed Cranberry Street all the way to the edge of town. They must have turned off along the way."

You would have spotted them, doll. Keep moving forward. Dollars to donuts, that dog was pulling a Rin Tin Tin.

"What do you mean?"

I mean that Sparky was obviously trying to give your boy a clue that something is very wrong. Once he got the kid's attention, the mutt took the lead, expecting your kid to follow.

"But follow where? We're way past the town center. We're practically in the woods—"

The road had narrowed with plenty of curves. During my back-and-forth with the ghost, the car crested a small hill. Suddenly I had to slam on the brakes.

A bicycle lay across the middle of the two-lane roadway. Spencer's bike! My insides turned colder than dry ice. I leaned over the steering wheel.

"Where is he, Jack! Where's my son?"

When I spotted Spencer on the shoulder of the road, I released a breath I didn't know I was holding. He was kneeling on the wet concrete, under a NO PASSING sign. He spotted me a second later and waved wildly. Sparky, who was crouching beside Spencer, jumped up and began barking as soon as I parked the car.

Only then did I realize someone else was with them. A figure swathed in a bright yellow hooded slicker lay unmoving on the pavement. I popped the car door and stepped out. Spencer jumped to his feet when I reached him.

"Mom!" he cried. "It's Mrs. Cunningham. I think she's alive, but I can't wake her up!"

CHAPTER 5

Mistress in Distress

I am I because my little dog knows me.

—Gertrude Stein

JANE CUNNINGHAM LAY on her side, arms outstretched, a phone resting in one limp hand. I didn't even see the form as human at first—the raincoat she wore was far too large for her slim frame, and with the hood still over her head, it enveloped her like a shroud. Jane's eyes were closed, her complexion waxy, as if death had already taken hold of her.

Spencer looked up at me with wide, frightened eyes. "Something's wrong, Mom!"

At the same instant, Jack and I both spotted the pool of blood forming on the damp ground under the woman's body. *The dame's been shot. That's what's wrong!*

I dropped to one knee and searched the stricken woman. I quickly located a small, ragged hole in the coat's water-proof fabric. When I gingerly opened the garment, I discovered a bleeding wound in Jane Cunningham's abdomen.

Sparky whimpered and dropped to the pavement, his worried eyes fixed on his unconscious mistress.

I handed my phone to Spencer. "Call 911 and tell them to—"

"Bring an ambulance! I know, Mom."

You better stop that red tide, Jack urged. *I saw enough of it during the war. Use the dame's scarf.*

While Spencer spoke to the police dispatcher, I followed Jack's good advice and tried to stop the bleeding. To my relief, the pressure slowed the blood loss, but I still worried because Jane never responded or stirred, even with all my jostling.

"Spencer," I called over my shoulder, "how soon before the ambulance arrives?"

"The dispatcher said help is less than a minute away."

I found that assessment optimistic. Our small town didn't have much in the way of emergency services, and the closest hospital was twenty miles from Quindicott.

Yet despite my doubts, help actually did arrive in record time.

A black BMW approached from the opposite direction. Instead of racing past us, the car pulled onto the opposite shoulder of the road. Seconds later, Quindicott's favorite physician, Dr. Randall Rubino, was kneeling at my side.

"I just got the call," he said, setting down his emergency medical kit. "What's happened to her?"

"My son found her like this, Doctor. She's been shot, I think."

Dr. Rubino bent low to check the woman's breathing. Abruptly he pulled back, his usually bland face registering surprise.

"That's . . . that's Jane Cunningham," he said.

"You know her, Doctor?"

"She's one of my patients . . ."

Rubino's voice trailed off as he shook away his shock and

went to work. The doctor yanked off his jacket and got down on the pavement, ignoring the damage that the oily surface was doing to his pressed khaki pants. With gentle hands, he turned Jane's head and grunted unhappily when he found another pool of blood on the pavement, this one from a deep scalp wound under her gray hair.

"That's not from a bullet, is it?"

"No, Mrs. McClure. It appears she hit her head when she fell."

He wrapped a compress around Jane's head wound to stop the bleeding. Then he moved my hand and lifted the scarf that I was using to stanch the blood loss from her bullet wound. After examining the entry point, he said, "Help me get her coat off, so I can check the exit wound."

As we slid her arms out of the coat, the contents of one pocket spilled onto the pavement—coins, a pen, house keys, and other items. I asked Spencer to scoop it all up, while the doctor and I carefully rolled Mrs. Cunningham onto her side.

Once again, Rubino blinked in surprise. "There's no exit wound."

"Is that bad?" I asked.

"The bullet could be lodged in an organ, or it could have struck a bone, which is the better of the two options, but neither is good."

Sparky, whose wide black eyes never stopped watching us, began to whimper again, as if the poor animal understood the doctor's words. Spencer stepped in to calm the dog, but Sparky just grew more unruly. Finally, my son was forced to drag the reluctant animal to the opposite side of the road.

"I gather that's Mrs. Cunningham dog," Rubino said.

"Sparky must have been with her when it happened. He ran to the bookshop to get help and led us back here."

"Then that dog saved her life . . . if she *can* be saved."

My throat tightened at those words.

Meanwhile, Rubino replaced the bloody scarf in my hand with a fresh white compress he'd retrieved from his kit.

"Keep the pressure on while I check her vitals."

With his thumbs, the doctor opened Jane's eyes; then he frowned. Next, he checked her blood pressure and pulse.

"The bullet must have come from a handgun or a small-caliber long gun."

"Why do you say that?" I asked.

"Because the bullet didn't have enough power to pass through Mrs. Cunningham's body."

As he spoke I glanced up, at the steel NO PASSING sign, and noticed several dents, which looked an awful lot like bullet holes.

"You seem to know a thing or two about gunshot wounds," I said as Rubino rooted through his first aid kit.

"Chalk it up to six years at Boston Medical," he replied. "Summer weekends in the ER gave me plenty of experience with this kind of trauma."

"So, who in the world would have shot her?"

"It must have been a hunter. This is deer-hunting season." Rubino scanned the woods around us. "On the other hand, no hunter in his right mind would be shooting this close to a residential area. Larchmont Avenue is just through those trees and across that meadow. And deer hunters typically use much larger-caliber bullets."

"What if it wasn't a deer hunter?"

"It might have been someone hunting birds or rabbits," Rubino conceded. "But a twenty-two-caliber bullet doesn't have a lot of range. The shooter would have been close enough to see where the bullet ended up. That is to say, the shooter would have seen . . ."

When his voice trailed off, I finished his thought.

"The shooter likely saw Mrs. Cunningham get struck."

"Most likely."

"Then why didn't they report it?"

Rubino frowned. "Perhaps the shooter panicked and ran."

I looked down at Jane Cunningham; then I pointed to the bullet-dented sign. "Don't those bullet holes suggest that someone was trying to hit her?"

Rubino shook his head. "This isn't New York City or LA, Mrs. McClure. I'm sure what happened here was a careless accident. We'll know more once we get her to an emergency room and dig that slug out."

Dr. Rubino moved my hand and checked under the compress again.

"The external bleeding has slowed, but I'm more worried about that head wound, to be honest. She needs a CT scan—"

He paused when the sound of a screaming siren echoed from a distance. A moment later, the flashing lights of an ambulance appeared.

Beside me, Dr. Randall Rubino sighed in relief.

CHAPTER 6

The Deer Hunter

I'm not very big. But I've got a big bark and a lot of heart.

—Sissy Spacek

THE AMBULANCE CAME with a QPD squad car. While Doc Rubino talked with the emergency crew, I faced the police.

As a small town, Quindicott operated a very modest police force. Years ago, my late father had been a member of it. My older brother, Peter—who was born with the same handsome ginger-haired features as my son—was planning on following in our father's footsteps. Fate made other plans, and I lost Pete to one of those foolish whims of youth.

Most of us survive our stupid decisions. My brother didn't. In an effort to impress a girl, he drove his hot rod in an illegal drag race.

Pete's best friend, Eddie Franzetti, who watched my brother literally crash and burn, was the one who took up the baton and joined the force. Now married with children, Eddie was a stable, intelligent officer who'd risen to become deputy chief of the department.

Because of his closeness with my late brother, Eddie always looked out for me, which is why I hoped he would be the one answering this call.

But I wasn't so lucky . . .

When I saw Chief Ciders lumber out of his vehicle with his big nephew, Officer "Bull" McCoy, my heart sank—and my blood pressure rose.

If it isn't your cornpone version of the Keystone Cops, Jack cracked.

I wouldn't go that far, I silently told the ghost. *Not yet, anyway . . .*

Why not? You know as well as I do, those ham-fisted yokels are no better than crossing guards with gats.

Gats?

Roscoes, Rodneys—

What?

Heaters. Weapons. Guns!

Oh! Right . . . Well, Jack, maybe they are no better than crossing guards with, uh, gats—but they're all we've got to work with at the moment. So let's give them the benefit of the doubt.

I doubt they'll be of any benefit. Knuckleheads always rub me the wrong way.

Then you better get ready for an unpleasant massage.

Ciders addressed me with his typically disgruntled expression on his bulldog-jowled face. "Mrs. McClure, what takes you away from that bookstore of yours?"

"Jane Cunningham's pet, Sparky," I replied. "He led us here, and we found Jane unconscious."

Ciders turned to the doctor with more questions, but Dr. Rubino had no time to give answers.

"I'm riding with my patient to the hospital," he said. "Mrs. McClure can fill you in on what I know. The rest will have to wait until Mrs. Cunningham is stabilized."

Trouble erupted when the volunteer paramedics loaded the injured woman's stretcher into the ambulance. Sparky broke free from Spencer's grip, leaped inside the cramped emergency vehicle, and crouched over his mistress in a misguided attempt to protect her.

Chief Ciders sharply addressed his nephew. "Get that mutt out of there!"

Sparky growled and bared white teeth in reply to the chief's harsh tone and Bull McCoy's scowling approach.

"That dog's a menace," the chief declared as he reached for his sidearm.

"No!" I cried, jumping between the dog and the lawman. "My son can control Sparky. Really, he can."

I glanced over my shoulder. "Right, honey?"

Spencer replied as I hoped he would. "Sure, Mom. Sparky and me are buds."

Spencer climbed into the ambulance and took hold of Sparky's leash.

"Come on, boy," he said, gently rubbing the dog's neck. "They're trying to help your mom. You have to let them do their work. You want Mrs. Cunningham to get better, don't you?"

Sparky stared at the unconscious form on the stretcher for a long moment, his large black eyes gleaming. Finally he allowed Spencer to pull him out of the vehicle. Then the ambulance doors closed, and the vehicle sped away.

As the siren faded in the distance, a heavy hand fell on my shoulder.

"Doc Rubino said you'd fill me in," Ciders reminded me.

I led the chief to the spot where Spencer had found Jane Cunningham. Bull McCoy was already there. He handed over purse, which he'd retrieved from the side of the road. As the chief rifled through it, he pulled out Jane's wallet and checked her driver's license.

Spencer kept his distance the whole time. Sparky clearly had no love for Chief Ciders. The dog curled his lips each time the man moved too close.

Thank goodness Spencer had wrapped the leash around one hand and gripped Sparky's collar with the other. My brave boy was determined to hold on to the unruly animal, no matter what.

When Ciders finished poking around in Jane's purse, I directed his attention to the blood on the ground, a stain that made the dirty road look even darker.

"We found Mrs. Cunningham lying here with a single bullet to the abdomen, no exit wound. She has a head injury, but it's not from a bullet. Dr. Rubino believes she hit her head when she fell."

"Anything else?" Ciders prompted.

"That's all I know. I don't have a clue why she was out here, walking on the side of the road."

"It's not a difficult deduction, Mrs. McClure." Ciders practically rolled his eyes. "Mrs. Cunningham was obviously out walking her dog. According to her ID, she lives on the north end of Larchmont Avenue, which is just across that meadow there."

Bull McCoy, his mouth slack, scratched his scalp under his policeman's cap. "Who do you think shot her, Unc— I mean, Chief?"

"Obviously, it was some stupid, careless hunter." Ciders shook his head. "Some trigger-happy jerk who probably missed his deer by a mile."

"Deer hunting?" I asked. "This close to Larchmont?"

"What else?"

The chief's explanation seemed unlikely, and I said so.

"Who in their right mind would shoot a gun this close to a residential area?" Before the chief could answer, I shared Dr. Rubino's theory about what caliber the bullet might be.

Ciders made a show of listening, but quickly shook his head. "The doc doesn't know what he's talking about, and neither do you. The bullet came from a hunter's rifle. It probably traveled a half a mile or more, which is why it wasn't powerful enough to rip through the woman's body. If you ask me, Mrs. Cunningham was lucky."

"What if more than one shot was fired?" I stepped up to the white NO PASSING sign and pointed to multiple bullet strikes. "Look at this sign. Bullets hit it, as well. What if someone took more than one shot at Mrs. Cunningham. Wouldn't that imply intent?"

A smirking McCoy burst out laughing. Ciders joined his nephew.

"Take a second look, Mrs. McClure," he said. "Those holes are ancient. Punk kids or drunks probably made them, popping off guns at night like they're in Vermont or something."

I took a closer look at the sign. Ciders was right. Two of the holes had brown rust around them; a third was rusted through. But when I looked at a strike just below the others, I saw naked, gleaming steel. I touched the hole, and tiny grains of white paint stuck to my finger.

There it is, Jack coaxed. *Proof you were right. Don't give up, doll. Try again!*

"Here!" I cried. "Come look. This bullet strike is fresh!"

Ciders and McCoy studied the hole. Finally, the chief grunted.

"No deer-hunting bullet made this. That hole came from a twenty-two-caliber bullet."

"You're missing my point," I told the chief.

That's right, honey, Jack urged me. *Tell him!*

I cleared my throat. "Dr. Rubino said if the shooter used

a twenty-two, they were likely close enough to see where their bullet hit. This sign has a fresh strike from a twenty-two, so if Mrs. Cunningham was hit with a twenty-two, then more than one shot was fired at the poor woman—and that doesn't sound like an accident to me."

"Now who would deliberately shoot an innocent woman walking her dog?" Ciders demanded.

I had no immediate answer—and neither did Jack.

Ciders folded his thick arms. "You know what I think, Mrs. McClure?"

"What?"

"Like a bad drug dealer, you're using your own stash."

"Excuse me?"

"You've been reading too many of those mysteries you peddle."

Jack cursed in my head, and I didn't blame him. I felt like cussing myself!

What is wrong with this yokel? You and the doc could be off, sure. But your theory should have occurred to him. Either way, it warrants an investigation. Even a rummy rookie would case the area for spent shells.

You're right, Jack.

I turned to the chief. "Shouldn't you mark some kind of perimeter around the area and look for spent shells and maybe the bullet that struck this sign—"

Ciders waved me off. "That would be a waste of time and manpower. If we need ballistics, we already have a bullet—inside Jane Cunningham."

"Are you sure? I mean, maybe if you called in the state police, they could take over and conduct a thorough—"

"This is a local matter," Ciders snapped back, "and we're perfectly capable of handling it. You mark my words, Mrs. McClure. The bullet they dig out of Mrs. Cunningham will be a thirty-aught-six fired from a deer rifle half a mile from here."

CHAPTER 7

A Friend in Need

You can take my heart, but I can't let you take my dog.

—Karin Slaughter, *Fallen*

I TOLD JACK there was no arguing with Chief Ciders. The man was a brick wall. Still, I said—

For all we know, he could be on the mark in this case. Even a broken clock is right twice a day.

Maybe, Jack replied. *But neither the clock or the cop is actually doing its job.*

While I debated my PI spirit, another police car arrived. Once again, I was hoping for my friend Eddie. Instead, Officer Welsh Tibbet swung his lean form out of the vehicle.

"No one answered at Mrs. Cunningham's door on Larchmont," Tibbet informed the chief. "After her husband died, she had that big house converted into apartments. One of her tenants there told me the lady lives alone, except for her dog."

"It's settled, then." Ciders turned to Bull McCoy. "I'm going back to the station with Welsh. You drive the old lady's mutt to a shelter."

"You serious?" Bull blurted out. "You want me to drive to Providence and back, on the clock, with an angry pooch in the back seat? Think of the upholstery, not to mention my overtime!"

"You don't have to drive *that* far," Ciders countered. "Take the dog to the shelter in Millstone."

I listened with mounting horror. Millstone was a dying town, and though they did have a shelter, the municipality could not afford to keep the animals around for more than a few weeks. And if Jane didn't recover and reclaim him, and no one else adopted him, Millstone could be a death sentence.

I was about to object when my son beat me to it.

"No way!"

Spencer's bold declaration interrupted the officers, and he didn't back down when they faced him, either.

"A shelter is no place for Sparky, Chief Ciders. Mrs. Cunningham is going to want him back when she gets better."

"But she may *not* get better—"

"She will!" Spencer insisted. "And Sparky will be waiting for her to come home."

"That's the problem," Ciders replied as he hitched up his sagging utility belt. "Right now there's no one at home to take care of Sparky."

Ciders spoke softly, displaying a modicum of sympathy for the first time since he'd arrived. To my surprise, he even made a counteroffer.

"Look, son, if you want, I'll drive Sparky to the no-kill shelter in Newport. They'll take good care of him."

"No!" Spencer shook his head, then thumped his thumb against his chest. "*I'll* take care of Sparky." He whirled to face me. "We can take him home with us, can't we, Mom?"

I hesitated, not because I didn't have a heart, but I'd never owned a dog before, and neither had Aunt Sadie. Like my aunt, I was a cat person. And speaking of cats, Bookmark was bound to have something to say about cohabitating with a canine. Unsure what to do, I was surprised to hear Jack exclaim—

What are you waiting for? The kid's right!

The ghost's reaction shocked me. Given his annoyance over all that loud barking on the Amber Breen call, I didn't think he liked dogs much. But I agreed with Jack. My son was on the side of the angels.

Mrs. Cunningham loved her dog. She would naturally want him back after she recovered, and I prayed she *would* recover. Sending Sparky, already in emotional distress, to some cold, impersonal shelter was not the act of someone with much faith—or heart.

"Yes, honey," I finally answered. "Absolutely. Sparky is coming home with us."

Any doubts I had vanished when I saw the look of happy relief on my son's face.

"All right, then." Chief Ciders threw up his hands. "You take the mutt."

As the police officers drove off, I turned and faced the floppy-eared dog. He cocked his head and stared back at me.

"Well, you heard the chief," I said, crouching down to gently pet his fur. "Welcome to our family, Sparky."

The dog seemed to understand because he practically bowled me over with doggy affection.

Arf-arf!

Arf-arf!

"See, Mom. Sparky likes you."

"I sure hope so. He must weigh eighty pounds!"

Spencer rubbed behind the dog's absurdly floppy ears. "Sparky wouldn't hurt a fly. Would you, boy?"

Sparky let loose with a yapping sort of growl that sounded eerily human.

"Don't worry, boy," Spencer told the dog. "We'll take

good care of you. Aunt Sadie is going to love having a dog around. Right, Mom?"

My reply was a grunt that was meant to sound noncommittal. Neither the boy nor the dog noticed. I pointed to the car.

"Come on, Spencer. Let's load your bike into the trunk and get back to the shop."

"Good idea, Mom. Let's show Sparky his new home!"

CHAPTER 8

Mail Call

Life, it turns out, goes on. There is no cosmic rule that
grants you immunity from the details just because you
have come face-to-face with a catastrophe. The garbage
can still overflow, the bills arrive in the mail . . .

—Jodi Picoult, *Perfect Match*

WHEN WE GOT back to Buy the Book, I asked Spencer to
take Sparky for a short walk while I had a talk with Sadie. I
entered the shop just as my aunt rang up Maria Patelli's
monthly haul of new releases.

"We missed you and your brother at the last Quibblers
meeting," Sadie chided gently. "We can't have an effective
business association without regular attendance."

"Fall planting season got in the way," Maria explained
with a swipe at her dark bangs. "Chick kept the garden center open until nine P.M. all month. But we won't miss the
next meeting. Scout's honor. And I'm looking forward to the
Pet Parade, and Amber Breen's book signing!"

"Glad to hear it. We'll see you then," Sadie replied with an approving smile.

Maria said goodbye, and Sadie immediately turned to me with a barrage of questions.

"Why were you gone so long? Did Spencer catch Sparky? Was Jane happy to get her dog back?"

When she saw my expression, my aunt's face fell, and I broke the disturbing news—

"We found Jane unconscious on the side of the road."

"What happened?! Where is she now?"

"Dr. Rubino is with her. She's on her way to the hospital."

"Was it a heart attack?"

"Nothing natural, I'm afraid. Jane was shot."

"Shot!"

"Chief Ciders believes it was a stray bullet from a hunter. She hit her head hard on the ground when she fell, and she didn't come around, not while I was with her. But she's alive, and Dr. Rubino is hoping for the best."

"The best . . ." Aunt Sadie angrily shook her head, even as she teared up. Grabbing a tissue, she swiped at her eyes. "Do you really think that frail woman can survive being shot?"

"Doc Rubino was hopeful. He said it could have been much worse."

"Let's call him right now and see if Jane is awake," Sadie insisted. "Or should we call the hospital first—"

"I think we should give it some time. Let the doctors and hospital do their job, and I'll follow up soon, okay?"

Sadie was about to answer when the shop bell rang, and a booming voice vibrated the bookshelves.

"Gather round, troops! Time for mail call."

A large man in a postal uniform headed our way with a friendly smile.

"Hello, Seymour."

"Hey, Pen!"

Seymour Tarnish was more than our local mail carrier and my longtime friend. A former *Jeopardy*! champ, Seymour was considerably smarter than anyone I knew, though following typical social norms was not his strong suit. Case in point: On this cool, overcast autumn day, he chose to belie the season by completing his rounds in his regulation US Postal Service *shorts*.

"It's getting nippy out there," he remarked with a mock shiver.

Seymour rolled his mailbag in front of our historical mysteries endcap and thrust an inch-thick wad of envelopes at me.

"The water and sewage bill, a form letter all the parents are getting from the PTA, the Great Courses fall catalog, and the rest is worthless physical spam I am actually paid to deliver."

Seymour noticed Sadie wiping her wet cheeks and frowned. "What's with the tears, Ms. Thornton? Have you been listening to NPR again?"

I told Seymour about the shooting—the who, what, where, and when. As to the why, I recounted Ciders's theory, based on his quick look around, that Jane Cunningham was the victim of a hunter's stray bullet.

Seymour grunted. "When it comes to the QPD, the word *investigation* should have quote marks around it."

"Do you think the chief is wrong?" Aunt Sadie asked.

"Some nearsighted hunter shot Jane Cunningham by accident?" Seymour snorted. "There are no hunters anywhere near Larchmont Avenue. It's the most expensive real estate in the area. The very idea is looney tunes!"

"But Larchmont *is* pretty isolated from the rest of town," I pointed out. "There's that big overgrown meadow, and all the woods surrounding the country club."

Seymour rolled his eyes. "It's not *Green Acres*, Pen. Remember, I've lived on Larchmont for a couple of years now. And Elmer Fudd is not hunting *wascally wabbits*. Sure, it's pastoral, but it's also—to quote Elmer—*vewy, vewy* quiet. I never once heard a rifle shot or glimpsed a hunting party. Heck, I never even spotted a deer."

"Do you know Jane Cunningham?" I asked.

"Not personally."

"But you know where she lives."

"Nope. Don't know her address, either."

"But you're a postal worker!" Sadie exclaimed.

"Yeah, one of many, and none of us mail carriers deliver on the street where we live."

Sadie blinked. "That's ridiculous."

"It's an unwritten code." Seymour lowered his voice. "They say it goes way back to the time when old Gantry Mullins took a load off on his route—you know, snoozing at his house during the workday."

"Well, I never—"

"I never do, either," Seymour replied with a shrug. "And that's why I don't know Mrs. Cunningham's address."

"Chief Ciders did study her driver's license," I said. "And although he didn't share her house number with me, he said it was across the meadow . . ."

I pulled out my phone to check Jane Cunningham's address on the Internet. But it wasn't publicly listed.

Seymour studied my anxious actions. "Are *you* looking for a person of interest, Pen?"

"Me? No, I'm not. I mean, when you consider the logic, how could I be? Mrs. Cunningham is a kind, upstanding member of the community. Nice people like Jane don't have enemies."

I noticed my aunt's face darken, and she looked away.

"What's wrong, Aunt Sadie? Do you know something?"

"Nothing . . . really."

"Sounds like something to me."

"You know I don't like gossip, Pen," she replied. "I don't know if I should even mention it—"

"Well, now you have to!" Seymour insisted. "Come on, dish."

Frowning, Sadie relented. "It was the other night, when Penelope took Spencer and me to dinner at Chez Finch. Remember, Pen? Bonnie Franzetti was tending the store by herself, and she informed me there'd been an incident."

"Wow, an incident." Seymour raised an eyebrow. "Could you be more vague?"

"Just listen. Bonnie overheard an argument after the Pawsome Pals meeting. She said a man was waiting on the sidewalk, beside Mrs. Cunningham's parked car. When he saw her, he started shouting at her—"

"At Jane Cunningham?" I interrupted. "About what?"

"I don't know the details. Bonnie said it was over quick. Then he left, and that was that. But in light of what's happened, perhaps you should ask her about it."

Did you hear that, Penny? Jack whispered in my head. *Listen to your old auntie and follow that lead.*

Maybe I will . . .

No maybe *about it. You're on the job now.*

I am?

We are. You and me. We're gonna crack this thing wide open.

What thing?

The case! The case of the doggone shooter.

I'm not as sure as you are that there is *a case,* I told the ghost, *or that we can do much about it. But thanks for the doggone reminder. I mean, about Spencer and the dog.*

"Say, where is Quindicott's own version of Lassie?" Seymour asked, and I realized I'd said those last few words to Jack aloud!

"Oh, um . . . you mean, Sparky?"

"Of course!" Seymour grinned. "I'd like to meet the amazing dog who saved his mistress."

"Yes, Pen, where is Jane's dog now?" Sadie asked.

"Actually, Aunt Sadie, I need to talk to you about that . . ."

CHAPTER 9

Sparky's Tale

A house is not a home until it has a dog.

—Gerald Durrell

"GO ON," SADIE prompted. "What about Jane's dog?"

"Well, you see, Chief Ciders was going to take the dog away. Put him in that shelter in Millstone."

"Oh, no."

"He didn't. We stopped him. Actually, it was Spencer who stood up for the dog."

"Spencer?" Sadie blinked behind her spectacles.

"Yes, he thought it might be better if he took custody of Sparky—just until Jane comes home, of course."

Seymour was positively giddy at this news.

"That's great, Pen! You can't get more Norman Rockwell than a boy and his dog. Just don't forget to take pictures. You'll regret it in your old age if you don't."

Unfortunately, Sadie did not look nearly as pleased.

"Do you really think this is a smart idea?" she asked

pointedly. "Spencer is just a child. Can he really handle the responsibility of taking care of someone else's dog? And neither you nor I have ever owned one, so we're not going to be much help—"

"I get it," Seymour interrupted. "You're cat people."

"I wouldn't say we're cat people exclusively," Sadie replied. "I have nothing against dogs in principle."

Seymour waved her explanation away.

"I honestly sympathize," he said. "As an employee of the United States Postal Service, I have a professional aversion to pets of the canine persuasion. And as a parrot person at this juncture of my life, I don't have a dog, cat, or ferret in this race. That said, there are certain advantages to having a dog around."

Aunt Sadie appeared dubious.

"For instance," Seymour went on, "it's nice to have a pet that actually comes when you call its name. Plus, no hair balls. And dogs aren't finicky like cats—"

"No, they eat everything in sight, including your slippers," Sadie said.

"See that!" Seymour cried. "You *do* know something about dogs!"

My aunt crossed her arms, and Seymour tried again.

"You can teach dogs to do fun tricks, like fetch—"

"Your slippers?" Sadie shook her head. "The dog already ate them."

"Dogs provide personal security," Seymour said, "though I admit the mutts in this town are too dopey to know the difference between a friendly mail carrier and a serial killer."

As Sadie countered every point he made, Seymour gamely continued to make them, but my aunt would not be swayed. Her doubts persisted right up to the moment a laughing Spencer blew into the shop, Sparky frolicking at his side.

"Look! It's Sparky the hero dog!" Seymour exclaimed, rubbing the dog's droopy ears. "Do you know how to shake, boy?"

Seymour thrust out his hand. "Shake, Sparky! Come on, shake."

To my surprise the dog tucked its right paw into Seymour's proffered hand.

Spencer was wide-eyed. "Wow. How did you know Sparky could do that?"

"Just a guess. I'm sure Mrs. Cunningham taught Sparky a few tricks. But you'll have to figure them out, Spence."

My son went down on one knee and hugged the dog. "You're going to teach me all the tricks you know, right, Sparky?"

As the dog licked my son's happy face, Sadie frowned, studying the pair. Then she shared a long glance with me, and I could see her heart had melted.

"You know what, Spencer?" she said. "Sparky is going to need a place to sleep. You'd better dig out that blue blanket at the bottom of the linen closet and see if he'd like a spot in the corner of the living room."

"Sure, Aunt Sadie!" Spencer turned to the dog. "Come on, boy. Let's go make your new bed!"

The pair raced through the door to the apartment upstairs.

"Thank you," I said, giving my aunt a tight hug.

Seymour shouldered his mailbag. "Well, now that all's right with the world, I can get back to work."

As Seymour went out, a chatty group of customers came in. I was ready to hop behind the counter when my aunt touched my arm.

"I'll take care of things here, Pen. You'd better run over to Koh's Market and grab some dog food. Cans and dry food, too. And you should buy a variety until we learn what

Sparky likes." After a pause, she sighed. "I certainly hope Seymour is right."

"About what?"

"That Sparky won't be as finicky as Bookmark."

"If he is, you might want to hide your slippers."

CHAPTER 10

Pizza the Puzzle

The world is full of obvious things which nobody by
any chance ever observes.

—Arthur Conan Doyle, *The Hound of the Baskervilles*

A QUICK STROLL down Cranberry Street took me first to
Koh's Market, where I sought out the pet food aisle. My jaw
dropped at the selection—and I wasn't the only one surprised.

Moist and meaty steak? Jack cracked. *Porterhouse? Filet
mignon in sauce? Mother Machree, Penny! Dogs in your
time eat better than I ever did.*

*If these labels are to be believed, they eat better than I
do!* I adjusted my glasses and took a closer look at a label.
Oh, I see. The small print reads steak *flavored. It's not
steak, Jack. It just tastes like it.*

Small print, the ghost echoed. *The flimflam's favorite
flavor.*

Excuse me?

A grifter's always happy to see a mark who needs glasses.

It's not flimflam, Jack. It's advertising.

Nothing new under the sun, honey. They called it that in my day, too.

Okay, Detective, I get your drift. Now, pipe down, so I can get this shopping done . . .

After dumping an assortment of Alpo Prime Cuts and Dog Chow Hearty Stews in my handbasket, I threw in a bag of Kibbles 'n Bits and a pack of T-Bonz porterhouse-flavor dog treats, in case I had to bribe the dog not to kill me.

While I was waiting in the checkout line—and wondering why dog food seemed so much heavier than cat food—Jack piped up again.

Now that you've reminded me I'm a detective, and you're nearly done with our doggy business, aren't you wondering what that bobby-soxer Bonnie is up to?

There's no wondering. Today she's helping out at her family's pizza shop—and I know why you're asking. You want to follow that lead.

I'm just thinking of you, doll. With all you've got going on, cooking dinner should be last on your to-do list.

And a Franzetti's pizza would solve all my problems?

Sure would. Ever hear of two birds with one stone?

Fine. You win, Jack. The thought of dragging this dog food back to the store is daunting enough as it is. I'll have Koh's deliver Sparky's food, while I pick up a pizza for the rest of us hungry entities.

What do you mean us, doll? You know I can't eat anymore.

I know, Jack. But you are hungry to get back to detective work, aren't you?

Touché, baby.

I left Koh's, crossed Cranberry Street, and strolled over to the most popular Italian eatery in Quindicott. As I'd hoped, I found Bonnie behind the counter. The air inside Franzetti's Pizza was perfumed by garlic, tomato sauce, and the yeasty aroma of baking dough.

I greeted Bonnie and asked if she wouldn't mind speaking with me in private. I explained why, and she quickly nodded.

"I was at the bookstore for the whole scene," she said, wiping her slick brow with the edge of her sauce-dappled apron. "Grab a booth, and I'll tell you all about it."

Like her big brother, Eddie, Bonnie possessed all the physical traits of the large Franzetti tribe—shiny black hair, big brown eyes, and a dazzling smile, which she flashed at me as she sat down with two fountain colas in her hands.

"Wow, you don't realize how hot those pizza ovens are until you step away from them!"

She lifted her dark ponytail with one hand and fanned the back of her neck with the other before inhaling a third of her drink through a paper straw.

"It sounds like things got pretty hot at the bookstore the other night," I prompted after my first sip.

Lips still curled around her straw, Bonnie rolled her brown eyes and nodded.

Does this dame talk? Jack asked as Bonnie continued to sip her drink. *Want me to goose her with a cold spot? She looks like she could use cooling off.*

Give her a minute, I warned the ghost.

But after a few more sips, Jack lost his patience. Suddenly, Bonnie cried, "Wow! The air-conditioning is strong over here. Feels great!"

I smiled tightly and tried not to shiver. *Dial it down, Jack!*

"Anyway," Bonnie went on, "the whole thing was ugly. I almost called the police . . ."

I already knew the background details. The Paw-some Pals met the last Tuesday of every month—public record, as our reading group schedules are published in the weekly *Quindicott Bulletin*. The Pals began that meeting at seven, and it lasted until Buy the Book's nine P.M. closing.

The group had a reputation for being a contentious bunch. Their arguments usually focused on the mystery novels they'd read and which books they should group-read next. Obviously, the confrontation the night before last had been a different situation entirely.

Bonnie told me the group had broken up and gone home. Mrs. Cunningham had stayed behind to help gather the cups and empty snack trays.

"What did you two talk about?" I asked.

Bonnie shrugged. "Just small talk. She told me she was looking forward to meeting Amber Breen. Then she asked me what book was hot. I told her one of the store bestsellers for the past few weeks was the latest in the Castle of Wishes series, *The Castle of Pearls and Wishes*, which I devoured in one weekend. But she told me she doesn't enjoy reading that young-adult-fantasy stuff. Zero interest. No sale."

"Then what?"

"Since it was past closing time, I had to unlock the door to let her out. When I did, I noticed a guy on the sidewalk, pacing near Mrs. Cunningham's parked car. I didn't think anything of it. She left, and I went around the counter to close the register. That's when I heard shouting outside. I went to the door and saw that very man yelling at Mrs. Cunningham."

"Was it a member of the Pals?"

Bonnie shook her head. "No one I'd ever seen."

"Can you describe him?"

Bonnie did, using both her hands and her voice.

"The guy was tall—" Bonnie stood and indicated the man's approximate size with one hand over her head.

"He had big strong arms—" Bonnie popped her biceps for me. "But he had a big beer belly, too." With both hands, she outlined an imaginary bulge over her own stomach; then she sat down again and hunched over. "And his shoulders were kind of stooped, like this.

"His hair was kind of brownish, but there were gray streaks. He was old—you know, forties maybe."

Geez, Louise, Jack marveled. *Your little friend just delivered the suspect's description in English and mime.*

I nodded, impressed but not surprised, as I reminded Jack—

Bonnie's big brother did rise to be deputy chief of the Quindicott Police Department.

Given the clowns in that three-ring flea circus, I wouldn't brag about it.

Okay, Jack. What else do you want to know?

Anything she can remember. Press her. Make her think.

I'll try . . .

"Bonnie, do you remember anything else about this man? What was he wearing?"

"Nothing special. No hat or anything. Jeans. No jacket. He wore one of those old wheelbarrow T-shirts they sell at the thrift shop."

"Wheelbarrow?"

Bonnie nodded. "A picture of a wheelbarrow loaded with fruits and veggies. The shirt was navy blue or maybe black, with white letters."

The description of that shirt rang a bell, but I pushed it aside and pressed on.

"How much of the argument could you hear?"

She frowned. "I couldn't make out most of what he said because the door was closed and locked. But I distinctly heard his threat—"

"Threat?" I leaned closer.

"This guy told Mrs. Cunningham that the next time he saw her dog on his property, he was going to shoot it."

I sat in stunned silence a moment. Jack, however, had some gloating to do.

I'm not the kind of guy who says I told you so, *Penny, but I won't stop you from saying it.*

Fine. I admit it. You were right. But what can we do about it?

Nothing yet. We don't know enough. Keep the bobby-soxer talking.

About what?

There must have been a motive for the threat. Get me?

I got you!

"Bonnie, why do you think this man threatened to shoot Mrs. Cunningham's dog? Did he say what made him so angry?"

She shrugged. "He complained about the dog wrecking his garden or his flowers. Something like that."

"I see. How did she respond to all this? Did she shout back?"

"That's the funny thing. Mrs. Cunningham is a pretty feisty lady. I know someone who lived in one of her rental properties, and he told me she has these strict rules. When it comes to her tenants, she lays down the law really firmly, and she won't put up with her rules being broken. But that night . . . she didn't yell back at the man. She didn't try to argue or deny anything. She just calmed the man down, and they spoke quietly for a minute or two. Then the guy turned his back and walked away like he didn't want to hear any more."

This is a whole different crossword puzzle answer from the one your Keystone Cop came up with, Jack said. *And it sure doesn't spell* stray bullet *or* careless hunter.

Then we have a suspect?

Sure, Penny. Now all we have to do is our legwork to find out exactly who our suspect is.

I asked Bonnie, "I don't suppose Mrs. Cunningham mentioned his name. First name? Last name? Middle initial?"

Bonnie shook her ponytail.

"What happened next?"

"I watched the guy drive away. He had an SUV—looked

like a Ford Explorer—parked across the street. It was hard to tell what color it was because of how the streetlights fool you at night. But it definitely wasn't black. Dark blue, maybe? I was too far away to read his license plate."

Bonnie turned pale. "He . . . he didn't come back to the bookstore, did he?"

I shook my head. "It's worse than that."

I gently told Bonnie about finding Mrs. Cunningham, unconscious and with a bullet wound, and the girl's shoulders sagged.

"I should have called the police. My brother was on duty. He would have handled this guy."

I reached across the table and squeezed Bonnie's hand. I told her not to blame herself. But in truth, I was sorry, too. That crazy, violent man might have tried to murder a poor defenseless dog and missed—

The same dog that was now living at my house.

CHAPTER 11

Cat-astrophe

Fighting should be left to dogs and cats and chickens, who can't reason.

—Margaret Deland, *The Kays*, 1926

WHEN BONNIE'S FATHER called her back to work, I ordered a pizza for delivery, wished her a good night, and left the restaurant. Jack didn't say anything. He didn't have to. As soon as my ankle boots hit the sidewalk, I dialed up Chief Ciders.

"It's you," Ciders said, his tone impatient. "So, you already regret taking that dog?"

"Sparky's fine. In fact, he's doing well, considering the poor dog has been marked for death."

I could imagine the chief rolling his eyes at that statement. Nevertheless, I reported everything Bonnie had told me.

"Do you want me to describe this angry man?"

"I've heard enough."

"So?"

"So this man you don't know was supposedly overheard threatening to shoot a dog, and not its owner—"

"Come on, Chief. You were the one pushing the stray-bullet theory. Don't you think this guy could have shot at the dog and hit the owner instead?"

Ciders sighed heavily. "Look, I'm still waiting for ballistics. I'll have Eddie talk to his little sister when he gets back. He can be the judge of whether she's credible or just a kid exaggerating for attention."

"Bonnie's not nine years old anymore, Chief!"

"Never did find the monster in Prescott Woods. She had the whole town up in arms. Remember?"

"Let's not get off topic—"

"Talk about crying wolf."

"And where is Eddie, anyway?"

"Rhode Island police chiefs annual conference in Providence. I sent him to represent the town. He likes all that glad-handing and new-technology talk—more than I ever did. Anyway, I'll make sure he gets all the details, and we'll look into it. Bye, now, Mrs. McClure."

"Wait, Chief! When exactly will Eddie be back from—"

Before I could finish my question, the chief ended the call. That was when I noticed the commotion in front of Buy the Book.

Three young women, all students from St. Francis University, were standing on the sidewalk, peering through our bookshop's glass door. And they were all laughing hysterically at something inside.

As I watched, another student exited the shop. Giggling, she joined the rest. Before the door closed, I heard a dog barking wildly and Spencer shouting—

"Sparky, don't—"

The note of distress in my son's voice was all I needed to send me cutting a swath through the cackling quartet like I was wearing a jet pack.

Bursting into the shop, I spotted an orange marmalade fur ball streaking toward me across the floor and taking refuge between my legs. Cowering at my feet, Bookmark the cat looked up at me with pleading eyes. Before I could lift her into my arms, another furry creature rushed me. This one was much larger, with floppy ears, a lolling tongue, and a tail wagging like a wind sock in a tornado

"Stop, Sparky! Please, stop!"

Spencer was doing his best to end the chaos. While pleading with the dog to behave, he kept an iron grip on Sparky's leash. Unfortunately, my son was also facedown on the floor with the dog dragging him down the center aisle and my frantic aunt chasing after them.

Bookmark reacted by climbing me like a tree and perching for a moment on my shoulder before leaping to the top of a nearby bookshelf. Tail puffed and thrashing, the cat peered down at the overexcited dog and let loose an outraged howl.

Sparky, determined to reach the freaked-out feline, rose onto his hind legs, his front paws scattering books hither and yon. Spencer, on his feet again, began tugging the dog back.

Meanwhile, Bookmark—who'd clearly forgotten all about lazing in our front window and merrily taunting the dog—now jumped to the next bookshelf. Arching her furry orange back into a spiky horseshoe, she spit-hissed louder than a cornered cobra.

"I've got Sparky now, Mom!" Spencer cried.

"Great! I'll grab the cat."

But Bookmark would have none of it. As I approached her, she raced across the rack until she reached the wall, and the end of the line.

"I've got her now," I said. "The center aisle is too wide for Bookmark to jump to the next shelf."

I didn't count on the cat's ingenuity.

As I lunged for Bookmark, she leaped again. Using the top of Sadie's head as a stepping stone, she bounded across the wide aisle. Tail thrashing, Bookmark raced along the top of the bookcase until she reached the children's section, where she dived into a hidey-hole behind the Dav Pilkey books.

With the cat out of sight, Sparky became controllable again. He calmed down even more when Spencer fed him some of the T-Bonz snacks that Koh's Market had delivered.

"How did this happen?" I asked.

"It's my fault, Mom," Spencer confessed. "I took Sparky to the event space, where Bookmark was sleeping. I . . . I just wanted to introduce them."

Jack's laughter echoed in my head.

So much for four-legged first impressions.

CHAPTER 12

A Boy and His Dog

A dog teaches a boy fidelity, perseverance, and to turn
around three times before lying down.

—Robert Benchley

I TOLD SPENCER to take Sparky upstairs.

"Dish him up some dog food. Aunt Sadie and I will put
the shop back in order—and try to coax Bookmark out of
her cat cave."

When things were back to normal, I faced my aunt.

"I wouldn't call it a disaster—"

Sadie sighed. "I would."

I would, too, Jack cracked.

"Let's hope we figure out a way for Bookmark and Jane
Cunningham's dog to get along," I told them both. "In the
meantime, the two will have to be kept apart. Bookmark
will stay down here in the shop. She likes to hunt mice at
night, anyway. And Sparky can sleep on his blanket in the
living room upstairs."

Sadie peered at me over her spectacles. "You do realize Bookmark is going to set off the motion detector? She always does when we leave her in the shop overnight."

"I guess we can't use that feature of the burglar alarm for now."

"So much for the security Seymour claimed a dog would provide," Sadie huffed.

"It's temporary, I promise. And if someone tries to break in, Sparky will no doubt make plenty of noise and wake us up. That's what Seymour meant."

Hours later we found out that we didn't need an intruder for Sparky to make noise.

At nine o'clock, Spencer took Sparky for his evening walk while I phoned Dr. Rubino to find out how Jane was doing. I got voice mail and left a message imploring the doctor to call me as soon as he had an update on her condition.

After Spencer and Sadie went to bed, I nodded off while (optimistically) reading a book on animal behavior. Suddenly, I was startled awake by an almost human cry of anguish.

Sparky, who seemed fine all day, had begun to whimper— quietly at first, but increasing in volume and intensity every moment. The sound was heart-wrenching and hauntingly familiar.

The poor dog's cries reminded me of my own, on the day of my mother's funeral. That was the first night—but certainly not the last—when I cried myself to sleep, missing the only mother I'd ever known and would never see again.

I swiped at a tear and crossed to the dog, who was so calm before but now cowering in the corner.

"Sparky, it will be all right," I said. "You're in a safe place. We'll take care of you. You'll see."

The whimpers became loud barks, then he began to whine. Sparky pushed his head so far into the corner, I thought he was going to chew a hole in the wall. Try as I might, I could not get the dog to quiet down.

Sadie appeared, her glasses and robe both askew. "Poor thing. He misses Jane. Perhaps we should get him that new antianxiety medication from the vet. I think they call it BlueSky."

"I've seen those BlueSky commercials, too. I can speak with Dr. Winnik about it, but that won't do us any good at this hour."

The dog's heartbreaking cries woke Spencer, too.

"What's wrong, Sparky?" he asked as he rubbed the sleep out of his eyes.

The dog's demeanor calmed when Spencer appeared. Cooing, Spencer sat down on the doggy blanket. Sparky tried to squeeze his ample body onto my son's inadequate lap. Then the dog rested his head on my son's shoulder and quieted at last.

After fifteen minutes with Spencer, the dog was nearly asleep. But as soon as Spencer rose to go back to bed, Sparky whimpered and whined again.

"He's lonely, Mom. I better sleep here and keep him company."

"You'll do no such thing," Aunt Sadie replied sharply.

The room went silent. Spencer froze and looked to me with big, pleading eyes.

My heart went out to my son, and I was about to argue on his behalf when I realized there was no need. We both misunderstood Sadie.

True, my aunt didn't want Spencer to sleep out here with the dog—only because she had a better idea. As we watched in surprise, she bent down, gathered up Sparky's blue blanket and carried it into Spencer's bedroom.

My son and I quickly cleared a corner, and Aunt Sadie created a comfy new dog bed. As Sparky happily settled on the blanket, Sadie smiled.

There was no more whimpering.

Thirty minutes later, I was ready to turn in myself when I peeked into Spencer's bedroom. The blue blanket abandoned, Sparky was now curled up beside my son on the bed, where they both slept like babies.

CHAPTER 13

Punchy Pillow Talk

A dog doesn't care if you're rich or poor, educated or
illiterate, clever or dull. Give him your heart and he
will give you his.

—John Grogan, *Marley & Me*

I COULDN'T SLEEP.

When I finally crawled under my bedcovers, it was after
midnight. I tried to read but couldn't concentrate, so I turned
out the light. All I did was stare into the shadows.

Those sad cries of Jane's dog nearly broke my heart. I
was relieved the pup took comfort in snuggling close to my
son, but even the sweet sight of Spencer and Sparky curled
up together failed to set my mind at ease.

I punched my pillows twice. Then I turned back and
forth until I heard that familiar voice in my head—

What's wrong, doll?

"Jack?"

Well, it ain't Clark Gable.

I smiled in the dark, imagining Gable on the silver

screen, with his cheeky grin, throwing a sly wink to the audience. Even so . . .

"I'm glad it's you, Jack."

That makes two of us. Now, tell me why you're flopping around on that mattress like a hooked marlin on a boat deck.

"It's Spencer. I know he loves Sparky, and I know he's old enough to understand why the dog will have to go back to its owner. My boy has a good heart, and I'm sure he'll want to see Sparky reunited with his rightful 'mom' again. The thing is . . . what if Jane Cunningham . . . what if she . . ."

I swallowed, not wanting to say the words.

Kicks the bucket? Jack blurted. *Bites the dust? Cashes in her chips? Catches the big chill?*

"I was going to say, *what if she doesn't pull through?*"

Listen, honey, there's no need to soft-pedal things with me. I'm not one of your small-town church ladies.

"Well, I don't see any reason to be crass. I mean, given your own . . . situation."

You mean, the fact that I'm dead? Or that I'm stuck in a bookshop in the middle of Cornpone-ville?

"Both, I guess. Only, you know I would never refer to my hometown that way."

Of course you wouldn't because you don't know what you're missing.

"Oh, yes, I do. You forget. Before my husband died, I lived and worked in New York City. I know all about the crowds, the crime, the chaos. You can have it."

I won't argue your three Cs, but the bright lights of the big city have three things this little burg never will.

"And what are they?"

Excitement. Energy. Edge.

"What are those, Jack? Your three Es?"

Yeah, and here's a fourth. New York offers an Education. One you could use.

"Why do you say that?"

Because you are not losing sleep over a boy and a dog.

"I'm not?"

No. What you're fretting over are feelings of helplessness. But you are not helpless. You got your wits—and you got me.

"My PI spirit?"

In more ways than one.

"Okay, fine. I'll indulge you. Just tell me what to do if Jane . . . you know, catches your big chill. I can't put Sparky in a shelter. It would break Spencer's heart—and mine. Do you think I should ask Seymour to take him?"

The moronic mailman? Why? Your boy loves the dog.

"Spencer may love Sparky, but Sadie and I have a business to run. Neither of us has experience handling a rambunctious canine. You saw what happened downstairs with poor little Bookmark."

That cat's nobody's poor little anything. She gleefully taunted that dog when it suited her. And when he showed her who was boss, she figured out how to save her own tail quick enough, didn't she? No harm done. In fact, that sleepy store of yours could use some excitement.

"You mean, other than mysteriously moving objects and drafts that goose customers?"

As to the problem of handling a canine, the ghost went on (ignoring my jab), *you need to take that one step at a time, and your first step should be looking for help from someone who does know a thing or two about the subject at hand—or on your hands, as the case may be. That's what I did when I was in your shoes.*

"What do you mean, in my shoes? Did you own a dog?"

I was in charge of one for a weekend. A very long weekend.

"You were dog-sitting for a friend?"

The dog was part of a case. I was hired to . . . Jack

paused. *You know what, doll? I'd rather show you than
tell you.*

"Well, tell me a little first," I said, snuggling under the
covers.

Jack agreed, and started his story . . .

*This crazy canine case began one night when I heard
strange sounds outside my apartment door. I remember it
was raining—*

"Like cats and dogs?"

*Yeah, as a matter of fact. And one of the latter ended up
in my building's hallway. I opened the door, and there she
was, with a little pink bow in her hair, looking up at me with
her pretty brown eyes.*

"A woman?"

A dog.

"Don't be insulting."

*I'm not. It really was a dog. A girl dog. See how nice I
soft-pedaled that for you? I could have said she was a
bitc—*

"Okay, I get it! And I believe you. You opened the door
to find a female dog. So, what happened next?"

The dog hired me.

"Come on, Jack. That I don't believe. What's the real
story?"

Like I said, I'd rather show you than tell you.

"All right, then. Show me."

*Glad to. You know the drill, honey. Close your eyes and
relax . . .*

Closing my eyes was easy. Relaxing, not so much. But
soon my limbs grew heavy, my breathing slowed, and my
anxious mind let go, descending, with the sound of Jack's
deep voice, into the world of his story.

CHAPTER 14

Nightcap

There was a sudden pool of darkness at my feet. I dived
into it and dropped . . . and dropped . . . and dropped.

—Raymond Chandler, "The Man Who Liked Dogs," 1936

New York City
Friday, April 18, 1947

I OPENED MY eyes to find myself standing in front of a
rain-streaked apartment window.

It must be late, I thought, peering down at the dark city
street. The stores were all closed, and the sidewalks deserted, except for three people. A pair of pedestrians hurried
along in overcoats and fedoras. And a blond woman was
climbing into a boxy yellow cab. She wore a bulky fur wrap
and a pillbox hat with a face veil in front and a vintage
snood in back—except the snood wasn't vintage, I reminded
myself. Not here, because I was no longer in my time.

Even the streetlights were different, far dimmer than in
my day.

Between the weak light and inky shadows on this rain-slick street, the few passing cars that I saw looked like they'd been liberated from an antiques road show, with every long, bulky vehicle carrying enough metal to arm a small tank.

On the corner, a shoeshine station stood next to an all-night newsstand with more newspapers and magazines than I could hope to count. Above the newsstand, a billboard proclaimed, LUCKY STRIKE MEANS FINE TOBACCO. Alongside the slogan was an image of a farmer in a straw hat and overalls, examining a tobacco leaf the size of a flat-screen TV.

Below the ad—one that would have been banned in my day—I noticed a hulking figure looking up at this very window. I couldn't make out his face, only the burning red end of his lit cigarette. As soon as the man noticed me staring, he faded back into the gloom.

For a moment I wondered if that mysterious figure was Jack Shepard, until I felt the warm breath of a living man speaking softly in my ear.

"Welcome to my world, baby."

I turned around to find myself finally facing him, though *facing* was far from accurate. The tall private detective with the acre of shoulders was standing so close, my nose was practically hitting his chest.

His bare chest.

"You okay, doll? You look like you've seen a ghost."

Jack was teasing, of course, but I didn't laugh. After the intimacy of hearing his voice in my head for so long, actually *seeing* this towering, vital man in his prime—which he'd been before his premature death—always gave me somewhat of a shock.

To top it off, I'd never before confronted Jack in this state of undress. Embarrassed, I stepped back and moved to touch my suddenly hot cheeks. That was when I realized my hands were wearing white cotton gloves. Glancing down, I saw my nightgown was gone, replaced by silky-feeling underthings, a white blouse with red polka dots, and a rust-colored pencil skirt that fell below my knees.

My glasses were gone, too, though I could see perfectly, and my auburn hair wasn't in its usual ponytail. Patting my head, I felt an expertly twisted French chignon. My legs were encased in stockings, and on my feet were peep-toed pumps.

Jack's feet, I realized, were bare, just like his chest, though he wasn't completely naked. (Thank goodness, for modesty's sake.) *At least the man is wearing pajama bottoms*, I thought, which was when I noticed he was also holding a gun.

"Jack, why are you—"

Ruff! Ruff! Ruff!

Before I could finish my sentence, a little dog ran up to me and began to sniff my stockings. The adorable cairn terrier was no more than fifteen pounds, with silky chocolate fur, black points for ears, a wet black nose, and bright brown eyes. A little pink bow was clipped to a tuft of fur at the top of her excited head.

Ruff-ruff-ruff!

"Hello, girl . . ." I reached down to stroke the little terrier's soft fur, glad to be distracted from my blushing reaction to Jack's half-clothed state. "What a cute little thing you are," I cooed.

Glancing up, I noticed the PI was staring, but not at the dog. His gaze was on me. And his head was tilted in a funny way.

"What is it?" I asked.

Jack's square jaw remained iron. The dagger-shaped scar on his chin appeared just as intimidating. But something in his gunmetal-gray eyes seemed to soften—just a bit.

"Cute," he replied. "I could say the same about you."

"Thanks," I said, then swallowed my reaction and changed the subject. "Is this the dog that supposedly hired you?"

"No supposing about it . . ."

As he moved to retrieve something from his coffee table, I took in the rest of the room.

Jack's apartment was small but surprisingly tidy with a big, lumpy (but comfortable-looking) sofa, an easy chair, and a couple of ceramic lamps with pleated linen shades. Against the wall stood a bar holding bottles of Scotch whisky, vodka, and bourbon. A vintage radio with a cathedral top sat between the room's two tall windows, and a bookshelf in the corner held paperbacks and a stack of pulp magazines. I saw a small kitchen through one door, a bedroom through another.

"Take a look at this."

Jack handed me an envelope. Inside was a letter that began:

*Dear Jack Shepard, I want you to find me
some answers . . .*

What followed was a list of typed instructions that made no sense—at least at first glance. No name. No address. Also inside was a hundred-dollar bill.

"The little fur hat was leashed to my doorknob. The envelope was slipped under its collar."

"Yes, but by whom?" I said. "Someone must have left the dog."

"By the time I opened the door, whoever left her was long gone."

"Did you check the street?"

I told Jack about the people I'd noticed outside: the two male pedestrians hurrying along; the hulking figure on the corner smoking a cigarette; and the blonde in the fur wrap climbing into a cab.

Jack raised an eyebrow. "That blonde sounds like a looker."

Now I raised my eyebrows. "Are you sure she wasn't visiting you? I mean, before I arrived."

"I'm sure."

"What night of the week is this, anyway?"

"Friday."

I glanced around the apartment again. "Really? Late Friday night at your apartment, and you're all alone? No female company?"

Jack shrugged. "You're not wrong. I typically would have some soft shoulders up here to join me for a, uh, shall we say, *nightcap*? But on this particular Friday, there was no lipstick left on my, uh, shall we say, *tumblers*?"

"Oh, you're hilarious. And your answer tells me absolutely nothing. Come on, Jack. What was the reason? Why no female company? And why in heaven's name are you holding a gun in your hand?"

"Same answer for both, Inspector." Jack set the gun on the coffee table and crossed his muscular arms. "When I heard the dog's heavy breathing and scratching at my front door, I thought it was an ex-con named Muggsy following through on a threat. That's the same reason I was flying solo this evening. If I was going to tangle with a Hell's Kitchen hothead, I didn't want some dame around to distract me — or be put in harm's way."

"Yes, but I'm here, and I'm a dame."

"No, Penny. Tonight you're not a dame."

"What am I, then?"

"You're my partner."

I liked the sound of that—and the way Jack looked at me when he'd said it. In fact, I liked it so much, I could feel the blush returning to my cheeks.

"Okay, *partner*," I said, "will you do me one favor?"

"Depends."

"On what?"

"On the favor . . ."

Jack stepped closer, so close that I could feel the heat coming off his half-naked body, a stark contrast from the ghostly cold of his typical presence—in my present, which this wasn't. This was Jack's past. His world. And I had to keep my reactions in check, because back here, Jack was the polar opposite of a disembodied voice. His heart was still beating, his breath still warm, and his vital, masculine energy still so palpable, it nearly overwhelmed me in that small space.

"Go on, honey," he said, his deep voice softening. "Tell mc. What's the favor?"

"Will you please put on a shirt!"

CHAPTER 15

Doggy Business

It's a sordid life, but I'm used to it.

—Raymond Chandler, *The Long Goodbye*

JACK AGREED TO my favor, though not without a moment of minor humiliation (entirely on my part).

"Sure," he said. "I'll put on a shirt for you. In fact, I'm flattered."

"Flattered? Why?"

He stood there a moment and looked down at me (and the blush on my cheeks), until finally he said, "I never had a partner in the PI game who couldn't control their animal attraction to me. Guess I'd better do something about it . . ."

With a wink, he headed into the bedroom.

"My request has nothing to do with animal attraction!" I insisted. "It's only a matter of propriety!"

"If you say so."

The smug reply was annoying enough to help me clear my head and refocus on—

Ruff-ruff-ruff!

By now the little terrier had abandoned sniffing up my stockings and turned her nose to smelling the rest of Jack's apartment (which, given the size, didn't take very long).

"Come here, girl. Let me have a look at you . . ."

Her chocolate coat was clean and shiny, her teeth were in good health, and her nails were clipped. She was certainly well taken care of. I examined her leather leash and collar; both appeared new, but there was no tag, no ID.

"What are you looking for?" Jack asked. As he returned to the living room, he was pulling a short-sleeved white undershirt over his head.

"I thought I might find a clue to who owns her. If this were my time, I would ask a vet to help me look for a chip."

Jack made an incredulous face. "How could a chippie be of any help with—"

"Not a chippie! A microchip. It's a form of identification, like your military dog tags, only very small and embedded under the skin with information that can be scanned at a veterinarian's office— Oh, never mind. Microchips won't be invented for another decade, anyway."

"Sorry. I can't help you find Mike Roe's chips, doll. Chippies, on the other hand, I can always locate."

"I have no doubt. But it won't do us any good tonight."

"Okay, then." Jack folded his arms. "What's your next move?"

"Let's take off the dog's collar," I suggested and proceeded to do just that. "You said the envelope was slipped underneath it. Maybe we'll find some kind of identifying information written on the underside of the— Jack, look!"

"What did you find?"

"A key!"

Jack lifted an eyebrow. "A key to the case?"

"An actual key. It's taped to the underside of the collar." I removed the key and examined the characters engraved in the metal. "LUDLOW-66. What does it mean, Jack? *Is* it a key to the case? What does this key open? You would know."

"Exactly, partner."

"I get it. You know, but you're not going to tell me, are you?"

"Nope. Any answers are for me to know and you to find out."

I sighed. This wasn't the first time Jack had attempted to put me through my paces. My trips into his past memories were almost always more than show-and-tell. They were his version of PI school, and today was a new lesson.

Unsure what to do next, I buckled the collar back on the dog. As soon as I did, she ran to the door, pawed it, and began smelling the floorboards.

"Jack, I think the dog needs to pee. Can we take her outside?"

"Right now we're better off inside—"

With a tilt of his head toward the windows, I realized the storm had picked up. Dark water was now streaming down the glass panes like a noir Niagara. A streak of lightning flashed, followed by a crack of thunder so loud, it made me jump—and the dog whine.

Glancing around, I tried to solve the problem at hand. "Do you have a newspaper you can trash?"

"Now that you mention it—"

Jack grabbed one of New York City's tabloid papers off the sofa and slapped it into my hand. I noticed it was turned to a particular story. "DOGNAPPED!" screamed the headline. "PRIZEWINNING POOCH IN PERIL!"

"That's funny," I said, staring at the photo next to the story. "This Pekingese looks familiar . . ."

Scanning the article, I realized that the award-winning dog was from one of Jack's cases. The story described a grateful society matron who had been reunited with her

kidnapped pooch, "without a single hair harmed" on its
pedigreed head due to the heroic efforts of one Mr. Jack
Shepard, "lover of creatures great and small."

The feature included Jack's office address, phone number, and a quote from Jack himself: "In this dog-eat-dog
world, I'll do anything to help my four-legged friends."

"You actually said that?"

"Does it sound like something I'd say? Or like a completely fabricated quote, compliments of a double-crossing,
liquid-lunch-guzzling, degenerate gambler who funds his
unsavory habits with yellow journalism?"

"You mean . . ." My gaze found the story's byline. "Right.
Timothy Brennan strikes again."

"Thanks to Brennan, my temporary secretary spent most
of her afternoon taking calls about my dog-walking services."

I hid my smile behind a white glove. "Well, I did notice
he failed to identify you as a licensed private investigator,
opting instead to declare you an expert in 'doggy business.'"

Ruff-ruff-ruff!

"Speaking of which . . ." I spread the newspaper down on
the floor, making sure Jack got the satisfaction of seeing
Timothy Brennan's byline get the treatment it deserved.
"Okay, girl, here you go . . . I mean, you can go!"

As she emptied her bladder on Brennan's prose, the dog
appeared to smile right along with Jack, and I couldn't help
observing—

"Now *that's* what I call yellow journalism."

Jack snorted. "Auditioning for vaudeville, are you?"

"Only if you go with me."

"Naw, I'd rather we do our double act in private, if you
don't mind."

"I don't mind," I said, and Jack sent me the sweetest look.
Then he clapped his hands and declared—

"All right, partner, what's next?"

Before I could answer, the terrier's furry little legs rocketed her into the kitchen. We followed to find her pawing at a cupboard.

Ruff-ruff-ruff!

I grabbed an empty bowl and filled it with water. She lapped that up and barked again.

"I think she's hungry, too . . ."

Unfortunately, with the exception of a few bottles of beer, Jack's icebox was completely bare.

"Really?" I scolded. "Nothing? Not even a quart of milk?"

"Why would I have a quart of milk?" Jack asked. "I take my coffee black and my meals at diners and dives."

"You never cook dinner here? Not even to entertain a lady friend?"

"Oh, I entertain them all right—and I get no complaints. Don't you recall our shall-we-say-nightcap conversation? Gee, for an educated doll, you sure have a short memory."

Ignoring Jack's goading, I checked his kitchen cupboards, but except for finding a tin of preground coffee, I had no luck. "You don't have anything for the dog to eat?"

"Not unless you count cigarettes and gum."

"You can't feed a dog that!"

"Then she'll have to wait till morning."

By now the dog was whimpering pitifully. "Aw, listen to her. Who knows when she had her last meal? Come on, Jack, there must be some solution?"

"There is, doll. Put your brain into it."

"Okay . . ." I tapped my chin. "There's no use suggesting Grubhub or DoorDash. Are there any food-delivery services around here at this hour?"

He shook his head.

"An all-night deli or diner?"

"Times Square, sure, but not in this neighborhood."

"Neighborhood . . . That's it, Jack! You have lots of neighbors on this floor, don't you? I'll bet someone owns a dog. If they do, I'm sure they'll lend you some food—and, hey, don't you want to canvas the floor, anyway? I mean, just because you didn't see who left the dog doesn't mean one of your neighbors didn't see something, right?"

"Not bad, partner. There's hope for you yet. . . ."

For the next few minutes, I grilled Jack on what he knew about his neighbors.

"Next to nothing," he confessed. "I haven't been here long, and I don't spend much time in this cracker box. When I do, it's so late, nobody's around."

"That's not much to go on. Have you ever *heard* a dog barking on your floor?"

"Yep," he said. "Somebody owns mutts. Don't know who, and chances are, at this time of night, most of my neighbors are already in dreamland. So how should we proceed?"

"I'm not sure. But give me a minute, and I'll give you a plan."

CHAPTER 16

The Mug Next Door

You're a sly dog. Hand in glove with the great detective, and not a hint as to the way things are going.

—Agatha Christie, *The Murder of Roger Ackroyd*

MY STRATEGY WAS simple. After putting the little terrier back on her leash, I trotted down the hall with her (Jack right behind us). Working systematically, I stood at each door and knocked lightly. If a tenant without a dog was already sleeping, I knew my light knock wouldn't wake them. On the other hand, if they *did* have a dog, I figured it would start to bark—and I would know to knock louder to get the neighbor to answer and (I hoped) help us out.

At the first three doors I tried, I heard no response. But when I lightly knocked on the fourth—

Arf-arf-arf-arf-arf! Arf-arf! Arf-arf-arf-arf-arf!

I turned to Jack. "Looks like we struck the canine mother lode!

Sure enough, when the door opened, three yapping lapdogs raced out—two long-haired Yorkies and a short-haired

Chihuahua. The adorable toy dogs excitedly circled our female terrier, and she joined in the enthusiastic greetings of touching noses and sniffing backsides.

Distracted by the activity on the ground, I assumed the owner would be some middle-aged matron with curlers in her hair.

I couldn't have been more wrong.

"Boys! Boys!" a deep voice scolded. "Mind your manners!"

My gaze moved from tiny toy paws to a pair of size seventeen slippers attached to two hairy tree trunks. The thick legs held up a giant barrel of a man, wearing a red silk robe, and his physique was taller and wider than any football linebacker I'd ever seen.

My neck strained backward, and I set eyes on a ferocious-looking whisker-covered face, framed by a wild mane of dark curly hair. My fight-or-flight response kicked in, and my body took an automatic step back, right into the solid wall of Jack's chest.

The second I hit that concrete curtain, I felt firm hands on my shoulders, and heard an encouraging whisper in my ear. "Don't quit now, Penny. You're finally getting somewhere."

Swallowing hard, I refocused on the business at hand.

"G-g-good evening, sir," I stammered, feeling less than steady in my peep-toed pumps. "We're sorry to disturb you—"

"Don't sweat it, sweetie!" The hairy giant waved his meaty hand. "Me and the boys were just listening to my Andrews Sisters records. They just slay me! Did you hear them this week on Jack Benny's radio show?"

Before I could reply, the giant's eyes grew wide, and he cried out. "Oh, my goodness—speaking of *Jack*, I see there's another one right behind you! Mr. Jack Shepard! How are you, buddy? Long time, no see!"

Jack's brow furrowed as he tried to remember the man.

"Donny? Big Donny Dalrymple? Is that you under all that hair?"

"Sure is! What brings you to my door with this copper-haired cutie-pie and her little terrier?"

"We'd like to speak with you if you don't mind . . ."

"Mind?! Are you kidding? I love company! Come on in! Would you two like a bowl of my homemade beef stew? I eat around the clock these days. Gotta maintain my wrestling weight."

"Wrestling?" Jack prompted.

"Sure! Haven't you heard? I'm Dogface Donny Danger now, a hit on the strongman circuit. What a year it's been!"

"Do tell . . ."

And Donny did. After we settled in at his polished dining room table, he dished out bowls of homemade stew for Jack, himself, and our little terrier (with a glass of sherry for me). Then he caught us up on everything that had happened to him since Jack had last seen him.

"When *did* you last see him?" I asked Jack.

"About a year ago," Jack said. "Donny was the biggest, scariest bouncer at the Aces High Club on Sixtieth."

"A nightclub?" I presumed.

Jack nodded. "A classy one. And only a stone's throw from the Copa."

"Working the club's door is how I got discovered," Donny explained.

According to the erstwhile bouncer, a booking agent and promoter of crooners and comedians was a regular at the club. The man also represented a stable of wrestlers worldwide. He took Donny on, taught him the wrestling ropes (literally), came up with his look and gimmick, and started booking him all over the tristate area.

"It's pure showbiz," Donny said. "Pretend fighting. Pratfalls and foot twisting, snarling, shouting, and dodging

breakaway furniture. My old boss at the Aces High— You
know him, Jack—"

"Sure, Paul Lambert."

"Yeah, Mr. Lambert didn't think much of my career
switch. But I tell you, Jack, I love it, the crowds love it, and
I'm making real lettuce. I'm even getting regular gigs as a
background palooka in those B movies they shoot in
Queens. And next month, I'm starting a sixteen-city wrestling tour! I'll miss my babies, but my auntie in Rhinebeck's
going to take good care of them . . ."

When Jack and Donny were finally all caught up, the
detective glanced my way. It was a signal, and I knew what
it meant. Time to get down to business.

"Donny," I began, "did you happen to take your three
boys out for a walk this evening?"

"Sure did. These little guys got a lotta energy. And I like
night air, even when the walk is just around the block."

"Did you happen to see anybody walking a cairn terrier
that looked like this one?"

"Like Toto from the *Wizard of Oz*, you mean?"

I glanced at Jack. "She does look like Toto, doesn't she?"

"Maybe we should call her Toto Two," Jack quipped.

For lack of another name, I didn't argue. Meanwhile,
Donny was taking a longer look at our dog.

"I *did* see a terrier like yours. A blond chickie was walking her."

"Do you remember anything else about her? What was
she wearing?"

"Bulky fur wrap—cheap fake fur. After years at the
Aces High, believe me, I can tell. Pillbox hat with a face veil
and one of those hair nets. What are they called, sweetie?"

"A snood."

"That's right. The odd thing is, with that veil and snood,
you'd think she was a matronly type, but I got a good look at
her under a streetlamp, and she was young. I mean bobby-

soxer young, fifteen, sixteen, maybe. One of those sunny, pert-faced, Doris Day–type blondes." Donny shrugged. "It was starting to rain, so I hurried home. I didn't see where she went."

Ruff-ruff-ruff!

Toto Two had finished her bowl of stew and was ready for another. Donny was more than happy to oblige. As he went into the kitchen with her bowl, I leaned close to my partner.

"Jack, that blonde with the face veil and fake-fur wrap that Donny described sounds like the woman I saw from your apartment window. She was climbing into a taxicab. She must have been the person who left Toto Two."

"Sounds like it," Jack said. He leaned back and wiped his mouth with one of Donny's fine linen napkins. "Now what?"

"Let's go back to your apartment . . ."

After Toto Two's second bowl of stew, we thanked Donny and headed back down the hall.

"Wait!" Donny said. "Here, take this." He handed us a flyer. "You two should come see me wrestle. Sunday night at the Majestic Palace on Fourteenth."

"The Majestic?" Jack said. "The old burlesque theater?"

"That's the one. They do radio shows there now, exhibition boxing, and wrestling matches—like mine! Ivan the Terrible and Dogface Donny Danger are going at it at eight P.M." He tapped the flyer. "What do you think? Do I look ferocious or what? I've been working on my ringside snarl, and I got a new gimmick I'm gonna try: chewin' on chair legs. This Sunday's crowd will be the first to see it!"

"We wouldn't wanna miss that, would we, Penny?" He threw a wink my way as he shook the big man's giant hand. "Thanks, Donny."

CHAPTER 17

Jack's Type

Nora: You got types?
Nick: Only you, darling—lanky brunettes with wicked jaws.
Nora: And how about the redhead you wandered off with . . . last night?
Nick: That's silly . . . She just wanted to show me some French etchings.

—Nick and Nora Charles in
The Thin Man, Dashiell Hammett

BY THE TIME we returned to Jack's apartment, the clock hands were hitting the wee small hours of the morning. Suppressing a yawn, I saw the terrier was tuckered out, too.

"Let's make a bed for her," I said. "Do you have an extra blanket?"

Jack pulled one from the closet, and I settled Toto Two in the corner of the living room. After turning round and round, she settled down but didn't sleep. Her curious brown eyes remained on me and Jack as we continued talking.

"Now we know the dog didn't hire you," I told Jack as he poured us each two fingers of Scotch.

He handed me a tumbler, settled on the couch, and put his slippered feet up on the coffee table. "I think we knew that already."

"Well, obviously. What I meant was, now we know who left the dog."

"We do? So what's your theory?"

I kicked off my heels and sat down next to him. "The very young blonde that Big Donny and I both saw must have read Timothy Brennan's tabloid article about you and decided to hire you. But for some reason she wanted to remain anonymous."

"Then why didn't she leave the dog at my office? Brennan published my office address, not this one."

"Good question," I said, sipping the whisky. It was strong, but I liked it. "Isn't your home address listed publicly?"

"Nope. I don't even get mail here."

"Then either someone followed you from your office, which is an awful lot of trouble, or they already knew your home address . . ." I reminded Jack of his penchant for inviting *dames* up here for nightcaps. "Could that blonde have been one of your previous . . . uh-hem, guests?"

Jack smirked. "First of all, I don't touch jailbait. Second, sunny blondes aren't my type. I prefer sharp redheads with curious minds—" He tossed me another wink. "On the other hand, I don't turn down sultry brunettes when they . . . like the look of me, if you get my drift."

"Like a tsunami. Let me see that letter again, the one that came with the hundred-dollar bill . . ."

I reread the note, more closely this time—

Dear Jack Shepard,

I want you to find me some answers.
First off, don't get hot under the collar!
You're looking for a dog.
The key is the key.
Follow the key and get the dog.
(You have an Ace in the hole.)
When you find the dog, break its legs, and the
mystery's solved.

I now understood the warning about not getting *hot under the collar.* Since I had *literally* found that key hidden under the dog's collar, it was obviously a clue. But the rest made no sense. There was nothing that revealed an identity, just terse instructions. Puzzling ones. And the final command for Jack was shocking.

"This last step is brutal, Jack. How can someone ask you to do such a terrible thing to an innocent animal?" I shuddered at the very idea. "You would never hurt a dog, would you?" I whispered.

"Of course not."

"Then what *did* you do?"

Jack raised an eyebrow. "You want me to say it again?"

"I know, I know—it's for you to know and me to find out."

Rising from the couch, I set my mind to the puzzle and began to pace back and forth in my stocking feet. The little dog must have thought it was playtime, because she suddenly got up to follow me—or else she was trained so well that she was trying to heel behind me.

Her behavior reminded me of that Pekingese show dog from Jack's case files—the one that Timothy Brennan had used to create his sensational tabloid story.

"That's it!" I whipped around to face Jack.

Ruff-ruff-ruff!

The detective's eyebrows lifted. "Sounds like you *and* Toto got an idea. One of you gonna tell me?"

I bent down to pet the pooch. "Brennan himself could be playing some kind of prank on you. You have to admit, this letter is bizarre, especially that last step of the instructions—"

I shuddered again at the thought of the violent act that it directed Jack to perform.

"I'll bet this is some scheme on Brennan's part to create a brand-new tabloid story. Seems to me he got a big reaction to the Pekingese piece. You said your secretary took messages all afternoon asking for your, uh—shall we say, doggy business?"

"You're a riot."

"But am I *right*? Did you confront Timothy Brennan about this alleged prank? Because, as next steps go, that's exactly what I would have done."

Jack didn't answer, but his little smile of approval made my knees go weak, which was suddenly more than a figure of speech. Feeling woozy, I sat back down on the sofa.

"Jack, I'm feeling light-headed, and it's not the whisky . . ."

"Easy, honey. Take a breath."

As I did, I realized that something was wrong with my eyesight. The detective's face, the dog, the entire room began to blur—as if I suddenly needed my glasses.

"Jack, what's happening?"

"You'll be okay, Penny." The detective put a firm hand on my shoulder. "Just remember what you learned tonight; neighbors can be a big help in the detection game. They sometimes see things, know things, and even do things that can crack a case wide open, or at least get you to your next good lead . . ."

Jack's lips kept moving, but all I could hear was the sound of the rain pounding on the window. It grew louder and louder, as loud a freight train.

"What are you saying, Jack?! I can't hear you . . . and I can hardly see you . . ."

Paralyzed on the sofa, I watched in helpless alarm as Jack's face faded away.

"Wait!" I cried. "Don't leave me! Please don't go!"

The only answer was the rumbling of rolling thunder, which quickly changed in tone and pitch until it became a strange vibration that shook the floor. Bzzz . . . Bzzz . . . Bzzz . . .

The incessant buzzing refused to stop!

Then the sheets of cold rain beating on the window broke through the glass. The noir Niagara streamed into the room in a frigid flow until a rising flood enveloped me. The water became a whirlpool, and I felt myself going round and round, then down and down, until a black abyss blotted everything out.

CHAPTER 18

Comings and Goings

I'm fine . . . Just fine. I'm going to have me a short nap now.

—Raymond Chandler, "The Man Who Liked Dogs"

BZZZ . . . BZZZ . . . BZZZ . . .

I opened my eyes to weak light coming through the curtains. My bedroom curtains. Disoriented, I fumbled for my glasses and heard them tumble to the floor, along with my vibrating phone.

I grabbed the digital alarm clock instead.

"Jack, who could be calling me at six thirty in the morning?"

Jack didn't reply. He couldn't. My ghost always disappeared after one of his dream adventures. I didn't know where he went, or how long he'd be gone, but showing me his past cost him a tremendous amount of energy, and whenever those nights were over, it was his turn to sleep.

Jack's absence left me with a hollow feeling—an acute sense of loss that made me want to stay in bed all day—until my phone buzzed again, and I realized it could be Dr. Rubino calling me back with a status report on Jane Cunningham. I picked my phone up off the floorwith such urgency, I didn't bother glancing at the caller ID.

"Dr. Rubino? How is—"

"Sorry, Pen. This isn't 'Randy' Randall Rubino. It's not Jonas Salk or Dr. Demento, either. Just your friendly neighborhood mail carrier."

"Seymour? Why are you calling me at this hour? What's the emergency?"

"No emergency. I came to work early to get that information you wanted."

"What information?"

"Jane Cunningham's address on Larchmont Avenue. You and Sadie made such a fuss yesterday, I figured you wanted to know."

"Yes . . . Of course!" I sat up in bed, excited.

As Jack's dream reminded me, questioning neighbors was a logical early step in any investigation; and with this address information, I could actually *do* something to help Jane. I could have a talk with her neighbors. Or in this case, one particular neighbor. If Sparky really had destroyed that angry man's garden, then he probably lived close by, possibly right next door.

I grabbed a pen and quickly scribbled down the address— on my forearm since I didn't have a pad handy. That's when I recalled something Bonnie mentioned last night. The shirt that nasty man was wearing.

"Seymour, do you remember that big farmers market and souvenir shop that used to be up on the highway back when we were kids?"

"The one with the three-dimensional sign with a wheelbarrow full of fruits and vegetables? Sure, Pen. You're talking about Slattery's General Store. I used to love their homemade goat's milk fudge."

"Do you know what happened to it?"

"The store burned down while you were living in New York City. I guess they decided not to rebuild."

"Could you tell me, by any chance, is there anyone with the name Slattery living near Jane's address on Larchmont?"

"Let me check . . . Yep, one Robert J. Slattery."

I added the second address to my forearm directory.

"Got to go," Seymour declared.

"Wait! I have one last question. Why in the world did you refer to Dr. Rubino as 'Randy' Randall?"

"It's the talk of the town, Pen."

"What talk? Who's talking? I never heard any talk. He's always been a perfect gentleman to me—and to all the women in this town, as far as I know."

"Oh, sure, when he's in Quindicott, he's the perfect family doc. Wears the halo of Saint Augustine. But scuttlebutt has it that our doctor of grace has a secret life."

"Scuttlebutt? You mean plain old gossip, don't you?"

"Gossip, scuttlebutt, or simple observation. Call it what you will. But Doc Rubino stopped his mail no less than three times in the past twelve months so he could go on different singles cruises—one south to the Bahamas, another north to Iceland. The big reveal was last month when he sailed to the Bay of Naples, the site of Caligula's pleasure palace in ancient times."

"I'm sure the Bay of Naples has more charm than some emperor's ruins."

"Yeah," Seymour replied slyly. "*Feminine* charms."

"Don't be silly," I countered. "Rubino is Italian. His family may come from that region. He was probably visiting relatives or sightseeing. Or maybe you and your gossipy friends are half right. Perhaps Dr. Rubino is looking for wife number two. The pool of single women of an appropriate age is small in Quindicott—"

"Tell me about it—"

"And I can see why Rubino would be reluctant to use a dating app. Can't you?"

Seymour snorted. "Yeah, I suppose it would be disturbing to see your daughter or sister swiping right on the Tinder profile of your trusted physician."

"I'm sure he's traveling single in a perfectly respectable bid to find someone special."

"Yet all he ever he comes home with is a really great tan. Nope, Pen. Mark my words. When Quindicott's own bronzed and toned Hippocrates is off our grid, he's a toga-party animal."

On that gossipy note (with classical references only a *Jeopardy!* champ would make), the mailman ended his call. I picked my glasses up off the floor and began my day—which started much sooner than expected. I'd hardly finished brewing my morning tea when the night bell rang downstairs.

"Pen, I just heard the bell," Sadie called from her room.

"I've got it," I cried over my shoulder as I hit the stairs.

What this could be I didn't know. We never got deliveries before business hours—then, in a heart-stopping moment, I remembered the security alarm had not been set.

Was it the QPD notifying us of a break-in?

I hurried into the bookstore—and felt a rush of relief.

At the front door, I spied a grinning woman with iron-gray hair in a single long braid flowing down her broad back. A huge knit bag hung over one arm, and a macramé cape was casually tossed over her shoulders to fend off the autumn chill.

Ms. Amber Breen, beloved author of the Kennel Club Mysteries, had arrived much earlier than expected. I unlocked the door, and the mistress of pet mysteries greeted me with a hearty bear hug.

"Penelope, it's wonderful to see you again! I don't think

we've met face-to-face since the Boston Book Fair two years ago."

I ushered her into the shop.

"The Finch Inn looks delightful, but their email said I couldn't check in until noon, so I came here instead. I hope I didn't wake you."

"No, our mailman already did that."

Sadie arrived, and the pair began to chat like old friends. I went upstairs and grabbed the tea to serve everyone. My yawning son followed me down with Jane Cunningham's dog romping beside him.

"Sparky needs to go for a walk," Spencer declared as he tried to leash the rambunctious canine.

"What a sweet creature!" Amber exclaimed, her face lighting up. "And Sparky is the perfect name for him. He seems so . . . electric."

Sparky loved the new attention. Tongue lolling, he rolled on his back.

"What a good dog," Amber cooed as she rubbed his tummy.

I introduced my son to Amber and explained her expertise. Now *his* face lit up.

"Do you know what kind of dog he is, Ms. Breen?" he asked.

Amber gave Sparky the once-over. "A Labrador is in there for certain. Those ears say a cocker spaniel mix, but Sparky is big, so he's probably part Labrador and part collie, which would make him a Lab collie."

"Lab collie? That's a funny name," Spencer said.

"That's how they name mixed-breed Labs. They just combine the breeds. It's not so odd, really. The German language combines words in the same sort of way."

Amber gave Sparky a peck on his forehead.

"And this guy's personality is friendly, and he's smart, too. Lab collies are the perfect mix for a family dog, though this one appears especially exuberant. Where did you find such a handsome fellow?"

"It's quite a story," I said, "and not a happy one, I'm afraid."

Amber gently took Sparky's leash from Spencer and easily linked it to the collar. "Well, Penelope, why don't we take this bright-eyed boy out for a walk, and you can tell me all about it?"

"What do you think, Spencer?"

"For sure. Let's go."

Amber handed the leash back to Spencer. "I'm not that familiar with your quaint little town. Where should we take our stroll?"

Spencer grinned. "That's easy! There's a dog walk in the town square!"

Arf-arf! Arf-arf!

Whether Sparky understood the words *dog walk* or simply reacted to Spencer's excited voice, Jane's Lab collie instantly bolted for the door. My son clung to the end of the dog's leash like an astronaut being towed by a rocket ship.

"Whoa, boy. Wait up!"

Amber tipped a glance my way. "Well, that's settled, isn't it?"

"Apparently so."

"Then off we go!"

CHAPTER 19

A Dog Walk in the Park

Without my dog my wallet would be full, my house
would be clean, but my heart would be empty.

—Anonymous

WHILE SADIE STAYED behind to open the shop, Spencer, Amber Breen, and I took Sparky on a stroll to Quindicott's premier green space. Along the way, I told Amber how we ended up taking care of someone else's dog.

When I finished the sad tale of finding Mrs. Cunningham in distress—thanks entirely to her dog—Amber Breen nodded knowingly.

"Sparky's heroics don't surprise me. Collies and labs are loyal, friendly, and smart. What Sparky did also speaks to his relationship with his mistress."

I considered her words as Amber and I watched my son romp with the dog.

"Sparky's a hero. Absolutely," I conceded. "But he's also a handful . . ." I told Amber about the battle with Bookmark inside our shop and noted, "Apparently it's not the first time he's caused trouble . . ."

Amber was shocked when I told her one of Jane Cunningham's neighbors had threatened to shoot Sparky for wrecking his garden.

"That's a monstrous threat!" she declared. "And I seriously doubt the veracity of the charge in the first place. No responsible dog owner would let their animal run loose and destroy property."

"I suppose Sparky could have escaped the house or slipped his leash."

"And what did he do the last time that happened?" Amber asked. "The dog ran to find help for his stricken mistress. And he couldn't have done better than finding you and your boy. No, I'm betting Sparky learned manners from Mrs. Cunningham."

"How can you be sure?"

"Let's find out!"

She slapped her knees and rose. With a wave, Amber summoned both boy and dog.

"Spencer, I want you to tell Sparky to sit."

My son seemed puzzled but shrugged and knelt down at Sparky's side.

"Sit down, boy. Come on, sit." He gently pushed on the dog's rump, but Sparky just slithered out from under his hand.

"He won't listen," Spencer said, frowning.

"Let's try it my way," Amber replied. "Stand right beside the dog, say his name in a firm voice—and for goodness' sakes, don't plead. Command! After you get his attention by saying his name, I want you to gently but firmly order him to sit."

Spencer tried it Amber's way. To my surprise, the dog reacted to my son's new, commanding tone and sat.

"Now, Spencer, tell Sparky he's a good boy. Give him

some positive reinforcement, and then we'll try some other commands."

For the next thirty minutes, the author introduced us to basic dog training—though, in this case, it was Spencer and I who were being schooled. Sparky (smart dog that he was) already knew most of the commands, and executed them perfectly.

Too soon the lessons were interrupted by the noisy bickering of a couple seated at the next bench. Both had pale skin and dark hair; the woman's was dead straight, while the man boasted an expert salon cut with a shock of brown curls on top and precise razor buzzing around the sides and back.

The way they were dressed caught my attention, as well. The man's spandex shorts and tank top, worn on such a cool morning, appeared calculated to show off his abundance of arm and leg tattoos. And the woman's tight black dress with a spiderweb collar, her dark nail polish, and her nose ring placed her as more Goth Boston than quiet, little Quindicott. Their ages were hard to guess, though they were far too old to be high school kids, despite their childish sniping.

Both held Cooper Family Bakery bags, and their visit to Linda and Milner's bakery appeared to be the subject of their squabbling.

"That clerk was so rude!"

"She didn't say anything, Gemma," the man countered. "How was she rude?"

"Come on, Troy. Didn't you see the way she looked at me?" the woman complained. "Like I said something ridiculously stupid."

"What did you say?"

"I asked if the oatmeal muffins were gluten-free."

Popping the lid off his coffee—and letting the wind carry it away—Troy snorted. "What do you expect! Small town. Small minds. Her mother and father were probably first cousins."

Overhearing them, Amber Breen made a grimacing face. "Do you know those two?"

"No," I replied in a lowered voice. "Our tourism has increased since we revitalized the town, but they don't sound like typical tourists. They could have drifted over from our local university, though they look too old to be undergrads. If I had to guess, I'd say they're remote workers from Boston or New York. We've seen an influx of them recently."

For a moment, I thought Amber was going to say something to the pair. But instead she looked kindly at me, Spencer, and Sparky, then slapped her knees again and said—

"Shall we go back to your store? I don't want Sadie to think we deserted her."

On the walk back, the dog seemed calmer. He trotted alongside Spencer, never once tugging on the leash as he had before. But the ultimate test came when we entered Buy the Book.

Bookmark was sprawled on the front counter, taking in the sunlight shining through the display window.

When the cat spied the dog, Bookmark's hackles rose, and her tail puffed to three times its size. On her tiptoes, the cat curled into a perfect marmalade-striped crescent moon.

"Meeeerrrowww!" she howled in bloodcurdling outrage.

Sparky's haunches tensed. The rocket ship appeared ready to launch until my son firmly declared—

"Sparky! No!"

The dog froze. Then he looked up at Spencer, his expression pensive.

"Stay!" Spencer commanded.

And Sparky did. He sat obediently by my son's side as Bookmark bounded away, heading in the direction of her hidey-hole.

As Spencer praised the dog, Aunt Sadie sighed in relief—and astonishment. "That was a miracle!"

No, I thought, *more like a revelation.*

I faced Amber. "You're absolutely right. Sparky's too well trained to destroy property. Now I'd like to ask another favor. An important one."

"Of course, Penelope. Anything."

"Would it be possible for you to know, by sight, whether a dog damaged a garden—vegetable or flower, I'm not sure which—versus destruction done by a deer, a rabbit, a gopher, or something similar?"

Amber smiled. "I'm not entirely sure. But I'd be happy to examine this mysterious garden and give you my opinion. Do you have a clue where it is?"

I lifted the sleeve of my jacket enough to expose the scribbled addresses.

"Look at that!" Amber declared, eyes wide. "It appears you have the answer up your sleeve."

CHAPTER 20

In the Garden

Good fences make good neighbors.

—Robert Frost, "Mending Wall"

"THIS STRETCH OF road is nicknamed Old Larchmont," I told my passenger. "Some of the oldest houses in the area are in this neighborhood."

We'd just crested the hill and passed a stand of the high conifer trees that gave Larchmont Avenue its name. The larch trees were already displaying their first traces of brown, signaling winter was coming, though the expansive lawns surrounding the large nineteenth-century homes were still lushly verdant.

"These old homes are stunning," Amber Breen marveled. "Have most of them been restored?"

"*Maintained*, I'd say. A lot of these houses have been in the same families for generations."

"Goodness! What's the story behind that spooky-looking place?"

I knew exactly what house she was talking about. "That's the home of our mailman, Seymour Tarnish."

"It could use a little maintenance," she said tactfully.

"Believe it or not, the whole *Addams Family* ambience is the aesthetic preference of its owner."

"Really? It's intentionally offbeat, then?"

"That's right."

"Hmm." Amber looked at the place with new eyes. "I'd love to meet this fellow. You say he's a mailman?"

How a humble mailman ended up living in the most affluent neighborhood in Quindicott was a story in itself, and I promised to share it with Amber Breen, but not today.

Right now we were on another mission—at the other end of Larchmont, where the homes, though still lavish, were of a more modern design.

I rechecked the address on my forearm. Finally, I spied one address and then another. The Slattery residence bordered an overgrown meadow. Next to it, Jane Cunningham's expansive home was within sight of the junction to Briar Patch Road, where the poor woman had been shot.

I stopped in front of Jane's sprawling two-story yellow brick residence, its gabled roof crowned by tall chimneys on either end. The elaborate structure featured an enclosed white-columned porch topped by a second-floor balcony on one side, and an attached two-story garage on the other. The house itself was fronted by four gigantic conifer trees and beautifully landscaped with manicured shrubbery.

"We could break the code of mystery novelists and knock on either door," Amber said. "But my inner Nancy Drew tells me we should snoop around first."

"Then you, I, and Nancy are all on the same page, pun intended."

I'll join you three dames to make it a quartet, Jack Shepard declared, speaking for the first time that day. *Sniffing around was my actual business, after all.*

I'm glad you're here, Jack. You're better than a blood-hound, and you don't need a leash.

Yeah, and I don't feel the need to mark telephone poles or fire hydrants, either.

I bit my cheek to keep from laughing, and realized Amber was staring at me.

"Pen?" she said. "Didn't you hear me?"

"I'm sorry. Did you say something?"

"I just asked—shall we go?"

"Oh! Of course!"

We exited the car into a deserted street. The air seemed cooler on the hill, and the wind came in chilly blasts—the kind that pushed dense clouds in from the Atlantic, darkening morning sunlight into the gloom of mock twilight with unsettling speed.

"Sparky was blamed for wrecking a neighbor's garden, which resulted in a death threat. The man who made the threat wore a Slattery's General Store shirt. And Mr. Robert Slattery happens to live right over there. The connection could be a coincidence, but maybe not . . ."

"Let's find out."

Amber and I quickly approached the two-story Victorian, an imposing old house constructed entirely of wood and painted maritime blue.

The front of the house was protected by a wrought iron fence overgrown with ivy. The front gate was locked, but free of growth. Through the rusty bars, we got a better look at the large house and the century-old oak tree towering over it. High among the branches—higher than the house itself—I spied a rickety-roofed tree house painted the same azure hue as the Victorian.

"All I see is that Tarzan tree house," Amber said.

"I see it, too. The tree is behind the house. That's likely where the garden is located, but Sparky would have had a tough time getting past this iron fence to get to it."

Amber pointed to the unkempt meadow that bordered the Victorian. The area was surrounded by a rotting wooden fence.

"A dog on the loose wouldn't even try to get to that house," she insisted. "Any canine worth its salt would be through that fence and frolicking in that meadow."

Unless old Sparky was chasing the Slattery's cat, Jack cracked. *I'll bet that mutt could leap over that fence in a single bound if it meant catching a feline.*

I thought of the incident with Bookmark and silently agreed, though I suggested a less extreme theory to Amber—

"You know, there might be a way onto this property from the meadow. Sparky may have found a way in from the field."

By silent agreement, Amber and I slipped between the horizontal fence posts and entered the overgrown field. Though blades of grass (up to our knees) dominated the landscape, a few poisonous plants had also taken root.

"Careful," Amber warned. "That tangle of weeds over there is poison ivy—and there's another patch."

As we negotiated the leafy minefield, we discovered my theory about the fence was correct. The sturdy wrought iron bars only fronted the property. The fence that bordered the meadow was mere chicken wire strung along a series of wooden posts.

Still, we couldn't see much beyond the wire because a thick screen of bushes masked the property. Doggedly (excuse the pun), we followed that fence until we found a section that had been smashed down and one of the support poles snapped in two.

"Would a dog do this?" I asked

"I doubt it," Amber replied. "A dog is more likely to jump over or dig under than knock down. They're not linebackers, and it would take a bigger dog than Sparky to do this."

Coincidentally or not, the fence was wrecked at a narrow break in the green screen of bushes. Together, Amber and I peeked through the opening.

"I think we found your elusive garden," Amber whispered.

The entire backyard between the house and the thick trunk of the massive oak had been landscaped into a secret garden paradise. A line of snow-white trellises bordered the edges. Ornate stone walkways wound through the ranks of manicured bushes, small fruit trees, and flowering plants. In the center of it all, a stone fountain bubbled beside a marble bench.

"Those Lemon Queens just bloomed." Amber gestured toward the tall sunflowers waving in the cool breeze. "I see goldenrod, too. And asters. And look—rosebushes. They're not in bloom now, of course, but . . ."

She paused for a full minute.

"I'm in awe," Amber declared. "This garden is a work of organic art, a showcase of the seasons. It appears to be landscaped so that something is in bloom no matter what time of year it is. Here, for instance . . ."

While Amber went on about the particulars of each plant and shrub, I took in the big picture. It didn't take long for me to spot something that was definitely not right in this Edenic place.

Somebody brought a bull in there, Jack said. *Or maybe a bulldozer.*

But not a bulldog! I doubt very much any four-legged friend would have done this much damage.

"Amber," I said, interrupting her marveling over the garden, "look over there, that area under the big oak. The place looks ravaged . . ."

Amber and I were so focused on our little investigation, neither of us paused to consider that we were entering private property. Without a glance toward the house or a single thought about its occupant, we moved across the broken fence into the private garden.

The temperature seemed to drop the moment we crossed the border. The constantly spraying fountain increased the humidity level, as well.

Clad only in a light jacket, I suppressed a chill as we walked along the stone path toward the massive oak tree. Flowers and bushes around the trunk had been mangled. What looked like blueberry bushes were flattened, sunflower stalks were broken, and other plants I couldn't identify seemed to have been trampled.

"Those poor blueberries and these ground orchids are completely ruined," Amber noted. "That Cassandra bush is hurting, and so is the purple catmint."

"A dog couldn't have done all this, could it?" I asked.

"Certainly not. Dogs dig. But the ground around here hasn't been disturbed. Only the plants are damaged. Trampled, really."

"Then Sparky is innocent!"

Amber nodded. "Perry Mason could not have stated it more succinctly."

That's when I heard it, a sharp metallic click that cut right through the white noise of the bubbling fountain. Amber heard it, too.

"Freeze, both of you," ordered a gruff voice somewhere behind us.

Amber and I exchanged worried glances, and together we turned around.

With simultaneous gasps, we found ourselves staring down the business end of a double-barreled shotgun!

CHAPTER 21

Gun Control

I have a very strict gun control policy: If there's a gun around, I want to be in control of it.

—Clint Eastwood

LISTEN TO MY every word, Jack commanded.

I stared at the twin gun barrels. *My attention is undivided.*

You are not to take one step in any direction. Do not blink or even breathe. Just slowly reach for the sky. And tell your pet-loving pal to do the same.

"Amber," I whispered, "raise your hands."

Good, Jack said as we both followed the ghost's advice. *What next, Jack?*

Keep reaching, doll, and flash this yahoo a friendly smile.

I studied the armed man—his disheveled brown hair, his unshaven face—but most of all the weapon he clutched in his hand.

There's absolutely nothing in this situation to smile about, Jack!

I know, honey. Try to think of it as making the boss happy, because the scattergun he's holding makes him the boss.

The sour smell of alcohol sweat wafted off the man. In the humid confines of the shaded garden, it easily overpowered the scent of the vegetation around us.

I think he's been drinking, I told the ghost.

Blotto he is, and dangerous, too, Jack warned.

So, I did what the PI suggested. Hands still raised, I smiled wider than a Halloween pumpkin.

"Why are you here?" The man's eyes shifted from Amber to me and back again. "What are you up to on my property?"

He sounded desperate and more fearful than angry.

"I'm sorry," Amber said. "My name is—"

As she spoke, the author inadvertently lowered her hands and stepped forward. The man jumped back and gestured with his shotgun.

"Stay back! Stay back, I say!"

Amber froze midstep and raised her hands again.

"Who are you people?"

Talk him down, Penny, Jack advised. *But keep it gentle, stay frozen, and don't stop reaching for the sky.*

"Hi, my name is Penelope," I said, forcing a tone as desperately cheerful as a beauty pageant contestant pleading for world peace. "And this is Amber. And you're Robert Slattery, right?"

He replied with an uncertain nod, and I thought fast—

"Amber and I are . . . canvassing the neighborhood in connection with a . . . uh, string of vandalism. We were wondering—"

"Are you one of them?" he demanded, addressing me specifically. "Why are you here in the daytime?"

"I'm not one of . . . well, anybody. I run the bookstore on Cranberry Street. Some of your neighbors complained about vandalism. We heard that you suffered damage—"

"In my wife's garden," he said, nodding again. "I try to keep the garden growing, but I don't have her gift. And then this happened."

His head jerked toward the wrecked patch.

"When did you notice the damage?" I asked.

The armed man shook his head, as if he didn't understand the question or he'd lost his train of thought altogether.

"Maybe I could speak with your wife?" I pressed. "It's her garden, you said? Perhaps—"

"No one speaks to Isobel! No one. You can't. No one can."

He stepped closer with the shotgun still aimed at my heart. "What are you doing here?"

Okay, Penny, listen to me. Sweet isn't working. Time for Plan B.

What's Plan B?

You have to disarm him—

What?!

He's juiced to the gills, and I doubt this lug has his head calibrated on the best of days.

How on earth can I disarm a drunk?

Say the word, and I'll distract him. When he looks away, you grab the barrel and point it at the sky. And remember to duck. He's got only two shells. Make sure the buckshot hits that tree house and not you or your four-legged-loving friend.

Or I could try kung fu, or maybe the Force. Come on, get serious, Jack! Do I look like someone who could disarm a shotgun-toting drunk?

You got a point, Penny. Try waltzing out, then. Nice and slow. . . . .

"Well," I said out loud, my stupid Joker grin still in place, "I think we'll be running along now. You're obviously busy doing . . . stuff. We'll just leave you to it."

Amber's head rocked up and down like a bobblehead doll's. Now all we had to do was step around the man with the gun and cross the expansive garden to the opening in the fence, and then struggle through the brush with one eye on the gunman at all times.

Doable, right?

Hands still held high, I wiggled my numbing fingers. The man's eyes widened in alarm. I tensed, ready to move if I had to.

Then a stern yet familiar voice interrupted us.

"That's enough, Robert. Lower that weapon right now."

The gunman blinked, and his aim wavered.

"Pointing a gun at people isn't going to bring Isobel back," Dr. Randall Rubino continued. The doctor stepped over the broken fence, pushed through the break in the bushes, and entered the garden.

"I came over as soon as I got your message, Robert. I'm sorry I'm late, but I was in surgery all night. You should have followed my instructions and called Dr. Isaacs in Millstone. He would have phoned in a prescription."

"I don't want pills, Doc. I want these people to leave. But they won't. They keep coming back. Every night—"

The doctor cautiously approached Robert Slattery until they stood toe to toe.

"You shouldn't be drinking, Robert. Alcohol doesn't mix well with the antidepressants."

Without hesitation, Rubino yanked the shotgun away from Slattery and cracked it open.

"It's not even loaded. What were you trying to do?"

"I wanted to scare them, Doc. I want them out of here. This was her special place. I don't want anyone else here."

Rubino put his hand on the man's sagging shoulders; then he locked his eyes with mine.

"Go out the way you came. I'll meet you in front," he murmured.

Amber and I scurried across the garden and over the trampled fence in a flash. We didn't speak much as we circled the property—and dodged the poison ivy.

By the time we got to the front of the old Victorian, Dr. Rubino was waiting for us at the now open gate, the shotgun still tucked under one arm.

"Are you both okay?"

To my surprise, Amber laughed—nervously, but she laughed.

"That wasn't the first time I've had a gun pointed at me. When your mission is to rescue abused animals, sometimes you have to face down the abusers."

"Well, Robert Slattery is no abuser," Rubino replied.

I cleared my throat. "Doctor, I was wondering, given Robert's last name, is he connected in any way to the old Slattery's General Store?"

"Same family. Robert is the only one left now. The general store was gone before I arrived in Quindicott, but Robert told me all about it, showed me photos."

"I remember it fondly," I said. "When I was a little girl, it was a treat to go to the general store."

"Did it close?" Amber asked.

"It burned to the ground," Rubino said. "That was probably a decade ago. Robert told me his family was heartbroken when they lost the place. The insurance didn't cover all their losses. They couldn't afford to rebuild, and they couldn't secure a loan, so the family sold the land to a developer."

"Is that why he goes around pointing a shotgun at people?" Amber asked.

Rubino sighed. "Robert is a man lost in grief so deep, he can't find his way back."

"He mentioned his wife," I prompted.

"Isobel. She died a few months ago, after a long fight with cancer. Robert blames himself—survivor's guilt, I think. But he has nothing to feel guilty about. I treated Isobel, and there was no way to save her. As I said, Robert Slattery is a disturbed and lonely man. All he has is that house, his wife's garden, and sad memories. He suffers from depression, and lately he's been showing signs of paranoia."

"I hate to bring this up, but Mr. Slattery *did* threaten to shoot Mrs. Cunningham's dog for wrecking his garden. Do you think—"

"That Robert shot Jane?" He shook his head. "That's impossible. This is the only gun he owns, and it's an antique that hangs over his mantel. Jane wasn't hit with buckshot, anyway. Her wound was the result of a single small-caliber round—a twenty-two caliber actually."

Despite his exhaustion, I detected professional pride in Rubino's next words. "I know because I was asked to assist the local surgeon. I have more experience with gunshot wounds than other doctors around here."

"What's Jane's situation?"

"The gunshot is not fatal. The bullet lodged in a rib, which mitigated the internal damage."

I remembered what the doctor had said the day before. That the short range of a small-caliber round meant the shooter likely *saw* his target.

"Then you think . . ."

"The person who shot Jane was close—likely near enough to know their round hit a human being. It *could* have been an accident, of course, a stray bullet from a hunter, but . . ." His words trailed off, and I finished for him—

"You think someone may have targeted Jane."

Rubino gave the slightest of nods, then quickly qualified his position. "If she was targeted, I have no proof of it. Chief Ciders made that clear enough when I spoke with him this morning. Until convinced otherwise, he's sticking to his hunting-accident theory."

"Let's hope Jane wakes up and tells us what really happened."

Rubino frowned. "That's what Ciders said. But Jane's still unconscious from her head injury—"

"Is that bad?"

"It's not good. But her vitals are strong, and we're hopeful she'll come around."

I sensed another shoe was waiting for its pratfall, and I was right.

"The thing is, if and when she does come around, Jane is likely to suffer short-term memory loss due to head trauma."

"You mean—"

"I mean Jane herself may not be able to give us many answers. It's a shame. Even if she did see the person who shot her, it's doubtful she'll remember."

CHAPTER 22

Out to Lunch

Well . . . there's nothing more to be done here. What about some lunch?

—Agatha Christie, *The Secret Adversary*

DR. RUBINO SEEMED willing to continue our conversation, until he noticed Robert Slattery staring at us from his front window. That was when he suggested we depart.

Given our all-too-recent memory of Slattery's double-barreled greeting, Amber and I bade the good doctor a quick farewell. Then we climbed back into my car, and I drove us out of Larchmont.

On the way, I noticed another of Jane's neighbors staring daggers at us from one of the arched front windows of her enormous, sprawling house. Though it took a moment to remember the woman's name, I recognized her as Ella Pruett, a Buy the Book customer and member of the Paw-some Pals—one of the more prickly ones, as I recalled.

After passing her house, I pulled over and considered making a U-turn to speak with her but thought better of it when I noticed something in my side mirror—a taxicab pulling into her driveway.

"Anything wrong, Pen?" Amber asked.

"No, I was just considering whether to visit another of Jane's neighbors."

But I was doing more than that. I was spying, and Amber knew it. True to her nature, she did the same!

From the car mirrors, we both watched as a man in his fifties, wearing jeans and a padded New York Yankees baseball jacket, climbed out of the taxicab. He had a lean build with a chiseled chin and a thick mop of Kennedyesque hair that had whitened to the color of dirty snow.

The cabdriver retrieved a Pullman suitcase from the trunk, and the man carried it up Ella's driveway. When she opened the front door and he walked right in, I assumed he was a relative arriving for a visit, and I said as much to Amber.

"Either that or a gentleman caller," she observed. "Are we turning around?"

"No," I said, and continued ahead.

I didn't want to intrude on Ella's welcoming her guest or friend or whoever he was. And since she was a member of the Paw-some Pals, I knew I'd be seeing her again soon enough.

Besides, it was already past noon, and I didn't wish to tax our guest author's patience any further. It was time I delivered Amber Breen to the Finch Inn.

TURNING DOWN THE long, scenic drive that led to Fiona and Barney Finch's grand Victorian bed-and-breakfast always cheered me up. The Finch Inn was a jewel of a Queen Anne, its meticulously restored facade stunningly reflected in "the Pond," as we called it, a body of water the size of a small lake, which was really a tidal estuary fed by a meandering stream that led through rustic wooded grounds to a breathtaking Atlantic beach.

After settling Amber into her lovely room, I treated her to a sumptuous lunch at Fiona's pride and joy, Chez Finch, the restaurant attached to the inn, where the doting innkeeper stopped by our table several times to chat—and make sure every bite of the chef's lauded coq au vin and sip of her personally selected pinot noir exceeded our expectations.

"I must say, Penelope, we had quite a morning," Amber remarked as we ate. "For a small town, Quindicott certainly has an unusual amount of drama."

Amber's pointed observation surprised me, especially considering her mystery-writing profession. Jack's response surprised me, too, given the ghost's typical attitude about the "dullness" of our little-town life—

Drama? he cracked. *Naw, Cornpone-cott's got no drama, unless you count trying to catch an attempted murderer who's still on the loose.*

I repeated a less sarcastic version of Jack's comeback to Amber, but the author was quick to dismiss the notion.

"I've found that mysteries, conundrums, and even a conspiracy or two happen frequently in fiction, but real life is seldom so interesting."

"That may be true," I countered (electing *not* to bring up the out-to-lunch business of the ghost in my head). "But you have to admit our trip today was rather *interesting*."

The author and I both laughed.

"I am sorry that we had no luck finding your shooter," Amber said sincerely. "But we did clear Sparky of any doggy wrongdoing, so our little sleuthing adventure accomplished something." Then Amber sighed. "I'm just relieved to know that poor grief-stricken man is getting help, and he wasn't involved in any violence."

"Yes," I said, "but if Mr. Slattery isn't to blame, who is?"

"When firearms are involved, accidents do happen," Amber pointed out. "Isn't that what your town's chief of police thinks?"

"Yes," I said, and left it at that for two reasons: One, I didn't wish to argue any further with our guest, and two, lunch was nearly over.

As Amber contentedly finished her chocolate mousse, she politely turned down my invitation to dinner, opting to turn in early instead. I didn't blame her. After she'd driven all night, held an impromptu dog-training class with my son, and survived a shotgun being shoved in her face, I respected the author's decision to spend a quiet evening resting or leisurely exploring the inn's scenic grounds.

"If you get lonely, just visit the inn's community room," I suggested. "Fiona loves to chat over tea and pastries with guests, and Barney often conducts parlor games."

"Will do, Penelope. I'll see you tomorrow." She shook my hand. "And never fear. I take my job as a contest judge quite seriously. I shall be bright-eyed and bushy-tailed for your Pet Parade!"

Oh, no, I thought, *the Pet Parade!*

I'd almost forgotten about this afternoon's parade-planning session with Professor Parker—J. Brainert Parker, to be precise. The parade was scheduled to begin and end at his Movie Town Theater on Cranberry Street. Though Brainert ran the place in partnership with his university, he was its primary manager and caretaker, and there couldn't have been a more dedicated one. Restoring our town's broken-down old movie palace to its former glory had been Brainert's lifelong passion, and I admired my old friend for his fortitude in achieving that dream.

During the festivities tomorrow, his theater would welcome the marchers, and host the awarding of pet prizes by our guest of honor (Amber Breen) along with a designated representative from the Paw-some Pals reading group.

Jane Cunningham had been slated to co-judge contestants with Amber, but that was impossible now. The Pals would have to name a substitute.

The thought of Jane missing the parade, and the reason why, sent my upbeat mood into the pits.

Jack was right. Whoever had put Jane in the hospital—whether by accident or design—was still walking around scot-free. The very idea made me more than sad. It made me angry.

I wanted very much to find Jane's shooter, but my strongest lead had been a dead end. What more could I do?

After checking the time, I headed for my parked car.

Our town's Pet Week celebration would soon be underway, and if I didn't get a move on, I was going to be late for the final planning meeting.

After texting a hasty "On my way!" message to Brainert, I quickened my steps, suddenly feeling like one of his students. If there was one thing our fastidious professor didn't abide, it was tardiness!

CHAPTER 23

Event Planning

When it's something you can't ever join but only watch, then it's a parade.

—Dean Koontz, *Darkness Under the Sun*

AS I PEELED out of the inn's parking lot, the ghost came back to life.

What's the hurry, honey? Got a new lead?

"What I've got is a meeting . . ." I filled Jack in on the details.

Pet Parade? he griped. *What in the Sam Hill is a Pet Parade? Hey, wait a second. Hold the phone!* Suddenly, the ghost's tone changed from annoyed specter to excited little boy. *Is it anything like that vaudeville show with poodles twirling in tutus, a momma bear and a poppa bear dancing a foxtrot, and tuxedo-clad monkeys playing baby musical instruments?*

I laughed. "Quit kidding, Jack."

I'm not.

"Come on," I said. "What you just described sounds more like a fever dream than a vaudeville act."

Shows what you know and what you don't. I saw that very show on Forty-second Street. Back in the twenties, when I was a kid, animal acts were the berries. Hell, the topliner at the Bijou was a show called Swain's Rats and Cats. *As a scrapper, I had to scrape together pennies to see it. You had to have a whole nickel for that ticket.*

"Well, our Pet Parade won't be as exciting as all that. Just a neighborly get-together where people will show off their animal friends."

Jack's grunt of disappointment chilled my car's interior. *Sounds like another day in dullsville. Guess I'll have to focus on the case.*

"Case? What case? There is no case."

Of course there is. I thought you were angry about what happened to that poor dame with the dog. Where's your sense of justice, Penny? Did the winey lunch go to your head?

"No, I still feel awful, but . . . Look, Jack, I'm fresh out of leads. And you heard Amber. She's a professional crime writer, and even she thinks what happened to Jane was an accident."

Then you no longer see eye to eye with Dr. Rube?

"The man's name is Rubino! And you're forgetting what he said back at Robert Slattery's place. Even if he believes someone targeted Jane, he has no proof of it."

So let's go find some!

"Where? How? There are no more leads, Jack, and I'm late for my meeting!"

The ghost spoke no more after my impatient outburst, but his supernatural chill lingered until I arrived at Buy the Book. I was practically shivering by the time I left the car!

"Come on, Jack, I know you're annoyed. And I'm sorry

for temporarily abandoning the case. But will you please tone down the arctic blast?"

Jack gave no reply, though the temperature around me did grow warmer as I rushed into my shop.

Thank you, I told the ghost. *I promise we'll talk later* . . .

Though I had minutes to spare, Brainert was early (no surprise!), and he brought Seymour Tarnish along (also no surprise). The two bickering buddies acted like frenemies on the surface, but underneath, they were closer than brothers-in-arms. In all the years I'd known them, there was never a time when they didn't have each other's backs—and mine.

"The Buy the Book event planner is in the building!" I announced as I hurried toward the register.

The slender professor was dressed casually this afternoon, that is, casually for Brainert, which meant he wasn't wearing a three-piece suit. Instead, his open-necked buttoned-down shirt, navy blazer, knife-creased khakis, and mirror-shined leather loafers told me his classes were over for the day.

I was happy to see him, but I frowned when I noticed the long line of customers and realized he was distracting my aunt from her checkout duties. His singular focus appeared to be explaining some unwieldy, hand-drawn diagram.

"Professor Parker, please step out of line and head to our back office," I firmly directed. "You, too, Seymour. Let Sadie and me help these customers, and I'll be with you shortly."

"Thank you," Sadie said gratefully.

"No," I whispered. "Thank *you* for humoring him!"

Once I'd helped my aunt get the checkout under control, I joined Brainert in our office space—really a corner of the stockroom in which we'd set up a desk, a computer, and file cabinets.

Seymour was there, too, of course, his postal uniform exchanged for worn blue jeans, black high-tops, and his favorite *Star Trek* T-shirt (*Beam me up, Scotty! There is no intelligent life here!*).

"I know you're enthusiastic about your diagram," I told Brainert, "but you shouldn't bother my aunt anymore with that stuff. She's going to have her hands full dealing with the Paw-some Pals—a job that's going to be even more complicated with their chairperson in the hospital. I don't know yet who'll be taking over for Jane Cunningham tomorrow, but we'll find out soon enough."

After I gave the boys an update on Jane's condition, Brainert unfolded his precious diagram.

"As you can see, I've divided the interior of the Movie Town into sections to keep order. There will be a velvet rope running down the center aisle to separate the contestants: dogs and their people on the right, and cats and cat people on the left—"

Seymour interrupted. "Hey, what about parrot people? And hamster people? And bunny people? Not to mention that guy Jeremy, who's been walking around Broad Street with a snake on his shoulders. You just *know* he's going to show up."

The professor pointed to a section of his map. "Specialty animals have accommodations in the rear. And *all* the seats inside of those designated pet zones will be covered with waterproof plastic—"

"Really?" I interrupted. "Are you certain that's necessary? I'm sure Quindicott's pets are housebroken."

He sniffed. "After last weekend's Marvel Movie Marathon, I'm not convinced Quindicott's *teenagers* are housebroken."

Seymour folded his arms. "And who is going to be the enforcer of your strict seating assignments?"

"Why, *you* are of course."

"Me? Why me?"

"You're big, you have a loud voice, and people fear you."

Seymour blinked. "Why would they fear me?"

"It's your profession. They're perpetually afraid you'll go postal. Face it, Tarnish," Brainert said, pointing to Seymour's *Beam me up, Scotty!* T-shirt. "You're halfway there already."

Seymour's face flushed, and he balled his fists.

"Listen up, Brainpan. I don't care what you've heard. This mail carrier does not have a temper! You got it?"

Good heavens, I thought. *Jack, are you there? I could use your help cooling things off, after all!*

CHAPTER 24

Puppy Dogs' Tails

It is one of the blessings of old friends that you can afford to be stupid with them.

—Ralph Waldo Emerson, *Emerson in His Journals*

THE GHOST FAILED to answer my request for an instant ice age to cool off my friends, but my son's sudden appearance in the stockroom doorway, with Sparky by his side, managed to provide a much-needed distraction.

"Hey, Mom, I taught Sparky a whole bunch of tricks!" Spencer shook the previously full box of doggy treats; it now sounded half empty. "Or maybe he knew them already and he taught me. Anyway, I want to march with Sparky in the Pet Parade tomorrow."

It was Seymour who sniffed this time. "Not in that dog's current condition, you're not."

"What's wrong with him?"

"Take a good look, kid. Sparky's feet are filthy, and his nails are caked with grass. And if you take a deep breath, you'll realize Sparky is a little ripe."

"Ripe?"

"Face it, buddy. This dog needs a bath."

My son frowned. "How am I going to give Sparky a bath?"

"Well, seeing as you don't have a backyard with a hose like some kid on a *Saturday Evening Post* cover, I'd put a little baby shampoo in the bathtub, drop the pooch in, lather him up, and rinse him with a bathtub sprayer—"

"We don't have a bath sprayer," Spencer said with an anxious frown.

"Hey, no problem. You can buy a rubber one that attaches to your faucet. Bud Napp stocks them at his hardware store. I bought one a couple of weeks ago—"

"And I can guess why," Brainert interrupted. "To drown that chattering bird of yours once and for all?"

"No, Brainiac. Waldo washes himself like a good bird. I bought the shower hose because I needed to clean my collection of monster statues. I'd been neglecting them, you see. It got so bad that cobwebs had formed between Frankenstein's outstretched arms! And there was so much dust on my Shin Godzilla, you could hardly see its atomic red markings. So, I put them all in the bathtub, soaked them down with the hose, and let them air-dry."

"Mom, can we get a shower hose?"

I'd gotten a whiff of the dog and agreed with Seymour. After promising to buy the hose, I sent Spencer upstairs to give Sparky "one can of food and one can only!"

"He's a hungry dog, Mom."

"He can have kibble later tonight. I can see you've already given him plenty of doggy treats. You don't want to return a fat dog to Mrs. Cunningham, do you?"

With the boy and the dog on their way upstairs, Brainert and I discussed a few details that had slipped the busy professor's mind. Most likely he'd been distracted by his quest for pet-poo protection, but his plan had glaring oversights.

I began on a positive note, applauding his thoughtfulness for providing pet water dispensers inside the theater.

"I had no choice," he said. "I certainly don't want animals drinking out of the human fountains!"

That was when I gently reminded him that a Buy the Book table should have been included in the lobby plan, so fans could purchase their favorite pet mysteries, including titles in Amber Breen's backlist.

Brainert quickly made the adjustment, though it forced him to scrap his plan to line up litter boxes like miniature porta-potties at a construction site.

"What were you going to do for the dogs," Seymour grumbled, "cover the rug with print editions of the *Quindicott Bulletin*?"

"That's not a bad idea," Brainert returned, "given that rag's penchant for peddling petty town gossip as local *news*."

When we finally finished our discussion, Brainert and Seymour began some serious book browsing, and Bonnie arrived for her evening shift—on the back of a motorcycle. The driver, a young man in jeans and a windbreaker, yanked off his helmet to reveal a lion's mane of golden hair pulled into a loose ponytail. He gave her a sweet smile and kissed her goodbye.

"Who was that?" I asked.

"Jeremy," she said dreamily. "He's such an amazing guy . . ."

As she helped me finish setting up the event space and store, including stocking the endcaps with an array of our theme-week pet mysteries, she filled me in on how cool Jeremy was. How he'd traveled all over the world. How he'd come to our area to crew on a sailboat with friends. And how she had met him at a bar on Broad Street.

"Broad Street," I repeated, remembering Seymour's comment. "Jeremy wouldn't happen to own a snake, would he?"

"Yeah. A boa. How did you know?"

"A postal birdie told me."

When we'd finished setting everything up perfectly, I went upstairs to check on Spencer before heading off to Bud Napp's hardware store on a quest for a shower hose.

I found my son in the kitchen, doing his homework at the table, Sparky at his feet, when I noticed some odd items scattered on the tabletop.

"Spencer, what are these?"

"Oh, that's the stuff that fell out of Mrs. Cunningham's pocket when we found her," he said.

I looked more closely at the collection. A Bic pen. A set of keys (more than a dozen) on a standard key ring. Honey lip gloss. A *second* set of keys, only two of them, both attached to a knight made of mock-pearl hard plastic. And a mini flashlight emblazoned with a strange-looking coat of arms.

I saw no name, address, or other identification on either set of keys. The large set most likely belonged to Jane. That made logical sense to me. She owned a lot of properties, hence a lot of keys. But the two keys attached to the plastic knight puzzled me.

Jane was outspoken about her lack of interest in fantasy and fairy tales, and it didn't seem like the sort of tchotchke she would carry around. Odder still, the knight and the odd coat-of-arms designs struck me as familiar, but I couldn't quite place them.

"And why two sets of keys?" I mused aloud.

Spencer grinned. "If you're wondering, you can always go to Mrs. Cunningham's house and test each key."

"Ha-ha. Very funny."

Very smart, you mean. It was the first time I'd heard from my PI spirit since we'd quarreled in the car.

If I didn't know better, Jack, I'd say you were a bad influence on my son, but—

Hey, the kid takes after his mom, smart as a whip and tough as seasoned leather.

That's generous of you to say, I told the ghost. *But even if comparing me to upholstery was the least bit flattering, it would still get you nowhere. I know what that one-track detective mind of yours is thinking. Let's hope we find out what happened to Jane before it comes down to breaking and entering—*

Entering, Penny. We already have the keys, so we don't have to break down the door. I promise I won't ask you to break anything. Scout's honor.

I don't know, Jack. Invading someone's home is not something I'm comfortable with.

You don't have to be. Because I am.

Let's not argue, I said, but the ghost was undaunted.

What have you got to do that's more important than catching Jane Cunningham's shooter?

I have to help out my son, okay? But . . . come to think of it, I may be able to help you out, too.

What do you mean?

Spencer wants to give Sparky a bath. To do that, we need a shower hose—and you're the one who advised me to talk to neighbors, right?

What does a shower hose have to do with—

Bud Napp has run our local hardware store for years, and he's the head of the Quibblers—you know, our Quindi-cott Business Owners' Association?

You mean, the bickering bozos? Those yahoos always give me a headache—and I don't even have a head.

Just listen. Bud was good friends with Jane's late husband. I don't know how well he kept up his friendship with Jane, but he might be worth talking to.

Jack agreed. *Getting background is never a bad idea.*

Then don't disappear on me, and we might both hear something worth pursuing.

Fine, doll. Just don't lose track of that dame's keys.

The keys! Right . . .

Thinking fast, I took the lone banana in our fruit bowl and handed it to Spencer.

"We'll be eating dinner a little later tonight," I told my son, "so pour yourself some milk, make your favorite peanut butter and banana sandwich. Then put Mrs. Cunningham's stuff in this empty fruit bowl and leave it on the table. We'll get it back to her when she's better. Right now I've got to go."

"Where to, Mom?"

"Sparky needs a shower hose, doesn't he?"

CHAPTER 25

Bed, Bath, and Beyond Hearsay

Gossip goes on about every human being alive . . . and about all the dead that are alive enough to be remembered.

—Booth Tarkington, *The Magnificent Ambersons*

BUD NAPP GREETED me wearing oil-stained overalls and his official Napp Hardware baseball cap. From the look of his whiskered face, he hadn't shaved, and in place of his usually curmudgeonly smile, Bud's mood was somber.

A few decades ago, Bud had opened his Napp Hardware shop inside the town's original icehouse. Since then, he'd expanded the place into a cavernous store, packed to the brim with everything a person needed to build a house, fix a car, or throw a lawn party. Though Bud had renovated several years ago, adding neat new shelves and orderly aisles, it wasn't long before the new hardware store resembled the jumbled mess of the old one.

Despite the chaos, Bud seemed to know where to find everything. Because he was as sturdy as a fifty-gallon drum, as spry as an electric lawn mower, and sharper than one of its blades, you'd never guess Bud was pushing seventy. Recently, Bud had even broadened his business to include contracting, and he assembled work crews (for painting, repairs, etc.) as needed.

He'd expanded his world in other ways, too. After his wife had passed away, my aunt Sadie reached out to him, recommending books as a distraction from his grief—one book discussion led to another, then to shared lunch breaks, and long walks. Before they knew it, the two were officially dating. Neither of those two busy, independent business owners seemed interested in pursuing marriage, but they definitely had a *thing* (my aunt's description of their ongoing relationship).

So it was no surprise to discover that Sadie had already informed Bud of Jane Cunningham's situation.

"I was shocked to hear about poor Jane," he said. "It's a terrible thing to happen to such a good person. Does anyone know yet who pulled the trigger?"

"The chief still has no clue. He insists a stray bullet fired by a hunter is to blame, but the ballistics are all wrong, according to Dr. Rubino."

I related as much as I knew.

When I finished, Bud fell silent a moment. "Maybe we should call a Quibblers meeting."

I heard Jack curse in my head.

Stay cool, Jack, I warned him.

Unfortunately, he took me literally.

"Are you feeling that odd draft, Pen?" Bud asked.

"I don't feel anything! Nope, nothing at all!"

Knock it off, Jack. It's been decades since this place was an icehouse!

"Strange. I just put in new insulation—"

"Anyway, Bud, I don't think we should bother the Quibblers right now, given that we're about to begin—"

"Yes, I know. Pet Week." Bud rubbed his stubbled chin thoughtfully. "Tell you what. I'll send out an email alert to the members and ask them to report any questionable activities: hunters roaming around, kids target shooting, the sound of gunfire—that sort of thing.

Now we're talkin'! Jack exclaimed. *Tell the geezer he's got the right idea!*

"That's a brilliant thought, Bud."

"Don't know about that." Bud shrugged. "More like a wild card. But who knows? Maybe we can solve this ourselves."

"I hope so," I said. "We really do need to find out what happened for the safety of the community. And—"

"And we owe it to Jane," Bud finished for me.

"Sadie mentioned you were friends with her late husband. Have you seen Jane much since he died?"

"Oh, sure." He nodded. "You can't manage as many properties as Jane owns without regular visits to a hardware store."

"Jane actually manages her properties by herself?"

Bud laughed at my surprise. "Don't let her sweet-widow-lady facade fool you. Jane may not do the heavy lifting, but she oversees every detail of every property. I helped her convert her Larchmont Avenue house into rentable units after Carl died. She said it made her feel bad—all that space and no Carl. And my work crews do painting and repairs on her other properties, too, though always at a discount."

"Why is that?"

Bud shrugged again. "Let's just say I owe her a personal debt."

"Sounds like a large one. Won't you tell me? I'd like to know."

"I already told Sadie, so . . . I guess you'd hear about it one way or another. See, when my wife died . . . well, I didn't have a clue where to turn. My wife did the account books for our business. She did our taxes, kept us up to snuff with payroll regs, and made sure we ended every year in the black. My pal Carl Cunningham suggested I sit down with his wife, so I went to Jane's CPA office for advice. It was Jane herself who set things straight and showed me how to keep them straight—and she never charged me a nickel."

"She's hand's on, then?"

"You bet. When Carl died, she closed her CPA office and took over managing his rental properties full time—" Bud caught himself. "No, that timing's wrong. She did all that just before Carl passed. I remember now. Jane did that after Stan took off."

"Stan?"

"Carl's kid brother. Stan was"—Bud made finger quotes—"*property manager.* He was also major trouble. In high school, he'd been a peacock. Star baseball player, you know? Got a scholarship to college and expected to make a career in the majors. But he wasn't disciplined enough, and he got kicked out of school for partying too hard—alcohol, drugs, ugly complaints from young women. You get the picture? When he came back here, his brother tried to help him out, but Stan was far from grateful. Just became a slacker and a bitter barfly, nurturing the chip on his shoulder for the *raw deal* he got dealt. I wasn't sorry to see his back. I do believe Carl was happy to see Stan go, too."

Bud told me all about Stan's drunken behavior and a notorious scene he'd caused at the girlie bar on the highway, which had led to Chief Ciders banning him from the place. Finally, Bud told me the ugly story of how Stan had betrayed his brother's trust by stealing money from their business. After Carl caught Stan embezzling thousands from an expense account, Carl fired him. The pair had a falling-out after that, and Stan left for parts unknown.

This guy Stan sounds like a real Father O'Reilly, Jack cracked.

Before I could ask what that meant, Jack proclaimed—

I'll bet he'd take a shot at your dog-loving friend if he could make a five-spot out of it. Find out if the creep is still lurking around.

I cleared my throat—and head—and asked Bud, "So . . . Stan never came back after that?"

"Not even for his older brother's funeral." Bud sighed. "He's out of the picture for good, I'd say."

"What else can you tell me about the Cunningham family? Does Jane have any close relatives nearby?"

"No, none. Her parents passed away long ago. She had an older sister who moved to California. Died a few years back. There's a niece she's visited. Very proud of the girl. Works in IT for some big drug company in San Francisco, but I don't think the girl has ever come here to Quindicott for a visit."

"How about her late husband, Carl? How did you two meet, anyway?"

"We went to high school together. Carl and I were on the football team. Jane was one of the cheerleaders."

"That's classic. So they'd been together since they were teenagers?"

"You'd think, right? But no. Back in high school, they never even glanced at each other. Carl was hot and heavy with Ella."

"Ella?"

"Ella Pruett. You know her. She's a regular customer at—"

"Our bookshop. Yes, of course. She's a member of our pet-mystery book club, and she's one of the core committee members organizing the Pet Week activities. But I never knew she and Jane's late husband were an item."

"We were all just kids back then. Our football coach was the one who got them together. Carl was flunking two classes, and Ella agreed to tutor him. Everyone thought Carl and Ella would be the ones who got married after graduation."

"What happened?"

"Ella graduated valedictorian, and she went off to college on the West Coast. Carl stayed here and took over his father's real estate business. By the time Ella got a handful of degrees and came back to Quindicott, Carl was married to Jane." Bud paused. "It was a better match, I thought."

"Why is that?"

"Well, I don't like to gossip—"

You're doing a real good job for an amateur, the ghost cracked.

Quiet, Jack!

"Go on, Bud. You were saying?"

"Well . . ."—he scratched his whiskers—"Ella was always pretty full of herself. Haughty, you know? Her family came from money, and she looked down on a lot of us, even her own high school boyfriend, though Carl's family was well-off, too—but she didn't think Carl was very smart. She was wrong about that. Carl Cunningham showed the whole town how smart he was when he doubled his father's business inside of a year *and* made a fortune on some shrewd investments. As a schoolboy, he just wasn't *book* smart, you know?"

"Sure, I know what you mean," I said. "But were there any hard feelings? When Ella came back from college, was she disappointed that Carl had moved on and married Jane?"

"That I couldn't tell you. Though Ella never married. Or did much of anything with her education. Not that I know of. She spent time in New York City, took quite a few extravagant overseas trips, cared for her wealthy parents as they got older. Of course, they're both long gone now, and she still lives in their big house on Larchmont." Bud shook his head. "If you ask me, that fortune her family relied on hasn't been doing so well lately."

"What makes you say that?"

"She's letting that valuable property of hers get awful run-down. I don't think she has much liquidity left. But you know what they say about sandals to sandals."

"What's that?"

"You never heard that saying? Sandals to sandals in three generations?"

"What does it mean?'

"First generation starts out lean and hungry. They work sunup to sundown to get somewhere. Their children build on that foundation and go even further, making their fortune and moving up the ladder. But *their* children, raised in the lap of luxury, are so removed from their grandparents' work ethic that they fritter away that hard-earned fortune and end their lives in poverty."

Bud paused. "You know, it's funny that Ella Pruett should come up in our conversation. I haven't seen her in months, yet just this morning, she came into the store."

"What was she looking for?"

"A bullhorn."

CHAPTER 26

Here Comes the Judge

Sometimes it's a dog-eat-dog world and the rest of the time it's the other way around.

—Lawrence Block, *A Dance at the Slaughterhouse*

THAT'S A SWELL rubber hose you got there, doll, Jack said as we left Napp's. *I knew a cop from Hell's Kitchen who sure knew how to use one of those.*

I glanced at the loop of rubber tubing clutched in my hand.

This is for bathing, Jack. Not beating a confession out of some poor suspect.

I'm simply pointing out that a rubber hose has more than one use . . .

On the short walk back to my shop, I anticipated my use for that one and worked out a strategy for Spencer and me to successfully bathe an eighty-pound dog.

I assumed that would be my most challenging task of the evening.

I was wrong.

When I'd left the shop, everything had been in hand, and we were all happily anticipating the fun festival to come. When I returned, I found Bonnie cowering behind the register, and a glowering Seymour Tarnish leaning against it.

"Welcome to occupied territory," Seymour said.

"What's going on? Where's Sadie?"

"There's been a regime change at the Paw-some Pals," Seymour informed me. "Ella Pruett called an emergency meeting and commandeered your event space. Right now Sadie, Brainert, and a few terrorized members of the Pals are listening to Ms. Pruett's last-minute *adjustments* to Pet Week."

"Why aren't you in there?"

"Because I've just been fired."

"What?!"

"I'm not surprised," Seymour said. "Ms. Pruett has had it in for me since I moved to Larchmont Avenue. Last year she tried to circulate a petition to force me to change the appearance of my unconventional abode to *fit the neighborhood*."

"Why am I just now hearing about this?"

"No big deal. I sicced my lawyer on her, and that was the end of it. But Ella Pruett has a memory like an elephant's—and as an added bonus, she carries a grudge the size of Jupiter."

Seymour jerked his head in the direction of the event space.

"One more thing. The new Princess of the Paws-somes requires your presence, *tout de suite*."

"She does, does she?"

I bolted across the shop with determined steps. I was not going to allow weeks of work and planning by Jane Cunningham to be upset by a woman I hardly knew—even if she did have a bullhorn!

Smart to go into this battle armed, Jack said.

I don't need a weapon to handle this.

But you have one, doll. You're still clutching that rubber hose.

So I was. And it was too late to put it down now.

Before I'd left earlier, Bonnie and I had finished setting up the event space for Pet Week. We'd prepared a book-signing table for our guest of honor, with stacks of Amber Breen's latest hardcover ready to go, and we'd put her back-list on a portable shelf.

We'd peppered the area with several of the standees that we'd kept from Amber's string of hardcover hits. Even better, the producer of the hit *Kennel Club* streaming series had been kind enough to send us posters promoting the new season, which was about to begin.

Now I entered our event space to find that the standees had been pushed aside, the portable shelf shoved into a corner, and the pristine copies of Amber's new hardcover stacked on the floor.

All of this was presumably done by the rail-thin sixtyish woman in low heels and a powder blue tailored suit who was now standing behind the author's table, on which sat one thing—a red bullhorn.

I was enraged, and I wasn't the only one.

"Who do you think you are to come in here and tell us how to run this event?" Hands on her hips, Sadie was facing down Ms. Pruett from the other side of the table. Her tone was as angry as I'd ever heard it, and Sadie was no one to mess with. Everyone in town knew it. Everyone except Ella Pruett, apparently.

"I'm a founding member of the Paw-some Pals and a ranking member of the Pet Week planning committee. That's who I am!" Ms. Pruett shot back.

"But you haven't shown up for a single planning meeting since the first one weeks ago. Jane has been our prime mover in organizing Pet Week."

The other woman sniffed. "It was clear that Jane was going to veto my every idea. And when your busybody niece backed Jane on inviting Amber Breen as our event's special guest instead of *my* author choice, I got the message. I know when I'm not wanted. But *now* the situation has changed."

"No, it hasn't," Sadie replied. "Jane may not be here to oversee things, but her plans are in place. Everything is under control."

Ella Pruett lifted her chin to peer down her sharp nose at my aunt. "I disagree. With Jane in the hospital, a new chairperson *must* oversee the events to ensure they go smoothly—and to resolve all the outstanding issues that are *obviously* going to cause problems. I have no choice but to step up."

And right now, I decided, *I have no choice but to speak up!*

"Excuse me," I interrupted. "Sadie and I are in charge of this room, the events that take place here, and the schedule."

"That's right," Sadie affirmed, "and there will be no changes."

"There'd better be," Ella Pruett threatened, "because my changes to the community events will surely interfere with Amber Breen's appearance here as well as with her signing schedule—"

Who does this broad think she is, Jack cracked, *the Queen of Sheba? You want me to scare her into next week?*

No, Jack! We'll handle it . . .

I cleared my throat. "Ms. Pruett, have you forgotten? The *primary* reason our guest of honor came to Quindicott in the first place is to meet her fans and autograph copies of her new book."

Sadie jumped in. "Pen's absolutely right. That's *why* Amber Breen is here. And Ms. Breen will not be going along with your last-minute changes. I'll make sure of it."

Ms. Pruett pursed her lips. "My word," she replied in a tone that conveyed about as much sweetness as a rotten lemon. "If you're going to be *that* inflexible and difficult to work with, we'll just have to let Ms. Breen's schedule stand as it is."

I couldn't help but share a triumphant glance with Aunt Sadie.

Unfortunately, the other woman was far from finished.

"Now, let's turn our attention back to our discussion of Professor J. Brainert Parker's theater. As I was saying earlier, I don't believe you have competent security, Professor—"

"Then perhaps you shouldn't have fired my head of security," Brainert tightly noted.

"Exactly my point, Professor. Mr. Tarnish is both unqualified and unsuitable." Ella rested a hand on the bullhorn in front of her. "If I must, I shall handle security inside the theater personally."

"Good luck with that," Brainert muttered.

"Another thing, Professor Parker. I insist that you return to the original sanitation plan you first submitted. The cat boxes must be inside the theater—"

"But that space has been reserved for a Buy the Book kiosk," Brainert protested.

"Sadie Thornton and her busybody niece can shill their wares during the author signings. I'm sorry but there is simply *no space* for them in the theater."

"Well, it's my theater. I manage it. And I insist that the book kiosk remains," Brainert replied.

"So do I," I added.

"There is one alternative, I suppose," Ella said in her strident voice. "We could erect a tent right outside the theater to serve as a cat comfort station."

Sadie spoke up. "I'm afraid that's not possible. We already have a permit for that space. It's reserved for the mobile veterinarian van—"

"Which I am subsidizing," Ella Pruett interrupted. She paused to examine her manicure. "Perhaps I should spare the expense and cancel—"

"You can't do that now," Sadie protested. "Jane's booked more than twenty appointments for the vet, and that doesn't count the walk-ins."

"Then there are really only two choices," Ella Pruett declared. "Either the veterinary van gets canceled and a pet comfort tent is erected, or the kitty litter boxes *replace* the bookstore kiosk inside the theater."

I glanced at Sadie. Frowning, she returned my gaze. We knew that Jane Cunningham had reached out to some of the less privileged pet owners in Quindicott and convinced them to have their animals checked out by a professional at a deeply discounted cost. I also knew she would not want to jeopardize that plan.

But it was my call, as store event planner, so Sadie left it to me. And there was really only one choice.

"Fine," I said. "The kiosk goes."

"I knew you'd see things my way." Ella Pruett sniffed.

With all that settled, Ella moved on to internal Paw-some Pal matters—which meant hectoring the members who'd shown up for this emergency meeting until they succumbed to her will.

The whole time, my fingers tightened on that loop of rubber hose with my barely suppressed rage.

I confess, Jack, you're right again.

I thought you'd come around, Penny.

I have. At this particular moment, I can think of only one use for this rubber hose. And it has nothing to do with personal hygiene!

CHAPTER 27

Wash Away Your Troubles

> I am sure there are things that can't be cured by a good bath, but I can't think of one.
>
> —Sylvia Plath, *The Bell Jar*

LATER THAT DAY, Sparky's cleanup went smoother than expected—until it didn't.

We waited until after dinner, ours and the dog's. While Spencer took Sparky on his evening walk, I dug through the storage closet in search of beach towels. I calculated that two of them would be enough to dry Sparky.

Our plan was to lead the dog into the bathroom, close the door to prevent his escape, and wrestle him into the tub. From there we expected a struggle, and Spencer and I were prepared to get as wet as the dog.

But Sparky stunned us both by hopping into the tub as soon as he saw it. Wagging his tail, he barked at the faucet until Spencer turned on the tap. Then the dog happily snapped at the flow and splashed his front paws in the rising water.

"Sparky's having fun!" Spencer exclaimed. "Look, Mom, he loves taking a bath!"

"He does!"

I didn't bother closing the door. Sparky liked the smell of the baby shampoo, and he appreciated his soapy rubdown. He didn't mind the shower-hose rinsing, either, though through sheer rambunctiousness, Sparky pulled the tube off the faucet twice, so he could snap at the gushing tap water.

Drying didn't go quite as smoothly. Sparky did the typical doggy thing and shook his whole body, causing a rainstorm in the bathroom. But despite his shake down, my two beach towels were quickly saturated—and still the dog felt like he'd just come out of the rain. Fortunately, the clean-smelling shampoo took care of any pungent wet-dog aroma.

"Let's try my hair dryer," I said, plugging it in. "Ready, Sparky?"

He wasn't.

Apparently, baths were old hat for Jane's dog, but Sparky had never heard the abrupt whine of an electric hair dryer. The dog panicked, bowled Spencer over, and was out the bathroom door in a flash, dragging a soggy beach towel in his wake.

In the hall, Sadie yelped and spilled her tea as the dog rocketed past her.

"Where did he go?" Spencer cried.

"To your room." Sadie pointed.

We found Sparky with his head under his blue blanket. Spencer coaxed him out with a T-Bonz snack, and in a few minutes, his tail was wagging again.

"Sorry, Sparky," I said as I stroked his moist fur.

Within fifteen minutes, the dog was sleeping, and Spencer was getting drowsy. I tucked them both in and headed to bed myself.

Despite his scare, Sparky was clean and carefree, and I

envied him. As I prepared for sleep, I wished that a simple bath could clean my mind along with my body.

What's got you in the dumps, doll? Jack asked.

Ella Pruett, I replied. *She's the most difficult woman I've dealt with since I left my publishing career in New York City.*

How so?

What do you mean, Jack? You were there! She's taken over Pet Week, and she's making a bunch of changes for no other reason than because Jane originally set everything up. And Ella shut down our kiosk just because I backed Jane instead of her on her guest-author suggestion.

You could have stood up to her. You had that rubber hose.

I could have stood up to her, and I didn't need a rubber hose. But all those veterinary appointments Jane made for the area's poorer pet owners— Well, I couldn't let one woman's nasty ego trip disappoint those folks.

That's how people like Ella Pruett always get their way, Jack said. *They squeeze everybody around them between a rock and a hard place.*

Ella Pruett is a difficult person, for sure. But now I wonder if there's more to it.

Are you putting a frame to this Pruett dame? Jack asked straight out.

Do I think Ella shot Jane? No, Jack. I can't see her shooting her rival over who gets a bullhorn or cats versus dogs. But there are things Bud told me—"

About her bobby-soxer romance with Carl Cunningham? Yeah, Elle coming back to town to find heartthrob Carl in wedded bliss could have been a shock that she never got over.

Maybe. But with Carl Cunningham dead and gone, I can't see that as a motive for attempted murder, either. And unless that man who arrived at Ella's place is a relative, she has had at least one gentleman caller.

I guess there's someone for everyone—even if they have a screw loose.

Very funny, Detective. But maybe not so funny. Maybe she is insane.

Nah, Jack fired back. *People like Ella are just a pain. A pain in your—*

I get the idea!

Okey-doke. But remember, difficult people *were my stock-in-trade—and last night, when you met that little* Wizard of Oz *terrier in my apartment—*

Toto Two, yes? The dog that hired you.

Good, you remember. Well, before we parted, you expressed interest in bracing the blab-sheet wordsmith who was a constant pain in my—

Timothy Brennan. I remember!

Good. Because tonight you're going to pay him a visit.

Which is what you did all those years ago, isn't it, Jack? Tell me, is he the one who left the dog with you? Was it some sort of prank or a setup for another tabloid dog story he could sell?

Like I said before, I'd rather show you than tell you. So, close your eyes and relax, and before you know it, we'll be right outside the Press Room . . .

CHAPTER 28

News Hounds

If a man whistles at you, don't turn around. You are a lady, not a dog.

—Niall Horan

JACK'S VOICE FADED, replaced by a whirling, whistling howl (not unlike the scream of my electric hair dryer).

Winds swirled all around me, sweeping me up and carrying me through a tunnel of rushing air. Then abruptly my high-heeled shoes clicked on solid ground again. I opened my eyes and gasped.

Before me stood a soaring, Doric-columned structure as massive, ornate, and impressive as a palace in ancient Rome, only this architectural masterpiece rose above Manhattan's crowded streets. It was late in the day, and the sun had fallen below the horizon, its fading rays backlighting the mammoth granite structure into an almost ghostly silhouette.

It was then I felt Jack's presence next to me. Still, I could not look away, though I managed to find my tongue.

"What is this place, Jack?"

"New York's Pennsylvania Station," Jack replied. "Don't tell me you never rode on a train?"

"Sure, I rode on trains. And from this very station. But in my time, the Penn Station railroads and waiting rooms were buried in a stifling, crowded, low-ceilinged dump." I shook my head. "How could anyone have torn down this magnificent palace and replaced it with a claustrophobic coffin?"

"You tell me."

"I guess it had something to do with the deals that were made to build a brutally ugly sports arena on its ruins."

"And the name of your new perspiration palace?"

"Madison Square Garden, but it's nowhere near Madison Avenue, and it's definitely not a garden."

Jack shrugged his wide shoulders under a tailored serge suit. (He was fully dressed now, so he was less of a distraction, though not entirely.)

"Things change, Penny," he said, "but they don't always get better."

Gawking at the magnificent proof before me, I couldn't disagree.

"Oh, Jack, would you take me inside? I would love to see it the way you did."

"Another time, Penny. I promise. Right now we have pressing business in the Press Room." He slipped his arm around mine. "Come on, partner. I've got a little job for you. And mind the mutt."

Only then did I realize that I held a leash in one white-gloved hand. Toto Two gazed up at me from between my peep-toed pumps. I was wearing the same polka-dotted blouse and pencil skirt, too.

"That's right," I remembered. "We're going to the press room. But for which newspaper? The *Times*? The *Post*? The *Daily News*? I'll bet you read newspapers I never even heard of."

"No newspapers, doll—we're here."

We'd barely taken twenty steps, but Jack wasn't kidding. The faded sign above the door to the shabby tavern did indeed read, THE PRESS ROOM, and it was certainly not what I'd expected.

Still, I was game, so I surged forward—only to have Jack drag me back.

"Whoa! You're not going in there cold, but you are going in there alone—"

"Alone! Why?" I squeaked, failing to mask my alarm. "I thought *you* wanted to see Timothy Brennan."

"I do, and he's in there. But the little weasel has an escape route. The second he spots me, he's gone. That's why you're going in—"

"Alone. Okay, I get it."

Jack smiled. "You'll do fine."

"I'm glad you have faith in me, but you'd better give me a clue. What exactly do you want me to do?"

A five-minute discussion was all it took, and I sashayed into the Press Room, displaying a confidence that I didn't feel. Toto Two didn't have that problem. The little terrier trotted happily beside me on her short but adorable legs, her head held high.

The place wasn't very crowded, and I recognized my target immediately. The young man was sitting right where Jack said he would be—at the end of the bar beside a grizzled older fellow with froggy jowls and sleepy eyes.

As instructed, I approached the scuffed and stained wooden bar, passing a table where a trio of men stared at me in silence. Jack had warned me that I would probably be the only woman in the place. And, sure enough, from somewhere in the darkened tavern, a man let loose with a loud wolf whistle.

Channeling the attitudes of the time, I tamped down my feminist outrage and forced a bland smile as I slid into a seat at the bar.

Toto Two hopped onto my lap and cocked her head at the bartender, who didn't blink an eye at a lapdog joining his mistress for a snort.

"What'll it be, honey?"

"Whisky, neat. Nothing for the dog."

He placed a glass in front of me and poured. I ignored the drink and loudly spoke the lines Jack had suggested.

"Say, you know *Jack Shepard*, don't you? The private detective? Has he been in tonight? I'm supposed to meet him here."

The bartender shook his head, but the target took the bait.

Out of the corner of my eye, I saw the younger man at the end of the bar exchange looks with the older fellow. Then, without a word, he quickly drained his glass, grabbed his hat, and shouldered through a pair of swinging doors at the rear of the bar.

Not five seconds passed before he was back—only now Jack Shepard was gripping the young newsman by the scruff of his neck and using the reporter's thick skull to bang open the swinging doors.

With a final push to the center of the bar, the detective released his grip.

"Hey, Jack," Timothy Brennan sputtered. "What do ya know? What do ya say?"

"I *know* I ought to give you a shiner for the crap you published about me in your scandal sheet," Jack growled. "And I *say* you're a jerk for hiring some teenage girl to ditch a *Wizard of Oz* dog at my doorstep."

Brennan gawked at Jack. "Are you blotto, Shepard? What are you talking about?"

Jack took hold of the reporter's head and turned it in my direction.

"You mean to say you never saw this mutt?"

"I've never seen that mutt. Or the shapely little tomato holding it, either. I'd remember a redhead like her—"

"Keep it scientific, newshound. She isn't the one who left the dog at my place. The way I hear it, the little blonde who left this mutt was young enough to be statutory."

Brennan's eyes went wide. "I don't know any jailbait, Jack! Honest."

"I don't believe one thing out of your lying mouth. You're an ambitious little underhanded schemer, a verifiable cad to the ladies, and a degenerate gambler who never pays his bar tab, which is why you've worn out your welcome at nearly every reputable joint in this town."

In a card sharp move, Jack flipped an envelope out of his lapel pocket. The same envelope that he'd found on Toto Two.

"So where did you get the C-note, Brennan?" Jack demanded, flashing the hundred-dollar bill between two fingers. "Get lucky with the ponies?"

The old guy with the froggy jowls and sleepy eyes suddenly laughed. "Lady luck has no love for Timmy, Jack. The kid hasn't got a nickel for a bowl of soup."

"Keene?" Jack said, blinking in the room's dim light. "You still got ink on your fingers? I thought you'd retired from the game."

Before the older man could reply, Jack faced me. "Penny, I want you to meet Morgan Keene, the sharpest crime reporter in this whole rotten apple—"

"Not anymore," Keene replied, moving down the bar to join us. "These days I'm dishing up romantic advice for spinsters at the *Tribune-Mirror*. My byline is Mildred Virtue."

"You kiddin' me?" Jack shook his head. "Brother, what a waste."

"Pays triple what I used to make," Keene said, a broad grin spreading from one ear to the other. "And I still keep my fingers on the crime pulse. How you been? I heard you went private. Ditched the uniform but kept the gun—and the nose for trouble, huh?"

Jack shrugged. "The war's over. What else am I gonna

do? Anyhow, I got a real strange case here. And since this clown's broke"—he jerked his thumb at Brennan—"I'm inclined to believe he had nothing to do with it. So, I'm back to square one, and it's a puzzler."

"Lemme see what you got."

Together Jack and the grizzled reporter examined the typed letter while Brennan struggled to peek over their wide shoulders. I already knew what it said . . .

Dear Jack Shepard,

I want you to find me some answers.
First off, don't get hot under the collar!
You're looking for a dog.
The key is the key.
Follow the key and get the dog.
(You have an Ace in the hole.)
When you find the dog, break its legs, and the
mystery's solved.

"Damn, Shepard, there's a real story here!" the young reporter blurted.

"Yeah, Brennan, and I know one thing for certain: You ain't writin' it."

"It's a puzzler, for sure," Keene said. "According to these instructions, you're searching for a dog. But you already got a dog. Someone left this little terrier at your door—"

Keene gently patted Toto Two's head, and she gave a happy little bark. As Keene gazed at the dog, he drummed his fingers.

"So what's the solution to this riddle? The letter tells you to *Follow the key and get the dog.* It says, *The key is the key*—"

The key!

I realized Jack had left something out of the story.

Without asking, I reached into his lapel pocket and grabbed the key I'd found taped to the underside of Toto Two's collar.

"Jack, don't forget this!"

Jack smiled his approval as I held the key high for the reporters to see. Brennan scratched his head, but Morgan Keene whistled.

Jack studied the older man. "What have you got for me, Keene?"

"This key is connected to one of the worst disasters to hit this town since the 1928 Times Square derailment."

It was Jack's turn to scratch his head. "What are you talking about?"

"That's right," Keene said. "You weren't here, so you wouldn't know."

"Know what?"

"When you were in Europe kicking the Nazis in the teeth, an airplane smacked right into the Empire State Building. People were killed and the fire was hellish. It was a miracle the department got it under control at that height."

"That's right," Brennan said, his tone grim. "Keene was there, Jack. I read all about it. Every feature. He was an eyewitness."

We all looked at Keene and waited. I was on the edge of my seat. And so was Jack—

"Go on," the detective said, waving the bartender over to refill Keene's glass. "Tell me your story."

CHAPTER 29

Key to Disaster

I know that I shall meet my fate
Somewhere among the clouds above . . .

—W.B. Yeats, "An Irish Airman Foresees His Death"

"IT WAS THE last Saturday in July, 1945," Morgan Keene began, "a little before ten A.M. I was on my way to the office because I had three hours to get my Mildred Virtue column to the editor's desk for the Sunday edition."

The bartender poured Keene a fresh drink, and he downed it.

"The morning was foggy. I mean, as thick as pea soup. I was on Thirty-fourth Street, right in front of the Empire State Building, when I heard this airplane, real low and getting closer. Before I had time to look up, there came an explosion. Seconds later, glass was falling like rain, mixed with chunks of metal and chips of granite. A hunk of burning something smashed through the hood of a taxicab and sent the driver scurrying for cover.

"I look up and see this yellow glow through the fog. It was hundreds of gallons of burning aviation fuel spilling into the building. The plane—a bomber from the Army Air Corps flying out of Massachusetts—had slammed into the seventy-eighth and seventy-ninth floors at two hundred miles an hour."

"Yeah," Brennan chimed in. "Lucky it was a Saturday. There were a few people on the observation deck, and they got quite a scare. But the offices were empty—"

"Not all of them," Keene interrupted. "There were ten sweet ladies and one man working at the National Catholic Welfare Council on the seventy-ninth floor. Nine of those women burned to death like that—" Keene snapped his fingers. "The man lingered for four days before he bought it, and one woman survived with horrible burns, but she ultimately succumbed."

"It was a twin-engine B-25 bomber," Brennan said. "One engine fell down the elevator shaft, snapping the cables. An elevator car dropped seventy-nine floors with the operator inside. Believe it or not the dame survived. I think she's living in Arizona now."

"The other engine went clean through the building and came out the other side," Keene said, staring into his glass. "It landed on an art studio and burned it to cinders."

"Fourteen people were killed in all," Brennan said, "including the pilot, copilot, and some unlucky Joe who was hitching a ride home for the funeral of a brother who was killed in the Pacific."

"You said there was a fire," Jack prompted.

"Yeah, a big one, too. But the fire department did a swell job." Keene's face brightened with that memory. "They put it out in under an hour. And no elevators worked above the sixtieth floor. Those boys climbed twenty flights of stairs, carrying all their gear, just to reach the inferno."

"What caused the collision?" I asked.

"Pilot error," Keene replied. "The pilot mistook the East River for the Hudson and made a wrong turn."

"Unbelievable," Jack muttered. "But then you should have seen the god-awful FUBARs I witnessed Over There."

The bar went quiet at that, until I finally broke the silence.

"If you don't mind, Mr. Keene, what exactly is the connection between that terrible Empire State Building disaster and this mystery key?"

The veteran reporter grunted. "Not everything made the papers. For instance, nobody wrote about the office on the seventy-eighth floor, right below those nice Catholic ladies."

"Whose office?"

"One Adrian Ludlow, certified public accountant."

I remembered the word and number etched on the key— LUDLOW-66! Now the Ludlow part was no longer a mystery. But what did the number mean?

Jack glanced at the etching on the key. "Okay, Keene, I'm all ears."

"Ludlow peddled his services to a particular kind of clientele—"

Brennan interrupted. "Yeah, *particular*—meaning, every bookie, low-life mobster, shady businessman, and crooked politician in the city."

Keene nodded. "A lot of them kept strongboxes in Ludlow's office. Maybe a hundred of them were stored there."

"Strongboxes!" I cried. "That's it, Jack. The sixty-six is the number of the strongbox." Excited, I gripped Keene's arm. "What did they keep in these strongboxes?"

Keene snorted. "Whatever they wanted to hide, honey. Cash. Bonds. Stock certificates. Jewels, gold, maybe a murder weapon or two. But after the collision and fire, not everyone got their strongbox back. Some individuals took that hard."

"The boxes were lost?" Jack asked.

"They were *immolated*. Or so that's the story," Keene replied. Then he lowered his volume. "However, I have some inside skinny . . ."

While the older man began confiding in Jack, I noticed the silhouette of a male figure sitting in a dark corner. Maybe it was the burning red tip of his cigarette, but for some reason, he reminded me of that man I'd seen lurking on the street corner and staring at Jack's apartment on the night I met Toto Two.

I would have called Jack's attention to the guy right away, but Keene was in the middle of conveying sensitive information, and I didn't want to interrupt the newsman, or miss anything!

Leaning closer to Keene, I heard him whisper—

"I happen to know one former safecracker who was paid to open a few boxes on the sly. Boxes without keys, if you get my drift."

"Boxes that didn't belong to the joe who wanted them opened," Jack assumed, and Keene nodded.

"All right, so who did this yegg work for?" Jack pressed. "And what did he find inside?"

"That he never told me. But you might shake it out of him if you ask personal. The ex-safecracker in question has been living on the up-and-up since he got out of Sing Sing ten years ago."

"Know where I can find him?"

"Sure. He runs a pricey jewelry shop inside Penn Station. Exclusive clientele only."

"You don't say."

Keene pulled a notebook and the stub of a pencil out of a pocket and began to write. That was when I stole a glance at that dark corner again, but the mystery man and his cigarette glow were gone.

With a loud rip, Morgan Keene freed his scribbled note and tucked it into Jack's pocket.

"Thanks," Jack said, doffing his fedora. "Can I spot you another drink before I go?"

"Nah, but if anything comes of this, I want the exclusive."

"You got it, Keene. And I bet it'll be a swell story, too."

CHAPTER 30

A Bowl of Riddles

There's no right answer to the wrong question.

—Ursula K. Le Guin, *Always Coming Home*

THE NEXT MORNING, Seymour didn't wake me. He didn't have to. By the time the mailman rang our service bell at seven A.M., I was not only up, but showered, dressed, and starting my morning tea.

Jack's dream had ended so abruptly that my eyes snapped open to a wide-awake state. Though my ghostly companion was gone again, off recharging his supernatural batteries, I now felt better about facing a new day, even if it meant dealing with Ella Pruett and her troublesome ego trip.

I had to admit, the way Jack dealt with Timothy Brennan (head-on, so to speak) certainly was effective. I never liked confrontations. And I wasn't planning on banging open doors with Ella's hard head, as much as I wanted to. But the trip to Jack's past—though it left him drained—filled me with new confidence. And for that, I was grateful.

In any event, with Seymour's arrival, I left my kettle on the stove and hurried downstairs to open the door.

"What's this?" I asked as Seymour rolled a loaded dolly into the shop.

"The books you were supposed to sell at the theater. Remember Queen Ella and her bullhorn? Since she scuttled Jane Cunningham's plans and kicked you out of the theater, Brainert didn't want anything to happen to your books, so here come those dreaded returns."

"Let's hope not."

"Brainert put out that line of cat boxes, just as Queen Ella demanded," Seymour said. "But I convinced him to cater to the canine crowd, too. He put a giant sandbox in the lobby. In the middle, there's a garden decoration in the shape of a fire hydrant—"

"Where in the world did you find one of those?"

"Chick Patelli's Garden Center," Seymour replied. "If you thought pink flamingos were tasteless, you wouldn't believe the junk people decorate their yards with nowadays."

"Roll the dolly over there and follow me upstairs. I don't want my kettle to boil over. Would you like some tea?"

Seymour mock-shuddered. "I never touch the terrible green herb. But if you have a cold Mountain Dew, that's different."

A few minutes later, we sat down at the kitchen table, and Seymour declared, "It's going to be a big day. People are already showing up with and without their pets, and the action doesn't even start for another two hours."

"Everything's ready?"

"On Cranberry Street, for sure." Seymour grinned. "Dr. Winnik and his mobile veterinarian van just pulled up in front of the theater. I saw a sign about the free doggy treats at the Cooper Family Bakery. Koh's Market replaced part of their outdoor produce section with a pet food super sale.

"For those favoring adult beverages over pet food, Donovan's Pub is serving a slew of animal-themed cocktails—Moscow mules, salty dogs, black cats, Colorado bulldogs, bee's knees. Even Leo Rollins got into the act. His electronics store is featuring dog and cat collars with GPS chips in them."

Seymour frowned. "Things are not going so well at Brainert's theater, however. Ella Pruett is making a mess of everything. That woman actually tried to change the Pet Week movie schedule."

"Why? Does she think *Lassie* is dog propaganda?"

"Good one, Pen." Seymour snorted. "Though the term would be *dog-o-ganda*, in the proper reductive Newspeak. But no . . . Queen Ella did not object to *Lassie*. She's protesting the Friday night showing of *Cat People*. Do you remember that Val Lewton classic from the 1940s? Ella thought the film showed cat owners in a bad light." Seymour shook his head. "I told Brainert he should replace it with the erotic R-rated reboot from the eighties. That would really bake her cookies."

"Brainert's not going to change his schedule, is he?"

"Nah. The only real power Ella has is inside of that group called the Paw-some Pals, and she sure knows what buttons to push on those people to keep them quiet."

"It's a dominance thing," I said. "I've been reading about animal behavior, and that's my conclusion."

Seymour shook his head in disgust. "A bully by any other name. And you're right about the call of the wild. You can dress people up in tailored duds or evening clothes, but that won't stop them from playing their parts in the animal kingdom. Giraffes go neck and neck, and may the best neck win. A rabbit will thumb one foot on the ground like a nervous Nellie. Sometimes they even scream, and a rabbit scream is nothing you ever want to hear."

(I didn't doubt it.)

"We all know chickens peck at one another," the *Jeopardy!* champ went on. "Hence the term *pecking order*. Wolves show who's boss by standing tall with their tails high while the rest of the pack slouches with their tails between their legs. But my all-time favorite is the Japanese honeybee. They get together in a gang and surround their foe. Then they vibrate their wings to increase the temperature until their victim is well done."

I lowered my voice. "I have reason to believe Ella held a long-standing *personal* grudge against Jane Cunningham, which is why I think her real goal today isn't so much changing Jane's plan to make it better but *undoing* everything she's accomplished. Like a child on the beach wrecking her friend's painstakingly built sandcastle out of jealousy and spite."

Seymour drained his Mountain Dew can and set it down hard. "It's disgusting. Some people don't care who they hurt, so long as they can thwart their rival in the process. Too bad Ella can't just thump her designer heels on the ground like an angry rabbit and be done with it. Or piss on something and sashay away. Then she'd have closure, and the rest of us wouldn't have to suffer. I mean, you should see poor, harried Brainert. And, of course, I wouldn't have been fired, and you'd still have your book kiosk."

"I guess Ella Pruett handed us each a raw deal, but there's no use moaning about it. Anyway, like you, I feel sorry for poor Brainert. He's going to have to put up with that woman—and her bullhorn—for the rest of the day."

"I predict chaos, followed by calamity." Seymour's face suddenly brightened. "It might be fun."

"You're going to the parade, then, and the theater afterward?"

"I wouldn't miss either for the world."

Seymour glanced at his watch. "Speaking of missing something, I'd better go. Ella Pruett is due to show up any minute at the Movie Town Theater, and I want to see what lunatic scheme she comes up with this time."

As he rose, Seymour bumped the fruit bowl, and Jane's stuff dumped out of it. He blinked, then picked up the mini flashlight.

"This is cool. Where did you get it?"

"This stuff belongs to Jane Cunningham. It fell out of her coat pocket the day someone shot her. I had Spencer gather it up for safekeeping."

"Wow," Seymour marveled, "who knew a mature woman like Jane Cunningham was a fan of the Castle of Wishes series."

"What? No. Jane is no fan. Bonnie told me that Jane has zero interest in the young-adult-fantasy stuff."

"But the coat of arms on this flashlight belongs to the Ice Queen. She's the mistress of the castle."

"Are you sure?"

"Sure, I'm sure. Can you name another coat of arms with a penguin and a polar bear? You can check yourself. And look at this—"

Seymour showed me the knight figure made of mock-pearl plastic—the one attached to the two keys.

"This is the Pearl Knight from the latest book, *The Castle of Pearls and Wishes*. In that one, a rival princess tries to take the throne away from the Ice Queen, and this knight rides up on a white dragon—"

I interrupted. "I don't get it. Bonnie specifically mentioned trying to sell Jane Cunningham that book—and Jane made it clear that she had absolutely no interest. No sale." I pressed Seymour. "How do you know about it? Have you been reading the series?"

"Not the books, but I've checked out the manga adaptations at the comic book store in North Kingstown. Those Japanese comics have great art, and I dig those girls with the Betty Boop eyes."

"I doubt Jane has read a comic book in her life, and she doesn't like young-adult fantasy, so why would she be carrying this Castle of Wishes swag?"

"Maybe you're asking the wrong question, Pen."

Seymour shook the two keys in my face, then pointed to the larger bundle still on the kitchen table.

"There are two sets of keys here. Maybe one of these sets is Jane's, but not the other—"

"So, you're saying—"

"Instead of asking why Jane Cunningham had swag from a series she would never read, you should be asking if this stuff even belonged to Jane Cunningham."

I slowly nodded. "You may be right . . . but if not Jane, then who?"

CHAPTER 31

Pets on Parade

Don't be alarmed. Don't be frightened. These are just some of my pets.

—Hugh Lofting, *The Voyages of Doctor Dolittle*

JANE'S MYSTERY KEYS and the Castle of Wishes conundrum rattled around in my mind for the rest of that day—and what a day it was.

The kickoff events for our Pet Week celebration drew people from Millstone, North and South Kingstown, Newport, Warwick, Providence, Woonsocket, and even Blackstone Falls. So naturally the crowd that gathered along Cranberry Street for the Pet Parade was larger than anyone, including our exasperated police department, had anticipated.

I spied Chief Ciders along the parade route. Looking haried, he was juggling a closed main street, tourist-jammed sidewalks, and parade security all at the same time.

The procession down Cranberry began with the high

school marching band striking up a shockingly loud version of Elvis Presley's "Hound Dog."

Bonnie Franzetti, Aunt Sadie, and I glanced at one another with bubbling, childlike excitement and raced to join the bystanders packing the sidewalk at the front of our shop—leaving Tommy, our St. Francis University grad student (who we'd hired for extra help this week), to watch the store.

Seymour arrived, squeezed in to join us, and reported that more than two hundred marchers had registered at the theater for the contest, and we'd see every one of them as they walked the half-mile, ten-block route.

"My pal Harlan Gilman is marching with his white Persian, Peepers," Seymour yelled over the noise.

"I hope that cat isn't as heavy as he is," Sadie blurted.

"Now, now, Ms. Thornton," the mailman replied, mock-scolding my aunt with a wagging finger. "Fat-shaming is verboten. But just between you and me . . ."—he leaned close—"Harlan's cat is only slightly smaller than the Goodyear Blimp."

Most of the marchers were happy and proud to simply strut their cherished dogs or beloved cats on a leash before an audience of animal lovers. But there were surprise showstoppers, too.

Our friendly local attorney, Emory Stoddard, and his assistant, Miss Tuttle, brought a magnificent hunting falcon named Razor. (Who knew?!) Perching regally on the young woman's leather-padded arm, the bird of prey ruffled its chest feathers to the awe and delight of the crowd.

Mona Evans, one of Seymour's neighbors on Larchmont, paraded her pet pig. Not surprisingly the porker was named Arnold.

"Yeesh!" Seymour cried. "I take back what I said the other day about Larchmont Avenue. Given the hobby farms, yahoos with shotguns, and now a pet pig named Arnold, it looks like *Green Acres* IS my home."

When I finally spotted Spencer marching with other students from his school, I'm not ashamed to say my heart swelled to see my son in his best (okay, only) suit, confidently waving to the crowd like a mini mayor. Sadie swiped a tear at the sight, and we weren't the only proud parents lining the parade route, either.

Spencer's schoolmates showed off pets ranging from birds to bird dogs—a pair of cute beagles, to be exact. I saw little cages with gerbils, hamsters, and a pure white, pink-nosed rabbit cradled in the arms of Susan Trencher.

The children's section was followed by a jolly pet store owner from South Kingstown who had a chimpanzee on his back. As they marched, the chimp tossed candy to the crowd.

More hobby farm animals followed: a calf with a big red ribbon around its neck, three sheep, a giant sheepdog, a billy goat wearing a straw hat, and two Shetland ponies (which thrilled every kid on the sidewalk).

Of course, Jeremy of Broad Street with the lion's mane of blond hair made an appearance. He'd put his hair up in a topknot today and slung his very large, very scary boa constrictor over his shoulders and around his tattooed arms. The youth and his pet certainly made an impression—if you call eliciting shudders and gasps from half the spectators an *impression*.

I wasn't surprised to see that Jeremy really did wow one attendee. When he appeared, our young clerk Bonnie Franzetti waved wildly and yelled out, "Yeah, Jeremy!"

Jeremy winked and waved back.

A massive serpent might have been a tough act to follow, but our guest of honor's charm won over the crowd. Amber Breen rode a platform strapped to the back of Chick Patelli's

Garden Center pickup truck. Behind the author was a large sign displaying the web address of her animal shelter beside a blown-up cover of her newest hardcover mystery, *Doggy Day Afternoon*.

Amber shared the float with her co-judge, Ella Pruett, who sat on her hands with a dour expression, while the author stood and blew kisses to the spectators.

When the parade ended, the marchers headed for the Movie Town Theater, where the pet talent show would take place. Little prizes would be awarded to all the participants. Bigger prizes to the winners. And all attendees would be included in a raffle with dozens of prizes donated by the Cranberry Street merchants, including a grand prize of a free weekend getaway at the Finch Inn with dinner for two at Chez Finch.

When the sidewalk crowds finally broke up, Seymour had his mind set on a jumbo blueberry muffin. He invited us along to the Cooper Family Bakery. But Sadie and Bonnie headed back to the store.

"We lost a good selling opportunity at the theater," Sadie said. "But this overflowing crowd is already pouring into our shop. We'd better get to it!"

Though a fresh-baked muffin sounded delicious, I had to pass. I was scheduled to introduce our guest author, Amber (and her co-judge, Ella), onstage at the Movie Town. After that, it was back to the bookstore, where I would start tag-teaming breaks for Sadie, Bonnie, and Tommy, so they'd each have a chance to enjoy some of the festivities.

When I got to Brainert's theater, however, a major bottleneck jammed up the entryway. I was standing at a distance from the crowd, waiting for things to move (and silently practicing my little speech), when an angry voice interrupted my concentration—

"What about me, Stoddard? When do I get something?"

Stoddard, I thought. That had to be Emory Stoddard, Esquire. But who would be picking a fight with the affable lawyer on today of all days?

I looked around, trying to catch sight of the attorney, and quickly spotted him in the crowd. He was about ten feet away, dressed impeccably as usual in a tailored gabardine suit. His assistant, Miss Tuttle, stood beside him with her hunting falcon still perched on her leather-gloved arm.

"You? What are you doing in town?" Mr. Stoddard said to the stranger.

Whatever the angry man said next, I couldn't make out. His back was to me, so I couldn't even read his lips, but I did overhear Mr. Stoddard's reply—

"I don't wish to argue, but if memory serves, you've taken enough from Jane Cunningham and her late husband . . ."

When the name *Jane Cunningham* was mentioned, I came fully alert. And so, finally, did my partner in crime solving—

What's this guy's beef, Penny? He sounds hot as a pistol.

Hello, Jack. I'm glad you're back. And I have no idea what this man is discussing with Emory Stoddard. Between the barking dogs and chattering crowd, I can't hear more than pieces of their conversation.

Jostled by the crowd, I nevertheless did my best to move closer to the pair. And when the angry man turned enough for me to see his familiar-looking chiseled chin and thick shock of Kennedy hair the color of dirty snow, I excitedly told the ghost—

I just saw this man yesterday. He's the guy who pulled up in a cab with a suitcase and waltzed right into Ella Pruett's house.

You mean, the prune-faced broad who gave you and your auntie all that trouble? The one who has a personal beef with Jane Cunningham, the very dog-loving dame now lying in a hospital bed?

The same, I told the ghost.

Then what are you waiting for?! Get your sweet keister over there, so we can listen in!

CHAPTER 32

Mystery Guest

The more one reads of it, the more shrouded in mystery the whole thing becomes!

—Agatha Christie, "The Affair at the Victory Ball,"
the first short story to feature Hercule Poirot, 1923

MOVING MY *SWEET keister*—as Jack had so tactfully put it—through the crowd of people and animals was no mean feat.

As I weaved my way through the gauntlet of legs, paws, hooves, and leashes, I got a better look at the mystery man. The day before, he'd been wearing a padded Yankee's baseball jacket, which had masked just how skinny he really was. Today, however, he wore a flannel shirt that was obviously too large for his thin frame. Hanging off his narrow shoulders, the material flapped like an oversized bathrobe at each furious gesture. He was tall, too, and he towered over the older attorney as they argued.

Not only that, but the mystery man's stature, which teetered like a high reed waving back and forth in the wind, made me realize something was off with this guy. Between his wide, staring eyes and his overbroad gestures, I wondered if—

He's up the pole, Jack cracked.

He's what?

Jingled, oiled, tanked to the wide. The man is blotto. You know, soaking up drink like blotting paper.

You mean, he's drunk?

No, he's stone-cold sober and ready to perform brain surgery.

I tried to wrap my mind around a relative of the prudish, judgmental Ella Pruett showing up at a public function in an inebriated state. *Maybe we shouldn't make snap judgments, Jack. He could simply be on prescription drugs —*

Yeah, sure. 750 milliliters of stagger juice from Dr. Jack Daniel's.

Whatever his problem, I agree there's an issue . . .

Unfortunately, just as I was close enough to hear more of the stranger's conversation with Stoddard, he grabbed the lawyer's elbow and pulled him to the side of the building. Stoddard didn't resist.

Again I hurried forward, trying to get closer, when a knot of excited kids rushed in front of me. At the center of the scene was a big, bearded man in a Stetson hat leading his two Shetland ponies closer to the theater entrance. The fan club of children, begging for rides, made it impossible for me to hear anything but squeals and shouts.

Thinking fast, I lifted my phone and took a photo. Everyone was taking photos of pets and kids, so I didn't look out of place. But now, at least I had an image of Ella Pruett's—What? Relative? Boyfriend? Accomplice?

When I finally got clear of the pony pileup, the conversation between the lawyer and the belligerent stranger was practically over.

"I'm not going anywhere until this is all s-settled,"

slurred the mystery man, shoving his finger into Stoddard's chest. "You'll see me again."

"Oh, I'll look forward to that," Stoddard returned dryly, and pushed past him.

Without the wit (or sobriety?) to deliver a comeback, the stranger simply wheeled around (which was more of a teetering spin) and stomped away.

What are you waiting for now, doll? Go after him! Jack demanded.

Are you kidding? I don't know this guy. He's angry and, as you pointed out, impaired.

Impaired?

Okay, blotto! So why would he talk to me?

You don't have to talk to him. Just see where he goes, what he does—

Well, I can't leave the theater. I have duties to perform!

All right, then you'll have to brace the lawyer. If Mr. Charming is a client, Stoddard won't give up much. But you can give it a try.

The prospect of pumping Emory Stoddard for info seemed a better bet (or at least a safer one), but as I moved back through the crowd to reach him—

"Mom! Mom!"

Spencer ran up to me, breathless, his tie askew, his shirt untucked, and an empty leash in his hand.

"Sparky got away from me. As soon as we got inside the theater, he just went nuts. Look—" Spencer displayed the leash. "He broke the chain."

"If he's in the theater, Sparky should be easy to find—"

Let the kid find the mutt, doll, Jack insisted. *We have a case to solve.*

Before I could reply to my son or my ghost, Seymour appeared, waving a half-eaten muffin.

"What's the problem, kid?"

Spencer brushed away a frustrated tear. "Sparky got loose in the theater, and I can't find him."

"Are you sure he didn't get out?" Seymour asked. "Because he should be easy to spot inside the theater."

"Not now!" Spencer pointed at the Movie Town entrance. "It's like a crazy house in there. Animals are everywhere. People are arguing—"

Seymour threw a knowing glance my way. "What about Ms. Pruett and her bullhorn?"

"She's yelling, but nobody's listening!"

With that, Seymour shoved the rest of his fresh-baked breakfast past his lips, brushed the crumbs from his shirt, and, through a mouthful of muffin, declared—

"We'll just see about that!"

CHAPTER 33

Animal Crackers

Speak softly and employ a huge man with a crowbar.

—Terry Pratchett, *Going Postal*

"MAKE WAY, COMING through!" the mailman bellowed.

Like a funnel cloud with elbows, Seymour plowed his way through the choking crowd of grumbling people and braying pets. Spencer and I followed in his considerable wake. When Seymour reached the door, someone tried to shut him out. Undaunted, Seymour simply barreled through, nearly knocking over the harried Movie Town ticket taker.

"Who do you think you are?" the outraged teenager demanded as he adjusted his usher's vest.

Seymour jammed his thumb in his own chest. "I'm the guy who's going to restore order, that's who."

The youth shook his head. "Good luck with that!"

As soon as we entered the lobby, Seymour spotted trouble. The cat boxes were all lined up, just as Brainert had promised—but more than one dog was also using them.

Well, sort of using them. Mostly, the canines just lifted their legs and wet the sides of the boxes.

Needless to say, the cat owners were not happy.

Seymour pointed to a college coed with a sun cap covering her honey blond hair. Her beautiful Irish setter was lifting its leg beside a litter box

"What is your dog doing here? This section is for cats."

The girl blinked. "Nelson has to pee, but there's only one hydrant and a really long line!"

"Only one hydrant!" Seymour smacked his own forehead. "I should have thought that one through."

Dismissing that problem, the determined mailman charged across the crowded lobby and into the auditorium. As the swinging doors closed behind us, Seymour took in the scene.

"Spencer's right," he declared. "It's a madhouse! A mad Animal House!"

Seymour wasn't exaggerating—much. Though the auditorium was only half full, no one had obeyed the seating instructions, and the result was borderline chaos.

The velvet rope that was supposed to separate the cats and the dogs lay twisted on the floor—except for a ragged section being chewed apart by a deranged Pomeranian.

If Sparky was indeed running around inside the theater, he wasn't the only dog gone wild. The young woman Seymour had chastised in the lobby was now chasing her Irish setter down the center aisle.

"Nelson! Bad dog!" She stomped her ballet flats. "You listen to Mommy and stop right now."

Nelson, meanwhile, dragging a spangled leash and in no mood to listen to *Mommy*, was in hot pursuit of a panicked poodle.

Dogs were climbing over seats and romping in the aisles. A black-and-white tuxedo cat named Miss Dingles hung by her claws halfway up the burgundy stage curtain, her owner trying desperately to coax her down. And—

Mother Machree! What is that thing in a straw hat chewing the upholstery?

"I'm no Old MacDonald, Jack, but I do believe that's a billy goat."

The sounds—both human and animal—were nothing short of deafening. Yapping. Squealing. Snarling—and those were the people! Meanwhile, dogs barked and cats yowled. I even heard Arnold the pig snort in indignation. Then a bloodcurdling scream like that of a crazed banshee from hell itself cut through the audio tidal wave.

"Yikes!" I cried, genuinely rattled. "What was *that*?"

"A rabbit," Seymour replied. "I warned you."

Somewhere in all that racket, Emma Pruett tried but failed to be heard. Her wavering voice boomed through her bullhorn, which crackled with feedback at every third word. And instead of keeping order in the middle of things, she stood rigidly in the center of the stage, firing off futile commands.

Beside her, Brainert waved helplessly for calm. His exasperated expression told me he'd pretty much given up trying to keep order, if not his dignity.

"Spencer," I said, "let's go find—"

But my son hadn't waited. He was already lost in the crowd and hunting for the elusive Sparky.

In a purely theatrical gesture, Seymour clutched his head with his hands. "Dogs and cats living together. Mass hysteria. And my best buddy being taken advantage of? This must all end!"

Damn, Penny, Jack quipped with a laugh. *This Pet Parade shindig is much better than you described. What a freak show! Do me a favor and tell the mailman not to throw a wet blanket on the fun.*

But Seymour was made of sterner stuff than all of us. Jumping to the center aisle, he power-lifted the velvet rope—Pomeranian and all—and reattached it to the pole.

Growling, the dog still hung on to the rope by its teeth as the mailman elbowed his way to the stage and bounded onto the platform.

"May I borrow this?" Seymour sarcastically asked as he yanked the bullhorn from a shell-shocked Ella Pruett. The mailman fiddled with the controls and stepped to the edge of the stage.

"Listen up!" his voice boomed. "There will be *no show* today!"

Suddenly, the human sounds faded as all eyes faced the mailman.

"Whatdaya mean, no show?" cried an irate voice from the seats.

"What I mean is, there will be no show UNTIL everyone TAKES A SEAT IN THE PROPER SECTION. Cats here, dogs there, specialty pets in the rear—that means the lady with the bearded lizard on a leash has to move back! Anyone not seated properly in TWO MINUTES will be EJECTED"—Seymour pointed to Harlan Gilman and his enormous cat in the front row—"BY THIS BIG DUDE AND HIS KILLER CAT."

There were nervous titters and some genuine laughter, but as I joined Seymour onstage, the situation in the auditorium actually began to right itself—with helpful hints, suggestions, and outright orders fired off by Seymour.

"All dogs on a leash or in laps. All cats on a leash or in laps. The rest of you, do whatever you do with your pets."

Seymour faced the tuxedo cat.

"Usher, lower the curtain so Mrs. Danbury can rescue Miss Dingles."

The kid with the vest blinked. "It doesn't lower, sir."

"Well, don't just stand there. Go get a ladder!"

"Yes, sir!"

"Oh, thank you, young man!" Mrs. Danbury exclaimed. "Hey, aren't you my postman?"

"Yes, ma'am. Neither snow nor rain nor deranged Pomeranian can stay this courier from his appointed rounds!"

After Seymour helped the grateful cat owner, he noticed more trouble brewing in the specialty-pet section. "Hey, Jeremy, I don't like the way your snake is eyeing that little girl's hamster. Would you move back a few rows, please?"

An unsettling screech again rattled the auditorium.

Brainert put a hand to his heart. "My God, what was that horrible sound?"

"Rabbit," I replied knowingly.

"Miss Trencher," Seymour bellowed, "if you cannot calm your unhinged bunny, I'm going to have to ask you to leave. Give it a treat or something!"

As the auditorium began to settle down, I spied Amber Breen in the wings gesturing me to come closer.

"What is it, Amber?" I asked. "What's wrong?"

"Nothing now."

She stepped aside, and I saw my son, Spencer, standing behind the author, with a panting Sparky on a leash again.

CHAPTER 34

Loyal to a Fault

Instinct is a marvelous thing. It can neither be explained nor ignored.

— Agatha Christie, *The Mysterious Affair at Styles*

"THANK GOODNESS, YOU found him!" I exclaimed—to both my son and our guest author. "I don't know what got into Sparky. Spencer said he just wouldn't listen."

"Loyalty," Amber Breen declared. "Sparky was looking for his mistress. Something about this situation convinced the dog that Mrs. Cunningham was somewhere around. It's instinct. He wants his mother."

Sparky whimpered when he heard his owner's name. Spencer frowned at the sound.

"What should I do to make him feel better, Ms. Breen?" my son asked.

"Take Sparky home with you. Did you make a special place for him?"

Spencer nodded.

"Good," said Amber. "Take him there and see if you can

calm him down. He may mope. If you have something that
belonged to Mrs. Cunningham, something that may carry
her scent, show it to Sparky. That might help him."

Once again, a rabbit scream echoed through the theater.

"Miss Trencher," Seymour bellowed through the bullhorn, "find a magician's hat and kindly make that rabbit
disappear."

Amber and I exchanged glances, and she said, "I've
never seen a man control a crowd so well. Is he a professional?"

"A professional postman. He also moonlights as an ice
cream vendor in a truck he bought with his *Jeopardy!* win-
nings."

Amber nodded, impressed. "So, dealing with unruly dogs
and sugared-up seven-year-olds is a typical day for him."

"Yes, but that only begins to describe all that is Seymour.
Remember that *Addams Family* house on Larchmont you
asked me about? He lives in it."

The author's look of curious interest blew up into a genuine grin. "I just knew I'd like him."

Just then I felt Ella Pruett's dagger-stare on us.

"I think your co-judge wants the show to go on," I told
Amber. "I'm going to make my introductions now."

Amber patted my shoulder. "Break a leg."

I met Ella center stage. As we waited for the auditorium
to finish filling up and settling down, she glanced at Spencer, who was leading Sparky up the aisle and out of the
theater.

"That's Jane Cunningham's dog, isn't it?"

"Yes, it is," I replied. "We've been taking care of Sparky
since the . . . incident."

Ella's brows knit in puzzlement. "Why doesn't her girl
take care of the dog?"

"Girl? What girl?"

"Oh, I don't remember her name," Ella said, frowning. "A young thing with light-colored hair and thick glasses. I don't know if she works for the Cunningham property company or if she's just a tenant, but I've seen that same girl walking Sparky along Briar Patch Road many times."

"I was near there yesterday," I informed her. "Actually, I was on your street, talking to your neighbor Robert Slattery. I think you saw me, didn't you? Amber was with me."

"What of it?"

"Before I drove away, I noticed you had a visitor arrive in a taxi. A good-looking older man with thick salt-and-pepper hair. He was wearing a New York Yankees baseball jacket. He's staying with you, I take it?"

"Penelope, let me stop you right there. You have a reputation of sticking your nose where it doesn't belong. And it does *not* belong in my personal business. So, do me a favor. Take that busy body of yours and busy it bothering somebody else."

And that was that. Ella's mystery guest continued to remain a mystery.

Jack, however, refused to remain quiet.

Don't quit now, doll. You didn't get the goods on the guy, but you did get something.

You're right, Jack. I did.

So? What are you waiting for? You heard the prune-faced broad. BUSY YOUR BODY WITH SOMEBODY ELSE.

Okay, okay!

With Jack as unrelenting as usual, I turned on the theater's standing microphone, made the official introductions of Ella and Amber, and then went to work.

As the show began, I made my way around the theater, questioning the Paw-some Pals members about the *girl* who took care of Jane's dog. No one knew she existed, let alone her name, with the exception of Mrs. Meyers, who recalled seeing a young woman walking Sparky along Larchmont just last week.

"A petite blonde," Mrs. Meyers said. "What they used to call a peroxide blonde because her hair is almost white. Cute girl. She wore those vintage tortoiseshell glasses. When I saw her, she was wearing jeans; a big, yellow slicker; and a T-shirt with some kind of dragon and castle on it."

It wasn't much, but Jack saw this mystery girl as a new avenue of investigation.

If she was walking Jane's dog, she's in pretty tight with the dame, Jack said. *That means, she might know something other people don't.*

Then why didn't she come forward?

Good question. And that's what investigations are for.

WHEN I FINALLY returned to Buy the Book, the shop was pleasantly busy. According to Sadie, they'd seen a steady stream of customers all day.

"And they didn't just browse. They bought," Sadie said with a satisfied wink.

Before I jumped behind the register, I went upstairs to check on Sparky.

As Amber Breen had predicted, something must have triggered the dog's memory of Jane. I found Spencer sitting beside the now sleeping Sparky.

"He's been moping since we got back." Spencer spoke quietly, like a doctor in a patient's room. "He whined every few minutes until he finally fell asleep."

Spencer and I tiptoed out of his room.

"Did you show Sparky the stuff in the bowl?"

"Sure, Mom. He sniffed it all, but he reacted only to that big set of keys. I put it beside him on the blanket, and he hasn't moved out of that corner since."

I pressed my son for an answer I'd already guessed. "You're sure he didn't react to anything else? Not the little flashlight? The plastic knight figure?"

Spencer shook his head. "No, Mom. Only that big fat set of keys."

CHAPTER 35

Family Affairs

Flocks, like families, have need of their black sheep . . .

—P. L. Travers, *The Fox at the Manger*

THE REST OF the day went well. Steady business with a big rush after the Movie Town Theater pet show finally broke up.

Seymour arrived to report that the winner of the talent segment was Paw-some Pals member Sylvia Meyers with her trio of pom-pommed poodles. The dogs had barked on cue to Patti Page's rendition of "How Much Is That Doggie in the Window?"

"Who won the sweepstakes?" Sadie asked.

"The guy with the chimp," Seymour replied. "My bet? That getaway weekend and intimate candlelight dinner for two at the Finch Inn will be him and that primate."

"How did Brainert react to the mess at his theater?"

Seymour sighed. "I doubt the Paw-some Pals will get their security deposit back."

During the dinner hour, we had our first lull in business, and I was able to call the hospital with questions regarding Jane, her condition, and a few other things.

After that, the town pretty much emptied out. The Pet Week activities had moved on to the St. Francis University chapel, where an evening of music and fellowship was scheduled. The traditional Blessing of the Animals would be held tomorrow, after the Sunday service.

I was relaxing in one of our overstuffed reading chairs, taking a well-deserved tea break, when Eddie Franzetti came through the door with his calm brown eyes, curly black hair, and signature Franzetti smile. Striding across the floor with an easy, athletic gait, he seemed untouched by the pressures of the day.

"Hello, Pen. Sadie. Is my sister here?"

The deputy chief of the Quindicott Police Department had come in uniform, so I knew his call was not social.

Bonnie poked her head above the stacks. "Hey, bro. What's up?"

"Chief Ciders said you witnessed a man menacing Jane Cunningham," Eddie said, his smile for us vanishing when he addressed his little sister.

Bonnie nodded. "I did."

"Would you care to tell me about it *now*, since you *didn't bother* to file a police report at the time?"

Geez, Louise! Jack's outraged voice exploded in my head. *Talk about slow on the draw. If the badges in this town were racehorses, you could clock them with a sundial!*

Oh, God, Jack. I forgot I'd reported that incident to Chief Ciders—

Yeah, and by the time these blockheads are getting around to investigating screwball Slattery, we already put him and his antique blunderbuss in our rearview mirror.

Yes, but I was the one who put Robert Slattery on the

*spot by mentioning him to the chief. Now that I know the
real story, I'd better set Eddie straight. I owe it to that poor
grieving man.*

"Eddie," I said firmly, "you need to talk to me, not just
your sister. We both have a story to tell."

I led Eddie and Bonnie to my office in the stockroom and
sat them down.

Eddie faced his sister. "So, a man came inside the store
and threatened Mrs. Cunningham's life—"

"He didn't come inside," Bonnie replied. "It happened
outside—"

"And he threatened her dog," I jumped in, "not Jane
herself—"

Bonnie nodded. "That's right. He—"

"His name is Robert Slattery," I interrupted. "He's Jane
Cunningham's neighbor."

"Hold on, now." Eddie threw up his hands. "Who is telling this story?"

"I am," Bonnie and I replied in unison.

Eddie sighed. "Please, start from the beginning."

"I'll start," Bonnie said.

"And I'll finish," I said.

For the next ten minutes, Bonnie told her story, and then
I told mine. I stressed that it was all a mix-up, that Robert
was no threat, and he certainly hadn't shot Jane with an
antique shotgun that had no bullets.

"Ask Dr. Rubino," I insisted. "He was there. He talked
Robert Slattery down and disarmed him."

Eddie sat back in his creaky chair and locked eyes with
his kid sister.

"You should have filed a police report, Bonnie. And, Pen,
Dr. Rubino had a duty to report a mentally unstable patient who was armed—even if, as you say, the gun wasn't
loaded—"

"It was a wall decoration," I said. "Dr. Rubino didn't think it would even shoot."

"Evaluating threats that involve firearms is our department, not yours." Eddie shook his head. "No matter how you slice it—"

"Is that a pizza reference, big brother?" Bonnie interrupted. "Because Dad and I thought you gave all that up to be a cop."

"It's a *saying*, Bonnie. And what I'm saying is that I owe it to the safety of our community to investigate this guy. I mean, think about it. A threat is made, followed by an actual shooting in the vicinity of this man's home. Circumstantially, it's hard to imagine anyone else being responsible."

Oh, no, I thought, and told him—

"Please, Eddie, don't jump to conclusions. You should speak with Dr. Rubino before you condemn that poor man."

"I will. First thing in the morning. And I'm not condemning anyone. But his threat to Jane Cunningham put him on our persons-of-interest radar. I have a job to do, and I'm going to do it."

"Then I hope you'll be gentle."

"To the doctor or his patient?"

"Both."

Sadie knocked on the open door. "Bonnie, Mrs. Chantilly is here. She said you reserved some new releases for her and promised to recommend some books for her daughter."

Bonnie jumped out of her chair. "Excuse me, *Deputy Chief*, but I have a job to do, too. And now I'm going to do it!"

When Bonnie was gone, her brother made a pained noise.

"Trouble, Eddie?"

"Yeah, her name is Bonnie. She's the youngest, and she was always the sweetest. She never rebelled or made trouble when she was a teenager—"

"Like you did."

Eddie scoffed. "I raised hell. There's a difference."

"And the difference is?"

"I'm a guy, and she's not."

"Really, Eddie? I'm surprised at you. I've known you almost all my life, and that's the most sexist thing I've ever heard you say."

"She's my kid sister. I don't see her the way you do."

"How so?"

"Not long ago, she was dating Kent Clark's oldest. Good kid, a bit slick, but it would have been nice to have a car dealer in the family. Now Dad tells me she's dating some transient with a motorcycle and a topknot—"

"He also has a boa constrictor, though I didn't catch the snake's name. The guy's name is Jeremy, and he marched in the Pet Parade today. Maybe you shouldn't judge a book by its cover."

Eddie made that pained sound again.

"Bonnie is a grown woman, Eddie."

"Then she should act like one, and not hang on the neck of some dubious stranger to our town, one with a snake fetish."

I suddenly remembered another stranger to our town from earlier today. "Speaking of dubious men, by any chance, can you ID this one?"

Eddie nodded as soon as he saw the photo. "That's Stanley Cunningham."

Well, well, well, Jack said in my head. *There's an interesting wrinkle!*

"Stanley Cunningham?" I echoed. "Carl Cunningham's black sheep brother? Eddie, are you sure?"

"Yeah, I'm sure. I arrested him myself years ago—on a drunk and disorderly. Why are you asking about that loser? Don't tell me Bonnie's thinking about dating him next."

"She can if she wants to. He's back in town. I took this photo earlier today . . ."

I told Eddie all about Stanley's (possibly drunken) confrontation with attorney Emory Stoddard.

"Well, if Stanley is really back, I'm guessing there's a trip to that girlie bar on the highway in my future. Before he took off, one of the dancers—Bashful Bambi is her stage name—got a restraining order against him. Knowing Stan, he'll violate it."

"Listen, Eddie, Stanley Cunningham may be involved in something far more serious than that. I saw him arrive yesterday morning in a taxi with a suitcase. He walked right into Ella Pruett's house on Larchmont Avenue. Don't you think that's odd? Suspicious?"

"Why would it be exactly?"

"Ella is Jane's neighbor, and there's bad blood between them. Could Ella and Stan be involved in an attempt to take Jane Cunningham's life?"

"That's a serious charge, Pen. What makes you think so?"

Lay it out for him, honey, Jack urged. *Now's the time for your legwork to pay off.*

"Okay, here it is . . ." I cleared my throat. "Bud Napp told me that Stan used to work for his older brother, Carl, who ran the Cunningham family's property management business. They had a falling-out when Carl caught Stan stealing thousands from an expense account. Carl never pressed charges, but he fired his little brother, and Stan left Quindicott. He didn't even come back for his brother's funeral.

"Meanwhile, Jane inherited the Cunningham business, and she runs it like clockwork. She has no children. Bud Napp mentioned an older sister in California who passed away, and a niece who works in IT for some big drug company, but she lives in San Francisco, so I doubt the young woman would have any use for a property management business in Rhode Island. I don't believe Jane has any other close relatives. So it's possible, upon her own death, Jane will leave the business and properties to Stan."

"Why would she do that if they're estranged?

"Jane's late husband might have wanted it that way, maybe out of guilt, since it was their father who started the company. Or maybe Stan believes he's got a good case to challenge whatever Jane's will says. Maybe he believes that he should inherit the business that his family started, a business he did help run at one time. At the very least, Stan's threat of a legal claim might earn him a fat settlement."

Eddie's frown deepened. "In other words, he may have a financial motive to see Jane dead?"

"Exactly. I don't know what his relationship is with Ella Pruett or how she might be involved. But I do know she was hot and heavy with Stan's brother, Carl, when they were in high school. And when she came back from college, she found him married to Jane."

"You think she's still bitter about that? After all these years?"

"Not about Jane marrying Carl. But she could be bitter about losing his net worth."

"But doesn't Ella Pruett come from money?"

"Bud Napp says Ella is letting her valuable home go to pot. He believes she's running out of her family's money while Jane is sitting on a fortune in property and business equity. Maybe in some twisted logic, Ella thinks the Cunningham fortune is rightfully hers. Maybe cozying up to Stan and helping him give Jane a premature end are her ways of exacting some kind of perverted justice for Jane 'stealing' Carl from her."

"I get it," Eddie said. "Stan Cunningham is nobody's knight in shining armor. But if he inherits his sister-in-law's properties and Ella Pruett marries him, then she's financially set again. Sure, I'll look into the pair, Pen—*after* I pay a visit to Robert Slattery. Do you, by any chance, have Slattery's exact address?"

I glanced at my arm.

"Sorry, Eddie. It washed off in the shower."

"Excuse me?"

"Never mind, but there is one more thing before you go . . ."

"What is it?" Eddie glanced at his watch.

I took a breath. His reference to a *knight* in shining armor jarred my memory of that Castle of Wishes knight that had fallen out of Jane Cunningham's coat pocket on the day she was shot.

I knew what I was about to say might mean nothing to a busy police officer, but in my bookseller's mind, this paradox continued to bother me: Jane was outspoken in her distaste for the young-adult-fantasy category in general and the Castle of Wishes series in particular. So why did she have swag from that series in her pocket? Unless it *wasn't* hers. Which is why I told Eddie—

"There's another important piece to this puzzle: a missing young woman. She's petite with hair dyed white blond, and she wears vintage tortoiseshell glasses. I don't remember seeing her around town. I asked Bonnie and Sadie, and neither of them remembered her, either. It seems this girl has kept a low profile for some reason. I don't know her name or where she went, but—by all accounts—she existed, and she was close to Jane."

"In what way?"

"She walked Jane's dog for her regularly, yet no one knows much about her. One of the Paw-some Pals remembered seeing her just last week on Larchmont. But not since. She never came forward to talk to the police, not as far as I know. And she never showed up here to ask about Sparky. Earlier today, I rang the hospital's IC unit. No one fitting her description has visited Jane. Don't you think that's odd?"

"What's odd about it?"

"Jane was shot walking her dog. Why wasn't the girl walking him? And where did this mystery girl go so suddenly? I believe Jane was even carrying some of the girl's personal items in her coat pocket."

"Too many questions. Not enough answers," Eddie said, sounding like Jack when he added, "And that's what investigations are for."

CHAPTER 36

A Sight to See

I have to go out every night. If I stay home one night I
start spreading rumors to my dogs.

—Andy Warhol

AFTER MY HECTIC day, I expected to fall asleep as soon
as my head hit the pillow. But there it was, nearly midnight,
and all I could do was toss and turn.

I was a juggler with too many glass balls in the air, waiting for them to drop and shatter. Half my mind was consumed with concerns about our retail sales and tomorrow's
schedule. The other half was wading around in the deep
conundrum of the Jane Cunningham affair.

And if that wasn't enough to burden my brain, why not
throw in a ghost?

Case, honey. It's the Cunningham case, Jack whispered
in my head. *An affair is something that leads to divorce
court.*

"Call it what you will, Jack. For me it spells insomnia."

Hmm. Then maybe it's time to shed those cutie-pie polka dots and slip into something with more class.

"Cutie-pie polka dots? What are you talking about?"

The outfit you wore on your last two trips to my time. You're going to need a new one.

"For what, exactly? I've got a lot on my plate right now, you know."

I know. That's why you need a little break. So, how about some sightseeing? You wanted me to show you the inside of Pennsylvania Station. I mean, the one in my time, not your current claustrophobic coffin buried below an ugly sports arena—as you put it.

"But what about your own canine case?"

Don't you worry, doll. We'll get around to it. But first you've got to close your eyes . . .

Suddenly drowsy, I did as Jack asked and felt myself dropping into a deep well, my body plunging through black space, falling faster and faster . . .

ABRUPTLY I LANDED on solid ground. Hearing voices and traffic noises around me, I opened my eyes to my own reflection.

I was standing on a city sidewalk, staring at a full-length mirror on a weigh-yourself-for-one-penny scale in front of a tobacco shop—and, *no*, I had zero interest in weighing myself in public.

But I did use the mirror. And Jack wasn't kidding.

The jejune polka-dot blouse was gone, and I couldn't help but admire the new outfit that had taken its place. The sophisticated suit dress was nicely fitted, with a perfectly tailored jacket that draped over my hips. The pencil-thin skirt ended midcalf, and the color was striking—

"It's Montezuma purple," Jack informed me at my side. "See I told ya. Classy, huh?"

"I like it, Jack. Very classy, as you put it . . ." I also sported a trilby hat, and my heels and handbag exactly matched the suit. "But why are we playing dress-up?"

"You and I are going to pay a visit to that jeweler Morgan Keene told us about. You remember the facts of our case, don't you?"

"Of course. We have yet to solve the mystery of *why* someone left you a dog with instructions to *find* a dog. But the letter that came *with* the dog advised you to follow the key."

"*Follow the key and get the dog*, is how it read," Jack noted.

"I remember. And the LUDLOW-66 key that we found in Toto Two's collar has led us here."

Jack nodded his approval. "Anything else?"

"Your crime reporter friend Keene was able to pass you the name of a safecracker for bad guys who opened those Ludlow boxes, the ones that were recovered after the Empire State Building disaster."

"That's right. The safecracker is legit now. Marcel is the name he goes by, and he runs a jewelry shop."

"So, why not walk through his store's front door, waltz right up to this guy, and give him the third degree?"

Jack smiled. "You're cute when you talk tough."

"I'm not trying to be cute. I'm merely asking, why the charade?"

"According to Morgan Keene, the shop is exclusive, so we've got to look like a well-heeled pair of cliff dwellers to get past the doorman. That's why I have this dapper new fedora, and Toto Two got a fancy new collar and leash."

The little terrier looked up and barked.

"I think she's learning her name, Jack."

"It's time for you to learn yours. This afternoon you are Constance Cabot."

"Constance? Oh, I like that. And who are you?"

"Why, Mr. Cabot, of course." Jack flashed an embossed business card belonging to one Denholm E. Cabot, attorney-at-law. "One of my former clients."

"What's the E stand for?"

"Ennui. The case was a bore, and so was the client."

"Are you sure Mr. Cabot won't mind you stealing his identity?"

"Borrowing," Jack countered. "And what Mr. Cabot doesn't know won't hurt him."

"So, I'm Mrs. Cabot, then?"

Jack slapped his lapels. "Right!"

He reached into his pocket, then took my left hand in his. Before I knew it, he'd slipped a simple yet elegant gold ring on my third finger.

"Nice fit," he said with a wink.

I held out my hand. The gold sparkled in the afternoon sun.

"It's lovely—"

"And it's real. You can't fool a jeweler with a fake—especially a jeweler who used to be a yegg."

"Jack, where did you get this?"

The PI cut me off with a gesture. "Story for another time."

"Now you've piqued my interest."

"Good. Keep it that way." With a wink, he offered me his arm. "Shall we go, Mrs. Cabot?"

Conversation ceased as we approached the busy Seventh Avenue entrance to Pennsylvania Station. Once again, I was in awe. Close up, I could see that the building's architect had borrowed from several classical styles. The interior arrangement was modeled after Roman baths, yet the classical Greek columns and exterior were inspired by the Acropolis—though this major transportation hub was far larger than anything the ancients had ever constructed.

Even more impressive on the inside, the sheer vastness of the high roof took my breath away.

"Jack, I've been to Notre Dame and St. Peter's Basilica, but I've never seen an interior space so big. It's like a hollowed-out skyscraper."

"It's the largest indoor space in New York City."

"I've got to see more!"

Jack fulfilled my wish, escorting me toward two massive Corinthian columns. Passing between them, we entered an indoor plaza flanked on two sides by plush waiting rooms for travelers. Everything there was pink granite, with a vaulted ceiling so high, I saw birds fluttering near the top.

The concourse itself was another imposing space. Capped by a high glass dome in a steel framework, the design allowed the afternoon sun to pour beautiful golden light into the station. Hanging under that dome, a clock at least ten feet across, with hands the size of a man, displayed the time—three thirty.

After indulging my shameless gawking, Jack pulled me aside for his version of sweet nothings—

"We've seen the sights," he whispered in my ear. "Now we've got to see a yegg about a strongbox."

Our destination was the indoor shopping arcade, which ran the length of the station from Seventh to Eighth Avenue—an entire city block! A wide walkway made navigating the busy marketplace possible, but not easy. There were hundreds of shoppers scurrying about with gift-wrapped boxes and fancy shopping bags in hand.

Exclusive stores lined either side of the corridor, and each had its own entrance and display windows. Though I knew those retailers represented the top of the line in Jack's time, I'd never heard of them: brands like Richard Hudnut, Bonnie Cashin, and John Cavanagh Hattery—

"We're here."

Jack stopped in front of a brightly begemmed display window for Fine Jewelry by Marcel. A tuxedoed man with a frozen smile opened the door from the inside.

"And whom shall I say is calling?" the man asked in a rather dubious English accent—as if he were a monarch's butler, and we were visitors at the palace.

Jack politely removed his fedora and slipped the man Mr. Cabot's business card.

"Ah, yes, come right in," the doorman said, his frozen smile melting as he stepped aside. "It's a pleasure to meet you, Mr. Cabot. My name is Thomas. Feel free to browse. Marcel is with another client, but he will serve you shortly."

Thomas's watchful gaze returned to the door.

Meanwhile, Jack and I made a show of examining the jewelry on display inside rows of glass cases.

"What a world," Jack whispered into my ear. "This whole thing is rich if you think about it. A reformed safecracker hawking ice to the kind of well-heeled square jills and johns he used to rob."

As we pretended to browse, Jack slowly edged us toward a small but elegant office behind the counter. The door was open, and an antique Tiffany lamp, on an ornate desk, illuminated the scene.

Sitting behind the desk was the jeweler, Marcel, a small, thin gentleman (with an even thinner mustache and a receding hairline) dressed impeccably in formal wear. Across from him sat his current customer: a trim, handsome man in his fifties. He had a thick head of slicked-back hair and wore a finely tailored double-breasted Wall Street suit. The man practically smelled of newly printed money.

In the chair next to Mr. Tycoon was a gorgeous blonde in a slinky dress. Half his age, she was wearing heavy makeup and smoking from a sterling silver cigarette holder while chewing gum at the same time.

We moved near enough to hear their voices, and when Jack heard Mr. Money Bags speak, he abruptly released my arm.

"Jack? What's the matter?"

In a shocking move, he abandoned our well-plotted charade—and barged right into the jeweler's office!

Thomas, the tuxedoed doorman, suddenly rushed toward me from the other end of the shop.

Good grief. Now what?

I didn't know what was going down, but I had to act fast, so I did.

Scooping up Toto Two, I followed the detective's lead—right into the Tiffany lamplit lion's den.

CHAPTER 37

The Swindler

Women can accept the fact that a man is a rotter, a swindler . . . and a general swine without batting an eyelash . . . Women are wonderful realists.

—Agatha Christie, *Murder in Mesopotamia*

"WHAT IS THE meaning of this?" The outraged jeweler rose to his feet as Jack entered his office.

"This isn't about you, Marcel," Jack assured him. "It's about this Cheating Charlie right here."

"Shepard." Mr. Tycoon spat out Jack's name as if he'd swallowed sour milk. Rising with indignation, he poked the broad-shouldered detective in the chest. "You've got a lot of nerve barging into my business."

"Your business?" Jack snatched a leather-bound checkbook from the man's sweaty hand. "Who are you impersonating these days, Herman?" He read the name on the top check. "Ah, Cecil P. Hagan, the Hollywood producer? Shooting for the big leagues, eh, Herman?"

By now Thomas was standing at the office door, looking uncertain about what he should do.

Marcel slammed his desk. "What is going on here, Mr. Hagan? Who are these people? And who is *Herman*?"

"Bad news, Marcel," Jack replied. "This is not the Hollywood mogul Cecil P. Hagan. Herman Hitch here has assumed the role. Behind the scenes, he plays the part of swindler extraordinaire."

Jack glanced at the slinky blonde, still seated, and shook his head. "I just testified at this guy's divorce trial."

"Why, you—"

Herman Hitch raised a fist. Jack swatted it aside and pushed the con artist into the arms of Thomas, who took a surprisingly firm hold of the con man.

Jack turned to the jeweler.

"I'll bet Herman here was about to pass a bad check for a few grand of your beautiful rocks." He jerked his thumb at the woman. "And I suspect you mistook this flapper for a Hollywood starlet, eh, Marcel?"

The woman, who appeared rather slow on the uptake, snapped her gum at Jack. Marcel sighed and pressed a button under his desk.

"Hold him for the police, Thomas. They should be here within minutes."

Finally getting a clue, the young woman jumped to her feet.

"Nooo!" she screeched, her face turning redder than her nail polish. "Not the police! Haven't you done enough to poor Herman?"

She lunged at Jack, her sharp scarlet nails extended like cat claws.

"I'm going to rip your face off, you lousy, two-bit shamus!"

Jack caught her wrists before she could inflict any damage,

but still she struggled and even tried to knee him. Poor Thomas couldn't act. He had his hands full with Herman.

"Please, calm yourselves!" Marcel commanded.

The woman kicked again, rocking the desk enough to tumble the Tiffany lamp. Horrified, Marcel caught it midair and clutched it to his heart.

"I'll get you, ya filthy rat!" the woman wheezed.

It was clear that the only way she would quit was if Jack slugged her. But his innate chivalry prevented it. I was not so hobbled, however.

After gently setting down Toto Two, who scurried beneath a chair in the corner, I swung my Montezuma purple handbag with all my might. There was a loud bang that bounced off the walls, and the woman dropped to the rug.

I pulled Jack's dazed and moaning attacker to her feet, and she stumbled through the office door. Abandoning her "poor Herman" to his fate, she quickly exited the store.

"Thanks, partner," Jack said, sending a wink my way.

"My pleasure."

While I moved to comfort poor little Toto Two, Jack did the same for the jeweler.

Still clutching the Tiffany lamp, Marcel sank back into his chair. Jack reached across the desk, took the antique out of his grip, and carefully set it back on the ornate desk.

"Are you a policeman?" Marcel asked, mopping his brow with a silk handkerchief. "I heard that awful woman call you a shamus."

"Private," Jack replied, flashing his PI license.

Marcel nodded. "To what do I owe your timely interruption, Mr. Shepard?"

"This," Jack announced, flashing the key.

Marcel took the object, studied it for a moment, then handed it back with a profound sigh. "My last questionable job, and it's come back to haunt me."

"Tell me all about it, Marcel."

The safecracker-turned-jeweler shooed Thomas out of his office. Then he reached into his desk, laid out three glasses, and filled them from a Jameson's bottle.

"It was back in forty-five, late August. Wartime was finally ending, and my jewelry business was taking off. Then these two gentlemen showed up at closing time. They had guns but told me it wasn't a robbery. They just wanted to take me for a ride—"

"To where?"

"I was blindfolded, so I can't say. Whatever the place was, we went in through a back alley, then down some stairs. I remember I heard live music playing, a big-band orchestra; and when they took the blinders off, I found myself in a basement with a pile of strongboxes in front of me. They told me they'd give me a grand for each box I could open, and I was to keep my mouth shut."

Marcel paused. "Now, these weren't safes, but strongboxes. Picking a strongbox lock can be tricky, but these guys handed me the proper tools and I got to work."

"Any luck?"

"Took me all night, but I picked every lock," Marcel said proudly. "They fed me coffee. After a while, the orchestra stopped playing, but I kept on working."

"What was inside those boxes?"

Marcel shrugged. "Cash, stock certificates, gold coins, gemstones, different valuables in every strongbox. It was like Cracker Jack, Mr. Shepard. I didn't know what I'd find, but I knew there would always be a prize."

Marcel poured himself and Jack a second round. I covered my glass with one gloved hand and rubbed Toto Two's ears with the other.

"Of course, I didn't pay too much attention to the contents of those Ludlow boxes because that would not have been conducive to a long and healthy life. So, I minded my business and did the job."

He drained his glass. "But I do remember one box was different. It was number sixty-six, the number on your key."

"Did you crack it?"

"Sure."

"And inside?"

"A wad of cash as thick as a brick, and a painted lead statue of a dog—"

"A dog!" Jack and I echoed together.

"Are you sure?" Jack asked.

"Sure, I'm sure. I remember because of my twin daughters. They're grown now, but when they were young, they fell in absolute love with the *Wizard of Oz* movie. Begged to see it several times. And it struck me how much the dog statue looked like the little dog in that movie—"

"You mean, the dog Toto?!" I blurted. "Like this dog here?"

"That's right, like your little terrier."

"And what happened to the dog statue?" Jack pressed.

"As I recall, the men who took me to that basement handled the contents of that box special. Someone ordered another man to take the stuff—dog and all—upstairs to Mr. Lambert's office—"

"Lambert? You mean, Paul Lambert? The manager at the Aces High Club?"

"Jack," I whispered, "isn't that the club where your neighbor Donny, the big wrestler, used to work as a bouncer?"

Jack nodded and turned back to Marcel. "So, *was* it the same Paul Lambert? The manager of the Aces High Club?"

"And is that where they took you?" I added. "The basement of the club? You said you heard a big-band orchestra."

Marcel shrugged. "I don't know for sure. I don't frequent those places, and I never met this fellow Lambert."

"What happened next, Marcel?"

"They paid me. Very well. Blindfolded me, put me back in the car, and dropped me off in front of Penn Station, just in time for me to open my shop the next morning."

A gentle tapping on the door interrupted us.

"It's Thomas, sir. The police are here."

"I'll be right out, Thomas," Marcel called. Then he rose, adjusted his tux, and addressed Jack.

"So, Mr. Shepard, do you wish to take a bow for catching Mr. Hitch?"

Jack shook his head and took my arm. "I'd rather me, the lady, and the dog exit out the back door."

A few minutes later, we were wending our way through Penn Station's early rush hour crowd.

"So, that's two mysteries solved," I told Jack, hurrying to keep up with his long strides.

"Yeah?" he said, looking down at me. "How do you figure?"

"The letter said, *You have an Ace in the hole.* That's got to be the Aces High nightclub. And now we know that the dog you're supposed to be looking for is a *statue*, not a real dog like Toto Two here."

Ruff-ruff-ruff!

"Yes, that's you!" I cooed to the dog trotting happily beside us.

"Glad you're keeping up, partner," Jack said with a wink, "in more ways than one."

"Yes, and I'm doing it in heels!"

We exited on Eighth Avenue, where Jack hailed a cab. As I climbed in, I started to feel a little woozy.

"Jack, I think the Jameson's is catching up with me."

Toto Two curled up on my lap and looked up at me with sweet affection in her big brown eyes. I yawned. I couldn't help it.

"Rest your head on my shoulder, honey. I'll let you know when we arrive."

"Arrive where, Jack? Where are we going next?"

"Can't you guess?"

I would have, but my limbs suddenly felt lighter than feathers as my mind floated away.

CHAPTER 38

The Aces High

> I was well aware that . . . the baser side of human nature frequently triumphed over the higher, and that the well-known rule of dog eat dog always applied.
>
> —Agatha Christie, "The Adventure of the Cheap Flat"

MY SENSE OF floating soon subsided, and I felt solid again. But where was I? Opening my eyes, I sat up and found myself in the back of a New York City cab far too spacious to belong to my century. And I wasn't alone.

"Ready for your night out?" Jack asked.

"Night out? To where?"

"The Aces High Club. We've got a rendezvous with Mr. Paul Lambert."

I was shocked to find day had turned to night and my outfit had completely changed. Long opera gloves now covered my arms, and blue silk draped my body down to my calves—with noticeable exceptions. My shoulders were nearly naked, except for the two thin straps attached to the cross-wrapped bodice of my gown, designed to make me look like one of those classical Greek statues honoring some Olympian goddess.

The severe plunge in the neckline was particularly troubling. As far as I could feel, there was nothing under the silk, so if I bent over, I feared I might spill out!

"Really, Jack? I'm half naked!"

Jack draped a lacy shawl over my shoulders. "How's that? Better?"

"I guess."

"Just remember to take the wrap *off* before Lambert sees you. I want you to make a distracting impression on him, since you're halfway there already."

"What do you mean?"

"I did jobs for Lambert this month, last month, and the month before. Each time he wanted me to check some references—"

"Work related?"

"Personal. Lambert hired me to make sure several young women—all curvy, all redheads—were on the up-and-up. One of those dames, a sweet gal from Canarsie, ended up riding Lambert's arm. Well, for a few weeks, anyway."

"Your point?"

"Obviously, Paul Lambert goes ape over redheads. *You're* a redhead, and curvy, and I sure find you worth going ape over—" There was that wink again. "So I figured—"

"You'd use me as bait to charm the man?"

Jack nodded. "I've always thought you were one smart cookie, and you prove me right every day."

"Funny how I'm smart, but *you* take the credit for being right."

"I am the instructor, doll, so the acclaim naturally falls on my shoulders."

"Naturally."

Suddenly I remembered. "Hey, where's Toto Two?"

"Don't worry. She's fine. Donny's taking care of her."

The cab rolled to a stop in front of two brass doors with four illuminated aces over the entrance. Jack tossed the cabbie a quarter, stepped out, and helped me exit the taxi.

Jack approached the uniformed doorman. "Hi, Frankie. Say, is Paul in?"

"Mr. Lambert is on the floor, as always."

Jack slipped Frankie a fin, and we were inside.

The big-band music of a live orchestra hit us like a wall of sound as we passed through the lobby and entered the club. I felt Jack gently pulling the lacy shawl off my shoulders. "As discussed," he whispered in my ear. Then a hostess showed us to a table and handed us menus.

"Is this a steak and lobster house, Jack?" I asked, scanning the selections.

"The menu over at the Copacabana features Chinese food. Paul thought steak and lobster would help set his club apart, but let's stick with the bubbly . . ."

Jack tossed our menus aside and ordered a bottle of champagne.

"You might have asked if I'm hungry."

"Dinner isn't on your menu tonight, partner. Bubbly is. I want you loosened up. And Paul hungry—for you."

"In other words, I'm the one on the menu?"

"What can I say?" Jack shrugged. "You're in my day now. And that's the play."

"It's all right. I always wondered what it would feel like to be dangling from a fishing line."

Jack laughed. "That's the idea. Hang with me and look like a fresh catch. When Lambert takes the bait, I'll ask the questions."

The champagne arrived, and it tasted so heavenly, I forgot my appetite. I also forgot my objections to my plunging neckline, which meant Jack was right again. The tingly, sweet bubbles really did loosen me up!

Sipping away, I checked out the decor—a paean to casinos

with the trappings of gambling painted on the walls or hanging from the ceiling: roulette wheels, giant playing cards, dice-shaped salt and pepper shakers. No actual gambling was going on (that I could *see*, anyway) since that would have been illegal. But I got the distinct feeling that backroom games were happening somewhere on the premises.

Jack noticed where my attention had gone, and he leaned close. "The look over at the Copa is tropical. Lambert wanted something different, and since he's a high roller . . ."

"I can't wait to meet this hoodlum."

"He's no hoodlum. Lambert is as clean as polished glass. That's why he's running this place, or so it *appears*. As for the guy Paul is *partnered* with? I couldn't tell you because I don't have a clue."

As he spoke, Jack refilled my glass. We watched the club's customers twirling on the dance floor, and listened to the orchestra. After a while, the band took a break, leaving only their pianist to play soft jazz in the background for the diners.

"Redhead up, doll. Here comes Paul Lambert, and"— Jack elbowed me—"it looks like he's got an appetite for you."

CHAPTER 39

Jack's Jackpot

His face had taken on an avid, hungry look. "Anything you say, but I have to meet her."

—Mickey Spillane, "The Girl Behind the Hedge"

"HELLO, MR. SHEPARD."

When he finally showed, Paul Lambert surprised me. Tall, with military bearing, the white-haired older man was elegant, eloquent, and instantly charming.

He greeted Jack with a smile and a slap on the back, but from the moment he arrived at the table, his eyes never stopped devouring me.

Jack rose and slid out the extra chair. "Take a load off, Mr. Lambert. Penny here would be delighted to meet you."

"Penny!" he cried. "Short for Penelope, I take it? My mother's name was Penelope—"

Jack blinked. "I thought it was Mabel, like that gal from Canarsie—"

"*Penelope* Mabel," Lambert quickly insisted.

He sat close to me, and when I offered to shake hands, he kissed my glove instead, and he didn't let go.

"You've never been to my club before, have you, Penny? I would have remembered a stunning smile like yours."

Okaaaay. I slowly extracted my hand and used it to finish my drink. Paul Lambert immediately called for another bottle, which arrived freakishly fast—as if this were a well-oiled routine.

"This place can be such a bore, Penny," he said, pouring me a fresh drink, "but you have certainly added a thrill to my evening . . ."

He continued greasing my gears until the band took their places again.

"The music is about to resume. Would you care to dance?"

Before I could reply, Jack set the Ludlow key on the table in front of the nightclub manager. Lambert paused midflattery to stare hard at Jack.

"Say, what is this?"

"I have a question for you, Paul. About a strongbox. A pile of money. And the statue of a dog."

Paul Lambert sat back. "Why do you want to know?"

"Because someone hired me to find that dog."

Lambert scoffed. "A worthless statue and not the money?"

"My client never mentioned the money, only the mutt. If it's so worthless, why not hand it over?"

"Because I don't have it. You have to believe me, Shepard. I was just the delivery boy on that one."

Jack was visibly disappointed. "Then who *does* have it?"

Lambert looked nervous now. "I can't say. I can *never* say."

"Listen, I have important news for the person who has that statue. Maybe life-and-death news—"

Jack was bluffing, and I knew it. I only hoped Lambert didn't. After a meaningful pause, Jack tried again.

"This is a warning I can only deliver face-to-face. Believe me, they'll be grateful to hear it. Give me something."

Lambert thought it over. Then he leaned close.

"Nobody knows where he lives, Jack. He makes sure of that."

"So how do I talk to him?"

"He'll be at the wrestling match on Sunday night—"

"On Fourteenth Street? Where Donny wrestles?"

Lambert nodded, sweat beading his brow. "There's an office he uses inside the theater. You can catch him there— if he'll see you."

The conductor struck up the band and Lambert rose.

"A pleasure," he said with a curt bow.

"That went well," I whispered, and turned to face Jack but found his chair empty.

"Jack? Where did you go . . ."

I stood up to search the crowd for him, but there was no crowd. All of the people had vanished. The tables, chairs, and dance floor were all completely deserted. I was alone in a ghost club, yet the music grew louder and louder despite the band shell being as empty as the rest of the place.

What in the world?

Feeling woozy, I nearly stumbled over my chair.

"Jack? Where are you? Can you hear me? Come back!"

If the detective replied, I couldn't hear him. The ghost band was playing so loudly, I had to cover my ears. The room grew brighter, too, until a painfully white spotlight threatened to blind me.

I closed my eyes to shut out the glare.

"Jack, don't go! Please, I need your help . . ."

But what I needed didn't matter.

When I opened my eyes again, I was lying in my bed, staring at the ceiling.

CHAPTER 40

Who's That Girl?

There are a lot of loose ends to be gathered . . . but this
pipe dream I just told you fits in with all the facts we
know . . .

—Dashiell Hammett, "One Hour," *Black Mask*, 1924

THE END OF Jack's dream was so disturbing, it haunted
me for hours. I rolled out of bed with the ghost band's music
still blaring in my head, which felt absurdly dizzy from too
much phantom champagne.

A long, hot shower washed away the woozy. As my head
cleared and I dressed for a new day, I realized Jack was
schooling me by example.

It was no coincidence that, like Jack, I needed to uncover
the identity of someone I did not know. We both needed to
hook up with a mystery person who held something we
sought. In Jack's case, it was a man who had a dog statue. In
mine, a young woman who (I believed) had information.

Last night, Jack had shown me how he'd stayed on the
scent, like a dedicated hound dog, sniffing out leads until he

found a trail to follow. At the Aces High nightclub, he hit the jackpot with Lambert, who told him how to stay on that trail.

Now it was my turn.

I knew I had to uncover a lead on the missing girl in Jane Cunningham's life, the one she trusted enough to walk her beloved dog. The one who had suddenly disappeared right after Jane was shot—while Jane herself was walking Sparky. And though I didn't have much to go on, I knew what Jack would say—

That's what investigations are for.

Unfortunately, my investigation was on temporary hold. As much as I wanted to sniff out more leads, I had a busy day ahead of me . . .

It began in earnest after our usual Sunday service at the First Presbyterian Church, where Jane's name was lifted up in prayers for healing.

Sadie, Spencer, and I then returned to Buy the Book to open the store and pick up Sparky. Leaving the shop in the hands of Bonnie and grad student Tommy, we took the dog to the nondenominational Blessing of the Animals at St. Francis University's chapel.

Amber Breen attended, and many marchers from the parade came. I was hoping to speak with attorney Emory Stoddard, but he didn't show. Neither did Jeremy or his boa constrictor.

I didn't miss the snake, but I was sorry I missed a chance to question Stoddard about his confrontation with Stanley Cunningham after yesterday's Pet Parade. As Jane's attorney, Stoddard might even know something about the missing young woman who walked Jane's dog.

Still, I wasn't a cop or professional investigator. Given the strictures of attorney-client confidentiality, I doubted Stoddard would be willing to share much with me . . .

When we returned to the shop, Bonnie reported that

business had been slow, and I hoped the situation would change that evening when Amber sat for her first bookstore signing.

Tomorrow, she was scheduled for a lecture at the university. On Tuesday, she was hosting a night of dog-themed movies at Brainert's theater. But on Wednesday evening, Amber would be back in our store for a formal author talk, Q&A session, and signing party.

That event included an appearance by the star actress playing Amber's amateur sleuth in the streaming show based on her books. It was a tickets-only evening and completely sold out, so I expected whatever books we didn't sell tonight would be cleaned out by Wednesday. At least I *hoped* so. After Queen Ella Pruett had killed our selling opportunity at the pet show, chances were, we'd end up stuck with unsold stock, even after Amber's two signing events.

"Linda called," Bonnie said, interrupting my retail worries. "She and Milner baked a giant sheet cake for the signing tonight. Linda said it was *a gift*, for all the business you brought to their bakery. All they ask is that we supply the paper plates and plastic utensils." Bonnie grinned. "I already set up the coffee urn in the event space."

"How wonderful," Sadie declared, turning to me. "Bonnie and I can handle things here. Why don't you drive over to Greene's for the supplies?"

"Sure, they have a great party section," Bonnie added.

I agreed to go but had an ulterior motive. If I took Briar Patch Road instead of the highway, I'd drive right past Jane's house on Larchmont.

I ran upstairs and changed out of my Sunday best. As I left, I grabbed the Pearl Knight key chain from that bowl on the kitchen table. Jack or no Jack, I was determined to find out the identity of the mystery dog walker. From what Mrs. Meyers had told me, I deduced that the girl (with the white-blond hair and vintage tortoiseshell glasses) must have been a tenant in Jane's big house, and one of the two keys probably unlocked her apartment door.

If I knocked on the door and the mystery woman was there, she'd no doubt be pleased to get her keys back—and, I hoped, would be willing to answer my questions. And if she wasn't there?

Well, I'd unlock that future when I got to it.

By the time I turned onto Larchmont, however, I could feel my resolve slipping and my thoughts fly off in a frenzy of dire predictions—

What if I set off a burglar alarm? What if Stoddard hired a security guard to stay at the house? Or, worse, what if the person who shot Jane is waiting there?

As Jane's sprawling yellow brick house came into view, a masculine voice firmly cut off my what-if party—

Mother Machree, Penny! What if you find out everything you need to know? That's a possibility, too. You could crack this case right now and be home for supper.

"Do you really think that's a possibility, Jack?"

There's only one way to find out. Just keep doing what you're doing and remember that every key opens a lock. The trick is finding the right lock.

My PI spirit's words buoyed my courage. I rolled into the driveway, cut the engine, and stepped outside.

As usual, the wind was strong on top of Larchmont Hill. The tops of the swishing conifer trees swayed as low clouds blocked the sun. Under my jacket, I suppressed a shiver.

No one was about, and there were no cars in the driveway. I quickly discovered the porticoed front porch led to Jane's portion of the big yellow house. I already knew that she'd converted the large home into separate apartments (with Bud Napp's help). But I didn't know how many, or anything about her current tenants.

Jane's property included a two-story, two-car garage,

which looked deserted. But on the other end of the house, there was a large, glass-enclosed porch, which I assumed led to those other apartments.

I followed a pebbled sidewalk to the back steps and found the porch door wide open. I stepped over the threshold. The area was large enough for a garden party, but the decor was Spartan—a cold stone floor, a few potted plants, and a pair of wrought iron chairs.

I crossed the sandstone floor to a second door, which led into the house. To my surprise, that one was also wide open. More promising, there were two doorbells and two mailboxes—one for someone named Troy Hanley, the other for a Gemma Osborn.

There, see that, doll?

See what?

An easy choice. I doubt the dame you're looking for is named Troy. Why, this is turning out to be a snap.

I pressed Ms. Osborn's bell and heard the muffled ring from inside an apartment. Three rings later, there was still no reply.

Should I . . . ?

What are you waiting for?

I called out a hello before entering the house. When the reply was silence, I moved into a wide carpeted hallway. A single low-watt bulb in a fixture was all that illuminated the area, so I couldn't see from outside that the short hall ended at a cul-de-sac with—

Three doors? How can there be three doors, Jack? Looks like we hit our first speed bump.

Speed bump? That doesn't even make sense. And you have the nerve to complain about my lingo.

Sorry, Jack. It means a hitch or a complication.

Okey-doke. But there's nothing complicated about a door. Pick one and knock.

None of the three entrances had a number or a name, so

I knocked on the door in the middle. Again, there was no response. Before Jack had a chance to hound me, I pulled the Pearl Knight with the attached keys from my pocket and shoved one into the lock. It didn't work, and when I tried the only other key on the chain, it wouldn't even fit.

I heard myself sigh. *Wrong door.*

You've got two more, Penny.

I moved to the one on the left side of the hall. I knew by sight that the key that didn't fit the last lock wouldn't fit this one, either, so I switched them. Unfortunately, I'd grown impatient and didn't bother to knock.

The tip of the second key had barely touched the lock when someone yanked open the door.

Sunlight streamed into the gloomy hallway, blinding me. Through blurry eyes I made out a male figure silhouetted against the glare. His arm was raised, and a knife was clutched in his hand!

CHAPTER 41

Remote Worker

You still fail to realize how this sort of talk sickens me.
Now please go.

—Iris Murdoch, *The Green Knight*

DUCK! JACK SHOUTED.

I was way ahead of the ghost. But I didn't duck. I jumped backward so fast, I slammed into the opposite door. Groaning, I was ready to bolt down the hall when my attacker froze in place, and I realized what I'd *thought* was a knife turned out to be a long, thin remote-control device.

"Who the hell are you and what are you doing here?" the man cried.

"Calm down," I said, showing him my palms. "My name is Penelope McClure. I run the local bookstore on Cranberry Street."

"What do you want?" he said, his tone more reasonable, though far from warm and cuddly. "You're lucky I didn't hurt you. My landlady just got shot."

"I know. Mrs. Cunningham is a friend."

His expression remained wary.

"I'm sorry I alarmed you," I said, "but I came here looking for someone."

"Who?"

"The young woman who walked Mrs. Cunningham's dog. I need to speak with her. I think her name is Gemma Osborn."

The man stared at me through distant, emotionless eyes for a few protracted seconds—long enough to make me uncomfortable.

Then he scoffed. "It wasn't *Gemma* who walked the landlady's dog. Gemma Osborn is allergic to dogs."

Only then did I recognize this man. I'd seen him in the town square two days ago—the morning Amber Breen taught Spencer how to handle Sparky.

I didn't immediately realize who he was because his elaborate arm and leg tattoos were now covered by baggy black sweatpants and a shapeless Brown University sweatshirt.

Close up, this man appeared even older than he had in the park. Despite the fashionable haircut (with that shock of dark brown curls on top and buzz-cutting around the sides and back) and the silver earring, he appeared to be at least thirty, maybe older.

"I'm sorry for the mistake," I said. "You see, I read the names on the mailbox out front and just assumed Gemma was the dog walker. Are you Troy Hanley—?"

"What's it to you?"

This guy needs a lesson in manners, Jack cracked. *Or maybe just a smack in the kisser.*

I took a breath. "I told you. I'm looking for the young woman who walked Mrs. Cunningham's dog. I thought it was Ms. Osborn, but if you say I'm wrong—"

"You're wrong."

Friendly sort, ain't he?

Hush, Jack.

"It doesn't sound like you can help me—"

"No," he replied snidely, "it doesn't."

Oh, brother. If I only had a fist.

"I don't suppose Ms. Osborn is around?"

He folded his arms. "She is not."

"I'd like to speak with her when she gets back. I presume you know so much about Ms. Osborn because you're friends—"

"I *work* with Gemma."

"In town?"

"Remotely," he replied, offering no further details.

I persisted. "You work right here, then? So that means you're on Larchmont Avenue most of the time, right? And you really don't know about the woman who walked Mrs. Cunningham's dog?"

Again, Troy Hanley gave me that far-off stare for a beat longer than necessary. Only this time I stared right back at him.

"Her name is Rebecca Wilkes," he said in a tone that sounded a lot like he was surrendering something.

"She lives here?"

"She did, but not anymore." Eyes on me, he tapped the middle door using his plastic remote. "Rebecca has moved on."

"Did she work with you, too?"

Smirking, he shook his head.

"Do you know where I can find—"

A young woman's voice, calling from the stone-and-glass porch, interrupted us.

"Hey, Troy, when I left this morning, the police—"

The young woman stepped into the hallway, then froze when she spied me.

Though her dark hair was now pulled into a tight bun on top of her head, and her Goth lipstick was so deep red, it looked almost black, I recognized her as the same young woman I'd seen with Troy in the park.

Unlike Troy, she seemed even younger up close, or perhaps it was her outfit. In a short black dress with a high Peter Pan collar and sleeves that ended with lacy white cuffs, she looked like a young-adult version of Wednesday Addams— if Wednesday wore black nail polish and had a nose ring. In each hand, the woman carried a Koh's Market shopping bag. And a copy of the *Quindicott Bulletin* was tucked under one arm.

"What were you saying about the police?" Troy demanded.

"They were up the block, in front of that weird blue house."

As she spoke, she eyed me, her puzzled expression almost comical. Finally, she asked, "Who are—?"

"She runs the bookstore in town," Troy snapped. "She's looking for Rebecca."

The girl's painted lips twisted into a smirk not unlike her coworker's.

"If you're looking for Rebecca of Sunnybrook Farm, you're in the wrong place. She—"

"Is gone," Troy interrupted. "I told her already."

He snatched one of the bags out of the woman's hand. "You were supposed to be here an hour ago, Gemma."

"It's Sunday—"

"So what?" he fired back. "The home office scheduled an emergency Zoom call. The site crashed—"

"Last night when you were out? Because I wasn't monitoring things."

"No, it happened an hour ago. I've been working on it. Come on, we're already running late for this call. We'll use my computer."

As Troy spoke, he muscled Gemma Osborn toward the half-open door.

"Excuse me, Ms. Osborn," I pressed. "I know you're in a

hurry, but can you tell me where Rebecca Wilkes might be? I really need to speak with her. It's urgent."

The girl shrugged even as her coworker urged her across the threshold.

"I don't have a clue," Gemma called over her shoulder. "Maybe you should ask Rebecca's friend, the pretty blond boy with the snake."

The door slammed in my face, but I just stood there, processing what I'd heard. *The pretty blond boy with the snake?* There was only one person I knew who fit that description. Could it be the same person?

I don't know, doll. How many blond boys with snakes are running around your Podunk town?

"I'm fairly sure Jeremy is it."

That makes your next move a walk in the park.

"Does it? I don't know Jeremy's last name or where he hangs his serpent at night. Seymour said something about Broad Street, but a lot of young people hang out on Broad Street."

You should brace the mailman, then.

Recalling my recent discussion with Eddie. I knew there was no need.

"We can leave Seymour out of this one, Jack. There's someone who knows Jeremy even better than the mailman— and I pay her salary."

CHAPTER 42

Where's That Girl?

It is sometimes difficult for a dog to find a scent, but once he has found it, nothing on earth will make him leave it! That is, if he is a good dog!

—Agatha Christie, "The Chocolate Box"

I RETURNED TO Buy the Book with a plan—along with shopping bags of paper plates, plastic forks, and disposable cups. Bookstore duty called, after all, and though Amber Breen's signing was two hours away, the shop was already filling up.

We couldn't just let everyone mill around the store aisles and block the shoppers, so I had Spencer bring out the brass (-looking) poles and velvet (polyester) ropes. After steering the autograph seekers into a line on the sidewalk, we mollified them with complimentary slices of cake and bottomless cups of free coffee.

When I took a restroom break, I found Bonnie Franzetti in the event space, preparing a third urn of joe. That was when Jack goosed me with a cold draft and his frank opinion of my event preparations—

Enough with the bookstore baloney! Time to put your plan into motion and get the bobby-soxer on board.

Okay, okay, I told the ghost. *Keep your spectral pants on!*

"Hey, Bonnie," I called in as innocent a tone as I could muster. "After we close this evening, are you free? Or are you scheduled to make pizzas at your dad's shop?"

"On a weekend?" She rolled her big brown eyes. "That's where I draw the line. Saturday and Sunday nights are mine."

"So, you have plans?"

She grinned and nodded.

"Plans that include a trip to Broad Street and a romantic interest named Jeremy, by any chance?"

Bonnie Franzetti flat-out blushed. "Oh, God," she cried in a pitch two octaves higher than I'd ever heard come out of her mouth. "Please, *please*, don't tell Eddie. If he suspects—"

"Oh, he suspects."

Bonnie made a pained sound not unlike her brother's.

"Listen, Bonnie. I'm not going to report your activities to the deputy chief, and I'm not planning on ruining your Sunday night. I just need to speak with Jeremy for a few minutes, and then I'm gone."

"But why?"

"Jeremy may have information that will lead me to a missing person. That person might know something about what happened to Jane Cunningham, maybe even who shot her—and why."

Bonnie blinked, puzzled. "I don't see how Jeremy can help."

"I'll explain everything on our way to Broad Street. We'll leave right after Buy the Book closes."

The signing went incredibly well. Amber showed up early and stayed late. We moved so many inscribed books, my worries about *unsold* stock turned into concerns about *lack* of it for her Wednesday event!

Sadie didn't blink. She swung into action, placing a rush online order for many more copies, to be delivered Tuesday.

"Wow. That's a big order," I said, looking at the computer screen. "After all the sales today, do you really think we'll move that many?"

"I know this business, Pen. Anything we don't sell, Amber and her streaming star can both autograph, and we'll offer the editions as *numbered collectibles* online with a photo we take of them signing together. How does that sound?"

"Perfect."

Before the night was over, Amber Breen asked me about the progress in the Cunningham case. I filled her in on Jane's condition (no change), but I withheld my thoughts about the mystery dog walker Rebecca Wilkes.

Frankly, I was flummoxed.

After the store closed—while Sadie handled the register and Bonnie tidied up the event space—I tried (yet another) Internet search on Rebecca Wilkes and came up with zero. I rechecked Facebook, Instagram, Twitter, and even TikTok, but I could find no one who used that name and fit the descriptions I'd been given.

Despite Jack's usual grumbles about my "Buck Rogers" tactics, I could tell the PI part of him was genuinely impressed.

In my day, there were only a few places for a PI to check out a name.

Let me guess. The telephone book?

That's right, doll.

And the others?

Local hospitals. Police departments. Hotel registers. And when all else failed, the obituary pages.

Well, unlike every other social-media-obsessed young

woman in America, our Ms. Wilkes appears to be off the grid.

Maybe she's shy, Jack replied.

What bugs me is that other people in this town saw her, met her, talked to her. But for me, Rebecca Wilkes of Quindicott, Rhode Island, does not exist.

It could be that the elusive Miss Wilkes is hiding out in Quindicott. Maybe that's why she's keeping a low profile.

But hiding from who or what? And why? And if she is hiding, and Deputy Chief Eddie can't find her, how am I going to do it?

Jack's hard-boiled answer: *There's always the obituary pages.*

This is a small town, I reminded the ghost. *If Rebecca Wilkes was dead, the gossip would have reached us before any journalist touched a keyboard.*

Unless nobody's found the body yet.

To that, I had no answer.

BY THE TIME I turned off our shop's lights, Amber was back at the Finch Inn, enjoying a "hot bath and hot toddy." Spencer had climbed the stairs to watch the Intrigue Channel with Sparky, and Aunt Sadie was settling next to them with a big bowl of buttered popcorn.

For Bonnie, me, and the ghost of Jack Shepard, however, a relaxing night of watching old *Jack Shield* episodes was not in the cards.

"I was supposed to meet Jeremy at nine thirty," Bonnie said. "We're already late."

"Give him a call. Tell him you're on your way."

Bonnie frowned. "I tried. He didn't pick up."

"Then we'd better get going."

I unlocked the car, and we both climbed in.

"Where to?" I asked, starting the engine.

"The Hound's Tooth. It's on Broad Street near the railroad tracks."

"I've never heard of that place."

"Hound's Tooth is kind of a dive bar, but pretty cool," Bonnie said, shaking out her thick dark hair and taking a brush to it. "It's mostly townies, but some students from St. Francis hang out there, too."

Meanwhile, Jack was practically giddy.

We're off to a gin mill on a weekend! It feels like the old days again. Down a shot or three for me, doll.

Nobody's downing any shots, Jack.

Ten minutes later we crossed the railroad tracks, and I spied the rickety two-story building with neon letters spelling out *Hound's Tooth* in the cracked and dirty front window. The bar certainly earned the title *dive*. Dimly lit, its decor was so out of fashion, it had become retro-trendy, which was evidently the appeal of the dingy establishment.

Fortunately, we didn't remain very long. Though we were late, we soon found out we hadn't missed Jeremy.

"Sorry, Bonnie," the bearded young bartender said. "Jeremy hasn't been here tonight. Someone else was looking for him earlier—"

"Who?" I interrupted.

He shrugged. "I never saw her before. Cute girl with short, white-blond hair and glasses. She asked if I'd seen Jeremy, and when I said no, she didn't stick around to wait for him to show."

I could tell by Bonnie's expression that she wasn't happy to hear about some "cute" young woman looking for her dream snake handler, but I was secretly thrilled. The woman's description sounded like Rebecca Wilkes!

I pressed the bartender, but he didn't know anything more—not the girl's name or why she was looking for Jeremy. Still, it was a clue that we were on the right track; and if we found Jeremy tonight, we might find Rebecca, too.

"We're not waiting for him here," Bonnie declared. "I know where Jeremy lives now. We should go there."

As we climbed back into my car, I grilled Bonnie. "You just said that you know where Jeremy lives *now*. You made it sound like he lived somewhere else recently."

She nodded. "He used to rent half of a two-family home on Shilling Street, until Jane Cunningham evicted him two months ago."

"I remember you told me Jane was very strict with her tenants. Were you talking about what happened to Jeremy?"

She nodded again.

"Did Jane object to his boa constrictor?"

Bonnie made a face. "Actually, she got mad because Jeremy did a little custom rewiring—"

"Rewiring? Of the electricity? Why?"

Bonnie shrugged. "I guess because Jeremy has a lot of computers and stuff. He has satellite dishes and everything."

I turned the ignition. "So, Bonnie, where are we going to find Jeremy tonight?"

"He's renting a trailer at the Wentworth Arms."

"The Wentworth Arms?"

I heard myself making that pained Eddie noise. But it couldn't be helped. The trailer park had an unsavory reputation, and I did not relish a trip there, especially at this time of night.

"I just hope Jeremy's home," I said.

"Me, too," Bonnie replied, scowling the scowl of a woman scorned. "And except for that snake, he'd better be there alone."

I didn't tell Bonnie, but I was hoping for the exact opposite.

CHAPTER 43

A Walk in the Trailer Park

I made what might have been a mistake. For a good
reason, of course, which is how the worst mistakes get
made.

— Spencer Quinn, *Heart of Barkness*

GRAVEL CRUNCHED UNDER the tires as I rolled my car
through the entrance to the Wentworth Arms.

When I was very young, this flat stretch of ground, just off
the highway, was known as the Wentworth Flea Market, a
lively outdoor swap meet that drew antiques dealers, vintage
clothiers, and artisans, along with hobbyists, collectors, and
pack rats from all over the region.

With the rise of Etsy, eBay, and global Internet markets,
sellers lost interest in spending their time, energy, and dollars schlepping physical goods to a rented table, and the flea
market was reincarnated as a mobile home park offering
short- and long-term leases for transients.

Someone with a keen sense of irony had added the word
Arms to the name—without bothering to add a heraldic coat

of arms to the sign, which was now as run-down as the large, weed-strewn lot and the worn trailers sitting on it.

"Jeremy's renting a big white trailer near the back of the park," Bonnie said. "You can't miss it. He hung twinkly lights all over his place."

We drove slowly, past rows of mobile homes. A few were unoccupied, their windows black or shuttered. Other windows were filled with lights and activity. I heard music and the sounds of blaring televisions. Garbage collection was spotty, with overflowing trash spilling out of rusty steel dumpsters.

Farther on, a half dozen men of various ages circled a bonfire roaring inside a steel drum. Empty cans of Narragansett Lager were scattered around them. As we passed, the smell of stale beer and burning wood permeated my car, and the men—every last one of them—leered our way. Their interest in two women driving alone through this half-deserted campground was a little too intense for my comfort level.

I noticed Bonnie shifting uneasily, as well.

"Just keep going, Mrs. McClure."

Listen to the bobby-soxer, Jack advised. *Keep the car moving and your eyes open.*

"Turn here," Bonnie said. "Jeremy lives at the end of this lane."

"I hope we don't run into more overly curious male tenants."

"Don't worry. We won't. Jeremy has the only occupied trailer on the whole lane. He values his privacy."

No sooner did I make the turn than Bonnie cried out, "Stop the car!"

I braked. "What's the matter?"

Bonnie managed to shake her head and shrug at the same time.

"Something's wrong."

She pointed to the big white mobile home at the end of a long row of darkened trailers. It was the only one with a satellite dish on top of it.

"All the lights are out at Jeremy's place. Even his twinkly lights aren't working, and they're *always* on."

Before I could stop her, Bonnie threw off her seat belt and exited the car. I cut the engine but left the headlights on. I also grabbed my flashlight from the glove compartment.

The night was cool, the air carrying the smell of woodsmoke and another odor I recognized as the skunkweed smell of marijuana. I heard the voices and laughter of those men by the fire and was relieved they sounded far off.

"The door is wide open," Bonnie whispered as we moved past the silent row of vacant mobile homes. "Why would it be open if all the lights are off?"

I strained to hear any sign of Jeremy being home, but beyond those faint voices in the distance, the only sounds came from the shifting gravel under our feet.

Just then a loud thump startled us—the sound of a heavy object falling. Bonnie and I froze, watching Jeremy's trailer rock.

"He *is* in there!" Bonnie exclaimed.

Grinning with happy relief, she opened her mouth to call out, and I immediately covered it.

"Shh! Stay quiet," I warned her. "That might not be Jeremy. Let's make sure before we announce ourselves."

I didn't remove my hand from Bonnie's face until she nodded.

As we crept closer, the glowing headlights from my car made strange shadows. Two heavy wooden Adirondack chairs, set up like lawn furniture in front of Jeremy's temporary home, looked like hulking monsters in the eerie night.

The twinkly lights that Bonnie had mentioned were all dark and hanging loose, their wires cut.

More wires—big ones—ran out of the mobile home's open window and up an old wooden utility pole beside it. A second satellite dish had been fixed on top of that pole, and a long cable, as thick as Jeremy's boa constrictor, dangled from a humming metal box on top of the pole. It was so long, it nearly touched the gravel.

"That looks dangerous," I whispered.

Jack agreed. *Like you, honey, that's a live wire. Steer clear, and keep the bobby-soxer out of the way, too. She tends to act dopey.*

Just then I heard a human sound, like a man grunting from exertion. It came from inside the darkened mobile home.

"See! Jeremy *is* in there!" Bonnie assured me, bolting forward.

"Bonnie, wait!"

Ignoring my warning (and making Jack's point for him), she foolishly headed for the open trailer door. I was thankful that she gave the dangling cable a wide berth—not because she'd noticed it, but because she couldn't wait to see Jeremy.

But it wasn't Jeremy inside. A fact she discovered when she nearly collided with a skinny vagrant, his scrawny arms struggling to balance a bulky metal box that I realized was the trailer's air conditioner.

She screamed.

He screamed.

Then the burglar lost his grip, and the heavy machine fell. Bonnie stumbled back as it smashed through the wooden steps leading up to the trailer door.

"Stupid girl!" the man roared, kicking out. "Look what you made me do!"

His filthy boot connected with Bonnie's stomach, and she cried out. Falling to the ground, she curled into a protective ball as the burglar came for her, his face a mask of rage.

"Stop!" I screamed with fury. "Don't you dare touch her!"

My warning worked. Seeing me with my Maglite raised like a weapon, the burglar changed his mind about pummeling Bonnie. Fists clenched, he lunged toward me.

Oh, hell no, Jack said.

In less than an instant, the air froze, chilling my spine as an arctic funnel cloud lifted one of Jeremy's heavy wooden lawn chairs and hurled it into the burglar's torso.

The force of the blow sent his body backward and directly into the live cable. For a brief second, the night lit up with a blue-white flash. The powerful charge sent the hapless burglar backward again, this time slamming him against the trailer.

The vagrant's body slid to the ground, and I blinked away light motes, watching dust settle back into the gravel like ash on a burned-out pyre. Slowly, the cold wind dissipated, and my spine warmed again.

"Thank you, Jack," I whispered.

But Jack didn't reply, and I wasn't surprised, given how much psychic energy he must have used to defend us.

Bonnie, still crouched in a ball, peeked out between open fingers.

"Oh, my God. Is he alive?"

The man was now a crumpled heap on the gravel. As I approached his still form, the smell of ozone and singed hair filled my nostrils, but I could see his chest rise and fall.

"It's okay. He's breathing."

I turned my flashlight's beam on the man's face, but I didn't recognize him, and neither did Bonnie.

"Are you okay?" I asked.

"I'm fine," she said. "And I'll be right back."

"Bonnie, stop!" I cried, seeing her enter the mobile home.

Fearing a second burglar might be hiding inside, I hurried toward the trailer's front door. Thank goodness, she quickly came out again (unharmed) and announced—

"Jeremy is gone. I don't know where or why. He even left his phone behind. What should we do?"

"Call 911," I replied, pulling out my own phone.

As I punched the numbers, Bonnie sighed.

"I sure hope my brother's not on duty."

CHAPTER 44

Shocking Developments

Got a better theory?

—Lilian Jackson Braun, *The Cat Who Could Read Backwards*

DEPUTY CHIEF EDDIE Franzetti stepped out of the looted mobile home, carefully avoiding the shattered steps. With a final glance over his shoulders, he shook his head and approached us.

With clenched fists resting on his gun-belted hips, Eddie spoke in a tight, controlled voice—a control he soon lost.

"Penelope, Bonnie . . . Could you tell me *just what the hell you were doing here?*"

I wasn't intimidated, but I felt for poor Bonnie. Before her brother arrived, she'd thought she was in the clear . . .

Since light shows were uncommon at the Wentworth Arms, our electrical display had grabbed immediate attention. A small mob had appeared at the end of the gravel lane.

The unidentified burglar had regained his senses around the same time that Bonnie and I had heard the wail of the approaching sirens.

It was Officer Bull McCoy (and not Eddie) who'd arrived at the scene first, along with the ambulance and a big white truck from the power company.

Bonnie had been relieved to see that Chief Ciders's nephew answered the call. She knew Bull wouldn't ask too many questions and would likely cut us loose rather than complicate his quiet Sunday night.

But before the paramedics could leave with the injured burglar, another QPD vehicle arrived—this one driven by Eddie Franzetti. When Bonnie spied her older brother, she made that pained sound I had come to know so well.

At first, the deputy chief ignored us both and grilled the burglar instead. After the ambulance departed, he spoke to the power company workers. Then he walked right past Bonnie and me and entered the trailer.

"When he comes out, let me do the talking," I whispered.

"Sure," Bonnie said with a shrug. "But it won't do a bit of good."

When Eddie exited the trailer, he finally approached us and asked that million-dollar question—

"Could you tell me *just what the hell you were doing here?*"

I held up my hand. "Eddie, I want you to know this whole thing is on me. I'm the one who pulled Bonnie into this. She's perfectly innocent."

"Is that so?"

"Yes. I dragged Bonnie here because I needed to see her friend Jeremy."

"The guy who lives in this trailer?"

"Lived!" Bonnie cried. "Now he's missing—"

"He had a very good reason to get out of town, Bonnie." Hands on hips, Eddie stood over his sister. "Do you know anything about Jeremy? Anything at all?"

"Jeremy is a nice guy—"

"He's been stealing power from the town grid," Eddie

interrupted. "And he's rigged a satellite dish to the top of that old utility pole and another on his mobile home's roof. He must have ten computers and I don't know what else in there. What was he doing, trying to contact aliens?"

Bonnie was defiant. "He said he had an online business!"

"With *what*, the CIA? And why is everything smashed up in there?"

"Ask that creep we caught robbing the place," Bonnie shot back.

"I did. His name is Norman Rice. He's a drug addict who lives right here at Wentworth Arms. For him, this was a simple crime of opportunity. He saw the door wide open and the place already ransacked. So he decided to take some things for himself."

Eddie sighed. "That trailer was wrecked more than twenty hours ago—just after four A.M. this morning, in fact."

"How do you know?"

Eddie tapped his head. "Brilliant deductive reasoning. There's a broken clock in there displaying the date and time."

"Oh."

"You still haven't told me why you're both here."

I spoke up. "I thought Jeremy might know something about Mrs. Cunningham's shooting. Actually, I thought he might know a *person* who may know something about that crime—and like Jeremy, this young woman is a *missing* person."

"I have no reports on any missing persons, Pen."

"I told you about her yesterday, Eddie. She's a dog walker for Jane Cunningham. And she just happened to vanish the same time that Mrs. Cunningham was shot. Earlier today, one of Jane's tenants told me her name is Rebecca Wilkes. No one knows what happened to her, and I have yet to track her down."

"You believe this Ms. Wilkes is a *suspect*?"

"Either that or a material witness—"

"To what, Pen?"

"To Mrs. Cunningham's life. She might know something about the person who shot her."

"Okay," Eddie said, clearly out of patience. "I can't fault you for your fanciful theorizing because you haven't heard."

"Heard what?"

"We have Jane Cunningham's shooter in custody. I arrested him this morning."

"Him?" I sputtered. "Who—?"

"Her neighbor on Larchmont Avenue. Robert Slattery."

"That's impossible. Slattery may be a bit unhinged, but I think he's harmless, and so does Dr. Rubino—"

"We have evidence, Pen, and a motive."

"Motive? Because of a vandalized garden?"

"Because of a long-running feud between the Slattery family and Carl Cunningham's real estate business."

"What does Jane's late husband's business have to do with anything?"

"The two families have been in a legal scuffle over a valuable piece of property for a decade, the land where Slattery's General Store burned down. That suit was finally settled in court and not to the Slattery family's benefit."

"Okay," I relented, "but what's your evidence?"

"Four spent twenty-two-caliber cartridges," Eddie replied. "They match the bullet that struck Mrs. Cunningham."

"Where did you find them?"

"In Slattery's tree house. I just got a hunch and climbed up there. It's rickety, but from that vantage point, you can clearly see Briar Patch Road and the exact spot where Mrs. Cunningham was shot."

"What about a weapon? Did you find the rifle?"

Some of the certainty faded from Eddie's face.

"Not yet, but Robert Slattery is a hoarder, and we really haven't begun a serious search. The state police agreed to send gun-sniffing dogs tomorrow, so it's only a matter of time."

"One last question, Eddie. Did you ever interview Stanley Cunningham and Ella Pruett?"

"I did. And they have alibis, Pen, solid ones."

"But what if—"

Eddie raised his hand. "They check out, Pen. At the time Jane Cunningham was shot, her brother-in-law, Stanley, was in New York City, where he works as a bartender, and Ella was in Providence, in a face-to-face meeting with a mortgage banker."

"You didn't let me finish," I replied.

Eddie folded his arms. "Go ahead."

"I was trying to say that with so much to gain if Jane were out of the picture, Stan and Ella could have hired *someone else* to do the shooting, which makes their *solid* alibis sound pretty convenient, if you think about it."

"Sorry, Pen." Eddie shook his head. "I have no time for elaborate conspiracy theories. I have a suspect. I have a motive. And I have solid evidence. In the next twelve hours, I expect I'll find the weapon, too. Case closed."

CHAPTER 45

Wrestle Mania

There is no honor in not fighting at all.

—Mark William Calaway aka the Undertaker (WWF/E, retired)

BY THE TIME I dropped Bonnie off at her dad's pizza shop, commiserated with the poor thing about her missing boyfriend, and climbed the stairs to my home above the bookstore, it was well past midnight.

Bookmark needed some love and attention, so I carried her upstairs and placed her on my bed. The poor cat soon got an earful, because I had nowhere else to vent my anger—and I was hopping mad.

"Case closed?" I muttered as I kicked off my shoes. "What makes Eddie so certain he's on the right track?"

I collapsed on the bed, flat on my back, still dressed. "I'm telling you, Bookmark, anyone could have climbed that tree and shot Jane."

Bookmark quietly crawled onto my chest and started kneading my sweater. I continued to rant—

"Unless the police find the weapon in Slattery's house, you can color me unconvinced."

Color you unconvinced? Jack said, speaking for the first time since the shocking incident at the trailer park. *Please tell me* unconvinced *is one of those high-fashion shades like Montezuma purple.*

"Jack! You're back! Thank goodness, but I could have used your help an hour ago when I was dealing with Eddie."

I heard your rant, doll. I just didn't have the juice to reply. But what do you expect? Police minds are basic. Most run on one gear, and they prefer not to shift.

"I expected more from Eddie."

Your friend Eddie is like every other cop. He likes to keep things simple, and he wants the case closed, preferably with an open-and-shut, straight-as-a-ruler bedtime story to tell a DA and jury.

Purring, Bookmark settled down contentedly beside me while I gently rubbed her ears.

"I can certainly understand Eddie's preference. I want this crime solved, too. And I want a nice, neat conclusion, but I still see too many glass balls in the air—and I'm still juggling. Now I have a mystery woman who's vanished. Jeremy went from *eccentric* to clearly sketchy. And I'm convinced a grieving, innocent widower has become a victim of circumstance—and was falsely arrested."

We'll work on your case, Penny. I promise. But right now it's past your bedtime, and you need to rest.

"I'll close my eyes, Jack, but I'm too upset to fall asleep."

Just close your eyes, honey, and I'll help you along.

"How are you going to do that?"

I'm gonna show you how I solved my own doggone mystery . . .

* * *

"I SAY, MOI-DAH da bum!"

Startled, I opened my eyes—and almost closed them again. A moment ago, I was lying in my bed, talking to my cat. Now I was sitting in a sea of screaming people, all shouting madly at two hugely muscled men squaring off inside a brightly lit wrestling ring below.

Suddenly jostled, I nearly lost my balance. Jack Shepard's solid arms caught me before I pitched headlong off the mezzanine and into the howling mob below. Protectively, he pulled me close—close enough for me to breathe in his fresh-smelling aftershave.

"I got you, doll! And I won't let go till you get your sea legs!"

Comforting words, if they hadn't been shouted at maximum volume, in a vain attempt to outvoice the throng.

Beside us, a woman in a plaid muumuu (that's right: a *plaid* muumuu) jumped to her feet, yelling at the top of her lungs.

"Tro him ovah da ropes!"

With all her might, she hurled something small and green at the ring below. *No, it couldn't be.* But it was—a gherkin from a pickle jar! She waved another in the air. And she wasn't the only one.

"Come on," she screamed. "*Pickle* him, ya palooka!"

Soon the mob around me took up the chant, until the whole arena echoed with the cry.

"Pickle him! Pickle him! Pickle him!"

I covered my ears to muffle the racket, though my eyes remained glued to the ring.

Just then the man in the green wrestling trunks ducked low, scooped up his opponent (in fiery red) and spun him over his head. With a loud BANG, he dropped the man on the canvas. Red Trunks bounced like a rubber ball, until the guy in green dived on top of him and pinned his thrashing opponent to the mat.

"He pickled him!" a man shouted gleefully. "He pickled him good!"

The ref counted to ten, and the man in green raised his hands in victory. The announcer stepped into the ring.

"And the winner of the third bout at our Majestic Palace Arena is Kirby Dill, the green man who gives the gals a thrill."

Pickles filled the air as shouts from boys, grown men, and (surprisingly) plenty of women assaulted my ears.

It reminded me of the evening Brainert, Seymour, and I watched *Gladiator* together on cable. *Jeopardy!* champ Seymour insisted that the biggest fans of the gladiatorial games in ancient Rome were women—housewives, single women, the privileged spouses of the elite, even vestal virgins all relished blood sport even more than their male counterparts.

I'd hardly believed it when Seymour told us. But it proved to be true, according to the encyclopedia I checked. And seeing all the screaming women around me, I now believed him on a whole other level.

"It's too bad you missed Donny," Jack cried over the roar. "He and Ivan the Terrible really went at it."

"Donny won?"

"No contest. Our Dogface Donny Danger took out the Russian in the fifth round, when he broke a chair over Ivan the Terrible's noggin."

"Oh, gee. I'm sorry I missed *that*."

"It *was* something," Jack replied with a little smile that told me he was intentionally ignoring my sarcasm.

Meanwhile, interest in the green man waned as the announcer moved on to the next bout, between Sam the Salamander Slayer and Kid Ballpeen.

I nudged Jack.

"So what are we doing here? I mean, what's the play? I remember the facts of your case. We're at Donny's Sunday night wrestling match, aren't we? The one he invited us to see at a converted theater called the Majestic Palace. You said it was an old burlesque house."

"That's right." Jack nodded. "What else do you remember?"

"The manager of the Aces High nightclub—your client with a fetish for redheads and Ludlow strongboxes—told you his silent partner, a gangster of some kind, has the dog statue you've been hunting for. And he's supposed to have an office here? Does he?"

Jack pointed to an alcove twenty feet away. Inside that darkened recess, I could just make out a shiny doorknob on an all-but-invisible door. A young tough guy in a flashy silk suit lingered watchfully beside the alcove.

"Paul Lambert's mystery partner hangs his shingle behind that door—a smart move."

"Why is that?"

"The man's underworld associates can waltz in and out of the theater on wrestling nights, and do their business with the big boss, without attracting undo attention."

"Any luck spotting this hoodlum or his *associates* tonight?"

"Not so far, but if you see a guy climbing those steps with his own entourage—" Suddenly, Jack craned his neck. "Someone's coming."

Jack and I watched as three nattily dressed toughs climbed the stairs to the mezzanine. They flanked a fourth man in evening wear. This one walked with a kingly smirk under lacquered black hair. He wore an oversized scarlet rose in his lapel and carried a leather valise that matched the color of the rose.

Jack tipped his head. "That's Joey Flowers. It's what they call him because he's always got one in his lapel. He's a big-time gambler and small-time promoter. It figures he'd wheedle his way into the wrestling racket. Wherever there's dough to grift, you'll find his shifty mitts."

As the waiting guard in the silk suit opened the door for his boss, Jack raised a pair of opera glasses. I saw a light snap on inside that secret room and Jack muttered a curse.

"What's wrong?"

The detective slipped me the glasses. Through the open door, I saw a small office with all the ambience of a prison cell. There was a big window with bars on it, and a sparse gathering of furniture: a few chairs and a cheap wooden desk. On that very desk sat a painted statue of a dog that looked exactly like Toto Two.

"We found the statue, Jack!"

After all that time digging, it felt like we'd finally struck gold. But the detective wasn't smiling.

"What's wrong?"

"We found it, Penny. But now we have to get it."

"It's just a lead statue. Practically worthless. Why not walk up to this Mr. Flowers and simply ask for it? Or make him an offer if he doesn't want to part with the thing for free? I'm sure he'll be reasonable about it."

"Joey Flowers reasonable?" Jack snorted. "You'll find glaciers in Hades first."

"You could try."

"There are two flaws in your plan, honey. You're correct when you say the statue has no real value, but that just means Joey Flowers kept it from its rightful owner out of spite."

"Why would he do that?"

"Because Joey is a gutter rat."

"Okay. What's the second flaw in my plan?"

"The last time Joey and I had an encounter, Mr. Flowers promised to fit me for a pair of cement shoes and dump me in the East River. And that, Penny, my sweet, is a direct quote."

"So you really were lying back at the Aces High when you said you had information for the person who had the dog statue."

"It was a poker play, and the bluff got me here, didn't it?"

"Sure. But what now? How do we get the statue?"

"The same way Joey got it. We steal it."

CHAPTER 46

Robbing Hoods

He who jumps for the moon and gets it not, leaps
higher than he who stoops for a penny in the mud.

—Howard Pyle, *The Merry Adventures of Robin Hood*

AFTER THE FINAL bout of the evening, most of the
crowd dispersed into the Manhattan night.

Jack challenged me to come up with a plan to get him
in—and out—of Joey Flowers's office without ending up at
the bottom of the East River.

As he disappeared to "do a little recon," he instructed me
to wait in the theater lobby, where I bumped into a wall of
hairy muscle.

"Donny!" I cried. "Congratulations on your victory. I
know the chair didn't survive, but I hope Ivan's okay."

Donny frowned. "Ivan's right here"—he jerked his thumb
at a crowd of overly muscled men gathered in a tight, grumbling knot—"but none of us are okay, Miss Penny."

"What's going on? You gentlemen look positively mis-
erable."

"You can say that again," Ivan groused as he stroked his long beard.

"We were cheated, miss," said a gentle giant I recognized as Kirby Dill, who gave the gals a thrill. He didn't seem very thrilled now.

"The promoter cleaned out the till," Donny explained. "He shoved all the box-office dough into a red valise."

"We were promised a C-note for tonight's fight," Ivan cried. "I got a chair broke over my head, and I didn't even make ten bucks."

"I don't like being cheated after all my hard work," Donny moaned. "Who would?"

Jack appeared at my shoulder. "So, there's a window in Joey's office that faces the alley. A fire escape leads to it, but it wouldn't do him any good in a real fire. He's got security bars on that window. They're welded to the frame. No way anyone's passing through them. So, what do you think, Penny? Got any ideas?"

I tapped my chin. "Fire escape, huh? And bars on the windows?"

"That's right."

"Well, what if there *was* a fire?"

Jack nodded his approval. "Interesting idea, partner. Tell me more . . ."

I told Jack what I had learned from the wrestlers. The night's receipts were stuffed inside Joey Flowers's red valise. The wrestlers gathered around as we spoke, until there were six big, scary-looking men who just happened to have a grudge against a certain promoter—a grudge I knew Jack and I could bank on (literally). And I whispered my idea into Jack's ear.

He nodded his approval and gathered everyone into a huddle.

"Gentleman, my partner has a plan to get the money owed to you, but we've got to do this smart. I need you guys to set the stage and do a little acting. Are you game?"

Donny and Dill both laughed, and the rest of the wrestlers nodded.

"Acting is what we do!" roared the Pickle Man.

"That's right!" Sam the Salamander Slayer cried. "We special-a-tize in it."

My plan was simple. And I knew from Jack's reaction it was what he'd come up with, as well. Unfortunately, it involved him walking into the lion's den. Recalling Joey Flowers's threat, I voiced my concerns and was promptly overruled.

"Sometimes that's what you have to do," Jack insisted. "You can't be afraid to face dangerous situations, not in this business, not if you want to get to the truth."

"All right," I said, surrendering. "I don't like it. Not one bit. But with all the tough guys surrounding Flowers, it's the only solution I can think of. So . . . where do you want me to be for this?"

"On the other side of Joey's window, where you'll have a front row seat for *my* wrestling match."

FIFTEEN MINUTES LATER the theater was practically deserted. Only the cleaning crew was left, to sweep up peanut shells, spilled popcorn, and soggy gherkins.

I was crouched below Joey Flowers's barred office window, three floors up, on a fire escape overlooking a dark, scary alley. I could hear the nasty gangster boss talking on his phone, and the low banter of his three young bodyguards.

I was waiting for Jack to execute our plan.

I didn't have to wait long.

Through the half-open window, I heard the office door open and a familiar voice call,

"Hiya, Joey, how's business?"

"Jack Shepard," Flowers growled. "You got a lot of guts coming here. Too bad you won't be leaving."

"Look, Flowers. I know you hate me and frankly the feeling is mutual. But tonight, I'm here to help."

"Help how?"

"I'm working for a client, and I found out something—"

"What client?"

"Privileged information. And it's what I found out that's important, not who I learned it from."

"Do tell us, shamus, before we finish you."

The toughs all laughed at the boss's humor. Jack didn't.

"Listen to me. All of you. I came here to *warn* you."

"About what?" Flowers demanded.

"This place is going to burn to the ground tonight, and you and your boys are going to burn with it."

The hoodlum's response was ruthless. "Grab him, boys."

I heard a scuffle and risked peeking through the window—in time to see two men hold Jack by his arms while a third smacked him in the jaw.

"You're making a mistake, Joey. I'm not lying— Ugh."

Jack's words were cut short by a punch to the gut. More blows followed, until I had to turn away.

Where are the wrestlers? I desperately wondered. *Did they chicken out? They should have started by now!*

Finally, inside the office, I heard one of the thugs cry out.

"Hey, boss. I smell smoke!"

"Me, too," said another.

"I warned you, Flowers," Jack grunted. "With those bars on your window, we're all gonna die unless we get outta here now!"

Outside, even I could smell smoke. But I already knew there was no fire—no real fire, anyway. The wrestlers had only started a perfectly safe, but horribly smelling, smoking fire in a trash can.

"You two, keep hold of that shamus!" Flowers barked. "Rocco, open the door and see what's going on."

The thug who'd been beating on Jack grabbed the door-knob.

"I can't open it. It's blocked! From the outside!"

Flowers rushed around the desk and pounded on the door. "Hey, let us out of here!"

"They've got you trapped, Flowers," Jack grunted. "You should have believed me!"

"Let him go!" Flowers cried. "And help me break down the damn door!"

The thugs released Jack, who clutched the desk to keep from falling.

On cue, everyone heard a loud scuffle outside, followed by a crash. Then the door was ripped off its hinges, and hulking Dogface Donny Danger was standing there, framed in billowing smoke.

"Some guys tried to bar your door," Donny declared. "Me and the other wrestlers chased them away! We saved you, but you've got to go *now*. The joint is on fire!"

In a blind panic, Flowers was out the door first, followed by the two thugs who'd held Jack for his beating. Rocco, the meanest of the bunch, was about to follow when I heard his coughing boss call from the smoke-filled hall.

"Get back there, Rocco, and grab the cash. It's in my valise!"

The gangster brutally shoved a dazed Jack aside and reached for the bag of money. Only Jack wasn't dazed. He'd been acting, too.

"Hey, Rocco, look out for that palooka!" he shouted, pretending another man had entered the room. "No, don't hit him!"

Rocco began to turn, and in one smooth move, Jack grabbed the lead dog statue and bashed the thug over the head with it.

The gangster pitched to the floor, out cold. Jack pulled

the valise from his hands, moved to the window, and slipped it through the bars to me, along with the dog statue.

In the distance, we heard sirens.

"Go!" Jack told me. "I'll meet you at the bottom."

It was an ingenious play. While everyone else in the building ran out the front doors, I moved down the fire escape and Jack slipped out the back. He knew it wasn't a real fire, so he simply covered his mouth and nose with a kerchief and moved *toward* the smoke in the stairwell, down to the basement, and out the back-alley door.

It was a cinch.

Even if someone had stopped Jack, he would have been caught with nothing on him. No dog statue, and no red valise stuffed with money.

When Rocco woke up, all he would remember was Jack Shepard, once again, trying to tell him about impending danger.

So if Joey Flowers wanted to blame anyone, the last person he'd consider fitting with cement shoes would be Jack Shepard.

"In fact," Jack said, "the next time I saw Flowers, he *thanked* me for trying to *warn* him."

"You're all right, Shepard," the less-than-brilliant gangster said. "Maybe next time you tell me something, I'll believe you."

"What now?" I asked Jack, handing him the dog statue and valise.

"Now we take a little trip across town."

"Where?"

Jack's answer, as ironic as ever, consisted of six words—

"Close your eyes, and you'll see."

CHAPTER 47

A Tale of Two Totos

"Remember, I've got no idea what this is all about,"
said the girl . . .

—Dashiell Hammett, "The Assistant Murderer," *Black Mask*, 1926

I OPENED MY eyes to find myself back in the Press Room,
that dingy, dimly lit watering hole near Pennsylvania Station favored by midtown's newshounds.

"To Jack Shepard!" Dogface Donny declared, raising his
glass high. "The man with the plan!"

His fellow strongmen joined in the toast, and plenty of
backslapping and carousing followed. No headlocks or chair
throwing (thank goodness), just raucous laughter and good-
natured bending of elbows.

By now Jack had ditched Joey Flowers's red valise and
passed the Robin Hood money to the men, who'd divvied it
up among themselves.

The wrestlers had exchanged their colorful trunks for
street clothes and gathered at the journalists' gin mill at
Jack's request, but no one would have mistaken these

muscle-bound giants with tattoos, wild hair, and weird beards for tabloid scribblers, section editors, or copyboys.

"So, Shepard, what's the story?"

The grizzled old crime reporter Morgan Keene (the one who'd given Jack that valuable tip on the Ludlow strongboxes) waited for Jack to fulfill his promise and come clean.

Jack bought Keene a fresh pour of whisky and settled on the stool next to him.

I sidled close and listened with interest as Jack quietly explained why, with a cutthroat gangster involved, he couldn't risk the details of his case going public. Before Keene could object, Jack held up his hand—

"How about another story—just as good, if not better?"

"And what would that be?" Keene asked skeptically.

"You're lookin' at it."

Jack regaled Keene with the colorful untold stories of the wrestlers celebrating in the bar.

"Take Dogface Donny over there. You'd never know that mean-looking machine is really a sweet guy who babies his three lapdogs. Danny was discovered while working as a bouncer at an exclusive Manhattan nightclub. Now he not only wrestles for packed crowds, but he also appears in pictures as a background tough guy."

Keene nodded. "Go on."

"All of these palookas have interesting tales to tell. Sam the Salamander Slayer came from a circus, Kid Ballpeen was a Broadway set painter, and the green giant there, Kirby Dill, actually started out as an opera singer. How's that for good copy?"

Keene smiled. "I can see it. And the pictures of these guys in their trunks should interest my female readers."

That was when I jumped in and mentioned how many *women* I'd seen cheering the wrestlers at the Majestic Palace. "Just like the days of the Roman gladiators," I added with a Seymour flourish. "As a woman, I can tell you, I believe it would make a fascinating feature, too."

"'The Ladies and the Strongmen,'" Jack said, sending a wink my way.

Keene's eyes lit up—the whisky helped. And so did his new beat as Mildred Virtue, the highly paid women's advice columnist, which had made the female angle lucrative for Keene.

"I'll do it," he told Jack, "but you still owe me."

"What do you want? Lettuce?"

"Hell, no. I want to know the end of your story!"

"Off the record?"

Keene crossed his heart. "You have my word."

"I don't know . . ."

"Oh, come on, Detective," I coaxed. "Let's finish this case. You know I'm dying to know, too. Who hired you? I mean, the dog obviously didn't. So who left Toto Two at your door with the C-note and letter full of riddles? Who wanted this dog statue so badly, they'd put you through all those hoops, including a run-in with a notorious gangster? What was this case *really* all about?"

Jack's answer was a single word—

"Him."

"Who?" Keene and I said together.

Jack tipped his head toward the far corner of the room, where a man sat alone, the red end of his cigarette burning through the bar's shabby light. It was the same hulking man I'd seen shadowing us and watching Jack's apartment window from the street corner on the very night Toto Two appeared at his door.

As the man approached us, I finally got a look at his scarred and pockmarked face. I recoiled not so much at his rough features and close-set eyes but the twisted grimace of his expression and the meanness in his gaze.

The silk-suited boneheads around Joey Flowers were

pretty guard dogs compared to this junkyard killer, a product of back alleys, rough streets, and prison yards, whose
aura of intimidation conveyed the frightening, teeth-baring
evidence of what it took to survive in such places.

Jack's reaction was automatic. He stood to confront the
ex-con.

"Back off, Muggsy. If I so much as see a glint of that handy
knife of yours, you're going straight back to the slammer."

Muggsy saw Jack's hand poised to dip into his double-
breasted suit, and quickly raised his palms.

"Take it easy, shamus. Keep your heater holstered. I'm
not gonna harm a hair on your head—or your pretty little
partner's here."

"Leave my partner out of it."

"Why? Seems to me she did as much legwork as you. If
you don't split my C-note with her, I'd call it a cryin' shame."

Jack's eyes narrowed. "How do you know about that C-
note?"

"Because I put it in the envelope for you. Along with that
letter. I'm the one who hired that bobby-soxer to dress up in
her mama's clothes and leave the little dog with the Ludlow
key under the collar."

"Jack, I still don't understand," I whispered. "What's this
all about?"

"What's this all about?" Muggsy looked at Jack and
laughed. Then he pointed to the shiner forming around the
PI's right eye. "Payback, that's what. Ain't I right, shamus?
I warned you it was coming, didn't I? Even left you a message with your little secretary . . ."

Before I could ask, that message appeared before me like
magic, the words floating in midair—

I'm out of the joint where you put me and back in town.
I'll be seeing you, Shepard. I owe you payback.
Expect me soon.

Muggsy laughed again, a big belly laugh. He laughed so hard and so long, he doubled over. That laughter grew louder and louder until it drowned out the noise of the bar.

I covered my ears with my white-gloved hands until I could hardly stand it anymore. "Jack, make him stop! Please, make him stop!"

That's when the earthquake hit (or what felt like one, anyway). The wooden bar began to shake, bottles broke, and pictures smashed to the ground. Then the walls began to crumble—

"Jack! What's happening?"

"Hold on, Penny. We need a change of scene—"

And that's when all the lights went out.

I OPENED MY eyes, but everything looked fuzzy.

"Jack, where am I now?" I blinked, rubbing away the blur to find myself sitting on a soft, lumpy old sofa, snuggled up against a hard wall of muscle.

"We're back at my apartment, honey. That's where we are. Back where we started . . ."

Jack was also back in his pajama bottoms, bare feet up on the coffee table, his arm around me.

"Sorry I cut things short, but I couldn't stand another second in that smug mug's presence."

"I don't blame you. But who exactly was that man? And why did he owe you payback?"

Jack told me about the horrible case of Muggsy Malone, and how he had helped put the man behind bars for knifing a teenage boy during a Hell's Kitchen street fight over a dice game.

"Turns out, Muggsy did time in the joint with a man named Kraft who was once in business with Joey Flowers, just like Paul Lambert, at the Aces High nightclub, only Kraft had partnered with Flowers in a dog-racing venture.

After a few good years, things went south when officials discovered the races were all fixed. Since Flowers was a silent partner, he walked away clean. It was Kraft who got the shaft."

"So Kraft went to prison and ended up as Muggsy's cellmate?"

"That's right. When Muggsy was about to get sprung, Kraft asked for a favor. He still had three years left on his own sentence, and he wanted something done on the quick. So he offered Muggsy a deal . . .

"Kraft told the street thug: 'Get my Toto dog statue back from that SOB Joey Flowers and deliver what you find inside to my little girl. If you're smart enough to figure out how to do that *and* you buy her a dog that looks just like that pooch from the yellow-brick-road picture, I'll set you up good with the boys in Cuba.'

"Muggsy knew Kraft had connections to a Cuban hotel casino where the work was easy, and he could lounge on the beach and sip rum cocktails for the rest of his life. Kraft planned on joining him there once he got out of Sing Sing.

"'Do this for me, and you'll have it made,' Kraft promised him."

"So what happened next?"

"Muggsy knew Joey Flowers would never just hand over that Toto statue for the asking. And if anyone did ask, or try to steal it, Muggsy figured they'd catch a beating, or worse. He owed me payback for sending him up the river, and he knew I occasionally did work for Flowers's partner at the Aces High Club, so he came up with the idea of *hiring* me. He figured with my connections and reputation on the street for doggedly working cases, I'd retrieve Kraft's statue for him—*and* get a beating in the process. Payback complete."

"But why leave Toto Two at your door? Why the mysterious note?"

"Are you kidding? Muggsy knew I would never take a

job from him. Not in a million years. He thought about using a dame to act the part of a client wanting to hire me, but he couldn't find any he could trust to pull it off. Then he read Timothy Brennan's doggy-business feature on me in that tabloid. He figured I had a soft spot for four-legged fur hats, so he bought a terrier that looked just like Toto—since Kraft asked him to get one for his little girl, anyway. Then he slipped a few bucks to a bobby-soxer to disguise herself and deliver it to my door."

"And you took the doggone case."

"Sure. I mean, a whole C-note for a weekend's work on some silly puzzle—why not? And I was more than a little curious to get to the bottom of who would set me up to work for a dog."

I took a breath to consider Jack's words—and all the crazy twists and turns we'd been through. "I guess if Muggsy set all that up, he really was smart enough to work for Kraft. What a way to pass a job interview! But where did he get the Ludlow key?"

"It was Kraft's strongbox in the first place, and he told Muggsy where to find the key. He'd gotten word in prison that Flowers had robbed some Ludlow strongboxes—including his own. He figured Muggsy would show the key to Flowers as proof that Kraft had sent him, but that's not what Muggsy did. Like I said, Muggsy knew Flowers would never just hand anything over for the asking. He knew that dog statue wouldn't be easy to get."

"But you got it."

"And a shiner in the process."

"Oh, Jack, that was so awful, watching you take that beating."

"Hey, the plan worked, didn't it? And Donny and his wrestling pals got the money Flowers stole from them."

"So, you weren't sorry you took the case?"

"Naw, not when I saw it to the end."

"What do you mean? What happened after Muggsy confronted you in that bar?"

"I finished the job."

"But how?"

"While Muggsy watched, I broke the dog's legs, just as his letter instructed—"

"Meaning the dog *statue*. Of course!"

"That's right. No harm ever came to Toto Two."

"Was there really something hidden inside?"

Jack nodded. "Stock certificates, and every last one was written in the name of Kraft's daughter, Sally. The certificates were worth a small fortune. You should have seen Muggsy's face. His eyes practically popped out of his head with glee. He stood there in that bar, laughing at my shiner—courtesy of Joey Flowers—and stuck his hand out, expecting me to just pass over those valuable stock notes. But I didn't."

"Why not?"

"I told the cackling hood, 'You hired me for a job, and I'm gonna finish it.'"

And that was exactly what Jack did. He quickly tracked down Kraft's little girl, though she was no longer little.

"When I caught up with Sally Kraft, she was nineteen and already a newlywed," Jack said. "Sally's mother had died years before. With her father in prison and no relatives willing to take her, she was placed into foster care, which is where she met the boy she married. She and her young husband were renting a cold-water flat in Greenwich Village. The two were happy together, but they were also dirt-poor— until I delivered the good news in the form of that golden paper."

"She must have been surprised."

Jack smiled. "She nearly fainted, partly because of the instant fortune. And partly because she was six months pregnant and a little unsteady. But her husband, Bobby

Breen, was thrilled. Bobby told me their dream was to move to New England, buy a pretty piece of property by a lake where they could live a quiet life. Sounded kinda nice, I have to admit."

"What happened to Toto Two?"

"I delivered the dog to Sally, just like Kraft wanted. She had tears in her eyes when she saw the little barker. She said *The Wizard of Oz* had been her favorite movie as a child. All during those sad and lonely years, she had wished for a dog like Toto to comfort her. Now she had that, too."

WHEN I OPENED my eyes the next morning, my mind was positively reeling from Jack's revelations, including the name of Sally's young husband—

"Bobby Breen," I whispered to my empty bedroom. "Could he be related to Amber Breen?"

That's when I recalled something our guest author had blurted out during our crazy phone conversation the day before she came to town: Amber Breen had called one of her dogs *Toto Seven*!

"Jack, is it just a coincidence?"

But there was no answer. After that doozy of a dream he'd given me, Jack the ghost was fast asleep.

CHAPTER 48

A Dangerous Doggy Business

Half of all criminal offenses occur in the victim's own neighborhood.

—Bureau of Justice statistic, 2020

WITHOUT ANY FURTHER answers, from Jack (on his case or my own), I rolled out of bed to start a new day. Rubbing the sleep from my eyes, I was glad to find Aunt Sadie in the kitchen, pouring me a fresh cup of good strong Irish breakfast tea.

"I'm sorry, Pen, but I'm afraid I indulged the boy last night," she confessed, handing me the piping hot cup.

"What happened?"

"The *Jack Shield* marathon on the Intrigue Channel. I let Spencer watch one too many episodes before I sent him off to bed."

And the result? It was nearly time for school, but Spencer was still snoring. And there was a new wrinkle in our daily routine called *walking the dog*. Right now that was out of the question, unless Spencer wanted to be tardy, and I wouldn't let that happen, despite Sparky staring at my son with big, desperate eyes, one paw resting on the boy's bed, the leash in his mouth.

"I have an idea," Sadie said. "You throw on some play clothes and walk the dog while I get Spencer up and off to school?"

I found myself making that pained sound I'd picked up from the Franzetti siblings. To be clear, the *walking* part of walking the dog wasn't what gave me qualms.

"Oh, pooh, Pen," Sadie said, reading my mind. "It's just poo."

She handed me a pair of disposable gloves and a plastic baggie.

"You clean Bookmark's litter box all the time."

"Yes," I countered. "But that only involves a shovel!"

Sparky seemed to understand and nudged me with his cold, wet nose. Finally, he dropped the leash on my feet.

Sparky can't be that smart, I thought. *It must be Pavlovian. The crinkle of the plastic must be (for lack of a better word) triggering.*

Sparky waited patiently while I found a suitable coat—it was much colder this morning than last night—and he behaved like a perfect gentleman when we got outside. The dog walked at my pace, only stopping to mark a pole or fire hydrant.

The dog had one annoying habit, however. Sparky liked to circle around his target, stepping off the curb to mark the lamppost or telephone pole while standing in the street. It wasn't safe, but there was no traffic, so I indulged the canine's whim.

The street was so quiet that a motion I caught out of the corner of my eye startled me. It was only someone sitting behind the wheel of a luxury SUV that I'd assumed was unoccupied. What I glimpsed was the top of the individual's hoodie as they bent over the steering wheel and vigorously scratched the back of their neck.

Sparky decided the dog walk wasn't for him. Instead, he headed in the opposite direction, toward Bud Napp's Hardware.

A brisk autumn wind gusted down Cranberry Street, and I tried not to shiver. It made me think of Jack, and I quietly called out to him—but my ghost was still sleeping off the dream he'd given me.

Finally, I grew impatient.

"Come on, Sparky, do your business. What are you waiting for? The stock market to open?"

Again, the dog seemed to understand. He immediately stepped off the curb beside a public trash can and squatted. I heard a car slowly roll down the street behind me. I glanced over my shoulder, and my paranoid alarm went off.

It was the same SUV I'd seen a moment ago on the *opposite* side of the street. The driver had moved to our side, rolled to a halt less than a block away, and kept the engine running.

Without seeming too obvious, I tried to make out the face behind the wheel but got nowhere. The windows were tinted, and the sun visor was down.

"Time to move along, Sparky—"

But there was no moving the dog now. Sparky was in the middle of a major transaction. Mercifully, the end came quickly. While I donned the gloves and unfurled the baggie, I took a final glance at the driver, whose head was turned away from me as they vigorously scratched their arm.

I decided I was paranoid and proceeded with the scooping.

"Smooth as silk, Sparky," I said proudly as I sealed the bag.

Once again, the dog had drifted off the sidewalk, to mark the trash can.

Suddenly, the driver threw the SUV in gear and hit the gas so hard that the tires squealed. The vehicle leaped forward, heading straight for Jane's dog!

"Sparky, come!" I shouted and pulled hard on his leash, even as the dog obeyed my command. Between my tug and the dog's momentum, Sparky hit me like a medicine ball. We both tumbled to the sidewalk as the SUV roared by.

Tires squealed again as the vehicle braked.

I was still trying to untangle myself from Sparky and his leash when the SUV went into reverse and stopped beside us with the driver's door already open. What happened next nearly paralyzed me

The driver lunged, but not at me. Sparky yowled in protest when the stranger's arms closed around him and tried to toss him into the vehicle!

"No!" I cried. Still holding the leash, I pulled with all my might—so hard I feared the collar might snap. Instead, Sparky clawed his way up and over the stranger's shoulders.

Whoever this person was, they had disguised themselves completely. Their form was hidden beneath a bulky coat, black gloves covered their hands, a hoodie was pulled fully over their head, and dark sunglasses and a black surgical mask obscured their face. In the terrifying seconds this all took place, the driver barely registered as a blur.

After climbing over the stranger's shoulder, Sparky hit the ground snapping, tearing a hole in the person's coat as he went. I moved to pull Sparky to safety and the dognapper wisely gave up, jumping back behind the wheel.

Still fighting mad, I swung with the only weapon I had.

The smelly bag burst, the door slammed, and the SUV was gone.

Seconds later, Bud Napp appeared at my side with a crowbar clutched in his fist.

"I heard you scream and came running! What happened, Pen?"

"An SUV almost ran me down and the driver tried to steal Sparky!"

Bud scanned the empty street. "Whatever happened, it's recorded," he said, gesturing to the CCTV camera over the entrance of his store. Then he took a step back and made a face.

"Toss what's left of that doggy bag in the trash and come inside," he said. "While we wait for the police, you can clean up."

CHAPTER 49

Case Overload

It's dangerous to know too much.

— Agatha Christie, *The Secret Adversary*, 1922

TO MY SURPRISE, Deputy Chief Franzetti responded to Bud Napp's 911 call. As soon as he came through the door, he spotted me, frowned, and scratched the back of his neck.

"Don't you ever sleep, Pen?"

"I could say the same about you."

"I got zero sleep last night," he acknowledged. "I've been on duty for nineteen hours straight, and the state police and their gun-sniffing dogs are due in two hours."

Eddie loosened his jacket. "So, what happened? Bud told the operator that someone tried to run you over."

"See for yourself, Eddie." Bud placed a laptop on the counter. "I called up the security footage."

Watching the replay, I was amazed at how fast things had happened. It took no more than thirty seconds. But Eddie agreed that the driver deliberately tried to run us down and attempted to snatch the dog.

Unfortunately, one important clue was left in doubt. I squinted at the image frozen on Bud's computer screen. "I can't read the license plate."

"Petroleum jelly was probably smeared on the plates," Eddie said. "Or they were covered in cellophane. It's a cute trick to dodge electronic tolls."

"That's a mighty nice ride," Bud observed.

"It's a BMW X5, and they don't come cheap." Eddie scratched his wrist. "It could be a rental. More likely it's stolen. I'll check the motor vehicle theft reports for the region and see what I come up with."

I glanced at Sparky, sprawled on the concrete floor. The dog was obsessively licking his front paw.

"Why would anyone want to harm Mrs. Cunningham's dog? There has to be a connection to the shooting—"

"Pen, we've been over that," Eddie replied. "The shooter's been charged. And you know his name: Robert Slattery, Jane Cunningham's neighbor. He's sitting in jail right now, awaiting arraignment—"

"But you haven't found the weapon."

"We will in a few hours, when the staties' gun dogs sniff it out."

I noticed Eddie absently scratching his wrist again. I was about to ask what was wrong—and then I recalled that the driver of the offending SUV was also scratching.

Allergic reaction, perhaps?

According to Troy Hanley, Gemma Osborn was allergic to dogs. Of course, the driver was itching long before they even tried to grab Sparky. But I read once that just the thought of exposure to an allergen can sometimes trigger an attack.

Could the driver of that SUV have been Gemma?

An intriguing thought, but I stopped myself from sharing it with the deputy chief. I'd already dropped Robert Slattery into hot water. I didn't want to incriminate Gemma on sheer speculation.

And yet it seemed to me that when I met her, Gemma knew more about the missing Rebecca Wilkes than her work partner Troy Hanley allowed her to say—which was a good reason to revisit Gemma, preferably when Troy wasn't around.

"Okay, Eddie, answer me this," I said. "If Robert Slattery is the shooter, and he's safely behind bars, then how do you explain the attack on me? On Sparky?"

"I don't know for sure, Pen." Eddie shrugged. "But what happened to you likely has more to do with the incident at the Wentworth Arms trailer park than the Cunningham shooting."

"What?"

"Someone may think you know too much about Jeremy."

"But I don't know anything about him! And who would care if I did?"

"Are you kidding?" Eddie said. "You can't imagine what I found inside that mobile home. I've been going through it most of the night. I wanted to learn what I could before the FBI or Homeland Security blocks access—"

"Homeland Security? What did you find, Eddie, a nuclear device?"

"No, but I did find at least twenty-five credit cards, all valid, all up-to-date, and all adding up to more than five hundred thousand dollars in credit."

"Who needs twenty-five credit cards?"

"More to the point, who needs twenty-five versions of their name?"

"What?"

"Every card has some version of the snake boy's name on it. But the first name was always different: Jeremy, Jerry, Jer, JJ, or just plain J." He paused. "When I made that crack about this crazy kid working for the CIA, I wasn't far off the mark. I also found thirteen valid drivers' licenses from six different states, along with a passport and student visas for three different countries."

"So, how does this lead to an attack on me?"

"You made a very public display of your curiosity about Jeremy. You may have stirred up a can of worms."

"But I was *searching* for Rebecca Wilkes—"

"A phantom, Pen. If she lived in Quindicott, she never registered to vote or received one piece of mail. After you mentioned her name last night, I looked into it."

My head was spinning now. Was Rebecca Wilkes somehow involved in Jeremy's dubious activities? Was that why she ran?

"What about Bonnie?" I asked. "Is she in danger? You know she's closer to Jeremy than anyone in town."

Eddie's frown deepened, and he furiously scratched his neck again, making me wonder if he'd developed an allergy to dogs, too.

"I called Ma and told her not to let Bonnie out of the house until I got there." He glanced at his watch. "That's where I'm going next."

"You didn't answer my question. Is Bonnie in danger. Am I in danger?"

Eddie zipped up his jacket. "Just keep watching your back, Pen, and I'll try to watch out for both of you."

After that, I thanked Bud for his help and headed for home—with one wary eye over my shoulder. The other was on Sparky, and I soon noticed that the dog was limping. I knelt and checked his paw.

I found blood.

Alarmed, I picked up all eighty pounds of dog and carried him down the street to the mobile veterinary van, which was still parked in front of the Movie Town Theater.

"SPARKY WILL BE fine," a smiling Dr. Winnik assured me. "He split his claw in that tussle, that's all."

"I panicked when I saw blood."

"Nothing to worry about, Mrs. McClure. I trimmed the broken nail and stopped the bleeding with a suture. The antibiotic shot will prevent infection but try to keep that bandage around his paw for a day or two."

I knew that would be a challenge. Sparky was already worrying the edges.

"Do you have anything to calm him? I've been seeing commercials for a new antianxiety medication for animals. Blue something—"

"BlueSky."

"That's it! What do you think?"

Dr. Winnik frowned. "I'm not using that product in my practice any longer."

The way he said it made me think something was very wrong. "Can you tell me why not?"

"Only unofficially. It's FDA approved, and the company BioQuill is considered reputable. They've marketed trusted human antidepressants for years. But I've been hearing troubling anecdotal reports of negative side effects from the BlueSky medication. Internal bleeding. Kidney and liver damage to the animals and other problems."

"Oh, my goodness, then let's skip it, by all means."

"I'll give you some dog chews with natural ingredients that promote calming. You might also try soothing music. Stroke or brush him and give him—"

"Lots of love."

The vet smiled. "I was going to say reassurance, but love will do."

"Of course."

The young veterinarian then slipped off his gloves and stroked his trimmed beard. "This is Jane Cunningham's dog, isn't it?"

"Yes, I'm watching him while Jane is in the hospital."

"I heard about the accident. It's a terrible shame. She's such a good person. It was her idea to have Cunningham properties subsidize our mobile van outreach here this week. It's a good tax write-off for her, of course, but it's also a helpful gesture to the community."

I blinked. "Are you telling me that *Jane's* company made the donation? Not Ella Pruett?"

"Ella who?"

Jack, did you hear that? The vet never heard of Ella Pruett. That woman lied to me, to all of us! She played on our own good intentions to make sure everything went her way—everyone else's interests and opinions, be damned!

I stared into space, waiting for Jack's response, but there was none. After last night's dream, my ghost was still sleeping.

Dr. Winnik touched my shoulder. "Mrs. McClure, are you all right?"

"What?" I shook my head clear. "Oh, I'm sorry. I'm fine, Doctor. You just surprised me with that information."

He frowned with concern. "Well, you should take some time to calm down, too. I'm sure what happened this morning was a shock."

"You mean, with Sparky?"

"Of course. When you came in, you said someone tried to steal him from you. Isn't that right?

"Yes, that's right."

"Let me check something, just to be on the safe side."

The vet dug out a handheld scanner, played it over Sparky's back. After a pause, he frowned in puzzlement.

"What's wrong?" I asked.

"Sparky has a microchip implant, but it seems to have malfunctioned."

"How is it supposed to work?

"A small transponder is inserted here." He pointed to the scruff of Sparky's neck. "The chip contains an identification number. If an animal is lost, a vet or shelter can scan the microchip with one of these." He displayed the scanner. "A number that's registered with a national pet-recovery service comes up. The service matches the number to the owner, and the animal can be returned to its home."

"It doesn't work like a GPS?"

Dr. Winnik laughed. "No, they don't have Apple AirTag implants for pets yet. Give science another few years, and I'm sure they'll be available. Meanwhile, when Mrs. Cunningham is back on her feet, let her know Sparky's chip went bad. She can make the decision whether to get it replaced."

I hurried back to the shop, happy it was after nine A.M. and plenty of people were crowding the sidewalks. Then I filled Sadie in on what had happened to me and Sparky. We weren't finished talking until it was time to open the shop at ten.

"Don't be surprised if Bonnie comes to work with a police escort," I warned Sadie.

"It's terrible, what happened to poor Sparky," Sadie said, hugging the dog's neck. "Did that bad driver hurt you?"

Sparky whimpered and rested his head on Aunt Sadie's welcoming shoulder.

"Hey," I said, "that bad driver knocked your niece on her posterior, too."

"Then come over here with Sparky and me for a group hug."

I spied Bookmark glaring at us from atop a high shelf.

"Come down, Bookmark," I called. "You can join our hug."

The cat turned her head and strutted away in disgust.

"Don't worry," Sadie said. "I have her favorite catnip treats under the front counter. With a shake of that bag, all will be forgiven."

I couldn't help but sigh. "If only human grudges could be soothed that easily."

CHAPTER 50

Return to Larchmont

The why must never be obvious. That is the whole point.

—Agatha Christie, *Five Little Pigs*

IT WAS NEARLY six P.M. when Sadie and I left the store in the hands of Bonnie and Tommy, and headed upstairs for a dinner break.

"You can take you break at seven," I told Bonnie, but she shook her head.

"I'd rather stay here. Eddie's coming over for dinner, and he's in a bad mood."

"Is he still upset about you and Jeremy?"

Bonnie shook her head. "Welsh Tibbet told me the sniffer dogs couldn't find a rifle in Mr. Slattery's house."

I wasn't surprised because I still believed the man was innocent.

Sadie went up to our apartment ahead of me. When I got to the top of the stairs, she pulled me into the living room to see "our little angels."

Spencer had fallen asleep in front of the television. He was curled up on the couch with Sparky beside him. And Bookmark was there, too. The marmalade cat had squeezed herself between Sparky's front paws, with her head resting right under the dog's chin. I swear there was a big smile on her little cat face.

"Peace at last," I whispered.

"It won't last," Sadie warned, "not unless we buy some pet food. We're down to our last cans."

"I'll run to Koh's after dinner . . ."

When our meal was over, Spencer started his homework and Sadie returned to the bookshop. Before I headed off to the market, I reminded Spencer that Seymour would arrive at around nine, and only then was he allowed to take Sparky for a walk. After the attempted dognapping this morning, I was taking no chances, and Mighty Mailman Seymour was the next best thing to a police escort.

The evening was cool but not cold, the streets busy for a Monday evening. A long line formed at the Movie Town Theater for tonight's supernatural canine-themed double bill, *A Dog's Purpose* and Tim Burton's *Frankenweenie*.

I stopped dead on the sidewalk when I noticed one moviegoer in particular. Troy Hanley was attending the cinema solo. I lingered long enough to watch him buy a single ticket, then fiddle with his phone while waiting with everyone else for the doors to open.

If remote worker Troy is here, I thought, moving closer, *then Gemma Osborn might be back at Jane's house on Larchmont doing whatever remote workers do. And without Troy there to intimidate her, Gemma might be more willing to talk about Rebecca Wilkes.*

Quick thinking, doll, Jack said, popping into my head so abruptly, I nearly tripped over my own feet. *Let's hit the road before the clock runs out.*

It's risky, Jack. What if Troy doesn't like the movie and

*leaves early? Or, worse, what if my suspicions are correct
and it was Gemma who tried to run me over this morning?
She was the one with the dog allergy—and the driver was
scratching as if they had some kind of rash.*

*Remember what I told you, Penny, and what I showed
you. You can't be afraid to walk into a dangerous situation,
not if you want to get to the truth.*

"You're right, Jack," I said aloud, eliciting stares from
people on the sidewalk. "I'm going to grab those keys—all
of them—and we're going for a ride."

In no time I was driving up Cranberry Street, breezing
through two yellow lights, including one at the junction to
Briar Patch Road. This was the same route I took four days
ago when I followed Sparky to his wounded owner, and
right now I felt the same sense of urgency.

A premonition?

To make my presence less obvious, I parked across the
street from the big yellow house. The wind gusts were
strong on Larchmont tonight. The tops of the trees in front
of Jane's house swished as I followed the pebble pathway to
the enclosed porch.

The porch door was open, and a single light burned near
the inner door. Around the fixture, a pair of moths flittered,
casting ominous dancing shadows.

I pressed Gemma Osborn's doorbell several times. There
was no response. I tried Troy Hanley's doorbell, thinking
Gemma might be working in his place. I still got nothing.

"She's not here, Jack. We've wasted our time. Should we
go home—"

*Nuts to that, Penny. You have a lot of keys rattling in
your purse. What's the point of dragging them around if you
aren't going to use them?*

But it's breaking and entering.

The law would call it trespass, *but who's going to know?*

I retrieved the large set of keys, and after several tries, I found the one that unlocked the building's outer door. The hallway was stuffy, and a bad smell hung in the air. I moved to the three doors at the end of the short hall and opened the one in the center. Troy had implied that door led to Rebecca's room, but all I found was a water heater.

I opened Gemma's apartment next. Once inside, I located the source of the vile odor.

When I'd first met her, Gemma had been carrying two grocery bags from Koh's Market. Bags just like them now sat on the floor inside the door. One contained ground meat, which had gone very bad.

So, where was Gemma? Clearly, something happened to the girl in the Wednesday Addams dress, and the full grocery bags told me it likely occurred yesterday, the very day I met her. Maybe right *after* I met her.

What do you think, Jack? Did Gemma leave because I came looking for Rebecca Wilkes? Or did she run after her failed attempt at vehicular homicide this morning? Or is there some other explanation for what certainly looks like an abrupt disappearance?

There's only one way to know, Penny. Toss the joint.

I did, but after a fairly thorough search of the woman's apartment, I found nothing incriminating.

What now, Jack?

You've got more keys and doors to try. In for a penny . . .

I locked Gemma's door behind me and found the key that unlocked Troy Hanley's apartment.

Troy's place was a mess, but his untidiness proved to be his undoing.

Jack, look at this!

On a coffee table I found a first aid kit, cotton balls, and a pink plastic bottle.

"Calamine lotion!" That was when it hit me. "A dog

allergy wasn't what made the driver scratch, and I'm sure Eddie has the same condition—"

Clue me in, doll.

"Poison ivy, Jack! The meadow adjacent to Robert Slattery's garden was riddled with the weed. I'll bet Eddie was scratching because he got exposed investigating Slattery. And this evidence suggests Troy Hanley got poison ivy, too. Did he get it on his way to that tree house? The same tree house where Eddie found the spent twenty-two-caliber shells? The same tree house the shooter must have used to target Jane Cunningham while she was walking Sparky? It would have been the ideal frame job, wouldn't it? With Slattery unstable and making threats, the setup was perfect."

I didn't know if Troy was really the shooter. But all doubts about the identity of the dognapping driver vanished when I discovered the hoodie and coat the perp was wearing that morning—I even found the hole Sparky tore while trying to bite him.

It was Troy all along, Jack. But I can't figure out a motive. If Troy was working with Stanley Cunningham and Ella Pruett to shoot Jane, why would he care about stealing Sparky? It doesn't make sense. Yet in my gut, I'm sure he's the shooter . . . and now it's got me wondering . . .

What are you thinking?

Jane was shot while she was walking her dog. Troy tried to steal the dog. Was he trying to shoot Sparky that day? Was Sparky the real target—a target he missed? And why? Why would he want to shoot Jane? Or her dog?

Don't worry about the motive right now. Try to find the weapon. That's all the proof the police will need.

Jack was tossing me possible hiding places for a rifle when we both heard the sound of a motorcycle rolling into the driveway.

"That's Troy," I whispered. "I've got to get out of here."

I locked the door behind me and hurried down the hall.

My plan was to duck behind some hedges until Troy passed me and went into the house. Then I would cross the street, hop into my car, and call the police.

But as I stepped off the porch and turned the corner, I smacked right into the dark silhouette of a man lurking there.

I screamed as we both tumbled to the pebbled walkway. And then I started fighting. . . .

CHAPTER 51

Motivationally Speaking

You scare too easy for a crook.

—Raymond Chandler, "The Man Who Liked Dogs"

"NO! OUCH! HEY! Wait! Please!"

Channeling Dogface Donny Danger, I was punching and kicking and ready to bite and scratch. But suddenly the man I was wrestling with on the ground broke free and jumped to his feet.

"Whoa!" he cried, backing away. "Don't *hurt* me!"

In the glow of a distant streetlight, I saw white teeth and a disheveled blond mane.

"Jeremy?"

He blinked, recognizing me. "Hey, you're Bonnie's boss, aren't you?"

Yeah! Jack laughed. *And the dame who just knocked you silly.*

Quiet, Jack, I told him. *Let me handle this.*

After Jeremy and I both caught a breath, we asked the same question in unison.

"What are you doing here?"

For a moment, Jeremy looked like he was ready to bolt. Instead he held his ground. "Ladies first."

How polite, Jack cracked. *Snake boy is a real gentleman.*

Ignoring the ghost, I said, "All right, I'll start. I'm a friend of Jane Cunningham, and I'm trying to find out who shot her and why. The last time I was here, I had a run-in with Troy Hanley, so when I saw him in town tonight, I came back, hoping to speak *alone* with his coworker, Gemma—"

"Coconspirator, you mean," Jeremy spat.

"I don't understand."

"I had a run-in with Troy myself. He showed up at my trailer—"

"Why?"

"He was looking for—" Jeremy suddenly stopped talking.

"Troy was looking for Rebecca Wilkes, wasn't he?"

Jeremy blinked in surprise, but he still wouldn't talk. In the light of the nearby streetlamp, I could see the conflicted expression on his face.

"Look," I said, "Bonnie trusts me, and you trust Bonnie. How about we trust each other?"

He studied me, the doubt continuing to shadow his face.

"Jeremy, *please*, clue me in. Your silence isn't getting either of us anywhere."

Maybe you should have brought that rubber hose, doll.

Give him a moment, Jack, I think he's coming around.

And he did. Surrendering to my logic, Jeremy sighed and finally spoke.

"I'm looking for Rebecca. She's hiding. She won't even use her phone because she's afraid they'll trace it and grab her. She's not wrong, either. They traced my phone and sent Troy Hanley to trash my trailer, so I know they can do it."

"Who's *they*?" I asked. "The FBI? Homeland Security?"

"A company called BioQuilll."

"The *drug* company BioQuill? The one that makes BlueSky?"

"They're endangering public health. Rebecca—which is not her *real* name, by the way—knows all about it. She plans to blow the whistle on them."

"And where is Rebecca?"

"Gone. And I don't know where."

"Well, if she's gone, why are you here, Jeremy?"

"Rebecca ran so fast, she left something behind. I was about to break into her apartment and find it before the BioQuill goons do."

"We won't have to break in. I have the key. But *where* exactly is Rebecca's apartment?"

"This way," Jeremy replied.

He led me around the back of Jane's house, along a concrete path and onto a small patio. With no streetlight to illuminate the scene, the yard was pitch-dark, and I tried not to give in to my worries. Was I walking into a bad situation?

Don't sweat it, honey, I've got your back.

You're right, Jack. After all, I came here for answers.

And so I continued to follow Jeremy—albeit with my eyes wide open *and* Jack watching my back.

We arrived at the house's garage, where two cars were parked. A wooden staircase led to a door on the second floor. With Jeremy in the lead, we began to climb. As we neared the top, I reached into my pocket for the Pearl Knight key chain.

Disturbingly, we didn't need it.

Jeremy abruptly halted on the stairs, then cursed.

The door to Rebecca's apartment was ajar, the locks obviously broken. Jeremy pushed his way into the large apartment with me on his heels. For a moment, he fumbled for the overhead light. Then he snapped it on, and I gasped at the sight.

The place had been torn apart: furniture slashed, the contents of the drawers violently scattered on the floor.

Jeremy groaned. "If it was here, they found it."

"If *what* was here? Tell me what's going on, and maybe I can help."

Now Jeremy seemed itching to talk, and he did.

"The girl who's now calling herself Rebecca worked at BioQuill as an assistant to the head of IT. Only the guy was a lazy SOB who never did his job. He gave Rebecca the password to his computer and let her do all the work.

"One day she found a confidential digital memo that outlined all the problems with the new veterinary drug BlueSky. How it caused liver and kidney damage to cats, heart problems in dogs, and miscarriage and birth defects in pregnant cats and dogs."

"Oh, my God . . ."

"That was Rebecca's reaction. She was so upset, she downloaded the memo and all of its attachments. For the next several months, she managed to find out more—like how BioQuill altered test results to hide negative data and then bribed an FDA regulator with a cushy job after the bureaucrat recommended approval for BlueSky, of course."

"What else?"

"Rebecca found out the company groomed a sales force to lie about the safety of the product. Pretty soon her boss began to suspect her, so Rebecca left San Francisco to live with her aunt Jane—"

"Jane Cunningham is Rebecca's aunt?"

"That's right. She agreed to hide her under the name Rebecca Wilkes, and I agreed to relocate to Quindicott to help Rebecca hack more stuff from BioQuill's computers."

"How did you hook up with Rebecca in the first place?"

"We met on the dark web. She found my posts about BlueSky. I vented my hate for BioQuill because of what they did to my dog."

"I thought you had a pet snake."

"That's Gordo. He's not mine. Gordo's the mascot at the Hound's Tooth tavern. I take him around town, but he's his own snake."

Jeremy's voice dropped an octave. "Once upon a time, I had a Siberian husky named Sonya. For years we traveled all over the country, just Sonya and me. When she was six, Sonya developed some anxiety issues. A vet prescribed BlueSky, and the drug killed her."

"I'm so sorry . . ."

"I hate to say this because I loved that dog more than life, but maybe it was for the best. If Sonya hadn't died, I never would have met Rebecca, and we never would have uncovered BioQuill's plan for the future of BlueSky—"

"Haven't they done enough damage?"

"Not hardly, Mrs. McClure. According to their rigged data, the drug works wonders for pets, so BioQuill is seeking approval for use by children."

Oh, Jack. If this is true, then these people—this company—they're monsters.

Jack did not reply, but I could feel the ghost's cold rage in the pit of my stomach.

"And Rebecca has proof of all this?"

"*Had* proof," Jeremy corrected. "When her aunt was shot, she ran and left it behind. You can't blame her. Rebecca was scared. She walked Jane's dog every day but that one, and when the weather was bad, she always borrowed Jane's big yellow slicker. So when her aunt was shot, Rebecca knew she was the real target."

"But *where* is this proof?"

"Before she ran, Rebecca texted me. Just six words and I never heard from her again. She said: *Protect Sparky and find the chip.*

"I knew Sparky would be protected when Bonnie told me you and your son were caring for him. I also knew Rebecca had put all the proof she'd found on a single microchip and hidden it. Why she didn't tell me where, I don't know—"

Suddenly, I did—because I remembered my conversation with our local veterinarian.

"Rebecca told you exactly where to find the chip, Jeremy. You just didn't understand the message."

"What do you mean?"

"Protect Sparky and find the chip. You were supposed to protect Sparky because he *has* the chip."

I told Jeremy about my talk with Dr. Winnik, and how he thought the identity chip in Sparky's neck had malfunctioned.

"But it didn't malfunction," I said. "I'm betting Rebecca replaced the ID chip with the data chip that contains her evidence."

Jeremy smacked his own forehead. "How could I be so stupid?"

I continued spilling to Jeremy, telling him all about Troy Hanley and why I believed he was the one who shot Jane and tried to kill or kidnap Sparky.

"The bastard is working for BioQuill!" Jeremy cried. "He's obviously some kind of corporate cleaner. This guy is really dangerous. He'll stop at nothing to—"

"Oh, no!" I cried. "How could *I* be so stupid? Troy is in town right now. I thought he was going to the movies. But I'll bet he's waiting for my son to walk the dog. If I'm right, that's when he's going to kill Sparky, and maybe everyone with him."

CHAPTER 52

Collision Course

A hero is no braver than an ordinary man, but he is
brave five minutes longer.

—Ralph Waldo Emerson

I RUSHED OUTSIDE to my car, speed-dialing all the way.

After three rings, Spencer's voice mail answered. My
son's phone was probably still in his backpack with the rest
of his school stuff.

I checked the time. Five minutes after nine. I still had
time to stop Spencer and Seymour from going outside. But
I knew the mailman would arrive at the bookstore any minute, if he wasn't there already.

I speed-dialed Seymour, but my call went to voice mail.
I stifled a scream.

Since when does Seymour not answer?!

When you need that knucklehead the most, that's when,
Jack replied. *Savor the irony and call your auntie.*

Sadie almost never used her personal phone at work, so I

called our bookstore—and got my own perky voice mail informing me that Buy the Book was closed.

This time I did scream.

Jeremy, who'd just hopped aboard his motorcycle, looked at me with alarm.

"No one will pick up their phone," I told him.

"Where will they walk the dog?"

"Probably the town square," I called as I crossed the street to my car. "The dog walk is open until eleven, and there will be other people." *I hope.*

"Meet you there," he replied.

Helmetless, Jeremy roared down Larchmont. I was right behind him.

I ignored the yellow light at the junction and turned onto Briar Patch Road, going well above the speed limit. It was a straight shot to Cranberry Street and the town square; I was probably going seventy when I passed Jeremy.

The next traffic light was green, but I would have blown through it no matter the color, just like I blew through the next two stop signs.

Tires squealed and a horn blared, but I was already gone.

My heart was pumping. I felt clammy with sweat.

I'm breaking every traffic law in the books, Jack. I'd actually welcome a little police attention.

Yeah, Jack echoed. *Where's a cop when you need one? On the other hand, sweetheart, you're not going to get any older if you don't slow down.*

And slow down I did, just as we reached the town square. The dog walk was well lit, and nearly empty. There was no sign of Spencer, Seymour, or Sparky.

"Sparky must have led them in the opposite direction, toward Bud Napp's hardware store."

I hit the gas, but I didn't get far before I spied two things at once.

My son and Sparky, along with Seymour and author Amber Breen, were about to step off the curb at the next block. And that same SUV that nearly ran me over was moving toward them. The driver had a red light, but he wasn't slowing down!

Hang on, Jack!

I hit the gas and shot between the oncoming SUV and its intended victims, hoping my Ford Escape would escape major damage.

It did. The driver spotted me and veered away at the last moment. Instead of our vehicles colliding, the SUV struck a trash can and a faux-Victorian lamppost—thankfully, nowhere near Sparky and his security entourage, or anyone else on the street.

The lamp snapped in two, the trash can flew through the window of Colleen's beauty parlor, and the SUV rolled up and over the stump of the broken lamppost, where it got stuck.

I braked and jumped out of my car in time to see Troy Hanley stumble out of his. He looked around as if dazed. Then he got his wits about him and ran!

He didn't get far. Jeremy blew past me on his motorcycle, his blond mane blowing wildly. As he reached the fleeing shooter, our golden boy stuck out his hand and straight-armed the corporate cleaner. Troy flipped end over end and hit the pavement.

He didn't get up.

Unfortunately, the strike threw Jeremy off-balance. His front wheel wobbled, then struck a fire hydrant. There was no fountain of water like in the movies, only the crunch of twisted metal as the motorcycle bounced sideways and annihilated itself on the facade of Franzetti's Pizza.

Bonnie emerged from her family's shop and screamed when she saw Jeremy lying in the street. He sat up just as

Bonnie reached him. She rained kisses on his face as Jeremy struggled to rise.

A crowd gathered, and I heard a siren in the distance.

"Mom!" Spencer called as he and Sparky ran toward me.

"It's okay, honey. You're safe now. And so is Sparky."

As I hugged my boy and his furry best friend, I whispered to the ghost—

It's over, Jack.

Yeah, and that's a crying shame.

Why would you say that?

I could almost see the ghost's glowing grin.

This was the most excitement Cornpone-cott has ever seen. I say we do it again tomorrow.

EPILOGUE

If you want to imagine the future, imagine a boy and a
dog and his friends. And a summer that never ends.

—Neil Gaiman and Terry Pratchett, *Good Omens*

Quindicott, Rhode Island
Eight months later

"THIS LOVELY LITTLE town is as peaceful as I remembered it," Amber Breen said with a caustic wink.

Recalling the last time we were all on Cranberry Street
together (and the chaos that ensued), Seymour and I had a
good laugh. Spencer joined in. Even Sparky's bark sounded
like a snicker.

This very morning, Amber had rolled back into our town
for a signing of *Doggy Day Afternoon*'s paperback edition.
On this beautiful Saturday in June, I was proud to show the
author how well our town had recovered from the crazy
events she'd witnessed last fall.

Now Amber, Seymour, and I were strolling down Cranberry's sidewalk with Spencer in front, strutting with Sparky, like he was leading his own private Pet Parade.

With a little spit and polish (and a lot of help from Bud Napp's work crews), our main street was once again shining like a rare jewel. Especially impressive was the new facade on Franzetti's Pizza.

Jane Cunningham had recovered, too—and with a brand-new outlook.

When she dropped off Sparky at the bookshop this morning, Jane was excited to finally meet Amber. And Amber was thrilled to shake hands with her number one fan.

"Jane Cunningham is such an incredible woman," the author gushed. "Meeting an admirer of my fiction who is so accomplished and so vital, and after she was hovering at death's door just eight months ago—it's humbling."

Humbled was how I felt the day Jane was reunited with Sparky. I watched with emotion as the dog leaped into his mommy's arms, licked her face, and wagged his tail so hard, it thumped the floorboards.

It was then I realized my son had done something profound by insisting we rescue that dog. Jane understood, too. She saw the bond that had formed between Sparky and Spencer and made sure my son would become her number one dog-sitter. Honestly, Jane practically let him share custody of the pooch.

At least three times a week, Spencer bicycled out to Larchmont to walk Sparky, and every Saturday, while Jane met with Bud Napp on their new business ventures, he and Sparky had a date for romping and playing on the town green.

But there were other beneficiaries of Jane's generosity, and as we strolled along the sidewalk, Amber Breen listened with rapt attention to all that had transpired since she'd last been to our little town . . .

After Jane awakened from her coma, and slowly made a

full recovery, she learned the whole story of what had happened to her—and everything that had been unearthed because of it. At first, she was devastated to hear from her lawyer, Emory Stoddard, the full extent of her two neighbors' bitterness toward her.

Ella Pruett, who'd been struggling to hide her own dire financial state, had been so filled with jealousy (and fear of ending up destitute) that she'd contacted Jane's estranged brother-in-law, Stanley Cunningham, immediately after Jane was shot.

"A nasty business," Seymour interrupted. "Ella promised Stan she would help him fight for control of Jane's properties upon her death, hoping he'd be grateful enough to help her with a big, fat piece of the inheritance."

"Instead, it was Jane who extended a helping hand to Ella," I said, "along with a solution to her financial problems."

Amber shook her head. "That's a big amount of forgiveness."

"Part of Jane's new outlook," I explained. "After coming so close to death, she told Bud, she wanted her years left on earth to be spent trying to help those around her—even Ella. Jane offered Ella a three-way partnership in the transformation of her family's spacious but neglected mansion into exclusive rental apartments. According to Bud, when Ella heard the plan, her wall of arrogance crumbled. There were tears in her eyes as she shook Jane's and Bud's hands."

"And what about Stanley Cunningham?" Amber asked. "He was quite a nasty piece of work himself."

"Jane made him a different kind of deal. She offered to pay for a top-notch addiction program. And if he completed the therapy and remained clean, she promised to employ him in the Cunningham business."

"How's he doing?"

"Surprisingly well."

"Not so surprising," Seymour said, "when you consider

how many addicts finally do reach a point when they realize bottoming out could send them six feet under."

"Stanley and Ella are now a couple," I told Amber, preferring to look on the bright side. "And so far, Stan seems like a changed man."

"Yeah," Seymour said. "He's even steered clear of the girlie bar on the highway."

"What about Jane's other neighbor?" Amber asked. "What happened to that poor, disturbed man who threatened us with a shotgun?"

"Robert Slattery? After he was released from jail, Jane made amends with him, too. Remember that secret garden and neglected meadow with poison ivy on his property? Jane convinced him to partner with her on transforming it all into a community park for Larchmont, which they could name after his late wife."

"How touching," said Amber.

"Yes, Robert liked the idea so much that he went even further after the park was completed. He asked for Jane's help in resurrecting the spirit of his family's dead business."

"And what was that?"

"A farmers market," Seymour replied. "They used to have the greatest goat's milk fudge. The new one is a different model. No fudge. And it's open only on the weekends. But they've still got amazing produce, plus baked goods, jams, local honeys, that sort of thing."

I nodded. "It's more of a rotating green market than what Robert's family originally ran, but Jane still insisted they call it Slattery's General Store. She even had a beautiful wooden sign made with the old wheelbarrow logo."

"Oh, I must plan a visit for the fall harvest!" Amber said, throwing a mysterious glance Seymour's way. "Perhaps in time for my next hardcover . . ."

I suppressed a little smile at that. Amber's new enthusiasm for Quindicott was certainly a boon for Sadie and me, but we both knew the author had an ulterior motive for her feelings.

Soon after we arrived in the town square, that motive become more than apparent.

Spencer spotted friends from school at the dog walk, and he took off with the frolicking Sparky at his heels. Then Seymour sat down on the bench with us, and I remembered a bit of news I wanted to share.

"I just booked Tad Zeus for a signing the first week of September. I know you like his thrillers, Seymour, so—"

"Sorry, Pen. I'll be out of town."

"Really? Where are you going?"

Seymour and Amber exchanged more glances.

"What are those looks about?" I teased.

"Oh, for goodness' sakes, tell her!" Amber cried.

"I'm going on a two-week cruise . . . with Amber."

I'd known Seymour since grade school, but I believe this was the first time I ever saw him blush.

"Scandalous, isn't it?" Amber said with a laugh.

I raised an eyebrow. "And just how many weekends have you spent in Maine since last fall, Seymour? I've been hearing gossip, you know. I think even swinging-singles cruise master Dr. Rubino made a remark."

"Ha-ha. Very funny," Seymour said, throwing up his hands. "And that's the last you'll get out of me. I refuse to fuel small-town gossip. I'm going to the bakery."

"Not without me you're not," Amber said, rising. "Would you like to come, Pen?"

"I'll stay here and watch Spencer, so you two can have a little privacy. But you *could* bring me one of Linda and Milner's jumbo blueberry muffins."

After they'd gone, I noticed a copy of today's *Quindicott Bulletin* on the bench. I turned to the single spread that carried state and national news. Sure enough, the BioQuill drug company indictments were featured. As I read the details, I felt a supernatural draft settle in beside me. And I knew what that meant—

So, what do you think, doll? Sounds to me like some slippery snakes in suits are finally going to the slammer.

"First, there'll be a trial," I told the ghost. "Or a plea bargain. Either way, you're probably right. Some of those bad actors will likely do time . . ."

In the days, weeks, and months after the criminal who called himself Troy Hanley was put in handcuffs, Justice Department attorneys worked to sort out the whole ugly mess.

Do tell, Jack prompted. *I never did hear all the facts of the case.*

"The local charges began with that stolen SUV," I informed the ghost. "The one that tried to run me and Sparky over. I told Eddie about the incriminating clothes I found in Troy's rented rooms, and his officers secured a warrant. When they searched Troy's place, they found the rifle those state gun dogs never did sniff out on Robert Slattery's property."

So the crazy guy with the antique shotgun really was as innocent as a newborn puppy?

"And just about as harmless, which is why I was happy to see Robert cleared. After that, Troy and Jeremy were deposed, which led to more truths being exposed. And in the end, Troy agreed to a plea deal in exchange for testimony as a witness for the prosecution in the case against BioQuill."

That's the way it worked in my day, too, Jack said. *Squeeze the little fish until he gives up the big shark.*

"Yes, and as you and I suspected, the shooting of Jane Cunningham came down to a case of mistaken identity. Jane's niece, the girl who called herself Rebecca Wilkes, had been walking Sparky regularly on Briar Patch Road. But that day, she was meeting with Jeremy, so Jane walked Sparky instead."

And they both wore the same coat?

"That's right. On all those chilly days, when Rebecca walked the dog, she wore Jane's oversized yellow slicker, a coat Sparky was used to. And because of the drizzly weather, Troy couldn't see who was under that big slicker's hood. With his rifle in hand, he climbed up to Robert Slattery's tree house—to intentionally frame the man—saw Sparky and the yellow slicker as usual, and thought he was shooting Rebecca."

And that's when the gal with the big whistle hit the road?

"Exactly. A powerful corporation seemed to be coming down on her with deadly force. and by then, she knew someone in the FDA had been corrupted. Rebecca didn't yet know who to trust in the FBI, the Department of Justice, or our local law enforcement. She was too afraid to even use a phone . . ."

Lying low is what saves your hide, but you can't stick your head up even once.

"Yes, and she did. Rebecca made one futile attempt to contact Jeremy a few days later at the Hound's Tooth bar. She was that cute blonde with short hair the bartender said came looking for Jeremy, and she quickly left again."

Smart felons would have snatched her then, for a real unhappy end.

"But we weren't dealing with smart felons. As we learned from Troy's deposition, Rebecca was wrong about the people chasing her."

How so?

"The BioQuill corporation wasn't after her. Her former IT boss was. He knew she'd stolen incriminating data—due to his own laxness (and laziness) in giving her his password to do his work. So, he secretly tried to cover his behind by personally hiring Troy Hanley on the dark web—"

Dark web? Jack interrupted. *Sounds like an eight-legged scheme for catching black flies.*

"Close. Let's just say it's not a place where you find up-

and-up players. And Troy was as sketchy as they come. He was supposed to clean up the IT boss's mess by finding Rebecca, recovering the data she stole, and using whatever means necessary to shut her up for good."

That I understand.

"I know you do. So, after tracking Rebecca to her aunt's home, Troy pretended to be a remote worker looking for lodging and rented the available rooms from Jane."

And what about his female sidekick? The one with the black lipstick?

"Troy hired Gemma to help him spy on Rebecca, but after Jane was mistakenly shot, and then I came sniffing around, the heat was too much. Troy told Gemma it was time to pull the plug on Larchmont and get out of Dodge. Gemma did, leaving so fast, she dropped the groceries where she stood while Troy stayed behind to continue cleaning up what he could.

"Fortunately, Troy wasn't nearly as competent as Rebecca's ally, Jeremy. Troy never found the evidence Rebecca took from BioQuill, or the additional files Jeremy had hacked. All he did find, after searching Rebecca's place, was a chip injection kit for pets."

So he knew the dog was the key.

"Not at first. Troy thought Rebecca used the kit to inject a chip under her own skin. That's why he went to Jeremy's trailer park, looking for Rebecca. He intended to kill them both, making it look like a break-in and murder. But Rebecca wasn't at the trailer, and after a scuffle, Jeremy fled. Troy grabbed the phone Jeremy had left behind and saw the warning text Rebecca had sent—*Protect Sparky and find the chip.*

"That's when Troy knew for certain where the incriminating data had been hidden. And he knew he'd have to kill Sparky, or run him over, expecting the dog's body would be buried or cremated and the evidence destroyed."

But that's not what happened, thanks to us, Jack said.

"And Jeremy," I pointed out. "And Jane's courageous niece, who was hailed as a bold whistleblower. She and Jeremy saved lives—that's for sure. No matter what happens with the trial, BlueSky is off the market for good.

"Of course, Rebecca's corporate career is over. After what she did, no company will ever hire her—not that she cares. Jane tells me her niece was relieved to put all that high-pressure insanity behind her and return to quiet Quindicott, where she now works for her aunt's expanding business."

A good ending for a brave dame, Jack said. *What about the golden boy, Jeremy? What happened to the snake handler?*

"You'll never guess. After the Department of Justice reviewed what he'd done, they recruited him for their cyber-crime division."

Electronic hat tricks get a whole division now?

"You bet, and they wanted Jeremy bad."

I guess his trailer park rewiring impressed them.

"Impressed? Jeremy hacked a corporate computer everyone thought was completely secure. Yes, Jack, they were impressed enough to move him to Washington and break Bonnie Franzetti's heart."

Aw, don't sweat it, doll. That bobby-soxer is tougher than you think, even if she does act dopey from time to time.

"Everyone acts dopey from time to time, Jack. They usually have their reasons." I suppressed a laugh. "I'm sure you felt like a dope when you found out it was that awful ex-con Muggsy who hired you to recover that stolen Toto statue—just to impress his gangster cellmate."

The worst client I ever had, if not my worst case. It still burns me up. I took a beating and that ex-con got the last laugh, earning a cushy casino job where he could lounge for the rest of his life on a Cuban beach, sipping cocktails and counting his money.

"Actually, Jack, that's not what happened."

Come again?

"From what I unearthed in old newspaper clippings, Muggsy did throw in with the crime bosses who were turning Havana into a tourist and gambling destination to rival Las Vegas. But it didn't last."

Lemme guess. The taxman came for them, just like Al Capone.

"Not even close. There was a revolution in Cuba, and the mob was driven out. Only some didn't make it. Muggsy wound up in a Cuban prison."

What do you know? I guess some jailbirds can't stay out of a cage.

"There's a happier ending for that young couple you helped. Did you know that?"

Can't say I did, doll. I got busy with other clients and then I got plugged. Without a pulse, I couldn't do much investigating—until I met you.

"Well, I did a little investigating on my own, and those two newlyweds *did* fulfill their dream. Because of the mystery you solved, and those stock certificates you handed to them, they were able to leave their shabby digs in New York for the greener pastures of central Maine, and they took Toto Two with them. But that's not the end of the story."

Really? Do tell.

"After chatting with Amber Breen, I discovered Quindicott's favorite pet-mystery author actually is the granddaughter of Sally Kraft and Bobby Breen. Not only that, but she also told me there are now many generations of Totos wagging their tails in Maine—all descendants of the little terrier you named Toto Two."

You don't say.

"Wait a minute. Is that sarcasm I hear? Okay, Jack, come clean. When you heard Amber Breen's last name, were you curious yourself? Is that the reason you told me your dog story?"

You're a bright Penny, the ghost said with a laugh. *What do you think?*

A child's happy shout snapped me back to the town green.

More people were there. Dogs and children were playing, birds were singing, and young couples and seniors were strolling about. On the other side of the park, two art students from the university were making elaborate balloon animals, taking pictures of them, and giving them away.

Just then I noticed my son waving me over to see one of Sparky's new tricks.

"Coming, Spencer!" I called.

Before I rose from the bench, I heard Jack's heavy sigh, and a chilling breeze made me shiver despite the brilliant summer sun. I knew what that meant, and I felt my heart tug.

Well, I see it's back to small-town life in Cornpone-cott. It's enough to put a spirit to sleep.

"So, you're leaving?"

Just for a little while. But I'll always come back to haunt you, Penny. And you know what that means . . .

Lowering his voice, he promised, *I'll see you in your dreams.*

And with that, the ghost of Jack Shepard retreated to my bookshop, fading back into the fieldstone walls that had become his home.

ABOUT THE AUTHOR

Cleo Coyle is a pseudonym for Alice Alfonsi, writing in collaboration with her husband, Marc Cerasini. Both are *New York Times* bestselling authors of the long-running Coffeehouse Mysteries —now celebrating twenty years in print. They are also authors of the national bestselling Haunted Bookshop Mysteries, previously written under the pseudonym Alice Kimberly. Alice has worked as a journalist in Washington, DC, and New York, and has written popular fiction for adults and children. A former magazine editor, Marc has authored espionage thrillers and nonfiction for adults and children. Alice and Marc are also both bestselling media tie-in writers who have penned properties for Lucasfilm, NBC, Fox, Disney, Imagine, Toho, and MGM. They live and work in New York City, where they write independently and together.

CONNECT ONLINE

CoffeehouseMystery.com

 CleoCoyleAuthor

 CleoCoyle

Ready to find
your next great read?

Let us help.

Visit prh.com/nextread

Penguin
Random
House

THE INDISPENSABLE GUIDE
TO THE WORLD'S BEST
CRAFT & TRADITIONAL BEERS

BEST
BEERS

STEPHEN BEAUMONT & TIM WEBB

MITCHELL
BEAZLEY

CONTENTS

A NOTE ABOUT BREWERY LISTINGS

We believe that brewery ownership matters. As such, where previously independent breweries have been purchased by much larger entities, we have listed the owning company in parentheses after the brewery name. Such is the pace and frequency of these deals today, however, that the odd acquisition may have escaped our notice and, of course, further purchases may have occurred between the finalization of the text and the moment this book reached your hands. Until such time as regulations require that the name of the company responsible for brewing the beer you buy be listed on the label, we can only advise careful research.

THE BEERS

INTRODUCTION

A VERY DIFFERENT BEER GUIDE FOR A VERY DIFFERENT BEER MARKET

No one today knows for certain exactly how many breweries are active throughout the world. We have estimates for various countries, but some of those, like the Brewers Association tally for the USA, are far better and more reliable than others, such as the "guesstimations" for Brazil and China.

Our own very conservative estimate places the global brewery total at over 20,000, but it is likely that there are many more than that. And if we take the equally conservative average of a dozen different labels per brewery, knowing that in this day and age of one-offs, special editions and collaborations any given craft brewery can probably boast in excess of 30, 40 or 50 brands, then the worldwide count of regular beers is fast closing on a quarter-million, and when one-offs are included, doubtless well beyond it.

In this context, the number of beers we assessed in the 2015 version of this book seems minuscule. For while 4,300 beer reviews is by any measure an impressive achievement, it represents but a very tiny fraction of the world's total beer supply.

So, you might ask, why create a book that features even fewer beers? The answer is focus.

We recognize that more people are enjoying more beer than ever before, and that in many cases they are also paying higher prices than ever before, from the special release that retails for $30 per highly coveted bottle to the extremely limited edition that sells for hundreds of pounds or yen or euros. We also recognize that when people open and drink such beers, they may be moved to quote the bittersweet refrain from the Peggy Lee standard "Is That All There Is?"

Hence this new approach. Rather than attempt to deliver a cross section of breweries spanning the globe, we have assembled a carefully selected group of what we firmly believe are the best minds in beer – you can meet them beginning on page 316 – and tasked them to deliver detailed reviews of the absolute best beers their native lands have to offer. Not the most talked about or the rarest or the most obscure, but simply the finest ales and lagers and mixed-fermentation beers that eager enthusiasts might actually be able to get their hands on. Star ratings have been dispensed with because all the beers we have featured are at the top of their class.

Along the way, we have tasted beers beside many of our experts to affirm that the high standards we have set are being rigorously maintained. Where possible, we have travelled with them to sample in situ, and where not we have assembled local and international beers to evaluate as one, making sure that just because a beer comes from a less developed beer culture, that doesn't mean it might disappoint a more seasoned beer aficionado.

We also introduce in this edition three categories of special merit: ICONIC BREWERIES, CAN'T-MISS BREWERIES and BREWERIES TO WATCH.

The ICONIC BREWERIES designation is in many ways self-defining and has been awarded in a most miserly fashion, as we feel is only proper. An Icon is not only a brewery that has to some extent perfected or even invented a style or styles, it is also one that brews splendid beer throughout its range and, most importantly, has acted as a major influencer in its national and, in many cases, international markets.

The CAN'T-MISS BREWERIES accreditation is reserved for those breweries that craft great beers across a variety of styles, with each being as good as or better than the rest of its portfolio kin. Essentially, it means what it declares, which is that if you buy a beer with this brewery's name attached, it is almost guaranteed to be a good if not great taste experience.

Finally, BREWERIES TO WATCH are those breweries under three years of age at the time of writing that show tremendous potential for the future. They can be already well-known operations or under-the-radar gems, but each and every one is a potential Can't Miss or even a future Icon, as chosen by our experts and vetted by ourselves.

And there you have it. You may not agree with every assessment of every beer mentioned in the following pages, taste being the subjective entity that it is, and it is equally likely that you will wonder why a favourite beer is absent or a cherished brewery denied Can't Miss status. But we can guarantee that the beers and breweries noted here will delight almost any beer enthusiast, from tentative novice to seasoned beer-hunting veteran, and that in the deliciously, delightfully crowded beer marketplace we face today, the selections we and our experts have presented will make your next beer-drinking experience just that much more interesting and enjoyable.

Cheers,

Stephen Beaumont and Tim Webb

BEER STYLES

The idea that a beer should be considered of a particular style was anathema to the 20th-century industrialists who forged the notion of the universal beer. For them, the ideal was light gold, grainy sweet, almost bereft of bitterness and served as cold as possible to hide flaws. The key was marketing.

The rise of modern craft breweries, on the other hand, has provoked a need for reliably recognizable terms to describe, distinguish and explain the myriad types of beer, old and new, that now adorn the shelves of bars, stores and home refrigerators around the world. The questions that remain are which terms to use and how to apply them.

We believe it was Michael Jackson, in his 1977 book *The World Guide to Beer*, who first attempted to catalogue global beer styles, introducing readers to such beer types as "*Münchener*", "*Trappiste*" and "(Burton) Pale Ale". His goal then was to provide a context through which to discover – or rediscover – these beers. Our challenge, although addressed to a more beer-aware public, remains in essence the same.

While we would love to report that we have solved all the issues surrounding the current confusion and can provide readers with a simple map of the major beer styles of the world, this is not currently possible and, we admit, may never be. What we offer instead is a rough guide on how to pick your way through a linguistic and conceptual minefield in a fashion that adds to rather than detracts from understanding.

START WITH TRADITION

We believe the most reliable stylistic imperatives to be those based on centuries of brewing tradition, and that most modern derivations are merely modifications of existing beer styles, however inventive or ingenious. Hence our first separation is according to method of fermentation.

Historically, the term **ale** has referred to a beer fermented at room temperature or higher, causing its *Saccharomyces* yeast to rise to the top of the wort, or unfermented beer, hence references to top-fermentation or, sometimes, warm-fermentation. In contrast, a **lager** was fermented at a cooler temperature, causing its yeast to sink, thus known as bottom-fermentation or, sometimes, cool-fermentation.

These main beer classes, comparable to red and white wine, still serve to define the overwhelming majority of beers, despite the temperature and yeast manipulation possible in a modern brewhouse. As a general rule, a beer fermented at warmer temperatures with a yeast of the family *S. cerevisiae* and conditioned at warm temperatures for a short period – an ale – should tend toward a fruitier character. Those fermented at cooler temperatures with a yeast of the family *S. pastorianus* and cold-stored (or "lagered") for a longer period at cold temperatures – a lager – should not. Combine ale yeast with a lager-style conditioning and you have the hybrid styles of **kölsch** and **altbier**, as well as the American cream ale. Flip it to lager yeast and ale-type conditioning and you have **steam** beer, also known as **California common beer**.

Beers that have no yeast added to them, most famously the **lambic** beers of Belgium, are said to undergo spontaneous fermentation, effected by a combination of airborne and barrel-resident microflora, including *Brettanomyces* and *Pediococcus*, which yield complex flavours from mildly lemony to assertively tart. Those fermented with the same types of microbes introduced deliberately are becoming known variously as wild beers, mixed-fermentation beers or, more crudely, sour beers.

ADD COLOUR

Colour is a powerful force in beer and often used to define beer by style, with some references to hue reserved exclusively for certain types of beer, such as "white" (*blanche, wit, weisse*) for **wheat beers**. "Pale" and "light" (in colour, not alcohol or calories) are also popular adjectives, yielding the now-international **pale ale** and **India pale ale**, or **IPA**, the German *helles* and the Czech *světlý*.

"Amber" in North America was and to some extent remains synonymous with otherwise ordinary ales or lagers with a blush of colour, while **"red"** has a questionable degree of Irish authenticity often used to describe a beer of uncertain style. The same tint trait among lagers may be termed *Wiener* or **Vienna**.

"Dark" is often also used in fairly random fashion in the English-speaking world, but retains validity in Bavaria where its literal translation, *dunkel*, should indicate a brownish lager of a style, *Münchener*, once strongly associated with Munich – unless it is combined with *weizen* or *weisse*, in which case the reference is to dark wheat beer. In the Czech Republic and across Europe's eastern half, the term is *tmavý*.

"Brown" implies the use of more roasted malts and is historically associated with **old ale**, a class of fairly winey ales aged in oak still seen in the tart, fruity *oud bruin* style from northern Belgium and the fresher English **brown ale**. Now, however, it is applied to a wide variety of creations, from sickly sweet to forcefully bitter, mild to alcoholic.

"Black" is usually reserved for **porters** and **stouts**, though also applied to bottom-fermented German *schwarzbier*.

CONSIDER STRENGTH

Brewers have for centuries used subtle nudge-and-wink systems to highlight alcohol content. One well-known remnant of this practice is the Scottish shilling system whereby ales are measured from **60 shilling**, or **60/-**, for the lightest, to **80/-** or **90/-** for stronger beers (*see* page 91), the last also referred to as **"wee heavy"** or **Scotch ale**. In the Czech Republic and elsewhere, the old Balling system of measuring wort gravity defines beers by degrees, from **8°** for the lightest to **12°** for a beer of premium strength and on up into fermented-porridge territory.

Few words are less useful to a beer description than "strong", the difficulty being context. In Scandinavia, strong beer (***starkøl***) is above 4.5–4.7% ABV, not far from where the British would place the definition were the word not banned from beer names. In contrast, few Belgians, North Americans and Italians would consider anything below 6–7% "strong".

The terms ***dubbel*/double** and ***tripel*/triple** are medieval in origin and have proved both durable and international, in the past used to indicate a beer fermented from a mash with greater malt content – often the "first runnings" of grain then reused to make a second beer. The modern context of *dubbel*/double generally indicates a beer of 6–8% ABV. Most eminently, it appears in reference to the malty and sweet Belgian abbey style *dubbel*, the German **doppelbock** and related Italian **doppio malto** (although use of the latter term appears to be waning) and the American **double IPA**, usually an ale of significant strength and aggressive bitterness.

The current use of *tripel*/triple owes its origins to 20th-century monastery breweries and typically describes a specific type of blond, sweet-starting but usually dry-finishing strong ale, although modern usage extends to **IPA** to suggest an even stronger and hoppier brew.

Quadrupel/**quadruple**/**quad** is a 21st-century affectation, the first variant originally used by the Dutch Trappist brewery La Trappe to designate its new high-strength ale in 1998. The Dutch spelling is employed to imply heritage.

Historically, the term **barley wine** was used to indicate a beer of wine strength, often undergoing some period of bottle-ageing. Modern interpretations vary from a high-hopped, fully carbonated US style to a virtually uncarbonated, fully attenuated Italian form that retains residual sugars and resembles Madeira made from grain. Barrel-ageing is increasingly common.

The adjective **"Imperial"** has experienced a recent transformation from its original deployment in **Imperial Russian stout** designating a strong, intense, sometimes oily stout to the suggestion that any style may be "Imperialized" by being made bolder and more alcoholic, sometimes also hoppier. Thus we find **Imperial pale ale** as a synonym for **double IPA** and confections such as **Imperial pilsner**, **Imperial brown ale** and so on.

FACTOR IN THE GRAINS

Besides the basic four ingredients of beer – water, barley malt, hops and yeast – numerous other grains are used with varying degrees of regularity, in all but a handful of specialized cases in combination with barley malt.

Wheat is the most common of these, creating whole categories of beer such as the German-style wheat beers variously known as *weizen* or *weisse*, prefixed *hefe-* when indicating that the beer is unfiltered and *kristall* when clear. Also included in this family are the derivatives

dunkelweisse and **weizenbock**, respectively meaning dark and strong wheat beers, and in an emerging category of hoppy versions pioneered by a US–German collaboration and known as **hopfenweisse**.

Different local traditions of light (typically 2.5–3.5%), quenching wheat beers have survived or been revived, such as **Berliner weisse**, made tart through lactic acidification and sometimes *Brettanomyces* during fermentation; salted, coriander-laced and tart *gose* (sometimes **Leipziger gose**); the smoked wheat **grodziskie** from Poland (*see* Style Spotlight, page 189) and northern Germany's tart, smoked **lichtenhalner**.

Spontaneously fermented Belgian **lambic** is by law a wheat beer, though more common in Belgium and elsewhere is **witbier** or **bière blanche** (white beer) brewed with unmalted rather than malted wheat and spiced with orange peel and coriander, sometimes in conjunction with other spices.

Once ubiquitous but now more seldom seen are simple **wheat ales**, blond beers that have been made lighter of body just through the use of malted wheat, although there is increased North American interest in well-hopped interpretations called **hoppy wheat beers**. Some craft brewers in the USA and elsewhere have started to make strong wheat beers called **wheat wines**, referencing barley wine.

Other grains in general usage include oats, which bring sweetness and a silky mouthfeel to **oatmeal stout**, and other, less conventional beers, such as: oatmeal brown ales; rye, which bestows a spiciness upon **rye pale ale** and **rye IPA**, as well as the odd lager-fermented **roggenbier** of German origin; buckwheat, blackened and used in the Breton beer style **bière de blé noir**; and an assortment of non-glutinous grains employed to create the growing class of **gluten-free beers**.

Malt and grain substitutes are mostly there for fermentable sugar to increase alcoholic strength, with or, more commonly, without adding flavour characteristics. The likes of maize (corn), rice, starches, syrups and candi sugar may bring balance to heavy beer by ensuring that it is suitably strong in alcohol, but are not seen as creating styles in their own right – though **Japanese rice beers** and a handful of related beers in the USA are having a go.

The exception to this rule is where unfermentable sugars are used with the intention of adding sometimes considerable sweetness without alcoholic strength, fructose creating **sweet stout** and lactose contributing to **milk** or **cream stout**.

HOPS AND OTHER FLAVOURINGS

Hops have been the primary flavouring agent in beer since the Middle Ages, but only in the last century or two have beer styles begun to be defined by the variety of hop used.

Perhaps most famously, what the world knows as the **Czech-style pilsner** is seasoned with a single variety of hop, the floral Saaz, grown near where the style was invented. Equally, the typical hops used in a **British best bitter** (*see* Style Spotlight, page 88) have always been Fuggle and Golding (with a wider variety employed in **Extra Special Bitter**, or **ESB**).

When what we now recognize as the **US-style pale ale** was established in the 1970s (*see* Style Spotlight, page 223), the hop used to give the beer its trademark citrusy bite was Cascade, although these days a variety of other so-called "C-hops" are considered acceptable, including Centennial, Chinook and Citra. By extension, these hops have also grown

to be emblematic of the **US-style IPA** and its rapidly developing family, including the double, triple and **Imperial IPA**; **black IPA** – a **hoppy porter** bereft of ample roastiness; lower-strength **session IPA**; fruit- and/or juice-fuelled **fruit IPA**; spicy **white IPA**; the yeast-defined **Belgian IPA**; and whatever else IPA-obsessed brewers and brewery marketing departments have developed since this writing.

More recent hop-defined beer styling includes the use of **New Zealand** to denote beers flavoured with grapey, tropical Kiwi hops, notably Nelson Sauvin and Motueka (*see* Style Spotlight, page 265), **Australian** for beers flavoured with Galaxy and its derivatives or **South Pacific** where these are mixed. As hop cultivation becomes increasingly scientific and additional varieties are created, more beers are being identified by the single hop variety used.

Hops can be considered a core ingredient of any beer, other flavourings being distinctly optional, including herbs and spices. While we still see the odd beer identified as *gruit* (sometimes *grut* or *gruut*), which is to say seasoned with a selection of dried herbs and flavourings but no hops, certainly the most famously spiced beer is the **Belgian-style wheat beer**.

Although all manner of herbs and spices were employed prior to the widespread use of hops in brewing – before Pierre Celis pitched coriander, cumin and dried Curaçao orange peel into the beers of Hoegaarden in 1966 – the extent to which brewers, Belgian or otherwise, spiced beers is questionable. Today, however, beers can be and frequently are flavoured with all manner of ingredients, to the extent that lumping them all into a single **spiced beer** category seems to us rather random. Unfortunately, in the absence of acceptable sub-categories based on which of these additives actually improves what beer, it remains the best available option.

Another area of contention is the addition of fruit syrups to beer. While cherries and raspberries have for centuries been steeped whole in Belgian lambic beers to create respectively **kriek** and **framboise**, the rash of beers made by adding juice, syrup, cordials or essence to ordinary lagers and ales is mostly a post-1980 phenomenon. Although these are collectively known as fruit beers, this can be a misnomer, as the additives are sometimes a considerable distance from their time on the tree.

Dark ales such as brown ale, porter and in particular stout are increasingly having vanilla, cocoa, liquorice and coffee added to them in formats that range from whole pods or stems to syrups and essences, with varying degrees of success. A recent outbreak of coffee-flavoured pale ales suggests that may be a future category to watch.

One of the most curious additives is salt, once commonly and still variously used in (Irish) **dry stout** to fill out the palate, achieved with greatest aplomb in the 19th century by filtering the wort through a bed of shucked oyster shells, hence **oyster stout**. East German *gose* is essentially a salted wheat beer.

Italian brewers have sought to make a style out of adding chestnut to their beer, whether in whole, crushed, honey or jam form, but have more recently, and more successfully, turned their attentions to **Italian grape ale**, indicating a beer flavoured with wine grapes, lees and/or aged in a disused wine barrel (*see* Style Spotlight, page 126). Japanese brewers evoke their own national drink with **sake-influenced beer** made with sake rice, fermented with sake yeast and/or conditioned in cedar sake barrels (*see* Style Spotlight, page 276).

Beyond these, there exists a multitude of other additives and seasonings currently in use – from root vegetables to nuts to flowers

and even Traditional Chinese Medicine herbs, known as TCM herbs. Whether these stand the test of time remains to be seen.

NATIONAL ADJECTIVES

Various national and regional markers have grown in recent years into beer-style descriptors. While some rankle – the term "Belgian" for a beer fermented by US-designated yeast that imbues a spicy or earthy character, for example – they do in most cases provide the buyer with useful information.

Thus **Belgian style** has come to mean a spicy or sometimes somewhat funky take on an understood beer style, as in **Belgian pale ale**, **Belgian IPA** and so on.

In contrast, **US** or **American** almost invariably refers to hop-forward styles in pale ales, IPAs (*see* Style Spotlight, page 223) and others seasoned with Cascade and other such related hops, and **New Zealand** (sometimes **Aotearoan**) pilsner and pale ale references those styles seasoned with Kiwi hops (*see* Style Spotlight, 265). **British** or **English** is usually used in conjunction with pale ale, IPA or barley wine, generally indicating a less aggressive hop character, but also a pronounced maltiness.

Scotch ale or **Scottish-style ale** suggests a beer of quite significant maltiness, with a strength of up to 8% ABV indicated by the former. Long-standing confusion about Scottish brewing methods means that beers so described sometimes also feature a potion of peated malt.

Other geographical qualifiers are more restricted. **Baltic porter**, for example, defines a beer that is not a porter at all, but rather a strong, dark and usually sweet bottom-fermented brew; **Irish red ale** is a popular

descriptor of questionable authenticity; **Irish stout** has both legitimacy and utility in describing a low-strength, dry, roasty form of stout; while **Bohemian** or **Czech style** generally modifies pilsner and suggests one more golden than blond, softly malty and floral; and **Bavarian** or **German** implies crisper, leaner and blonder when referencing pilsner, clove-y and/or banana-ish when applied to a wheat beer.

SEASONAL OFFERINGS

Before 1870 and the coming of affordable large-scale refrigeration, much of mainland Europe enjoyed a brewing "season" that lasted from Michaelmas (29 September) to St George's Day (23 April), fermentation in the summer months being rendered unsound by infestation and insect life. The need for beer during the non-brewing months of summer led historically to the creation of somewhat related styles such as *märzen* in Germany, *bière de garde* in France and *saison* in southern Belgium, each brewed to last the summer months and deploying increased hopping for preservative effect.

Come harvest, German, Austrian, Dutch and Norwegian brewers would clear the stocks of malt from the previous year's barley by brewing a dark *bok* or *bock* and an additional Christmas beer (Scandinavian *Juløl*). This custom was mirrored in the spring in all but Norway with a pale *maibock* or *lentebok* that might see off grain felt unlikely to survive the summer untainted.

There are also beers named after other occasions or seasons, including winter ales, summer beers and harvest ales, suggesting general character traits – heavier in winter, lighter for summer – but little else.

AND LOCAL BREWS

The great unsung charm of German beer is the host of local variants, typically on blond lagers, which are only partially filtered. Sometimes known collectively as *landbier*, they include types that are simply cloudy (*zwickelbier*), some that are cellar-conditioned (*kellerbier*) and a few in which carbon dioxide is vented during lagering (*ungespundetes*).

Franconian brewers claim a slice of history by perpetuating the use of wood-smoked malt in their *rauchbier* – at the same time inspiring a host of new wave smoked beers from Alaska to Poland.

Finnish and Estonian farmhouse brewers create respectively *sahti* (*see* Style Spotlight, page 160) and *koduōlu*, beers filtered through juniper boughs and fermented with bread yeast, served by necessity young and fresh for the lack of hops.

Lithuanian brewers celebrate their curious history with *kaimiškas* (*see* Style Spotlight, page 185), individualistic for a number of reasons, but most notably for adding "hop tea" to rapidly fermented wort post-mashing.

Finally, the craft brewing renaissance has witnessed the emergence or re-emergence of a cacophony of new methods of beer making, both authentically recreated and imagined. In the first group we place **barrel-aged** and **barrel-conditioned beers**, beginning in a multitude of styles and spending time in a variety of different barrels, including those that previously held wine, bourbon, single malt whisky, Cognac, Calvados or, in at least one case, barrels previously used to age maple syrup. Of particular interest in this area, we find, is what Brazilian brewers are currently doing with the exotic woods of the Amazon and Italian brewers with disused wine barrels.

In a similar vein, fresh or unkilned hops are used in a new class of **wet hop beers**, mostly ales and primarily in the USA, but otherwise of almost any hop-driven style the brewer wishes to brew.

At this stage in the development of beer, we see no end to new inventions and possibilities.

SUSPECT STYLES & TENUOUS TRENDS

Very few observers in the mid-1990s would have predicted the rise of IPA as the dominant craft beer style of the new millennium thus far. Too bitter, most would have said – as many did – and in a culture where healthy eating and increasingly moderate drinking were the dominant themes, surely a 7% alcohol content would be considered too high?

What did they know? *What did we know?*

The fact is that beer trends have become pretty much unpredictable over the last two or three decades. Just when you think that IPAs may have maxed out their strength and bitterness, along come double IPAs. Imagine that every long-forgotten beer style that could be revived has been, then sit back and watch the rise of an obscure Polish beer called *grodziskie* (*see* Style Spotlight, page 189). Figure that so-called "sour beers" are too laborious and time-consuming to create in large quantities, and no sooner do brewers develop kettle souring to make the cruder flavours of a months-long process achievable overnight.

That said, craft beer is not immune to the fads, fashions and flights of fancy that have long beset mass-market beer (remember ice beer?). And those, it must be noted, are usually a bit easier to identify.

FRUIT IPA

Occasionally it is possible to place the credit – or blame – for a beer trend at the feet of a single brewery, and so it is with fruit IPAs. For while some might argue that Vermont's Magic Hat Brewing actually kicked things off with their apricot-flavoured "not quite pale ale" #9, it was in fact California's Ballast Point Brewing that really started the ball rolling when they brought out a grapefruit-charged version of their Sculpin IPA in 2013.

It is still unknown if the grapefruit was originally added as a substitute or supplement to the citrusy hops that characterize regular Sculpin (*see* page 221), but either way the modified beer was an immediate hit. In short order, Grapefruit Sculpin went from being a novel curiosity to the sort of beer that sold out the same day a keg was tapped at the local beer bar.

Other fruit IPAs naturally followed, and then the onslaught began. Soon, it was not only commonplace for US breweries to have one, two or more fruited IPAs in their portfolio, but the trend spread to Canada, England, Continental Europe and even Australia.

The problem is that the "style" has now gone from the natural progression of adding grapefruit peel or juice to already grapefruity IPAs to the addition of all sorts of not-necessarily-logical fruits, from pineapple to mango to kiwi. Some of these odd interpretations work, but many more fall out of balance and wind up tasting like bitter fruit beer rather than well-rounded fruity-hoppy ale, which may well signal that this is a trend that will burn itself out sooner rather than later.

KETTLE SOURS

Only a few years old, kettle souring is the process of inoculating wort with various bacteria to lower its pH and then boiling it so that further bacterial growth is inhibited. This brings a level of tartness to the fully fermented beer and so has become a popular short cut, fuelling the growth of the so-called "sour beer" market. In particular, the process has proved popular in the production of low-strength styles such as *Berliner weisse* and *gose*.

The problem with kettle sours, however, is two-fold. On the one hand, many such beers are being sold for the same sort of elevated prices

commanded by beers that spend many months in oak barrels to achieve a similar effect, while on the other, the process has a tendency to result in beers that are relatively simple in their profiles, with chemically slanted lactic flavours and negligible complexity.

And indeed, when compared with the depth and nuance of a beer that undergoes months or years of conditioning in wooden barrels, a kettle-soured beer cannot help but appear as a "one-trick pony" of acidity and little else. Given enough time, it is likely that even those beer drinkers who explore beyond their first couple will tire of such brews, particularly if they continue to be sold at inflated prices.

EXTREME TURBIDITY

With some exceptions, German and Belgian-style wheat beers most prominent among them, cloudiness in modern beer has been generally frowned upon. In fact, since the advent of transparent glassware, clarity, or what is known in beer circles as brightness, has been prized above all as an indication of a well-made beer.

Then came the New England IPA, sometimes known as the NEIPA or the Vermont-style IPA, a much more extreme version of what started out as "unfiltered" blond lagers in Europe some decades ago (their principle being that a bit of flour in the body of the beer added to the otherwise less impressive flavour). These new interpretations are turbid in the extreme and nothing like that which has gone before.

Typically cloudy in appearance and loaded with fruity esters from both hopping and fermentation, New England IPAs rose to fame on the back of a beer called Heady Topper from The Alchemist brewery in northern Vermont (*see* page 209). Other northeastern US and central Canadian breweries soon started to emulate the massively successful beer, and from there this new style spread westward and eventually overseas.

Along the way, the appearance of these beers gradually evolved, growing first densely cloudy, then turbid and finally reaching something resembling orange juice with a head on it. As the "turbidity stakes" grew hotter, it came out that some breweries were adding flour and fruit purées to increase the cloudiness and "juicy" character of their beers.

Surprisingly, the principal difficulty with such ales is not that their appearance might put drinkers off – a dense cloudiness has, in some circles, come to be perceived as a mark of quality – but that some of these ales lack the flavour stability necessary in a market where competition is growing and kegs or cans of beer might not wind up being consumed within an optimal time frame. As such competition grows further and the bloom starts to come off the turbid beer rose, it seems likely that this will become an even greater issue.

THE TWO WORLDS OF BEER

The division of beer into the two broad categories of fast and industrial versus traditional and craft – dull versus interesting, if you prefer – began in earnest with the commencement of a consumer backlash against homogeneity that started building in the 1970s.

Since then, more than 60 countries have seen the revival, or increasingly the arrival, of a vibrant, local beer culture, often boosted by a growing import–export market. But how much impact is this having?

By 2017, the schism between these two philosophies of beer making seemed more pronounced than at any time in its commercial history. Global beer giants continue to see the job of a beer company as to spend as little money as possible making stuff that people can be persuaded to buy through branding and marketing.

In contrast, the massively growing number of craft or traditional brewers, be they tiny local concerns or companies now producing beer in brew runs the size of an Olympic swimming pool, concern themselves more with offering flavour, choice and authenticity – aims contrary to cost-cutting culture.

In 2016, the value of the US domestic beer market was around US\$106 billion or 1.5% of the USA's GDP. Of this amount, over US\$23 billion constituted "craft beer" as defined by the US Brewers Association, a figure matched in growth and significance by the sales of imported beers. Sales of both continue to rise impressively year on year despite the overall volume of beer consumed falling. The brunt of the fall was borne by mostly well-known industrial brews.

A similar pattern exists around a world in which the number of commercial breweries has risen from roughly 4,000 in 1977 to more than 20,000 in 2017.

It is hard to define the proportion of beer produced that might be termed non-industrial, for three main reasons.

Firstly, what actually counts as craft, traditional or special beer? Does one include a blond lager simply because it is made by a small brewery that has existed since before 1960? In the UK and Germany, it is clear that some longer-standing and traditionally inclined producers are engaged in a race to the bottom on price, hiding behind pedantic definitions of quality rather than challenging consumers with the sort of more assertive flavours that are one of the hallmarks of the craft beers that are shaking up the market everywhere.

Secondly, should we be considering the proportion of total beer volume or of total sales, and if the latter, should this be the amount received by the brewers or by the end-point sellers? Craft beers tend to be both stronger and more labour intensive, factors that contribute significantly to the fact that the same measure of a craft beer will probably cost 30–50% more than an industrial brew. Which is not to deny that some retailers have a propensity to pimp the c-word in order to raise their margins.

Thirdly, there is the question of ownership versus intention. Can a global brewing company with a business built around shipping vast volumes of consumable liquids cheaply be expected to make carefully crafted beers in small quantities? Or if a global brewer buys a craft brand, is it ever going to be likely to retain craft production principles long-term?

Staking out how much of the beer in the world should now be considered "craft" is a matter of educated conjecture, though one Californian market analyst suggested early in 2017 that current global sales at the brewery gate stand at around US$85 billion per annum – a figure

that in many countries will quadruple by the time the beer hits the glass – and projected a six-fold rise by 2025, based on current global trends.

In less than 15 years, craft and traditional beers have switched from being quaint niche products to mainstream commodities, acknowledged as an essential and prominent part of the portfolio of any beer-selling company that wants to stay in business. Not bad for a small industry born out of taste, hope and individuality.

Meanwhile, AB InBev has now become the world's largest brewer by far, by January 2017 holding 30% of global production and 50% of the profit from beer making, and posting a projected EBITDA (earnings before interest, tax, depreciation and amortization) of 38%. Yet in reality, the volume of industrial beer being drunk is falling steadily in most established markets and even in places like China, once seen as the key area of hoped-for expansion. The African market, a large percentage of which was acquired through the bank loans that enabled it to buy SAB Miller in 2016, is in effect their last throw of the dice.

Be in no doubt that we live in interesting times.

THE BEERS

WESTERN
EUROPE

BELGIUM

Long considered a Mecca for beer aficionados, Belgium's brewing greatness lies in the sheer variety of what is brewed within its borders, from spontaneously fermented lambics to monstrously strong and complex dark ales. A new generation is now appearing on the scene to evolve and define further the country's brewing culture, which is a delightful bonus.

IV SAISON

Jandrain-Jandrenouille, Jandrain-Jandrenouille, Wallonian Brabant; 6.5%

Arriving fully formed at the inception of its brewery in 2007, IV Saison is the beer that enhanced the most popular Wallonian *saison* style by using US hop varieties.

ALPAÏDE

Nieuwhuys, Hoegaarden, Flemish Brabant; 10%

Just up the road from Hoegaarden's only independent brewery is a small brewhouse serving the family pub and a few distributors, creating a highly accomplished, strong and dark brown unclassifiable brew.

AMBRÉE

Caracole, Falmignoul, Namur; 7.5%

Arguably the classic contemporary take on an old-fashioned Wallonian *ambrée*, managing a neat balance of subtle fruity flavours, some with light caramel and a slightly burned edge.

ARDENNE STOUT

Bastogne, Sibret, Luxembourg; 8%

A strong stout that offers remarkably easy drinking by being softened with spelt, then smoothed out further in oak casks. The best of a good range from a rising star of the Ardennes.

AVERBODE

Huyghe, Melle, East Flanders; 7.5%

A brewery renowned for its massive range of gimmick beers has managed to epitomize the so-called abbey style in this clean and direct, unmistakably Belgian, medium-strong pale ale.

BLACK

Bellevaux, Malmedy, Liège; 6.3%

Dark winter ale based on the brewery owner's taste memory for the UK brew Theakston's Old Peculier from way back in 1975. And it comes eerily close.

BLACK MAMBA

Sainte-Hélène, Florenville, Luxembourg; 4.5%

This slowly evolving tiny Ardennaise brewery is finally settling down after playing about for 20 years. Progress is typified by this US-hopped, UK-styled simple but tasty stout.

BLOSSOMGUEUZE

Lindemans, Vlezenbeek, Flemish Brabant; 6%

This seventh-generation brewery has engulfed the family farm, turning it over to making lighter, sharp lambics that now include both a basil version and this one, with elderflower.

BRUNE

Abbaye des Rocs, Montignies-sur-Roc, Hainaut; 9%

Complex all-malt, delicately spiced ale that starts sweet but gains depth down

ICONIC BREWERY

WESTMALLE

Malle, Antwerp

The first and largest of the breweries that operate within the walls of a Trappist abbey, overseen by members of the Order and for the purpose of supporting the Order and its charities. Important to the development of the modern *dubbel* and *tripel* styles of Belgian ale. Best known for its deep, roasted, medium-strength **Westmalle Dubbel** (7%) and the heavier, cellar-evolving, almost honeyed golden blond **Tripel** (9.5%), but also able to craft **Extra** (4.8%), a delightfully simple blond ale once reserved for the abbey's refectory.

ICONIC BREWERIES

CANTILLON

Anderlecht, Brussels

Not the largest or oldest lambic brewery, but by far the most expressive, notable for their provocative style, originality in new products, openness to brewery visits and sheer persistence. Beers, mostly bottled, include fermented-out old lambic **Grand Cru Bruocsella** (5%); the rule-breaking, all-malt and spontaneously fermented **Iris** (6.5%); a delightfully delicate cherry-steeped **Kriek** (5.5%); and the ground-breaking **Saint Lamvinus** (6.5%), steeped with grapes from Bordeaux.

RODENBACH [BAVARIA]

Roeselare, West Flanders

The largest-remaining creator of historically commonplace, recently near-extinct oak-aged brown ale, housed in large oak tuns for expert blending with younger brews. A work of distinctively Flemish preservation best expressed in sharp and caramelly, filtered and bottled **Rodenbach Grand Cru** (6%); upstaged occasionally in the single-cask **Vintage** (7%); and joined by cleverly cherry-steeped variants, including the recently revived **Alexander** (6%).

the bottle. Made by one of Belgium's first "new wave" breweries, founded back in 1979.

BUFFALO 1907

Van den Bossche, Sint-Lievens-Esse, East Flanders; 6.5%

Pure nostalgia drives the support for this authentic early-20th-century burned variant on a routine brown ale, from a fifth-generation family brewery better known for its stronger exports.

BUSH PRESTIGE

Dubuisson, Pipaix, Hainaut; 13%

Dubuisson has brewed an English barley wine since 1933, and Bush Prestige (aka Scaldis Prestige in some markets) is the late-bottled variant that spends an additional six months in oak casks before bottling to smooth out and evolve its character.

CUVÉE DES JACOBINS ROUGE

Omer Vander Ghinste, Bellegem, West Flanders; 5.5%

Created by injecting cultured wild yeast into a beer that then spends 18 months in oak, and originally only a mixer beer used in blending, it was released raw when a US importer tasted its potential.

CUVÉE VAN DE KEIZER BLAUW

Het Anker, Mechelen, Antwerp; 11%

Brewed annually on 24 February, the birthday of Hapsburg Emperor Charles V, who grew up in the town. No-holds-barred brewing makes a strong dark ale that improves on cellaring for a decade at least.

DE KONINCK

De Koninck [Duvel-Moortgat], Antwerp; 5.2%

The beer of the city of Antwerp is this light, sweetish pale ale that dates back centuries. It is always best when drunk locally and on draught in its synonymous glass, known as a *bolleke* (pronounced "ball-e-ke").

EXTRA BRUIN

Achelse Kluis, Hamont-Achel, Antwerp; 9.5%

The standout beer from the newest of Belgium's six Trappist breweries. A hearty, near-black winter ale noted for its intense malt, a little sherrying and a dab of hop.

GOUDENBAND

Liefmans [Duvel-Moortgat], Oudenaarde, East Flanders; 8%

Now brewed elsewhere but still matured at the Liefmans warehouse to create a somewhat sanitized yet evolving recreation of the softer type of aged brown ale.

GRAND CRU

St-Feuillien, Le Roeulx, Hainaut; 9.5%

Famed for making beers in huge bottles and able after decades to be self-sufficient, this massive but strangely delicate, golden-blond top-of-the-range ale is the must-try brewery statement.

GRANDE RÉSERVE

Chimay, Baileux, Hainaut; 9%

The bigger-bottled version of Chimay Blue, the strongest and consistently best regular beer from Belgium's second-largest Trappist brewery.

GULDEN DRAAK

Van Steenberge, Ertvelde, East Flanders; 10.5%

Try to ignore the white plastic bottle wrapping and get to the ruby-brown strong ale inside to find, from an ardently Flemish brewer, a lusciously near-sweet brew of balanced ferocity.

HERCULE STOUT

Légendes, Ellezelles, Hainaut; 9%

A modern Belgian classic from the range produced at Légendes's smaller brewery, this strong, dry stout dominated by roasted malt is probably unspiced yet incorporates billowing spicy aromas.

HOP RUITER

Scheldebrouwerij, Meer, Antwerp; 8%

This Dutch-spirited brewery is parked next to a beer hypermarket and distribution centre on the Belgian side of the border. This hybrid *tripel*-cum-double IPA is the best in the range thanks to complex hopping.

JAN DE LICHTE

Glazen Toren, Erpe-Mere, Flemish Brabant; 7.5%

One of the most accomplished newer small breweries in Flanders that concentrates on making fulsome takes on classic beer styles, like this stronger, more citrus, doughier take on a Belgian wheat beer.

KAPITTEL PRIOR

Van Eecke, Watou, West Flanders; 9%

Watou's smaller brewery is also the Leroy family's smaller one. Deep, dark, pear-dropped Prior is the second strongest in the Kapittel range. At its best from a 75cl bottle that has been cellared for a decade.

KRIEK MARIAGE PARFAIT

Boon, Lembeek, Flemish Brabant; 8%

The honorary professor of lambic culture and the story of beer, Frank Boon produces this top-of-the-range cherry lambic by adding his best cherries to his best lambic casks and then waiting until its time has come.

KRIEKENLAMBIK

Girardin, Sint Ulriks-Kapelle, Flemish Brabant; 5%

The raw draught cherry lambic produced on this old Payottenland farm is still found at local bars like De Rare Vos in Schepdaal, baffling beer lovers with its absurd classical beauty.

LUPULUS

Les 3 Fourquets, Bovigny, Luxembourg; 8.5%

One of a host of well-run small craft-orientated breweries in Wallonia making a range of hop-forward Lupulus beers, among which this original blond version is arguably the best.

MALHEUR BIÈRE BRUT

Malheur, Buggenhout, East Flanders;11%

Applying similar techniques to making beer that the wine growers around Épernay employ in producing their local plonk creates this golden malt wine that manages to be light, ultra spritzy and heady.

MANO NEGRA

Alvinne, Moen, West Flanders; 10%

Strong black ale, nearest to an Imperial stout, sometimes pepped up by spirits-cask exposure. The most consistent beer from a brewery dominated by experimentation.

ORVAL

Orval, Villers-devant-Orval, Luxembourg; 6.2%

Once unique and still rare, presented in a beautiful bottle, this pungent Trappist brew from deep in the Ardennes is the result of dry-hopping a well-made pale ale and refermenting it with *Brettanomyces*.

CAN'T-MISS BREWERIES

BLAUGIES

Blaugies, Hainaut

Family-run farmhouse brewery creating a unique range of beers to their personal preference. The star is yeasty buckwheat **Saison d'Epeautre** (6%); dry blond **La Bière Darbyste** (5.8%) is more elusive; heavy, earthy **La Moneuse** (8%) is a *saison* of sorts; while US collaboration **La Vermontoise** (6%) is a mid-Atlantic *saison*-IPA combo.

DE RANKE

Dottignies, Hainaut

Great beer designers revered by other brewers for bringing hops to Belgian ales and reviving *versnijsbier*, or "cut" beer, blended from lambics and ale. Summery pale ale **XX Bitter** (6%) is crammed with hops, delicately; **Guldenberg** (8%) succeeds in up-hopping a *tripel*; equally potent **Noir de Dottignies** (8.5%) defies easy styling; while **Cuvée de Ranke** (7%) ladles heavy lambic overtones onto sound pale ale.

DOCHTER VAN DE KORENAAR

Baarle-Hertog, Antwerp

On the Dutch border in many different ways, capturing the new Dutch spirit with a Belgian twist in internationally modern **Belle Fleur IPA** (6%); newer doubled-up **Extase** (8.5%); dry, vanilla stout **Charbon** (7%); and pan-Belgian amber-brown **Embrasse** (9%). Oak-aged and spirits-cask versions also appear.

DOLLE

Esen, West Flanders

Pioneering revivalists in the 1980s now producing singular beers like the perfectly complex, sharp, dark and messy keeper **Oerbier** (9%); best fresh, golden hoppy blond **Arabier** (8%); lush light amber Easter brew **Doskeun** (10%); and heavy, succulent Christmas stunner **Stille Nacht** (12%). Special reserve editions matured in spirits casks crop up, too.

DRIE FONTEINEN

Beersel, Flemish Brabant

Passion-fuelled producers of classic Payottenland lambics. **Lambik** (5%) and **Faro** (5.5%) are only found on draught regularly at the café–restaurant in Beersel and at the nearby, brewery-run Lambikodroom. The authentic cherry beers, **Oude Kriek** (5%) and original **Schaerbeekse Kriek** (6%), along with their gueuzes, travel the world in bottles.

CAN'T-MISS BREWERIES

DUPONT

Tourpes, Hainaut

Squeaky-clean, eco-enthusiastic brewery in an idyllic farm setting. Responsible in part via importation for the US beer revolution, with beers such as the authentic light *saison* **Biolégère** (3.5%); the pioneering, genre-defining **Saison Dupont** (6.5%); the strong blond, faintly rustic, cleverly balanced **Moinette Blond** (8.5%); and the outstanding, dry-hopped Christmas-beer-turned-mainstay **Avec les Bons Voeux de la Brasserie Dupont** (9.5%).

RULLES

Rulles, Luxembourg

Village visionary from La Gaume, making near-perfect local beers that travel the world on merit. Fragrantly hopped **Estivale** (5.2%) lights up the summer; the practice-perfect **Blonde** (7%) is possibly the best in Belgium; as is the **Triple** (8.4%). **Stout Rullquin** (7%) is what happens to their brown ale when spiked with 10% of Tilquin lambic.

DE LA SENNE

Brussels

Attitudinally inventive, challengingly straightforward multi-talented brewers who lead a generation. Ever-so-simple **Taras Boulba** (4.5%) is their hoppy light ale; **Stouterik** (4.5%) is the multi-award-winning, standard light stout; **Jambe-de-Bois** (8%) is the cosy triple with a complicated aftertaste; and the 100% *Brettanomyces*-fermented **Bruxellensis** (6.5%) pushes all the buttons put there by ancient Orval.

ST. BERNARDUS

Watou, West Flanders

Originally created to make beers for Trappist Westvleteren Brewery, now expanded to serve the world. Their **Wit** (5.5%) is most expressive of the Belgian style; **Prior 8** (8%) is brown, fruity, complex and good-looking; **Abt 12** (10%) is the heavyweight, fruity, bittersweet, self-styled *quadrupel*; and **Christmas Ale** (10%) is the dark and spicy winter warmer.

STRUISE

Oostvleteren, West Flanders

Determinedly boundary-pushing show-offs with a lot to show off about. Famed for long-aged, strong and soured heavy beers like heavy, dark **Pannepot** (10%), the lighter-hued and aged winter ale **Tsjeeses** (10%), an absurdly strong Imperial stout **Black Albert** (13%) and more recently for the cask-aged **Ypres** (7%). Ageing in reused casks is common.

OUDBEITJE

Hanssens Artisanaal, Dworp, Flemish
Brabant; 6%

The lambic world's only authentic
strawberry lambic loses the fruit's
flavours within weeks, but retains a
haunting and unmistakable aroma that
cuts across the natural sourness of the
lambic underlay.

OUDE KRIEK

Oud Beersel, Beersel, Flemish Brabant;
6.5%

Created largely from bespoke brews
made at Boon (see page 42) and
steeped to a unique recipe, this darker
than average, earthy and rustic bottled
cherry lambic is one of the classics of
the style.

OUDE LAMBIEK

De Cam, Gooik, Flemish Brabant; 5%

This small gueuze blender and lambic
steeper matures other brewers'
lambics to create beers of distinctly
different character. Bottling at the end
of maturation creates this ultra-dry
single-cask lambic.

PETRUS AGED PALE

De Brabandere, Bavikhove, West
Flanders; 7.3%

Arguably crude but unquestionably
important, this was the first oak-aged
mixer beer to be allowed out on its
own, having been formerly used only
in the creation of lesser blends.

PILS

Strubbe, Ichtegem, West Flanders; 5%

Founded in 1830, the same year as
Belgium itself, this sixth-generation
small family business creates almost
every style of beer in Belgium, including
perhaps the country's hoppiest and
tastiest blond lager.

PORTER

Viven, Sijsele, West Flanders; 7%

Commissioning their beers from the
Proef brewery at Lochristi and seeking
unashamedly international flavour
profiles, this drinks distributor has the
best range of Belgian-made US-style
beers, including this hoppy stout porter.

QUETSCHE

Tilquin, Bierghes, Wallonian Brabant;
6.4%

The lambic world's new star has pushed
the envelope wisely with this clever and
delicious, sharp-edged yet sumptuous
plum lambic. Expect variants using
other plum varieties.

ROCHEFORT 10

Abbaye Notre Dame de Saint-Rémy,
Rochefort, Namur; 11.3%

One of three beers made in a classic
copper-kettled brewhouse beneath a
crucifix. A many-layered, heady, dried-
fruit and caramelled elixir, demanding
room-temperature service.

BREWERIES TO WATCH

BRUSSELS

Beer Project, Brussels

Brewing mostly at Anders in Limburg, to create modern Belgian takes on IPA **Delta** (6.5%), black IPA **Dark Sister** (6.5%) and strong *hefeweizen* **Grosse Bertha** (7%).

BZART

Niel-bij-As, Limburg

Beer club experimentalists maturing mostly Oud Beersel brews on Champagne yeast for their **Kriekenlambiek** (8%), **Session Triple** (6.3%) and **Geuze Cuvée** (8%).

DE LEITE

Ruddervoorde, West Flanders

Jobbing new waver now developing prowess with new brews such as lactic **Fils à Papa** (6.5%), herbal **Enfant Terrible d'Hiver** (8.2%) and vinous **Cuvée Mam'zelle** (8.5%).

DE PLUKKER

Poperinge, West Flanders

Hop-farm brewery using local varieties in regular pale **Keikoppenbier** (6.1%) and annual specials **Single Green Hop** (5.5%) and **All Inclusive IPA** (8%).

EN STOEMELINGS

Brussels

Shoestring adventurers creating off-centre ales like **Noirølles** (5%) porter and unclassifiable pale **Curieuse Neus** (7%).

HOF TEN DORMAAL

Tildonk, Flemish Brabant

Hit-and-miss creators of myriad one-off, barrel-aged **BA Project** creations based on solid dark **Donker** or **Blond** ales (10–12%).

LIENNE

Lierneux, Liège

Husband and wife team gaining confidence and skills, best demonstrated in delicate hoppy **Grandgousier** (5%), **Noire** (5.5%) porter and heavier **Brune** (8%).

VERZET

Anzegem, West Flanders

Three young friends making waves with variants of oak-aged **Oud Bruin** (6%), **Golden Tricky IPA** (7.5%) and stronger **Rebel Local** (8.5%).

VLIEGENDE PAARD

Nomadic, West Flanders

Award-winning contracting brewer creating beers under the **Préaris** label, including the single-hopped **Session Ale** (4.5–5%), **Quadrupel** (10%) and variously barrel-aged **Grand Cru** (10%), mostly at the Proef brewery.

SAISON

Cazeau, Templeuve, Hainaut; 5%

Better known for its Tournay brands of more classical Wallonian beer styles, this twice-revived brewery also makes this spritzy summer variant on a *saison*, with added elderflower.

SAISONNEKE

Belgoo, Sint-Pieters-Leeuw, Flemish Brabant; 4.4%

The lightest, simplest and catchiest beer from a talented Payottenland ale brewery that had been practising elsewhere for some years.

SCOTCH

Silly, Silly, Hainaut; 8%

This long-established Wallonian village brewery derives its most interesting beer from a pre-1914 version of a Scotch ale or wee heavy. It is sometimes enhanced by whisky-cask-ageing, but is always dark, sweet, rich and playful.

SPECIAL

De Ryck, Herzele, East Flanders; 5 5%

This small-town family brewery, more famous for its Arend brands, also makes this masterpiece of sophisticated innocence, the supreme example of the easy-drinking *special* or *spéciale* style of pale ale.

STRAFFE HENDRIK HERITAGE

Halve Maan, Brugge, West Flanders; 11%

The gradual regrowth of the Vanneste family's brewery in Bruges has now expanded to include some exceptional beers, such as this strong black ale that is developed in oak for a year before being bottled.

TRIPEL KLOK

Boelens, Belsele, East Flanders; 8.5%

A brewery in a drinks merchant's premises that began by making honeyed beers and has gone on to create this exceptional and ever-evolving interpretation of a *tripel*, with not a bee in sight.

STYLE SPOTLIGHT

GUEUZE – THE WORLD'S MOST UNLIKELY HERITAGE BEER

First, mash a grain bill designed for wheat beer; then brew with old hops that have lost aroma and bitterness but retained preservative qualities; next, cool and inoculate with wild yeasts overnight in a shallow metal cooler; and in the morning filter it into oak barrels or tuns and let sit for six months to three years. Decant and blend, bottle and wait.

An *oude* or *vieille geuze* or *gueuze* should shock the nose with its strong aromas of old books, musty leather or a hay barn in late summer, then confuse the palate with its spritzy mouthfeel and tart, invasive edges set off against a base redolent of grain. Approach its sharper forms as if they were a sparkling wine in a beery cloak and ignore your immediate reaction. Hold back judgement for your next encounter, too, as it can sometimes take years to properly understand an unlikely type of beer fermented only by wild yeast that happens across its path.

The best proponents of this brewing art form are all from Brussels and the surrounding region, the Payottenland. Cantillon with their light citrus **Gueuze** and best blend **Lou Pepe**; Drie Fonteinen with **Oude Geuze** and long-cellared **Vintage**; Boon (*see* page 42) with **Oude Geuze** and his upscale **Mariage Parfait**; Girardin's **Gueuze 1882** when sporting a black label; Lindemans light and lemony **Oude Gueuze Cuvée René**; and four non-brewing blenders – Tilquin with bottled **Oude Gueuze à l'Ancienne** and draught **Gueuze** lambic; De Cam with **Oude Geuze**; Oud Beersel for their **Oude Geuze**; and Hanssens Artisanaal **Oude Gueuze**.

TROUBADOUR MAGMA

The Musketeers, Ursel, East Flanders; 9%

One of the longer-standing teams of beer designers acquired their own brewery recently to make this, their triple-strong, Czech-hopped IPA, among others.

VALEIR EXTRA

Contreras, Gavere, East Flanders; 6.5%

Hard-working but fairly conservative small family brewery in the Schelde valley making a typically Flemish Valeir range, extra to which is this standout, cleverly hopped, Belgian-influenced IPA.

VICARIS GENERAAL

Dilewyns, Dendermonde, East Flanders; 8.5%

In 2010, the four Dilewyns sisters were gifted a state-of-the-art brewery by their father, where among other Vicaris beers they make this hefty, rich and fruity red-brown ale, dedicated to their grandma.

VICHTENAAR

Verhaeghe, Vichte, West Flanders; 5.1%

Better known for their Duchesse de Bourgogne, the Verhaeghe brothers' lighter, less-well-travelled, oak-aged brown ale is sharper and probably truer to the old local Kortrijk styles.

WESTVLETEREN BLOND

Sint-Sixtusabdij, Westveleteren, West Flanders; 5.8%

A rustic pale ale that is the simplest and best-made beer from this Trappist brewery, which bears its mostly unwelcome and partly unearned adulation with dignity. Best when drunk fresh at the on-site abbey café.

WITKAP PATER STIMULO

Slaghmuylder, Ninove, East Flanders; 6%

A close look at this old family brewery reveals most of its range to be off-centre, none more so than this yeasty, grassy, slightly citrus blond ale, best in the bottle or else locally on draught.

GERMANY

There is probably no country as universally synonymous with beer as Germany. The latter part of the 20th century was not, however, kind to the birthplace of lager and Oktoberfest, as a lessening appetite for beer coupled with some industry consolidation resulted in declining brewery numbers and tougher times for those that remained. Thankfully, that situation has now changed and German breweries are not only once again growing in size and quantity, but also expressing renewed creativity in both the creation of new beers and the revival of old, almost forgotten styles.

7:45 ESCALATION

CREW Republic, Unterscheißheim, Munich, Bavaria; 8.3%

Of the regular beers from this 2011 *kraft* pioneer, the most challenging to Bavarian brewing orthodoxy is this powerful and strong IPA, resinous with US hops yet managing reasonable balance despite its bitterness. Sacrilegious but arty.

1838ER

Ferdinand Schumacher, Düsseldorf, North Rhine-Westphalia; 5%

Created for the brewery's 175th anniversary in 2013 as an up-market *altbier* with more aroma and fruitier hopping, this proved popular enough

to stay in the range. Whether other new takes follow remains to be seen.

ABRAXXXAS

Freigeist Bierkultur, nomadic; 6%

A "free spirit" operation that since 2010 has been reviving defunct styles and pushing others to extremes, as with this smoky, pepped-up take on the north German, light and lactic style of wheat beer called *lichtenhainer*.

ALT

Im Füchschen, Düsseldorf, North Rhine-Westphalia; 4.5%

One of the four classic *altbier* brewers that can be found in the old city, or Altstadt. Perhaps the most aromatic, but also earthier than others of its ilk, it is best sampled in its heavily food-slanted taphouse.

ALT

Zum Schlüssel, Düsseldorf, North Rhine-Westphalia; 5%

Another of the four historic brewers that preserve the *altbier* tradition in Düsseldorf's Altstadt, where gravity-feed, same-day-service casks dispense a precise, light-copper-hued beer with a bit of caramelly sweetness.

ASAM BOCK

Weltenburger Kloster, Kelheim, Bavaria; 6.9%

A frequently prize-winning *doppelbock*, all the more surprising for having to punch well above its weight. Sweet and intense, but filled with endless nuances of flavour, from a former monastery on the banks of the Danube.

AUFSESSER DUNKEL

Rothenbach, Aufseß, Bavaria; 4.7%

Not the punchiest beer from this village *brauereigasthof*, or guesthouse brewery, but an alluring, dryish, oddly maroon-coloured, roasty-toasty quaffer that sets you up for the rest of the range.

BAMBERGER HERREN PILS

Keesmann, Bamberg, Bavaria; 4.6%

One of the lightest-coloured lagers in the world, more *helles* than pilsner with its delicate, floral, grassy and innocent-

ICONIC BREWERY

G SCHNEIDER & SOHN

Kelheim, Bavaria

The family brewery that re-invigorated Bavarian white beer back in 1872, recreating a style that predated the *Reinheitsgebot*. From the complex and spicy **Mein Original** (5.4%), also known as Tap 7 or, more colloquially, simply Schneider Weisse, they pushed forward to luscious, spicy wheat *doppelbock* **Mein Aventinus** (Tap 6; 8.2%) and on to the absurdly but deliciously intense **Aventinus Eisbock** (12%). A collaboration with the Brooklyn Brewery (*see* page 208) yielded the fresh, aromatically hopped **Meine Hopfenweisse** (Tap 5; 8.2%), which has gone on to become a style unto itself (*see* page 17).

ICONIC BREWERIES

HELLER-BRÄU TRUM (SCHLENKERLA)

Bamberg, Bavaria

The family brewery responsible for the global fame of Bamberg brewing, the survival of smoked beers and their modern-day renaissance. The **Aecht Schlenkerla Rauchbier** range includes the unmistakable if indelicate smoke-sweated brown **Märzen** (5.1%); barbecued, sweet-cured autumnal **Urbock** (6.5%); heavyweight and heady, local Easter treat **Fastenbier** (5.5%); and winter's oak-smoked **Eiche Doppelbock** (8%), an exquisite strong lager that legitimizes smoked malt at the highest level of brewing achievement.

UERIGE

Düsseldorf, North Rhineland-Westphalia

The brewery at the heart of Düsseldorf's Altstadt that creates the epitome of the local lagered ale known simply as *alt*. The uncarbonated, auburn and bready **Uerige Alt** (4.7%) served in its taphouse is now captured in the spritzier, bottled **Nicht Filtriert** (4.7%). Brewed only for the city's annual carnival special, the availability of the stronger **Sticke** (6%) is now prolonged by bottling. In recent years it has been joined by *alt–bock* fusion beer **Doppelsticke** (8.5%) as, swan-like, the style begins to spread its wings.

looking countenance. Always more delicious when drunk at the brewery's handsome taphouse.

BERLINER KINDL WEISSE

Schultheiss [Oetker], Berlin; 3%

The Berlin-style wheat beer that survived the era of standardization by losing character while heading mainstream is (very) slowly regaining its light, hazy, lactic, thirst-defeating individuality.

BLACK IPA

Heidenpeters, Berlin; 5.6%

From a small brewery located in the cellar of the German capital's Markthalle Neun, this occasional release boasts a plummy nose with blackberry tones and similarly fruity body, with date and light citrus notes alongside a moderate bitterness.

BOCK

Kneitinger, Regensburg, Bavaria; 6.8%

One of the south's best bocks, deep ruby brown and full of Vienna malt that comes through at every stage from the aroma to the toffee-sweet follow-through, so much so that the hopping is barely noticeable.

BOSCH BRAUNBIER

Bosch, Bad Laasphe, North Rhineland-Westphalia; 5%

A beer not necessarily loved by the new beer cognoscenti, this simple, workaday, resinous and nutty brown offering is in an old local style from a brewery with heart as well as technical excellence.

CURATOR DOPPELBOCK

Ettaler, Ettal, Bavaria; 9%

A modern brewery and distillery based in and part of a Benedictine monastery near Oberammergau, creating numerous beers of superior quality and character, including this deep, heavy, multi-toned dark lager intended for nights of quiet contemplation.

DER DUNKLE REH-BOCK

Reh, Lohndorf, Bavaria; 7.1%

An interesting dark *bock*, with both sweet and dry aspects, the former hitting maple-syrup notes and the latter in a surprisingly harsh finish, due we think to being Franconian rather than flawed.

DIPLOM PILS

Waldhaus, Waldhaus, Baden-Württemburg; 4.9%

What some might consider a fairy-tale German pils – light, crisp, floral, beautiful in the glass and profoundly quaffable. It really does exist, but you will have to take a walk in the southern Black Forest.

DOPPEL-ALT

Giesinger, Munich, Bavaria; 7%

For time out from *helles* in a beer garden, try this modern southern interpretation of a northern

hausbrauerei and its cheekily contrived, potent take on an *altbier*, amber with notes of toast and dried fruit.

DUNKEL

Kreuzberger Kloster, Bischofsheim an der Rhön, Bavaria; 5.4%

Light golden-brown *dunkel*, made within the grounds of an inhabited Franciscan abbey. Slightly stronger than many, allowing a more intense light caramel flavour to pervade.

DUNKEL NATURTRÜB

Schöre, Tettnang, Baden-Württemburg; 4.8%

Locally famed guesthouse brewery in hop country, which cracks out some classic brews on a small scale, like this well-constructed, dark, traditional *Münchener* that barely needs its local hops.

DUNKLES

Goldener Engel, Ingelheim, Rhineland-Palatinate, 4.8%

After spending a lot of money constructing and beautifying their exceptional modern brewpub, the Winkelser family made it a worthy destination by creating this clean, tar-laced, black *dunkel* with a lingering finish.

DUNKLES KELLERBRÄU

Seinsheimer, Seinsheim, Bavaria; 4.9%

Technically just outside Oberfranken, but spiritually at its heart, the flagship

CAN'T-MISS BREWERIES

AYINGER

Aying, Bavaria

Unusual for being independent and family owned yet relatively well known internationally. The brewery's range is broad, if traditional, led on the global stage by the molasses-accented, gently bitter **Celebrator Doppelbock** (6.7%). Stellar wheat beers include the blond **Bräuweisse** (5.1%) and amber, yeasty and equally exemplary **Ur-Weisse** (5.8%), while the centenary of the brewery in 1978 is still celebrated in the form of the firmly malty **Jahrhundert Bier** (5.5%).

BAYERISCHE STAATSBRAUEREI WEIHENSTEPHAN

Freising, Bavaria

Regardless of whether this Bavarian state-owned brewery truly is the world's oldest in continuous production, it unquestionably makes some of the nation's finest session beers, like mousse-topped, cloudy blond, banana-laced **Hefeweissbier** (5.4%) and its auburn equivalent **Hefeweissbier Dunkel** (5.3%). It can also go serious with the intensely focused and amplified dark *weizenbock* **Korbinian** (7.4%) or its equally ornate golden dance partner **Vitus** (7.7%), making this a reference brewery for any wheat beer producer.

CAMBA BAVARIA

Truchtlaching, Bavaria

Almost iconic for its insistent infusion of the IPA concept into the long-

established Bavarian beer culture, with beers like the gently questioning **German IPA** (6.5%), the stronger, assertive and slightly cocky double IPA **Ei Pi Ai** (8%) and just plain ballsy "Imperial black IPA" **Black Shark** (8.5%). It is, however, with the placing of a tropical-fruity hop in an otherwise traditionally banana-ish wheat beer to make **Nelson Sauvin Weissbier** (5.2%) that the wickedness of their inventive streak is best revealed.

GÄNSTALLER

Hallerndorf, Bavaria

Arguably modern German brewing's best brewing talent. Good enough to pioneer Mandarina Bavaria hops in a striking **Kellerbier** (5.3%) and craft a stellar **Zwickelpils** (5%) that is head and shoulders above the sea of others sharing the same moniker, but also comfortable with big beers such as chewy, rich wheat bouillon **Weizenator** (8.1%) and the ground-breaking 10 layers of smoked-powered nuance in **Affumicator** (9.6%).

of this small-town brewery is a ruddy-brown *kellerbier* with great balance that finds room for a barnyardy aroma and apple-pie notes within a sound mainstream *dunkel*.

EXPORT HEFE WEIZEN

Wolferstetter, Vilshofen, Bavaria; 5.5%

A full-on yet nicely balanced cloudy wheat beer, dominated by neither clove nor banana but led by a bready and fresh grain character. Made by a well-established and sound local brewery.

FASSBIER

Krug Geisfeld, Geisfeld, Bavaria; 4.9%

The name means "draught beer", which is how it is at its best, preferably drawn by gravity. Golden amber in colour, it is rustic, herbal-hoppy and oddly caramelized, far from a *helles* but neither *dunkel* nor Vienna.

FESTBIER DUNKEL

Stern-Bräu Scheubel, Schlüsselfeld, Bavaria; 5.5%

Increasingly in regular, year-round production, this quite delicately smoked dark lager, from a Franconian "farm brewery in a village" with strong rural values, is certainly deserving of more widespread recognition.

GÖRCHLA

Höhn, Memmelsdorf, Bavaria; 4.9%

Classically Franconian in its way, this light, hazy, dryish and earthy *landbier* is the effective centrepiece of a small village brewery that has developed into a polished, traditional guesthouse and local restaurant.

HAUSBRÄU

Kommunbrauhaus Seßlacher, Seßlach, Bavaria; 4.1%

A sort of *dunkel landbier* brewed in the spirit of *zoigl* (*see* page 63), if not the method. Herbal and earthy with enough sweetness to appeal to the mainstream drinker, this is a beer for quaffing rather than sipping.

HEFE-PILS

Winkler, Velburg/Lengenfeld, Bavaria; 4.7%

With an obvious name for a *zwickelbier*-cum-*kellerbier*, this delivers exactly what the name suggests – slight haziness, with grassy, earthy edges to its sweet floral maltiness and a satisfying hop bite in the finish.

HELIOS

Braustelle, Cologne, North Rhine-Westphalia; 4.8%

This pub brewery has since 2001 been pushing envelopes and changing perceptions, but its best beer is a blond lagered ale in the local style, a *kölsch* that, for now at least, will not speak its name.

HOCHFÜRST PILSENER

Hacklberg, Passau, Bavaria; 5%

A crisp, light and hoppy well-made blond lager that retains its bitterness throughout. Dominant in its home town, located next to the Austrian border in the far southwest, but still known elsewhere.

HOPFENPFLÜCKER PILS

Pyraser, Thalmässing, Bavaria; 5%

What could very well be Germany's best intensely hoppy beer is an annual indulgence, packed as it is with freshly harvested green hops and many-layered. It is produced by a brewery that makes a wide range of other fine beers year round.

HOPFENSTOPFER INCREDIBLE PALE ALE

Häffner, Bad Rappenau; Baden-Württemburg; 6.1%

One of the regulars from this otherwise conventional brewery's "hop shot" range, which appears in myriad forms through the year, highlighting the use of style-specific hop experiments, in this case Taurus, Saphir, Nelson Sauvin and Cascade.

INSELHOPF

Feierling, Freiburg, Baden-Württemberg; 5.2%

The main and often only beer from this *hausbrauerei* and *biergarten* that brought new life to the site of the family's former brewery. Freshly hoppy, solidly malty, light and hazy, it is among the country's best *zwickelpils*.

KELLER BIER

St Georgen, Buttenheim, Bavaria; 4.9%

The house brew of an elegant village brewery, beers from which travel more often and to greater distances than do most. Bready and nutty malt flavours are consistent, but its fairly assertive hop streak sometimes vanishes on leaving Franconia.

KELLERBIER

Eichhorn, Dörfleins, Bavaria; 5%

Another of those Franconian *kellerbiers* that are best when drunk on the premises – a short bus ride out of Bamberg – but are quietly impressive in a grassy, yeasty, not-quite-defined sort of way in the bottle, too.

KELLERBIER

Griess, Geisfeld, Bavaria; 5.1%

The most distinctive of the beers made at this small family concern in the Franconian brewery belt east of Bamberg. Citrus leanings in the nose and body, and a tad herbal and yeasty, yet quite refreshing and hard to dislike.

KELLERBIER

Lieberth, Hallerndorf, Bavaria; 4.8%

From a small Franconian brewery that also makes a couple of neat blond lagers comes this one-of-a-kind house brew, pinging dried-fruit, herbal and citrus lightning forks into a breadily toned beer.

CAN'T-MISS BREWERIES

KLOSTERBRAUEREI ANDECHS

Andechs, Bavaria

A Benedictine monastery with one of the most picturesque *biergartens* in Bavaria and a wide assortment of excellent beers with which to enjoy its Alpine views. **Spezial Hell** (5.9%) is an easy-to-overlook refresher with emphasis on a luscious yet dry maltiness, while **Doppelbock Dunkel** (7%) is the showstopper with dense maltiness and a drying, warming finish. On the wheat beer side, **Weissbier Dunkel** (5%) adds appley and tropical-fruit notes to the expected aromas and flavours, while the **Weissbier Hell** (5.5%) tends toward the crisp and yeasty aspect.

RIEGELE

Augsburg, Bavaria

Augsburg's brewers have long played second fiddle to their colleagues in Munich, but this fifth-generation family brewer has no equal there.

With beers like blond **Feines Ur-Hell** (4.7%), it acts the local brewer, and with top heavyweight **Speziator** (7.5%) *doppelbock* it joins other leading Bavarians, while the chocolaty **Robust Porter** (5%) makes it a modernist and the **Biermanufaktur** range of specialties, including the intense, triple yeast-fermented **Magnus 16** (12%) and the fruit-forward **Simco 3** (5%), plus other unconventional, potent and barrel-aged offerings, defines it is an exponent of modern *kraft*.

SCHÖNRAM

Petting, Bavaria

The first long-established Bavaria family brewery to project itself into the era of craft beer, covering both traditional German styles and "new era" ales. Its across-the-board high quality Schönramer range is diverse enough to include fresh hop showboat **Grünhopfen Pils** (5%); both basic and barrel-aged versions of **Imperial Stout** (9.5%); hop-edged but classic **Dunkel** (5%); and the best-in-class, crisp light *helles*, **Surtaler Schankbier** (3.5%).

BREWERIES TO WATCH

BRAUKOLLECTIV

nomadic

Four young brewers cracking out beers at a couple of local breweries, highlighted by the Chinook, Cascade and Columbus hop-fuelled **Jacques West Coast IPA** (7.9%) and **Horst California Brown Ale** (6.2), which finds common ground for US and German hops.

BUDDELSHIP

Hamburg

Clear vision, an artistic eye and the ability to articulate in words and deeds has meant that even the dull Hamburg beer scene has been impacted by beers as diverse as session IPA **Deichbrise** (3.9%), *schwarzbier* **Kohlentrimmer** (5.3%) and Imperial stout **Doktor Schabel** (8%).

KELLERBIER

Roppelt, Stiebarlimbach, Bavaria; 4.9%

This classic Franconian house beer from near Forchheim is impossible to classify, but has citrus character throughout,with a hazy golden appearance that nudges amateurish yet ends up superbly complete on draught, albeit less so in the bottle.

KNUTTENFORZ SCHWARZBIER

Lüdde, Quedlinburg, Saxony-Anhalt; 4.9%

Deep brown with a tan head, the brewery takes the roasted malt route to building a *schwarzbier*, with hoppiness in relatively little evidence. This off-centre pub-based brewery also makes its own low-alcohol *malzbier*.

KÖLSCH

Gaffel Becker & Co, Cologne, North Rhineland-Westphalia; 4.8%

Oft-maligned for the sin of being both well marketed and widely available – even in cans, no less – this is probably the driest, arguably the hoppiest of its kind, with a quenchingly bitter finish.

KÖLSCH

Päffgen, Cologne, North Rhineland-Westphalia; 4.8%

From perhaps the most dedicated of the city's remaining *kölsch* brewers, this straw-blond beer boasts a full and aromatic hoppiness that is fresh and floral without being overly bitter.

KRÄUSEN-PILS

Elzacher Löwenbräu, Elzach, Baden-Württemberg; 4.9%

Beautifully balanced unfiltered pils from a small-scale family brewery in the Black Forest brewing a good range of other styles besides. Starts softly with a floral Tettnang hop character and builds to a long, balanced finish.

KYRITZER MORD UND TOTSCHLAG

Klosterbrauerei Neuzelle, Neuzelle, Brandenburg; 7.2%

An adventurous and almost *bock*-like take on coal-black *schwarzbier*, roasted to the extreme without acridity, arguably begging the designation of a *doppelschwarz* style.

LAGER BIER

Greifenklau, Bamberg, Bavaria; 4.9%

The best of the range from Bamberg's least immediately impressive, greyish taphouse is this solid, no-nonsense *helles*, forgoing subtlety, gimmickry or anything distinctive, yet a beer one could stick to all night.

LAGERBIER HELL

Augustiner-Bräu, Munich, Bavaria; 5.2%

Of the six big Munich breweries dominating the city and its Oktoberfest, this is the only true independent and its light, crisp but smooth and fulsome blond lager is the quintessential *Münchener helles.*

LOFFELDER DUNKEL

Staffelberg-Bräu, Loffeld, Bavaria; 5.2%

There is a wisp of smokiness and decidedly savoury character to this dark lager brewed just north of Bamberg, with sweet grain, tobacco and roasted-chestnut notes combining in the body and an off-dry finish.

MAI-UR-BOCK

Einbecker, Einbeck, Lower Saxony; 6.5%

The paler (*heller*), springtime offering from the brewery most associated with the stronger north German lager tradition. Gold of hue with a honey-ish, toffee maltiness that plays host to rising and drying hoppiness.

MEMMELSDORF STÖFFLA

Drei Kronen, Memmelsdorf, Bavaria; 4.9%

A seasonal beer evolved into a regular offering, this deep amber *rauchbier* has a smoky aroma and smoked caramel body, sweet upfront but slowly drying to a wood-smoke finish.

MÖNCHSAMBACHER WEINACHTS-BOCK

Zehendner, Mönchsambach, Bavaria; 7%

Rightly famed for its *kellerbier*, this village brewery, located west of Bamberg, also makes this indulgently fulsome golden Christmas *bock* with bready, floral maltiness and touches of spice without spicing.

MÜHLEN KÖLSCH

Malzmühle Schwartz, Cologne, North Rhineland-Westphalia; 4.8%

Considered by many to be the definitive *kölsch*, this clever blond lagered ale has a rustic, gently fruity maltiness and mellow hop character. Best enjoyed in situ at the brewery's genial beer hall.

NANKENDORFER LANDBIER

Schroll, Nankendorf, Bavaria; 5.2%

Golden brown in colour, this has an earthiness to its aroma that translates well into the body, which is possessed of a richness beyond its alcohol content. Sweetish and caramel–chocolaty with a gentle nuttiness in the finish.

OKTOBERFESTBIER

Hofbräu München, Munich, Bavaria; 6.3%

The notion that there are two sorts of Oktoberfest *märzen* – a traditional, toastier one and a modern, sweetly malty one – is supported by this marvel of balance with a floral nose, sweet honeyed start and mildly bitter finish.

ORIGINAL LEIPZIGER GOSE

Bayerischer Bahnhof, Leipzig, Saxony; 4.5–4.6%

One of the early revivals of a style of beer originally from the north but popular in the city before 1919, based on wheat but dried by salting, although not really salty; tangy, a bit tart and spiced with coriander.

ORIGINAL RITTERGUTS GOSE

nomadic; 4.7%

Far from being *Reinheitsgebot*-compatible yet claimed by its commissioners to have been in production since 1824. Brewed for some years in Chemnitz. Global imitators of the style have tended to ape its malty, sourish and lightly spiced character ahead of its Leipziger counterpart.

PILS

Bischofshof, Regensburg, Bavaria; 4.7%

A typical Bavarian pils boasting perfumey aromas of noble hops and pilsner malt, looking polished with a chef's-hat mousse, promising and delivering a crisp, clean and deceptively direct blond lager.

PILSISSIMUS

Forschungsbrauerei, Perlach, Munich, Bavaria; 5.5%

An unusually fruity, aromatically hoppy blond lager from an early-20th-century family brewery on Munich's outskirts.

BREWERIES TO WATCH

HANSCRAFT & CO

nomadic

One of the more energetic groups of beer marketers, punching out impressive brews like **Single Hop Kellerpils** (4.9%) and IPA **Backbone Splitter** (6.6%), but with style and marketing high on the list of priorities.

INSEL-BRAUEREI

Rambin auf Rügen, Mecklenburg-Vorpommern

As close to Copenhagen as it is to Hamburg, this island brewery displays more Scandinavian creativity than German traditionalism in beers such as the off-dry, mocha-ish **Baltic Dubbel** (8.5%) and the lactic, sweet-and-sour **Seepferd Wildsauer** (6%).

KEHRWIEDER

Hamburg

Running before they can walk, perhaps, but thus far yet to stumble badly, with red ale **Hamburger Rot** (5%), **Rogger**

Roggen IPA (6.5%) rye IPA and **Kogge** (6.9%) Baltic porter. Hamburg's second scene-stirrer.

SCHNEEEULE

Berlin

Set up in 2016, this staunch and yeast-obsessed brewer is focused on perfecting traditional north German light and sour beers, beginning with the dry and enticingly subtle *Berliner weisse* **Marlene** (3%) and its elderflower-flavoured sibling **Otto** (3%).

STONE

Berlin

A European base for the US producer of Arrogant Bastard (*see* page 200), testing the *wasser* with a UK-style "strong ale" **Little Bastard** (4.7%), honestly named **Berliner Weisse Prototype** (4.7%) and jet-black **Imperial Belgian IPA** (10.1%).

Very gentle carbonation and Bohemian in its rather rounded mouthfeel, if not in its hopping.

PINKUS PILS

Pinkus Müller, Münster, North Rhine-Westphalia; 5.2%

From a brewery that tried its hand at everything comes a great organic, or "bio", beer with grassy and bready edges, though lacking the sharp hop presence of a northern pils.

POTSDAMMER WEISSE

Forsthaus Templin, Potsdam, Brandenburg; 3%

A cheekily named light, lactic, lemony *Berliner weisse* that some consider is too tart and even one dimensional, but we consider challenging to orthodoxy.

RAUCHBIER LAGER

Spezial, Bamberg, Bavaria; 4.7%

Unavailable outside of a 15-kilometre (9-mile) radius of the brewery – or so it is claimed – this is a masterpiece of smoky nuance and understated maltiness, delivering whiffs of sweet, caramelly smoke rather than a trip to the smokehouse.

RÄUCHERLA

Hummel, Merkendorf/Memmelsdorf, Bavaria; 5.5%

The darker, more frequently made, smokier *rauchbier* from this Franconian village brewery. Its name references "incense smoke", but after the aroma

of a granary fire passes, a well-balanced smoked *märzen* follows.

SCHLOTFEGERLA

Weyermann, Bamberg, Bavaria; 5.2%

Germany's most famous malting facility has a tiny brewhouse for the creation of sample brews, among which the regular is this dark, sweetly bitter and earthy *rauchbier*, the smokiness of which is designed to showcase their smoked malt.

SCHWARZBIER

Eisgrub-Bräu, Mainz, Rhineland-Palatinate; 4.9%

A jet-black *schwarzbier* with more dark chocolate flavours than most, the malt residing principally on the nose rather than in the body. As with many of this eastern German style, it tastes thinner that its colour implies.

SCHWARZBIER

Altstadthof, Nürnberg, Bavaria; 4.8%

More a dark Bavarian *dunkel* than an eastern-style *schwarzbier*, with more sweet caramel maltiness than coal-dusty roast, from a large and popular Nürnberg brewpub.

STETTFELDER PILS

Adler, Stettfeld, Bavaria; 5%

The most striking beer from a solid brewery near Bamberg, illustrating the southern tradition of pale pilseners with a solid hop character, but accompanied by a crisp and hoppy edge.

STYLE SPOTLIGHT

ZOIGL – MORE A WAY OF LIVING THAN A BEER STYLE

It may be argued, particularly by those who consider that a beer style must be fermented by yeast from a specific range, that *zoigl* should not be regarded as one. We disagree. The tradition of the *kommunbrauhaus*, or communal brewery, is probably as old as commercial brewing itself. Shared town breweries existed in Bohemia by the 11th century and have brewing rights in Bavaria that pre-date the *Reinheitsgebot*.

The principle is that a group of local people or a town council fund a brewhouse where citizens brew to create wort that, after cooling overnight in a *kühlschiff* – a large, shallow, open vat – is taken away to be fermented and lagered by one or more stakeholders in different ways, who eventually sell their finished beer from their *zoiglstube*, usually a bar or small restaurant that is an extension of a home and traditionally identified by a hanging six-pointed *zoigl* star.

These beers vary according to the brewery, the brewer, the batch and who conditions it, but typically lie somewhere between an earthy infant lambic and a herbal *kellerbier*.

The tradition survives in the Oberpfalz region of eastern Bavaria – in Eslarn, where **Beim Ströhern** serves its eponymous rustic, hazy orange, multi-dimensional light brew; in Falkenberg, where the brewhouse makes golden, grassier and lemony beers like **Kramer-Wolf** and the darker, clearer, sweeter **Schwoazhansl**; in Mitterteich's brewhouse where a tranche of beers is crafted, among which the best is the cidery-tart, yeasty yet honeyed **Oppl**; in Neuhaus an der Waldnaab, where the brewhouse serves seven *zoiglstuben*, and in the most active brewery at Windischeschenbach, which yields a range from soft, full, more "normal" **Weisser Schwann** to earthier, nuttier **Posterer**.

STRALSUNDER TRADITIONSBOCK

Störtebeker, Stralsund, Mecklenburg-Vorpommern; 6.5%

A dark and heavily roasty *bock*-meets-Baltic-porter from a Baltic Sea coast brewery that has revived a huge range of beers, with this being the pre-eminent head-turner.

UNGESPUNDET HEFETRÜB

Mahrs, Bamberg, Bavaria; 5.2%

From a brewery that is a favourite among beer-savvy Bamberg tourists, this lightly carbonated, yeasty lager is grassy and grainy in equal degrees, and most of all refreshing. Now bottled, but best enjoyed at the brewery.

UNGESPUNDETES LAGERBIER

Wagner-Bräu, Kemmern, Bavaria; 4.5%

The gravity-poured beer from the brewery tap is a rich and herbaceous

take on the more cellar-aged style of blond lager, its gently rising bitterness culminating in an appetizing finish.

VETTER'S WEIHNACHTSBOCK

Alt Heidelberger, Heidelberg, Baden-Württemberg; 6.2%

Brewed each year for Christmas, this relatively understated, caramel-malty, amber *bock* is typical of the excellent seasonal offerings from this popular *häusbrauerei*, better known for its barley wine.

VOLLBIER HELL

Heckel, Waischenfeld, Bavaria; 5.5%

Vollbier translates metaphorically as "house brew" and this herbal, grassy, hazy, tangy-edged and delightfully disjointed copper-blond lager is typical of the local talent for the imprecise. Unusual for Franconia in that it can crop up in far-flung places.

WEIHERER RAUCH

Kundmüller, Viereth-Trunstadt, Bavaria; 5.3%

Deep gold in colour, with a sweet and relatively soft smokiness to the aroma. That reserve is also evident in the body, which neither whispers nor screams its balanced, smoky maltiness and gradually drying caramel sweetness.

WEIZEN-BOCK

Jacob, Bodenwöhr, Bavaria; 6.5%

Part of the winter offering from this busy, small-scale family brewer of wheat beer specialties. The liquid equivalent of partly burned toast spread with banana paste.

WEIZEN-BOCK

Karg, Murnau, Bavaria; 7%

An accomplished beer from a wheat beer specialist that is like a classically proportioned Bavarian *weizen*, only bigger. To banana and clove characteristics add overripe peaches in the aroma and a dab of caramel toffee in the body.

WEIZENBOCK

Gutmann Tittinq, Bavaria; 7.2%

Arguably the best and certainly the most intense of the range offered by this wheat beer specialist, emphasizing the house flavour characteristics of banana and sweet fruit set against a full, malty backbone.

WEIZLA DUNKEL

Fässla, Bamberg, Bavaria; 5%

All the beers from this atmospheric *hausbrauerei* (and hotel) are to a greater or lesser degree classics of their kind, but this fruity, aromatic, banana–malt dark wheat beer stands out for being the best from Bamberg.

WITZGALL-BIER

Witzgall, Schlammersdorf, Bavaria; 5.2%

By whichever name it is marketed – Lagerbier, Landbier or Kellerbier – this straw-golden local beer, with its faintly citrus-zingy hop bite, is held by many to epitomize Franconian brewing – laissez-faire on style, precise on delivery. This is best enjoyed as fresh as possible.

WÖLLNITZER WEISSBIER

Talschänke, Jena, Thuringia; 4.2%

Of a style that combines smoked malt, wheat and lactic fermentation, known as *lichtenhainer*, this sole product of a 1997 guesthouse brewery is tart, cloudy, a bit smoky, citric and just rustic enough. Truly a beer of myth and legend.

ZWICKELBIER

Lübeck Brauberger, Lübeck, Schleswig-Holstein; 4.8%

One of the few north German gravity-feed cask beers, delicately hopped, possibly containing some wheat. Highly quaffable at the brewery taphouse, if less impressive in the bottle.

AUSTRIA

Austria, having long resided in Germany's sizeable shadow and despite laying claim to some historic brewing advances (*see* Schwechater, page 68), is now well ahead of its much larger neighbour in terms of craft brewing development, while still supporting the country's many traditional breweries.

BOCKBIER

Augustiner, Kloster Mülln, Salzburg; 6.5%

Seasonal brew from the monastery-owned brewery with Austria's largest beer halls just outside Salzburg's city centre. Bold and somewhat bready in the nose, it's a stronger version of the *märzen* that is available all year.

BONIFATIUS BARRIQUE

Handbrauerei Forstner, Kalsdorf bei Graz, Styria; 9.5%

Belgian-style strong ale from one of Austria's smallest breweries, aged in red wine barrels that add intense raspberry notes, plus hints of almonds and kiwi

fruit. Sweet on the palate, dry and bitter in the aftertaste.

CARINTHIPA

Loncium, Kötschach-Mauthen, Carinthia; 5.6%

Orange-coloured ale with fruity aromas (mango and grapefruit), relatively highly carbonated, medium body and moderately bitter from start to finish.

EISBOCK

Rieder, Ried im Innkreis, Upper Austria; 10.3%

From a storeyed brewery, this is a concentrated (through freezing) version of their 6.5% *weizenbock*. The warming result has aromas of almonds and roses, and finishes with a long-lasting banana- and nut-like aftertaste.

FLANDERS RED

Brauwerk, Vienna; 7.2%

Ruby red with aromas of sour cherries and red wine, and refreshing acidity in the body that helps hide the beer's strength.

GOLD FASSL PILS

Ottakringer, Vienna; 4.6%

Grassy aromas of Tettnang hops characterize this classic German-style pilsner, brewed at Vienna's largest brewery. Straw in colour, the medium-weight body is crisp and refreshing with a dry finish.

GOLDBRÄU

Stiegl, Salzburg; 4.9%

Mildly hopped, medium-bodied golden lager with a grainy malt aroma from Salzburg's most famous brewery, which still operates in 19th-century buildings.

GÖSSER DUNKLES ZWICKL

Falkenstein, Lienz, Tyrol; 5.7%

Nut-brown unfiltered lager with a caramelly aroma and some sweetness, balanced by a hint of roastiness and a generous hoppiness in the surprisingly dry finish.

GRANITBOCK ICE

Hofstetten, St Martin im Mühlkreis, Upper Austria; 11.5%

The strongest lager in Peter Krammer's Granitbier series, this *eisbock* features the caramelly, smoky and burned taste of the base beer, plus notes of dried plum, chocolate and coffee.

GREGORIUS

Engelszell, Engelhartszell, Upper Austria; 9.7%

Austria's first Trappist beer is usually bottled very fresh, tasting sweet and unbalanced when young, but

CAN'T-MISS BREWERY
•••••••••••••••••••••••••••••••••••

1516

Vienna

Close to 20 years in, this is still the only US-style brewpub in Austria. It rolls out new beers on a regular basis, including at least one highly aromatic yet refreshing **Wit Series** (~4.8%) in the summer, often using different citrus fruits, and a chilli-spiced and chocolate-flavoured **Tovarich Sanchez Bourbon Cask Matured Imperial stout** (9.7%) in winter, in addition to their full-bodied and citrusy regular **Victory Hop Devil IPA** (7%), brewed in cooperation with Victory Brewing of Pennsylvania since 2004.

ICONIC BREWERY

SCHWECHATER [HEINEKEN]

Schwechat, Vienna

Vienna-style lagers – and, in fact, industrial-scale lager brewing – were invented at this brewery by Anton Dreher in 1841, but all buildings from that time are gone. Now part of the Heineken empire, it is responsible for beers such as the golden **Schwechater Bier** (5%) with a nutty, mildly bitter taste; the straw-coloured, very hazy **Zwickl** (5.4%) with a herbal hoppiness, a creamy body and a distinctively bitter finish; and the recently revived, reddish-amber **Wiener Lager** (5.5%) with a cake-like aroma.

developing complexity after a year or more. The evolution brings a plum-like fruity aroma, with the sweetness balanced by a chocolaty bitterness.

HADMAR

Weitra, Weitra, Lower Austria; 5.2%

Vienna-style lagers were revived in 1994 in Austria's oldest brewing town – dating from 1321 – with this dark amber, roasty and full-bodied yet well-hopped organic beer.

HOPFENSPIEL

Trumer, Josef Sigl, Obertrum, Salzburg; 2.9%

A hop-dominated, light version of the pils style that Trumer is famous for, with a trio of hops adding enough flavour for the beer to taste more full bodied than one would expect.

HUBER BRÄU SPEZIAL

Familienbrauerei Huber, St Johann, Tyrol; 5.4%

Golden *helles*-style lager with a full white head, aromas of malt and Tettnang hops, high carbonation, medium to full body with an almost creamy mouthfeel and a dry, bitter finish.

MÄRZEN

Murauer, Murau, Styria; 5.2%

In Austria, *märzen* is typically lighter both in colour and alcohol than the German versions. This example from Styria is golden, highly carbonated and combines full body and a nutty, medium bitterness.

BREWERIES TO WATCH

BREW AGE

nomadic

Four itinerant brewers from Vienna who brew award-winning ales such as the fruity (dried plums, raisins, blackberries, walnuts) barley wine, **Nussknacker** (10%) and the resinous, citrusy and off-dry **Affenkönig Imperial IPA** (8.2%) at different small breweries.

COLLABS

nomadic

Originally meant to supply the Hawidere pub in Vienna but now brewing in Austria and England, responsible for the extremely hoppy **Domrep Pils** (5.2%), the acidic, sorrel-flavoured *Berliner weisse* **Sauer? Lump!** (3%) and the vinous **Burgen** (5.6%).

CRAFT COUNTRY

Hall, Tyrol

Small brewery started in 2015 and brewing a series of bold ales such as the coconut-ish **Miyamato Japanese Pale Ale** (5.5%), alongside their standard **da'Hoam** pale lager (5%).

NEXT LEVEL

nomadic

Founded in late 2015, this Vienna-based company has put out rather extreme beers like the **Bitter Freak** (7.5%), which claims to have 200 IBUs, and the herbal-aromatic **Lemon Thyme** (4.9%), a *gose* with a distinct acidity, a sweet body that underlines the taste of thyme and a dry, very salty finish.

MORCHL

Hirter, Micheldorf, Carinthia; 5%

Chestnut-brown lager with a caramelly aroma and some residual sweetness that combines well with roasted nuttiness and hoppy bitterness. A style-defining beer for Austrian dark lagers.

NO. 4 BELLE SAISON

Schleppe, Klagenfurt, Carinthia; 5.4%

Light gold, fruity and rose-like, this is the fourth in a series of ales from the centuries-old Schleppe brewery that has been resized to brew small batches of craft beer.

OND BEVOG

Bad Radkersburg, Styria; 6.3%

Robust smoked porter with a distinct smoke aroma and a full, roasty body from a rapidly growing micro on the Styrian–Slovenian border.

ROGGEN BIO BIER

Schremser, Schrems, Lower Austria; 5.2%

Orange-coloured, unfiltered organic rye ale, aromatically grainy and doughy, with a full yet refreshing body carrying rye-bread notes and gentle bitterness.

SAMICHLAUS BARRIQUE

Schloss Eggenberg, Vorchdorf, Upper Austria; 14%

Most recent addition to the range originally brewed by Hürliman in Zurich, once the world's strongest beer. Mahogany coloured with subtle carbonation, sweet, ripe fruit, warming and a mere hint of the wooden casks.

SAPHIR PILS

Zwettler, Zwettl, Lower Austria; 5.3%

While the Zwettler brewery usually favours local ingredients, they employ the citrusy German Saphir hops for this straw-coloured, spritzy and moderately bitter German-style pilsner.

SCHWARZBIER

Wieselburger, Wieselburg, Lower Austria; 4.8%

Black in colour, caramelly and roasty in the nose, but bitter with just a hint of sweetness on the palate. Packaged in flip-top bottles that the brewery reserves for its speciality brews.

DIE SCHWARZE KUH

Gusswerk, Hof bei Salzburg, Salzburg; 9.2%

Deep black with a slightly sweet, fruity malt character, this organic Imperial stout shows a hearty bitterness with notes of coffee and hops in a beer that has good balance and a long-lasting, roasty finish.

SILBERPFEIL

Raschhofer, Altheim, Upper Austria; 5.3%

Once known for their inexpensive lager, in recent years this brewery has added a range of more interesting beers to their repertoire including this pale ale with a fruity, grapefruit-like aroma and a moderate bitterness.

URTYP

Zipfer, Zipf, Upper Austria; 5.4%

One of Austria's bestselling premium lagers, brewed with whole hops. Although rice was dropped from the grain bill in 2016, this straw-coloured beer is still spritzy and crisp, with a slightly herbal bitterness at the start, a medium to full body and a dry finish.

WEISSE HELL

(Baumgartner, Schärding, Upper Austria; 5.4%

Golden *hefeweizen* from a town that belonged to Bavaria until 1779, with just the right amount of banana, vanilla and clove aromas, a faintly sweet body, lively carbonation and a medium bitterness in the finish.

SWITZERLAND

Having got off to a slow start in craft brewing, Switzerland now counts among the global leaders in terms of breweries per number of residents, although the national practice of licensing those who are little more than home-brewers skews the numbers somewhat. Still, the growth and improvement of Swiss beer in general begs exploration today.

523 INDIA PALE ALE

523, Köniz, Bern; 7.2%

Does just what it promises on the label, which is a straightforward, clean, quaffable and fragrant IPA, brewed by a tiny operation in the suburbs of Bern that is also notable for its constant stream of one-off beers.

BÄRNER JUNKER

Felsenau, Bern; 5.2%

A good example of a Swiss take on pilsner, especially in its unpasteurized draught form – flowery, fragrant and with a crisp final bitterness underpinning an almost honey-ish malt base.

L'AMBRÉE

Jorat, Vuillens, Vaud; 6%

The standout brew of an otherwise fairly pedestrian brewery; a smooth, balanced, subtly smoked amber ale, marrying caramelly malt, beech smoke and meaty notes.

BIÈRE DE TABLE

Virage, Plan-les-Ouates, Geneva; 3%

A fine example of the low-gravity ales that are growing in popularity among Swiss craft breweries. The recipe for this shape-shifting beast changes with every new brew, but the beer remains dry, quenching and fruity.

GALLUS 612

Schützengarten, St Gallen; 5.6%

Originally brewed for the city's 1400th anniversary, this is a juniper-infused, light brown, dry, spicy and moderately fruity ale, the brewery's first foray beyond Germanic orthodoxy.

MERCURY SAISON

Blackwell, Burgdorf, Bern; 4.2%

One of the core beers in Blackwell's prolific range of seasonals, collaborations and one-offs, dubbed a "*saison de table*" and brewed with rye to a dry and quaffable character.

OROINCENSO

Officina della Birra, Bioggio, Ticino; 8%

Initially a Christmas seasonal, an ale that has become pretty much the flagship of this pioneering brewery established in 1998. Dark and dry, it showcases beautifully a healthy dose of chestnut honey, including its bitter edge.

PACIFIC PIONEER PORTER

Sudwerk, Pfäffikon, Zurich; 6%

Very smooth, chocolaty and medium-bodied, this is a stylish interpretation of porter by a brewery whose range focuses on British and US beer styles.

PALE ALE

Müller, Baden, Aargau; 5.9%

A creditably spicy, orangey, caramel-edged take on British-style pale ale brewed by a family brewery otherwise known for its conservative lagers. It is mostly available in cans across German-speaking Switzerland.

PILGRIM TRIPLE BLONDE

Kloster Fischingen, Fischingen, Thurgau; 10%

A dangerously quaffable, lingering and warming abbey-style *tripel* that pushes all the right spicy–peachy–orangey buttons, brewed at Switzerland's lone brewery located on monastic premises at the St Iddazell Abbey.

SCHWARZER KRISTALL

Locher, Appenzell, Appenzell Innerrhoden; 6.3%

Impressively smooth, rounded, roasty and rich, this creamy black beer comes with a hint of smokiness, leaving it somewhere between a *schwarzbier* and a Baltic porter.

SKINNY DIPPER

Storm & Anchor, nomadic; 6.1%

Brewed at Doppelleu by itinerant brewer Tom Strickler, this IPA showcases his sizeable talent for creating hop-accented, US-style beers with rich peach, watermelon and bitter-orange notes.

TEMPÊTE

Docteur Gab's, Savigny, Vaud; 8%

From a pioneering craft brewery founded in 2001, this is a typical example of a Swiss take on a *tripel* that errs on the dry, quaffable side of the style.

CAN'T-MISS BREWERIES

BIER FACTORY

Rapperswil-Jona, St Gallen

Possibly the first craft brewery to venture off the Germanic beaten path in eastern Switzerland, it has seen its range thoroughly overhauled for the better following the arrival of Katie Pietsch at the brewing helm. Grassy, slightly citrusy, dry **Rappi Gold** (4.8%) is their golden ale in response to local pale lagers, **Blackbier** (5%) is a smooth, dry stout with chocolaty notes, while **Oh IPA** (6.7%) is a powerfully fragrant, fruity ale in the US style.

DES FRANCHES-MONTAGNES (BFM)

Saignelégier, Jura

Craft brewing pioneer founded in 1997 and widely credited with single-handedly putting Switzerland on the world beer map. Its flagship label is **Abbaye de Saint Bon-Chien** (11%),

a tart, dark-red, fruity, oak-aged beer also available in a variety of usually singular "Grand Cru" versions. **Cuvée Alex Le Rouge** (10.3%) is an idiosyncratic spicy "Imperial Jurassian stout", while dry, bitter, fragrant, sage-infused **La Meule** (6%) is the most distinctive in BFM's core range.

TROIS DAMES

Sainte-Croix, Vaud

Raphaël Mettler was the first to brew authentically British-style beers in Switzerland and his citrusy, peppery, earthy but smooth **India Pale Ale** (6.5%) has been an eye-opener for many a Swiss drinker. Smooth, rounded, fruity, rich **La Pasionaria** (9%) was the first double IPA released in quantity in Switzerland, while old brown **Grande Dame** (7%), a blend of strong stout and spontaneously fermented apricots, has paved the way for what is now a whole programme of wild fermentations and barrel-ageing worth watching.

BREWERY TO WATCH

LA NÉBULEUSE

Renens, Vaud

Youthful and not afraid of growth, this potent brewery is responsible for **Stirling** (5.3%), a fragrant, citrusy, dry steam beer; **Embuscade** (6.7%), an IPA bursting with orange and grapefruit notes; and the vanilla- and bourbon-infused porter **Malt Capone** (7%).

GREAT BRITAIN

With the march of craft beer in full swing, British beer orthodoxy, in large part inspired by the work of the Campaign for Real Ale (CAMRA), has had a difficult time accepting the new world of brewing, even as it has thrived and wildly expanded within the country's borders. A massive expansion of the market led by a rather remarkable growth in the number of new breweries, however, has the potential to drag British beer well into the 21st century, kicking and screaming or not.

ENGLAND

6X

Wadworth, Devizes, Wiltshire; 4.1%, cask

An amber bitter with treacly malt, rounded fruit and a slightly nutty almond note in a herbal coating finish, this isn't as ubiquitous as it once was, but is still a solid ale from an important Victorian survivor.

1872 PORTER

Elland, Elland, West Yorkshire; 6.5%

This much-lauded erstwhile Champion Beer of Britain is a meaty, toasty liquorice-tinged mouthful based on a historic recipe, from a brewery merged from two predecessors in 2002.

AGELESS

Redwillow, Macclesfield, Cheshire; 7.2%

Grapefruit, burned toast, sesame oil, lavender and pineapple waft through this, one of the UK's best modern IPAs, which comes from a former home-brewer who turned pro in 2010.

AUDIT ALE

Westerham, Westerham, Kent; 6.2%

One of a growing number of conventionally brewed beers that have been treated to remove gluten imperceptibly, this recreation of a pre-Second World War strong ale is rich and vinous, with the bitter orange tang of locally grown hops.

AXE EDGE

Buxton, Buxton, Derbyshire; 6.8%

There are numerous beers worth trying from this Peak District producer, but among the standouts is this smooth, zesty IPA with tangerine, passion-fruit and mango notes, and a comfortably bitter finish.

BABY FACED ASSASSIN

Roosters, Knaresborough, North Yorkshire; 6.1%

Modern IPA from a brewery that championed New World hops in the 1990s. Vividly flavoured but delicate, with hints of fresh mango and papaya, and an emerging peppery bitterness on the finish.

BAD KITTY

Brass Castle, Malton, North Yorkshire; 5.5%

Full-bodied, creamy and complex vanilla porter finishing with gentle rooty hops and roastiness, from a brewery

ICONIC BREWERY

FULLER'S, SMITH & TURNER

London

Long-standing independent family-led brewery on a wisteria-clad Chiswick riverside site with evidence of brewing from the 16th century. Well known for exemplary cask beers like style-defining marmalade-tinged **ESB** (5.5%), but gaining new respect for historical revivals, wood-aged beers and bottle-conditioned specialities such as biscuity, slightly smoky amber ale **1845** (6.3%) and outstanding annually released barley wine **Vintage Ale** (8.5%), which becomes magnificently complex and port-like with age. Gentle yet crisp **Chiswick Bitter** (3.5%), sadly now only an occasional special, and medium-bodied but assertively roasty **London Porter** (5.4%) are also highly rated.

ICONIC BREWERY

THORNBRIDGE

Bakewell, Derbyshire

Hailed by many as Britain's leading 21st-century brewery, set up with the help of Kelham Island's Dave Wickett (*see* page 84) at the eponymous Peak District stately home and since expanded to nearby Bakewell. Flagship is the resinous but approachable **Jaipur IPA** (5.9%), one of Britain's first in the new transatlantic style, while the rest of an imaginative and consistently impressive range includes the intense and fragrant double IPA **Halcyon** (7.4%), toasty Vienna lager **Kill Your Darlings** (5%) and unique dark, sweet and spicy honey beer **Bracia** (10%).

that started in a garage in 2011 and deservedly expanded six months later.

BARNSLEY BITTER

Acorn, Barnsley, South Yorkshire; 3.8%, cask

Flowery, fruity and resinously dry local favourite, resurrected with the original yeast following the demise of the old Barnsley brewery by an outfit that has also ventured into contemporary single-hop pale ales.

BEARDED LADY

Magic Rock, Huddersfield, West Yorkshire; 10.5%

One of Britain's most successful and respected new US-influenced craft brewers makes a range of punchy beers, of which this charred ooze of an Imperial stout is arguably the standout.

BEAST

Exmoor, Wiveliscombe, Somerset; 6.6%

Deeply grainy and coffee-ish dark brown beer with chocolate and fruit on the finish, from a brewery established in 1990 on the site of the historic Hancocks brewery.

BEDE'S CHALICE

Durham, Bowburn, County Durham; 9%

Big, sweetish, orange-liqueur-tinged *tripel*, rich in creamy fruit and herbal hops, from an older micro that has long been a reliable source of strong bottle-conditioned ales inspired by its home city's ecclesiastical heritage.

BIG BEN

Thwaites, Blackburn, Lancashire; 5.8%

US-style brown ale with a fusion of fruit and herbal hops and chewy malt, from a 210-year-old brewery that in 2015 unexpectedly downsized to "craft" scale, farming out its cask-conditioned beers to Marston's (see page 84).

BISHOPS FAREWELL

Oakham, Peterborough, Cambridgeshire; 4.6%, cask

Soft strawberry, lime and passion-fruit sustain over a firm cereal base in this hoppy but not too bitter golden ale from an early UK adopter of New World hops, founded in Rutland in 1996.

BLACK ADDER

Mauldons, Sudbury, Suffolk; 5.3%

From a historic brewery reinvented in 1981, this slightly tarry and tart stout has elements of cocoa, black coffee and cola, with almond-like bitterness on a smooth finish.

BLACK DOG FREDDY

Beckstones, Millom, Cumbria; 3.9%, cask

Multi-award-winning dark mild with caramel and blackberry flavours and a notably bitterish roast note, from a small brewery in good walking country founded by an ex-InBev drayman.

BLUEBIRD BITTER

Coniston, Coniston, Cumbria; 3.6%, cask

Popular and influential lime- and ginger-tinged golden bitter, from a modest plant behind the Black Bull pub. Also worth trying in its US-hopped and bottle-conditioned versions.

BODGER'S BARLEY WINE

Chiltern, Aylesbury, Buckinghamshire; 8.5%

Gracefully ageing, smooth, substantial and spicily honeyed chestnut-coloured ale with salted-olive notes, from a well-established farmhouse brewery.

BRIGSTOW BITTER

Arbor, Bristol; 4.3%, cask

Now one of the oldest of Bristol's new wave of breweries and noted for fresh contemporary styles, but also for this delightfully grainy, honeyed and orange-tinged bitter using English hops.

CHARRINGTONS IPA

Heritage, Burton upon Trent, Staffordshire; 4.5%, cask

Heritage London pale ale with a fine blend of toffee, toast, nuts and a very dry bitter finish, resurrected by legendary ex-Bass brewer Steve Wellington with its original yeast at the National Brewery Centre.

COHORT

Summer Wine, Holmfirth, West Yorkshire; 7.5%

"Double black Belgian rye IPA" from a determinedly modern operation, with herbs, pineapple and citrus successfully layered over a base of dry chocolate and soothing caramel.

COOLSHIP

Elgood's, Wisbech, Cambridgeshire; 6%

A remarkably successful, spontaneously fermented lambic-style beer from an old family-owned brewery, made in a long-disused coolship, with sherry-like tones, tart jam and biscuit sweetness and a mild lactic sourness.

CUMBRIAN FIVE HOP

Hawkshead, Staveley, Cumbria; 5%, cask

Notes of floral peach and sweet onion lead this firmly bitter but refreshing, contemporary pale ale from a brewery that began in a Lake District barn, but soon expanded on the success of numerous beers of similar quality.

DARK RUBY

Sarah Hughes, Dudley, West Midlands; 6%, cask

Benchmark strong Black Country mild from a brewery revived in 1987 when the current owner rediscovered his grandmother's recipes, with notes of brown toast, caramel, port and cherries, and a decidedly dry finish.

DOROTHY GOODBODY'S WHOLESOME STOUT

Wye Valley, Stoke Lacy, Herefordshire; 4.6%

Excellent creamy and medium-bodied stout with a notably dry and ashy Irish-inspired roast-barley bite, long a mainstay of this reliable rural small brewery in hop country.

DOUBLE MAXIM

Maxim, Houghton-le-Spring, Tyne and Wear; 4.7%

Distinctive heritage brown ale in the dry northeastern style, with citrus, caramel and raspberry notes, and a bitter, slightly resinous finish.

DOUBLE MOMENTUM

Hopshackle, Market Deeping, Lincolnshire; 7%

Exemplary double IPA from an often-overlooked, ahead-of-its time brewer, with honey, pollen and roses on a firm malt palate and an assertive yet controlled, peppery-bitter finish.

FLAGSHIP

Hook Norton, Hook Norton, Oxfordshire; 5.3%

A rare, revived strongish IPA with English hops from a village-based, Victorian-era brewery that is still partly steam-powered, with notes of spring meadows, orange, honey and plum, and a chewy lettuce finish.

GADDS' FAITHFUL DOGBOLTER

Ramsgate, Broadstairs, Kent; 5.6%, cask

Mildly roasty porter with orange-marmalade and liquorice tones, this was the celebrated mainstay of the Firkin brewpub chain during the 1980s, resurrected by brewer Eddie Gadd at his brewery on the Isle of Thanet.

CAN'T-MISS BREWERIES

ADNAMS

Southwold, Suffolk

Long-established, family-dominated independent brewery and wine importer in a particularly pretty Suffolk seaside town. Revered for benchmark cask ales like **Southwold Bitter** (3.7%, cask), with complex marmalade and peppery flavours, and recently revived and rich, classic bottled barley wine **Tally-Ho** (7.2%), which improves with ageing. Successfully cultivating a contemporary edge under the Jack Brand label with beers such as earthy but tropical-fruit-tinged **Innovation IPA** (6.7%).

BURNING SKY

Firle, East Sussex

Eagerly anticipated solo project from one of Britain's most influential brewers, Mark Tranter, from a rural setting on the South Downs. Hit the ground running in 2013 with a succession of outstanding, often seasonally influenced beers, including the fruity, grassy and refreshing **Saison à la Provision** (6.5%); a vividly flavoured **Devil's Rest IPA** (7%), with melon, mint and tobacco notes; and the grape-ish, oaky, lightly phenolic barrel-aged dark **Monolith** (8%).

HARVEY'S

Lewes, East Sussex

Revered independent brewery on the south coast, best known for its old-fashioned, dryish, beautifully balanced and slightly toffee-accented **Sussex**

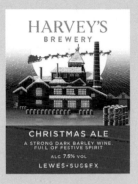

Best Bitter (4%) and, internationally, for the benchmark grainy, leathery, slightly sour and long-ageing **Imperial Extra Double Stout** (9%). Numerous cask and bottled specialities, often in endangered styles, include an indulgently sweet and complex **Christmas Ale** (7.5%).

THE KERNEL

London

Perhaps the most influential and respected of the new wave London breweries and the inadvertent founder of the Bermondsey "beer mile". Equally adept at artisanal **Pale Ale** (~5.5%) made with ever-changing hops – the Mosaic and Simcoe versions have been particularly fragrant, fresh and balanced – and strong heritage stouts and porters such as the complex, velvety and tobacco-tinged **Export Stout London 1890** (7.2%). In contrast, **Table Beer** (3.3%) is a cheerfully light and citric refresher.

CAN'T-MISS BREWERIES

MARBLE

Manchester

The brewery that arguably kicked off Manchester's current brewing renaissance, founded in 1998 in the Marble Arch heritage pub just north of the city centre, though since relocated to a bigger site nearby. **Chocolate Marble** (5.5%, cask) is a strong mild with berry notes and a rich, indeed chocolaty finish, while creamy, delicately flowery **Manchester Bitter** (4.2%, cask) was inspired by Boddingtons at its best. Among highly recommended specials are complex but beautifully integrated **Earl Grey IPA** (6.8%), originally a collaboration with Dutch brewer Emelisse (*see* pages 115 and 119), and deep, plum-cake-tinged Imperial stout **Decadence** (8.7%).

SIREN

Finchampstead, Berkshire

Probably the UK's most consistently high-achieving new-style craft brewery, founded by a Home Counties home-brewer in 2012. Red ale **Liquid**

Mistress (5.8%) expertly blends chewy, toasty, cherry-like malt with spicy hops, while smoky, coconut-tinged and indulgent sweet stout **Broken Dream** (6%) is also available in wood-aged versions. **Calypso** (4%) succeeds in laying peach and lychee hop notes over a refreshingly lemony *Berliner weisse* base.

ST AUSTELL

St Austell, Cornwall

The last-surviving Victorian independent in Cornwall, deploying a canny contemporary sensibility by supplementing its regular cask bitters with beers like **Proper Job** (4.5%, cask), a flavourful strawberry- and citrus-tinged IPA, and richly biscuit-malty, lightly fruity **Admiral's Ale** (5%), brewed from a malt specially kilned to the brewery's specifications. New stout **Mena Dhu** (4.5%) deploys a dose of smoked malt in a lightly sweet, liquoricey and easy-drinking brew.

GAMMA RAY

Beavertown, London; 5.4%

Vivid but balanced pale ale bursting with flavours of pineapple, lemon marmalade and grapefruit, this is deservedly one of the most successful new London beers, from an ambitious outfit that has pioneered the use of cans in the UK market.

GOOD KING HENRY SPECIAL RESERVE

Old Chimneys, Market Weston, Suffolk; 11%

Sought-after but rare, oaked Imperial stout from a tiny farm brewery, with a heady whisky–sherry–blackcurrant aroma and candied fruit, marzipan and oaky tannins in the body.

HARVEST ALE

J W Lees, Middleton Junction, Manchester; 11.5%

Seasonal barley wine using the harvest's ingredients to give a nutty, sherried and slightly salty, olive-imbued complexity to an ale that often benefits from a degree of ageing.

INDIA PALE ALE

Harbour, Kirland, Cornwall; 5%

Resinous and grapefruity, but comparatively restrained transatlantic-style IPA with subtle tropical-fruit and apricot notes from an impressive US-influenced set-up launched in rural Cornwall by a former Sharp's brewer.

INDIA PALE ALE

Shepherd Neame, Faversham, Kent; 6.1%

Revival of a 19th-century recipe from the archives of what is probably Britain's oldest brewery, situated in hop country on the north Kent coast. Characterized by nutty malt, orange cream and earthy resins, with seedy aromas.

JJJ IPA

Moor, Bristol; 9%

One of the UK's best double IPAs, from one of its persistently ground-breaking brewers, heading up the rapidly emerging Bristol beer scene with increasing aplomb. Citrus and hay aromas, biscuity, white wine and coconut flavours and a long tannic, peppery finish.

LONDON KEEPER

Truman's, London; 8%

Brown sugar, toasted coconut, tart rosehip and a gently roasty finish mark out this complex export porter, revived from an 1880 recipe using US hops. Still maturing splendidly.

LONDON PORTER

Meantime [Asahi], London; 6.5%

Reliably fine and complex 19th-century-inspired porter, with sappy blackcurrant and chocolate mousse flavours and earthy hoppiness, from London's second-biggest and second-oldest brewery.

LURCHER STOUT

Green Jack, Lowestoft, Suffolk; 4.8%

Soft, chocolaty and very sessionable stout with a taste of spicy black grape, from Britain's most easterly brewery, whose founder has brewed locally since 1993.

MAD GOOSE

Purity, Great Alne, Warwickshire; 4.2%, cask

Arguably the tastiest choice from a reliable and popular producer of clean-tasting and consistent session ales, filled with hoppy perfume and orchard-fruit aromas over generous maltiness in a satisfying golden ale.

MARY JANE

Ilkley, Ilkley, West Yorkshire; 3.5%, cask

Lots to admire at this rapidly expanding brewery located on the edge of the Yorkshire Dales, but this cheerful and supremely quaffable pale ale with gentle citric and earthy bitterness makes a great go-to beer.

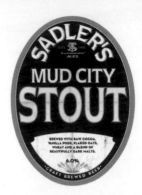

MIDNIGHT BELL

Leeds, Leeds, West Yorkshire; 4.8%, cask

Lightly treacly, vermouth-tinged but very approachable strong mild, the calling card of a highly professional and ambitious 2007 set-up, now filling a niche in the city where Tetley was king until closed by Carlsberg.

MUD CITY STOUT

Sadler's, Lye, West Midlands; 6%

Chocolate liqueur, coconut, dark malt and a relatively bitter finish characterize this strong stout flavoured with cocoa and vanilla, brewed by an operation revived by a new generation of Sadlers in 2004.

MILK SHAKE STOUT

Wiper & True, Bristol; 5%

Lactose-dosed, not at all oversweet, fruity–vanilla sweet stout that is a fine example of a revived local speciality and the flagship of acclaimed brewers who acquired their own premises in 2015.

MUTINY

Stringers, Ulverston, Cumbria; 9.3%

Slightly yeasty pear notes add interest to this Imperial stout, rich with dark chocolate and cakey malt, and capable of bottle-ageing, from a small brewery on the edge of the Lake District.

MOROCCO ALE

Daleside, Harrogate, North Yorkshire; 5.5%

Unusual spiced ale slightly reminiscent of red vermouth, with flavours of ginger and cough drops supported by rich cakey malt, based on a recipe allegedly brought back from Morocco by a Crusader.

NINKASI

Wild, Evercreech, Somerset; 9%

Spicy, fruity and extraordinarily complex big blond ale tinged with vanilla, fenugreek and tropical fruit, made with local apples and wild and Champagne yeasts by a confidently innovative 2012 farmhouse-based team.

NORWEGIAN FARMHOUSE STRONG ALE

Poppyland, Cromer, Norfolk; 7.4%

A near-still rye bread-, eucalyptus- and treacle-tinged brew made with authentic Norwegian *kveik* yeast by a tiny and highly experimental seaside brewery, worth looking out.

OLD FORD EXPORT STOUT

Redchurch, Bethnal Green, London; 7.5%

Arguably the best of a strong range of older English beer styles from this bottle-conditioned specialist, dark as Hades and rammed with burned malt, coffee and bitter chocolate character.

OLD NO. 6

Joule's, Market Drayton, Shropshire; 4.8%, cask

Historic dark amber winter brew, with flavours of toffee, burned vine fruit and chocolate, and building bitterness in the finish, from a once-revered local name closed by Bass and resurrected in 2010.

OLD PECULIER

Theakston, Masham, North Yorkshire; 5.6%

Named after the medieval privileges exercised through a so-called "peculiar" (or "peculier") court such as Masham, this rich and famous old ale turns remarkably dry after a complex and sweetish, molasses-accented start.

OLD THUMPER

Ringwood [Marston's], Ringwood, Hampshire; 5.6%, cask

A substantial, reddish-brown bitter, with blackcurrant and almond flavours and a nutty, resinous finish, this is the signature beer of a brewery founded by late craft brewing pioneer Peter Austin.

OLD TOM

Robinsons, Stockport, Cheshire; 8.5%

Classic barley wine from an 1899 recipe illustrated with a cat's face, tasting of rum, chocolate and red wine with a rounded spirity finish turning dry and tannic. The flavoured brand extensions are best avoided.

OMERTA

Fixed Wheel, Blackheath, West Midlands; 7.5%

Gentler take on an Imperial stout from a 2014 Black Country start-up created by cycling enthusiasts. Its grainy, chewy body has hints of ash and rum over sweet chocolate.

ORACLE

Salopian, Hadnall, Shropshire; 4%, cask

Dry, creamy golden ale with tantalizing tropical-fruit and grapefruit notes and an oily, spicy but not too bitter finish, from a brewery already ahead of its time when founded in 1995, now gaining overdue respect.

BREWERIES TO WATCH

BULLFINCH

London

Former sound engineer Ryan McLean branched out in 2014 to produce beers such as fruity and moreishly drying **Born to be Mild** (3.3%), and the refreshingly lemon-tinged and spicy **Milou** (6%) *saison*.

CHORLTON

Manchester

Specialist in tart German styles and *Brettanomyces* fermentation, best known for the surprisingly successful hop-forward take on a *Berliner weisse* **Amarillo Sour** (5.4%), while **Citra Brett Pale** (4.5%) does what it says on the can, and rather well.

CLOUDWATER

Manchester

Manchester's most ambitious new brewery offering charming seasonally rotating **Session IPAs** (~4.8%) and well-hopped lagers, plus a varied series of **DIPAs**, each highly anticipated.

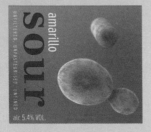

ORIGINAL

Dark Star, Partridge Green, West Sussex; 5%, cask

Toasty and autumnal tart dark ale recreating the first "microbrew" to win Champion Beer of Britain in 1987, from a renowned brewery that began in Brighton's Evening Star pub, also famed for hoppy brews.

OSCAR WILDE

Mighty Oak, Maldon, Essex; 3.7%, cask

Rare and impressive southern mild from a brewery founded in 1996 by an ex-Ind Coope brewer, with a full malty caramel palate, some blackcurrant fruit, a touch of roast and bracing hops around the edges.

PALE RIDER

Kelham Island, Sheffield, South Yorkshire; 5.2%, cask

Lively golden ale brimming with lychee, pineapple and citrus, and a prickly finish, the best-known beer from a revered pub brewery founded by the late Dave Wickett, one of the architects of the British beer revolution.

PEDIGREE

Marston's, Burton upon Trent, Staffordshire; 4.5%, cask

The only beer still fermented using Burton Unions at the last-surviving historic, non-multinational brewery in England's brewing capital, this is a toffee-ish pale ale with gently spicy–orange hoppiness, apple notes and a delicately drying finish.

PENNY LANE PALE

Mad Hatter, Liverpool, Merseyside; 3.9%

Fine modern-style pale ale that is the brewery's flagship brand, with orange and mango aromas and peppery bitterness within a sweetish body.

THE PORTER

Anspach & Hobday, London; 6.7%

A home-brew competition victory with this luscious, complex, tangy fruit and chocolate porter prompted Paul Anspach and Jack Hobday to turn commercial as one of the highlights of London's Bermondsey "beer mile".

REPUBLIKA

Windsor & Eton, Windsor, Berkshire; 4.8%

Impressively authentic Bohemian-style pilsner with flowery, grassy notes and a firmly bitter edge, created with Czech assistance by ex-Courage brewers in the shadow of the famous royal castle by the Thames.

RUBY MILD

Rudgate, Tockwith, North Yorkshire; 4.4%, cask

Firm grainy malt, brown sugar, dark fruit and quite a bracing hoppy, chalky finish on an award-winning dark mild from a brewery founded in 1992 that does well at both traditional and contemporary styles.

BREWERIES TO WATCH

TORRSIDE BREWING

New Zealand/
New Mills Pale

**West of
the Sun**

SACRE BREW

Wolverhampton, West Midlands

New York City native Gwen Sanchirico conjures highly inventive beers including semi-regular rye *saison* **Man on the Oss** (4.7%), and Belgian-style golden ale **Dracunculus** (4.8%).

TORRSIDE

New Mills, Derbyshire

Brewery commanding immediate attention on its late 2015 launch with beers like the accomplished session IPA **West of the Sun** (4.5%), with white grape and floral notes, and **Sto Lat** (2.8%), a rare British *grodziskie*.

SAISON RHUBARB AND GINGER

Partizan, London; 3.9%

One of numerous often-changing Belgian-inspired beers, this elegant and refreshing brew skilfully integrates subtle ginger and rhubarb flavours and fruity yeast notes with a light lactic edge.

SBA

Donnington, Stow-on-the-Wold, Gloucestershire; 4.4%, cask

Smooth, dry premium bitter tinged with caramel, fruit and sometimes buttery tones, from a small, picturesque Cotswold independent with its own trout lake.

SINGLE HOP

Mallinsons, Huddersfield, West Yorkshire; 3.9%, cask

Series of fine, clean golden ales showcasing various hops that have steadily enhanced the reputation of this notably small outfit. The Galaxy-hopped version is grassy and citric.

SNECK LIFTER

Jennings [Marston's], Cockermouth, Cumbria; 5.1%, cask

Signature dark ale, rich with flavours of treacle toffee, burned toast and tangy orange peel, from a classic Victorian small town brewery on the northwestern edge of the Lake District.

SNOW TOP

Old Dairy, Tenterden, Kent; 6%, cask

Cakey, creamy and chocolaty award-winning winter special dark ale lifted by quite a dose of spicy and fruity hops, from an unassuming but reliable farm-based brewery opened in 2010.

SONOMA PALE ALE

Track, Manchester; 3.8%

Session pale ale from a railway arch behind Manchester Piccadilly Station occupied by an ex-Camden Town brewer late in 2014, with focused floral, fruit-salad and citrus aromas and flavours, most courtesy of Mosaic hops.

SOUR GRAPES

Lovibonds, Henley-on-Thames, Oxfordshire; 5.4%

Wine-barrel-aged sour beer that began as a mistake but went on to win a medal in international competitions; zesty, tartly fruity and floral, with a balanced lactic character.

STOUT

Titanic, Stoke-on-Trent, Staffordshire; 4.5%

Intense, roast- and mocha-tinged stout successfully developed as alternative to the Irish variety by a consistently high-achieving brewery in the home city of the captain of the SS *Titanic*.

STRANNIK

Northern Monk, Leeds, West Yorkshire; 9%

Assertively rich, near-black Imperial stout with marzipan, port and sherry flavours, and a roasty rosehip-tart finish, from a youthful and inventive team with great promise.

STRONG SUFFOLK

Greene King, Bury St Edmunds, Suffolk; 6%

Unique blend of Old 5X, a strong, vinous and slightly sour stock ale aged in oak vats, and a malty, sweetish Burton ale, neither of which is regularly available separately. The best-kept secret from Britain's biggest non-multinational brewer.

SUBLIME CHAOS

Anarchy, Morpeth, Northumberland; 7%

Punchy coffee stout with blackcurrant, liquorice, honey and fruity New Zealand hop notes, and a surprisingly gentle, chocolaty finish, from what is one of northeast England's most acclaimed contemporary breweries.

SUMMER LIGHTNING

Hop Back, Downton, Wiltshire; 5%, cask

This lovely golden ale, from a former brewpub, galvanized British brewing in the 1990s by successfully taking a swipe at the premium lager market. Still a zesty, perfumed delight, with a long finish for the style.

T.E.A.

Hogs Back, Tongham, Surrey; 4.2%, cask

Popular and very English bitter from a farmhouse brewery perched atop a chalk ridge, with notes of plum, autumn fruit and tobacco, and earthy hops on a mellow, sweetish finish.

THREEONESIX

Grain, Harleston, Norfolk; 3.9%, cask

Excellent low-strength refresher, parchment pale but gloriously fruity, brewed from pilsner malt and Amarillo hops at a farm brewery opened in the Waveney Valley in 2006.

TRINITY

Redemption, London; 3%, cask

Citrus and rose notes and lightly bitter resins over a decent malty body characterize this masterclass of a low-gravity, high-flavour light ale, made from three malts and three hops by one of the earliest (2010) and still one of the best of London's new wave.

STYLE SPOTLIGHT

CASK BITTER AND MILD

Britain remains the only country where draught beer that continues fermenting in its cask has survived as a mainstream commercial format. Known as cask-conditioned or sometimes "real" ale, the beer is served without additional gas pressure, straight from the cask or via a handpump. Its quality relies on competent and conscientious retailers, and not all are up to the challenge.

A variety of economic and cultural factors contributed to cask's survival in Britain, along with the fact that the subtle flavours and aromas of the low-strength session bitters and milds that increasingly dominated British drinking habits after the First World War were enhanced by cask-conditioning, but obliterated by kegging.

When the industry attempted to dump this format in the late 1960s, a consumer movement led by the Campaign for Real Ale (CAMRA) arose to resist it. Even in today's market of diverse and distinctive beers, there remains something special about a top-quality cask bitter or mild in peak condition, gently carbonated and cellar cool.

To fully appreciate this, try **Holden's Golden Glow**, sweetish and light-coloured with subtle hopping; **Black Sheep Bitter**, a blackcurrant-tinged classic; or the lightly peppery and resinous **Butcombe Bitter**. An unapologetically old-school, chalky-dry pint with a gingery note is **Timothy Taylor's Landlord**.

Mild is an object lesson in how to squeeze maximum flavour from a low-strength beer, evident in the lightly tart, chocolaty **Hobsons Champion Mild**, or subtly nutty amber-coloured **Banks's Original**. Other beers particularly recommended in cask are highlighted elsewhere in this section.

TRIPLE CHOCOHOLIC

Saltaire, Shipley, West Yorkshire; 4.8%, cask

Accomplished stout featuring chocolate malt, chocolate syrup and cocoa nibs (hence the name), but supported by nutty malt and tart citric fruit.

UNFILTERED HELLS

Camden Town [AB InBev], London; 4.6%

Flagship of a craft brewer plucked up by AB InBev in 2015 for its solid street cred. The hazy version of this London lager has plenty of juicy malt, crisp polleny hops and a slightly citrus finish.

VINTAGE

Bristol Beer Factory, Bristol; 6.6%

Annually produced old ale usually blended from oak-aged beers, with rich malt, cherry and tobacco notes. One of many strong options from a Bristol stalwart based on the historic Ashton Gate brewery site.

WHERRY

Woodforde's, Woodbastwick, Norfolk; 3.8%, cask

Popular, cheerfully light, slightly astringent but satisfying blackcurrant-tinged golden bitter, called after a traditional style of sailing boat.

WORKIE TICKET

Mordue, North Shields, Tyne and Wear; 4.5%, cask

Deliciously autumnal malt-forward dark bitter with a waft of blackberry fruit, named with a local dialect term for a troublemaker.

WORTHINGTON'S WHITE SHIELD

Molson Coors UK, Burton upon Trent, Staffordshire; 5.6%

Historic bottle-conditioned pale ale with a taste of fresh apricot jam, nutty grainy maltiness and quite a pursing hop note at the finish. Cellar-worthy despite its low strength. One of the UK's most authentic heritage ales.

XB

Batemans, Wainfleet, Lincolnshire; 3.7%, cask

Chewy best bitter with hints of russet apples and almonds, from a picturesque family-owned brewer that excels at traditional bitters, milds and other quaffable styles.

XXXX

Hydes, Salford, Manchester; 6.8%

Notes of mint toffee, whisky and brown sugar characterize this spicy seasonal barley wine from a brewer once known as the most conservative in the UK, with some recipes unchanged for 50 years, yet now refreshed.

YORKSHIRE STINGO

Samuel Smith, Tadcaster, North Yorkshire; 8–9%

Oak-aged, bottle-conditioned old ale packed with flavours of nutty malt, spiced toffee and red fruit, this is a standout entry in a range of bottled specialities from Yorkshire's oldest and most eccentric brewery.

YOUNG'S WINTER WARMER

Charles Wells [Marston's], Bedford, Bedfordshire; 5%, cask

With its rich malted-milk body layered with coffee, liquorice and cola, this seasonal is arguably the best cask beer from Charles Wells, which absorbed the brands of former London stalwart Young's in 2006 before itself being purchased by Marston's in mid-2017.

ISLE OF MAN

BITTER

Okells, Kewaigue; 3.7%, cask

Classic amber bitter with a twist of Muscat-like fruitiness from New World hops over a soft but dry, biscuity base, from the only surviving historic independent brewery located on the Isle of Man.

NORTHERN IRELAND

BREWERY TO WATCH

BOUNDARY

Belfast

Proving that Ireland's burgeoning craft beer scene knows no borders, Boundary's beers include a fragrant **American Pale Ale** (3.5%) and a more obviously **Irish Export Stout** (7%), plus Belgian styles and mixed-fermentation brews.

BALTIC PORTER

Farmageddon, Comber, Co Down; 10.8%, bottle

The most ambitious brew so far from a young co-operative based near Newtownards and typical of new beer in the north. Pushes the coffee a bit, along with the definition of Irish porter, but warming and mellow with huge presence.

BELFAST ALE

Whitewater, Newry, Co Down; 4.5%, cask

Delightful reddish amber ale, substantial and distinctive with crisp malt and mineral tones, from the province of County Down's second-largest and oldest brewery, producing quality ale since 1996.

SCOTLAND

5AM SAINT

BrewDog, Ellon, Aberdeenshire; 5%

The UK's most successful brewery in a century, influential and rapidly expanding, producing a huge range that includes this reliable, flavourful and quaffable red ale with elements of pine, lemon tea and biscuit malt.

80/-

Belhaven [Greene King], Dunbar, East Lothian; 4.2%, cask

Once dubbed "the Burgundy of Scotland", this rare surviving traditional "80 shilling" ale is richly malty but dry, suffused with nutty notes and a light touch of sulphur.

80/-

Stewart, Loanhead, Edinburgh; 4.4%, cask

Spot-on traditional Scottish session ale, lusciously malty and comforting with tobacco and dark fruit flavours, from one of the few new Scottish breweries conserving such retro styles.

BEARFACE LAGER

Drygate [C&C], Glasgow; 4.4%

Fruity, hazy, hop-forward but balanced and crisp contemporary lager from inventive craft brewery and taproom outside the gates of Glasgow's historic

ICONIC BREWERY

TRAQUAIR HOUSE

Innerleithen, Scottish Borders

The oldest-inhabited stately home in Scotland, where the late laird revived the 16th-century brewhouse in the grounds in 1965 to create what was in effect the UK's first microbrewery. Signature revivalist **Traquair House Ale** (7.2%) is a dark delight of rich malt with tart-fruit and vermouth tones, while **Jacobite Ale** (8%) is sweetish, complex and liquoriced, its name reflecting the family's historic loyalties.

Tennent's lager brewery, a joint venture with Williams Brothers.

BROCKVILLE DARK

Tryst, Falkirk; 3.8%, cask

Chocolaty, husky, roasty and slightly briny Scottish mild from a reliable producer named after Falkirk's historic cattle market, offering several other imaginative choices.

DARK ISLAND RESERVE

Orkney [Sinclair], Quoyloo, Orkney; 10%

This well-established northern island brewery supercharges its Dark Island ale to create this fruity, peaty whisky-barrel-aged delight, with rich, smooth sultana and chocolate-cake malt, rosehip tartness and a faint whiff of seaweed.

FRAOCH

Williams Brothers, Alloa, Clackmannanshire; 5%

The beer that changed perceptions of Scottish brewing in 1992, using local heather to create lavender and ginger-like notes over tartly fruity malt in this light amber ale.

HOPCLASSIC BELGIAN IPA

Six° North, Stonehaven, Aberdeenshire; 6.6%

An IPA fermented with Belgian yeast, yielding notes of ripe apricot pastry and raspberry, and a bittering but persistently fruity finish, from a brewery so named because it is six degrees of latitude north of Brussels.

JARL

Fyne, Cairndow, Argyll and Bute; 3.8%, cask

One of the UK's most flavourful contemporary golden ales, boasting zesty lychee and kiwi fruit supported by crisp malt, from a farm-based brewery overlooking Loch Fyne.

OLA DUBH 18

Harviestoun, Alva, Clackmannanshire; 8%

One of Scotland's oldest craft breweries ages already notable oaked porter Old Engine Oil in ex-whisky barrels to create this complex, spicy, malty delight, labelled according to the age of the previous Highland Park whisky contents.

ORKNEY BLAST

Swannay, by Evie, Orkney; 6%

Fruit salad, peach and grapefruit dominate this nectarish strong pale ale with a peppery-sulphur note, from a small but reliable operation also known as the Highland Brewery.

ROGUE WAVE

Cromarty, Cromarty, Highland; 5.7%

Cheerful contemporary pale ale with flavours of lime, raspberry jam, elderflower and cracked pepper, and a bitter quinine quality, from a family-run brewery in a far-flung coastal location northeast of Inverness.

CAN'T-MISS BREWERY

TEMPEST

Tweedbank, Scottish Borders

Always interesting, this multiple award-winning team progressed to greatness via garage brewing in New Zealand and a gastro-brewpub in the Scottish Lowlands to a new 30-hectolitre brewhouse that opened in 2015. The stalwart is tropical-fruity pale ale **Long White Cloud** (5.6%); the charmer is more piney but balanced IPA **Brave New World** (7%); the masterpiece is beautifully balanced mocha porter **Red Fye Flight** (7.4%); and the explorer is burned, short of smoky, Imperial stout-cum-wee heavy **Old Parochial** (10%).

WALES

DARK MATTER

Vale of Glamorgan, Barry, Vale of Glamorgan; 4.4%, cask

Award-winning dark brown porter with rich layers of chocolate, blackcurrant and roasted malt tones from a 2005 brewery with a growing reputation and food-friendly leanings.

OCHR DYWYLL Y MWS/DARK SIDE OF THE MOOSE

Mŵs Piws/Purple Moose, Porthmadog, Gwynedd; 4.6%, cask

Unusually hoppy dark ale with citrus and pineapple notes set over a coffee and cola body, from a small brewery on the coastal strip of the Snowdonia National Park.

BREWERIES TO WATCH

HOPCRAFT

Pontyclun, Mid-Glamorgan

A gathering collective of South Wales talent is now boosting a project creating hoppy beers like Citra-hopped cask pale **Citraic** (5.2%), black IPA **Devilfish Ink** (5.8%) and versions of toffee–grapefruit brown ale **Diggin' up the King** (4.6–5.4%).

LINES

Caerphilly

Experimental brewer focused on eco-friendly production and developing six "lines" of beer, impressing early with light ale **Munich Table Beer** (2.8%), **Farmhouse IPA** (6.1%) and Imperial stout **Primary Brett** (9.5%).

RAMNESIA STRONG ALE

Penlon Cottage, New Quay, Ceredigion; 5.6%

Complex, nutty and plummy strong ale with a mellow stab of hops in the finish from a brewery that began on a farm in 2004 and is noted for an eclectic bottled range.

SA

Brains, Cardiff; 4.2%, cask

This curious mid-gold bitter, dry and seedy with autumn fruit and a gooseberry-tart finish, is arguably the most distinctive regular from one of only two surviving old-established Welsh independents, soon to move to a new site.

CAN'T-MISS BREWERY

TINY REBEL

Newport

Youthful craft brewery rocketing to prominence since 2012 with bold and flavourful beers like the raspberryish red ale **Cwtch** (4.6%), Champion Beer of Britain in 2015; **Dirty Stop Out** (5%), a complex but well-integrated oatmeal stout with a dash of smoked malt; and the floral and fruity flagship ale **FUBAR** (4.4%). The brewery also has a pair of fine pubs in Cardiff and Newport.

REPUBLIC OF IRELAND

While many, indeed perhaps most, beer drinkers still think of stout when the term Irish is mentioned, Ireland's brewers have in recent years made great strides in brewing all manner of styles, including many new variants of porter and stout.

BLACK LIGHTNING

9 White Deer, Ballyvourney, Co Cork, 6.5%

The most hop-forward of Ireland's regular black IPAs, making great use of Simcoe hops for flavours of orange candy and lemon peel, plus a balancing dry, roasted finish.

BLACK ROCK

Dungarvan, Dungarvan, Co Waterford; 4.3%

Though it was first brewed as recently as 2010, this dry stout is as classic as they come with all the signature roasted flavours of the style, plus an added fruity complexity from its bottle-conditioning.

BLOND

White Gypsy, Templemore, Co Tipperary; 4%

A light take on a Bavarian *weissbier*, pale and hazy yellow with a highly refreshing crispness and gentle celery hop flavours. Perfect easy-going, summertime fare.

BLUE JUMPER

Western Herd, Kilmaley, Co Clare; 6.2%

An IPA to remind you why you first fell in love with the style, this offers the classic US combination of palate-scrubbing grapefruit bitterness and rich warming toffee set on a rounded, filling body.

CARRAIG DUBH

West Kerry, Ballyferriter, Co Kerry; 6%

A big porter from West Kerry, one of the country's smallest breweries, delivering luscious rich chocolate with a fun, fresh herbal character resulting from the unorthodox use of German hop varieties.

CASTAWAY

YellowBelly, Wexford, Co Wexford; 4.2%

At a time when breweries everywhere seem to be turning out *Berliner weisse*, this one really grabs the attention, with a strong, refreshing tartness balanced by massively juicy, and real, passion-fruit. No half measures here.

COALFACE

Carrig, Drumshanbo, Co Leitrim; 5.5%

Fruit-forward black IPAs are rare, but this fits the bill. The hops bring zesty citrus notes, enhanced by a sweet

chocolate flavour from the dark malt, resulting in the unusual marriage of warming satisfaction and refreshment.

CONNEMARA PALE

Independent, Carraroe, Co Galway; 6%

Loaded with more pine-and-citrus US hops than most Irish IPAs, this is dominated by a dry and sharp bitterness. The addition of rye to the grain bill adds an extra vegetal spice.

FRANCIS' BIG BANGIN' IPA

Rye River, Celbridge, Co Kildare; 7.1%

Despite the jokey name, this is a seriously good multi-award-winning US-style IPA, part of the brewery's McGargles range; pale gold, light-bodied and popping with citrus bitterness, tropical fruit and a slight savoury complexity.

GRAFFITI

Trouble, Kill, Co Kildare; 3.6%

The campaign for hop-forward low-strength beer in Ireland was hard fought and Graffiti was one of the first. It remains one of the best examples, with big pine and grapefruit notes in a smart little package.

GUINNESS FOREIGN EXTRA

Diageo, Dublin; 7.5%

A classic since records began, with vital statistics essentially unchanged since the 1820s. Balancing dry roast against smooth treacle and seasoned with a signature lactic sharpness, this stout is complex yet accessible.

HEAT SINK

Metalman, Waterford, Co Waterford; 4.9%

A playful take on Irish porter, incorporating smoked malt and cayenne pepper. The smoke is little more than seasoning, while the chilli starts mild but builds pleasantly on the chocolate malt flavour as it goes.

IRISH PALE ALE

Galway Hooker, Oranmore, Co Galway; 4.3%

Ireland's original hop-forward pale ale, taking its cue from Sierra Nevada (*see* page 206). You get a taste of traditional Irish crystal malt biscuit with the bright, fresh grapefruit notes of US hops.

KENTUCKY COMMON

Wicklow Wolf, Bray, Co Wicklow; 4.8%

It is unclear why Wicklow Wolf picked this obscure southern US style, but it's great that they did. Jet black in colour, it mixes the light caramel of brown ale with the refreshing dry roast of porter.

LAGER

Boyne Brewhouse, Drogheda, Co Meath; 4.8%

A lightly carbonated lager in the *Dortmunder* style, this full-bodied beer is given a bold fresh-mown-grass flavour from the Saaz hops used.

O'HARA'S LEANN FOLLÁIN

Carlow, Bagenalstown, Co Carlow; 6%

"Revered" is not too strong a word for how this export-strength beer is treated by Irish stout connoisseurs. The texture is weighty and warming, while the generous hopping gives it an invigorating old-fashioned bitterness.

PORTER

J W Sweetman, Dublin; 4.8%

A simple name belies an immensely complex beer, mixing rich chocolate, bright floral perfume and sharper tar and tobacco. Despite all this, it never tastes busy, staying smooth and satisfying to drink.

THE PREACHER

O Brother, Kilcoole, Co Wicklow; 4.6%

Badged as a session IPA by the brewery, this delivers an authentically US taste experience. Pine and lemon peel are delivered by the West Coast hops, with the Wicklow water giving it a chalky mineral base.

RAIN CZECH

Rascals, Rathcoole, Co Dublin; 5%

Jaw-dropping pilsner is rare outside of central Europe, but Rascals have managed to score one for Ireland with this summer seasonal loaded with Saaz hops for a sumptuous and soft damp-grass flavour.

SHANCO DUBH

Brehon, Carrickmacross, Co Monaghan; 7.7%

A bruiser of a strong porter, packing in all the signature flavours – bitter coffee, high-cocoa dark chocolate and unctuous caramel. This uncompromising jet-black beer rewards slow sipping and savouring.

SHERKIN LASS

West Cork, Baltimore, Co Cork; 4.4%

Originally a cask exclusive, though now available in bottles, this makes superb use of the natural conditioning process to create a soft effervescence with bright apricot notes. Best enjoyed at the source – Casey's Hotel in Baltimore.

SPAILPÍN SAISON

Killarney, Killarney, Co Kerry; 5.5%

A perfect rendition of Belgian *saison*, lightly crisp with a refreshing pepperiness. The name, pronounced "SPAL-peen", is the Irish-language equivalent of *saisonnaires*, the farmhands who gave *saison* its name.

SPRING BOCK

St Mel's, Longford, Co Longford; 5.6%

An authentic-tasting German-style lager, rich gold in colour with a full body and a flavour that perfectly integrates smooth honey malt with the peppery greenness of German hops.

WESTERN WARRIOR

Black Donkey, Ballinlough, Co Roscommon; 4.6%

This farmhouse brewery has a *saison* as its flagship beer and this lager is brewed to an identical recipe, but with a different yeast. The result is crisp and clean with a wheaty cereal wholesomeness.

WESTPORT EXTRA

Mescan, Westport, Co Mayo; 9.3%

The brewery is a little bit of Belgium in rural west Ireland, and this is its strongest beer to date, broadly a supercharged *tripel* that is dark gold in colour with enticing spices and tropical fruit.

WORLD'S END

Blacks, Kinsale, Co Cork; 8.5%

An Imperial stout for the winter months, this adds cocoa and vanilla pods to a smooth and rounded base. Sweet without being cloying, it makes for a superb dessert beer.

WRASSLERS XXXX

Porterhouse, Dublin; 5%

The biggest and boldest of Ireland's drinking stouts, holding a full hand of Galena hops for a bitter green punch on top of the leather-and-tobacco rich roast malt. Best when on draught, though a slightly different bottled edition is available.

BREWERIES TO WATCH

HOPE

Dublin

So far just limited-edition brews from head brewer Mark Nixon – ex of Trouble Brewing (*see* page 96) – but watch this space.

WHITE HAG

Ballymote, Co Sligo

Revolutionizing with US-inspired styles like session IPA **Little Fawn** (4.2%) and Imperial oatmeal stout **Black Boar** (10.2%), plus Irish *gruit* ale **Beann Gulban** (7.5%).

CAN'T-MISS BREWERIES

EIGHT DEGREES

Mitchelstown, Co Cork

Their mastery of hop-forward styles is beyond dispute, with **Full Irish IPA** (6%) expertly blending the citrus and tropical sides of the hop flavour equation. **Big River IPA** (5.3%) celebrates the brewers' Antipodean roots, piling in Australian hops for fresh and refreshing juicy melon and guava elements alongside assertive pine and herbs, while **Amber Ella** (5.8%) offers a chewy biscuit malt base and notes of peach, plum and tangerine. Watch also for frequent specials and one-offs.

GALWAY BAY

Galway, Co Galway

Highlights of this prolific brewery's range include the multi-award-winning **Of Foam and Fury** (8.5%), a perfect rendering of American double IPA; classic porter **Stormy Port** (4.8%); and a more recent addition to the line-up, **Harvest Altar** (5.6%), a sumptuously smooth autumnal brown ale. For something different, there is **Heathen** (3%), Ireland's only black *Berliner weisse* – a refreshingly tart palate-scrubber.

KINNEGAR

Rathmullan, Co Donegal

A tiny farmhouse brewery (rhymes with "vinegar") with big plans. **Rustbucket** (5.1%) rye ale is universally adored for its combination of peppery, grassy rye flavours with mouth-watering New World hop bitterness. A rarer black IPA version, **Black Bucket** (6.5%), adds liquorice and espresso notes to this, while the brewery explores the sour side of the spectrum with beers such as **Sour Grapes** (5%), lightly acidic and softly fruity, like a fine Sauvignon Blanc.

FRANCE

The French have always enjoyed beer, and indeed pre-First World War, France was awash in breweries, several thousand of them. The 20th century proved almost fatal to French brewing, however, and even at the start of this century one would have been hard pressed to predict the boom in *les bières artisanales* that has occurred since. The culture is still in its infancy, but having seen the rise of many hundred breweries across every *département* in the land, an observer would be equally imprudent to doubt that at least flashes of greatness shall surely follow.

3 MONTS

St-Sylvestre, St-Sylvestre-Cappel, Nord; 8.5%

From what was once viewed as the producer of many of France's finest ales, this flagship *bière de garde* is soft and slightly appley in aroma, full-bodied with dried-fruit and slight vinous flavours, finishing off-dry and warming.

ALPINE

Galibier, Valloire, Savoie; 4.8%

From the highest-altitude brewery in France comes this US-style pale ale with the hop emphasis on aroma rather than bitterness, hints of white wine in the aroma and tropical-fruit flavours defining its dry and lingering nature.

AMÈRE NOIRE

L'Agrivoise, Saint Agrève, Ardèche; 6.5%

A black IPA from a brewery noted for its well-hopped ales, this has an aroma of well-kilned malt and singed wood mixed with liquorice and pine, and a powerful, grassy bitterness that finishes quite dry.

BARBE BLEUE

Mélusine, Chambretaud, Vendée; 7%

A dark brown ale seasoned with aniseed and alchemilla, the latter a herb sometimes used in tea. Almost stout-like, it has a roasty, vanilla-ish aroma and flavours of coffee and liquorice with hints of banana.

BARRICADE RAMPONNEAU

La Canaille, Sail-sous-Couzan, Loire; 6%

From a brewery housed in a former mineral water plant comes this brown ale made with smoked malt and hot peppers, resulting in a nuanced smokiness, roasted maltiness and a note of spicy heat that balances everything out.

BIÈRE DE BRIE BLANCHE

Rabourdin, Courpalay, Seine-et-Marne; 4.5%

Named after the region renowned for its famed cheese, this farmhouse brewery beer demonstrates wonderfully the French take on the Belgian-style wheat beer, with exquisite balance between malt, hops and spice, and a slight sweetness in the aftertaste.

BIÈRE DE GARDE

ArtMalté, Annecy, Haute-Savoie; 6.5%

The product of a young female brewer respectful of traditional styles, this *bière de garde* is fermented with a *saison* yeast and maturated for eight weeks, delivering peppery flavours with fudge and coffee notes in the finish.

BIÈRE DES SANS CULOTTES

La Choulette, Hordain, Nord; 7%

So called in recognition of the heroes of the French Revolution, this golden *bière de garde* has a yeasty, spicy aroma with tones of honey and fruit, and a caramelly malt body layered with notes of brown spice and dried fruit.

BITTER

Joli Rouge, Canals, Tarn-et-Garonne; 5.5%

Hopped with an Alsatian hop called Barbe Rouge, this malt-driven French interpretation of the English bitter has a citrusy nose with hints of berries and a quenching body with grassy bitterness.

BM SIGNATURE

Rouget de Lisle, Bletterans, Jura; 11%

A barrel-aged Imperial stout that has cherries added three months prior to bottling, giving it a vinous character and flavours of chocolate and cherry. From a pioneering brewery that boasts one of the top brewery barrel rooms in France.

BORIS GOUDENOV

Corrézienne, Curemonte, Corrèze; 10.5%

An Imperial stout with a powerful toasted malt aroma boasting notes of dried fruits, with a full and balanced body offering elements of coffee, wood, dark chocolate and candied fruit balanced by floral hoppiness.

CABÉO'LUNE

de la Pleine Lune, Chabeuil, Drôme; 5.2%

Brewed entirely from barley grown and malted locally, this light bitter has an aroma that emphasizes the grains used, along with light citrusy notes and a body that does the same but becomes bitter as it progresses.

ICONIC BREWERY

THIRIEZ

Esquelbecq, Nord

For 20 years a leader in French *bière artisanale*, this brewery near Cassel is best known for its Kent Bramling Cross-hopped *saison* **Etoile du Nord** (5.5%). Other noteworthy beers include the red wine barrel-conditioned, Flemish-style **Vieille Brune** (5.8%); a revivalist French "table beer" created with the US brewery Jester King **Petite Princesse** (2.9%); **Dalva** (8.5%), a complex and nuanced double IPA with tropical-fruit and nutty notes; and **Ambrée d'Esquelbecq** (5.8%), a *bière de garde* boasting a fine balance between hops and caramelly malt.

CERVOISE LANCELOT

Lancelot, Le Roc-Saint-André, Morbihan; 6%

First brewed in 1990, this light amber ale is said to be in an ancient Gauloise style, seasoned with seven herbs, one of which is hops, to create a spicy–herbal palate with a honey-ish aroma and toasted-malt backdrop.

CHARLY'S BEER

Gilbert's, Rabastens, Tarn; 9.1%

A wonderful barley wine with aromas of candy cane and candied fruit, and a balanced and mouth-coating body with candied-orange and tangerine notes, powerful bitterness and caramelly malt, all leading to a long and hoppy finish.

LA CHIMÈRE DE CENDRE

L'Antre de l'Échoppe, Narbonne, Aude; 4.8%

An atypical stout in the French style, with powerful roasted malt aromas and flavours, some ashy dryness and complex hoppiness from Alsatian Triskel, Strisselspalt and Aramis hops.

CUVÉE DES JONQUILLES

Au Baron, Gussignies, Nord; 7%

From a brewery–restaurant on the Belgian border comes this *bière de garde* that blurs the line between its style and *saison*, with a refreshing, sparkling character, balanced bitterness and dry finish.

DUCHESSE DE LORRAINE

Les Brasseurs de Lorraine, Pont-à-Mousson, Meurthe-et-Moselle; 5.5%

A mahogany ale made with smoked malt and sassafras, with a fruity and spicy aroma, a slight sourness and oaky aspects to the body and a bright, refreshing effervescence.

EAU DE PIERRE

Entre 2 Mondes, Mouthier-Haute-Pierre, Doubs; 6.2%

A copper ale made from seven malts, hazy with a grassy nose, rich body and floral, well-balanced flavour leading to a more bitter finish with spicy notes.

L'EXILÉE

L'Excuse, Mauzevin, Hautes-Pyrénées; 6.5%

From a youthful and promising brewery, this amber ale is seasoned with cardamom and star anise for an aroma and flavour that are spicy but well balanced with malt and hops, having a firm but gentle bitterness and dry finish.

EXTRA STOUT

Les 3 Loups, Trélou-sur-Marne, Aisne; 6.9%

A deceptively approachable strong stout with a powerful aroma of chocolate and roasted malt and a creamy body balancing bitterness with hints of cocoa and spice.

FLEUR DE MONTREUIL

La Montreuilloise, Montreuil, Paris; 5–5.5%

A summer beer produced by a cooperative teaching brewery that emphasizes a local, organic approach. Flavoured with elderflowers, this is a biscuity ale with slight acidity and fruity, blackcurrant notes.

FRAMBRUNETTE

La Barbaude, Nîmes, Gard; 5.4–5.7%

Infused with local strawberries, this stout boasts an aroma that is unsurprisingly like gourmet chocolate-covered strawberries, although the body tends more to chocolate and floral blackberry flavours with a bitter finish.

GAILLARDE BRUNE

La Gaillarde, Gignac, Hérault; 9%

A strong and deep brown ale aged on oak chips, this has a chocolaty, spicy dried-fruit aroma and a taste to match, with dark fruits dominant and mocha, spicy vanilla and liquorice in support.

CAN'T-MISS
BREWERIES

LA DÉBAUCHE

Angoulême, Charente

The brewery that has become a reference point for others wishing to create strong dark ales or barrel-aged beers in France, characterized by **Nevermore** (9.5%), an intense and full-bodied Imperial stout with strong notes of chocolate and vanilla, and **Cognac Barrel** (9.5%), a self-describing ale boasting flavours of candied fruit and raisins. More experimental beers include **Amorena** (14%), an Imperial stout flavoured with almond paste and Amarena cherries and then barrel-conditioned on a bed of either cherries or raspberries.

DES GARRIGUES

Sommières, Gard

Pioneer of ultra-hoppy beers in the land of wine, boasting brands like **La Frappadingue** (7.5%), with powerful bitterness and citrus notes on a caramelly malt base, and **P'tite Frapp'** (3.8%), a light but still amply hopped variation. Other beers include the seasonal barley wine **Sacré Grôle** (12.6%); **La Ribouldingue** (4.5%), a wheat ale seasoned with local herbs; **La Belle en Goguette** (6%), a spicy wheat pale ale; and **La Bière du Coing** (5.5%), a tangy seasonal ale flavoured with quince.

GOSE'ILLA

Sulauze, Miramas, Bouches-du-Rhône; 5%

From a farmhouse brewery with a biodynamic approach to farming and brewing comes this refreshing take on the *gose* style, complete with minerally aromas and a suitably tart and refreshing character.

GRÄTZER

du Haut Buëch, Lus-la-Croix-Haute, Drôme; 3.4%

A specialist in obscure beer styles, brewer David Desmars enjoys developing wheat beers in particular, as with this hazy, light gold *grätzer* with smoked-meat aromas and a dry, highly effervescent and tangy character.

HOME OUTLAND

Fontenay-sous-Bois, Paris; 5.4%

Brewed on the outskirts of Paris, this US-style pale ale is bright gold with an aroma of lemon, mandarin and hints of cooked fruit and a dry, firm bitterness in the body.

HOUBLONNÉE À CRU

de la Plaine, Marseille, Bouches-du-Rhône; 5.5%

An organic pale ale dry-hopped to a full and floral aroma of white flowers and peach, with a refreshing and herbal bitterness holding flavours of tropical fruit and wild flowers.

INDAR JOKO

Etxeko Bob's Beer, Hasparren, Pyrénées-Atlantiques; 4.5%

A deep black dry stout in the Irish style produced by an English brewer in the Basque part of France, with notes of coffee and a gentle bitterness leading to a quaffably dry finish.

INSOMNUIT

La Rente Rouge, Chargey-lès-Gray, Haute-Saône; 7%

An annual release aged six months in Nuits-St-Georges wine barrels, emerging with a predictably winey character, an earthy, tobacco-ish aroma and notes of red fruit and oak in the creamy and rich body.

IPA

Parisis, Épinay-sous-Sénart, Essonne; 6.2%

A US-style IPA brewed in the Île-de-France region near Paris, this has an intense aroma of citrus, peach and honey and a rich malty–grainy flavour, with significant bitterness and hints of honey. The lingering finish is dry and fruity–bitter.

CAN'T-MISS BREWERIES
● ● ● ● ● ● ● ● ● ● ● ● ● ● ●

DU MONT SALÈVE

Neydens, Haute-Savoie

An impressive range of styles and sometimes audacious experiments are turned out by this brewery near the Swiss border. **Tsarine** (13%) is a powerful Imperial stout with espresso notes and a spicy bitterness in the finish; **Mademoiselle Aramis** (6%) is an IPA that highlights the Alsatian hop of its name alongside orange, pineapple and peach tones; **Tourbée** (5.5%) is a quaffable smoked malt ale with flavours of dark fruit and liquorice; and **Berliner Weisse** (3.3%) is tangy, wheaty and lemony.

SAINT GERMAIN

Aix-Noulette, Pas-de-Calais

A countryside brewery near Arras emphasizing the use of local hops and barley in their "Page 24"-labelled beers, such as **Réserve Hildegarde Blonde** (5.9%), a hoppy blond with sublime balance. Other terroir-focused efforts include **La Rhub'IPA** (6.9%), using local rhubarb to produce a floral, tangy and fruity flavour, while among the more limited-run brands are **Imperial Stout Whisky Barrel** (9.5%), boasting hoppiness in harmony with whisky and wood notes, and **Sour Ale** (4.9%), which displays a keen acidity on a sweet citrus-accented malty base.

CAN'T-MISS BREWERY

- - - - - - - - - - - - - -

DE LA VALLÉE DU GIFFRE

Verchaix, Haute-Savoie

A young brewery with a wide range of styles and ongoing experiments. Their smoked malt beer, **La Petite Fumée** (4.8%), offers strong elements of roast and chimney, while the soft double IPA **Alt Sept 65** (8.3%) brings forth a resinous and lasting bitterness, and **La Rioule** (5.8%) is a single-hopped IPA that changes hop regularly – the version made with Alsatian Mistral hops was breathtaking. Also of note is the highly aromatic **Du Bout du Monde** (4.7%), a *saison* refermented with *Brettanomyces*.

IPA CITRA GALACTIQUE

du Grand Paris, St Denis, Seine-Saint-Denis; 6.5%

The result of a "union Franco–Américaine", this is a startling expression of the Citra hop, with a big mix of citrus, pine and tropical fruit on the nose and a dry and bitter body with lasting fruitiness.

JENLAIN AMBRÉE

Duyck, Jenlain, Nord; 7.5%

Widely regarded as an iconic *bière de garde*, this copper ale has a caramel and toasted bread body with earthy bitterness and gentle nutty tones. So successful in the 1990s that the brand changed from the family name Duyck to Jenlain.

KERZU

An Alarc'h, La Feuillée, Finistère; 7%

A seasonal Breton Imperial stout – the name means December in the Breton language – that is thick, rich, creamy and somewhat sweet, with notes of strong coffee and smoky wood.

MONGY TRIPLE

Cambier, Croix, Nord; 8%

From the brewery's line dedicated to the northern French engineer Alfred Mongy, this complex *tripel* has a fruity, spicy grain nose and a near-perfect balance of crisp maltiness, grassy bitterness and spicy fruitiness with just a hint of juniper.

NOIRE

Ninkasi, Tarare, Rhône; 6.6%

A revival of a 19th-century city beer style known as noire de Lyon, this sweet dark ale is similar to a porter, with caramel, coffee, fig, chocolate and toasted breadcrumb aromas and flavours, and a light bitterness.

PLANCHE ODE À LA VIE

La Franche, La Ferté, Jura; 7%

This hazy copper-gold ale is aged in barrels that were previously used for Jura's famous *vin jaune*, emerging with a powerfully vinous aroma and a tart and spicy body filled with yellow fruit, white wine and walnut.

RODÉO +

Bendorf, Strasbourg, Bas-Rhin; 10%

Made with apricot juice and aged in oak barrels for three months, this malty *tripel*-style ale combines the taste of apricot nectar with a light bitterness and leafy and fruity flavours from the local Triskel hops, finishing with a gentle sweetness.

SALAMANDRA

de l'Être, Paris, Paris; 6.5%

Located near the Gare de l'Est, this brewery brings "green" brewing to the French capital with, among other brands, this aromatically fruity, organic malt *saison* with spicy notes in the nose, a firm maltiness and drying bitterness on the finish.

SANGUINE

Iron, Montauban, Tarn-et-Garonne; 4.5–5%

From one of France's youngest and most promising brewers, David Garrigues, comes this hibiscus-flavoured wheat beer with an intense red hue, slightly lactic aromas of red berry and citrus and a tart, fruity and floral body.

BREWERY TO WATCH

PERLE

Strasbourg, Bas-Rhin

After years of brewing abroad, Christian Artzner returned to France to revive the 19th-century Perle brand with beers like the herbaceous, Strisselspalt-hopped **Perle Blonde** (5.4%) alongside grape ale **La Perle dans les Vignes** (7.7%) and the US-style **IPA** (6.6%).

SEIGLÉE

La Caussenarde, Saint-Beaulize, Aveyron; 6%

A unique ale made from barley both grown and malted on the farm where it is brewed, grainy with considerable spiciness, fruity notes and a long and lingering hop bitterness.

SYLVIE'CIOUS

Le Paradis, Blaiville-sur-l'Eau, Meurthe-et-Moselle; 5.5%

A "session-strength" version of the brewery's P'tite Sylvie IPA, this has a fragrant and fruity citrus aroma and sweetish, malty front that starts fruity but dries to a refreshing, hoppy finish.

TRIPLE

d'Orgemont, Sommepy-Tahure, Marne; 8.5%

In a brewery located not far from the Champagne capital of Reims, a different sort of golden elixir is produced, strongly Belgian influenced with spicy, peppery tones on a toasty, yellow, fruity malt base.

TROBAIRITZ

de Quercorb, Puivert, Aude; 6%

Brewed in the foothills of the Pyrenees, this *saison*-style blond ale boasts an appealing grassy aroma and a pale malt-driven palate with notes of citrus fruit and spice and a refreshing, herbal hop finish.

VOLCELEST ÉLEVÉE EN BARRIQUE

de la Vallée de Chevreuse, Bonnelles, Yvelines; 9.5%

Aged three months in French oak, this Imperial stout is aromatic with chocolate and blackberry notes and boasts fruity chocolate flavours in the body, but finishes dry and reminiscent of a spiced coffee.

LUXEMBOURG

In contrast to its more prolific neighbours, craft beer culture is developing slowly in the "lux" portion of the Benelux, but some small progress is nonetheless being made.

BLACK WIDOW

Stuff, Stoinsel; 6.5%

Created by two young brewers with arguably the country's first real new wave craft brewery, this lightweight, very drinkable porter has blackcurrant notes and hints of bitter chocolate and dried fruit that veer it toward a black IPA.

IPA

Simon, Wiltz; 5%

The first attempt by a Luxembourg "major" at something approaching craft is a quaffable, gently bitter and citrusy pale ale that is deliberately restrained to break a nation gently into a global phenomenon for which it may not quite be ready.

SATELLITE

Grand, Luxembourg City; 4.9%

Previously known as Capital City, the expat Kiwi owner was brewing at Simon (see left), but is switching to his own installation in 2017 to create his easy-drinking range, which includes this hoppy, fruity and citrusy golden-blond session IPA.

THE NETHERLANDS

Arguably no European beer scene has improved as remarkably over the past 10–15 years as has that of the Netherlands. From what was once a landscape dominated utterly by a small cabal of mighty breweries has emerged one of the Continent's most vibrant and creative craft beer markets.

58 HANDLANGER

Kompaan, The Hague, South Holland; 8.2%

An ultra-dry, slightly grassy triple-hopped golden-blond Imperial IPA with a fresh hop taste, medium bitter finish and an easy, quaffable drinking quality belying its strength.

400 VOLT VANILLE

Eindhoven, Eindhoven, North Brabant; 10%

This heavyweight Imperial stout has the inky black, viscous appearance of crude oil and is infused with Madagascar bourbon vanilla, which gives a sweet edge to balance the strong alcohol and bitter finish.

1818

Maallust, Veenhuizen, Drenthe; 10%

Sold as a limited edition in 75cl bottles, this full-bodied almost stout-like winter barley wine has hints of raisin, cocoa, aniseed and banana that keep the waves of warming alcohol in check.

AMSTERDAM PALE ALE

Amsterdam Brewboys, nomadic; 5.2%

Despite the geographically precise name, these brewers use various locations to brew hop-forward beers such as this crisp, floral and fruity US-hopped amber pale ale, which is dry-hopped to give a lingering bitter finish.

ARMADA

Pelgrim, Rotterdam, South Holland;
11%

Based in Rotterdam's historic
Delfshaven district, this brewer makes
consistently reliable ales that include
this complex, full-bodied Imperial stout
with notes of dried fruit, chocolate and
cocoa and a bitter finish. Also sold in
barrel-aged versions.

BEA

Kaapse, Rotterdam, South Holland;
6.5%

Four-hopped and double dry-hopped
for extra aroma and bitterness, this
full-bodied black rye IPA is a melting
pot with hints of cocoa, coffee, roasted
malt and citrus fruit, and a strongly
bitter finish.

BIG BLACK BEAVER

Pontus, nomadic; 7.6%

This Amsterdam-based brewer
creates beers with an assured touch
at De Naeckte Brouwers in nearby
Amstelveen (see page 117), in this
case a richly rounded export stout with
alcohol to the fore balanced by sweeter
chocolate/cocoa notes.

BLACK BIRD

Brouwpact, nomadic; 7.4%

The brewer Brouwpact uses brewery-
for-hire Loonbrouwerij in Cothen to
make beers such as this balanced,
dark and bitter black IPA, with rich
roasted-malt and coffee flavours giving
it porter-ish qualities.

BROEDERLIEFDE

De Moersleutel, Heiloo, North Holland;
8%

New arrivals on the Dutch beer scene
have made an instant impression with
their early offerings, including this
delightfully rich, bitter and superbly
balanced golden-blond double IPA.

BRONSTIG

Eem, Amersfoort, Utrecht; 6.5%

A superior example of an autumnal
Dutch *bock*, this chestnut-brown ale
has a bittersweet balance of caramel
and burned malt boosted by light
Centennial hopping. This formerly
nomadic brewer established his own
self-built brewery in 2017.

BRUTUS

Maximus, Utrecht; 6%

A superb and deeply appealing, rich,
fruity–hoppy US-style amber lager that

is practically an IPA, with malty notes upfront and an intensely bitter finish, brewed with European hops for a nod toward subtlety.

CALF

LOC, Tilburg, North Brabant; 9.5%

A malty and bitter Imperial milk porter with added everything – espresso beans lending an intense coffee flavour, and Madagascar vanilla pods and cocoa nibs providing depth and sweetness to balance the bitter finish.

CEAUX CANE

Ceaux, nomadic; 10.5%

Created by an Utrecht-based brewer using various locations, "Cocaine" is a warming, strong amber Imperial IPA with added sugar cane and smoked peppers to create a lightly bittersweet and very smoky brew, not unlike a German *rauchbier* on steroids.

DE RUMOERIGE ROODBORST

Bird, nomadic; 5.8%

A bright and crisp, copper-coloured US-style amber ale containing malted rye with hints of tropical fruits and a little caramel balancing the light bitterness. Brewed at Jopen (*see* page 116) by this Amsterdam-based outfit.

DIRTY KATARINA

Two Chefs, Amsterdam, North Holland; 10.5%

Two formerly nomadic brewers now have their own installation with which to make their range of impressive beers, including this strong, rounded and bitter-finishing Imperial stout that hides its strength well.

DOERAK

Van Moll, Eindhoven, North Brabant; 6.5%

A city-centre brewpub making a wide variety of usually excellent beers, including this assertive, full-bodied, golden-blond IPA that balances a basket of tropical- and citrus-fruit flavours with a bitter finish.

EN GARDE!

Oersoep, Nijmegen, Gelderland; 6.5%

This lovely, light, dry, refreshing and (variously) single-hopped and fruity *saison* comes from a brewery known for using innovative fermentation to make a reliably great range of cutting-edge beers.

EXTRA STOUT

Praght, Dronten, Flevoland; 8%

Also seen as Stout Weesje Extra Stout, this lovely dark ale has background raspberry aromas, bittersweet chocolate and roasted malt in the body and a dry bitter finish.

GAJES

Bruut, nomadic; 8%

Brewed at Praght by two Amsterdam-based friends, this golden-blond abbey-style *tripel* has fruity notes and a floral perfumed sweetness balanced by gentle bitterness, and is one of the finer Dutch examples of its class.

GREEN CAP

Butcher's Tears, Amsterdam, North Holland; 6%

Brewed by a Swedish expat, this bitter and flowery golden-blond pale ale has a smooth, dry finish and restrained earthiness from the use of Eastern European rather than trendier US hops.

HEER VAN GRAMSBERGEN

Mommeriete, Gramsbergen, Overijssel; 12%

A beer that has evolved over time from a barley wine into a full-bodied dark Imperial stout, with dominant notes of roasted malt, coffee and chocolate, and background hints of vanilla.

HOP ART

VandeStreek, nomadic; 5%

These two talented Utrecht-based brothers brew their beers mainly at nearby De Leckere, including this lightly citrusy, dry and refreshing blond session-style IPA.

HOPFEN WEISSE

Oldskool, nomadic; 8.2%

An Eindhoven-based brewer making beers at various locations in German and British styles, including this hoppy amber *dunkelweizen* with strong and sweetish banana overtones kept in check by bitter single-hopping in changing varieties.

ICONIC BREWERY

DE MOLEN

Bodegraven, South Holland

A powerhouse brewery that effectively began the Dutch craft beer revolution and remains one of its leading pioneers. Known for its hundreds of experimental special releases as well as hard-hitting Imperial stouts, the permanent range includes a full-bodied amber IPA **Vuur & Vlam** (6.2%); the balanced and easily accessible **Hel & Verdoemenis** (10%) Imperial stout; a more complex Imperial porter **Tsarina Esra** (11%), which is even better in its oak-aged Reserva form; and the rich, chewy and powerful **Bommen & Granaten** (15.2%) barley wine.

HOUTGERIJPTE ROOK DUBBELBOCK

Duits & Lauret, Everdingen, Utrecht; 7.5%

This subtly smoked, wood-aged dark *bock* has hints of dried fruit and a dryly bitter finish, plus peaty notes throughout, like a diluted Islay malt. One for fireside chats on long winter evenings.

IMPERIAL OATMEAL STOUT

Oproer, Utrecht; 9.5%

From a brewery created by the merger of Ruig and Rooie Dop, this rich bittersweet stout is a heady mix of roasted-malt, chocolate, oats and prune flavours that give way to a light bitterness in the finish.

IPA

Lowlander, nomadic; 6%

This Amsterdam-based brewer makes beers at Jopen (*see* page 116), using his roots designing botanicals at a gin distillery to create unusually spiced ales, such as this refreshingly citrusy, hoppy and bitter amber IPA with notes of coriander, white tea and spice.

IPA

Troost, Amsterdam, North Holland; 6.5%

This dry, bitter and fruity US-hopped golden-amber ale has improved greatly since its 2013 launch, and comes from a growing empire of brewpubs that currently numbers two in Amsterdam with a planned third in Utrecht.

JOLLY ROGER

Raven Bone Hill, nomadic; 6.6%

Three brewers based in Maassluis but making beers at Ramses in North Brabant, including this eminently quaffable black IPA-meets-porter, with notes of coffee and chocolate and a touch of chilli and vanilla.

KOUD VUUR

Bax, Groningen; 6.3%

A fruity, bitter, dry-edged and impenetrably black smoked porter given depth and a sweet edge by malted oats, with plentiful hints of bonfire, but remaining balanced and subtle enough not to frighten the smoke-averse.

LA TRAPPE QUADRUPEL

Koningshoeven, Berkel-Enschot, North Brabant; 10%

This amber barley wine has banana esters that are characteristic of this Trappist abbey's output, but avoids sweetness and improves with cellaring, as does its deeper and richer Oak Aged sister.

MESTREECHS AAJT

Gulpener, Gulpen, Limburg; 3.5%

A sweet-and-sour, wood-aged ale in the style of a Belgian old brown with a richness belying its slight strength. Mainly available only in the Maastricht area, although an unsweetened and stronger version is sold in the USA.

CAN'T-MISS BREWERIES

BRONCKHORSTER

Rha, Gelderland

Formerly known as Rodenburg, this expat British brewer creates his beers with across-the-board assuredness. Standouts include the beautifully rounded and fruity smoked *altbier* **ALTernative** 6.5%); **Hoptimist** (9.5%), a spicy, fruity and seductive double IPA; the characterful and dark **Nightporter** (8%), with bitter hints of coffee and dark chocolate; and Nightporter's richer, darker, spicier and altogether bossier Imperial, evening-ending sister **Midnight Porter** (11%).

HET UILTJE

Haarlem, North Holland

This young brewer with a growing international reputation makes experimental, occasionally uncompromising, but usually great beers, including the fruity, quaffable summer session IPA **FF Lekker Met Je Bek In Het Zonnetje** (3.6%); the easy-drinking black IPA **Bosuil** (6%),

which balances hoppy bitterness with coffee and cocoa tones; the fresh and outstandingly bitter, five-hopped and dry-hopped **Big Fat 5 Double IPA** (8%); and the barrel-aged, take-no-prisoners heavyweight Imperial stout **Meneer de Uil** (~12%).

KEES

Middelburg, Zeeland

The brewer responsible for building Emelisse's (*see* page 119) global reputation, now making great beer in various styles at his own self-titled brewery. Standouts include refreshing golden-blond **Pale ale Citra** (4.6%), with grassy hop notes; fruity, bitter and full-bodied **Farmhouse IPA** (6.5%); rich, malty **Export Porter 1750** (10.5%) that packs a punch and tastes barrel-aged but isn't; and the whisky malt **Peated Imperial Stout** (11%), the smokiness of which is balanced by dark chocolate and prune sweetness.

RAMSES

Wagenberg, North Brabant

The eponymous brewer uses his experience in US brewing to create a range of consistently great single-hopped ales, usually with dry-hopping involved. Examples include the dark, fruity and attractive **Mamba Porter** (6.2%) using Galena hops; dark amber, Centennial-infused **Den Dorstige Tijger** (6%) IPA with fruity aspects and an intensely bitter finish; and cocoa-tinged **Shire Stout** (8.9%), which adds British Pilgrim hops and is sometimes sold as the wood-aged **Met Hout**.

MILK STOUT

Prael, Amsterdam, North Holland; 4.9%

This delightful black milk stout has cocoa overtones, a burned caramel edge, hints of coconut macaroon and a sharpness coming from the added lactose to bring balance to all the sweetish elements.

MOOIE NEL IPA

Jopen, Haarlem, North Holland; 6.5%

This slightly hazy, golden-blond and award-winning ale is aromatic, fruity and full-bodied with a subtle bitter finish. Sold internationally as North Sea IPA, it is considered by some as the flagship "Dutch IPA".

MORSPORTER

Leidsch, Leiden, South Holland; 6.1%

With chocolaty cocoa and coffee notes to the fore, backed by raisins, dark fruit and a bitter finish, this highly accomplished, pitch-black porter is named after an old city gate dating from 1669.

NIEUW LIGT GRAND CRU

Hemel, Nijmegen, Gelderland; 12%

This cellared version of the already excellent Nieuw Ligt, from a craft pioneer with 30 years of history, is a warming and rounded barley wine with a bitter astringency that balances both alcohol and sweetness.

NOT TOTALLY BLACK IPA

Hilldevils, nomadic; 6.7%

A dry black IPA with roasted malt in the nose and a tart fruity finish, created by brewers from the North Brabant village of Wouwse Plantage who make beers at the Pimplemeesch brewery in Chaam.

QUADRUPEL POORTER

Kleiburg, Amsterdam, North Holland; 10.7%

This intense and lovely deep black porter offers a witches' brew of chocolate, coffee and raisins, and comes from talented formerly nomadic newcomers with their own brewery since early 2017.

ROOK IN DE KACHEL

Gulzige Gans, Coevorden, Drenthe; 10%

From a very small house brewery, this rich, strong and hazy dark amber winter ale uses smoked malt to create a sharp, peaty, smoky bitterness that perfectly balances the nutty notes and the sugary sweetness.

SAENSE KRACHT

Breugem, Zaandijk, North Holland; 11%

A dark ruby, full-bodied, rich and sweetish but well-balanced barley wine with a mildly bitter finish. Its occasional limited-edition sister, Saense Kracht Houtgerijpt, is aged with aromatic South American Palo Santo wood.

SAISON

Schans, Uithoorn, North Holland; 7%

An enigmatic brewer whose beers are sometimes hard to find but always worth the effort, including this delightful, golden-blond farmhouse *saison* that balances banana, peach and touches of clove with a bitter, almost peppery finish.

SCHÔON MÈDJE

KraftBier, Tilburg, North Brabant; 6.2%

An aromatic, hazy, golden-blond "white IPA" wheat ale that uses both German and US hops to create a blend of citrusy and herbal flavours with a strongly bitter finish.

SHAKTI

Walhalla, nomadic; 8.8%

A new Amsterdam-based brewer making beer at various locations. The label range is still developing but includes this dryly bitter, golden double IPA, with a floral and fruity mixed bag of aromas coming from a cocktail of US hops.

SHIPA

De Naeckte, Amstelveen, North Holland; 6.8%

Ever-changing hop varieties result in minor taste fluctuations in this golden-blond single-hopped IPA, but the quality is seldom less than great and is occasionally spectacular, as in the case of the Sorachi Ace version.

SMOKEY THE BARRACUDA

Kromme Haring, Utrecht; 7.5%

This lovely rich and rounded smoked porter balances earthy peat, tar and liquorice notes with a slight chocolate sweetness. Brewed by a formerly nomadic American–Dutch team now at their own brewpub.

SOOTY OTTER

Neobosski, nomadic; 8.5%

Made by a pair of Utrecht-based brewers at nearby Loonbrouwerij, this tangy black IPA has hints of black treacle but avoids sweetness, while adding flavours of roasted malt and liquorice that edge it toward a stout or porter.

STORMBOCK

Texels, Oudeschild, North Holland; 10%

A heavy-hitting, ruby-brown winter barley wine from one of the country's largest craft breweries, with dark fruit, burned sugar and a slight but not intrusive caramel sweetness balanced by a lightly bittersweet finish.

BREWERIES TO WATCH

NEVEL

Nijmegen, Gelderland

Young brewers making low-alcohol experimental ales under the Katjelam brand such as the floral–spicy, slightly sour *saison* **Pepper Rebellion** (5.4%), the malty, chocolaty **London Porter** (4%) and the subtly sour **Bloei** (5%) *Berliner weisse*.

TOMMIE SJEF WILD ALES

Den Helder, North Holland

Outstanding young brewer cellar-ageing to produce sharp, tart ales such as the fruit-heavy **Cassis-Braam** (5%), *gueuze*-like **Cuvée** (5%) and citrusy blond **Sici** (5%).

STOUT + MOEDIG

7 Deugden, Amsterdam, North Holland; 7%

This dry and lightly bitter dark stout is made using three types of malt, and comes from a brewer known for adding unusual herbs, although in this case the adjunct is merely coffee.

STRUIS

I J [partnership with Duvel Moortgat], Amsterdam, North Holland; 9%

One of the early creations from Amsterdam's longest-running craft brewery, this pleasing, dark brown, full-bodied and lightly bittersweet English-style barley wine has notes of caramel and rich dark fruit with hints of chocolate.

TANKARD

Frontaal, Breda, North Brabant; 3.9%

This highly accomplished and quaffable light golden-blond US-style session ale uses four American hop varieties to create a strongly aromatic, hop-forward and bitter ale that doesn't taste as light as it is.

THAI THAI

Oedipus, Amsterdam, North Holland; 8%

From a quartet of brewers with a growing reputation for bold, experimental beers, such as this Belgian-style *tripel* given a Thai-spiced edge by added galangal, lemongrass, chilli and coriander, balanced by generous hopping.

US HEIT ELFSTEDENBIER

De Friese, Bolsward, Friesland; 8%

A dark, quaffable and strong Belgian brown ale with a bittersweet balance of malt, nuts and fruit and warming tones in the background, brewed for the winter months by an early pioneer of Dutch craft brewing.

VREDESGIJT

De Natte Gijt, Weert, Limburg; 6.8%

A hazy gold smoked rye IPA with a subtle smokiness that doesn't overpower fruity hoppy notes or the lingering bitter finish, created by two talented brewing brothers with a taste for hop-forward ales.

WATERGEUS

Vandenbroek, Midwolde, Groningen; 5–7%

This softly sour and refreshing blond *gueuze*-style beer is 100% spontaneously fermented with wild yeast, then oak-aged, adding a fruity counterpoint to the sourness. Hard to find, but highly recommended.

WHITE LABEL SERIES

Emelisse, Kamperland, Zeeland; ABV varies, usually 11%

An ever-changing range of usually barrel-aged Imperial stouts, seldom less than world class, created by a once-iconic brewery currently in a state of flux following the departure of its star brewers.

XTREME BALTIC COFFEE CHOCO MOCCA PORTER

Klein Duimpje, Hillegom, South Holland; 9%

The name signals a beer trying too hard to be all things at once, but this Baltic porter largely succeeds and is subtler than expected, despite having coffee and cocoa in abundance.

ZUNDERT

Kievit, Zundert, North Brabant; 8%

The single offering from the second Trappist brewery in the Netherlands is a richly rounded amber ale that has gained in confidence since its 2013 origins, with elements of toffee in the nose and taste, and a bittersweet balancing finish.

ZUSTER AGATHA

Muifel, Oss, North Brabant; 10%

This ruby-brown barley wine hints at being an abbey-style *quadrupel* with no ecclesiastical connections, and has background notes of sour cherry and dark fruit combined with a light bitterness to keep its caramel sweetness in check.

ZWARTE SNORRE

Berghoeve, Den Ham, Overijssel; 11%

This heavy-hitting darkly black Imperial stout with a handsomely dark brown foam is brewed with five malts to create an intriguingly complex blend of dark fruit and liquorice with a warming alcoholic glow in the finish.

ITALY

In its early days, the Italian craft beer scene was characterized by ornate bottles at elevated prices, sometimes dodgy consistency and a peculiar fascination with chestnut beers. As the first decade of the 21st century gave way to the second, however, Italian brewers uniformly upped their game, improving standards of quality, combining seasonings in the most sublime and imaginative ways and developing a beer style all their own, borrowed from the country's long history of wine production.

LA 5

L'Olmaia, Montepulciano, Tuscany; 5.5%

Moreno Ercolani is always in search of quaffability and this golden ale is testament to that quest, with a fragrant aroma and a light, malty sweetness well balanced by hops.

10 E LODE

Opperbacco, Notaresco, Abruzzo; 10%

Inspired by Belgian strong and dark ales, this is a powerful, lavish masterpiece, rich with vinous, spicy aromas and a smooth and balanced flavour completed by a warming, fruity–chocolaty finish.

A.KOLSCH

Borderline, Buttrio, Friuli-Venezia Giulia; 4.8%

From a publican-turned-brewer comes this successful take on a *kölsch*-style beer brewed with US hops. Fragrant, floral, bready and dry.

AMERICAN IPA

Canediguerra, Alessandria, Piedmont; 6.7%

Brewer Alessio Gatti worked for Toccalmatto (*see* page 128) and Brewfist (*see* page 127) before landing at Canediguerra, where his US-style IPA has an intriguing piney, balsamic note and a sharply citrusy, bitter finish.

AMERICAN MAGUT

Lambrate, Milan, Lombardy; 5%

The oldest brewpub in Milan has expanded its portfolio in recent years, including this pilsner dry-hopped with US hops for a citrus and mango nose, grain and white-bread body and dry and thirst-quenching character.

AREA 51

Free Lions, Viterbo, Lazio; 5.4%

A quaffable and sessionable US-style pale ale with a rich bouquet well balanced between tones of exotic fruit, malt and honey, a medium-weight body and a pleasant, bitter finish.

ARSA

Birranova, Triggianello, Apulia; 5.5%

An unusual smoked porter made from grano arso, the wheat left on the ground after the harvest and the burning of the stubble, and smoked malt from Bamberg, Germany. Toasted notes and hints of dried plums in a light body.

BABÉL

Foglie d'Erba, Forni di Sopra, Friuli-Venezia Giulia; 5%

A highly quaffable pale ale made with a blend of six different hops for a complex aroma of citrus, tropical fruit and resin – gentle rather than aggressive – and medium-weight, malty and sessionable body.

ICONIC BREWERIES

BALADIN

Piozzo, Cuneo, Piedmont

Teo Musso may be a brilliant self-promoter, but he is also a great visionary brewer, from **Nazionale** (6.5%), a quaffable all-Italian ale with a light aroma of coriander and bergamot, to the powerful dark **Leön** (9%), rich with flavours of dried fruit, toffee and liquorice. Then there are the experimental creations, such as **Xyauyù** (14%), a silky, intentionally oxidized beer with a complex bouquet of figs, sweet fortified wines and soy sauce, and **Lune** (11.5%), matured in white-wine barrels for a rich bouquet of walnuts, dried apricots and vanilla.

ITALIANO

Limido Comasco, Como, Lombardy

With his fragrant, herbal **Tipopils** (5.2%), Agostino Arioli created a benchmark in Italian craft beer and gave notice to the world that Italian beer was ready to be taken seriously. Arioli also loves to explore new frontiers in brewing, with beers like fruity and slightly vinous **Cassissona** (6.5%), made with cassis, **Scires** (7.5%) with Vignola cherries, perfectly balanced between sweetness and sourness, and **Inclusio Ultima** (7%), a softer version of Tipopils refermented in bottle with hops, part of a new project called Barbarrique.

BREWERIES TO WATCH

EBERS

Foggia, Puglia

Skills across a variety of styles are shown in beers like **Blanche** (5.3%), refreshing and elegant with citrus and coriander notes, and **Hopsfall** (7%), a black IPA with floral and resinous tones and a persistent bitterness.

HAMMER

Villa d'Adda, Lombardy

Menaresta alumnus Marco Valeriani indulges his love of hops with **Wave Runner** (6.5%), an IPA with exotic aromas and well-balanced bitterness, and **Black Queen** (7%), an earthy, grassy black IPA with a toasty finish.

HILLTOP

Bassano Romano, Lazio

Irish expat Conor Gallagher is one of Italy's most promising brewers, crafting beers like the toasty, brackish **Gallagher Stout** (5.5%) made with smoked seaweed, and the dry-finishing **Barry's Bitter** (4.2%).

VENTO FORTE

Bracciano, Lazio

Helmed by a surfer-brewer, this operation is garnering praise for beers like **Follower IPA** (7.1%), with a tropical-fruit aroma, hidden strength and dry, clean finish, and **Amber Oatmeal** (4.5%), floral and smooth with hints of white chocolate.

BB BOOM

Barley, Maracalagonis, Sardinia; 9%

The father of the Italian Grape Ale style, Nicola Perra, is still at work, his latest featuring Vermentino *mosto cotto*, or cooked must, resulting in a full-bodied, slightly sour and balanced ale with a floral, green-grape aroma.

CHOCOLATE PORTER

Perugia, Pontenuovo di Torgiano, Perugia, Umbria; 5%

An impressive brewery growing in quality year after year, as seen in this porter with a persuasive aroma of chocolate and roast, and a creamy and slightly bitter palate.

COFFEE BRETT IMPERIAL STOUT

Carrobiolo, Monza, Lombardy; 11%

Pietro Fontana is a talented brewer with no fear of experimentation, hence this beer as a meeting point between coffee and *Brettanomyces*, the former dominant but accompanied by an earthy wildness.

CORVINA

Mastino, San Martino Buon Albergo, Verona, Veneto; 10%

Corvina, one of the grapes used in Amarone wine, brings a vinous, wooden bouquet to this sour ale and accents of alcohol-soaked cherries to its flavour.

D-DAY

Decimoprimo, Trinitapoli, Puglia, 5.5%

A hoppy, elegant pale ale with a subtle citrus and tangerine aroma and an initially malty body that is quickly overwhelmed by aromatic bitterness from a combination of British and US hops.

DUE DI PICCHE

Menaresta, Carate Brianza, Lombardy; 6.8%

A black IPA with a hoppy, toasty aroma holding notes of burned caramel and red fruit. The body is deceiving in its ability to hide its strength, presenting an approachably fruity and toasty body before a pleasingly bitter finish.

DUNKEL

Batzen Bräu, Bulzano, Trentino-South Tyrol, 4.9%

With rich toasted and caramel notes, a rounded body and well-balanced finish, this dark lager is the highlight of the brewery's accomplished, German-inspired portfolio.

FLEUR SOFRONIA

M-C77, Serrapetrona, Marche; 5%

From one of the most interesting young microbreweries in Italy comes this Belgian-style wheat beer flavoured with hibiscus flowers for a pink hue, an elegant, floral aroma and a touch of acidity to keep it all refreshing.

GERICA

Birrone, Isola Vicentina, Veneto; 4.5%

From a brewery equally inspired by German traditions and US hops comes this "Cascadian lager", well balanced between herbal and citrus aromas and highly thirst-quenching in the body, with a long and lingering, bitter finish.

HELLER BOCK

Elvo, Graglia, Piedmont; 7.2%

From one of Italy's finest lager breweries, a classic German style beer well balanced between the sweet honey and fruity malt in the body and a dry finish that hides its strength well.

LATTE PIÙ

Retorto, Podenzano, Emilia-Romagna; 4.8%

The name pays tribute to Stanley Kubrick's *A Clockwork Orange*, but the effects of this "Milk Plus" Belgian-style wheat beer are refreshing rather than dangerous, with distinctive orange notes and hints of coriander evident in the finish.

CAN'T-MISS BREWERIES

32 VIA DEI BIRRAI

Pederobba, Veneto

Consistency is key to the success of this operation helmed by Belgian–Italian Fabiano Toffoli, who structures all his beers with optimal balance. **Oppale** (5.5%) is a hoppy ale with a distinctive herbal, fruity aroma and a round body, while **Curmi** (5.8%) is a refreshing floral and spiced *witbier* with a slight spike of acidity, and **Admiral** (6.3%) is a Scotch ale with toasted and caramel notes, smooth and persistent.

ALMOND '22

Loreto Aprutino, Pescara, Abruzzo

Jurij Ferri has a surgical hand with ingredients, creating beers that are well structured and original. **Blanche de Valerie** (4.5%) is a *witbier* spiced with black and pink pepper, floral and elegant with a slightly dry finish; **Pink IPA** (6%) is a personal interpretation of the style made with pink peppercorns for a delicate, tangerine-accented flavour; and **Maxima** (6.9%), brewed with acacia honey, is a strong ale with a warm aroma of biscuits and a light body.

LOVERBEER

Marentino, Piedmont

A true explorer of flavour, Valter Loverier loves to push the limit. His uniformly excellent beers include **BeerBera** (8%), spontaneously fermented with Barbera grapes to a vinous, fruity and wonderfully balanced body; **BeerBrugna**

(6.2%), made with Damaschine plums and wild yeasts, fruity and citrusy with well-balanced acidity; and **Saison de l'Ouvrier** (5.8%), with a woody, vinous, red-fruit bouquet and a very dry body.

MONTEGIOCO

Montegioco, Piedmont

Riccardo Franzosi is a multi-tasking brewer known for his creative side, which brings us **Quarta Runa** (7%), a fruit beer made with Volpedo peaches that boasts an amazing bouquet of flowers, almonds and peach, the vinous and minerally **Tibir** (7.5%), with Timorasso grapes, and **La Mummia** (5.2%), a cask-aged blended ale with complex notes of wood, wine, citrus and honey in outstanding harmony.

MARRUCA

Amiata, Arcidosso, Tuscany; 6.5%

The Cerullo brothers are brewers strongly connected to their region, brewing with local chestnuts, saffron and, as with this ale, honey. Warming and full-bodied with tones of caramel, toffee and honey in the aftertaste.

MOLO

Ivan Borsato, Camalò, Treviso, Veneto; 5.5%

An unusual porter characterized by a small amount of port wine added for bottle fermentation, creating a silky, warming ale with round notes of coffee and bitter chocolate.

NADIR

Il Chiostro, Nocera Inferiore, Campania; 10%

Rested for two years in US oak, this silky, fruity and warming ale with a big aroma of tobacco, wood and red fruit is testament to Simone Della Porta's fruitful love affair with wood-ageing.

'NDO WAISS

Hibu, Burago di Molgora, Lombardy; 5.5%

A solid interpretation of the *weizen* style with honey and fruit on the nose and slightly spicy banana and candied apple in the body. Quaffable with a light bitterness drying out the finish.

NOBILE

dell'Eremo, Assisi, Umbria; 5%

A delicate, bready and herbal aroma introduces this highly sessionable golden ale, while a crispy, clean and quenching palate completes the picture.

NOCTURNA

Kamun, Pedrosa, Piedmont; 5.4%

An oatmeal stout brewed with a portion of smoked malt that stays apparent throughout but never grows overwhelming, with bitter chocolate and coffee notes in both the aroma and the smooth, persistent flavour.

ORANGE POISON

Pontino, Latina, Lazio; 7%

A very Italian take on a pumpkin ale, this adds almonds and three different kinds of pepper to the pumpkin for a complex bouquet of dry fruits, spices and pumpkin in the background.

PECORA NERA

Geco, Cornaredo, Lombardy; 4%

Seven different malts form the backbone of this milk stout with an appealing cappuccino-esque aroma and

STYLE SPOTLIGHT

THE WINE-INFLUENCED BEERS OF ITALY

The 2016 edition of the Italian national beer competition, Birra dell'Anno, saw the introduction of a category entitled, in English, Italian Grape Ale. This inclusion was an acknowledgement of a skill at which Italian brewers have been excelling for years, specifically the careful use of grape must in their beers.

In winemaking, must is the term used to denote freshly pressed grapes, which includes seeds, skins and some stems. From a brewing perspective, "must" can mean exactly that, or simply juice that is added during primary or secondary fermentation. Wine-influenced beer could also be said to include beers conditioned in wine barrels or aged on top of winemaking lees, which is to say the seeds and skins left behind after juice extraction. By whatever definition, it is a practice that Italian brewers are rapidly adopting as their calling card to the world.

Proponents skilled at this practice include LoverBeer, with **BeerBera** and **D'uvaBeer**; Montegioco, brewer of the excellent Barbera-barrel-aged **La Mummia**; Brùton, whose **Limes** is fermented with Verdicchio grape juice; the AB InBev-owned Birra del Borgo, with the multi-award-winning **Equilibrista**, made from 50% grape must; and Pasturana, whose **Filare!** is juiced with the white Piedmont grape Cortese di Gavi.

more coffee and cocoa elements in the smooth and highly approachable body.

PIAZZA DELLE ERBE

Ofelia, Sovizzo, Veneto; 4.9%

A spiced ale with readily apparent yet also balanced and clean notes of cardamom accenting a light, refreshing body, with a gentle touch of acidity grafted to its maltiness.

PIMPI

BAV, Martellago, Veneto, 7.2%

This wonderful pumpkin ale gets its unique flavour boost from fruit that is caramelized prior to brewing and just a pinch of coriander, resulting in a beer that is mildly pumpkin-y, round and very well balanced.

PUNKS DO IT BITTER

Elav, Comun Nuovo (Bergamo), Lombardy; 4.3%

The flagship brand of this fast-growing brewery is dry-hopped with Mosaic and Cascade hops for an intense citrus and grapefruit aroma, although the body remains light, dry and enjoyable with a thirst-quenching finish.

REALE

del Borgo [AB InBev], Borgorose, Lazio; 6.4%

Unchanged thus far by its acquisition, the del Borgo brewery continues to produce excellent beers like this original ale with a delicate grapefruit and orange aroma, a subtle hint of black pepper and great quaffability.

REGINA DEL MARE

del Forte, Pietrasanta, Tuscany; 8%

Belgian beer-inspired Francesco Mancini is the brewer of this rich dark ale with notes of caramel, candied orange and dried fruit on the nose and the palate, and a silky, clean and well-balanced character.

RODERSCH

Bi-Du, Olgiate Comasco, Lombardy; 5.1%

Brewer Beppe Vento has always prized drinkability in his beers, as witnessed by this *kölsch*-style beer with a light citrus and herbal aroma, dryly malty body and pleasant hoppy finish.

SALADA

Lariano, Sirone, Lombardy; 5%

Inspired by the *gose* style, this has pure Sicilian salt and some coriander in its recipe, giving it a refreshing and well-balanced flavour profile with a gentle, savoury note in the aftertaste.

SCARLIGA

Rurale, Desio, Lombardy; 8.5%

A powerful but well-balanced double IPA seasoned entirely with European hops for an intriguing aroma and a sneaky-strong body with a dryly hoppy, clean finish.

SLURP

Soralama', Vaie, Piedmont; 4.8%

A pilsner dry-hopped with US hops for a floral, citrusy aroma and a light, quenching body leaving an enjoyable and lingering bitterness; quite persistent and dry.

SPACEMAN INDIA PALE ALE

Brewfist, Codogno, Lombardy; 7%

A combination of Citra, Columbus and Simcoe hops gives this IPA a perfumed aroma of citrus and tropical fruit and a powerful mid-palate bitterness. A favourite among Italian hop fanatics.

STONER

Brüton, Lucca, Tuscany; 7.5%

An intensely fruity bouquet with notes of apricots and candy signals the arrival of this rounded and very well-balanced golden ale with fruity and honey tones on the palate.

SUN FLOWER

Valcavallina, Endine Gaiano, Lombardy; 4.3%

Delicate honey, citrus and exotic-fruit aromas introduce this light and highly aromatic golden ale, with the citrus and tropical fruit carrying through to the complex palate.

TEMPORIS

Croce di Malto, Trecate, Piedmont; 6.8%

A fascinating interpretation of *saison* style with a complex, expansive aroma that begins fruity and grows spicy, elegant and very well balanced on the palate, with a subtle spicy finish.

TERZO TEMPO

Argo, Lemignano di Collecchio, Emilia-Romagna; 4.4%

Perfectly balanced and thoroughly enjoyable, with a floral bouquet and a malty body, this cream ale is a much-appreciated rarity on the Italian craft beer scene.

TRE FONTANE

Abbazia Tre Fontane, Rome, Lazio; 8.5%

The one and only Italian Trappist brewery is located in Rome where the monks began brewing in 2015. Their *tripel* is made with eucalyptus, which gives it an elegant balsamic element in both aroma and taste.

TRIPLE

Maltus Faber, Genoa, Liguria; 8%

This classically styled *tripel* possesses an intensity and controlled strength that makes all the difference, with fruit and citrus notes apparent in the aroma and a slightly spicy, smooth and persistent palate.

TUPAMAROS

Ritual Lab, Formello, Lazio; 8%

Young but promising brewery making waves primarily due to this double IPA with an intense aroma of resin and grapefruit, powerful hoppiness and a punchy, bitter finish that mellows as it lingers.

L'ULTIMA LUNA

del Ducato, Soragna, Emilia-Romagna; 13%

A barley wine matured 18 months in Amarone barriques, this emerges with an aroma of vanilla, leather and cocoa, with a rich, sweet intensity and complexity in the body supported by soft tannins. One of many great beers from Giovanni Campari's brewery.

YELLOW DOCTOR

Black Barrels, Turin, Piedmont; 5.2%

Renzo Losi pioneered mixed fermentation in Italy with his Panil Barriquée, and now he is at work in Turin creating beers with tart complexity and light alcohol, like this refreshing, thyme-accented, slightly sour summer ale.

ZONA CESARINI

Toccalmatto, Fidenza, Emilia-Romagna; 6.6%

The flagship label of the brewery features a blend of hops from Japan, Australia, New Zealand and the USA, yielding an IPA with notes of tropical fruit, citrus and apricot that progress from nose to palate, ultimately finishing quite dry.

GREECE

Like much of the Balkans, Greece is still finding its feet where craft brewing is concerned, but a few lights are nevertheless beginning to shine, some even brightly.

ORA STOUT

Patraiki, Patras, Western Greece; 7%

There is a hint of Foreign Export Stout about this creamy and roasted Greek stout. Vanilla, mocha and chocolate notes make their mark alongside a peppery hoppiness. A complete and satisfying beer.

PILSNER

Nissos, Vagia, Tinos, Cyclades; 5%

Fifteen months after first being brewed, this crisp Czech-style beer won its first international medal. Flurries of soft lemon waft from its aroma, while the crisp body and bitter finish pair wonderfully with fried Greek food.

RED DONKEY

Santorini, Meso Gonia, Thira (Santorini); 5–5.2%

This island brewery produced the first Greek IPA in 2011, but its soft and sensuous red ale with a chewy mouthfeel, joined by caramel, vanilla and a dry, hop-fringed finish, is more memorable.

W DAY

Septem, Orologio, Euboea; 6%

Fragrant and fruity from Southern Hemisphere hops and bearing hints of banana and clove, this "wheat IPA" is a quaffable fusion of two styles with a slight sweetness in the finish, from one of the most adventurous new wave Greek breweries.

SPAIN & PORTUGAL

The adjoining nations of the Iberian peninsula began their journey to brewing respectability without any great brewing heritage to recreate. Spain got the jump on its neighbour with its culinary creativity influencing many of its better beers, following an Italian path to growing excellence, including early flaws and inconsistencies. Portugal, meanwhile, has taken longer to get going, but is now making steady strides towards joining Europe's family of brewing nations.

SPAIN

APOKALYPSE

Reptilian, El Vendrell, Catalonia; 11.5%

Black as night, this Imperial stout is dense and intensely toasty, with chocolate and coffee tones, warming strength and hints of vanilla, nut and grain. Also made in versions aged in Málaga, port and brandy barrels.

BLACKBLOCK

La Pirata, Súria, Catalonia; 11.2%

The brewery's second release set the course for this renowned brewery.

Dense and dark, with chocolate, brandy, nutty and dried-fruit notes, plus an impressive flavour balance of sweet and bitter. Also available in a bourbon-barrelled version.

CHOC INFESTED PORTER

Vic, Vic, Catalonia; 6%

This pitch-black porter has an attractive hoppy profile reminiscent of orange zest and strawberry, an intense toasty character, gently caramelly maltiness and a pleasing hint of cocoa in a creamy body.

CLAUDIA

BlackLab, Barcelona, Catalonia; 7%

The flagship of this brewpub by the city's seaside, this US-style IPA is aggressively hopped, as per its fresh, juicy, tropical-fruit and citrus aromas, but with a strong malty balance as well.

DOUBLE DRAGON II

Falken, nomadic; 10%

Known and revered for the retro video-game imagery of their beers, this dark brown wee heavy is intense yet also mellow, with a rich toffee and caramelly character holding notes of biscuit and ripe fruit leading to a warming finish.

EX 1 IPA SEVE-BORIS

Sevebräu, Villanueva de la Serena, Extremadura; 7%

Created in partnership with renowned master brewer Boris de Mesones, this intense ale delivers citrusy, grassy and piney aromas, with a nice caramel and nutty malt character for balance.

FRANCESKA

Art, Canovelles, Catalonia; 5.2%

From a brewery of great personality comes this "steam pilsner", made with Czech malts, Kiwi hops and Californian yeast for a mild citrus and tropical-fruit character, a light spiciness and crisp, quenching demeanour.

GALAXY FARM

Instituto de la Cerveza Artesana (ICA), Barcelona, Catalonia; 7.5%

A contemporary take on the *saison* style single-hopped with Galaxy. Fruity with aromas ranging from citrus to passion-fruit, and pleasantly peppery, yeasty and slightly musty.

GOMA 2

Caleya, Rioseco, Asturias; 6.3%

With the name of an industrial explosive, this IPA is designed to target its aim at the drinkers' taste buds with an explosion of tropical fruits, peach and citrus, all on a soft and malty base with refreshing bitterness.

GRECO

Domus, Toledo, Castilla-La Mancha; 8.2%

Evoking the marzipan for which Toledo is famous, this gently sweet ale spiced with almond, saffron, lemon and cinnamon has a herbal character throughout, with almond accents and a steadily growing hoppiness that finishes slightly bitter and vaguely nutty.

GREEN MADNESS

NaparBCN, Barcelona, Catalonia; 6%

Naparbier's brewpub was launched
in 2016 and quickly became one of
the reference breweries for the city.
This hazy, heavily hopped IPA is full of
juicy citrus flavours and aromas, with
a residual malt presence.

HAPPY OTTER

Dougall's, Liérganes, Cantabria, 5.6%

Bright amber-gold with an intense and
fresh hoppy aroma, this pale ale delivers
all sorts of fruity notes from peach
to grapefruit to tropical fruit, all with
a firm and pleasant malt backbone to
keep it quite quaffable.

HOPTIMISTA

Edge, Barcelona, Catalonia, 6.6%

This crystal-clear amber ale is very
American in style, with citrus zest,
grapefruit, pine and orange in the

aroma and a lightly caramelly body.
Dry, medium-bodied and resinous.

HØRNY PILSNER

La Quince, nomadic; 5.2%

Best known for their innovative
collaborations with some renowned
national and European brewers, these
brewing nomads offer a hoppy pilsner
that is fresh and lively, with a tropical
and citrus-fruit nose followed by a
bitter, dry finish.

IMPARABLE

Basqueland, Hernani, Basque Country;
6.8%

An impressive recent arrival brings this
hazy amber beer with a wide range of
hoppy aromas from citrus to pine to
mango, balanced with a moderately full
maltiness producing an effect that is
both sweet and bitter.

IPA ANIVERSARI

Montseny, Sant Miquel de Balenyà,
Catalonia; 6.4%

Released on the brewery's fifth
anniversary and brewed ever since,
this amber IPA offers aromas of pine,
grapefruit, dried apricot and grapes,
with a biscuity, lightly caramelly malt
base for balance.

JULIETT

L'Anjub, Flix, Catalonia; 6.2%

A long-time favourite among local
drinkers, this strong stout is deep black
with a roasty aroma combined with
hints of prunes and liquorice and a

coffee-ish body with dry, herbal notes from the northern Spanish hops used.

MORENETA BRUNE

Barna, nomadic; 5.5%

Designed to evoke the flavours of *rom cremat*, a Catalonian rum and coffee drink, this cinnamon-spiced *dubbel* has a roasty body with mocha and spice notes and a richness that belies its modest strength.

PORTER

Arriaca, Yunquera de Henares, Castilla-La Mancha; 5.9%

Black and intensely flavoured, this offers aromas of coffee, dark bitter chocolate and liquorice, along with a bit of dried fruitiness and boozy warmth despite its relatively low strength.

RINER

Guineu, Valls de Torroella, Barcelona, Catalonia; 2.5%

In existence since almost the start of Spanish craft brewing, this low-strength hoppy beer was a trailblazer with its zesty apricot and orange hoppiness, and delicately bready, yeasty body.

ROYAL PORTER

Nómada [Mahou San Miguel], nomadic; 10%

Now brewed on Mahou's pilot facility, this full-bodied and boozy, roasty ale offering chocolate, raisin, fig and vanilla notes is one of the reasons the larger brewery bought a 40% stake in the much younger company.

BREWERIES TO WATCH

GARAGE

Barcelona, Catalonia

A modern, exciting brewpub founded in 2015 that launched a new production brewery in 2017, meaning that the fruity session IPA **In Green We Trust** (4.7%) and the more assertive, citrusy IPA **Slinger** (5.8%) will reach a wider circle of palates.

JAKOBSLAND

Santiago de Compostela, Galicia

This newcomer Galician brewery is rapidly spreading through the Iberian Peninsula with its impressive hop-forward beers, such as the Citra-hop-fuelled **Dumbstruck** (6.3%) and the tropical-fruity double IPA **Fix for the Fits** (9%).

MAD

Madrid

The recent arrival of this brewpub was very good news for sometimes beer-challenged Madrid, thanks to their impressive early offerings like **Trigo Hoppy** (5.2%), a hopped-up wheat ale, and **Red** (7.1%), a caramelly, spicy strong ale.

SETEMBRE

Ales Agullons, Sant Joan de Mediona, Catalonia; 5.5%

The brewery's single-hopped pale ale blended with young lambic and aged for two years, half in oak, this earthy and woody ale has a mild hoppiness, notes of tart red fruits and a distinctive *Brettanomyces* mustiness.

SIDERALE

Cotoya, Santo Adriano, Asturias; 6.2%

Brewed once a year and typical of the brewery's fruit-infatuated approach, this pale ale is flavoured with cider apples to delight drinkers' palates with its sweet fruity character, mild tartness, tannins, malty base and dry, bitter finish.

WHITE IPA

BIIR, nomadic; 6.8%

These wandering brewers with a Belgian inclination made their debut with this hybrid ale offering rich, fruity aromas from its Australian and US hopping, and a nice spicy profile coming from the coriander and orange peel also used.

ZENDRA

Zeta, Alboraia, Valencian Community; 7.8%

From a brewery that has truly conquered local palates, this smoked rye *bock* is medium-bodied with spicy, caramelly malt complemented by herbal hoppiness and a lovely, lingering smoked malt aftertaste.

ZZ+ AMBER ALE

Naparbier, Noain, Navarra; 5.5%

The catalyst for the growth in popularity of hoppy ales in Spain. The caramelly and biscuity malt base gives structure to this hop-forward beer, with juicy aromas of orange and mango, resin and jam. Medium-bodied and lively.

PORTUGAL

BLIND DATE 2.0 IPA

Passarola, nomadic; 6.5%

A somewhat restrained IPA when compared with the explosion of fruit in the brewer's Chindogu IPA, with a piney, slightly caramelly nose and a resiny hop body that sits atop biscuity malt. Quaffably bitter without being overwhelming.

CREATURE IPA

Dois Corvos, Lisbon; 6.5%

One of the first hazy, "New England-style" IPAs brewed in Portugal, this has a fruity nose with ample pineapple and other topical-fruit tones, and a slightly less fruity body with grassy, piney notes and an off-dry finish.

BREWERY TO WATCH

AMNESIA

Oeiras, Lisbon

Started when the owner won a home-brewing competition with the prize of being able to brew at Mean Sardine (*see* below), this impressed immediately with its debut **Juniper Smokin'** (8.5%), a smoked ale with juniper, and the newer double IPA **Amnesia You Talkin' To Me?** (7%).

IMPERIAL STOUT BY PEDRO SOUSA

Post Scriptum, Trofa, Porto; 11.6%

From one of Portugal's most accomplished breweries, this massive beer drinks more like a medium-strong stout, with toffee and ample hop in the aroma and a dense body filled with flavours of coffee and toffee.

MALDITA WHEATWINE

Faustino, Aveiro; 8%

Copper-coloured, this has a strongly malt-forward aroma with a near-ideal combination of toffee and caramel malt leading to a surprisingly soft but well-rounded body with toffee-ish sweetness and herbal bitterness. Best of a very good range.

URRACA VENDAVAL

Oitava Colina, Lisbon; 6%

From the "eighth hill" (*oitava colina*) of Lisbon, this is a well-constructed and copper-hued IPA with a fresh, piney, citrusy aroma and earthy, fruity (citrus and pineapple, plus some other tropical fruit), grassy body carrying full bitterness.

VORAGEM

Mean Sardine, Ericeira, Mafra; 7%

From one of the country's up-and-coming star breweries, this black IPA has a resinous aroma with some alcohol and coffee notes and a citrusy, earthy body holding hints of grapefruit and pine to a lively, lingering finish.

SCANDINAVIA

DENMARK

There is no common ground in Danish brewing these days, with some breweries emerging from basement home-brewing operations, others part of slickly designed city centre brewpubs and, perhaps most famously, still others gaining fame through beers produced by breweries-for-hire both within and outside of the country. There is no questioning the success of this multi-pronged approach, however, as the country has become both Scandinavia's undisputed craft beer leader and a bold and confident innovator.

ALSTÆRK

Munkebo, Munkebo, Funen; 9.4 %

An impressive tribute to the strong Scotch ale known as wee heavy. Low in bitterness and high in the roasted maltiness from seven types of malt, this is full-bodied with notes of toffee and raisins.

BEER GEEK BRUNCH WEASEL

Mikkeller, nomadic; 10.9%

Ignore the gimmick of making the beer with kopi luwak coffee, the most expensive in the world, and focus instead on an impressive Imperial oatmeal stout with flavours of cold coffee, dark chocolate and red berries.

BLACK MONSTER

Aarhus, Aarhus, Jutland; 10%

A deep black, full-bodied and syrupy Imperial stout aged first in rum barrels, then in a steel tank with oak chips and finally dry-hopped. Expect roasted maltiness with dark-chocolate, oak, whisky and vanilla tones.

CARIBBEAN RUMSTOUT

Hornbeer, Kirke Hyllinge, Zealand; 10%

An award-winning beer and new beloved Danish standard. Notes of rum, vanilla and oak from the barrel-ageing are prominent, with roasted malt flavours and hints of smoke, espresso and dark chocolate.

CHRISTIAN BALE ALE

Dry & Bitter, Gørløse, Zealand; 4.6%

More bitter than dry, this single-hop (Mosaic) session-strength IPA is easy-going with sharp bright flavours of grapefruit, peach, melon and tropical fruits, followed by a snappy bitter finish.

CLUB TROPICANA

Rocket, Haslev, Zealand; 5.2%

A fruity pale ale with tastes of grapefruit, mango and papaya accented by tart and peppery characteristics, creating in the process a quaffable and light orange-hued beauty.

COLUMBUS ALE

Det Lille, Ringsted, Zealand; 7.8%

Explore this hoppy ale and you will first be rewarded with a rich bitterness, followed and supported by malty fruitiness heavy on the mango notes.

DARK SIDE OF THE MOON

Kissmeyer, nomadic; 9.5%

From veteran brewer Anders Kissmeyer comes this Imperial porter loaded with flavours of dark chocolate, espresso, whisky and vanilla, accented by a refreshing cherry-ish tartness.

DOPPEL BOCK

Krenkerup, Sakskøbing, Zealand; 8.3%

A traditional Bavarian-style *doppelbock* with a lovely and warming mouthfeel, caramel flanked by chocolate and dried fruit and a subtly hoppiness on the finish.

EXTRA PILSNER

Jacobsen [Carlsberg], Copenhagen; 5.5%

From Carlsberg's craft beer sub-label, this organic pilsner with added sea buckthorn is well hopped in the Bavarian style with a full rather than crisp body given added tartness from the berries.

ESB

WinterCoat, Sabro, Jutland; 6.1%

A strong, dark amber-coloured English-style bitter in which caramelly and biscuity malt are the predominant flavours, accented by floral hop and red-berry notes and culminating in a notably bitter finish.

FOUR

Coisbo, nomadic; 10%

A strongly floral Imperial stout – rich in lavender – with a massively malty mix of roasted and chocolaty flavours with prune notes, yet with unusual quaffability and an appealing dryness.

FROKOST

Fur, Fur, Jutland; 2.6%

Despite its low strength, this simple and refreshing pale ale offers an ambitious bitterness surrounding elements of biscuity malt, citrus and elderflower. Refreshing and highly, perhaps surprisingly, satisfying.

HØKER BAJER

Hancock, Skive, Jutland; 5%

As fine an example of a simple, refreshing Czech-style pilsner as you will find in Denmark, full in body with a round rather than crisp maltiness and a floral character from the use of exclusively Saaz hops.

HUMLEFRYD

Skands, Brøndby, Zealand; 5.5%

A fine crossover of a Czech and Bavarian approach to pilsner, crisp, clean and lively with a taste of mildly sweet malt, grass and hay, with the hoppiness pairing perfectly with the malt sweetness.

LE SACRE

Ebeltoft, Ebeltoft, Jutland; 6.7%

A light orange-hued *saison* with considerable wild yeast characteristics, such as notes of barnyard, hay, leather and sour apples, plus a rustic tartness and hints of strawberries and banana.

LIMFJORDSPORTER

Thisted, Thisted, Jutland; 7.9%

A smooth, oily and rich stout brewed with liquorice and smoked malt, with

CAN'T-MISS BREWERIES
●●●●●●●●●●●●●●

AMAGER

Copenhagen

Brewer of bold and mostly forcefully hoppy ales, although with rising interest and proficiency in Imperial stouts. In the former class is **The Lady of Cofitachequi** (7%), an IPA with grassy, resinous and grapefruity aromas and flavours, while **Double Black Mash** (12%) leads the latter camp with an elegantly warming, chocolate and coffee character. Others on the IPA side include **Todd The Axe Man** (6.5%), with understated maltiness and tropical-fruit hoppiness, and **Winter in Bangalore** (6%), a modest, crisp and very well-balanced IPA with caramel and grapefruit notes in perfect harmony.

BEER HERE

nomadic

Founder Christian Skovdal Andersen can seem at times like the most gifted and versatile brewer in Denmark. Testament to his skills are beers like the hearty and creamy milk stout **Ammestout** (6.5%); **Nordic Rye** (8%), a rustic, dark ale loaded with fresh maltiness; and **Kama Citra** (7%), a brown ale well seasoned with its signature hop. **Infant Øl** (2.8%) derives low-alcohol complexity from six different malts, while **Hopfix** (6.5%) relies on a mix of hops for its resinous flavours of grapefruit, mango and pineapple.

CAN'T-MISS BREWERIES

BØGEDAL

Vejle, Jutland

Situated on an old farm and employing ancient brewing techniques, this may be the most charming brewery in Denmark, producing equally charming beers that are each unique and often difficult to define by style. **No. 505** (7.7%) is a rich dark ale with added liquorice root, full of fresh malts and only discreet bitterness; **No. 459** (8.1%) is a light, strong ale with considerable maltiness and greater hoppiness than that usually found in the brewery's beers; and **Hyld** (6.6%) is seasoned with elderflower. **Jul#1** (6.7%) is a dark-brown Christmas ale with a solid base of malt and flavours of orange, coffee and caramel.

HERSLEV

Herslev, Zealand

An organic and terroir-focused brewery from farmer–brewer Tore Jørgensen, one of the pioneers of the Danish beer revolution. Cider-ish **Mark Fadlagret** (11%) is an unhopped ale fermented with wild yeast cultivated from hay; Czech-style **Økologisk Pilsner** (5.5%) is strongly malty, but neither does it lack any refreshing crispness; **Økologisk Stjernebryg** (9%) is a powerful but smooth, milk-chocolaty Christmas beer spiced with star anise and coriander; and **Birk** (5.5%) is a Belgian-wheat-beer-ish brew made with every part of a freshly harvested birch tree, from bark to sap to leaves.

flavours of dark chocolate, roasted malt, liquorice, smoke and tobacco all accenting a mouth-coating character.

MDXX DET STOCKHOLMSKE BLODBAD

Kongebryg, Næstved, Zealand; 11%

An almost flat mahogany barley wine with elements of roasted malt, caramel, sherry, dried plums and cherries. Composed of a grain bill that includes malted rye and oats.

MØRK MOSEBRYG

Grauballe, Silkeborg, Jutland; 5.6%

A dark, reddish brown Scottish-style ale from Grauballe with subtle tones of smoke hidden among the dunes of exquisite roasted maltiness and flavours of chocolate and dark fruits, with hops only providing balance.

PÁSKA BRYGGJ

Föroya Bjór, Klaksvik, Faroe Islands; 5.8%

This amber-coloured and highly quaffable Easter beer is an easy-going *bock* with sweet maltiness in focus, rich with caramel maltiness and raisin notes.

PERIKON

Kølster, Humlebæk, Zealand; 5.7%

An amber ale brewed with malt from the brewery's own malt house, seasoned with St John's Wort foraged from the surrounding forest. A solid base of fresh, rustic maltiness with herbal and bitter elements and hints of liquorice and hay.

BREWERIES TO WATCH

ALEFARM

Køge, Zealand

The brewery's fast journey to cultish status is due to its takes on IPA and saison, hazy and juicy beers loaded with interesting accents and tropical-fruit flavours, exemplified by **Funk Orchard Farmhouse Ale** (7%) and **Kindred Spirits Lactose** IPA (6%).

BRUS

Copenhagen

A brewpub concept from To Øl (*see* page 142) with a great variety of beers heavy on hip and hoppy styles, such as **Walk'n the Park** (4.8%), a pleasant IPA packed with Citra and Mosaic hops, and **Das Fruit** (8.4%), a sneaky strong, cleverly hopped double IPA.

WARPIGS

Copenhagen

A collaboration between Mikkeller (*see* page 137) and 3 Floyds designed to "bring a US-style brewery to Denmark", featuring many one-offs and regulars like the tropical-fruity IPA **Lazurite** (7.4%) and berry-ish, hoppy ESP **Illuminaughty** (6%).

PHISTER DE NOËL

Flying Couch, Copenhagen; 6.7%

A Christmas Imperial stout brewed with a touch of vanilla and dark sugar. A deep black and creamy body offers flavours of dark chocolate, roasted malt, vanilla and lactose.

RAVNSBORG RØD

Nørrebro, Copenhagen; 5.5%

From a near-legendary brewpub that has perhaps seen better days, this organic red ale is roasty with notes of dried fruits, caramel and pine.

RAZOR BLADE

Ghost, nomadic; 10%

Flavours of pine, grapefruit and tropical fruits are ever present in this black IPA, though they are the supporting cast to those of roasted malt, liquorice and candied sugar with hints of coffee, all leading to a dry and bitter finish.

RED ALE CELEBRATION

Ugly Duck, Nørre Aaby, Funen; 8.6%

A reddish-brown Imperial with notes of roasted and bready malt, caramel, fruit syrup and woodiness. The sweetness of this barrel-aged and dry-hopped ale has a tart edge to it.

ROUGH SNUFF II

Midtfyns, Årslev, Funen; 9%

A mahogany-coloured, Belgian-inspired strong ale with complex flavours of caramel, liquorice and tobacco accented by notes of tar, raisins and seaweed.

ROULV

Frejdahl, Assens, Funen; 9%

A full-bodied, creamy and sweet porter, slightly smoky with blackcurrant and rum hints mixing alongside more prominent elements of chocolate and raisins, all leading to a lasting bitterness in the finish.

SORT DESSERT ØL

No5, Holbæk, Zealand; 14%

What happens when *schwarzbier* meets barley wine; deep brown and evocative

of a fine port stuffed with flavours of prunes, plums and raisins, and accented by tones of coffee and chocolate.

SORT MÆLK

To Øl, nomadic; 10.6%

The added lactose is the key to this deep brown and very full-bodied Imperial stout aged in whisky barrels. The notes of cream from the lactose blend perfectly with intense flavours of roasted malt, tobacco, toffee and coffee.

SPELT BOCK

Indslev, Nørre Aaby, Funen; 7%

A dark brown *bock* with a twist, brewed not only from barley malt and spelt, but also rye and wheat. A fresh and grainy maltiness introduces the beer, and notes of coffee and chocolate carry through the body.

VADEHAV

Fanø, Nordby, Fanø, Jutland; 6.5%

A masterful take on the challenging task of brewing a delicate brown ale, smooth and close to full-bodied with flavours of fresh roasted malt, lightly sweet caramel and mildly bitter nuttiness.

NORWAY

Spurred forward by the success of Nøgne Ø in 2002 (*see* page 145), Norwegian brewers convinced their country's beer drinkers to pay well above the already high price of local, uninspired lagers for beers of character and depth, and in so doing took one of Europe's more hidebound beer markets and evolved it into one of the most exciting.

A DAMN FINE COFFEE IPA

Ego, Fredrikstad, Østfold; 7.4%

Hazy and deep copper in colour, this unique IPA has an aroma that balances tropical fruit and coffee, while the body positions notes of papaya and mango on top of flavours of dark roasted coffee, chocolate and caramel with a dry, hoppy finish.

ALSTADBERGER KLOSTERGÅRDEN,

Tautra, Frosta, Nord-Trøndelag; 6.5%

A unique Norwegian-style ale known as *stjørdalsøl*, which is brewed with smoked local barley malt. The smoky,

foresty aroma also boasts tones of freshly tanned leather, while the body adds caramel, smoked grain, honey and vanilla to the mix.

APARTE

Hadeland Håndverksbryggeri, Gran, Oppland, 4.5%

An unusual take on a *hefeweizen* fermented with *kölsch* yeast to a spicy, green-grape-accented aroma and grassy, malty body, all leading to a balanced, medium-dry finish.

BELGISK GYLLEN

Færder, Tønsberg, Vestfold; 8.5%

A forcefully fruity Belgian-style strong blond ale with dried fruit, raspberries, strawberries, mango and sweet lemon on the nose, and a vibrant fruitiness with red apple, honey, melon and mango in the body, finishing rather astonishingly dry.

BERGEN PALE ALE

Balder, Leikanger, Sogn og Fjordane; 5.7%

The joke here is that with no plans to export to India, the brewery named this US IPA-style beer after the west coast town of Bergen, where they do sell a considerable amount of beer. Hoppy in aroma, well balanced and refreshing.

BIPA

Aja, Drammen, Buskerud; 4.7%

The "B" stands for "Belgian", which is the yeast used to ferment this low-strength session IPA to its spicy, fruity, tea-leaf-accented aroma and dry, nutty body carrying notes of leather and nutty prune.

BIRKEBEINER

Rena, Østerdalen, Hedmark; 4.7%

A classic Norwegian light lager in the pilsner style from a small brewery located in the deep woods. A fresh, dry and hoppy aroma introduces a beer that is much the same, with light maltiness and easy-going hops. Well balanced.

BLÅBÆRSTOUT

Austmann, Trondheim, Sør-Trøndelag; 6%

A stout brewed with Norwegian wild blueberries, black in colour with a predictably blueberry-ish aroma

accented by dark chocolate and coffee, and a body that follows suit, ending medium-dry.

BLÅND

Trondhjem, Trondheim, Sør-Trøndelag; 4.7%

A US-style blond ale, slightly hazy with aromas of fruit candy, spice and wheat. The body features a soft, wheaty graininess and elements of melon and white gooseberry, with hoppiness growing to the finish.

BOCK

Aass, Drammen, Buskerud; 6.5%

Long-surviving Scandinavian *bock* with a deep reddish-amber colour, notes of roasted walnut and chocolate in the nose and a complex but quaffable palate of caramel and mocha accompanied by tones of prune and fig. A Norwegian classic.

BØKERØKT

Larvik, Larvik, Vestfold; 7.2%

A smoked malt, dark ale brewed by a small brewery established in 2011. Aromas of open fire, roasted malt, wet earth and leather lead to flavours of coffee, chocolate, caramel and nuts.

BOKKØL

Borg, Sarpsborg, Østfold; 6.6%

An award-winning, copper-brown *bock* with a roasted aroma of chocolate and coffee, a taste of caramel, bitter chocolate and dark roasted coffee and a slightly sweet and faintly fruity finish.

BOKKØL

Frydenlund [Ringnes-Carlsberg], Gjelleråsen, Oslo; 6.5%

A classic Norwegian *bock* beer, deep reddish brown in colour with an aroma of chocolate, dried berries and coffee. The berry notes carry through to the body alongside roasted malt, finishing with dark chocolate and coffee.

BØVELEN

Kinn, Florø, Sogn og Fjordane; 9%

This deep gold and hazy Belgian-style *tripel* has a fruity aroma of white melon, honey, orange peel and almonds, with a body of orange-peel marmalade, honey and exotic spices leading to a complex and warming finish.

BRETT FARMHOUSE

Lindheim, Gvarv, Telemark; 7%

Part of this fruit farm brewery's Farmer's Reserve series, this sees the regular, *saison*-style Farmhouse Ale conditioned with *Brettanomyces* and apple fruit to a complex fruitiness and an off-dry and hoppy finish.

CORVUS

Nøisom, Fredrikstad, Østfold; 10.2%

Aromas of port wine, blackberry, chocolate and espresso characterize this cross between a *saison* and an Imperial stout by Nøisom, with a rich and forceful body carrying flavours of fig, prune, berries, dark chocolate, coffee and caramel.

ICONIC BREWERY

NØGNE Ø [HANSA BORG]

Grimstad, Aust-Agder

The most award-winning craft brewery in Norway, founded by Kjetil Jikiun of Bådin (*see* page 147), who left the company not long after its purchase by Hansa Borg in 2013. It is still acknowledged as a Norwegian craft beer market leader, and highlights from the lengthy portfolio include **Imperial Stout** (9%), with notes of espresso, dark chocolate and roasted nuts; **#100** (10%), a barley wine of impressive complexity; the lightly smoky, apricot-ish **Tiger Tripel** (9%); and **#500** (10%), a double IPA crafted from five malts and five hops to commemorate the brewery's 500th brew.

CROW'S SCREAM ALE

Crowbar, Oslo; 4.7%

In the steam beer style, this hazy and orange brew has a gently fruity hoppiness on its aromatic nose and a palate of grapefruit, orange and caramelly malt, finishing dry and hoppy.

DRENGENS DEBUT

Moe, Trondheim, Sør-Trøndelag; 4.7%

A hazy golden and quite floral ale with citrus on the nose, and a refreshing, malt-led body with elements of sweet lemon, green apple and gooseberry, finishing off-dry.

FISH & SHIPS MARITIM PALE ALE

Grim & Gryt, Hareid, Møre og Romsdal; 4.7%

A light copper-coloured and very fruity pale ale from an all-organic brewery on the Norwegian coast, this offers notes of peach and grapefruit in the nose and a citrusy mix of peach, apricot and melon in the body.

HAAHEIM GAARD RØYKT IPA

Lysefjorden, Ytre Arna, Hordaland; 7%

This amber-hued, smoked malt IPA offers aromas of wet wool, wood smoke, roasted malt and caramel to introduce a smoky body carrying flavours of chocolate, caramel, date, fig and dried blueberries.

HARDT STYRBORD

Baatbryggeriet, Vestnes, Møre og Romsdal; 6.4%

A strong version of the brewery's 4.6% Styrbord pale ale, this is amped-up and citrusy, with plenty of hoppy fruit in the nose and spicy pine added to the mix in the malt-forward body.

HELVETESJØLET QUADRUPEL

Geiranger, Geiranger, Møre og Romsdal; 10%

Brewery-aged for over six months, this strong Belgian-inspired abbey-style ale exudes aromas of banana, raisin, nougat and nutty marzipan, with a complex palate of fruity chocolate and caramel, and a long and warming finish.

HUMLEHELVETE

Veholt, Skien, Telemark; 8.5%

A double IPA from an award-winning, family-owned farm brewery. Pine and tropical-fruit notes on an otherwise grapefruity nose, and a complex and warming body with roasty and caramel malt buttressed by fruity flavours of citrus, mango and pear.

HVETEØL

Reins Kloster, Rissa, Sør-Trøndelag; 4.6%

A *hefeweizen* brewed on an ancient farm that was for centuries also a monastery. Aromas of banana, wheat and lemon introduce this lean and quaffable beer, with tones of melon, banana and tropical fruit in the body.

IPA

Telemark, Skien, Telemark; 6.5%

Very much in the classic US style, this cloudy orange IPA has tropical-fruit aromas, including papaya, pink grapefruit and melon, and a richly malty and citrusy-fruity body that finishes very dry and hoppy.

JULIE INDIA SAISON

Amundsen, Oslo; 6%

A successful brewpub, now expanding to brew greater quantities of beers like this tropical-fruity *saison* with a full and floral, citrus-and-tropical-fruit and moderately dry finish.

KJELLERPILS

Sundbytunet, Jessheim, Akershus; 4.5%

A German-style *kellerbier* brewed in small batches by the award-winning brewer Frank Werme. Lightly cloudy with a balanced aroma of malt, florals and fresh hops, and a faintly fruity palate of grain, honey and apples at the finish.

KJETIL JIKIUN INDEPENDENT STOUT

Bådin, Bodø, Nordland; 8.5%

A black and oily stout with complex aromas of nuts, dark bitter chocolate, roasted coffee and dried berries, and a body of strong coffee, dark fruit, cherries and vanilla.

KNURR

Tya, Øvre Årdal, Sogn og Fjordane; 7%

A single hop – Centennial – US-style IPA with a grapefruity aroma holding notes of papaya and a balanced body with marmalade tones layered over dry maltiness.

KØLA-PÅLSEN

St Hallvards, Oslo; 6.2%

Porter with a complex aroma of herbs and chocolate, coffee and liquorice, and a luscious body of coffee and dried dark fruits, made by a crowd-funded brewery with its very own fields of barley and hops.

KVERNKNURR

Små Vesen, Valdres, Oppland; 6.5%

From a defunct brewery revived in 2015, this British-style ESB is dark copper in colour with an aroma of caramel, dry toffee and dark fruit, and a balanced body of chocolate and caramel, vanilla and honey that finishes medium-dry.

KVITWEISS

Inderøy, Inderøy, Nord-Trøndelag; 4.5%

This *weissbier* pours a hazy light gold with a rich collar of foam and tones of wheat and banana in the aroma. The refreshing body offers bright notes of red apples, honey and melon, leading to a medium-dry finish.

LØKKA SITRONGRESS SAISON

Grünerløkka, Oslo; 6%

A *saison* brewed with added lemongrass, this has a spicy, grassy nose accented by lemon and tropical spices, and a fresh and vibrant body with elements of lemon and grain, finishing hoppy and off-dry.

MELKESTOUT

Eiker, Mjøndalen, Baskerud; 5.5%

The name translates to "milk stout", which is precisely what this sweet, nutty and caramelly stout is, with roasted coffee and cream notes on the nose, and chocolate and those of vanilla adding to the flavour.

NAKENBAD

Atna, Atna, Hedmark; 4.7%

Unpasteurized and unfiltered organic pilsner brewed in a small village in central Norway. The aroma is floral and lightly grainy, while the body offers soft bready malt tones and a moderate hoppiness.

NEPTUN

Berentsens, Egersund, Rogaland; 4.7%

A Belgian-style wheat beer that is very light of hue with a fruity aroma

of orange peel, grapefruit, coriander and pine needles, and a fresh and fruity body balanced between fruity and wheaty notes, ending with a slight hoppiness.

OREGONIAN

Voss Fellesbryggeri [Norbrew], Voss, Hordaland; 6%

A US-style pale ale, as evidenced by its name, with a deep copper colour, a hoppy, fruity, spicy and slightly bready aroma and a fine balance between its malty tropical fruitiness and reserved hop flavour.

PALE ALE

Nua, Mandal, Vest-Agder; 4.7%

A light and refreshing pale ale, with a fruity nose of fresh grass, floral citrus, papaya and mango, and a medium body with tropical-fruit notes leading to a dryly hoppy finish.

RATATOSK

Ægir, Flåm, Sogn og Fjordane; 9%

A double IPA produced by a brewery located on a fjord, this is emblematic of the brewery's many successes, with a richly fruity aroma and a complex, fruity and malty body, loaded with hoppiness on the finish.

ROASTY ROAST

Schouskjelleren, Oslo; 6%

A popular brewery located at a historic brewing site making impressive ales like this espresso- and vanilla-scented stout with a full, moderately sweet body carrying notes of coffee, chocolate and gentle liquorice and finishing with a burst of hoppiness.

SJEF

Skavli, Evenskjer, Troms; 4.7%

A US-style amber ale with a fruity aroma of berries and a balanced body weighing out roasted malt, honey, fig and red berries. Brewed by the lady of the house.

SLOGEN ALPE IPA

Trollbryggeriet, Liabygda, Møre og Romsdal; 4.7%

A deep golden IPA with a light character and sessionable strength, tropical fruit, pine and grapefruit in the nose and a fresh citrus–spicy body with a hop-fuelled finish.

SPITSBERGEN STOUT

Svalbard, Longyearbyen, Svalbard; 7%

From the world's northernmost brewery hails this strong stout with rich aromas of nut, caramel, chocolate, toffee and dark rum, and a malty, roasty body with chocolate, liquorice and nutty flavours. Well balanced with a creamy finish.

STEAMER

Oslo, Oslo; 4.7%

The bestseller at the first craft brewery established in Scandinavia, in 1989. Aromas of dried forest berries, plum and caramel characterize this take on the steam beer style, with a lightly roasty maltiness, more fruity berry notes and moderate hoppiness in the body.

CAN'T-MISS BREWERIES
●●●●●●●●●●●●●●

HAAND

Drammen, Buskerud

One of the first successes among craft breweries in Norway, established in an old knitting factory inherited by the founder Jens Maudal. **Norwegian Wood** (6.5%), probably the brewery's best-known beer, is a smoked malt ale with a malty body of smoke, charred wood, whisky and dry caramel, but also not to be missed are **Dark Force** (9%), an Imperial wheat stout; **Tindved** (7%), a tangy ale rich with Norwegian berries; and **Ardenne Blond** (7.5%), a Belgian-style strong blond ale with tropical-fruit elements and a rich hoppiness.

LERVIG

Stavanger, Rogaland

An accomplished brewery on the southwest coast well known for its **Rye IPA** (8.5%), a hazy, amber ale with complex notes of spicy rye grain, dried fruit and berries. Other stellar picks from the brewery's lengthy portfolio include **Konrad's Stout** (10.4%), a rich, full and complex Imperial stout; **Galaxy IPA** (6.5%), single-hopped with Galaxy for a full, tropical fruit character; and **Lucky Jack** (4.7%), a citrusy, sessionable US-style pale ale.

STORHAVET

Lauvanger, Tennevoll, Troms; 4%

A brown ale brewed with seaweed, this unusual Lauvanger beer has a lightly smoky nose with elements of wood, caramel and roast, while the body brings interesting tones of smoked almonds and roasted caramel.

STOUT

Smøla, Smøla, Møre og Romsdal; 4.7%

A young brewery on a western island is responsible for this coffee-ish, dark chocolaty stout with hints of liquorice in the nose and vanilla and caramel in the body, finishing dry, roasty and bitter.

TRAA

Voss, Voss, Hordaland; 4.7%

An unfiltered blond ale with a slightly fruity and yeasty nose, lightly malty and gently fruity body and enough hoppiness to make it eminently quaffable.

TYST

Fjellbryggeriet, Tuddal, Telemark; 4.75%

A light and refreshing *saison* of the type one might want to drink when working the fields, with fresh grass and floral citrus on the nose, and a crisply malty body that grows spicy toward its dry finish.

ULRIKEN DOUBLE IPA

7Fjell, Bønes, Hordaland; 8.5%

Although relatively light in strength for the style, this double IPA displays all the

hoppy notes of its type, with grapefruit and pine in the aroma and a fruity and dry body with elements of orange peel, pine resin, papaya and mango.

VIKING WARRIOR

Lindesnes, Lindesnes, Vest-Agder; 7.2%

Brewed at the southern tip of Norway, this is a rich and heavy IPA designed for Norwegian cuisine, with exotic fruit on the nose, a malty and fruity body featuring dried berries, fig and plum and a strongly hoppy finish.

WINTER WARMER BATCH # 1

Backyard Hero, nomadic; 7.1%

Riffing on the famous BrewDog slogan, this *doppelbock* brewed at Grünerløkka and aged three months in aquavit barrels is billed as "Beer for Underdogs". Complex with flavours of coffee, caramel, dried plum and chocolate.

SWEDEN

The sometimes shocking cost of beer in Sweden has not dampened the enthusiasm of its brewers, who have created one of the most dynamic markets in Europe despite the price hurdles. Certainly of some benefit is the state liquor store system, which is quite supportive of craft breweries, although the rest is all grit, determination and apparently boundless imagination.

AMARILLO

Oppigårds, Hedemora, Dalarna; 5.9%

This citrusy, quaffable IPA, from a brewery that has grown organically into a major operation, is one of the mainstays of the Swedish beer scene and a go-to IPA for many.

BARONEN

Hantverksbryggeriet, Västerås, Västmanland; 9–12.7%

A deeply malty barley wine with some variation between the annual releases. Intense raisiny malt character combines with mild peppery heat in a beer that ages with grace.

BIG BLIND

All In, nomadic; 7.9%

This beer is a real hop feast, delivered by an up-and-coming contract brewer with high ambitions. Passion-fruit, lychee and mango notes grab all the attention in this double IPA with unusually high quaffability.

BLACK JACK

Monk's Café, Stockholm; 7.5%

Chocolate and liquorice meet blackcurrant in a dense version of an Imperial porter made by a prolific brewpub that over the years has attracted at one time or another some of the country's top brewing talent.

ICONIC BREWERY

NÄRKE KULTURBRYGGERI
– med anor från allra första början –

Kaggen!

STORMAKTS PORTER 2008

Kraftig och värmande Imperial Stout bryggd med ljunghonung från Närke och lagrad på ekfat i 2,5 månader. Serveras med fördel i små kupor vid lägst 14°C. Den bryggdes i december 2008 och går bra att lagra i många år.

OG 1.112   Öl är Konst!   ABV 9,5%

NÄRKE

Örebro

With a curious sense of humour and an experimental mindset, but still deeply in touch with brewing traditions, Närke announced its arrival on the global beer scene with **Kaggen! Stormaktsporter** (10%), an outstanding heather honey Imperial stout. While that particular beer has since been retired, variations such as **Kaggen Stormaktsporter Börb'nåhallon** (9%) continue to be brewed and are complemented by **Tanngnjost & Tanngrisnir XXX** (9.5%), a juniper wood-smoked strong ale brewed in *Gotlandsdricke* tradition; **Jontes Atgeir** (4.7%), a well-hopped pale ale named after the brewer's son; and **Mörker** (4.9%), a mellow yet rich porter.

BLACK RYE IPA

Sälens Fjällbryggeri, Sälen, Dalarna; 6.5%

Liquorice and citrus notes dominate this partially rye-based black IPA, designed as a peppery *après ski* warmer at this resort brewpub. The chocolaty, rounded malty body enhances the experience.

BLACK SOIL IPA

Sigtuna, Arlandastad, Stockholm; 7.5%

Blackcurrant, tar and liquorice combine with grapefruit zest and treacle in this full-flavoured and hoppy black ale, brewed in, of all places, a shopping outlet in the vicinity of Arlanda Airport.

BOURBON MASH BEER

Rådanäs, Mölnlycke, Västra Götaland; 6.7%

An unconventional beer from an otherwise conventional brewer – strong ale brewed from malted barley, rye and corn, using bourbon-soaked oak chips during fermentation to deliver evident oaky tones while remaining relatively light.

BYSEN NO:1

Barlingbo, Visby, Gotland; 5.5%

A turbid amber beer, loosely based on the brewing traditions of the region, made by one of many new breweries on this Baltic island. Phenolic banana and other yeast-induced flavours meet light juniper smoke.

CASSIS

Brekeriet, Landskrona, Skåne; 5.2%

This mainly *Brettanomyces*-fermented ale, refermented with blackcurrant, took the market by storm upon release. While this was the first from a brewer solely brewing "wild" beers, it is widely regarded as their best.

CHRISTMAS ALE

Åre, Järpen, Jämtland; 7.3%

A spiced, medium-strength ale evidently modelled after that of California's Anchor Brewing (*see* page 201), crafted by a tiny brewer near Sweden's premier skiing resort, and delivering a punch of nutmeg and cardamom atop a toasty body.

FOR REAL ALE

Klinte, Klintehamn, Gotland; 5.8%

Tangerine, key lime, gooseberry and mango meet the nose at first encounter with this pearl of a US-style pale ale. A seductively creamy maltiness is followed by a distinctly piney bitterness.

GOLDEN ALE

West Coast, Gothenburg, Västra Götaland; 4.5%

A crisp and light golden ale with rich tropical-fruit hop character and a highly refreshing quality from one of several promising upstart breweries in Gothenburg.

HALF IPA

Örebro, Örebro; 5%

A juicy, but fairly light ale, packed with papaya, tangerine and dill flavours from a brave new brewery located in Örebro with high ambitions and a fiercely progressive attitude.

HALF THE STORY

Södra Maltfabriken, Handen, Stockholm; 7%

A suburban brewery provides this malty strong ale with evident inspiration from Britain. Designed to complement Jura whisky, it is doing that astonishingly well in an unexpected way. Rather than delivering smoke and awe, it relies on rich maltiness and mild hay-like hops.

HERRGÅRDSPORTER

Skebo Bruksbryggeri, Skebobruk, Uppsala; 5%

An English-style porter from Sweden's finest producer of cask ales. Mildly earthy with some liquorice flavours, and as soft and pleasant as you would get from traditional English brewers.

HOLD THE BUNS

Költur, Hölö, Stockholm; 5.9%

A coffee stout rich with the taste of espresso, yet treacherously mild with a seamless, soothing flavour profile, made by a tiny brewery on the far outskirts of Stockholm.

H W SÖDERMANS PILSNER

Ångkvarn, Uppsala; 4.6%

The one fixed entry on an otherwise ever-rotating taplist at this new brewpub is a solid, smooth, malty Czech-style pilsner with mild grassy notes.

IDJIT

Dugges, Landvetter, Västra Götaland; 9.5%

A concentrated, potent, relatively dry Imperial stout with plenty of coffee, liquorice and vanilla in the taste from a long-standing craft brewery, edgeless and harmonious in spite of its richness.

KB STOCKHOLM STOUT

Kungsbryggeriet, Älta, Stockholm; 4.5%

A velvety, chocolaty dry stout from a start-up brewery. Despite concentrated coffee and chocolate flavours, it retains the desired quaffability for a beer of its style.

LEUFSTA BLONDE

Leufstabruk, Lövstabruk, Uppsala; 6%

Immigrant Wallonian brewing traditions persist in the mining areas in northern Uppland, where family-brewing roots can date back centuries. This Belgian-style blond ale is a harmonious, down-to-earth beer with mild yeasty bubblegum notes.

LJUS BELGO

Ryentorps, Falun, Dalarna; 9.6%

A seductive, treacherously strong golden ale where Belgian yeast character and peppery heat are emphasized. Its balance and depth make it stand out among Belgium-inspired ales in Sweden.

LUNATOR

Grebbestad, Grebbestad, Västra Götaland; 7.9%

An annually released seasonal, this nut-brown *doppelbock,* which is rich with sticky malt accented by notes of fig, toffee and grass, is practically a west coast institution.

MÄLARÖ KYRKA

Adelsö, Adelsö, Stockholm; 10%

A sherry-barrel-aged Imperial porter from a small brewery in the inland archipelago. Featuring liquorice and oak flavours, it has the expected depth of a well-made high-strength beer and a warming, peppery finish.

MÖRK LAGER JULÖL

Nääs, Ydre, Östergötland; 5.3%

Dark Christmas lagers are traditional in Sweden and this updated interpretation features citrusy hops rather than the more usual spices, all on a delightful toasty malt base.

CAN'T-MISS BREWERIES

MALMÖ

Malmö, Skåne

A brewpub and production brewery that a few years into existence suddenly started putting out world-class beers. **Canned Wheat** (7%) is a citrusy hop bomb partially based on wheat malt. **Limpic Stout** (12.2%) and **Acoustic Porter** (14.2%) cater, with their sweet and heavy richness, for those in need of warmth in the wet Scandinavian winters. **Grand Crew** (6.2%) is a lambic-style ale, aged in Cognac barrels, complete with cobwebs and citric acidity.

NYNÄSHAMNS

Nynäshamn, Stockholm

One of the oldest craft breweries in the country, with one foot solidly in the British tradition and the other in the US genre. The marmalade-ish house character is evident in **Bedarö Bitter**

(4.5%), the brewery's most popular beer, and the British influence runs deep in **Bötet Barley Wine** (9.1%) and **Smörpundet Porter** (5.9%). **Pickla Pils** (4.8%), a summer favourite, breaks with the brewery's standard approaches and embraces instead central European traditions.

QVÄNUM MAT & MALT

Kvänum, Västra Götaland

Rural, somewhat rustic ales produced at a farm on the fertile plains between Sweden's largest lakes, including hearty **Ambassadörsporter** (7.8%), an earthy Imperial porter; the peppery, phenolic **Helgas Hembrygd** (7%), an ale brewed from local barley, rye, oat and spelt, using only local hops; **Jonsson** (5.8%), a spicy ale, brewed with rye from the neighbours' fields; and the Czech-influenced **Q Lager** (5.1%) with bready malt and a touch of butteriness.

OKTOBERFESTLIG ÄNGÖL MÄRZEN

Ängö, Kalmar; 5.8%

An amber-coloured Oktoberfest beer with lovely creamy, deep malt character, balanced sweetness and subdued grassy–spicy bitterness. Obviously designed for gulping rather than sipping.

OUD BRUIN

Stockholm (Sthlm) Stockholm; 6%

A copper-coloured, woody and vinous *oud bruin* with notes of oak and lemon and light grape-stone bitterness from an inner-city brewer that in 2016 defied local legislation to open a taproom.

PALE ALE

Electric Nurse, nomadic; 4.6%

A nicely citric US-style pale ale with lychee and grapefruit flavours from a successful contract brewing operation run by a young couple, he an electronic designer and she a nurse, made at the Dugges brewery, which is owned by the nurse's father.

PALE ALE

Skäggalösa, Växjö, Kronoberg; 5.3%

A dry and zesty pale ale with citrus, blackcurrant and a long, piney bitter finish, produced in a tiny village in the Swedish forests of the deep south.

PERDITION

Tempel, Uppsala; 8.3%

A sour raspberry stout with balsamic vinegar elements made by a brewer

NEBUCHADNEZZAR IIPA

Omnipollo, Stockholm; 8.5%

An immensely popular, intensively citrusy, full-bodied IIPA. Combining the design and marketing talents of this contracting brewer with the clinical execution of Belgium's Proef brewery.

NYA TIDENS IPA

Pite, Piteå, Norrbotten; 6.9%

A small brewery from the northern Bothnian coast produces this straightforward, bronze-coloured IPA with ample hoppy notes of grapefruit and hay atop a solidly malty body.

OATMEAL PORTER

Jämtlands, Pilgrimstad, Jämtland; 4.8%

From a small village deep within the taiga forests, this wonderfully crafted, light but roasty porter brought the modern Swedish beer scene to life in the mid-1990s.

focusing solely on so-called "sour" beers. Fresh cherry tartness balances liquorice and tobacco flavours.

PILSNER

Lycke, Mölnlycke, Västra Götaland; 5%

A crisp and distinct north German-style pilsner from a youthful brewery in Gothenburg's suburbs. Grass and citrus notes combine with a dry and grainy breadiness for a refreshing experience.

THE RED SLOPE

Remmarlöv, Eslöv, Skåne; 8.5%

Copper coloured with a bold and forthright maltiness and a wealth of Seville-orange, tea and caramel flavours, this is possibly the best Swedish example of modern US-style strong ales.

RÖKÖL

Helsinge, Söderhamn, Gävleborg; 5%

A *rauchbier* from a brewery focusing solely on German beer styles, an unusual entity in Sweden. With a very traditional approach and relatively subtle smoke, it is aiming for approachability.

RÖTT MEN INTE SÖTT – BARREL AGED

Sahtipaja, Sätila, Västra Götaland; 4.4%

A juicy modern-style *Berliner weisse* with lots of raspberries, subsequently aged on bourbon barrels with vanilla pods and cinnamon. Despite an onslaught of concentrated flavours, it remains curiously harmonious.

BREWERIES TO WATCH

STIGBERGETS

Gothenburg, Västra Götaland

It took only a year for this brewery to jump from solid, well-made beers to outstanding hop-heavy examples such as the IPA **GBG Beer Week 2016** (6.5%) and malt-focused gems like **Wee Heavy** (10%).

WENNGARN

Sigtuna, Stockholm

A new microbrewery situated at the ancient Wenngarn Castle, starting out in valiant fashion. Among the early releases are **De la Gardie Porter** (9.5%), a rich Imperial porter rested in bourbon barrels, and **Lager Nr. 1** (5.2%), a hoppy *zwickelbier*

SVAGDRICKA
Hjo, Hjo, Västra Götaland; 2%

One of a handful of remaining traditional examples of a "table beer" style once produced by hundreds of brewers and consumed in quantity, this showcases restrained sweetness and accessibility.

SVARTKROPP
Modernist, Stockholm; 8.4%

Mildly peaty with a full body replete with chocolate, liquorice and leather notes, this is a relaxed, yet full-flavoured Imperial stout with personality.

T-56 STOUT
Fjäderholmarnas, Lidingö, Stockholm; 8%

Potent and chocolaty, this warming stout from a brewpub located on an islet in the harbour inlet to Stockholm leaves distinct impressions of liquorice and citrus.

TREUDD SAISON INSIDIEUX
Nyckelbydal, Ekerö, Stockholm; 7.2%

A tart, blond ale brewed true to the Wallonian *saison* traditions by a small family brewery. Elegant and mildly spritzy with harmonious, focused flavours of curaçao with honey and a mild tartness.

TRIPEL
Eskilstuna Ölkultur, Södermanland; 9%

A full-bodied and fruity *tripel*-style ale with bubblegummy and mildly peppery heat, evocative of a fine brandy. It is best enjoyed in situ at the scenic riverfront brewpub.

WEE HEAVY
Octabrew, Fagersta, Västmanland; 8.7%

A mature and mellow strong ale with a mildly warming finish, this Scottish-inspired beer boasts rich maltiness with notes of bread, toffee, prune and ripe fruit.

WHAT THE DUCK!
Klackabacken, Kristianstad, Skåne; 7.8%

Although it is packed with flavour, including elements of blueberry, liquorice, dark chocolate and coffee, this Imperial porter never grows overwhelming, remaining instead concentrated and delightful.

FINLAND

Facing the highest alcohol taxes in the European Union, a government store system that has exclusivity to the sale of all beers greater than 4.7% ABV and an attitude that can be hostile toward small breweries, together with a flood of cheap beer arriving daily aboard the Estonian ferries, it takes a lot to make it as a Finnish craft brewer. Still, many have prevailed, and despite it all, Finland's craft beer making scene is not only surviving but bordering on thriving.

BLACK PILS

Mallaskosken, Seinäjoki, Southern Ostrobothnia; 5.5%

A hybrid between *schwarzbier* and pilsner, with the label emphasis on the latter, there is a rich roastiness to this beer, even hints of coffee, but in the end it is the hoppiness that has the last say.

BLACK TIDE

Hopping Brewsters, Akaa, Pirkanmaa; 6.4%

While billed as a black IPA, this ale has a toasty, almost burned roastiness with notes of dark fruit and liquorice more reminiscent of a stout, all balancing and occasionally dominating its not-insignificant hoppiness.

BREWER'S SPECIAL SAISON

Salmaan, Mikkeli, Southern Savonia; 6%

Quite floral and perfumey with hints of citrus and fresh-cut grass on the nose, this light and refreshing ale offers the drinker a wheaty, fruity and faintly peppery palate.

BUSTER-JANGLE

Radbrew, Kaarina, Southwest Finland; 7%

With a wealth of citrus notes from the Cascade and Mandarina Bavaria hops used, this US-style IPA offers a firm, caramelly maltiness and a quaffability disproportionate to its strength.

STYLE SPOTLIGHT

SAHTI – POSSIBLY THE ULTIMATE FOLK BEER

Sahti entered public awareness outside Finland after beer scribe Michael Jackson began exploring and writing about it in the 1970s and 1980s. Sometimes described as the closest thing to what the Vikings drank and possibly as old as Nordic civilization itself, it was once purely a farmhouse brew, mashed in a hollowed-out tree trunk and heated with the addition of red-hot stones.

The defining feature of the beer, which is made from barley malt and up to 50% or more rye, is arguably less its grain make-up than the juniper boughs through which it is filtered, the berries and the branches acting as both flavouring and antibacterial agent. Or perhaps the more important characteristic is the baker's yeast typically used for fermentation. Or maybe it is the freshness that is all but essential to its enjoyment.

The flavour of most sahtis will tend toward the highly fruity, with banana notes frequently dominant and a spiciness also key to its character. The majority will also be higher strength, as with **Lammin Sahti**, a rich though mellow mélange of fruity, honey-ish and juniper tones. Closer to what traditional "feast" versions of the drink would have been is the **Finlandia Sahti**, full of toffee and banana flavours with a more biting juniper spiciness, while harder to find but a classic is **Hollolan Hirvi Kivisahti**, a full and velvety *sahti* still heated with hot stones according to traditional techniques.

CAN'T-MISS BREWERY

PLEVNA

Tampere, Pirkanmaa

Though it started by simply breathing some life into simple lager styles, this brewery–restaurant has moved with the times and demonstrated that it can master a variety of styles. The succulent **Amarillo Weizen** (5%) is a full-bodied and hoppy *weizen*, blending the signature hop's fruitiness with that from the yeast; **Petolintu** (5.4%) is a bready lager high in both hop aromatics and bitterness; **Weizenbock** (7.5%) is rich with banana esters; and **Siperia** (8%) is a massive Imperial stout with unusually high hop aroma and bitter hopping.

HELSINKI PORTTERI

Suomenlinnan, Helsinki, Uusimaa; 5.6%

A respectful nod to the classic English porter, this chocolaty interpretation may seem on the light side, particularly for a Scandinavian beer, but reaches its zenith when occasionally found in cask-conditioned form.

HUVILA ESB

Malmgård, Malmgård, Uusimaa, 5.2%

Richly malty with a gentle East Kent Golding hop bitterness, this remains true to its English extra-special bitter designation with a fruity malt character tempered by its hops.

ISOPORTTERI

Pyynikki, Tampere, Pirkanmaa; 7.3%

A rich, chocolaty porter with a gentle touch of both smokiness and woodiness, and a dryness and bitterness that exceeds those of many — perhaps most — other Finnish strong porters.

JULMAJUHO

Teerenpeli, Lahti, Päijänne Tavastia; 7.7%

With sweetish and slightly woody aspects that are almost reminiscent of barrel-ageing, this smoked porter is a marvel of malt construction, with a mellowness that belies its strength and a peaty and liquorice-ish finish.

KIEVARI IMPERAALI

Laitilan, Laitila, Southwest Finland; 9.2%

An Imperial stout with a roasty, plummy and raisiny aroma accompanied by a

body that is sweet, burned and even a touch phenolic, evoking thoughts of baked raisin cookies.

KOFF PORTER

Sinebrychoff, Kerava, Uusimaa; 7.2%

Stands out as unusual among Baltic porters today as a top-fermented beer, in contrast to the lagers now typical, with a rich and oily mouthfeel, chocolate–caramel notes in a full body and a roasty, bitter finish.

MALTAAN HAUKKA

Olutpaja, Laitikkala, Pirkanmaa; 4.7%

Brewed to the *altbier* style, this has a sweet and bready maltiness holding a touch of nuttiness and a soft, drying rather than bittering hoppiness.

MOOOD

Maistila, Oulu, Northern Ostrobothnia; 5.8%

A mellow and balanced stout that comes with a sweetness evocative of double cream and a cakey and quaffable body holding notes of burned sugar and hints of raisins.

MUFLONI SINGLE HOP SIMCOE

Beer Hunter's, Pori, Satakunta; 3.5%

One of a wide range of single-hop and lower-alcohol beers from the brewery, this fruity and resiny session IPA delivers plenty of character and avoids the wateriness of some of its style.

PASKA KAUPUNNI

Sonnisaari, Oulu, Northern Ostrobothnia; 7.1%

Made with four malts and six varieties of hop, this IPA is packed with tropical-fruit notes in the aroma and a rich and full maltiness in the body, with a lingering, resinous hoppy finish.

PILS

Helsinki, Helsinki, Uusimaa; 4.5%

Crafted by a German head brewer, this is a perhaps surprisingly malty pilsner with bready tones and a well-balanced herbal bitterness.

PILS

Rousal, Rosala, Southwest Finland; 4.6%

With citrusy, peppery hoppiness, this pilsner deviates slightly from convention, but satisfies nonetheless with a crisp and refreshing body culminating in a long and lingering bitter finish.

PLÄKKI

Hiisi, Jyväskylä, Central Finland; 6.3%

With a "hotness" that makes it seem stronger than it actually is, this shippable black IPA has a highly chocolaty roastiness contrasted by a notably citrusy hoppiness.

SAVU KATAJA

Vakka-Suomen, Uusikaupunki, Southwest Finland; 9%

With both a fair proportion of smoked malt and added juniper, this could easily be an overwhelming ale. It is, however, designed to be more approachable and satisfies with its luscious, rich palate, which ends in a sweet, smoky finish.

SAVU PORTER

Maku, Tuusula, Uusimaa; 5.9%

Although made with smoked malt, the smoky aspect of this balanced beer is kept mellow and accessible by a rich and chocolaty maltiness culminating in a drier and more roasted finish.

ULTIMATOR

Stadin, Helsinki, Uusimaa; 8%

From one of Finland's oldest modern craft breweries, this rich *doppelbock* is fruity with citrus and pine notes when young, but develops a raisiny hint as it ages and has a beautiful winey and woody flavour either way.

VEHNÄ

Koulu, Turku, Southwest Finland; 5.4%

From a brewery–restaurant built in a former school near the city centre, this well-executed *hefeweizen* has a decidedly wheaty, malty character, with banana and citrus notes providing the refreshment.

ICELAND

Although very late to end the country's extended flirtation with Prohibition, with full-strength beer made legal only as recently as 1989, and even later to join the craft beer movement, Iceland has been moving forward quickly to establish its own space within the world of beer. Some of its brewery creations have been little more than cries for attention – smoked whale testicle ale, anyone? – but many more have been genuinely interesting, uniquely Icelandic takes on the world of brewing.

ICELANDIC NORTHERN LIGHTS

Steðja, Borgarnes, Western Region; 5.3%

From the brewery responsible for the notorious whale testicle beer comes this significantly more conventional brew – a crisp, deep amber lager flavoured with liquorice to a sweet, smooth and well-balanced character.

ICELANDIC TOASTED PORTER

Einstök, nomadic; 6%

Having its beers brewed at Viking Ölgerd in Akureyri allows this export-driven company to focus on the clever marketing of some occasionally impressive beers, including this coffee-accented porter with vaguely smoky chocolate elements.

LAVA

Ölvisholt, Selfoss, Southern Region; 9.4%

Named after an active volcano visible from the brewery, this smoked malt Imperial stout has a sweet, roasted malt smokiness, on the line between subtle and assertive, with dark, dried-fruit notes and hints of liquorice.

PALE ALE

Gæðingur, Skagafirði, Northern Region; 4.5%

Brewing on Iceland's northwest coast, a fair distance from the population centre of Reykjavík, this young operation has managed to craft some of the country's deftest hoppy beers, including this clever pale ale with an approachable, floral character.

CAN'T-MISS BREWERY

BORG

Reykjavík

Although not the first Icelandic brewery to make an impression outside of its home country's borders – that title goes to Ölvisholt (*see* above) – this offshoot of the Ölgerðin beer and soft drinks producer and distributor has certainly made the biggest noise. Brands identified by number include **Nr. 3 Úlfur India Pale Ale** (5.9%), with its spicy–grassy–citrusy balance; the raisiny, walnutty **Nr. 19 Garún Icelandic Stout** (11.5%); the chocolaty, faintly herbal **Nr. 13 Myrkvi Porter** (6%); and the herbal, heathery and slightly mossy **Nr. 32 Leifur Nordic Saison** (6.8%), among many, many others.

CENTRAL & EASTERN EUROPE

THE CZECH REPUBLIC

The current explosion of independent small breweries in the Czech Republic is comprised mostly of pub breweries, more often than not focused on traditional lager styles that, even in small brewhouses, often undergo the laborious process known as decoction mashing, considered by many an essential component of Czech lagers. Meanwhile, ale traditions are regrowing, with early stages of fusion styles emerging that appear to give pale ales, porters and wheat beers a distinctively Czech edge.

12° SVĚTLÝ LEŽÁK

Rezek, Zásada, Liberec; 5.5%

A pils with presence – a little stronger, a little louder, with a heavier charge of hops than usual, yet very well balanced and almost surprisingly grown-up for a beer that comes from a young brewery big on attitude.

450

Svijany, Svijany, Liberec; 4.6%

Something Czech drinkers value the most in a pale lager is its *říz*, roughly translating as "zest". The best way to understand what that means is with a pint of this rich gold and floral, Saaz-hopped lager, brewed to celebrate the brewery's 450th anniversary.

ALBRECHT INDIA PALE ALE 19%

Frýdlant, Frýdlant, Liberec; 7.9%

As classy as the restored brewery that makes it, this IPA boasts a wonderful blend of complexity, balance and approachability, with intense notes of orange peel and tangy tropical fruit that will captivate even wine drinkers who have never before encountered an IPA.

ASFALT

Zhůřák, Zhůř, Plzeň; 7.2%

An Imperial stout as dark as its name implies stands out not only thanks to its impressive quality but because it is made by a Californian brewer in a small village near the cradle of pale lager, Pilsen.

B:DARK

Budějovický Budvar, České Budějovice, South Bohemia; 4.7%

While its pale sibling gets all the attention, in part due to its US Budweiser doppelgänger, this *tmavý ležák* (dark lager) has a roasted, drier character and towers above the competition from the larger Czech breweries.

BESKYDIAN BANDIT

Beskydský Pivovárek, Ostravice, Moravia-Silesia; 5.4%

This brewery from the far east of the Czech Republic is better known for its range of pale ales, but they also know how to lager, as this rich, unctuous, nutty *polotmavé* shows with great panache.

BLACK I.P.A.

Permon, Sokolov, Karlovy Vary; 5.7%

Anyone insisting that black IPAs are just hoppier stouts may find support in the roasted flavours of this one. Others will simply find a solid, well-balanced beer that gets everything right, from one of the best Czech ale brewers.

BŘEZŇÁK 12°

Velké Březno [Heineken], Velké Březno, Ústí nad Labem; 5.1%

The Czech subsidiary of Heineken makes this superb *světlý ležák* with a crisp mouthfeel and notes reminiscent of sweet herbs and fresh grain in a brewery they have kept as a sort of living museum.

ICONIC BREWERY

MATUŠKA

Broumy, Central Bohemia

When Martín Matuška opened his brewery in 2007, it became one of the first widely distributed new Czech breweries. When he was joined by son Adam, it also became one of the first famous for the quality of its ales, including **Raptor IPA** (6.3%), almost a national benchmark for the style; **Apollo Galaxy** (5.5%), a US-style pale ale with flavours that are both balanced and intense; **California** (5.3%), an elderflower-accented ale that speaks to its namesake state; and **Černá Raketa** (6.9%), a powerful black IPA that equally evokes Oregon.

ICONIC BREWERY

ÚNĚTICKÝ

Únětice, Central Bohemia

Restored in 2011 after over 60 years of idleness, the brewery was an immediate success thanks to their only two year-round beers, both pale lagers: **10°** (3.8%), providing proof that, in good hands, ordinary-seeming beers can pack flavour and character; and **12°** (5%), with all a proper Bohemian pils should have and then some. Seasonals include the almost criminally quaffable **Masopustní Bock** (6%), brewed for the outdoor winter revelries of the Czech Mardi Gras; and **Posvícenský** (4.6%), a rye amber lager with a complex blend of malts taking centre stage, brewed for the village's Parish Fair.

BRNĚNSKÁ 11

Hauskrecht, Brno, South Moravia; 4.5%

From the former brewmaster at a major brewery, now running his own business, comes this *světlý ležák*. Nothing innovative – just sweet grains with fragrant herbs and flowers making it a classic Bohemian pils done as it should be.

ČERNÁ SVINĚ

Šnajdr, Kostelec nad Černými lesy, Central Bohemia; 5.2%

If anyone were to be given this blind and told that it was an English-style porter, nobody could fault them for believing it, even though it is, in fact, a dark lager with notes of prune, hints of liquorice, roast and chocolate and a full quaffability.

ČERNÝ LEŽÁK

Bernard [co-owned by Duvel Moortgat], Humpolec, Vysočina; 5.1%

Renowned in several countries, this lager has become a true classic and remains one of the best available in the country, coming across like a lightweight Baltic porter able to keep a firm grip on your palate.

CHOTOVINSKÝ STOUT

Chotoviny, Chotoviny, South Bohemia; 5.3%

A beer to bring to mind a block of bitter chocolate dissolved in a cup of strong and very good espresso. Complex and rewarding, and the sort of stout that begs for your palate's attention.

DALEŠICKÁ 11°

Dalešice, Dalešice, Vysočina; 4.3%

Classic and traditional are overused words, but it is hard to find better ones for this bready pale lager boasting notes of dandelion honey and embodying all the attributes of a classic and traditional Czech beer.

DUŠIČKOVÝ STOUT

Falkenštejn, Krasná Lípa, Ústí nad Labem; 5.7%

Brewed each year for early November, when Czechs honour their dead, it brings everything you expect from the style, with an intriguing yet warming note of freshly ground black pepper.

ESO

Konrad, Vratislavice nad Nisou, Liberec; 4.6%

In the darker side of the *polotmavý* spectrum, this conversational amber lager from Northern Bohemia demands to be drunk in half-litre portions so that you can fully appreciate its subtle harmony of caramel, hazelnuts and herbal bitterness.

FABIÁN 12°

Fabián, Hostmice, Central Bohemia; 4.6%

Made by the former head brewer of Dalešice (*see* above) in a resurrected brewery located not far from Prague, this is a textbook example of how round and floral a proper *světlý ležák* can be, with hints of honey and far from boring and bland.

FLEKOVSKÝ LEŽÁK

U Fleků, Prague; 4.6%

Ignoring any possible modern trend, Prague's oldest pub brewery produces only one beer, the same since 1843 or so they claim – a superb dark lager full of notes of chocolate, sweet coffee, dried fruit and history.

GYPSY PORTER

Kocour, Varsndorf, Ústí nad Labem; 7.1%

Born from a collaboration with an English brewer brokered by a local beer writer, the success of the first batch convinced the brewery to add it to its regular portfolio. Muscular, complex and weighty.

H8

Hendrych, Vrchlabí, Hradec Králové; 3.3%

The brewery produces a solid range of beers, but it is in this case in particular that the brewer shows his craftsmanship by brewing a lightweight pale lager with enough flavour to keep you entertained for either one glass or the whole day.

HIBISCUS

Krkonošský Medvěd, Vrchlabí, Hradec Králové; 6.8%

A *weizenbock* infused with hibiscus flowers and lemongrass, the flowers bringing principally the beer's pink colour, while notes of the herb appear almost fleetingly toward the finish, contrasting with the flavour and inspiring curiosity.

HRADEBNÍ TMAVÉ

Měšťanský Pivovar v Poličce, Polička, Pardubice; 3.9%

A *tmavé výčepní* that calls to mind a dark mild, with notes of dark fruit and sweet coffee and hints of roast. An exception within a style mostly associated with the sweet, uninspired products of macro breweries.

HUBERTUS PREMIUM

Kácov, Kácov, Central Bohemia; 4.7%

Inexpensive doesn't have to mean low quality where Czech is concerned, as proven by this *světlý ležák* produced in a small regional brewery near Prague. It is a terrific quaffer, with grassy, honey-ish and bready malt notes.

JANTÁR 13°

Vinohradský, Prague; 5.5%

This *polotmavý* (amber lager) is an all-evening quaffer that makes you wonder whether it is possible to make an infusion of silk and dose it with a dash of summer fruit and the nectar of autumn flowers.

JISKRA

Radniční, Jihlava, Vysočina; 3.8%

When it first came out, this citrusy session ale tasted like a beginner's home-brew project. Its massive improvement is a testament to the dedication and perseverance of its brewers, who took the criticism as a motivator and not a deterrent.

KANEC

Břeclav, Břeclav, South Bohemia; 5%

Tasting of everything you could desire in a *světlý ležák*, this offers a solid, almost croissant-like malt base and confident yet subdued notes of noble hops. Perfect.

KLOSTERMANN

Měšťanský, Strakonice, South Bohemia; 5.1%

First brewed in 2008 to honour its namesake Austrian-born writer, this is a full-bodied *polotmavé* packing caramel-coated nuts and dried apricots with a pinch of roast and herbs in a very attractive finish.

KOUNIC

Uherský Brod, Uherský Brod, Zlín; 4.6%

Anton Dreher (*see* page 68) would probably love this superb Vienna lager with a round and smooth body supporting subtle notes of caramel and nuts that slowly open the path to an aromatic and floral finish.

KRÁLOVSKÁ ZLATÁ LABUŤ

Dvůr Zvíkov, Zvíkov, South Bohemia; 11.8%

After spending up to 15 months in the cellar, this bottom-fermented interpretation of the barley wine style with an appealing mahogany colour feels almost like drinking a mildly carbonated amontillado sherry or tawny port.

CAN'T-MISS BREWERIES

ANTOŠ

Slaný, Central Bohemia

A brewery making lagers and ales with equal skill at two locations. **Slánský Rarach** (4%) is a near-perfect *desítka* to tempt even the most conservative drinker; **Polotmavá 13%** (5.5%) boasts a blend of floral, autumn fruit and nut flavours; **Tlustý Netopýr** (7%) is a rye IPA that brings appealing spiciness to the mix; and **Choo-choo** (7.8%) is a powerful and complex black IPA that completes an interesting and rewarding beer voyage.

BŘEVNOVSKÝ KLÁŠTERNÍ

Vojtěcha, Prague

Located within the walls of the oldest monastery in Bohemia, the beers are sold under the Benedict name, including **Klasická Dvanáctka** (5%), a *světlý ležák* seasoned with Saaz hops from a 75-year-old hopyard, and **Imperial Lager** (8.5%), with a quaffability that belies its strength. **Klášterní IPA** (6.5%) has more of an English character with juicy tropical-fruit notes, while **Russian Imperial Stout** (8.5%) drinks like a study on the style, also coming in a whisky-barrel-aged version.

KLÁŠTERNÍ

Strahov, Prague

One of the Czech Republic's best, brewing under the Svatý Norbert name. Year-round beers include: **Jantár** (5.3%), a *polotmavé* with a stunning balance of malt and hops; **Speciální Tmavé** (5.5%), almost chewy and full of roastiness, but with a surprisingly hoppy finish; and the truly world-class **IPA** (6.3%) on top – intense and aromatic, but perfectly balanced. Of their many other brews, two autumn beers stand out, **Antidepressant Ale** (6.3%) and **Antidepressant Lager** (6.3%), brewed from the same dark malt bill, though with different hopping.

KRUTÁK 12°

Továrna, Slaný, Central Bohemia; 5%

When beer snobs complain that Czech pale lagers "lack personality", they are not thinking of this beer with freshly kilned grain notes supporting a bouquet of summer flowers.

MAGOR

Zichovecký, Zichovec, Central Bohemia; 6.2%

Fortunately, it doesn't honour its name – Czech for "lunatic" – but carefully and sanely chooses the best bits of Vienna lager, *märzen* and *bock* to create an impressive strong *polotmavé* that qualifies as dangerously quaffable.

PARDUBICKÝ PORTER

Pernštejn, Pardubice; 8%

It might be the novelty of "foreign" styles or because it is a classic everyone takes for granted, but this Baltic porter doesn't get the attention it deserves. Smooth, rich and reminiscent of tawny port with a drop of umami.

PILSNER URQUELL

Plzeňský Prazdroj, Plzeň; 4.4%

They say it is a shadow of its former self, perhaps with some justification. But it's still the most iconic Czech beer and, doubters notwithstanding, remains the benchmark of *světlý ležák* (pale lager), one that few smaller breweries are able to reach.

PODLESKÝ LEŽÁK

Podlesí, Příbram, Central Bohemia; 5.5%

Full flavoured, smooth and floral – adjectives that, while accurate, don't do justice to a beer sufficiently impressive that it will make you want to travel to a suburb of an ugly former mining town.

POLOTMAVÉ VÝČEPNÍ

Bakalář, Rakovník, Central Bohemia; 4.5%

A beer named after and of a style native to the Czech lands, yet so rare as to be almost unknown. Subtle notes of nuts coated in caramel, dark bread crust and herbs; simple and complex at the same time.

POLOTMAVÝ 11°

Všerad, Všeradice, Central Bohemia; 4.6%

You don't need big, bold flavours to make a beer with interest and complexity, and this example provides ample proof. Full appreciation requires contemplation and more than a sip or two, but rewards with peppery, herbal and malty elements.

POLOTMAVÝ LEŽÁK

Bašta, Prague; 4.8%

Once this brewpub found the god of consistency, their beers fulfilled all the promises of those first batches, and this subtle, caramelly amber lager with notes of stone fruit and nuts and a flowery finish became something to pursue.

PORTER

U Bulovky, Prague; 6.1%

An English-style porter that in one pint will take you back to the late Victorian age, while a second will have you return to the present enjoying its malty mix of roast, black sugar, prunes and dried figs.

PORTER

Uhřiněves, Prague; 6.8%

Baltic porter is an underrated style all over the world, and the Czech Republic is no exception. Which is a shame, as we need more dark lagers like this one, which brings to mind Christmas fruitcake soaked in amontillado sherry.

POSTŘIŽINSKÉ FRANCINŮV LEŽÁK

Nymburk, Nymburk, Central Bohemia; 5%

The Nymburk brewery was the birthplace of writer Bohumil Hrabal, whose face adorns the label of this excellent, everyday drinker, with a fuller body than usual for the style, but no less quaffability.

PREMIUM TMAVÝ LEŽÁK

Bohemia Regent, Třeboň, South Bohemia; 4.4%

Criminally underrated and almost forgotten in favour of the wave of new breweries and styles, this classic boasts chocolaty notes that masterfully walk the fine line between sweet and roasty without missing a step.

CAN'T-MISS BREWERIES

● ● ● ● ● ● ● ● ● ● ● ● ● ●

KOUNICKÝ

Kounice, Central Bohemia

Owned by the renowned malting company Klusáček, which naturally produces the excellent Bohemian floor malts that are the foundation of the brewery's beers. **Světlý Ležák 12%** (4.9%) proudly displays the quality of these house-made malts, complemented by the finest Saaz, while the ginger-infused **Ginger Ale** (5%) uses Premiant hops to make a surprisingly quaffable beer. **Rauch** (5.6%) is smoked beer for introducing people to the style, while **Melon 15°** (6.5%) is one of a changing line of ales, each brewed from pilsner malt with a single hop variety and named after the hop.

KOUT NA ŠUMAVĚ

Kout na Šumavě, Plzeň

Brewery with an almost cult-like status among fans of proper lagers, which is all that they brew. **Koutská Desítka** (4.2%) is a pale lager that laughs in the face of the category's stereotype of bland and boring beers, with **Dvanáctka** (5%) being a contender for the title of ultimate *světlý ležák*. The dark **Koutský Tmavé** (6%) pumps up the volume with strength and complexity, while **Tmavý Speciál** (8.2%) could be considered the Tmavý on steroids.

BREWERIES TO WATCH

CLOCK

Potštejn, Hradec Králové

Principally an ale brewery, although also making lagers, with beers such as the textbook US-style pale ale **Clock** (5%); **Twist** (6.2%), a reddish IPA; and **Rišaví Zmikund** (7.8%), a massive and muscular red ale that feels like falling asleep in a basket full of summer.

RAVEN

Plzeň

Australian-led ale specialist making excellent beers like the nutty, soothing **Brewhemian Cream Porter** (6.3%); a balanced, light-on-the-palate **White IPA** (6.3%); **Laid to Waste** (8.2%), a strong ale named after a heavy metal band; and **Gunslinger** (6.4%), an IPA that shoots.

PRINC MAX X

Vysoký Chlumec, Vysoký Chlumec, Central Bohemia; 4%

In the upper gravity range of the *desítka* pale lager category, this has a fuller body than most, dominated by freshly dried cereal notes. The hops are solely to provide some balance to the relatively generous maltiness.

PŠENIČNÝ SPECIÁL 16°

U Vacků, Chlumec nad Cidlinou, Hradec Králové; 6.4%

A *weizenbock* by any other name, with all the warm, autumnal characteristics of the style and a surprising flash of wild strawberry by the finish that will make you crave another round.

RAMPUŠÁK

Dobruška, Dobruška, Hradec Králové; 4.9%

Made with the brewery's own floor maltings, it offers the sensory gamut of a proper *světlý ležák* – freshly baked white bread, flowers, herbs, grain, honey and caramel –with a subtlety that will reward every sip.

RYCHNOVSKÁ KNĚŽNA

Rychnov, Rychnov nad Kněžnou, Hradec Králové; 5.2%

At first encounter, it seems no different than any other decent *světlý ležák*, but a sharper bitterness than most sets it apart and will have the drinker hurrying for another round.

SEDM KULÍ

Ferdinand, Benešov, Central Bohemia;
5.5%

Named after the seven bullets that
whacked Archduke Franz Ferdinand,
founder of the brewery, this *polotmavý*
infused with herbs doesn't pack a
murderous punch, but a range of subtle
yet complex flavours that seem to
change with every sip.

SINGLE HOP

Velický Bombarďák, Velká nad Veličkou,
South Moravia; 5%

Single-hop beers are becoming popular
among Czech brewers, often with
mixed results, but not in this case. Each
beer in the series brings out the best
of the hop used without neglecting the
other ingredients.

SMOKED AMBER ALE

Mordýř, Dolní Ředice, Pardubice; 5.5%

Smoked malts often get lost in hop-
forward beers, but not here, with bacon
appearing at the end of the first sip and
gaining intensity with each subsequent
mouthful yet never overwhelming the
fragrant Cascade hops.

STALKER IPA

Falkon, nomadic; 6.9%

Jakub Veselý, the young brewer
behind this beer, is proud of his "flying
brewery" and has impressed from the
start – which happened to have been
this IPA – with bold hopping of varying
varieties depending on what Veselý
can get his hands on.

STAROKLADNO 10,8°

U Kozlíků, Kladno, Central Bohemia; 4%

At the strong end of its generally
low-alcohol style, this *desítka* will have
you believing that you are drinking
something considerably stronger.
Full and richly flavourful for a lager
of its diminutive strength, session beer
hardly gets any better than this.

ŠTĚPÁN SVĚTLÝ

Dům, Prague; 5%

From one of the first craft breweries
in the Czech Republic comes this still
solid *světlý ležák*, full of herbal notes
on a solidly malty base, which remains
one of the finest examples of the
Czech-born style.

SVĚTLÝ LEŽÁK

Poutník, Pelhřimov, Vysočina; 5%

A slice of freshly baked white bread –
without the crust – spread with a thin
layer of mild honey with bitter spring
herbs. Beautiful in its simplicity.

SVĚTLÝ LEŽÁK

Purkmistr, Plzeň; 4.8%

When you are making a pale lager in
Pilsner Urquell's town, it had better be
damn good, as is this one, with grain,
honey and floral notes dialled up a
notch, almost as if the brewer were
trying to show the creator of the style
how it should be done.

SWEET JESUS

Sibeeria, nomadic; 8%

When an Imperial stout is designed and commissioned by a bar called BeerGeek, you know subtlety won't be one of its features. Still, there is surprising balance and complexity provided mostly by the blend of malts.

TAMBOR 11°

Tambor, Dvůr Králové nad Labem, Hradec Králové; 4.5%

A classic, working-class Bohemian pils, unpretentious, grassy, a bit drier than the average and a beer to build an evening around.

TEARS OF SAINT LAURENT

Mamut/Wild Creatures, Mikulov, South Moravia; 6%

An unremarkable South Moravian brewery run by winemakers who decided to make the first Czech "lambic", maturing this one for two years with Saint Laurent grapes in casks used for that same wine and yielding remarkable results.

TMAVÝ SPECIÁL

Herold, Březnice, Central Bohemia; 5.3%

The best way to describe this Bohemian dark lager is a blend of the best of stout, *dunkel* and *schwarzbier*, with typical Czech character. A beer that doesn't demand attention, but will reward anyone who will pay heed.

TORPID MIND

Bad Flash, nomadic; 10.5%

An Imperial stout that is brewed with a grain bill that includes smoked wheat malts and proves that contract brewing can produce unique beers, especially when commissioned by two pub owners who understand beer as well as many brewers.

TRIBULUS

U Dobřenských, Prague; 6%

Named after the herb it is brewed with – *Tribulus terrestris*, also known as puncturevine – this has the quality of a pale ale brewed with exotic hops. The flagship of a brewery specializing in herbal ales.

VÍDEŇSKÝ SPECIÁL

Harrach, Velké Meziříčí, Vysočina; 6.2%

A couple of sips of this reddish-amber-coloured lager makes one wish there were more brewed exclusively with Vienna malts. Silky, with notes of dark honey and lightly toasted white bread, and a pinch of floral hoppiness.

WILD CREATURES

Tears of Saint Laurent

VIMPERSKÝ SVĚTLÝ

Ležák Šumavský, Vimperk, South Bohemia; 4.9%

Brewed by the same person who teaches secondary school children in Prague how to brew, this is, naturally, technically perfect. A beautiful, flowery, smooth, rewarding Czech pils from start to finish.

WEIZENBIER

Primátor, Náchod, Hradec Králové; 4.8%

One of the oldest wheat beers still on the market, and the first to come out in bottles, with classic notes of banana and clove and a smooth mouthfeel that can compete as an equal with the best Bavaria has to offer.

YERBA MATE'S 13°

U Bizona, Čižice, Plzeň; 5.25%

This amber lager is an excellent example of how to use an unconventional ingredient — yerba mate or *Ilex paraguariensis*, a member of the holly family — while avoiding the gimmick. Anyone familiar with Argentina's national beverage will recognize it at once; the rest will be intrigued by its earthy tones.

ZAJÍC 12°

Kynšperský, Kynšperk nad Ohří, Karlovy Vary; 5.2%

Resurrected breweries are a Czech phenomenon and tend to produce very good, mostly classic beers, and this *světlý ležák* is no exception, featuring notes of crushed dried flowers, herbs and slightly sweet bread.

ESTONIA

Rife with influence from Scandinavia – the three largest breweries in Estonia are all owned by Scandinavian brewing concerns – Estonia was perhaps well set to become one of the first Baltic states to fully embrace craft brewing, beginning with Põhjala (*see* opposite) and evolving quickly from that pioneering operation.

DR. JONES

Anderson's, nomadic; 6.5%

Very much a classic example of modern IPA, this offers jammy and juicy fruitiness upfront and a lovely zesty aspect to the finish. Citrusy and full of character, yet still refreshing and quaffable.

EV98 PORTER

Must Lips, Tallinn, Harju; 7.7%

This was originally brewed in 2016 for the 98th anniversary of the Estonian Republic and the number will be adjusted accordingly. What will not change is the rich and chocolaty roastiness and smooth palate that disguises its strength.

GAMBRINUSE ÕLLEPOOD RADIAATOR

Vormsi, Norrby, Lääne; 7.5%

This rich *doppelbock* was brewed initially for the Gambrinuse beer shop in Tartu, but is now widely available. It showcases bold, sweet, bready malts, dryly bitter hopping and a raisiny element that stands up well to cellaring.

HOP TVOYU MAT

Käbliku, Palutaja, Põlva; 7.9%

Introducing Belgian yeast to a double IPA recipe, this beer offers a potent mix of fruity, rich hoppiness in the aroma and body with a sweet, caramelly malt backbone, rounded off by a drying bitter finish.

MÄRZEN SPEZIAL

Beer House, Tallinn, Harju; 4.4%

This is a crisp and refreshing unfiltered lager that belies its relatively low strength with a solid bready maltiness and generous hopping. Characterful but, like all of this brewpub's offerings, remaining true to tradition.

MÜNCHEN VASKNE

Sillamäe, Sillamäe, Ida-Viru; 6.3%

A full-bodied amber lager worthy of the city mentioned in its name, Munich, this is gently hopped with light herbal notes, but its standout characteristic is a rich grainy taste that brings the phrase "liquid bread" to mind.

ÖÖ

Põhjala, Tallinn, Harju; 10.5%

This potent Imperial stout, billed as a Baltic porter but ale-fermented with roasty, chocolaty maltiness and a drying finish, is the grandfather of the Estonian craft beer scene, providing inspiration for a family of variants, including heady barrel-aged versions.

PIHTLA ÕLU

Taako, Pihtla, Saare; 7.6%

Similar to a Finnish *sahti*, this is filtered through juniper branches, which gives it a herbal bite and strong yeastiness. However, without any rye content, it is more bready and wheaty. A true Estonian farmhouse brew.

CAN'T-MISS BREWERY
● ● ● ● ● ● ● ● ● ● ● ● ●

PÜHASTE

Tartu

Nomadic until 2016, one of the earliest craft brewers in Estonia now has a brewery of its own and is building a strong reputation. Notable beers include the fruity **IPA Mosaiik** (6.9%), dry-hopped with the Aussie hop newcomer Vic Secret; **Patt** (6.6%), a rich and chocolaty porter; and the suitably named **Dekadents** (11.2%), a strong and sweet Imperial stout aged on raisins and rum-soaked vanilla pods. A new arrival is **Sosin** (6%), a black IPA with richness from rye and other darkly roasted malts alongside a spruce-tip and citrusy hoppiness.

OAK AGED PORTER

SUUR PAKS MASTIF

Lehe, Keila, Harju; 9.6%

This barley wine in the English tradition is rich, sweet, raisiny and nutty, matured for a full year prior to release and with the potential for much more ageing.

RUKKI KUNINGAS

Õllenaut, Saue, Harju; 7.7%

From the brewery recognized for its mastery with malts, this rich rye beer is cakey with hints of dried fruit and mellowed by long maturation. An excellent dessert beer.

WINTER GORILLA

Sori, Tallinn, Harju; 7%

A soft, velvety porter with a hint of liquorice to its roasted maltiness, this is dosed with enough coffee to notice, but not so much that it becomes the overwhelmingly dominant trait.

SAUNA SESSION

Tanker, Vaida, Harju; 4.7%

Brewed with birch leaves, this is intended to evoke thoughts of the sauna with its unique aroma and atmosphere, offering a pleasant herbal character at a quaffable strength ideal for sauna sessions.

HUNGARY

Following a mid-1990s boom in brewing, Hungary saw the majority of its new and hopeful breweries close by the turn of the century. Today, however, the comeback is well underway, buoyed by beer fests like Budapest's Főzdefeszt and the establishment of a small brewers association, Kisüzemi Sörfőzdék Egyesülete.

BLACK ROSE

Szent András, Békésszentandrás, Southern Great Plain; 9%

The oldest bottled craft beer in Hungary is this *doppelbock* from Szent András in the southeast, slightly fruity in its sweetish aroma and medium-bodied with a gentle, sweet maltiness and warming finish.

BRETTANNIA BRUT SOUR ALE

Legenda, Budapest; 5.3%

A highly fruity ale broadly in the Flemish red style, with cherry and other berry notes in the aroma and a hint of balsamic vinegar in its complex, sweet-and-sour body.

FORTISSIMA IMPERIAL STOUT

Széles & Széles, Balassagyarmat, Northern Hungary; 9.5%

So called after the nickname that the city earned in the First World War, "the bravest", this has a pleasing aroma of roasted malt and mocha backed by fruity hoppiness and a full, slightly oily body with a lingering finish.

FRANKY FOUR FINGERS

MONYO, Budapest; 13%

A British-style barley wine brewed from renowned Maris Otter malt aged in the bottle for a year prior to release. Toffee-ish in the aroma with notes of

CAN'T-MISS BREWERY

. . . .

BORS

Győrzámoly

One of the old-style "microbreweries" from the 1990s, surviving well into the new century with core beers inspired by the legend of Robin Hood, such as **Tuck Barát** (7.7%), a heavily malty *dubbel* with notes of dried fruit; **Maid Marian** (6%), a honey-ish *hefeweizen*; and **Sherwood** (6.5%), a slightly sweet, earthy stout. Most promising are the beers of the emerging Seven Sins series, such as **Wrath** (5%), a well-hopped black IPA with a creamy, rounded mouthfeel.

dried fruit, and medium-rich on the palate with impressive complexity.

FREAKY WHEATY GRIBANC

armando_otchoa, nomadic; 7%

A spin-off from this contracting brewer's flagship Grabanc IPA, this is brewed without wheat but fermented with a *hefeweizen* yeast, then infused with raspberries for a delicately tart, creamy and citrusy body.

GREYJOY DOUBLE IPA

Balkezes, nomadic; 9%

Infused with bergamot oil and Earl Grey tea, the focus of this quaffable, tea-like brew is balance and harmony between tea, hops, malt and citrus elements, which it accomplishes admirably.

INSTEAD OF INNOCENCE IPL

zip's, Miskolc, Northern Hungary; 6.5%

A full-bodied "Imperial pale lager" with tremendous hop complexity, mixing herbal-resiny, citrussy and fruity flavours, supported by a firm maltiness and leading to a sweetish, lingering long aftertaste.

ISOTONIA

Hedon, Balatonvilágos, Southern Transdanubia; 5.3%

A refreshing, pale-gold summer seasonal *gose* with a wheaty aroma sporting light coriander notes, a spritzy, slightly grassy and faintly salty body and a touch of thirst-quenching sourness on the finish.

JAM 72

Mad Scientist, Budapest; 7.2%

Although billed as American in style, this IPA opens with a fruity aroma that is more tropical than citrusy, a characteristic that continues in the medium-full, slightly sticky body and lingering, moderately bitter finish.

MAIBOCK

Rizmajer, Budapest; 6.5%

A seasonal homage to Germany, this has a sweet and biscuity aroma backed by herbal hop notes and a well-balanced character with just enough hop to support the sweet, bready maltiness.

ONE NIGHT SEDUCTION

Synthesis Brewlab; Budapest, 8.2%

A creamy, chocolaty, biscuity Imperial stout made with malted rye, there is a delicate and fruity hoppiness and notable rye-derived spiciness to this beer; truly seductive.

ROMANOV RUSSIAN IMPERIAL STOUT

Fóti, Fót, Budapest; 12%

Not quite black in colour with a sweet and spicy aroma accented by liquorice and a whiff of alcohol. The body is multi-layered and complex, with molasses and sweet coffee notes and a warming finish.

TÁVOLI GALAXIS

Köthbeer, Nagykovácsi, Budapest; 6.1%

As the name suggests, this IPA is hopped with Galaxy only, giving it a tropical-fruit and citrus aroma and a flavourful, hoppy-fruity body supported by an elegant maltiness.

BREWERY TO WATCH

HOPTOP

Budapest

The first Hungarian brewery to earn a medal at the European Beer Star competition, with beers like **Green Zone** US-style IPA (6.4%), spicy with a earthy maltiness, and the award-winning, chocolaty **Midnight Express Foreign Extra Stout** (6%) boding well for its future.

LITHUANIA

While breweries have for several years now been seen starting up in Lithuania, particularly in the capital, Vilnius, the country is perhaps more rewarding to the adventurous beer trekker who is willing to venture into the countryside in search of the fascinating, indeed challenging authentic beer style of the land.

GREEN MONSTER IPA

Apynys, Kaunas; 6.3%

This likeable, fruity take on a US-style IPA is the most accomplished beer yet from a small brewery of growing confidence in the country's second city.

IMPERIAL STOUT

Sakiškių, Vilnius; 9.2%

Rising star already making spot-on beers in straightforward styles at their self-built brewhouse near the capital, including this rich, balanced and misleadingly quaffable strong stout.

PORTERIO

Aukštaitijos Taruškų, Trakiškis, Panevėžio; 6%

The best new beer from the recent amalgamation of Aukštaitija breweries is this occasional limited-edition fusion of herbal-edged folk ale and light, well-attenuated Baltic porter.

STYLE SPOTLIGHT

KAIMIŠKAS

The *kaimiškas* beers of northeastern Lithuania were hidden for decades from Soviet officialdom, their production method becoming along the way unique, including: a grain bill that can encompass most cereals; hops boiled separately in sealed containers, sometimes in underground cellars, making a concentrated tea that is added after mashing; and a rapid fermentation by naturally selected yeasts that have survived reuse for a century or so.

The result is not so much a beer as a cultural entity, ill-fitted to a world that celebrates the clean character of its great ales. This beer is earthy, edgy, technically flawed and created for low-paid locals. Their lone "export" market is seen as the cluster of bars called Šnekutis in Vilnius. Variants include brews that veer toward mead and ales called *keptinis*, made from caked spent grain.

On a faltering journey from traditional to modern, better examples of the former are the enigmatic **Jovaru** by the brewery of the same name and its honeyed variant **Medumi**, while prized among the newer breed are Joalda's semi-rustic **Joniškėlio Respublika 1919** and the plainer **Seklyčios** from Piniavos. A recent amalgamation of five Aukštaitija breweries has seen **Aukštaitijos Bravorų** appear in stoppered flagons and a revival of the sweetish, darkish **Kupiškėnų Keptinis**.

CAN'T-MISS BREWERY

DUNDULIS

Panevėžys

The driving force and inspiration behind the country's revived brewing culture, creating beers in global craft styles, traditional local ones and a few fusions from two breweries in the same town. A tasting journey begins with ruddy-brown, burned-toast **Kurko Keptinis** (5.2%), thence to the tidy, refreshing Anglo-American **Humulupu IPA** (5.5%), the bravely authentic, sweetish **Syrne** (6%), made with pea flour, and ending with a tar-black, peat-smoked and unrelenting stout, **Kovarnių** (6%).

POLAND

New Polish brewing has advanced beyond the ubiquitous IPA variants to build on its Baltic porter tradition, old ways of brewing with rye, the practice of mashing with smoked grain and a revival of local session styles like *grodziskie* (*see* page 189) and perhaps *schöps*. An unusually high proportion of flashier new players are nomadic, but some are putting down roots.

AFICIONADO

Kingpin, nomadic; 7%

At the avant-garde end of pale ale, this is a beer that survives a chaotic recipe. Aromatic from Ethiopian coffee and smoky from peated malts and pine-smoked Lapsang Souchong tea, it has a remarkably appealing finish.

ALBERT

Wąsosz, Konopiska, Silesia; 4.9%

One of the own-brand beers from a southern brewery that also makes ales for over a dozen nomadic craft brewers. This clove- and banana-tinged *hefeweizen* would pass as classic Bavarian were it not for its splash of Mosaic hop.

BIO HAZARD

Hopkins, nomadic; 7.5%

A "whisky" porter from Gdynia on the Baltic coast that is the best of a range of black beers from a beer designer that has proved it has mastered the art. Its intense peaty aroma heralds a well-delivered smoky character.

DYBUK

Golem, nomadic; 6.5%

This reliably excellent rye porter has a touch of cola behind its sweet chocolaty aroma and wider-ranging, coffee-tinged and more caramelly taste, from a sometimes hit-and-miss range commercialized by a craft beer pub in Poznań.

FUNKY WILD FRUIT WIŚNIA BA

Jan Olbracht Rzemieślniczy, Piotrków Tyybunalski, Łódź; 5.6%

This is the cherry beer from the Piotrek z Bagien series. Fruit-steeped beer is barrel-aged with cultured *Brettanomyces*, creating horse-blanket aromas and a sour taste, but a nice cherry character. Refreshingly new and wild!

HOPFACE KILLAH

Piwne Podziemie, Chelm, Kuyavia-Pomerania; 6.4%

One of the lasting brands from a prodigiously inventive husband-and-wife brewery near the Ukrainian border, influenced by 10 years in Atlanta, as tasted in this intensely hopped, bitter but drinkable IPA.

NAFCIARZ DUKIELSKI

Brokreacja, nomadic; 6.3%

A uniquely designed beer named after the oil miners of Dukla. Whisky malt and rye are brewed into a double brown recipe and porterized with Goldings to create a full-bodied ale with a peaty, almost diesel aroma and oily texture.

PORTER BALTYCKI WEDZONY 24°

Gościszewo, Sztm, Pomerania; 9.6%

Another huge Baltic porter, in this case from the 55 series from a northern brewer of numerous top-quality beers. Subtly smoked to create a cacophony of flavours vying for attention, but none dominant.

ICONIC BREWERY

KORMORAN

Olsztyn, Warmia-Masuria

Among the first of the new wave breweries established in 1993, Kormoran has kept steadily to a line of making off-mainstream beers, its grand cru exemplars appearing as Podróże Kormorana brands. Experiments with different cereals, hops and fruits has led to a range of well-balanced beers respected by consumers, connoisseurs and competitors alike. Among the best are IPA **Plon Niebieski** (6.2%) made with fresh Sybil and Marynka hops, which are also found in "noble" blond lager **Warmińskie Rewolucje** (5.2%). At the heavier end are multi-award-winning straight Baltic porter **Warmiński** (9%) and **Imperium Prunum** (11%), an aged variant lavishly flavoured with heavily smoked dried plums.

CAN'T-MISS BREWERIES

ARTEZAN

Błonie, Masovia

The first of Poland's nomadic craft brewers to have their own brewery, opened in 2012 west of Warsaw. Its dizzying scatter of interesting one-off beers has topped 100, complementing the regular pilsner are the clean, exotically hopped, solid **Pacific Pale Ale** (5%), hoppy, spicy-wheat **Białe IPA** (5.6%), barrel-aged rye porter **Kazimierz** (6%) and Christmas's chocolate-orange stout **Too Young to be Herod** (8%).

PINTA

nomadic

The release of robustly hopped US-style IPA **Atak Chmielu** (6.1%) in March 2011 marked the start of the craft beer revolution in Poland.

Remaining a trendsetter, highlights of its wide offer today include gentle birch-sap-infused wheat beer **Son of a Birch** (3%), high-hopped and lactified "double India sour" **Kwas Epsilon** (6%) and authentically constructed *sahti* tribute act **Koniec Świata** (7.9%).

PRACOWNIA

Modlniczka, Lesser Poland

Set up in 2013 on the outskirts of Kraków and developing a reputation for collaboration brews, it nonetheless keeps faith with its own beers, like cleverly nuanced, grassy wheat beer **Hey Now** (3.8%), classically Polish smoked stout **Cent-US** (4.7%), dark herbal *saison* **Magic Dragon** (5.9%) and pitch-black, coffee–chocolate and tobacco-toned Imperial stout **Mr. Hard's Rocks** (9.5%).

BREWERIES TO WATCH

MARYENSZTADT

Zwoleń, Masovia

Rapidly expanding small brewery near Warsaw producing the fruity, Mosaic-hopped pilsner **Wunder Bar 13** (5.4%); **Polish Hop(e)** (5.5%), an amber ale brewed from locally sourced ingredients; and the coffee-fuelled Imperial stout **RalSa Espresso** (9.4%).

URSA MAIOR

Uherce Mineralne, Subcarpathia

An ambitious small brewery with a developing range of two dozen beers, including the citrusy wheat beer **Rosa z Kremenarosa** (4.8%), spicy, toasty "Indian summer ale" **Carynki z Caryńskiej** (5.2%) and malt-driven IPA **Pantokrator** (6.5%).

ROWING JACK

AleBrowar, nomadic; 6.2%

One of the first US IPAs on the Polish market back in 2012. This is beer well done, with new wave hops, 80 IBU of bitterness and nice citrus and resinous aromas, yet managing to retain drinkability.

THE SPIRIT OF SONOMA

Widawa, Chrząstawa Mała, Lower Silesia; 6.2%

New Polish beer has advanced far enough to host this US-style IPA dry hopped and aged in Sauvignon Blanc barrels, one of the more successful creations from an inconsistent but inventive and talented brewer.

SZCZUN

Szałpiw, nomadic; 8.1%

Unashamedly flashy and eye-catching operation creating beers in a wide variety of styles, from whisky-soaked quadrupels to light session beers via this ester-popping, slightly phenolic Polish take on a US-hopped Belgian-style *tripel*.

ŻYWIEC PORTER

Zamkowy Cieszyn [Heineken], Cieszyn, Silesia; 9.5%

This is a huge beer from a huge brewery group, made at one of its smaller breweries. Typical of the Polish take on Baltic porter – deep ruddy brown, heavy and grain dominated with some hop balance.

STYLE SPOTLIGHT

GRODZISKIE – RISING STAR FROM A BYGONE CULTURE

Grodziskie is like a little-known 19th-century watercolourist whose work has been rediscovered and is now found in modish galleries and auction houses. Identical to German *grätzer*, it probably originated in the Polish town of Grodzisk Wielkopolski near Poznań.

For 500 years, across much of central Europe beer was defined as brown or white, the latter referring to wheat beers. This bright, yellowish and highly carbonated variant is light in body and low in alcohol, but stands out for its oak-smoked grain mash.

Supporters of *grodziskie* hail it as a distinctive old-fashioned summer quencher, while detractors see it as a beer for another era. Known since the 14th century, it was out of production between 1993 and 2010, but today **Grodzisku Wielkopolskim Piwo z Grodziska** is brewed in the town and **Nepomucen Grodzisz** up the way in Jutrosin, with **Profesja Mnich** and **Olimp Sophia** also impressing.

RUSSIA

If there is a "Wild East" in global craft beer, it is in Russia. With some nomadic brewers operating out of several different breweries and even outside of the country, others appearing overnight and disappearing almost as quickly, and still others brewing quantities so small as to be almost insignificant, even the most informed of the local beer cognoscenti have no idea of how many breweries are in operation. What they do agree upon is that, despite overall beer production numbers falling steadily since 2008, they will witness continued craft beer growth for the foreseeable future.

BALTIC PORTER

Knightberg, Saint Petersburg; 6.8%

Almost black in colour with a light tan head, this offers an aroma of spicy, roasted malt that translates into the body, with flavours of cinnamon, chocolate, light citrus and ripe fruit along with earthy notes.

BASTILSKIJ PORTER

ID Jons, nomadic; 7%

"Bastille Porter" is in fact a Baltic porter first brewed on the French Bastille Day holiday, with roasted malt and a hint of chocolate in the nose, and a sweet, slightly burned-tasting body that lends itself to quaffability.

COWBOY MALBORO

Plan B, Yaroslavl; 6.5%

A deep gold US-style IPA with bright, fresh, bready aromas of orange and earth, from a combination of Mosaic and Citra hops, and a formidably hoppy, citrusy and floral body with a lingering and bitter finish.

CRAZY MOOSE

Konix, Zarechny, Penza Oblast; 5.5%

A very citrusy, medium-bodied US-style pale ale with tropical-fruit tones in the aroma and a spicy, grassy flavour accented by notes of grapefruit, bitter orange and pine.

ЭНС 28% — АЛК 13,2%

ЛЕНИНГРАДЕЦ

ОВСЯНО-ЯЧМЕННОЕ ВИНО

БАКУНИН

ПИНТА МЁБИУСА

INVISIBLE PINK UNICORN

Mager, nomadic; 10.5%

An old ale made from both honey and barley malt in the style of a braggot, this is amber-red with a toasted malt aroma and medium-bodied with sweet flavours of caramel, berries, herbs, honey and smoke.

KRÜGER PREMIUM PILS

Томское (Tomskoe), Tomsk; 5%

From a Prussian brewery founded in 1876 by Carl Krüger, this is, in Russian terms, an unusually hoppy pilsner, with a bold flavour profile comparable to Germany's best.

LENINGRADER (ЛЕНИНГРАДЕЦ)

Bakunin, Saint Petersburg; 13.2%

A deep red barley wine with an aroma of dried fruit, caramel and fruit jam introducing a sweet, medium-full body

CAN'T-MISS BREWERY

● ● ● ● ● ● ● ● ● ● ●

МОСКОВСКАЯ ПИВОВАРЕННАЯ КОМПАНИЯ)

Mytishchi, Moscow Oblast

Large but reliable brewery creating traditional beers like **Zhiguli Barnoe (Жигули Барное**; 4.9%), an award-winning Bohemian-style pilsner, so successful that illegal knock-offs are sometimes found, and the solid, clean pale ale **Shaggy Bumblebee (Мохнатый Шмель**; 5%). Craft division Wolf's Brewery (Волковская пивоварня) gets more creative with the slightly nutty, moderately sweet porter Port Arthur (**Порт Артур**; 6.5%), the Mosaic-hopped Belgian-style wheat beer **Blanche de Mazay (Бланш де Мазай**; 5.9%) and **American Pale Ale** (5.5%), fresh and fruity with mango and tropical-fruit notes.

BREWERIES TO WATCH

JAWS

Zarechny, Sverdlovsk Oblast

One of the earliest craft breweries of Russia with exciting beers including **Nuclear Laundry (Атомная прачечная**, 7.2%), a golden amber IPA with notes of tropical and citrus fruits, and **APA** (5.2%), a floral, hoppy pale ale with balanced bitterness.

STAMM

Krasnaya Pakhra, Moscow

Creative brewery making diverse beers like the outstanding Imperial stout **Urals** (10%), chocolaty with hints of vanilla, liquorice and blackcurrant; **Red River** (5.5%), a fruity pale ale; and the US-style IPA **Hop Gun Eldorado & Citra** (7%), seasoned with the hops of its name.

with notes of red berries, warming alcohol and a touch of citrus.

LOBOTOMY 777 (ЛОБОТОМИЯ 777)

AF Brew, Saint Petersburg; 12.7%

This coffee-infused Imperial stout pours a dark brown and offers aromas of coffee, chocolate and toffee and a sweet, creamy mouthfeel with flavours of coffee, roasted malt and oak.

MIDNIGHT MOSCOW IPA

Zagovor, Moscow; 5.6%

Golden and quite hazy in appearance, this brightly hoppy IPA is hugely fragrant with its Amarillo, Simcoe and Centennial hops, but more malty in the body with a light sweetness accented by citrus and spruce notes.

PORTER

Afanasy, Tver; 8%

A solid, rich, deep brown Baltic porter with a bready aroma holding soft liquorice notes and a medium-weight, sweet body with an elegant bitterness and a hint of sourness in the aftertaste.

PRYANIK STOUT 5.0 EDITION

Salden's, Tula; 6.5%

A dark brown stout with a spicy, caramelly aroma accented by coriander, ginger, cinnamon and nutmeg and a flavour that follows suit with ginger cookie, milk chocolate and hints of clove, finishing dry and spicy.

VICTORY ᴀʀᴛ BREW

Red Machine IPA

OG 1.068   IBU 65   Alc 6,9

RED MACHINE IPA

Victory Art Brew, Ivanteevka, Moscow Oblast; 7%

This US-style IPA from a most prolific brewery is double dry-hopped but remains nevertheless balanced with a herbal, citrusy hoppiness on a broad, caramelly maltiness and a moderately bitter finish.

RYZHAYA SONYA (RED SONYA or РЫЖАЯ СОНЯ)

Odna Tonna, Zhukovskiy, Moscow Oblast; 6.2%

An IPA that is flavoured with ginger, this amber-coloured ale has a floral, herbal aroma of tropical fruit and a lightly spicy and citrusy body with moderate bitterness.

RIZHSKOE BEER (РИЖСКОЕ ПИВО)

Vyatich, Kirov; 4.9%

This pilsner from a brewery founded in 1903 by the German brewer Carl Otto Schneider was formerly a favourite beer of the Soviet elite. Delicate and floral on the nose, but more assertively hoppy in the body.

ZOLOTOJ YARLYK (GOLD LABEL)

Velka Morava, Moscow; 5.4%

A revival of an old Russian variety of *märzen* made by the Trekhgorny brewery, honoured at the time by Tsar Nicholas II. Biscuity and slightly fruity on the nose, with caramel and citrus on the palate leading to a hoppy finish.

REST OF CENTRAL & EASTERN EUROPE

While proceeding at a much slower pace than that of many of their surrounding countries, these nations are nevertheless making forward strides into modern craft brewing, usually centred in the cities and sometimes led by expat brewers from the Western world, both tendencies that are increasingly common in emerging beer lands.

CROATIA

ALJAŠKI MRGUD

Vunetovo, Hvar, 5.9%

Named after the brewer's dog, an Alaskan malamute, this black IPA boasts notes of roasted malt and slightly herbal citrus on the nose and a somewhat mellow, dark malt-led body with herbal and fruity hop flavours.

FAKIN IPA

Medvedgrad, Zagreb, 7%

Well-established brewery producing a solid line-up of dependable beers, including this flagship IPA with an aroma of overripe fruit, a malty body with a slightly medicinal quality and a grassy, citrusy finish.

PALE ALE

Zmajska, Zagreb, 5.3%

A quartet of hops gives this amber-hued US-style pale ale a fruity nose with plenty of grapefruit and lemon notes, while a light caramelly maltiness in the body provides great balance to a moderately bitter, fruity hoppiness.

LATVIA

GAIŠAIS

Užavas, Užava; 4.6%

A refreshing and bready lager with crisp grassy hopping and delicate floral-honey sweetness. Packaged unfiltered and always at its best when served as fresh as possible.

LENTENU KĀVĒJS

Labietis, Rīga; 7.2%

A beer with the name "Tapeworm Slayer" had best be good to avoid ridicule, and this black IPA accomplishes the task with chocolaty roastiness and tingling citrusy hops combining to produce a deceptive quaffability.

TREJLEDUS

Valmiermuižas, Valmiermuiža, 8%

Occasionally tipping the scales at up to 9%, this *eisbock* is a caramelly and fruity classic, with sweet raisiny notes that are reminiscent of barley wine and a woody bitterness that keeps the sweetness in check.

CAN'T-MISS BREWERY

MALDUGUNS

Rauna

A versatile brewery working well in many styles, including **Stokholmas Sindroms** (6.3%), a soft, rich porter with a mocha twist and a tempting hint of chilli; **Lauvas Pacietība** (8.9%), a piney, citrusy double IPA with great balance; and an ongoing series of single-hopped IPAs, **Zaļā Bise** (6.3%), where emphasis is always on hop character and approachability. A seasonal pumpkin beer, **Pa Ķirbi** (7.7%) adds pumpkin flesh and spice notes to a luscious porter base.

SERBIA

BREWERY TO WATCH

KABINET

Nemenikuče, Sopot

The consensus leader in Serbian craft brewing, this still-young operation is making waves with beers like the hemp-fuelled **Rufaro** (5.2%); a series of single-hop pale ales and IPAs including **Mozaik** (5.2%); and the flagship **Kolaboracija 02** caramel stout (10%), aged six months in apple-brandy barrels.

SLOVAK REPUBLIC

ANCIKRIST IPA

Hellstork, Senica; 6–6.5%

Even with a supposed bitterness of 66.6 IBU, this is a nicely balanced IPA with tropical-fruit notes defining the aroma and an earthy maltiness in the body to support its bitterness. Dangerously drinkable, perhaps, but hardly evil.

PETER SVETLÝ ALE IPA

Wywar, Holíč; 5.7%

Australian Galaxy hops yield a full and tropical-fruity hop aroma that travels through to the body in a moderate and balanced way, blending nicely with crisp and elegant hoppiness.

STRANGE LAND IPA

dUb, Bratislava; 6%

The founder of this accomplished brewery pub had at publication left the operation, so it is only hoped that this spicy–citrusy ale built on a firm, biscuity malt base does not change except for the better.

CAN'T-MISS BREWERY

LANIUS BREWERY

Trenčín

Built in a 17th-century butcher's shop, this tiny operation brewing in 200-litre (44-gallon) batches is turning out some of the Republic's most interesting beers. Nutty, dark **Mild Ale 9°** (4%) demonstrates the brewer's dedication to traditional styles, while the raisiny, dried-fruit character of the *eisbock* known simply as **Eis 36°** (17%) shows an adventurous side. **Belgian Abbey Tripel 21°** (10%) boasts a spicy–sweet body with a dryly hoppy finish, and **Red Rye IPA** (6.9%) offers plenty of spicy rye character and a moderately bitter finish. Many other beers are made on a rotational basis.

SLOVENIA

BATCH #50 IMPERIAL STOUT

Reservoir Dogs, Nova Gorica; 9%

With the brewery transitioning from a hotel-based brewery to a stand-alone one, it is hoped that this liquorice-accented stout with notes of tar and bitter chocolate will only get better.

QUANTUM DIPA

Pelicon, Ajdovščina; 8%

An impressively nuanced double IPA from a young and rapidly improving brewery, this has an aroma of ripe fruit and a flavour that layers yellow fruit with citrus and caramelly malt, all leading to a hop-edged finish.

CAN'T-MISS BREWERY

HUMANFISH

Vrhnika

Slovenia's leading craft brewery since 2008, run by an Australian expat, this operation southwest of Ljubljana has branched out from basic ales like their crisp, aromatic **Pale Ale** (4.5%) and chocolaty, creamy, medium-bodied **Stout** (4.5%) to more adventurous beers such as the formidable **Russian Imperial Stout** (8.2%), with rich aromas of molasses and dark chocolate and a jammy, oily palate, and **Combat Wombat** (4.8%) session IPA, with an earthy, citrusy aroma and a malt-driven creamy body.

NORTH AMERICA

USA

At the start of 2017 the USA was home to more than 5,000 breweries, most of which were the small, artisanal operations known as craft breweries. When and where this number will reach saturation is the subject of much debate, but with a market share of over 12% and a dollar volume stake in excess of 20%, there is little question that US beer drinkers are shifting their beer preferences in droves, fuelling not just the expansion of the craft brewing industry but also the growth of beer specialist bars, brewery taprooms and domestic beer-focused tourism.

2X4

Melvin, Alpine, Wyoming; 9.9%

A ginormous wallop of hops grabs hold of you and never lets go. Luckily, it is perfectly balanced and paradoxically delicate despite the Imperial IPA's heft, layered with juicy citrus, resiny pine, orange zest, grapefruit and mango.

5 BARREL PALE ALE

Odell, Fort Collins, Colorado; 5.2%

Perhaps best described as a pale ale with a foot in each world, this sophisticated quaffer has a citrusy, US hop character layered over a more British-style, earthy–biscuity malt base.

ADAM

Hair of the Dog, Portland, Oregon; 10%

The brewery's first release and still its unlikely flagship, this traditional ale takes the drinker from a gingerbread start through a subtly spicy, roasted apple and raisin mid-palate to a long, warming and lingering finish.

ALPHA KING PALE ALE

Three Floyds, Munster, Indiana; 6.66%

Once considered the king of ultra-hoppy beers, the recent IPA bitterness arms race has lessened the impact of this ale's notable US hop character, but has done nothing to detract from its balance and beauty.

ANGEL'S SHARE

The Lost Abbey, San Marcos, California; 12.5%

From southern California's barrel-aged beer specialist comes this massive ale named after the alcohol lost from the cask in a distiller's warehouse. Complex, densely malty with vanilla threads and a warming, dried-fruit finish.

ARCTIC DEVIL BARLEY WINE

Midnight Sun, Anchorage, Alaska; 13.2%

Monstrously malt-forward and vanilla-accented from its time in oak barrels, this northern legend combines earthiness with fruity malt for a kaleidoscope of flavours that mix and mingle for what seems an eternity.

AROMA COMA

Drake's, San Leandro, California; 6.75%

One whiff should put the most ardent hophead into a summer slumber, with complex aromas of citrus, pine, grapefruit, herbs and flowers. This summer seasonal IPA hits you with fresh hop flavours, big fruit notes and great balance.

ARROGANT BASTARD ALE

Stone, Escondito, California and other locations; 7.2%

One of the first craft beers to combine copious quantities of malt with high hoppiness and significant strength, this ale did, and still does, it brilliantly, with shocking balance and high quaffability for such a potent brew.

AUTUMN MAPLE

The Bruery, Placentia, California; 10%

An autumn seasonal of a different ilk, brewed with large quantities of yam, various spices and maple syrup for a sweet, clove-ish and spicy, earthy beer with nutty hop notes and a long, soothing finish.

BARNEY FLATS OATMEAL STOUT

Anderson Valley, Boonville, California; 5.8%

A revivalist stout from the earlier days of California craft brewing. Deep black and silky smooth, with a gently porridge-y sweetness and mild roasted-malt character carrying notes of soft berry fruits and coffee.

BARREL AGED SHIPWRECK PORTER

Arcadia, Kalamazoo and Battle Creek, Michigan; 12%

Aged 10 months in bourbon barrels, this is a heady brew redolent with aromas of roasted malt and vanilla, chocolate and plum, along with chocolate, rum-soaked raisin and vanilla in the body.

BEAR WALLOW BERLINER WEISSE

Arizona Wilderness, Gilbert, Arizona; 3.2%

This beer highlights both local ingredients, some foraged, and the wild yeast character of kettle souring. Delightfully complex combination of fruity elements; decidedly tart, though softened by white Sonora wheat.

BED OF NAILS BROWN ALE

Hi-Wire, Asheville, North Carolina; 6.1%

A toasted malt aroma introduces this wonderfully balanced, mid-weight brown ale from Hi-Wire. Brown sugar and date notes leading to a slightly winey, dry finish.

BEING THERE

Right Proper, Washington, DC; 5%

Although this newish brewery has a well-deserved reputation for mixed fermentations and the use of botanicals, it is hard to resist the unpretentious beauty of this *kellerbier*; floral, bready, spicy and dry.

BENDER

Surly, Minneapolis and Brooklyn Center, Minnesota; 5.1%

English ale yeast and oatmeal soften this somewhat silky brown ale with notable complexity, the roasty coffee-and-cream nose giving way to a chocolate, caramel and tart-fruit body.

BERNICE

Sante Adairius, Capitola, California; 6.5%

A golden straw colour with a pillowy white head, this US take on a Belgian farmhouse ale is brightly effervescent, with a wonderfully sophisticated mélange of tart lemon and zesty spices, soft flavours and a dry finish.

ICONIC BREWERY

ANCHOR [SAPPORO]

San Francisco, California

By most accounts, US craft brewing got its start when Fritz Maytag bought the floundering Anchor brewery in the late 1960s and, with zero background in brewing, set about reversing its course in dramatic fashion. First came the revival of **Steam Beer** (4.9%), which mixes ale and lager characteristics in a most refreshing fashion, followed by **Liberty Ale** (5.9%), arguably the first modern American IPA, and equally pioneering **Old Foghorn Barleywine Style Ale** (8–10%). Still eagerly anticipated is the annual **Christmas Ale** (6.5%), a spiced beer brewed to a different recipe for each of its more than 40 years.

ICONIC BREWERIES

BELL'S

Kalamazoo and Comstock, Michigan

First known for its oversized portfolio of porters and stouts, numbering about a dozen, Bell's has gone on to claim adherents on several fronts, including those who await the summer arrival of the spicy–hoppy wheat beer **Oberon** (5.8%), and others who swear by the complexly fruity bitterness of their IPA **Two Hearted Ale** (7%). For the rest, there are such delights as the leafy hop-driven and underrated **Amber Ale** (5.8%), the plum and cinnamony **Third Coast Old Ale** (10.2%) and, not to forget the dark stuff, the densely fruity, oily and complex **Expedition Stout** (10.5%).

BOSTON BEER

Boston, Massachusetts and elsewhere

The largest craft brewery in the USA, responsible for often good, sometimes great and occasionally just okay beers grouped under the Samuel Adams brand name. Pay little heed to the gimmicky Nitro Project ales and focus instead on the dry and toasty original **Boston Lager** (5%); "Barrel Room" beers like the winey *tripel* **New World** (10%); the robustly flavourful seasonal **Octoberfest** (5.3%); and, of course, the outstandingly complex and almost ludicrously strong **Utopias** (28%), blended to a differing intensity every year or two.

BITTERSWEET LENNY'S R.I.P.A.

Shmaltz, Clifton Park, New York; 10%

Named after the late comedian Lenny Bruce, this potent rye IPA packs considerable spicy punch into a beer that is as complex as it is warming, and which is worth storing in the cellar for a year or two.

BLACK BAVARIAN LAGER

Sprecher, Glendale, Wisconsin; 5.86%

The picture of balance in a black lager, this is both one of the first US-brewed *schwarzbiers* and among the oldest continually brewed brands in this Germanic specialist brewery's portfolio.

BLACK TULIP TRIPEL

New Holland, Holland, Michigan; 8.8%

While New Holland is better known for its Mad Hatter line of IPAs, this gently spicy–herbal Belgian-inspired strong ale is at least as deserving of note, particularly given its smooth progression to a dry, lightly bitter finish.

BOAT BEER

Carton, Atlantic Highlands, New Jersey; 4.2%

This American Pale Ale looks and smells like exotic fruit juice; juicy hops, including flavours of grapefruit, pineapple and mango, are balanced by resin and pine. Soft malt middle notes slide easily into a dry finish.

BOURBON COUNTY BRAND STOUT

Goose Island [AB InBev], Chicago, Illinois and other locations; 13.8%

One of the earliest bourbon barrel beers in modern America, this remains a complex, chocolate–vanilla–spice beauty despite some infection issues in 2016.

BUTT HEAD BOCK

Tommyknocker, Idaho Springs, Colorado; 8.2%

This reddish-brown ale has the strength of a *doppelbock*, but the gentle malt profile of a lighter *bock*, with spicy caramel in the nose, a floral–spicy toffee body and a warming, off-dry finish.

CAMPFIRE STOUT

High Water, Stockton, California; 6.5%

Imagine you are in the woods, beside a roaring campfire over which you have just roasted marshmallows to put with chocolate pieces in between two graham crackers. Now imagine that s'more were a beer.

CAPELLA PORTER

Ecliptic, Portland, Oregon; 5.2%

A stellar porter from the former long-time Full Sail brewer John Harris, this is more London than West Coast USA, with chocolate and liquorice in the nose, nutty cocoa along with a drying bitterness in the body and a faintly spicy finish.

CAVATICA

Fort George, Astoria, Oregon; 8.5%

A standout Imperial stout from the brewery that celebrates Stout Month every February. Smooth and silky, with notes of dark chocolate, coffee and char, this black beauty is named after the spider in E B White's children's classic, *Charlotte's Web*.

CERASUS

Logsdon, Hood River, Oregon; 8.5%

This barrel-aged Flemish-style red ale sees two pounds (a kilogram) of sweet and tart local cherries added per US gallon (3.8 litres) of beer, contributing a lovely burgundy colour and anticipated cherry tones to complement oak and balsamic flavours.

CHERRYTREE AMARO

Forbidden Root, Chicago, Illinois; 9%

Brewed as an homage to the Italian herbal liqueur amaros, a wide range of botanicals including cherry stems, bitter orange peel, lemon peel, cinnamon, coriander, basil and almond flavour this still highly beer-like beer, as with the other beers in the portfolio.

CHING CHING

Bend, Bend, Oregon, 4.5%

Pomegranate and hibiscus lend a stunning pink hue and contribute a gentle, tasteful tartness to this beautiful, gently wheaty take on a *Berliner weisse*.

CHINGA TU PELO

5 Rabbit Cerveceria, Bedford Park, Illinois; 4.8%

This former Trump Hotel exclusive had a rebirth and name change following Donald Trump's negative comments about Mexicans, emerging a splendid and solid golden ale quaffer with a slightly rude Spanish name.

CITRA DOUBLE IPA

Kern River, Kernville, California; 8%

A big beer with a bright amber colour. It pours a generous white head and boasts a pungent Citra nose, with signature floral and citrus aromas and tropical-fruit flavours nicely balanced with a honeyed malt backbone.

CITRAHOLIC

Beachwood, Long Beach, California; 7.1%

A standout IPA from a brewery that has burst onto the scene with a remarkable range of quality offerings, this one blending four varieties, emphasizing Citra, into a beautifully nuanced and balanced hop monster.

CITY WIDE

4 Hands, St. Louis, Missouri; 5.5%

A pale ale brewed to benefit the city of St. Louis and sold only in St. Louis in a can decorated by the city's flag. Showcases US hops balanced properly by moderately sweet malt.

COUNTER CLOCKWEISSE

Destihl, Bloomington, Illinois; 3%

Demand for German-style sour beers like this one has fuelled brewery expansion. Refreshingly wheaty, smelling of yogurt and lemon and pleasantly tart on the palate.

CRASH LANDED

Begyle, Chicago, Illinois; 7%

Billed an "American pale wheat ale", this medium gold beer has an approachability that contrasts favourably with its strength, its tropical fruitiness being tamed to an appealing dryness by herbal hoppiness.

CUVEE DE CASTLETON

Captain Lawrence, Elmsford, New York; 7%

Barrel-ageing, muscat grapes and *Brettanomyces* transform the brewery's popular Liquid Gold into an enormously complex experience, with juicy tropical fruit at the front of all the flavours expected in a "wild" beer.

DAILY WAGES

Saint James, Reno, Nevada; 6.7%

Goldenrod in colour and pouring a thick, pillowy head with great lacing, this big, Americanized *saison* is funky and herbal, with tart citrus notes and spiced with green peppercorns.

DAISY CUTTER PALE ALE

Half Acre, Chicago, Illinois; 5.2%

Flagship brand from this now landmark Midwestern success story, with a floral and fragrant, citrus-filled aroma and likewise grapefruity and lemony body with solid balancing malt.

DAYLIGHT AMBER

Track 7, Sacramento, California; 6.25%

Clear copper colour, with toffee and toast aromas. Malt-forward with toffee, caramel and soft biscuity character, but balanced with aggressively big, spicy and grapefruit hops.

DEAD CANARY LAGER DORTMUNDER-STYLE EXPORT

Ol' Republic, Nevada City, California, 4.8%

Light gold colour with a biscuit malt nose and delicate aromas of light sweet corn, honey and whole-grain bread. Crisp, refreshing flavours that are mildly sweet with a clean, noble hop finish.

ICONIC BREWERY

NEW BELGIUM

Fort Collins, Colorado and Asheville, North Carolina

Now a misnomer, since this brewery's impressive portfolio features many beers well outside of the Belgian style set, including hop-forward but soft-finishing **Voodoo Ranger IPA** (7%) and gluten-reduced **Glütíny Pale Ale** (6%). For their best, however, one should still explore the limits of the Belgian-inspired oeuvre, like the pleasingly estery **Trippel** (8.5%), the caramelly **Abbey** (7%), cast in the style of a well-executed *dubbel*, and the tartly fruity, complex **La Folie** (7%), aged one to three years in the large oak barrels known as foeders.

ICONIC BREWERY

SIERRA NEVADA

Chico, California and Mills River,
North Carolina

A powerhouse brewery that dates
as one of the earliest of the craft
beer renaissance and remains one of
the best. Beers include the definitive
US-style pale ale **Sierra Nevada Pale
Ale** (5.6%); a more recent IPA arrival
Torpedo Extra IPA (7.2%), which
portrays hop complexity brilliantly;
the seminal hop-forward barley wine
Bigfoot (9.6%); **Nooner Pilsner**
(5.2%), a crisp lager that can stand with
Germany's best; and a host of special
releases, collaboration brews and
seasonal brands.

DEATH AND TAXES

Moonlight, Santa Rosa, California; 5%

Some say this is a *schwarzbier*, while
others think it's a black lager. But given
that few things in life are certain, we
can attest that this light-bodied, highly
drinkable beer with a taste of iced
coffee is always delicious.

DOG ATE MY HOMEWORK

West, San Pedro, California; 7%

Deep purple colour with a full pink
head. Yeasty *saison*-like nose with
strong blackberry fruit aromas.
Well-integrated tart fruit flavours,
lightly spiced, with blackberry jam
and vinous notes, finishing dry.

DORTMUNDER GOLD LAGER

Great Lakes, Cleveland, Ohio; 5.8%

The late beer-writing maven Michael
Jackson described the Dortmund style
of lager as bigger and sweeter than a
pilsner, but drier than a *helles*, which
pretty much describes this refreshing
lager to a tee.

EASY UP PALE ALE

Coronado, Coronado, California; 5.2%

One of the San Diego area's best-
balanced beers, this medium gold ale
offers a dry, leafy aroma with hints of
citrus and a round, more citrusy and
highly quaffable, dry body accented
by slight peppery tones.

ELEVATED IPA

La Cumbre, Albuquerque, New Mexico; 7.2%

Although the La Cumbre brewery makes a more pungent IPA called Project Dank, the flagship is brimming with US hop character – complexly fruity with tongue-coating resins, and robust bitterness that balances all that hop flavour.

EXPONENTIAL HOPPINESS

Alpine, Alpine, California; 11%

Even in a brewery known for its hop monsters, this beer stands out exponentially, with fresh hop aromas and tastes; herbal, pine, blood orange, apricot and grapefruit, yet surprisingly smooth and well balanced throughout.

EXTRA PALE ALE

Summit, St. Paul, Minnesota; 5.2%

Thirty years old and considered an English-style pale ale these days, EPA is distinctive without being overpowering, citrusy at the outset with toasted malt and fruity character mid-palate and a firmly bitter, lemon-scented finish.

FIELD 41 PALE ALE

Bale Breaker, Yakima, Washington; 4.5%

Hailing from the hops motherland of the USA, this light and refreshing pale ale stands out among the brewery's other delicious hoppy offerings for its smooth, balanced bitterness of grapefruit, tangerine, honeydew and pine.

FIREBRICK

August Schell, New Ulm, Minnesota; 5%

A classic Vienna lager from the USA's second-oldest family-owned brewery, showcasing toasted malt from start to finish. Rich, almost regal, but clean and crisp, balanced by firm hop bitterness.

FIRST FROST WINTER PERSIMMON ALE

Fullsteam, Durham, North Carolina; 10%

The brewery rewards patrons who forage for persimmons with this caramelly, cinnamony winter warmer that grows better with a year or more of ageing.

FIST CITY

Revolution, Chicago, Illinois; 5.5%

Bright gold with a very floral aroma, this quencher offers crisp fruitiness mixed with brown spice and a drying, medium-bitter finish. Like a fine ESB, except seasoned with US rather than British hops.

FLORA RUSTICA

Upright, Portland, Oregon; 5.2%

From this Pacific Northwest Belgian and French style specialist comes their particular take on a *saison*, a hazy blond ale brewed with yarrow and calendula for a floral–peppery aroma and complex, spicy–herbal flavour.

CAN'T-MISS BREWERIES

ALLAGASH

Portland, Maine

Unabashedly Belgian-centric in its approach to brewing, this East Coast stalwart has been turning out sometimes unexpectedly excellent beers since 1995. Mainstay is the superbly balanced Belgian-style wheat beer **White** (5.1%), the success of which enables the production of more "out there" beers, such as the surprisingly subtle, oak-aged *tripel* **Curieux** (11%), also stunning in non-barrelled form as the regular **Tripel** (9%), and the spicy, pear-accented **Saison** (6.1%). An ongoing spontaneous-fermentation project has yielded such impressive results as the plummy–oaky–herbal **Coolship Resurgam** (6.3%).

BOULEVARD [DUVEL MOORTGAT]

Kansas City, Missouri

This early achiever in the heart of the Midwest has progressed from an early wheat beer, now the refreshing **Unfiltered Wheat Beer** (4.4%), to the tangerine-accented **Single-Wide IPA** (5.7%). Along the way, a line of more esoteric beers called the Smokestack Series was developed, producing such beers as the fruity, tart and much sought-after **Love Child No. 7** (8–9.5%) and the spicy and misleadingly quaffable **Tank 7 Farmhouse Ale** (8.5%).

BROOKLYN

Brooklyn, New York

Born from contract brewing, this East Coast mainstay has gone on to become a pivotal force in craft brewing, partly thanks to its charismatic head brewer, Garrett Oliver. Mainstay **Lager** (5.2%) is an underrated Vienna lager with a dry finish, but greater excitement is generated by regulars like the slightly nutty **Brown Ale** (5.6%); seasonals such as the deeply rich, chocolaty **Black Chocolate Stout** (10%), the flavour of which is all from malt; and big-bottle releases like the botanically influenced **Improved Old Fashioned** (12.8%).

FORTUNATE ISLANDS

Modern Times, San Diego, California; 5%

Think hybrid wheat IPA, aggressively hopped with Citra and Amarillo. The result is a massive tropical-fruit nose and hop flavours of mango, guava and passion-fruit smoothed out wonderfully by the wheat malt.

FREAK OF NATURE

Wicked Weed [AB InBev], Asheville, North Carolina; 8.6%

Loyalists were up in arms when this stellar operation was sold to AB InBev in early 2017, and it is hoped that changes do not befall beers such as this intense, herbal–citrus double IPA with plenty of oily hoppiness and sufficient malt to hold it all together.

FÜNKE HOP FARM

Sudwerk, Davis, California; 6.5%

For a brewery that is best known for its lagers, this funky wild one is brewed with three yeasts and aged on different wine barrels, giving it amazing complexity with soft fruit and a tart farmyard earthiness.

GRAND CRU

Alesmith, San Diego, California; 10%

If you choose not to age this immensely cellar-friendly ale, your experience will be one of spicy raisin, cocoa and brown spice on the nose and a body filled with massive dried-fruit notes and bittersweet chocolate.

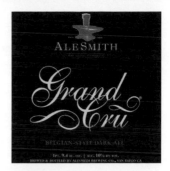

GREEN PEPPERCORN TRIPEL

The Brewer's Art, Baltimore, Maryland; 10%

Effervescent, nuanced, subtle banana and floral pear skins are played against peppery phenols and peppercorns, and brightened by lively acidity.

HEAD HUNTER

Fat Head's, Middleburg Heights, Ohio and other locations; 7.5%

An IPA that other brewers judge their own against, beginning with the citrus/ tropical hop punch at the outset. Hop bitterness and flavour are perfectly intertwined.

HEADY TOPPER

The Alchemist, Stowe, Vermont; 8%

One of the original New England cult beers, folks still line up to buy this double IPA with a perfume of florals in its aroma and citrusy, spicy, lightly tannic hoppiness held just in check by robust orange–caramel malt.

HEFEWEIZEN

Live Oak, Austin, Texas; 5.3%

The beers here lost none of their Old World character when the brewery began packaging in cans in 2016. This one is wheat-rich with a harmonious blend of banana, clove and vanilla.

HEFEWEIZEN

San Tan, Chandler, Arizona; 5%

Built for the southwest heat with a bright carbonation and a light wheat body showcasing classic Bavarian character alongside notes of pear and lemon-lime, which add complexity to expected banana aroma and flavour, matched by peppery cloves.

HELL OR HIGH WATERMELON WHEAT

21st Amendment, San Francisco/San Leandro, California; 4.9%

Only available during the warmer half of the year, fresh watermelon juice is added to wheat beer for a second fermentation, creating a uniquely refreshing fruit beer that is delicate and not overpowering.

HELLES

Kansas City, Kansas City, Missouri; 5%

Great beers in the *helles* style have aromas of perfumey grain and gentle, malty sweetness on the palate, like this fine lager. Arguably a touch fuller than the style would dictate, but no less refreshing for it.

HUNAHPU'S IMPERIAL STOUT

Cigar City [Oskar Blues], Tampa, Florida; 11%

The brewery has built a festival around the release of this beer, a truly Imperial stout infused with and flaunting the flavours of cacao nibs, vanilla pods, Ancho and Pasilla chillies and cinnamon.

IMPERIAL COCONUT HIWA PORTER

Maui, Kihei, Maui, Hawaii; 9.4%

A rich mocha head rises out of this ash-black beer, with a nose redolent of coffee roast and, naturally, fresh coconut. With a very smooth and creamy mouthfeel, the beer maintains its balance in spite of being loaded with coconut flavour.

INCEPTUS

Three Taverns, Decatur, Georgia; 6%

A "Georgia Wild Ale", fermented with yeast captured during a rare snow storm and then aged for several months in wine barrels, creating complex fruity and grapey flavours before a brightly tart finish.

JET STAR IMPERIAL IPA

No-Li, Spokane, Washington; 8.1%

Pine forest meets toasted lemon peel in the aroma of this big beer that deftly combines biscuit and British-style maltiness with US hop-forwardness, producing a malty–citrusy–peachy ale with an off-dry finish.

KATY

2nd Shift, St. Louis, Missouri; 5.4%

Fermented and aged in barrels inoculated long ago with a strain of *Brettanomyces*, Katy is beholding to no style. Brightness from zesty lemon at the outset leads to lightly bready, stone-fruit elements adding complexity mid-palate and a tart finish.

KILT LIFTER

Four Peaks [AB InBev], Tempe, Arizona; 6%

The brewery's flagship, showcasing its UK influence in a Scottish ale that is rich and malty throughout, with a taste of caramel and toffee and a hint of smoke on top.

LA GUARDIA RUBIA

Cruz Blanca, Chicago, Illinois; 6.8%

An early success from this *cerveceria* owned by celebrated chef Rick Bayless, this is a spicy, medium gold-hued treat based on the *bière de garde* style, with food-friendly citrus accents and a mildly bitter finish.

LE PETIT PRINCE

Jester King, Austin, Texas; 2.9%

Those who complain about the difficulties of getting full flavour from a low-alcohol beer have never met the Little Prince. With a citrusy floral aroma, this sublime thirst-quencher is peppery and mildly bitter, and finishes bone dry.

CAN'T-MISS BREWERIES
● ● ● ● ● ● ● ● ● ● ● ● ● ● ●

DESCHUTES

Bend and Portland, Oregon

One of the handful of early Pacific Northwest breweries to emerge as a national leader, Deschutes seems to excel at almost everything they turn their hands to. Flagship **Black Butte Porter** (5.2%) sets the standard for American porters, while **Mirror Pond Pale Ale** (5%) is a laudably floral take on the style pioneered in California. Cocoa-accented, spicy **Jubelale** (6.7%) is a much-anticipated winter seasonal, while special Reserve Series releases like the intense anniversary ale **Black Butte XXVIII** (XXIX in 2017; 11.5%) and liquorice-accented Imperial stout **The Abyss** (11.1%) are not to be missed.

FIRESTONE WALKER [DUVEL MOORTGAT]

Paso Robles, California

Founded as the meeting place of British and US brewing, the flagship Double Barrel Ale, now **DBA** (5%), marks the territory marvellously, with a rich yet refreshing mix of fruit and caramel malt drying finely on the finish. **Union Jack IPA** (7%) continues the brewery's cross-continental ways with juicy fruit upfront and citrusy hop bitterness in the back, while the quenching, spicy **Pivo Hoppy Pils** (5.3%) demonstrates the brewery's skills in lager fermentation. Yearly **Anniversary Ale** (12.5–13.5%) releases are always complex blends and are seldom less than exceptional.

LIL' HEAVEN

Two Roads, Stratford, Connecticut; 4.8%

Brewed with four designer hops, producing the exotic tropical aroma and rich juicy taste expected of a modern IPA on a satisfyingly firm malt base, despite its lower alcohol and "session IPA" label.

LITTLE JUICE IPA SMOOTHIE EDITION

Three Magnets, Olympia, Washington; 6.6%

Joining the cloudy IPA craze, this hazy offering delivers on the promises of its aromas of tropical-fruit cocktail and oranges, later bringing a citrus-peel note and residual juicy, fruit flavours intermingled in a slightly creamy body.

LOOSE CANNON HOP3

Heavy Seas, Baltimore, Maryland; 7.25%

From the brewery formerly known as Clipper City comes this hops cocktail of an IPA, brimming with tangerine, grapefruit and pine aromas and flavours, lightly toasted bread slathered in alcoholic orange marmalade.

LUPULIN LUST

Rip Current, San Marcos, California; 9%

Referred to as a San Diego-style IPA, this light golden-hued ale has all the anticipated grapefruit and tangerine aromas with floral notes. It is also easy-drinking, being beautifully balanced with a dry, bitter finish.

CAN'T-MISS BREWERIES

FOUNDERS

Grand Rapids, Michigan

Fame may have come to the company on the back of their rich and complex Kentucky Breakfast Stout, renamed **KBS** (11.8%) following a Kentucky-based lawsuit, but this is a brewery solid throughout their portfolio. From the single-hop, grapefruit–apple–redcurrant **Centennial IPA** (7.2%) to the dark rye breadiness of **Red's Rye I.P.A.** (6.6%); and the wonderfully aromatic, raisin-and-fig **Old Curmudgeon Ale** (9.8%) to the well-named, quenching **All Day IPA** (4.7%), it's hard to go wrong with a Founders brew.

NEW GLARUS

New Glarus, Wisconsin

The bestselling brand is the slightly chewy, quaffable **Spotted Cow** (4.9%), yet fame resides in its many only-in-Wisconsin brands including balanced fruit beers like the whole-cherry-flavoured **Wisconsin Belgian Red** (4%) and the apple–cherry–cranberry **Serendipity** (5.1%). Seasonals bring further highly deserved accolades, as with the strong, clove-and-pepper **Dancing Man Wheat** (7.2%) and nutty brown ale **Fat Squirrel** (5.5%). Some of the finest spontaneous fermentation in the USA results in occasional releases such as the **R&D Vintage 2015** (5%).

MAD ELF

Tröegs, Hershey, Pennsylvania; 11%

Cherries and local honey take a strong Belgian ale literally to 11 (% ABV), imbuing it with a menagerie of fruity and spicy aromas and tastes that glow a bright dark red.

MÄRZEN

Gordon Biersch, San Jose, California; 5.7%

Bright amber orange in colour with aromas of toasted pretzels, dried fruit and sweet malt. Refreshingly authentic version of a German Oktoberfest beer with clean, rich malt flavours and a caramel sweetness balanced by classic noble hop character.

MÉLANGE À TROIS

Nebraska, Papillion, Nebraska; 11.3%

Six months in Chardonnay barrels add all the flavours you would expect to an already rich and fruity blond Belgian ale, as wood tannins merging with peppery phenols and residual wine provide a crisp acidity.

RUSSIAN RIVER

Santa Rosa, California

Run by the husband and wife team of Vinnie and Natalie Cilurzo, the brewery excels in both hoppy and so-called sour beers, producing the definitive double IPA **Pliny the Elder** (8%), on the former side, and mixed-fermentation, barrel-aged beers such as the wine-ish, sour cherry **Supplication** (7%) and surprisingly nuanced blond ale **Temptation** (7.5%) on the latter. Dryly fruity **Damnation** (7.75%) is an homage to the Belgian ale Duvel, while **Blind Pig IPA** (6.25%) is a solid and sturdy India Pale Ale.

CAN'T-MISS BREWERY

• • • • • • • • • • • • • •

VICTORY

Downingtown, Pennsylvania
and other locations

Brewing multiple styles since before it
was cool, Victory has long exhibited skill
in both ale and lager fermentation, their
deliciously crisp **Prima Pils** (5.3%) and
deftly hopped, piney **HopDevil India
Pale Ale** (6.7%) being among their
early successes. A similarly early foray
into Belgian influence yielded the fruity,
almost nectar-ish **Golden Monkey**
(9.5%), while more aptitude on the
Germanic side is shown in the newer
Helles Lager (4.8%).

MIAMI MADNESS

J Wakefield, Miami, Florida; 3.5%

The state's brewers have staked out
Florida weisse, a Berliner beer infused
with fruit, as their own style. This
version, one of several that the brewery
makes, balances mango, guava and
passion-fruit sweetness and lemonade-
like tartness.

MODUS HOPERANDI

Ska, Durango, Colorado; 6.8%

From a musically minded brewery in the
south of the state, this IPA offers the
familiar mix of citrus and pine aromas
and flavours typical of its style in the
USA, but with a softening finish that
accentuates its refreshing character.

MONK'S INDISCRETION

Sound, Poulsbo, Washington; 10%

Consistently award-winning Belgian-style
strong ale that nods to its West Coast
upbringing, with tropical-fruit flavours
canoodling alongside more conventional
banana, herbal, spicy and lemon notes,
leading to a pleasantly dry finish.

MOSAIC SESSION IPA

Karl Strauss, San Diego, California; 5.5%

This relatively restrained IPA, at least
for the West Coast, is still loaded with
grapefruit and tropical-fruit aromas.
Satisfying mouthfeel with mango,
tangerine and guava, plus a noticeable
malt presence underneath it all.

MOTHER OF ALL STORMS

Pelican, Pacific City, Oregon; 14%

A world-class barley wine from a consistently award-winning brewery, aged in bourbon barrels for deep flavours of toasted malt, bourbon and oak, with a sublime finish of vanilla, toffee, caramel and a touch of alcoholic warmth.

MT. NELSON

Cellarmaker, San Francisco, California; 5.4%

This American pale ale stands atop the mountain of impressively hoppy offerings at which Cellarmaker excels, and its single hop, Nelson Sauvin, manages to introduce a complex array of flavours, from grapes and lemon to guava and mango.

MULLET CUTTER

Revolver [Molson Coors], Granbury, Texas; 9%

An unusual take on an American double IPA with spicy rather than citrusy hops dominating the nose and an earthy, spicy–herbal and slightly resinous body, culminating in a citrusy hop finish.

NOYAUX

Cascade Barrel House, Portland, Oregon; 9.29%

A blend of blond ales aged in white wine barrels on raspberries and apricot stones produces a sublime, almondy–berry-ish beer with a tart and drying palate of great fruity complexity and a rosé Champagne-esque finish.

OAK AGED YETI IMPERIAL STOUT

Great Divide, Denver, Colorado; 9.5%

One of several versions of the brewery's trademark Imperial stout, this one rounds off the borderline sharp roastiness of the regular Yeti with whiskey-barrel-derived vanilla notes and a softened hop bitterness.

OKTOBERFEST

Real Ale, Blanco, Texas; 5.7%

One of the best Oktoberfest märzens brewed in the USA, this has a bready, toasted-grain aroma and a caramelly, off-dry maltiness in the body that effectively bridges the gap between traditional and modern styles.

OLD RASPUTIN RUSSIAN IMPERIAL STOUT

North Coast, Fort Bragg, California; 9%

A "gentle giant" of an Imperial stout, with luscious chocolate- and coffee-accented maltiness and just enough hop to keep the sweetness in check. Deservedly an iconic American stout.

PALO SANTO MARRON

Dogfish Head, Milton, Delaware; 12%

Ageing in vats made from Paraguayan woods gives this brown ale a nose of cinnamon, vanilla and other aromatic spices, while a load of malt bestows flavours of chocolate fudge and rum-soaked raisins.

PEEPER ALE

Maine, Freeport, Maine; 5.5%

Certainly a beer that is not shy about its US hopping, this golden Maine pale ale has nonetheless a deep and rich maltiness that instead evokes the British approach to brewing hop-forward beers.

PETIT DESAY

de Garde, Tillamook, Oregon; 5%

This wild-fermentation brewery uses the coastal region's microflora to ferment its beers traditionally in a *koelschip* before transferring to barrels. A refreshingly tart farmhouse ale with notes of apricot and pineapple, a touch of oak and a lemony finish.

PIKE IPA

Pike, Seattle, Washington; 6.3%

In 1990, there were few IPAs brewed in the USA, but there was this beer, built on a solid base of dry, caramelly malt and floral, citrusy hoppiness with an almost note-perfect balance between the two.

PILS

Heater Allen, McMinnville, Oregon; 4.9%

Brewed in wine country, this earthy, spicy take on a Bohemian-style lager is slightly more golden in colour and rounder in body than many versions, while finishing dry. No wonder it's a favourite among local winery workers.

PILS

Lagunitas [Heineken], Petaluma, California; 6%

The brewery's typical irreverence is set aside for this foray into Czech-style *světlý ležák*, which offers a classically floral aroma, firm maltiness and crisp refreshment, albeit with more bitterness and strength than is typical.

PILS

Trumer, Berkeley, California; 4.9%

Pale golden, bright and clear, with a dense white head. Signature Saaz hop nose and classic German-style pilsner flavours make this one of the best authentic pilsners brewed in the USA using a centuries-old Austrian recipe.

PILSNER

Marble, Albuquerque, New Mexico; 4.7%

Unfiltered, and a frequent award winner in international competitions as a *zwickelbier*. Floral and spicy hops create a delicate perfumey aroma and persist into the taste, blending seamlessly with bready malt, finishing dry and bitter.

PIPEWRENCH

Gigantic, Portland, Oregon; 7.8%

Ageing Gigantic's already tasty IPA in
Ransom Old Tom gin barrels creates
an entirely different entity that is
surprisingly refreshing, with bright
citrus and fruity notes alongside
juniper, spice and oak.

POINT REYES PORTER

Marin, Larkspur, California; 6%

Inky black with a tight tan head, a nose
thick with chocolate and coffee aromas
and a creamy mouthfeel. The flavour
profile is dry with rich espresso and
chewy chocolate character, finishing
cleanly with a velvet smoothness.

PORTER

The Duck-Rabbit, Farmville, North
Carolina; 5.7%

Robust dark malt flavours from a
dark beer specialist, with creamy
middle notes (perhaps from the
addition of oats) creating an intriguing
juxtaposition with dry chocolate and
roasted coffee bitterness.

PORTER

Stoneface, Newington, New Hampshire;
5.5%

With an aroma of chicory-accented
mocha plus a whiff of liquorice, this
solid and sessionable black beer from
Stoneface boasts elements of raisin
and date mixed with a hint of espresso
toward its off-dry finish.

PRAIRIE STANDARD

Prairie Artisan, Krebs and Oklahoma
City, Oklahoma; 5.6%

Not as strong as most of its stable
mates, this *saison*-style ale shares
much of its relatives' complex
funkiness, stone and citrus fruits and
spicy finish, in this case with a bit of
lime zest thrown in.

PSEUDOSUE

Toppling Goliath, Decorah, Iowa; 5.0%

An American pale ale that serves as
an advertisement for the Citra hop, the
only variety used to make it, checking
all the boxes for bold citrus-, tropical-
and stone-fruit aromas and flavours.

PUMPKIN LAGER

Lakefront, Milwaukee, Wisconsin; 5.8%

Pumpkin sceptics may be forgiven for
approaching this beer with trepidation,
but Lakefront makes it all work with
soft spice in the aroma and a clove-
accented body boasting soft, creamy,
vaguely peppery richness.

RACER 5 IPA

Bear Republic, Healdsburg, California; 7.5%

Atypically brewed from malted barley and wheat, which adds a fragrant and floral, even slightly spicy aspect to the US hops that otherwise shine their citrusy light throughout this quaffable ale from Bear Republic.

RASPBERRY EISBOCK

Kuhnhenn, Warren, Michigan; 15.5%

With outrageous complexity and massive fruit flavours, this very big lager is no shrinking violet, mixing raspberry notes with chocolate cream and orange brandy. Delicious on release, but also highly cellar-worthy.

THE REVEREND

Avery, Boulder, Colorado; 10%

The nose of this massive deep purplish burgundy *quadrupel* is dark fruit – raisins, dates, prunes, currants – while the body is rich and intense, with molasses, plum, burned raisins and chocolate, as warming as a thick blanket on a cold night.

ROBUST PORTER

Reuben's, Seattle, Washington; 5.9%

A spot-on porter from a brewery known for its flawless interpretations of styles. Rich caramel, roasted coffee, cocoa and a hint of liquorice, with a dry, cracker-y finish.

ROBUST PORTER

Smuttynose, Hampton, New Hampshire; 6.2%

While decidedly chocolaty in its aroma, this full and coffee-ish ale is drier than one might expect and, in fact, quite dry in its mocha-ish finish. A tasty mixture of US and British approaches to the porter style.

ROGGENWEISSWINE

Coachella Valley, Thousand Palms, California; 10%

Made from wheat and rye malts comprising an astonishing 96% of its grain bill, the nose is full of spiced plum, vanilla and charred oak, while the palate brings boozy lemon peel, dried fruits and peppery spice.

THE RUSTY NAIL

Fremont, Seattle, Washington; 13.2%

A beer so deeply complex that it begs hours of contemplation, with a base of Imperial smoked oatmeal stout aged on cinnamon bark before spending 15 months in 12-year-old bourbon barrels. Delicious at release, it promises to improve with age.

RYE PALE ALE

Terrapin [Molson Coors], Athens, Georgia; 5.3%

The brewery came to life around this beer, one of the USA's original rye ales. Spicy rye enhances an impression of dark bread, earthy and citrusy bitterness leading to a dry finish.

SAHALIE ALE

Apothecary, Bend, Oregon; 9–10%

Flagship wild ale from this rustic, mixed-fermentation brewery where mashing, open fermentation, conditioning and dry-hopping all take place in oak, resulting in notes of pineapple, apricots and citrus that dance sublimely with pithy, earthy and herbal undertones.

SAISON

Casey, Glenwood Springs, Colorado; 5.5%

The base beer for other wildly popular brands such as the Fruit Stand series stands up just fine on its own, with aromas and flavours of funky fruitiness, wet hay and bright citrus backed by fresh, tart and lively acidity.

SAISON ATHENE

Saint Somewhere, Tarpon Springs, Florida; 7.5%

The first beer that this smallish brewery bottled is brimming with house character – a bit wild, spicy lemon zest on the nose, stone fruits lingering beneath, mingling with grainy malt. Ultimately tart and dry.

BREWERIES TO WATCH

BAERLIC

Portland, Oregon

With a name meaning "of barley" in old English, this young outfit shows great promise with unusual brews like the creamy **Eastside Oatmeal Pilsner** (6%), classics including the porridge-y **Noble Oatmeal Stout** (6.3%) and a straight-up, spicy, dry-finishing **Invincible India Pale** (6.7%).

BAGBY

Oceanside, California

Multiple award-winning brewer Jeff Bagby turned a former car dealership into a brewpub, where he brews a dizzying line-up, from Belgian-style mini blond **Yvankë** (4%) to tropical-fruit-forward **Dork Squad IPA** (6.8%) and the dark chocolaty **Reconnoiter Porter** (7.4%).

BIG DITCH

Buffalo, New York

Brewery–restaurant that is part of downtown Buffalo's ongoing renaissance, with beers ranging from **Low Bridge** (4.8%) "hoppy golden ale" to the intense **Deep Cut Double IPA** (8.5%).

BREWERIES TO WATCH

BLACK PROJECT

Denver, Colorado

Wildly experimental brewery devoted to spontaneous fermentation in varied forms, producing beers like the lemony, solera-style **Dreamland** (5.7%) and the dry and dry-hopped **Jumpseat** (6.2%)

CENTRAL STANDARD

Wichita, Kansas

There are big ambitions from this young outfit formed by five friends, who are brewing such diverse beers as the creamy **Extra Medium Pale Ale** (5.3%), the tangy and quenching **Wally Funk** (7%) and the floral, gingery **Red Cicada** (4.5%) gose.

CLOUDBURST

Seattle, Washington

Former Elysian brewer Steve Luke has released completely new and different IPAs every two weeks since opening his new brewery in January 2016, along with other gems like "bastardized German Pilsner" **Happy Little Clouds** (5.1%) and "toasted brown ale" **Two Scoops** (5.8%).

SAISON DE LIS

Perennial, St. Louis, Missouri; 5%

The addition of camomile flowers adds a tea-like twist to a fruit-and-spice character central to many of the often adventurous beers made here at Perennial. Lively, floral, earthy, complex but never overbearing.

SAISON DU FERMIER

Side Project, Maplewood, Missouri; 7%

No longer just a side project, the intense stouts and lively *saisons* from this brewery generate equal excitement. Fermented and aged with local cultures in Chardonnay barrels and wrapped in a fog of fruity funk finished by bright acidity.

SAISONHANDS

Tired Hands, Ardmore, Pennsylvania; 4.8%

First known as FarmHands, this is a tribute to farmers and a nod to four grains – barley, rye, wheat and oats – in the grist. Brightened by lemon zest and stone-fruit aromas, with yeasty funk adding satisfying complexity.

SARA'S RUBY MILD

Magnolia, San Francisco, California; 3.8%

The inspiration for Magnolia's mild came during an English vacation; malt-forward throughout, it has a silky mouthfeel. Especially fine on cask, with lightly roasted malt, dark fruit and delicate flavours.

SAWTOOTH ALE

Left Hand, Longmont, Colorado; 5.3%

The brewery's original flagship beer, a not-so-simple amber ale combining toasty biscuit malt with sweet chocolate and caramel notes, finished with citrus-tinged bitterness and mineral-like dryness.

SCALE TIPPER IPA

Bosque, Albuquerque, New Mexico, 6.5%

Part of a family of IPAs that quickly established hop-forward intentions here. A fresh, tropical bouquet along with hints of pine and camphor leads to a firm, bready maltiness balanced by lingering bitterness.

SCULPIN IPA

Ballast Point [Constellation], San Diego, California; 7%

A near-perfect West Coast IPA, especially when fresh, with a mountain of hops that somehow still manages to maintain great balance. With strong grapefruit aromas and flavour, it is lightly spiced and highly drinkable.

SCURRY

Off Color, Chicago, Illinois; 5.3%

Deceptive in its chocolate, liquorice and molasses aroma, which is akin to that of a bigger ale, this honey beer has a creamy brown ale character, chocolaty with notes of hazelnut and an off-dry, food-friendly finish.

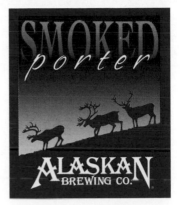

SLESS' OATMEAL STOUT

Iron Springs, Fairfax, California; 8%

Strong, smooth stout with aromas of dark chocolate and roasted coffee. Velvety mouthfeel, delightfully softened by the oats, with flavours of bitter dark chocolate, espresso and a hint of liquorice.

SMOKE & DAGGER

Jack's Abby, Framingham, Massachusetts; 5.6%

An outstanding *rauchbier* from New England's lager specialists, mahogany hued with a lean, softly smoky nose that is reminiscent of smouldering balsawood and a complex, lightly smoky body with hints of black liquorice and burned walnut.

SMOKED PORTER

Alaskan, Juneau, Alaska; 6.5%

From a first batch made with malt smoked at a local salmon smokehouse

BREWERIES TO WATCH

CREATURE COMFORTS

Athens, Georgia

An almost instantly popular brewery that struggled early to keep up with demand for **Tropicália** (6.6%), a tropical (of course) and juicy IPA, but **Athena** (4.5%) *Berliner weisse* and several fruited versions thereof are equally impressive.

DOVETAIL

Chicago, Illinois

An oddball but so far outstanding brewery producing a wonderfully Munich-esque **Lager** (4.8%) and outstanding **Rauchbier** (5.3%) downstairs, while upstairs it conditions barrels of spontaneously fermented beers for much later release.

GRIST HOUSE

Pittsburgh, Pennsylvania

Destination brewery in the city's Millvale neighbourhood, making solid, straightforward ales like **Gristly Bear** (5.8%) American brown and **Camp Slap Red** (5.8%) American IPA.

to a craft beer legend, this slightly oily, smoky and utterly enticing and wonderfully balanced ale has changed little through the years, thankfully.

SMOKESTACK HERITAGE PORTER

East End, Pittsburgh, Pennsylvania; 5.7%

A smoked porter that is sublime in its smokiness, mixing with dark chocolate and raisin in the nose and dried fruitiness – prune, dates and raisins – in the body, with a refreshingly dry finish.

STICKY HANDS

Block 15, Corvallis, Oregon; 8.1%

Also known as The Hop Experience Ale, this double IPA, from which numerous variants are made, continues to draw fans, thanks to its aromatic blast of tropical fruit and citrus and an assertive yet balanced bitter finish.

SUE

Yazoo, Nashville, Tennessee; 9.2%

The first legal high-strength beer sold in Tennessee scrimps on nothing, with cherrywood-smoked malt dominating a big porter long on chocolate flavour and roasted bitterness, with dark figgy fruit providing complexity.

SUPER SAISON

pFriem, Hood River, Oregon; 9.5%

A beautiful meringue-like head floats atop juicy notes of pineapple, papaya, peppercorns and kiwi fruit that are well balanced with a touch of wood, citrus, barnyard funk and a slightly mineral finish.

STYLE SPOTLIGHT

AMERICAN PALE ALE & IPA

No beer has dominated the conversation since the start of the new millennium as much as has US-style IPA. And so it is easy to forget that as little as two decades ago it barely existed.

The US interpretation of India pale ale, or IPA, was born not out of the British original but as a spawn of the less-hoppy, weaker American pale ale, pioneered by Sierra Nevada Brewing and characterized by the citrusy twang of US-grown Cascade hops. As US-style pale ales, sometimes known as APAs, rose in popularity through the 1990s, they gave rise to the bigger, bolder, even more citrusy IPAs that would dominate the US craft beer market for the 2000s and 2010s.

Today, US-style IPAs are multitudinous and cross a vast range of flavour profiles and sub-styles, while after serving years as a distant second fiddle to their bolder stylistic offspring, American pale ales appear to be in fashion again. Classics among the former camp, not counting those already mentioned elsewhere in these listings, include Cigar City's flagship **Jai Alai** from Florida, with melon and peach notes joining the citrusy party, the fiercely aromatic **Susan** by Hill Farmstead of Vermont and the resinous **Pernicious** from Wicked Weed, in Asheville, North Carolina.

In the pale ale camp, established mainstays such as Missouri's subtle, nuanced **Schlafly Pale Ale** and the fragrant, quaffable Philadelphia standard **Yards Philly Pale Ale** are joined by more recent arrivals like the Boston area's tropical **Night Shift Whirlpool** and the floral-citrus **Bone-A-Fide** from Oregon's Boneyard Beer.

SURETTE

Crooked Stave, Denver, Colorado; 6.2%

From a brewer who wrote his master's thesis on *Brettanomyces* comes this dusty, herbal, modestly tart and earthy *saison* with controlled fruity acidity and impressive depth. Changes slightly from batch to batch.

SWEET POTATO CASSEROLE

Funky Buddha, Oakland Park, Florida; 7.9%

One of the funkiest beers from a brewery known for unique flavours, in this case "fresh out of the oven" spiced sweet potatoes and marshmallows swimming in a strong ale.

TEN FIDY

Oskar Blues, Longmont, Colorado and Brevard, North Carolina; 10.5%

One of the first strong beers to appear in a can, this pitch-black Imperial stout bears its potency proudly, with molasses and raisin on its boozy nose and a warming roastiness throughout.

TINY BOMB

Wiseacre, Memphis, Tennessee; 4.5%

An immigrant beer, drawing on Czech and German tradition, but adding local wildflower honey to create an American pilsner. Floral and spicy hops complement cracker-like honey malt and provide crisp bitterness.

TRINITY TRIPEL

Community, Dallas, Texas; 9%

Belgian in inspiration but indisputably New World in character, this strong and moderately hoppy ale boasts a unique and appealing mix of fragrant orange and tropical-fruit notes, with yeasty spice bringing it all together.

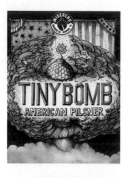

TRIOMPHE BELGIAN-STYLE INDIA PALE ALE

Vivant, Grand Rapids, Michigan; 6.5%

More sublime than most so-called Belgian IPAs, this beer has notes of sweet and floral apple throughout, with a restrained spiciness and bittering hop rising to the drying finish.

TRIPLE WHITE SAGE

Craftsman, Pasadena, California; 9%

Long before craft brewers were throwing everything but the kitchen sink into their beers, Mark Jilg was foraging wild white sage to bring a tremendously appealing peppery–herbal character to his dryish take on a *tripel.*

TROPIC KING

Funkwerks, Fort Collins, Colorado; 8%

A well-named *saison* with a rich and tropical-fruity aroma – notes of floral mango, papaya, pineapple and kiwi fruit, and a likewise richly fruity body that grows both spicier and drier as the flavour progresses to its peppery finish.

TRUTH

Rhinegeist, Cincinnati, Ohio; 7.2%

From the historic Over-the-Rhine brewing district, a very New World IPA, weaving fruit flavours such as grapefruit, pineapple and melon throughout, finishing dry and resiny.

URBAN FARMHOUSE

Commons, Portland, Oregon; 5.3%

Proving that less can be more, this mildly *Brettanomyces*-affected golden ale has a delicately floral aroma with musty notes and a gently fruity body with hints of funk upfront and a lengthy dry finish. Quenching and appetizing.

VELVET ROOSTER

Tallgrass, Manhattan, Kansas; 8.5%

A seasonal take on the *tripel* style, this light golden ale is dryly fruity of aroma, round and fruity with peppery spice in the body and with a super-dry finish, bringing it very close to the textbook ideal for the style.

VIENNA LAGER

Devils Backbone [AB InBev], Lexington and Roseland, Virginia; 5.2%

Delivers on the promise of the label, with rich, toasty Vienna maltiness paired with subtly spicy hops. A clean and crisp product of patient lagering.

WEE MAC SCOTTISH-STYLE ALE

Sun King, Indianapolis, Indiana; 5.3%

A beer some might argue exceeds what the Scots themselves are brewing in the style, this canned ale has an attractive sweetness that never grows cloying or sticky, but always invites another sip.

WEEDWACKER

Saint Arnold, Houston, Texas; 4.9%

A unique mash-up from the oldest craft brewery in Texas, its Fancy Lawnmower

BREWERIES TO WATCH

MANTRA

Franklin, Tennessee

Exciting operation founded by television chef Maneet Chauhan, crafting beers such as **Saffron IPA** (6.2%) and **Sun Salutation** *witbier* (4.8%) designed to complement Indian cuisine.

THE RARE BARREL

Berkeley, California

Calling themselves a "sour beer company", they take wort from nearby breweries and create liquid masterpieces in their home barrels, such as the dark **Ensorcelled** (6.2%), aged with raspberries, or **Soliloquy** (5.4%), a golden sour aged with rose hip and orange peel.

THE VEIL

Richmond, Virginia

An instant cult favourite helmed by much-lauded brewer Matt Tarpey. Early and exciting beers include **Crucial Taunt** (8%), a sneaky-strong double IPA, and the hugely aromatic, double dry-hopped **Broz Broz Day Day** (4.8%).

(*kölsch*) grist fermented with a *hefeweizen* yeast, the result hinting at banana bread but finishing crisp and peppery.

WEST COAST IPA

Green Flash, San Diego, California; 8.1%

Despite the audacity to call their IPA "West Coast", it does deliver on that promise, hitting all the right notes; with a big herbal and citrus hop nose, along with juicy hop flavour lasting for days.

THE WHALE

Community Beer Works, Buffalo, New York; 5.9%

A US take on the northern English brown ale (*see* page 13), this beer has a slightly austere maltiness, but in a way that really works for its flavour mix of burned nut, toasted malt and raw cocoa.

WITTE WHEAT ALE

Ommegang [Duvel Moortgat], Cooperstown, New York; 5.2%

It took Ommegang many years to brew up a *witbier*, but they nailed it when they did with this dryly spicy, wheaty brew offering whispers of fresh lemon juice and peel and a fully dry, peppery finish.

XQST KÖLSCH

Ruhstaller, Sacramento, California; 5%

Nice Californian interpretation of a German classic, with bright straw-gold colour and lasting lacing on a frothy white head. Biscuity malt and light floral hop flavours combine with a zesty and effervescent mouthfeel to make this satisfyingly refreshing.

XS OLD CRUSTACEAN BARLEY WINE

Rogue, Newport, Oregon; 10.6%

One of the early classic American barley wines, this presents a complex aroma of mixed berry fruit and spicy cigar tobacco, and a body that is aggressively hoppy and bitter. Will mellow with ageing.

ZONKER STOUT

Snake River, Jackson, Wyoming; 6%

A US standard-bearer for foreign-style stout, robust without being overbearing, hop bitterness balancing rich mocha-tinged malt. Pleasingly dry finish.

ZWICKEL

Urban Chestnut, St. Louis, Missouri; 5.2%

Unfiltered and hazy as per the style, this wonderfully yeasty lager is everything a *zwickel* should be, with a fresh and floral aroma, bready maltiness and a dryly bitter, refreshing finish.

CANADA

Canada came to what was then "microbrewing" not much later than the USA – the first modern brewpub in North America was actually Canadian – but lagged behind for some time due to the conservative nature of its brewers and, frankly, its citizenry. In recent years, however, the stereotype of the "cautious Canadian brewer" has been flipped on its head and the country has begun producing exciting, creative beers in almost every province.

AMNESIAC DOUBLE IPA

Phillips, Victoria, British Columbia; 8.5%

A spicy mix of citrus fruit, apricot and gentle nuttiness, this powerhouse-that-sips-softly is both one of the first and one of the best Canadian west coast double IPAs.

BACK HAND OF GOD STOUT

Crannóg, Sorrento, British Columbia; 5.2%

A wonderfully named and pleasingly roasty stout with hints of tobacco leaf from the BC interior's leading organic farm brewery, now also a resource for home hop-growers.

BEST BITTER SPECIAL

Granite, Toronto, Ontario and Halifax, Nova Scotia; 4.5%

The survivor Maritime brewery is now overshadowed by its Toronto offspring, from whence originated this deliciously appetizing, leafy and dry-hopped cask-conditioned best bitter, the equal of England's finest.

BLACK LAGER

Silversmith, Virgil, Ontario; 5%

This young wine-country brewery made a great first impression with this earthy, slightly liquorice-accented *schwarzbier* with hints of black pepper and burned citrus oil. Pleasingly roasty, dry-finishing and immensely satisfying.

BOB LEBOEUF

Brasseurs du Petit Sault, Edmundston, New Brunswick; 5.2%

There is considerable spiciness to this unspiced blond ale, with a brown-spice hoppiness in the nose and body that mixes favourably with just off-dry toffee-ish malt. Big flavours in a relatively small beer.

BOCK ME GENTLY

Big Rig, Kanata, Ontario; 7%

The name is a riff on a song by 1970s Canadian warbler Andy Kim, but this Big Rig beer is all business, with a dry toffee aroma and an off-dry body that is as soft and smooth as it is flavourful and warming.

BOSON DE HIGGS

Hopfenstark, L'Assomption, Québec; 3.8%

A stylistic mash-up of *rauchbier*, *Berliner weisse* and *saison* that this eccentrically minded brewery somehow manages to make work, with predictably smoky, tart flavours complemented by a yeasty spiciness.

LA BRITISH

À la Fût, Saint-Tite, Québec; 4.7%

Although nut free, there is a profound nuttiness to this bright brown ale crafted very much in the English tradition, with a hazelnutty aroma and off-dry body with faint chocolate notes upfront and a dry, nutty, roasty finish.

BRONAN IPA

High Road, nomadic, Ontario; 7.1%

A hazy-to-cloudy IPA in the so-called "Vermont style", meaning deeply fruity and, usually, turbidly cloudy, this draught-only beer is a refreshingly restrained take with citrus and mango notes, made for now at the Niagara College brewing school facilities.

LA BUTEUSE

Trou du Diable, Shawinigan, Québec; 10%

Sold in both regular and barrel-aged versions, this is a loose interpretation of a *tripel*, with a spritzy character and ample fruitiness subdued in the second half by peppery spiciness and a growing hoppiness. Wonderfully warming.

DECEPTION BAY IPA

Tatamagouche, Tatamagouche, Nova Scotia; 6.2%

From a promising young brewery, this is a hugely fragrant IPA offering mixed-citrus and tropical-fruit aromas and a similarly fruity, bitter body that is the picture of aromatic complexity in an IPA.

DOUBLE TEMPEST

Amsterdam, Toronto, Ontario;
11.9–14%

Variable from year to year, this weighty
version of Amsterdam Brewing's
Imperial stout is aged in bourbon barrels
to a fruity and mocha mix that is as
soothing as it is intoxicating.

FARM TABLE MÄRZEN

Beau's All-Natural, Vankleek Hill,
Ontario; 5.5%

A full and rich take on the style with
a toasted caramel and lightly nutty
character and a warming note of alcohol
on its mild to moderately bitter finish.
An autumn seasonal very well suited
to its season.

FARMHAND SAISON

Driftwood, Victoria, British Columbia; 5%

A spiced *saison* for those who dislike
spiced saisons, its black pepper does
present itself in both aroma and body,
but always in gentle harmony with the
orangey notes of the body and dryness
of the finish.

GLUTENBERG BLONDE ALE

Brasseurs Sans Gluten, Montréal,
Québec; 4.5%

From a brewery dedicated to gluten-
free beers comes this testament to
creativity with different grains, thin and
citrusy but with enough spiciness that
you almost forget the fact.

ICONIC BREWERY

UNIBROUE [SAPPORO]

Chambly, Québec

More than any other, the brewery that
brought Belgian brewing sensibilities to
Québec and, eventually, Canada, and
mercifully little has changed since its
purchase by Japan's Sapporo. Known
for a quenching and coriander-ish
Blanche de Chambly (5%); the spicy,
food-friendly strong amber ale **Maudite**
(8%); and a fine and fruity *tripel* that
was among the first brewed in North
America, **La Fin du Monde** (9%). Not to
be missed is the intense, almost brandy-
like *quadrupel* **Terrible** (10.5%).

CAN'T-MISS BREWERIES

CENTRAL CITY

Surrey, British Columbia

Perhaps better known as "Red Racer" after the name that adorns many of the brewery's brands, including the grassy, citrusy **Red Racer Pale Ale** (5%), one of the best in its style in Canada. Big brother **Red Racer IPA** (6.5%) is more aggressive, but no less appealing, while **Red Racer ISA** (4%) has a balance and structure much bigger than its moderate strength. Southern BC's rainy winters are made more tolerable by the arrival of the complexly spicy, orange-tangerine maltiness of the rich barley wine **Thor's Hammer** (11.5%).

DIEU DU CIEL!

Montréal and St-Jérôme, Québec

An impressive Montréal brewpub that expanded to a production facility north of the city, this is one of Canada's earliest and best beer innovators. Widely varied successes include the summery, hibiscus-flavoured wheat beer **Rosée d'Hibiscus** (5.9%), the densely fruity kumquat IPA **Disco Soleil** (6.5%) and the intense, coffee-accented strong stout **Péché Mortel** (9.5%). Seasonal releases include the stunningly balanced, black pepper-spiced rye beer **Route des Épices** (5.4%) and the dryly fruity, impressively reserved barley wine **Solstice d'Hiver** (10.5%).

HOYNE

Victoria, British Columbia

Helmed by veteran brewer Sean Hoyne and located in a rather industrial part of the generally pretty provincial capital, this is a brewery skilled in many styles. Highlights at the bottom of the fermenter include the lightly sweet, eminently quaffable **Pilsner** (5.5%) and the firmly malty **Helios Dortmunder Golden Lager** (6%), while ale fermentation yields the authentically British-style **Appleton Extra Special Bitter** (5.2%) and lean and sophisticated porter **Dark Matter** (5.3%), the last given a cold, lager-like conditioning for smoothness.

SIDE LAUNCH

Collingwood, Ontario

The offspring of Toronto's once-landmark Denison's Brewing, the plain names of this brewery's beer belie their frequent brilliance. **Wheat** (5.3%) is a lovely and fairly fruity example of the Bavarian *hefeweizen* style, while **Dark Lager** (5.3%) is a similarly authentic, toasty-nutty take on a Munich *dunkel* and **Mountain Lager** (4.7%) a superbly quenching *helles*-style beer with soft malty sweetness balanced by herbal hoppiness. Visit the brewery taproom for occasional treats like the deliciously spicy **Colossus Dunkelweizen Dopplebock** (8%).

GOLDEN ALE

The Exchange; Niagara-on-the-Lake, Ontario; 7.6%

A lovely example of the studious use of oak-barrelling to achieve a lighter beer style, mixing musty tones of *Brettanomyces* yeast in with pineapple, melon and pear fruitiness, finishing dry and gently warming.

GRAND BALTIC PORTER

Garrison, Halifax, Nova Scotia; 9%

A big-flavoured, deep purple beer from a stalwart of the "second wave" east coast craft brewing scene, suitably unfruity, rich and coffee-ish finishing in a pleasantly sweet, burned-sugar character. Thoroughly enjoyable.

HELLER HIGHWATER

Kichesippi, Ottawa, Ontario; 4.8%

From a brewery whose fortunes improved after the hiring of peripatetic brewer Don Harms, a nearly spot-on *helles* lager with a perfumey aroma and gentle malty sweetness.

KELLER PILSNER

Persephone, Gibsons, British Columbia; 5%

Only slightly hazy, but with a fresh, bright, wild-flower aroma and a grassy-bitter mid-palate with steadily advancing dryness. Lovely structure in a beer occasionally released in special single-hop versions.

KING HEFFY IMPERIAL HEFEWEIZEN

Howe Sound, Squamish, British Columbia; 7.7%

Even those with naught but distain for "Imperial" versions of traditionally lower-alcohol beer styles must appreciate the spice-accented roasted banana and tangerine of this sweet but never cloying beauty.

KITCHEN PARTY PALE ALE

Big Spruce, Nyanza, Nova Scotia; 5.8%

A copper-coloured ale with a perfumey aroma discernible from a foot away, rich with apricot, peach and tangerine. Add to that a mix of fruity toffee and faint, resinous herbals in the body and you have yourself a winner.

LEO'S EARLY BREAKFAST IPA

Dunham, Dunham, Québec; 6.2%

A successful collaboration with Danish brewer Anders Kissmeyer that has become a Dunham mainstay, this tropical-fruity, citrusy and spicy IPA is made with the addition of Earl Grey tea and guava purée.

LONDON STYLE PORTER

Propeller, Halifax, Nova Scotia; 5%

This is as English a porter as you are likely to find outside of the UK, with a slightly burned chocolate aroma and a dark chocolaty, toffee-ish body leading to an off-dry finish.

MAD TOM IPA

Muskoka, Bracebridge, Ontario; 6.4%

An IPA that speaks first to nose, then to palate, this brewery flagship offers a full, leafy, slightly forest-y aroma and a flavourful hoppiness that is a fragrant perfume, then a mouth-shattering bitterness, finally finishing dry and moderately bitter.

MITCHELL'S EXTRA SPECIAL BITTER

Spinnakers, Victoria, British Columbia; 5.2%

Long-standing mainstay at Canada's oldest craft brewery, very much in the character of an English ESB with a floral hoppiness and full and fruity malt profile. Usually even better in cask-conditioned form.

NECTAROUS

Four Winds, Delta, British Columbia; 5.5%

Billed a "dry-hopped sour", this enigmatic ale offers fresh tropical-fruit notes on the nose and a tangy mid-palate of complex tropical and citrus fruits. A beer to linger over, perhaps for several bottles.

NUT BROWN ALE

Black Oak, Toronto, Ontario; 5%

Aptly named and a survivor in a market not particularly enthusiastic about brown ales, this has a robustly nutty aroma, principally hazelnut, a just off-dry, slightly winey and still nutty flavour and a satisfyingly bitter finish.

OLD DEUTERONOMY BARLEY WINE

Alley Kat, Edmonton, Alberta; 10.3%

Released annually in frustratingly small amounts, this cellar-worthy ale has a slightly variable strength and complexity, but always features ample malty fruitiness and a lengthy, warming finish.

PILSNER

Steam Whistle, Toronto, Ontario; 5%

The lone product of this downtown brewery is a good one, more toward the *helles* than the pilsner style. Fragrant and floral in its aroma, with a gently sweet and grainy body that is well tempered by a drying hoppiness.

PORTER BALTIQUE

Les Trois Mousquetaires, Brossard, Québec; 10%

Almost jet black, this sweet espresso-scented beauty has a chocolate-raisin front leading to a complex mix of cinnamon-led spiciness and more dark

chocolate. Occasionally released in spirits-barrel-aged versions.

RED HAMMER

Paddock Wood, Saskatoon, Saskatchewan; 6%

Reddish copper of hue, this slightly strong Vienna lager/*märzen* quaffer has a caramel apple-ish aroma with a whiff of nutmeg and a nutty, faintly spicy toasted-malt body. Lovely structure with an appetizingly dry finish.

ROBOHOP IMPERIAL IPA

Great Lakes, Toronto, Ontario; 8.5%

With an aroma of fruit cocktail mixed with pine tar, this is a big and unapologetic ale that still manages to cram in sufficient malt that the bitterness never grows overwhelming. The picture of balance in a double IPA.

ST-AMBROISE OATMEAL STOUT

McAuslan, Montréal, Québec; 5%

One of Canada's longest-surviving craft stouts is all that an oatmeal stout should be – pitch black with a silken mouthfeel and a whisper of mocha sweetness to balance the roasted malt.

STOUT

Postmark, Vancouver, British Columbia; 4.8%

Deep brown and highly quaffable, this excellent, not-too-dry stout has a chocolate-brownie aroma and a nutty, faintly burned and gently bitter body

BREWERIES TO WATCH

BLACK BRIDGE

Swift Current, Saskatchewan

Solid new arrival to the relative beer desert of the Prairies, with the perfumey, herbal–citrus–piney **IPA!** (7%) and spicy caramel **Rye Ale** (5.3%), among several others.

BRASSEURS DU TEMPS (BDT)

Gatineau, Québec

Long-standing brewpub that broke ground on a full production brewery in early 2017, aiming to bring its summery **La Saison Haute** (8.5%) and resinous **Diable au Corps** (10%) double IPA to a wider audience.

DAGERAAD

Burnaby, British Columbia

Belgian-style specialist in the Vancouver suburbs, featuring a **Blonde** (7.5%) cast in the Duvel genre and an appetizingly spicy **Lake City Farmhouse** (5.2%).

BREWERIES TO WATCH

NEW LIMBURG

Simcoe, Ontario

Brewery run by a Belgian family transplanted to southwestern Ontario, producing home-country-inspired ales like the peppery **Belgian Blond** (7.2%) and plummy **Dubbel** (6.5%) with a dry finish.

TOOTH AND NAIL

Ottawa, Ontario

Within its first year, this brewery managed to create contenders for both Canada's top pilsner with the crisp, dry-finishing **Vim and Vigor** (5.2%), and best *saison* in the spicy, four-grain **Valor** (6%).

UNFILTERED

Halifax, Nova Scotia

Irreverent outfit helmed by irascible veteran brewer Greg Nash, specializing in hop-forward beers like the richly fruity but decidedly balanced pale ale **Hoppy Fingers** (4.8%) and flagship double IPA, the grassy-fruity, citrus-and-spice **Twelve Years to Zion** (8%).

accented by traces of star anise and espresso, finally finishing quite dry.

SUMMIT SEEKER

Banded Peak, Calgary, Alberta; 6.5%

Unusual for a Canadian IPA, this moderately bitter ale is defined as much by its malt as it is by its hops, with a deep amber colour and a mix of berry, citrus and toasted caramel in the taste.

LA VACHE FOLLE IMPERIAL MILK STOUT

Charlevoix, Baie-Saint-Paul, Québec; 9%

A bold take on a usually gentle style, sweet with notes of burned brown sugar in the aroma, with a chocolaty body boasting elements of sugary espresso and burned caramel and a warming, slightly bitter finish.

WITCHSHARK

Bellwoods, Toronto, Ontario; 9%

The opening of a second brewery in late 2016 brings hope for more regular production of popular brews like this inspired double IPA with a fruit basket of citrusy aromas and flavours backed by dryly toffee-ish malt.

YAKIMA IPA

Le Castor, Rigaud, Québec; 6.5%

A Québécois favourite, the late and dry-hopping of this beer has it exploding with fruity–floral aromas, while the body begins with fruit-cocktail sweetness before sliding into a more hoppy and bitter, citrus-accented body.

LATIN AMERICA

MEXICO

Due to the oligopolistic tendencies of Mexico's two largest brewers, it took quite a while for craft beer to establish a firm footing in the country. Eventually, though, Guadalajara and Baja California began to see a rise in breweries, followed in short order by the capital city. Aided by some changes in federal law, Mexican craft beer is now not only thriving but improving at an almost exponential rate.

ASTILLERO

Agua Mala, Ensenada, Baja California; 8.5%

Citrus fruit abounds in this bright copper-coloured IPA, with spicy orange backed by lemon zest in the nose and a crisp, lemony and grapefruity body buttressed by herbal notes that carry through to the finish.

BÁGHA SUPER IPA

Propaganda, Monterrey, Nuevo Leon; 9%

Mexican breweries such as this are still feeling their way where highly hopped beers are concerned, which makes this double IPA with a big peppery, orange-citrus aroma and flavours of tropical fruit, citrus zest and lemon oil all the more impressive.

BOCK

La Blanca, Guadalajara, Jalisco; 7.3%

Mexico's leading and perhaps only wheat beer specialist, this heavily German-influenced operation crafts several fine ales, including this *bock* with a fragrant banana nose and lightly phenolic, sweetish body.

BRUTAL IMPERIAL STOUT

Border Psycho, Tijuana, Baja California; 10.5%

Over-the-top brewery making over-the-top beers such as this dense and rich stout with a tar-ish maltiness, cocoa- and aniseed-accented body and restrained sweetness.

CROSSOVER IPA

Urbana, Mexicali, Baja California; 6.5%

From Cerveza Mexico's large brewery of the year for 2016 comes this well-balanced IPA with broad floral and citrus notes in the aroma and a body that is hop-forward and grapefruity without being overdone.

HÁZMELA RUSA

La Chingonería, Mexico City; 7%

Another in the country's growing range of cocoa-and-spice Mexican Imperial stouts, this is also among the best, with a large nose of molasses, dark chocolate and port wine, and a subtle pepper element within a robust chocolate flavour.

LÁGRIMAS NEGRAS

Rámuri, Tijuana, Baja California; 10%

Billed as an oatmeal stout, the elevated strength and chocolaty intensity of this

CAN'T-MISS BREWERIES

● ● ● ● ● ● ● ● ● ● ●

CALAVERA

Tlalnepantla, State of Mexico

Located in the suburbs of the capital, this brewery turned heads early with solid Belgian abbey-style ales, including the milk chocolaty **Dubbel de Abadía** (6.4%) and slightly candied but dry-finishing **Tripel de Abadía** (9%), as well as what might have been the country's first **Mexican Imperial Stout** (9%), with lovely smoked chilli notes accenting flavours of dark chocolate. Not to be overlooked are the brewery's solid quaffing beers, like the tropical fruit and citrus **American Pale Ale** (5.4%).

MINERVA

Zapopan, Jalisco

Low-key brewery located near Guadalajara and producing solid interpretations of mostly classic and lower-strength styles. Typical of this approach are **Viena** (5%), a lovely quaffer with toasted malt tones throughout, and **Rila** (4.88%), an occasionally brewed burgundy-hued ale with notes of toasted malt, berry and cinnamon. Veering slightly from the brewery's norm are the also fine **I.T.A.** (7%), or Imperial Tequila Ale, with a distinctly peppery body, and a rather restrained, slightly astringent **Imperial Stout** (6%).

CAN'T-MISS BREWERY

• • • • • • • • • • • • • • •

PRIMUS

San Juan del Río, Querétaro

Brewers of two lines, the original Tempus range of ales and a pair of lagers under the Jabalí name. Of the former, **Alt Clásica** (5.2%) is well named, being classically enough of its *altbier* style that it could be at home in Düsseldorf; **Doble Malta** (7%) has a similar appeal but with richer yet still balanced hops and malt; and **Dorada** (4.3%) is a golden ale with an appealingly light peachy fruitiness. In the Jabalí family, the **Hellesbock** (8.1%) stands out with its biscuit malt and creeping warmth.

beer make it more akin to an Imperial stout, albeit one with a rich and silken mouthfeel. Cherry and vanilla notes round out its appeal.

LA LUPULOSA

Insurgente, Tijuana, Baja California; 7.3%

Five varieties of hops are used in this highly fruity, berry-ish IPA with a chewy maltiness and a drying, bitter and somewhat grapefruity finish. One of Mexico's best straightforward IPAs.

MAÍZ AZUL

La Brü, Morelia, Michoacán; 4.2%

A special beer developed to highlight the local blue corn, which quite unsurprisingly gives it a distinct yet also distinctive corn flavour, backed up by a light spiciness.

MERCEDES FAUNA

Mexicali, Baja California; 5%

From one of the northwest's most accomplished brewers comes this wonderfully earthy brown ale with a cinnamon-accented aroma and an appealing dryness that lasts from the molasses front to the roasted nutty finish.

MEZCAL IPA

Chaneque, Mexico City; 6.5%

Ageing beer in tequila and mezcal barrels could be a growing trend in Mexico, and if they all turn out like this superbly balanced ale with a smoky, dryly fruity and spicy hop character, so much the better!

BREWERIES TO WATCH

COLIMA

El Trapiche, Colima

Fast-growing brewery south of Guadalajara, known for flagships like the floral, quenching **Colimota Lager** (4.2%) and the perfumey, citrusy **Páramo Pale Ale** (5.2), as well as a number of collaborations.

WENDLANDT

Ensenada, Baja California

Multi-award-winning brewery and pub south of Tijuana, excelling at a variety of styles including **Harry Polanco** (5.5%), a dryly hoppy aperitif red ale, the best bitter-ish **Vaquita Marina Pale Ale** (5.2%) and forcefully aromatic **Perro del Mar India Pale Ale** (7%).

SPORT LOBA

Guadalajara, Jalisco; 5%

A classically fashioned Belgian-style wheat beer with a lightly sweet, aromatic and orangey nose and balanced, faintly acidic and refreshing body. Brewed with the hot Jalisco summers in mind.

BRAZIL

Although recent economic and political woes have certainly not made it easy for Brazil's craft brewers, the number of breweries populating the country continues to grow, and so does the quality of the beers being produced. All of which adds up to a rosy picture for beer drinkers from the Amazonian north – source of many of the interesting fruits and woods making their way into a steadily increasing proportion of Brazilian beers – through to the more German-leaning south.

3 LOBOS BRAVO AMERICAN IMPERIAL PORTER

Backer, Belo Horizonte, Minas Gerais; 9%

Aged in amburana wood, this seductive, pitch-black porter has an aroma of spicy vanilla mixed with sweet espresso and a flavour of spice, cinnamon, chocolate and aniseed with hints of roasted chestnuts.

1516

Verace, Nova Lima, Minas Gerais; 4.8%

Bright, light gold in colour, this German-style pilsner has a floral hop aroma, delicate maltiness, well-balanced and assertive bitterness and a dry, refreshing finish.

AMBURANA LAGER

Way Beer, Pinhais, Paraná; 8.4%

One of the first Brazilian beers to employ the flavours of the Amazon, this full-bodied lager uses ambarana wood in conditioning for a cinnamony, spicy, slightly chocolaty and intensely rich-tasting result.

BLACK METAL IPA

Maniba, Novo Hamburgo, Rio Grande do Sul; 7.2%

A black IPA designed for hop lovers, this assertive brew is strongly citrusy on the nose and intensely bitter in the body with balancing roasted malt and a dry and hoppy aftertaste.

CAFETINA

Landel, Barão Geraldo, São Paulo; 5.2%

This seasonal, coffee-enhanced porter is brewed when only the best beans are available. Fresh floral and fruity notes from the coffee are in full harmony with the caramel and chocolate malt flavours.

FELLAS

Dama, Piracicaba, São Paulo; 9%

A coffee-flavoured double IPA, this combines strongly fruity aromas from both the hops and the coffee beans, balancing them with caramelly maltiness in a velvety body with a warming finish.

FOREST BACURI

Amazon, Belém, Pará; 4.1%

From a brewery specializing in beers flavoured with Amazonian fruit, this pilsner has a sweet and faintly tart aroma and sweetish palate that turns tangier and more gooseberry- and pineapple-accented toward the off-dry finish.

CAN'T-MISS BREWERIES

● ● ● ● ● ● ● ● ● ● ●

BAMBERG

Votorantim, São Paulo

One of Brazil's most well-established breweries and one very much influenced by German brewing traditions. The citizens of Bamberg would be proud of the gently smoky **Rauchbier** (5.2%), while Müncheners would approve of the fragrant, honey-ish **Maibaum** (6.5%) seasonal *maibock* and the mellow, lightly roasty *dunkel* **München** (5%). Düsseldorf also gets a shout-out in the form of the slightly sweet but dry-finishing **Altbier** (5%).

BODEBROWN

Curitiba, Paraná

Brewery born out of a brewing school operated by Samuel Cavalcanti and popularized on the back of Brazil's first, and still arguably best, double IPAs **Perigosa** (9.2%), and occasional supercharged offspring **Double Perigosa** (15.1%). The big beers sometimes overshadow other fine creations, such as the strongly Scottish-influenced **Wee Heavy** (8%), with attractive cinnamon and molasses notes, and subtle, quenching **Blanche de Curitiba** (5.5%). Inspired creations like **4 Blés** (11.7%), made from four types of wheat and boasting a highly complex, herbal–dried-fruit character, make sporadic appearances.

GORDELÍCIA

Urbana, São Paulo; 7.5%

An intense and warming Belgian-style strong golden ale, this beer has a strongly spicy and fruity character, notably banana and yellow fruit, which is medium- to full-bodied and pleasantly sweet.

HOLY COW 2

Seasons, Porto Alegre, Rio Grande do Sul; 7.5%

First brewed in collaboration with the US brewery Green Flash (see page 226), this IPA is intensely hopped to a tropical-fruit aroma, featuring passion-fruit and pineapple, a striking bitterness and a dry finish.

HORNY PIG SESSION IPA

Blondine, Itupeva, São Paulo; 4.5%

This light amber IPA – with a slightly rude label – features a fresh tropical-fruit aroma and a light, refreshing and moderately bitter body with commendable balance.

MADALENA DOUBLE IPA

Premium Paulista, Santo André, São Paulo; 7.5%

At the low end of strength for the style, this ale manages a nice balance between citrusy and resiny hops and ample malt sweetness in a full, strongly bitter body.

MÄRZEN RAUCHBIER

Bierbaum, Treze Tílias, Santa Catarina; 4.6%

Brewed in the "most Austrian city in Brazil", this Bamberg-style smoked beer has a malty sweetness and biscuit notes that are not overwhelmed by its pleasantly balanced smokiness.

MONJOLO IMPERIAL PORTER

Tupiniquim, Porto Alegre, Rio Grande do Sul; 10.5%

Also available on occasion in a whisky-barrel version, this warming, velvety porter embraces the drinker with aromas and flavours of toffee and chocolate, accented by notes of vanilla and roasted malt.

PETROLEUM

DUM, Curitiba, Paraná; 12%

One of Brazil's most recognized beers, originally brewed as a collaboration with Wäls (see opposite), this is as inky and black as its name would suggest,

with a silken mouthfeel and chocolaty character from the oats and cocoa used in its making.

RUSSIAN IMPERIAL STOUT

Bierland, Blumenau, Santa Catarina; 8%

This strong stout brewed in the beer capital of southern Brazil has a cheeky sweetness reminiscent of a chocolate liqueur, but in a roasty and dense body that speaks to its "Imperial" status. A thoroughly enticing ale.

SEXY SESSION IPA

Barco, Porto Alegre, Rio Grande do Sul; 4.3%

Hopped with Citra, Simcoe and Centennial, this features citrusy aromatics, an assertive bitterness and a dry, refreshing finish.

SORACHI BERLINER

Perro Libre, Porto Alegre, Rio Grande do Sul, 3.4%

Conditioned on lemon zest and dry-hopped with Sorachi Ace hops, this well-balanced *Berliner weisse* is highly aromatic with predictable lemon notes, pleasantly tart in character and very thirst quenching.

TRIPPEL

Wäls [AB InBev], Belo Horizonte, Minas Gerais; 9%

As traditional a *tripel* as probably exists in Brazil, this boasts a spicy, dryly lemony aroma and a body that begins orange–herbal, proceeds to tropical fruit and finishes with an earthy, drying hoppiness.

CAN'T-MISS BREWERY

●●●●●●●●●●●●●●●

MORADA CIA ETÍLICA

Curitiba, Paraná

Not a nomadic brewery per se, but rather one sharing a facility with other breweries, this home-brewer-turned-professional operation impresses with a wide variety of beers. Their foundational brand is the clever **Double Vienna** (7.6%), a big-bodied take on the Vienna lager style, while newer **Hop Arabica** (5%) impresses with layered coffee and hop flavours. Clean and faintly fruity **Kölsch** (5%) is designed for the Brazilian summer heat, and **Gasoline Soul** (6.7%) is an amber ale drawing inspiration from the Brazil Motorcycle Show.

BREWERIES TO WATCH

DOGMA

São Paulo

Born in 2015, the brewery was earning plaudits early for beers such as the self-explanatory **Mosaic Lover IPA** (8.5%), the double IPA **Rizoma** (8.3%) and **Sourmind** (4.4%), a refreshing *Berliner weisse* with guava and mango juice.

HOCUS POCUS

Rio de Janeiro

A young and innovative brewery that is already considered among Brazil's best whose accomplishments include the spicy, Belgian-esque **Magic Trap** (8.5%), the caffeinated amber ale **Coffee Hush** (5.5%) and newer **Overdrive** (8.2%), a cloudy, fruity double IPA brewed with oats.

VELHAS VIRGENS MR. BROWNIE

Invicta, Ribeirão Preto, São Paulo; 5%

An English-style brown ale brewed with vanilla pods, this mahogany ale boasts caramel, toasted bread and chocolate notes in its aroma and a good balance between toasted malt and sweetness on the palate.

VIENNA LAGER

Da Mata, Embu das Artes, São Paulo; 4.9%

A fine amber-coloured lager that balances a fine spicy–leafy hop aroma with a body that highlights toasted malt without becoming overly sweet, drying with gentle bitterness to its dry finish.

VIXNU

Colorado [AB InBev], Ribeirão Preto, São Paulo; 9.5%

With a nose reminiscent of fruit salad steeped in brandy, this double IPA attracts the drinker into a fruity (apricot especially) and spicy body that turns progressively bitter toward a lingering bitter and warming finish.

VÓ MARIA E SEU LADO ZEN

Avós, São Paulo, São Paulo; 4.9%

Perfectly suited to the strong heat of the Brazilian summer, this golden, well-hopped hoppy lager features balanced bitterness and a pleasant citrusy hop aroma in an impressively refreshing quaffer.

ARGENTINA

Argentina is unusual in that craft brewing first gained its foothold not in any of the country's major cities but rather in the Lake District of northern Patagonia. As breweries have come and gone through the years, however, more and more have made a home in the nation's capital and it is there that we now find the greatest promise for the future.

AMERICAN IPA

Sir Hopper, nomadic, 7.2%

Brewed with imported US hops rather than Argentina-grown versions, this has a pungent, citrusy-fruity aroma and full, citrus and tropical-fruit hoppiness in the body leading to a lingering and dry finish.

BARLEY WINE

Antares, Buenos Aires and other locations; 10%

This brewpub chain, now bottling their beer as well, was a pioneer in Argentina and is still a leader with beers like this boozy, fruity, round and full strong ale with sugary notes and a long finish.

BEAGLE NEGRA CREAM STOUT

Fueglan, Ushuaia, Tierra del Fuego; 6.2%

A full, sweetish, caramel roasted and well-balanced stout, with dabs of chocolate, coffee and bitter hop, made at the tip of the Andes in the world's most southerly brewery.

BLACK MAMBA

Grunge, Buenos Aires province; 6.5%

Perhaps a bit light in strength for its "Foreign Stout" billing, this nonetheless enticing beer combines dark chocolate, dried fruit, coffee and a hint of liquorice on the nose with a complex, full and chewy body and off-dry finish.

BRIGIT

Kraken, Caseros, Buenos Aires province; 5.6%

Billed as an "Irish red", this is appropriately amber in colour with a clean caramel and toffee aroma that extends to the palate as well, although there combined with hints of coffee and a drying yet still caramelly finish.

CHOCOLATE PORTER

Anna-C, Llavallol, Buenos Aires province; 6.5%

Brewed with coffee beans as well as cocoa, this has a forcefully chocolaty nose backed by coffee notes and a mildly bitter, velvety, chocolaty body.

DUBBEL 6

Abdij Deleuze, Avellaneda, Buenos Aires province; 7%

From a brewery crafting exclusively Belgian styles of ale comes this convincing take on an abbey *dubbel*, with a toasty and caramelly aroma backed by hints of prune and a rich, sweet and full palate.

GROSA

Jerome, El Salto, Mendoza; 9%

An unapologetically big beer that spends 18 months inside a wine barrel prior to its release, emerging with a grapey palate, spicy finish and lingering warmth. Ownership of the brand is unclear – it is variously attributed to the company "Cerveza Grosa".

MIVER

Darwin, Buenos Aires; 5.5%

A lovely looking *weissbier* with a good balance between banana and clove notes, accented by light citrus and acidity that enhance the dry finish and overall refreshing character of this beer.

OAK AGED DOPPELBOCK

Juguetes Perdidos, Caseros, Buenos Aires; 10.5%

Aged in barrels previously used for Malbec wine, this offers elements of cherry, vanilla and coconut on the nose, and a full and sweet body accented by hints of orange peel and apricot, leading to a warming finish.

OLD ALE

Berlina, Bariloche, Río Negro; 7.5%

A nice coppery brown ale with complex aromas balanced between fruity and caramel notes. Rich and malty in its viscous mouthfeel with good structure and balance.

RUSSIAN IMPERIAL STOUT

Nihilista, Cipolletti, Río Negro; 9%

Aged at the brewery for six months prior to its release, this gold-medal-winning stout from Nihilista boasts a sherry-ish nose with prune, raisin and mocha tones and an oily, complex and robustly bitter body.

CHILE

Having spent years as the number three craft beer country in South America – after Brazil and Argentina – at last Chile now seems poised to make a bigger name for itself. If a more stable supply of fresh hops can be found, the sky may wind up being the only limit for its increasingly creative brewers.

BLACK IPA

Zigurat, Santiago; 7%

A complex mix of cocoa, chocolate and piney hoppiness characterizes the aroma of this ale, while further intrigue is provided by the blend of coffee, dried fruit, liquorice and spice in the body.

IMPERIAL STOUT

Hernando de Magallanes, Punta Arenas; 7%

The country's southernmost brewery produces this sweet and blackcurrant-y stout that adds port wine and prune notes in front of a creamy, slightly roasty and warming finish.

IPA

Kross, Curacaví, Santiago; 6.5%

An interesting mix of aromas in this beer – passion-fruit, melon, floral, pine and citrus. Together with a quenching bitterness and a good malt backbone, they produce a beer that is creamy, balanced and refreshing.

RAUCHBIER

Grosse Gerste, Pirque, Santiago; 5%

A deep copper lager with balanced smokiness on the aroma, the body strays to the sweet side but does so with a keen understanding of the beer's smoky character, the overall effect being that of a nicely structured smoked malt beer.

CAN'T-MISS BREWERY

● ● ● ● ● ● ● ● ● ● ● ● ● ●

GRANIZO

Olmué, Valparaíso

Located in the Reserve of the Biosphere La Campana-Peñuelas (UNESCO) and using solar energy, Granizo has won awards for beers such as **Tue Tue** (10.5%), a deeply complex and robust black ale fermented in French oak barrels that previously held Pinot Noir; **IRA** (7%), a refreshing India Red Ale flavoured with rosemary; **Foxy Lady** (12.1%), an Imperial stout also fermented ex-Pinot Noir oak but with additions of Puta Madre chilli peppers; and **Quercus** (8.5%), a complex strong ale fermented and matured in French and US oak previously used in Syrah wine production.

BREWERY TO WATCH

HESS

Valparaíso

Dedicated to creating highly hopped ales fashioned in the US style, including the strongly hoppy **Bozko Barakus Brown Ale** (7.5%) and the creamy, balanced stout **Lykantrop** (7%).

SESSION IPA

Jester, Santiago; 4.6%

New for the summer of 2016, this is full of piney, resinous and tropical-fruit aromas with the flavour following suit and adding herbal and citrusy hop notes leading to a dryly bitter finish.

STOUT

Emperador, Santiago; 6%

Impressive and still-improving stout with an almost clotted-cream-like aroma accented by chocolate and soft roasty notes, and a similarly sweet and creamy body with more chocolate and a slight burned woodiness.

STOUT

Szot, Talagante, Santiago; 5.8%

Deep mahogany with a roasty, biscuity aroma holding hints of vanilla and chocolate, this nicely rounded ale has a strong roasted malt character to it, finishing dry, roasty and slightly boozy.

TÜBINATOR

Tübinger, Pirque, Santiago; 8%

The almost port-like sweetness of this intensely ruby-coloured ale is complemented well by the dried fruit and nuttiness of the nose, Christmas cake and sweet plum flavours and warming, toasted brown sugar notes in the finish.

URUGUAY

Only a few years ago, an aficionado of flavourful beer would have had a hard time slaking her thirst in Uruguay, so sparsely populated was the country's craft beer market. But lately, breweries have been opening at a fairly fierce rate, and furthermore, some have been producing ales and lagers of impressive quality.

BELGIAN DARK ALE

Volcanica, Las Toscas, Canelones, 8%

A gorgeous mahogany brew with a fruity, slightly spicy aroma with hints of caramel, toffee and chocolate. Brewed from Belgian malt and fermented with Belgian yeast, it will only get better as it ages.

BELGIAN DUBBEL WITH ARRAYÁN

Oceánica, Playa Hermosa, Maldonado; 6.5%

Brewed with foraged native *arrayán* berries, this blends the spicy, caramel characteristics of a Belgian *dubbel* with the fruity yet slightly minty taste of *arrayán*, producing vivacious flavours that dance in the mouth.

CAN'T-MISS BREWERY

DAVOK

Montevideo

Chief brewer Alejandro Baldenegro is a pioneer in the Uruguayan craft beer scene and generally regarded as a catalyst for the growth in quality of Uruguayan craft beer in general. The brewery's thirst-quenching, superbly balanced **American IPA** (6.2%) is a local icon, while the deep copper **Barley Wine** (12%) is a full-bodied, malty yet not overly sweet beer, brewery-aged for at least six months after bottling. The new flavour bomb, **Choco Canela Stout** (7%), with oatmeal, cacao, US oak chips and cinnamon, is a superlatively chewy beer.

BREWERY TO WATCH

INDICA

Montevideo

A young duo of former home-brewers producing hoppy beers that frequently sell out within a week of arriving at stores. Their citrusy, tropical-fruity **West Coast IPA** (6.8%) and award-winning **Californian Common** (5.2%) are both ground-breaking entries to the local market.

CITRA HIBERNATION

Oso Pardo, Montevideo; 5.3%

Produced by a newcomer to the Uruguayan beer scene who is making very hoppy beers very well, this single hop (Citra, as per the name) US-style pale ale has a strong passion-fruit aroma and a quaffable and highly sessionable character.

DRY STOUT

Montevideo Brew House, Montevideo; 4.7%

Sold exclusively at Uruguay's only brewery–restaurant, this dry stout will transport the drinker instantly to Ireland with its black hue, dense and creamy head and aromas of coffee with dark chocolate undertones.

GUAYABO BLONDE ALE

Ibirá Pitá, San Luis, Canelones; 5%

Produced on a small, family-run farm, this organic pale ale is brewed with an indigenous fruit called *guayabo del país*, resulting in a quince and tropical-fruit aroma and a refreshing flavour of hoppy bitterness mixed with fruity tartness.

REST OF LATIN AMERICA

Outside of the larger countries, craft brewing has come to Latin America in fits and starts, with tourist-oriented breweries here, home-brew clubs there and everywhere a mix of fly-by-night operations, which open only to close almost as quickly, and more stable, long-term-leaning breweries, often helmed or assisted by ex-pats from the USA and elsewhere. Here we present some of the brighter lights.

COLOMBIA

SEPTIMAZO IPA

Bogotá Beer Company [AB InBev], Tocancipá, Bogotá; 6%

An IPA characterized by a thick and enduring collar of foam. Its citrusy, piney aroma presages a citrus–herbal quality in the body and a balanced, clean and dry finish.

COSTA RICA

FUNKY JOSEPH

Calle Cimarrona, San José; 7.2%

A well-integrated mix of aromas with notes of peppercorn, fruit and *Brettanomyces*, supplemented on the palate by spicy, oaky and winey flavours. An interesting and complex beer with a good balance of sweetness and tartness.

MAMACANDELA

Treintaycinco, San José; 7.8%

A deep black stout from Treintaycinco with a creamy and persistent head and attractive aromas of roasted malts, dark fruits, cacao and coffee. The flavour follows suit, with an intense and complex balance of chocolaty malt, fruity esters and floral hops, all finishing with a pleasing warmth.

SEGUA RED ALE

Costa Rica's Craft Beer, Cartago; 5%

From the country's leading small brewery, a coppery-orange ale with an aroma of walnut and ripe apricot and mango, and a nutty, bready, faintly spicy palate that finishes mildly bitter and off-dry.

ECUADOR

HELLER WIEZENBOCK

Páramo, Quito; 5.8%

Golden with an enduring ivory foam, this not-so-strong *weizenbock* offers rich malt, caramel and bready notes in the nose and a full and malt-forward body with balanced banana and clove flavours.

IRISH RED ALE

Santana, Quito; 5.2%

A complex mix of caramel, biscuit, toffee and toasty maltiness can be found in both the aroma and flavour of this red ale, with hops providing a drying bitterness and dark malts bringing a roasty character to the finish.

WEE HEAVY

Sinners, Quito; 10%

Intense chilli, caramel, toffee and floral aromas introduce this original take on a strong Scottish-style ale, with the heat in the body well integrated with the sweet maltiness and dried fruit character. This is a fine balance of spice and malt.

PANAMA

COCO PORTER

La Rana Dorada, Panama City; 5%

A rich and satisfying variation on the brewery's core line-up porter, this has expressive aromas of chocolate, coconut, vanilla and toasted malts, with a toasty, fruity, coconut-accented body and mild to moderate bitterness.

TULIVIEJA

Casa Bruja, Panama City; 8.4%

An intense double IPA from Casa Bruja with a resinous aroma carrying notes of tropical fruit and citrus, a balanced flavour profile of caramelly malt and moderate, citrusy hoppiness and finally a warming, dry finish.

PARAGUAY

ESPRESSO PALE ALE

Sajonia, Sajonia, Asunción; 5.5%

A special version of the brewery's citrusy Pale Ale, fuelled with coffee from the local Café Consulado for a surprisingly refreshing, coffee-forward and lightly resinous result.

PARAGUAYAN ALE

Herken 1885, Cañada de Ybyray, Asunción; 4.7%

Brewed with cassava, *kapi'i cedron* (a herb similar to lemongrass) and *upepú* (a sort of sour orange), this is a well-constructed, bright golden, strongly citrusy and highly quaffable ale.

PERU

CH'UNPI SOUR

Valle Sagrado, Pachar, Cusco; 4.6%

An interesting mix of fruity (berries), floral and caramel aromas precedes a complex mélange of maltiness, bitterness and sourness on the palate and a very dry finish.

SHAMAN IPA

Sierra Andina, Huaraz, Ancash; 8%

On the nose this shows a classic citrusy US hop profile, while the flavour adds floral and tropical-fruit notes to the citrus, creating a clean, refreshing and dry-finishing beer.

AUSTRALASIA

AUSTRALIA

Although Australian brewers have gone through a rather halting progression with respect to their craft beer evolution, all indications suggest that they are now firmly set in full-speed-ahead mode. Future developments may well find their raison d'être in the nation's emerging indigenous hop culture, led by the Galaxy hop but with numerous others following.

AMBER ALE

Prancing Pony, Totness, South Australia; 5%

An amber that tips its hat to the USA with multiple hop additions layering textured bitterness over a complex caramel malt.

BALTIC PORTER

Redoak, Sydney, New South Wales; 8.7%

Old rope, rich dark chocolate, figs and demerara sugar all figure in the aroma and flavour of this highly awarded version of a beer style that the brewer discovered in a Polish café early on in his brewing career.

CHEVALIER SAISON

Bridge Road, Beechworth, Victoria; 6%

One of the first locally brewed versions of a *saison* (see page 23) and still a reference point for this classic style. Spicy and dry with a grassy hop character and very quenching.

CLOUT STOUT

Nail, Bassendean, Western Australia; 10.5%

First brewed to celebrate the brewery's 10th anniversary and now an annual special release, this chocolate-, aniseed- and tobacco-redolent beast is a yearly highlight from Nail.

CRANKSHAFT

BentSpoke, Braddon, Australian Capital Territory; 5.8%

As with many Australian IPAs, this carries mild bitterness for the style, but still delivers on flavour with a resiny blend of five hops producing notes of tropical fruit salad carried along by caramel malts.

ENGLISH ALE

3 Ravens, Thornbury, Victoria; 4.5%

A classic English-style pale ale, made from Maris Otter malt and Fuggles hops and first brewed for cask-conditioning. Earthy and slightly jammy hops mix with a base of gentle toffee-ish malt edging toward chocolate.

FORMER TENANT

Modus Operandi, Mona Vale, New South Wales; 7.8%

Mosaic and Galaxy hops lend strong tropical aromas to this savoury red IPA, which won the title of Champion Australian Craft Beer in 2014 just three months after the brewery opened.

GOLDEN ALE

Two Birds, Spotswood, Victoria and contract; 4.4%

Highly approachable but still nuanced and rewarding, delicate stone fruits mingle with a honey malt profile in this summery ale from Australia's first female-owned brewery.

GROWLER

2 Brothers, Moorabbin, Victoria; 4.7%

One of the first US-style brown ales commercially brewed in the country and still one of the best, with American-grown Cascade hops adding aromatic light to a crystal-malt shade.

HAZELNUT BROWN

Bad Shepherd, Cheltenham, Victoria; 5.9%

There is no mistaking the nut in question in this rich brown ale, made with hazelnuts, hazelnut extract and even Frangelico with a touch of vanilla. It all works beautifully, right to the smooth, dry finish.

HEF

Burleigh, Burleigh Heads, Queensland; 5%

Classic banana and clove aromas define this award-winning and stylish *hefeweizen*, followed by a light and spritzy mouthfeel and classically refreshing finish.

HIGHTAIL ALE

Mountain Goat [Asahi], Melbourne and Laverton, Victoria; 4.5%

Pioneering beer and brewery, now Japanese-owned but still delivering earthy malt characters and spicy hop bitterness in an ale that should be considered a modern classic.

HOP HEAVEN EASY IPA

Barossa Valley, Tanunda, South Australia; 4.8%

Australia's climate and punitive alcohol taxes see brewers creatively getting more flavour into lower-strength versions of popular styles, including "session IPAs" such as this lemon-tinged zinger from Barossa Valley Brewing.

HOP HOG

Feral, Swan Valley and Bassendean, Western Australia; 5.8%

There are many hoppier pale ales on the market these days, but few better than this perennial critical and consumer favourite. Burnished gold, it assaults the nose with citrus and pine.

HOPSMITH

Akasha, Five Dock, New South Wales; 7.2%

An IPA in the US West Coast style, triple dry-hopping with Amarillo and Simcoe gives a lifted aroma to an already hop-heavy but stylish ale.

IPA

Fixation, Byron Bay, New South Wales; 6.4%

An independent offshoot of Stone & Wood (see page 259) produces this robustly hopped ale delivering a pronounced grapefruit aroma and punchy bitterness over a solid malt base, bold yet emphasizing aroma and flavour over sheer aggression.

ICONIC BREWERY

COOPERS

Adelaide, South Australia

Family owned since its foundation in 1862, and for the second half of the 20th century a bulwark against brewery consolidation despite many fluctuations in fortune, Coopers kept alive Australia's only indigenous beer style, the sparkling ale. Now enjoying a renaissance, that historic **Sparkling Ale** (5.8%) remains the gold standard for the now-resurgent style, joined in the brewery's line-up by its younger, cloudier sibling **Pale Ale** (4.5%), the rich classic **Extra Stout** (6.3%) and an annual highlight **Vintage Ale** (7.5%), which showcases interesting hop character when fresh, but is brewed for ageing.

LITTLE DOVE

Gage Roads, Palmyra, Western Australia; 6.2%

From Australia's only publicly listed craft brewery – with a 25% share recently repatriated from shopping giant Woolworths – comes this fine "New World pale ale" boasting pineapple and orange aromas over a sweet malt body.

LOVEDALE LAGER

Sydney, Lovedale, New South Wales; 4.7%

While Australia loves lagers, its craft brewers have tended to eschew them, a notable exception being Sydney Brewery's luscious Munich-style *helles*, with complexity from three malts and an elegant bitterness.

MOONSHINE

Grand Ridge, Mirboo North, Victoria; 8.5%

With its delicious mélange of burned sugar, dried fruit, chocolate, caramel and just a hint of Vegemite on the nose, this richly malty ale has been delighting Australian beer drinkers for more than 20 years.

NINE TALES

James Squire [Kirin], Camperdown, New South Wales; 5%

The marketing stories may be tortured and contrived, but this English-style brown ale is still highly worthy and rewarding with its rich toffee maltiness and nutty finish.

PALE

Mornington Peninsula, Mornington, Victoria; 4.7%

This rock-solid version of a very common style – pale ale – witnesses passion-fruit and pine aromas atop a refreshing malt base, lightened with wheat malts and a quenching hop bite.

PALE ALE

Little Creatures [Kirin], Fremantle and other locations, Victoria; 5.2%

The brewery's purchase by Kirin in 2012 has seen no loss of quality in this solid and spot-on US-style pale ale from a pioneer of the Australian craft movement.

PENNY PORTER

Green Beacon, Brisbane, Queensland; 6.1%

Subtropical Brisbane's climate makes it an unlikely home to such a delectable porter, with coffee, mocha and liquorice notes mingling on the palate in advance of a drying finish.

PILSNER

Hawkers, Reservoir, Victoria; 5%

With floral and grassy hop characteristics, a bready and honey-ish malt base and a beautifully clean finish, this lager needs little more description than "classic German-style pilsner".

RAMJET

Boatrocker, Braeside, Victoria; 11.4%

Coffee and tobacco are softened with more than a hint of figs and vanilla in this whisky-barrel-aged Imperial stout from one of the country's most extensive barrel-ageing programmes.

ROBERT

Stomping Ground, Collingwood, Victoria; 8.9%

A straight-up-and-down double IPA, with classic pine and grapefruit notes, elevated by the sublime balance for such a big beer.

SEEING DOUBLE

Brew Boys, Croydon Park, South Australia; 8%

A solid whack of peated malts gives this Scotch ale a fair reek of smoky iodine with Vegemite and banana over a syrupy malt base.

STOUT

4 Pines, Brookvale, New South Wales; 5.1%

While it is reputedly being tested to become the first beer to travel into space, for the terrestrial-bound this is a classic dry stout with coffee and chocolate aromas and flavours, and a touch of aniseed at the finish.

TEMPTRESS

Holgate Brewhouse, Woodend, Victoria; 6%

A classically styled porter tricked up with Dutch cocoa and vanilla pods to add caramel smoothness to a sharply espresso-accented body, from a regional brewery that is one of the country's "must-visit" venues.

CAN'T-MISS BREWERIES

● ● ● ● ● ● ● ● ● ● ● ● ●

LA SIRÈNE

Alphington, Victoria

Few Australian breweries attempt Belgian-inspired beers and fewer do it well, which makes La Sirène unique. Launching with a sublime **Saison** (6.5%), and following with several variations, the brewery also excels at other styles, including malt-driven **Farmhouse Red** (6.5%), infused with fresh rose buds, hibiscus and dandelions, and **Praline** (6%), a Belgian-style stout brewed with organic vanilla pods, cacao nibs and hazelnuts.

STONE & WOOD

Byron Bay and Murwillumbah, New South Wales

When others were turning out bitterness-driven pale ales, Stone & Wood launched **Pacific Ale** (4.4%), an aromatic New World take on a British-style summer ale, helping to popularize the indigenous Galaxy hop. **Jasper** (4.7%) is a twist on the German *altbier* and a core brand, while the annual **Stone Beer** (6.4%) is a dark, malty delight and **Cloud Catcher** (5.5%) riffs on the Australian pale ale style while maintaining the brewery's love of colouring outside of the stylistic lines.

THANKS CAPTAIN OBVIOUS

BrewCult, nomadic; 5.8%

Citra, Centennial and Simcoe give a classically citrusy US-style IPA edge to this mainstay of Australia's leading brewery without a home.

TWO TO THE VALLEY INDIA PALE ALE

Newstead, Newstead, Queensland; 5.9%

A tight bundle of Citra, Centennial, Cascade and Simcoe hops serves up an assertive and bold bitterness beneath a grapefruit and melon cloud, while a healthy amount of biscuity malt keeps it all in check.

WEST COAST IPA

Batch, Marrickville, New South Wales; 5.8%

The only permanent offer from this inner-city Sydney operation sees Mosaic, Centennial and Chinook hops pound out a pineapple beat driving malt rhythm in this encore-demanding ale.

WILLIE WARMER

Seven Sheds, Railton, Tasmania; 6.3%

Cassia bark and star anise add greater depth to the already complex and mocha-ish maltiness of this densely rich, rustic and warming dark ale, structured with a nod toward Belgian brewing traditions.

XPA

Wolf of the Willows, Cheltenham, Victoria; 4.7%

The style space between pale ale and IPA has proved a sweet spot for a number of Australian brewers, and this wolf prowls it well. Australian and US hops with Maris Otter and wheat malts provide a cleverly balanced ale.

BREWERIES TO WATCH

BALTER

Currumbin, Queensland

The first release from this brewery – founded by a quartet of champion surfers – a fragrant and balanced pale ale called **XPA** (5%), and the follow-up brown ale **ALT** (4.8%), immediately quashed concerns about image possibly besting quality.

PIRATE LIFE

Adelaide, South Australia

Influenced by Scotland's BrewDog (*see* page 91), where the brewers apprenticed, hoppy ales abound here, with **Throwback IPA** (3.5%), **IPA** (6.8%) and **IIPA** (8.8%) each pushing the lupulin limit while managing a measure of balance.

NEW ZEALAND

If ever there were a craft beer market that has embraced its own uniqueness, it is that of New Zealand. It has defined its style through the use of native hops, welcomed nomadic or contract brewing in order to further the market in a logistically challenging land and, in the early 21st century at least, grabbed the Australasian craft brewing lead from its much larger neighbour. This combination of audacity and creativity is what has made New Zealand a potent force in Southern Hemisphere brewing.

AMBER

North End, Waikanae, Wellington; 4.4%

A New World twist on a quaffable US style amber ale made by substituting local hops for US ones, creating a beer that is surprisingly full-bodied with dominant notes of caramel, coffee, marmalade and grapefruit.

(NUCLEAR FREE) ANZUS IPA

Croucher, Rotorua, Bay of Plenty; 7%

Named after a defunct defence alliance, this ale employs hops from the three participants – Australia, USA and New Zealand. Hop-forward and resinous, with an early taste of toffee followed by grapefruit, mango, more toffee and pine.

BOOKBINDER

Emerson's [Lion], Dunedin, Otago; 3.7%

The first beer from this veteran and venerated brewery is still a bestseller. Inspired by English best bitter and named after an early customer, Booky (as it known) is soft and balanced, with touches of caramel and stone fruit.

CAPTAIN COOKER

The Mussel Inn, Nomadic; 5%

Easily one of the most distinctive and interesting beers produced in New Zealand, enhanced with tips from the native manuka tree for a unique flavour combination of Turkish delight, honey, rosewater, caramel and ginger.

CITRA

Liberty, Riverhead, Auckland; 9%

Sharing space with Hallertau (*see* page 264) in scenic Riverhead, Liberty's Joseph Wood has developed a brewing style that is unabashedly about big aromas, flavours and bitterness, as demonstrated by this Imperial IPA behemoth exuding grapefruit, orange peel, resin, passion-fruit and pine.

COALFACE STOUT

Eagle, Christchurch, Canterbury; 6.2%

A decadent stout that utilizes nine malts, US and Kiwi hops and the famously pure Canterbury water. Roasted coffee on the nose and in the body, joined by chocolate, burned toast crusts and dark fruit.

DEADCANARY

ParrotDog, Wellington; 5.3%

Despite the outrageous name, DeadCanary is a contemporary Aotearoa pale ale (APA; *see* page 265) combining English malt with Kiwi hops, yielding ample aromas and flavours of tropical fruit, caramel, digestive biscuits and citrus zest.

DEATH FROM ABOVE

Garage Project, Wellington; 7.5%

Super-creative and prolific brewery making this "Indochine Pale Ale", which is brewed with mango, chilli, Vietnamese mint and lime juice. Fascinating flavour combination of orange, lime and herb garden, underwritten by a warming heat.

DUMP THE TRUMP

Behemoth, nomadic; 7.2%

Brewed as a protest against the US President, but this beer is no gimmick. A well-balanced US-style pale ale with a landslide of grapefruit and mango hoppy notes before a strong, clean finish.

THE DUSTY GRINGO

Deep Creek, Silverdale, Auckland; 6.8%

A rare New Zealand example of an India brown ale, with chocolate, toffee and nutty sweetness from the malt upfront, and hoppy citrus, lemongrass and fresh grass as complements.

ENFORCER

Baylands, Petone, Lower Hutt, Wellington; 6%

Balanced black IPA from a brewery that started in a suburban garage. First come notes of chocolate, vanilla and coffee along with a whiff of smoke, before a late charge of citrusy hops completes the equation.

CAN'T-MISS BREWERIES

8 WIRED

Warkworth, Northland

Brewing in a style described as "New World interpretations of Old World styles", this once New Zealand Champion Brewery pushes boundaries with beers like **iStout** (10%), a big Russian Imperial stout, luxurious with notes of chocolate, liquorice, smoke and citrus hops; **The Big Smoke** (6.2%), a porter brewed from Bamberg (Germany) smoked malt that shouts chocolate, molasses and smoke; **Tall Poppy** (7%), a balanced caramel, nutty, food-friendly red ale; and **Super Conductor** (8.88%), a punchy grapefruit and ripe orange double IPA. Look for vintage and barrel-aged releases – a speciality.

EPIC

nomadic

Making "really hoppy beers for the world to enjoy", usually with US hops, and lots of them. **Pale Ale** (5.4%) is a genuine ground-breaker with tangerine and pine, while **Armageddon I.P.A.** (6.66%) ups the ante with a gorgeous combination of grapefruit, orange and ginger over a long, dry finish. Only a 90 IBU **Hop Zombie** (8.5%) double IPA will survive Armageddon, protected as it is by layers of grapefruit, pine and toffee, while a decided change of pace is provided by **Epic Lager** (5.4%), which is balanced with floral, citrus and grain prominent.

TUATARA [DB BREWING]

Paraparaumu, Wellington

Started in a farm shed, it became the first two-time Champion Brewery of New Zealand and was purchased in early 2017. Highlights include **Mot Eureka** (5%), a fruity, grassy pilsner using four hops from the Motueka region; US-style pale ale **Tomahawk** (5.6%), which showcases orange peel and pine needles; dark hoppy ale **Amarillo** (5%), which emphasizes chocolate, peach and coffee instead; and **ITI** (3.3%), from the Maori for "small", a leader in the mid-strength category with a surprisingly flavourful character boasting tropical-fruit and toffee notes.

Blue Flower tea to create a dry and quenching brew, with grapefruit, lemon and, naturally, bitter tea to the fore.

HOPHEAD IPA

Brew Moon, Amberley, Canterbury; 5%

Operating near the small North Canterbury township of Amberley, Brew Moon is known for producing English-inspired beers. Hophead has notes of smooth orange marmalade with balance at a time when many others are going heavy on the hops.

KAURI FALLS

Hot Water, Whenuakite, Waikato; 5.2%

From a brewery located near the popular Hot Water Beach, the first Kiwi operation only to can its beer, this Aotearoa pale ale bursts with grapefruit, pine, orange and caramel flavours while remaining balanced.

FOR GREAT JUSTICE

Kereru, Upper Hutt, Wellington; 4.5%

Chris Mills created this "Wood-Fired Toasted Coconut Porter" as a celebration of beer and pizza. Pizza-oven-roasted coconut results in a mix of flavours of chocolate, burned toast and surprisingly subtle toasted coconut.

GOLD MEDAL FAMOUS

Fork & Brewer, Wellington; 4.9%

Veteran brewer Kelly Ryan is highly regarded, and his Aotearoa golden ale is a showcase for his talents, featuring punchy Kiwi hops that deliver notes of grapefruit, mango skin and pine.

LONGBOARDER

McLeod's, Waipu, Northland; 5.2%

With a name that reflects the area's surf culture, the flagship of this small brewery winning big awards is a crisp and quenching lager with subtle fruitiness, a biscuity malt backbone and lingering bitter finish.

GUNNAMATTA

Yeastie Boys, nomadic; 6.5%

Brewed partly in light-hearted protest against the proliferation of coffee beers, this "Tea Leaf IPA" uses Earl Grey

LUXE

Hallertau, Riverhead, Auckland; 4.5%

Sometimes called Number 1 because it was the first beer produced, Luxe is a very rare example of a New Zealand kölsch-style beer, straw coloured with grassy notes, biscuity malt and floral hops.

MILD

mike's, Urenui, Taranaki; 4%

Once lauded by Michael Jackson on a tour of the country, this long-standing dark mild is subtle and silky and certified organic, with flavour tones of coffee, nuts and toffee.

OH LORDY!

Funk Estate, Grey Lynn, Auckland; 5.5%

Funky name and funky branding for a seriously funky brewery. This Aotearoa pale ale is made with local NZ hops for a balanced and quaffable brew complete with prominent notes of passion-fruit, grape skin, grapefruit, pine needles and malt biscuits.

OYSTER STOUT

Three Boys, Christchurch, Canterbury; 6.5%

A beer that the brewer often struggles to convince people contains actual oysters, and the famous Bluff oyster at that. Complex with elements of coffee, liquorice, chocolate, smoke, molasses and leather, but never salty.

STYLE SPOTLIGHT

AOTEAROA PALE ALE

A debate rages over the proper name for pale ales made solely with New Zealand hops, contenders being Kiwi pale ale (KPA), New Zealand pale ale (NZPA) and Aotearoa (the Maori name for New Zealand) pale ale (APA; confusingly also a popular designation for the US style of pale ale).

There is, however, agreement on the critical element – the use of unique New Zealand hops, described as the key to the present and future of New Zealand craft beer. Enjoying the mild climate, rich soil and natural resistance to pests and disease, hops have flourished mainly on the South Island, including new breeds such as Nelson Sauvin, Riwaka, Motueka and Wakatu, all with notable tropical-fruit characteristics. New Zealand hops are globally popular, the amount exported having doubled in recent years.

Tuatara Kapai uses four Kiwi hops to produce notes of orange peel, grapefruit and pine, the name being Maori for "good". One of the first and best Aotearoa pale ales is **8 Wired's Hopwired** with flavours of orange, lime and the country's famous Sauvignon Blanc. **Townshend's Aotearoa Pale Ale** highlights dark stone fruit and grape skin, while **Behemoth CHUR!** bursts with grapefruit, lemon and sherbet, its name being New Zealand slang for "cheers".

PITCH BLACK

Invercargill, Invercargill, Southland; 4.5%

The country's southernmost brewery is renowned for its darker beers, including a *bock* made from malt smoked over native manuka wood. This creamy stout, on the other hand, offers flavours of burned toast crusts, milk chocolate and chewy caramel.

RED IPA

Hop Federation, Riwaka, Tasman; 6.4%

Brewers fled the rat race of Auckland for the idyllic country town of Riwaka to create this wonderfully balanced, rich mahogany brew showcasing caramel, passion-fruit, resin, melon and citrus.

RESURRECTION

Galbraith's, Auckland; 8.7%

New Zealand's first modern brewpub is renowned for traditional cask ales served on handpump. However, Resurrection is a strong, dark, abbey-style ale with a distinctly fruity, spicy Belgian nose and resplendent with burned caramel, raisin, sugar and spice.

SPARKLING ALE

Good George, Hamilton, Waikato; 4.5%

From a brewer also working for the Green Dragon pub in the "Hobbiton" *Lord of the Rings* attraction, this sparkling ale is balanced and sessionable with notes of lime peel, warm malt biscuits and fresh nectarine.

SPRUCE

Wigram, Christchurch, Canterbury; 5%

Using the 1771 recipe of Captain James Cook, explorer and first to brew in New Zealand, this is an unhopped ale flavoured by manuka and spruce. A unique and challenging beer with strong pine, molasses, honey and sherry elements.

BREWERY TO WATCH

ROCKY KNOB

nomadic

Husband and wife Stu and Bron Marshall brewing big-tasting beers like **Snapperhead** (7.4%), a double IPA rich with grapefruit and passion-fruit; **Oceanside Amber** (5.6%), with citrus and straw notes; and IPA **Hop Knob** (6%), with flavours of peach, currant and passion-fruit.

SUTTON HOO

Townshend's, Upper Moutere, Nelson; 4.7%

Previously a one-man operation that famously won the Champion Brewery of New Zealand award, but could not attend because he was working. The brewery is now growing and its amber ale offers a treasure trove of caramel, vanilla, sweet orange and nuts.

ST JOSEPHS

Moa, Blenheim, Marlborough; 9.5%

Located next to the family's Scott vineyard and helmed by Josh Scott, this larger New Zealand craft brewery produces this *tripel* with a classic flavour profile of banana, cloves, spice, caramel, citrus and funky Belgian yeast.

THREE WOLVES

Mac's [Lion], nomadic; 5.1%

Part of the Mac's range of beers, the craft brand of industry giant Lion. Approachable rather than extravagant, this accessible US-style pale ale offers notes of tropical fruit, pine and caramel.

STONECUTTER

Renaissance, Blenheim, Marlborough; 7%

Incredibly complex Scotch ale from a former Champion Brewery of New Zealand, pouring pitch black with intriguing aromas and flavours of coffee, chocolate, whisky, tanned leather, vanilla, oak, cigar ash and plum.

TWISTED ANKLE

The Twisted Hop, Wigram, Christchurch, Canterbury; 5.9%

In 2011 this brewpub had to move after the devastating Canterbury earthquakes, but it is thriving in its new location. Styled as an old ale, this pours an attractive chestnut and exhibits complex notes of roast coffee with hints of toffee and citrus.

SUPERCHARGER APA

Panhead Custom Ales [Lion], Upper Hutt, Wellington; 5.7%

Explosive growth saw the brewery purchased in 2016. Quality remains high with this flagship using US hops to produce a quaffable, bitter but balanced ale with lashings of orange peel, grass and grapefruit.

THE WOBBLY BOOT

Harrington's, Wigram, Christchurch, Canterbury; 5%

Silky-smooth, dark English-style porter from a sizeable brewery that consistently produces the largest range of beers in the country. The Boot (as it is known) exudes chocolate, cocoa and a gentle nuttiness.

ASIA & THE
MIDDLE EAST

JAPAN

For most of its almost century and a half of existence, Japanese brewing has been dominated by German methods and styles, all concentrated in the hands of an ever-shrinking coterie of large breweries. That all changed in the mid-1990s, however, when an alteration in the law allowed the establishment of smaller breweries, and since that moment two waves of craft beer expansion and innovation have transformed the land of "dry beer" into Asia's most interesting beer market.

BAY PILSNER

Bay Brewing Yokohama, Yokohama, Kanagawa, 5%

A Bohemian Pilsner with crisp Saaz hops almost balancing the rich, biscuity malt. The most impressive beer so far from a small brewpub that is soon to be a much larger brewery.

BENIAKA

Coedo, Kawagoe, Saitama; 7%

Labelled an "Imperial Sweet Potato Amber" and using locally grown Kintoki sweet potatoes, Coedo's most original year-round ale is sweet and rich, with caramel and sweet potato flavours balanced mostly by the slightly high alcohol content.

BLACK ONYX

Devil Craft, Shinagawa, Tokyo, 4.8%

This oatmeal stout is one of more than 60 beers made in the first year by this trio of US brewers. Full but light, it has smooth chocolate and coffee flavours and a perfect level of roast.

CALIFORNIA COMMON

Brimmer, Kawasaki, Kanagawa; 5%

Released as an autumn seasonal, this offering from Brimmer is a rather hoppy, full-bodied version of the steam beer style, with a malty, bready nose leading to lemony hoppiness and a dry, pleasantly bitter finish.

CHAMOMILE SAISON

Talmary, Yazu, Tottori; 4.8%

Brewpub and bakery opened in 2016 in which all bread and beer is made using wild yeasts. The beers are not sour, but display a barnyard spiciness perfect in Belgian styles, as in this balanced, crisp *saison*.

CHRISTMAS ALE

Minami Shinshu, Komagane, Nagano; 7.5%

This deep amber-coloured English-style strong ale is very malty and rich, with lots of caramel, cherry and dried-fruit flavours, becoming even silkier in its aged versions.

COFFEE AMBER

Marca, Osaka; 4.7%

This brewery started in 2015 and has shown promise with IPAs and saisons, but this deep brown aromatic ale has been the most consistently impressive. Sweet notes of caramel and chocolate are enhanced by cleanly infused coffee.

CORIANDER BLACK

North Island, Ebetsu, Hokkaido; 5%

A rich stout with flavours of chocolate, coffee and tart fruit accentuated by just the right amount of coriander. A roasty and sweet but well-balanced treat from Hokkaido's most innovative brewery.

EISBOCK

Otaru, Otaru, Hokkaido; 13.5%

Oak barrel-aged to a rich, fruity and port-like character with soft carbonation and high quaffability. Brewed only for the New Year.

FRAMBOISE

Atsugi, Atsugi, Kanagawa; 8%

Established as the Japanese leader in abbey-style beers, Atsugi turned to spontaneous fermentation, beginning with this not-quite-authentically lambic-style beer. Raspberries surround a lightly sour, lactic base with a bit of emergent barnyard funk.

FUYU SHIKOMI PORTER

Oh! La! Ho, Toumi, Nagano; 5%

A hotly anticipated winter seasonal that punches far above its weight. Its hoppy, fruity aroma leads to a chocolate malt taste with cherry and grape notes and a slight roastiness.

GOYA DRY

Helios, Gushikami, Okinawa; 5%

From the largest craft brewery in Okinawa, this original lager uses local bitter melon to complement its hops,

resulting in a massive bitterness that is not for everyone, but ideally suits the Okinawan climate.

GRYESETTE

Songbird, Kisarazu, Chiba; 4.5%

Spicy, crisp *saison* with rye and some barnyardy notes, from a tiny two-year-old brewery producing mainly Belgian-inspired beers that extend to the very funky.

HARE NO HI SENNIN

Yo-Ho, Karuizawa, Nagano; ~9%

English-style barley wine from Japan's largest craft brewery, it changes every year but is typically sweet and malty with notes of toffee and treacle and light English hops. Finds its way into various barrels for ageing as well.

HARU URARA

Moku Moku, Iga, Mie; 5%

Made at an agricultural park between Nagoya and Kyoto, this is labelled an "American-style Hefeweizen". It is creamy and fruity, fragrant with citrus hops and has a crisp hoppy finish that keeps everything in order.

HEIHACHIRO

Locobeer, Sakura, Chiba; 7.5%

A rich, full-bodied Baltic porter with lots of chocolate-fudge flavour accented with cherries, soy sauce umami and a touch of smoke, from a brewery experimenting with almost every style imaginable.

BREWERIES TO WATCH

KYOTO

Kyoto

Run by three non-Japanese brewers, this brewery adeptly blends US and Belgian influences, as in **Ichii Senshin** (6.5%), IPA-like but with a Belgian sensibility, and **Ichigo Ichie** (5.9%), a well-hopped *saison*.

Y. MARKET

Nagoya, Aichi

Their abundant use of dry-hopping took Japan by storm in 2014. **Purple Sky Pale Ale** (5.6%) has a big citrus and grassy nose, while **Meiyon Lager** (5.2%) proves they can handle hugely dry-hopped lagers, too.

YOROCCO

Zushi, Kanagawa

Small but expanding brewery focused on hoppy ales like **Skywalker IPA** (5.9%), and Belgian-inspired saisons such as **Cultivator** (6%), also with standout hopping.

IMPERIAL CHOCOLATE STOUT

Sankt Gallen, Atsugi, Kanagawa; 8.5%

Released for Valentine's Day, although with no added chocolate. Six malts and four kinds of hops give a luscious chocolate and coffee taste with an exceptionally strong hop bite.

IMPERIAL STOUT

Swan Lake, Agano, Niigata; 10%

This is an impressive and surprising powerhouse from a brewery that usually does low-alcohol ales to perfection, exhibiting lots of chocolate and berry flavours with rather light roastiness and some gin-like notes.

IMPERIALITY

Anglo Japanese (AJB), Nozawa Onsen, Nagano; 9.5%

English husband and Japanese wife opened the barrel-ageing-orientated AJB in 2015, and this Imperial stout has been the star of a so-far fascinating line-up. Aged in bourbon barrels, with elements of chocolate, vanilla, coffee, pears and soy sauce.

INNKEEPER BITTER LAGER

Outsider, Kofu, Yamanashi; 6%

A brewer well known for barley wines, but this rich, full pilsner, well hopped with Tettanger hops, is the best of their everyday beers, with a herbal, grassy nose and a prickly, bitter finish.

IPA

Oze no Yukidoke, Tatebayashi, Gunma; 5%

Deep golden colour, huge grapefruit hop nose and light, crisp malts made this a winning session IPA before the style was even named. Easier to find in the USA than Japan lately.

KAGAYAKI WHEAT 7

Johana, Nanto, Toyama; 7%

The first super-hoppy beer from a brewery specializing in colourful fruit blends, this convinces with a rich, wheaty backdrop to big grapefruit, orange and tropical-fruit hop aromas and a long, bitter finish.

KARUMINA

Hida Takayama, Takayama, Gifu; 10%

From a little-appreciated brewery in a popular tourist town, this is a black barley wine with Belgian yeast, a spicy and flowery nose and flavour notes of raisins, ginger, orange, chocolate and a touch of liquorice.

IMPERIALITY

BOURBON BARREL AGED
RUSSIAN IMPERIAL STOUT

KAZAMATSURI STOUT

Hakone, Odawara, Kanagawa; 7.5%

A potent winter stout from just outside the Hakone National Park near Mount Fuji, with creamy chocolate and coffee tones, faint hints of tart berries and a moderately strong hop bitterness.

KIN'ONI

Oni Densetsu, Noboribestsu, Hokkaido; 5%

Brilliantly hoppy and fruity American Pale Ale, pale of hue with a crisp malt character. New batches are made with different hop combinations and can be fun to compare.

LUSH HOP IPA

Ise Kadoya, Ise, Mie; 6%

From a very experimental brewery, this ale uses US hops for huge fruitiness, spanning citrus to tropical to stone fruits, while a light sweetness and medium bitterness make it very lush and quaffable.

MAROYAKA HYUGANATSU

Hideji, Nobeoka, Miyazaki; 5%

From a brewery that focuses more on yeast and local fruits than hops, and lagers more than ales, this citrus-fruit lager exemplifies their keen ability to harmonize fruity additions with a rich, bready lager base.

CAN'T-MISS BREWERIES

BAIRD

Shuzenji, Shizuoka

Brian Baird has been brewing US ales the Japanese way since 2000. **Suruga Bay Imperial IPA** (8.5%) is a perennial favourite among Japanese hop fanatics, double dry-hopped and fermented to total dryness, while **Natsumikan Summer Ale** (6%) shows Baird's brilliance with fruit, as mandarin orange enhances the ale rather than overwhelming it. **West Coast Wheat Wine** (10%) is sweet, fruity and wine-like, but finishes dry and strong.

FUJIZAKURA HEIGHTS

Kawaguchiko, Yamanashi

From *weizen* to *rauchbier* to pilsner, no one in Japan does German beer styles better than Hiromichi Miyashita at Fujizakura. **Weizen** (5.5%) is creamy and sweet, fruity and spicy, whereas **Roppongi Draft #1** (6.6%), a pale *weizenbock*, is hoppier with notes of orange and peaches, and winter seasonal **Rauch Bock** (7%) is smoky, sweet and meaty. A new taproom in Tokyo's Roppongi district makes the brewery easily accessible to travellers.

MIOBIKI WHEAT IPA

Ushitora, Shimotsuke, Tochigi; 6.4%

Ushitora made over 150 mostly dry and hoppy beers in its first two years. This wheat IPA, while bursting with tropical-fruit aromas from the hops, is set apart by its juicy sweetness and fuller body.

MUISHIKI NO SHOUNIN

Kazakami, Kawasaki, Kanagawa; 8%

"Unconscious Assent" is a generously spiced Imperial porter from a young brewery specializing in strong and mostly spiced beers. Christmassy with notes of chocolate brownie, clove and orange.

NAGOYA AKAMISO LAGER

Kinshachi, Inuyama, Aichi; 6%

A *dunkel* with local miso paste added, it tastes lightly roasty and meaty with lots of umami and body from the miso.

NINE-TAILED FOX

Nasu Kohgen, Nasu, Tochigi; 11%

This expensive, long-aged barley wine has a sherry-like aroma with caramel and lots of fruity esters. Remarkably smooth with an alcoholic heat that diminishes with ageing.

NIPPONIA

Hitachino Nest, Konosu, Ibaraki; 6.5%

Golden lager made with native Kaneko Golden barley and Sorachi Ace hops, with a lemony, oaky, vanilla character. Perhaps the best of this well-known

brewery's originals, and one of the first beers to popularize the hop.

OYSTER STOUT

Iwate Kura, Ichinoseki, Iwate; 7%

First and best of the Japanese oyster stouts, this is a creamy, velvety brew with ample umami from the oyster meat and shells in the boil. Silky and full mouthfeel, with elements of coffee, chocolate and cream.

PHARAOH SMOKED PORTER

Bell, Tokorozawa, Saitama; 5.5%

Whoever thought that malt-produced flavours of bacon, smoked salmon and chocolate could go together so well? A beer with strong smoke, great umami and high drinkability from a brewery opened in 2015.

PILSNER

Inuyama Loreley, Inuyama, Aichi; 5%

A sake maker that started with German-style beers and is now also making US-style ales, but whose best beer is still this standard pilsner, with lemony, grassy noble hops supported by a bready malt backbone.

PILSNER

Nihonkai Club, Noto, Ishikawa; 5%

A very Bohemian-style pilsner made by a Czech brewer at the tip of the Noto Peninsula. Rich biscuity malt character via decoction mash is balanced excellently by the aroma of plentiful Zatec hops.

CAN'T-MISS BREWERIES

MINOH

Minoh, Osaka

Kaori Oshita and her two sisters have been brewing Osaka's best-loved home-town beers for 20 years, including the soft, chocolaty, multi-award-winning **Stout** (5.5%). **W-IPA** (9%), pronounced "Double IPA", was the first high-alcohol hoppy beer in Japan, and its caramel maltiness is still convincing. **Yuzu White** (6%), a *witbier* made with locally grown citrus, is a fruity winter favourite.

SHIGA KOGEN

Yamanouchi, Nagano

Has been making dry, hoppy beers in US and Belgian styles since 2004. **Sono Juu** (7.5%), their 10th Anniversary IPA, uses Miyama-nishiki sake rice (*see* page 276) for a crisp, light palate that lets the hops shine. **Takashi Imperial Stout** (9%) is dark and fruity, with notes of soy sauce and chocolate; versions aged in Ichiro's Malt barrels are especially coveted. **Yamabushi Saison 1** (6.5%), sold in 75cl bottles, has Miyama-nishiki replacing Belgian candi sugar and is also made in occasional, and much-desired, fruit-, brett- and barrel-aged versions.

SHONAN

Chigasaki, Kanagawa

Based at the Kumazawa Sake Brewery, Shonan makes three German-style beers year round, but their vast array of seasonals and one-offs is more in the US mould. **Imperial Stout** (8%) carries a big punch, with roasted, oily, umami-laden malts and a burned, bitter finish; **Belgian Stout** (7%) is a bit milder, focusing more on sweet chocolate and balanced spicing; and **IPA** (6%) appears variously in different guises, with over 35 versions mixing hops, yeasts and even grains and fruits.

STYLE SPOTLIGHT

JAPANESE BEERS WITH A SAKE INFLUENCE

Sake, the original beer of Japan, has been made from rice for over 2,000 years, yet even as drinkers around the world are discovering today's better-than-ever sake, it is losing market share domestically. Hence the reason that many sake breweries are expanding into craft beer, leading to the emergence of a new domestic style of sake-influenced beers.

Various aspects of sake making can be employed in beer production. Possibly the easiest is the use of sake rice as an additive, where it plays a more prominent role than when employed as an adjunct in industrial lagers. **Yago** from Daisen G is made with sake rice and Belgian yeast for a crisp, spicy and fruity take on a *witbier*. Similar is **Konishi Howaka**, a delicate and fruity low-alcohol *wit*. Sake yeast can ferment beer as well, imparting distinct flavours in the process, as in **Umenishiki Sokujo**, which uses ginjo yeast with barley malt and tastes more like a sake than a beer. **Orochi**, a "rice barley wine"

from Shimane Beer Company, uses both sake rice and yeast, the brewery collaborating annually with a different sake maker to produce a startlingly different brew each time. **Hitachino Nest Japanese Classic Ale** is an IPA aged in cedar sake barrels, and in the extreme case, sake and beer can be blended, as in **Kuninocho Kijo Gold**, wherein dry-hopped junmai sake is added to their golden ale.

In the near future, sake-influenced beers may well be seen as the first original Japanese beer style.

PLUM WHEAT

T.Y. Harbor, Shinagawa, Tokyo; 4%

An older brewery that is making waves with fruit beers and kettle-soured ales. Although traditionally fermented, the plums provide a tart juiciness similar to that of a *Berliner weisse* balanced by mild, fruity sweetness.

PORTER

Campion, Asakusa, Tokyo; 4.9%

This small brewpub in touristy Asakusa serves British-style ales straight from bright tanks, low in carbonation and very authentic, like this black, light porter with a bit of tangy fruit and roasty chocolate malt.

PRINZ

Bayern Meister, Fujinomiya, Shizuoka; 5%

Made close to Mount Fuji by a Bavarian brewer who does all things German well, this flagship pilsner is in the southern German style with rich, sweet, bready malt being well balanced by grassy hoppiness.

RASPBERRY

Harvestmoon, Maihama, Chiba; 6%

An original fruit beer, dry but not sour, that uses Champagne yeast in a secondary fermentation. Its rich, jammy raspberry nose becomes unexpectedly dry, clean and minerally with just enough fruit sweetness to keep it fun.

RAUCH

Tazawako, Senboku, Akita; 7.5%

Nearly *bock*-like richness and body make this one of the nicest rauchbiers in Japan, with a smoky caramel and molasses aroma and a lovely smoky, woody flavour. Ageing renders it as smooth as silk.

SAKURA KOBO ALE

Chateau Kamiya, Ushiku, Ibaraki; 7%

Fermented with yeast from cherry blossom, this is fruity and also funky, with cherry notes and a wild, tart, barnyard character. Cherry yeast beers are multiplying in Japan.

SEYA NO KOMUGI

Yokohama, Yokohama, Kanagawa; 5.5%

An ale using local wheat, this is neither exactly German, Belgian nor US in style, with clove notes from the yeast, biscuity wheat malt, and citrus from the hops.

SHIMANOWA

Kure, Kure, Hiroshima; 5%

A lager hopped as an IPA from a brewery adept at lagers of all sorts, the lemon, orange and peach aromas coming from US hops, which are backed up by crisp, crackery pilsner malt.

STEAM LAGER

Aqula, Akita, Akita; 5%

From a brewery adept at both lagers and ales, hybrid fermentation reveals deep orange, grapefruit and peach flavours in a relatively full-bodied beer that showcases spicy, peppery hops.

STOUT

Chatan Harbor, Chatan, Okinawa; 4.5%

From a promising brewery that opened in 2016 at a beach resort near Japan's US military base, this thick oatmeal stout has a full body with rich chocolate and soy sauce notes, making it seem stronger than it really is.

TROPICAL WEIZEN STRONG

Mojiko Retro, Kitakyushu, Fukuoka; 7.5%

A massively fruity blond *weizenbock* from a brewery doing German styles well. Rich tropical-fruit flavours from generous amounts of Nelson Sauvin and Cascade hops are almost shocking in their ability to blend with banana and clove tones.

URSUS

Baeren, Morioka, Iwate; 7%

A velvety smooth blond *weizenbock* with rich notes of cream, melon, banana and clove. This northern Honshu brewer is a local favourite that is an expert with German styles, and experiments with many others as well.

VOLCANO

Kisoji, Kiso, Nagano; 9.7%

Strongest beer made to date from this brewery in a hot springs hotel, toffee-apple red with sweet cherry and citrus tones and a hugely bitter and earthy finish. The one-year-aged version is silkier and less sweet.

WEIZEN

Zakkoku Kobo, Ogawa-Machi, Saitama; 5%

This "Miscellaneous Grains" brewery uses home-grown rye and millet to give a tart, grainy edge to their rich wheat beer's typical banana and clove notes.

WHEAT WINE

Daisen G, Saihaku, Tottori; 9%

A winter special from Daisen G in western Honshu, this golden brew is wine-like and powerful, with spicy aromas of wheat, pears, bananas and cloves, and a strongly hoppy finish to balance its sweetness.

WORLD DOWNFALL STOUT

Thrash Zone, Yokohama, Kanagawa; 7.6%

As yet the only dark beer from a thrash metal bar and brewery specializing in IPAs. A roasty, chocolaty foreign-export-sized stout with sweetness upfront and a roasted, bitter finish.

YUKYU NO TOKI

Akashi, Akashi, Hyōgo; 5%

A creamy, dry *schwarzbier* from a brewery right on the Seto Inland Sea specializing in German-style beers. With lots of chocolate and coffee flavour, this finishes dry and softly bitter.

CHINA

The world's largest producer of beer by a great margin, brewing as much as the next three largest brewing nations combined, China is also potentially the great disruptor, since the country's per capita consumption is still low compared with the developed beer lands. If the initial stirrings of craft beer interest blossom into more widespread appeal, the strain it could put on hop and malt supplies might be considerable.

CAPTAIN IPA

Urbräu, Handan, Hebei; 6.8%

An IPA built in the classic US style, this has a complex, hop-fuelled aroma featuring floral and citrus-spicy notes before a body that boasts a soft maltiness, layered over the top with crisp hop bitterness.

DUGITE VANILLA STOUT

The Brew, Shanghai; 5%

Black in colour, this creamy stout mixes a rich maltiness with flavours from real vanilla pods to produce a smooth, full-bodied, creamy vanilla character with hints of dark chocolate to round it all out nicely.

CAN'T-MISS BREWERIES

● ● ● ● ● ● ● ● ● ● ●

BOXING CAT [AB INBEV]

Shanghai

China's first and still most influential craft brewery, and also the country's first international medal winner, with the toffee-ish **Ringside Red** (5%) amber lager winning a silver medal at the World Beer Cup 2016. Other year-round beers include **Contender Extra Pale Ale** (4.9%), golden and lightly hopped with a fruity character; the light and thirst-quenching **Right Hook Helles** (4.5%), with a pleasingly soft bitterness; and **TKO IPA** (6.3%), aromatic and, for Chinese beer, both strong and well hopped.

SLOW BOAT

Beijing

One of the Chinese capital's first breweries – the main brewery is on the city's outskirts, the newer brewpub and taproom both more central – and one of its most reliable. Regular brands include the sweet, floral and dry-finishing **The Helmsman's Honey Ale** (6%), flagship **Captain's Pale Ale** (5.5%), with preserved-lemon notes and a very dry finish, and **Monkey's Fist IPA** (5.75%), with mango and other tropical-fruit tones. Watch for seasonal specialities like densely cocoa-ish **Sea Level Chocolate Sea Salt Stout** (7.1%).

KOJI RED ALE

Jing-A, Beijing; 5.5%

Innovative approach by a pair of expat brewers, one American and the other Canadian, using koji rice, wasabi and ginger to create a unique, lightly sweet, earthy, spicy-peppery ale.

KUDING PALE ALE

Panda Brew, Beijing; 6.5%

Made with the Traditional Chinese Medicine herb that gives the beer its name, this has a strongly herbal aroma and a fascinating bitterness, different than one would get from the use of hops alone.

KUNGFU PEPPER

Zinnbath, Jinan, Shandong; 5.2%

An unusual lager brewed with Chinese Sichuan peppers to produce a unique peppery aroma and a clean and

BREWERY TO WATCH

SHANGRI-LA HIGHLAND

Shangri-la, Yunnan

Producing six different beers at over 3,300 metres (10,800 feet) above sea level, including **Yalaso** (3.1%) and **Son Gha** (5.2%), both lagers brewed from heirloom Qingke barley.

surprisingly unpeppery, malty palate accompanied by medium bitterness.

LITTLE GENERAL IPA

Great Leap; Beijing; 6.5%

Made with whole cone hops from China, of a variety known as Qingdao Flower, which give it a vaguely citrus-peel but mostly floral hoppiness that blends well with the fruity malt.

TENGYUN WHEAT ALE

Fengshou, Chengdu, Sichuan; 5%

A gentle fragrance of banana and coriander announces this summery thirst-quencher, with yeasty notes of bitter orange and other strongly aromatic fruits occupying the body.

TIAO DONG HU

No 18, Wuhan, Hubei; 5.5%

Award-winning US-style IPA featuring tropical-fruit hop aromas and fruity malt supporting a gradually growing hop bitterness that culminates in a flavoursome bitter and lingering finish.

SOUTH KOREA

Hampered for years by laws that limited their number rather severely, South Korean craft breweries have flourished since the repeal of those laws and are now beginning to catch up in terms of quality, consistency and creativity as well. A bet against the country's beer scene yet developing into one of Asia's most interesting would be ill-advised indeed.

KUKMIN IPA

The Booth, Seongnam-si, Gyeonggi-do; 7%

Born as a small alleyway pub with a single contract-brewed beer, this growing operation now boasts an expanding portfolio of own beers and collaborations, including this IPA with a crisp malt palate that lets its well-structured hoppiness shine.

MOONRISE PALE ALE

Galmegi, Suyeong-gu, Busan; 5%

This brewery with four taprooms in Busan is known for its uncompromisingly hoppy beers, but credit is also deserved for their well-balanced pale ale with a peppery citrus nose and zesty, quenching palate.

SLOW IPA

The Hand and Malt, Hwado-eup, Gyeonggi-do; 4.5%

At the high end of strength for its declared "session IPA" style, this is nonetheless a fragrant, appealingly floral and eminently quaffable ale from an already sound and still fast-improving brewery.

STOUT

Gorilla, Gwanganhaehyeon-ro, Busan; 6.3%

In any young craft beer culture there is a need for breweries that present straightforward beers like this somewhat light-bodied, well-structured ebony ale with mocha notes layered over a simple base of roasted maltiness.

THE LAST TRAIN

Magpie, Jeju-si, Jeju-do; 8%

Born a nomadic brewer, Magpie found a permanent home for their fine ales in a disused fruit packaging plant on Jeju Island in 2016, including this silky, rounded, sweetly chocolaty and stronger take on their core Porter.

BREWERY TO WATCH

GOODMAN

Guri-si, Gyeonggi-do

A young brewery outside of Seoul making creative beers from the get-go, such as a Pinot Noir-barrel-aged **Garden Saison** (5.5%), a chocolate–caramel, London-style **Seoul Porter** (5.1%) and an aromatic **Table Beer Pale** (3.1%) made with a rotating schedule of hops.

TAIWAN

Of all Asia's still-underdeveloped beer lands, Taiwan and perhaps South Korea hold the greatest promise for the future, with active and collaborative home-brewing cultures giving rise to ambitious commercial-brewing concerns. That said, Taiwan is also, like most of Asia outside of Japan, significant more for its potential than for its creative and impressive present.

#1 PALE ALE

23, New Tapei City; 5.5%

From an expat US brewer, this offers tea-like hop aromas with earthy qualities and a citrusy, floral complexity with a firm, lingering bitterness – although deliberately made slightly less bitter to suit the Taiwanese palate.

AMBER ALE BREWED WITH DRIED LONGAN

55th Street, Taoyuan City; 5.5%

One of Taiwan's smallest breweries produces this amber ale with prominent smoky fruit flavours from the use of smoked and dried longan fruit. Smooth and nutty in its maltiness, with a pleasant minerality in the finish.

THE CACAO FOUNTAIN CACAO PORTER

Indie Brew, Taoyuan City; 6.9%

A well-crafted porter from Indie Brew providing layers of roasted malt and complex chocolate notes, a rounded mouthfeel and a sweetness that avoids becoming cloying.

GOKUAKU WHEAT BEER

Shodoiji, Taoyuan City; 5%

This slightly hazy wheat beer pours with a generous foam and bready aromatics. Despite a slightly grainy profile, it is well balanced with medium acidity and a somewhat creamy texture.

HONEY LAGER

Dingmalt, New Taipei City; 7%

Companion to the brewery's German-style *kellerbier* specialities, this lager is deep gold with alluring honey aromas, piney, fruity complexity and a warming finish.

LONGAN HONEY LAGER

Radiant, New Taipei City; 6%

Made in small quantities due to the limited availability of the speciality honey used in its recipe, this has a fragrant and floral nose, firm yet smooth bitterness and a drying, thirst-quenching finish with long, honeyed malt flavours.

MANEKI NEKO PUMPKIN ALE

Sunmai, New Taipei City; 5–5.5%

From Sunmai, one of the leading brewers in Taiwan, this beer has a spicy complexity, yet remains refreshingly light for the style – a summery interpretation of an autumnal beer.

PANGU ALE

Prost 12, Zhubei City; 6.7%

Slightly hazy with fresh citrusy hop aromas, this offers firm bitterness in balance with gentle malty flavours and fruitiness, drying on the finish with grapefruity notes. Crisp, delicate and highly quaffable.

PASSION MOSAIC

A Brewers Team, nomadic; 5.6%

Created under contract by a talented home-brewer, this summer thirst-quencher has attractive citrusy and passion-fruit aromas, gentle herbal tones and a light, refreshing body with firm fruitiness in the finish.

WAXY RICE ALE

Taiwan Ale, New Taipei City; 4.5%

From a brewery with a focus on creating original recipes using local ingredients, including various kinds of rice, comes this ale with a smooth and creamy texture, fruity and bready body and lingering, off-dry finish.

WOO BEER – SANDALWOOD FLAVOUR BEER

North Taiwan, Taoyuan City; 6%

Initially brewed for the Woobar cocktail lounge bar and made available commercially, this speciality amber ale has smoky, woody, spicy complexity, and is remarkably refreshing.

REALITY AMERICAN PALE ALE

Beer Farm, Taoyuan City; 5.5%

Based on a home-brewing competition winner, this is a refreshingly light pale ale with citrusy and piney hop flavours, moderate bitterness balanced by biscuit malt and a drying, lingering finish.

SOUTH GATE SCHWARZBIER

3000 Brewseum, Hengchun, Pingtung; 4.9%

Produced at a brewpub below a beer museum, hence the brewery name, this is refined, balanced, long and complex, close to a world classic in quality and one of Brewseum's best.

TAIWAN RAUCHBIER

Taiwan Head Brewers, nomadic; 5.5%

With refined smoky flavours well balanced by sweet and nutty maltiness, this beer finishes dry without any undue harshness from the smoke and a lingering minerality.

VIETNAM

Alongside traditions of brewing "yellow" and "black" beers, effectively interpretations of *světlý ležák* and *tmavý ležák* imported from the Czech Republic, and the country's own light, fresh *bia hoi* beers, Vietnam is now beginning to witness impressive growth in craft brewing. While it is still early days, we will watch anxiously to see what distinctly Vietnamese beers may yet emerge.

BIA HOI

HABECO, Hanoi, 3.5%

The name for both Vietnam's famous light beer, brewed from malt, rice, sugar and hops, and the street-side establishments that serve it. One of the best of the many brands available in Vietnam.

BLACK BEER

Goldmalt, Hanoi and other locations; ~5%

For over 10 years, this company has been opening small brewpubs around the country, now 20 in number, all of them brewing this Czech-inspired lager with notes of coffee and chocolate and a dry, nutty finish.

CAN'T-MISS BREWERY
• • • • • • • • • • • • • • • •

FURBREW

Hanoi

Opened in 2016 and with plans for up to 40 different beers in 2017. Danish brewer Thomas Bilgram produces experimental beers like the seasonal **Yuletide 2016** (8.3%), complex with sweet maltiness and a spicy nose, and **Boston Rose** IPA (7.3%), flavoured with rose pellets for Valentine's Day, as well as more conventional ales, such as **Hoa IPA** (7.3%) with lightly malty and citrus notes, and nine other regular offerings.

BLONDE LAGER

Hoa Vien, Hanoi and other locations; ~5%

From a brewery producing Czech-style lager in multiple locations; amber and floral with hints of grapefruit.

FAR EAST IPA

East West, Ho Chi Minh City; 6.7%

A full-bodied IPA with aroma and flavour notes of citrus, tropical fruit and pine, courtesy of the Nelson Sauvin and Centennial hops used.

FARMER'S WEIZEN

Barett, Hanoi; 5.5%

From Siebel-Institute-educated brewer Quang Van comes this fruity and effervescent *hefeweizen* with a light body, fruity character and lemongrass and apricot finish.

BREWERY TO WATCH

EAST WEST

Ho Chi Minh City

Head brewer Sean Thommen's US roots are evident in beers like **Coffee Vanilla Porter** (7%), with toffee-ish coffee and vanilla flavours, the darkly fruity **Independence Stout** (12%) and raspberry and citrus **Saigon Rosé** (3%).

JASMINE IPA

Pasteur Street, Ho Chi Minh City; 6.5%

As true to type an IPA as Vietnam has to offer; malty with notes of citrus and a bitterness that you expect from a US-style IPA.

LOST-AT-SEA DOUBLE IPA

Lac, Ho Chi Minh City; 8.5%

A rare Vietnamese double IPA, this juicy ale is suffused with hops for an aroma and flavour thick with lemony, grapefruity and orangey tones.

LÙN MÀ LÁO BLONDE ALE

BiaCraft, Ho Chi Minh City; 5.2%

The name translates to "Short but Arrogant", which sums up the gentle yet firm approach of this golden ale with a lightly malty body and floral hop notes.

PALE ALE

Platinum, Ho Chi Minh City; 4.6%

One of Vietnam's first widely available craft beers, initially marketed in trendy clubs, this is an approachable ale with a light body and modest hoppiness.

PATIENT WILDERNESS WHEAT ALE

Heart of Darkness, Ho Chi Minh City; 4.5%

A recent arrival to the local beer scene, one of this young brewery's first efforts was this banana-y *hefeweizen* with a gentle bitterness and fruit-forward flavour.

ISRAEL

For obvious reasons, there is not a lot of brewing underway in the Middle East. Of what relatively little there is, however, Israel is the undisputed leader, its way paved over the past decade or so by US-influenced breweries like Dancing Camel.

ADMONIT

Malka, Yehiam, Upper Galilee; 5.5%

One of Israel's most popular and widely available craft beers, this quaffable, medium-bodied pale ale has considerable caramel malt sweetness, mellow bitterness, lively carbonation and a touch of coriander.

BAZELET PILSNER

Golan, Katzrin, Golan Heights; 4.9%

This German-style pilsner from Golan Brewery is crisp and refreshing, with a floral aroma, clean malt flavours, sharp but tamed bitterness and a light body. Not completely filtered and highly thirst quenching.

BLACK

Alexander, Emek Hefer, Central Israel; 7%

This acclaimed robust and chocolaty porter is a winter seasonal that carries a full body, creamy texture and a couple of international gold medals. Rich malt character and earthy hops help define this hearty beer.

DARK LAGER

Jem's, Petach Tikva, Central Israel; 5%

This amber-hued Munich-style *dunkel* is light-bodied and balanced, with pleasant toasty and biscuity malt flavours and a gentle noble hop aroma. Clean, mellow and quaffable.

DARK MATTER

HaShakhen, nomadic; 5.5%

Even with occasional hop substitutions based upon availability, this black IPA features a bold but well calculated hoppy character, balanced with highly roasted malt flavours and an agreeable approachability.

EMBARGO

Herzl, Jerusalem; 6%

A unique porter based on an award-winning home-brew recipe, brewed with Cuban tobacco leaves. Loaded with cocoa and vanilla aromas, powered by fresh herbal flavours and with a moderately full body.

JACK'S WINTER ALE

Shapiro, Beit Shemesh, Jerusalem; 8.2–8.5%

Probably the country's most anticipated winter seasonal is a strong Belgian-inspired ale conditioned on Jack Daniels-soaked oak chips. Lots of woody and bourbon-ish flavours add complexity to the rich maltiness and fruity banana esters.

PATRIOT

Dancing Camel, Tel Aviv; 5.2%

A citrusy US-influenced pale ale brewed since the very early days of this first-ever Israeli craft brewery. Rich with American hop aromas and flavours, backed by a clean biscuit body.

PUMPKIN ALE

Galil, Moran, Lower Galilee; 5.1%

This sought-after autumn seasonal from Galil Brewery is Israel's only pumpkin beer, released once a year on Hallowe'en. Brewed with baked pumpkin chunks, pumpkin-pie spices and floral hops, it is sweet without being cloying and highly enjoyable.

RONEN THE UGLY BEER

Srigim, Li On, Jerusalem; 6.5%

A heavily hopped IPA that combines the attractive fruity and piney aromas of US hops with high bitterness and enough caramel malt to support it all. Intentionally somewhat out of balance, but quite irresistible.

REST OF ASIA & THE MIDDLE EAST

Most Asian nations aside from those already featured are notable more for their potential than their current craft beer reality. They range from countries with nascent though laudably ambitious brewing markets, such as India, to those with established, superior mass-produced brands that may in time beget the growth of even more interesting beers from a new generation of craft breweries, for example Cambodia. Until such potential is realized, we highlight a few of the important existing labels.

CAMBODIA

ABC EXTRA STOUT

Cambodia [Heineken], Phnom Penh; 8%

Brewed under licence to varying strengths in at least five Asian countries, this thick, sweet, somewhat burned-tasting and aniseed-accented stout paved the way for similarly styled beers from several as yet not as accomplished breweries.

SRI LANKA

STOUT

Lion (Ceylon), Biyagama, Western
Province; 8.8%

Widely exported, this inky black stout is
characterized by notes of tar in the aroma
and a sweet, faintly lactic body offering
flavours of chocolate, aniseed and burned
herbs. Also known Sinha Stout.

THAILAND

DUNKEL

Tawandang, Bangkok; 4.5%

The best of the trio of beers produced at
this showstopper brewery and beer hall
with three locations of varying enormity.
Chocolaty and off-dry, it has a broadly
toasty character with a nuttiness that
emerges as the beer warms.

LEBANON

LEBANESE PALE ALE

961 Beer/Gravity, Mazraat Yachoua,
Mount Lebanon; 6.3%

Brewed with Lebanese flavours such as
sumac, sage and mint, the dry, almost
woody entry of this unique pale ale leads
to a balanced body with a bracing, herbal
dryness and a nutty maltiness.

AFRICA

SOUTH AFRICA

Far and away the African continent's leader in brewing, South Africa is not only the birthplace of part of what is now the world's largest brewing company – the former SABMiller part of AB InBev – but also the sole African nation that can boast rapidly developing craft beer culture. Hopes are that its influence will continue to spread north.

1912 APA

Clarens Brewery, Clarens, Free State; 4.5%

Of the extensive range of beers served in this small-town brewpub, this US-style pale ale, with peach, passion-fruit and toffee flavours vying for top spot, is the most memorable.

BONE CRUSHER

Darling Brewery, Darling, Western Cape; 5.2%

Of the vast range produced at this ·not-to-be-missed brewery, the well-spiced *witbier* stands out for its heady perfumed aroma.

COCONUT IPA

Afro Caribbean, Cape Town, Western Cape; 6%

While experimental, one-off beers are the speciality here, and their flagship ale, with plenty of body, a subtle hit of toasted coconut and a long bitter finish, is the go-to pint.

EXTRA PALE UIL

Aegir Project, Noordhoek, Western Cape; 3.8%

The lightest and perhaps cleverest of a strong range from a small husband-and-wife team with real talent. A hoppy, surprisingly full, fruity summer ale.

GUARDIAN PALE ALE

Citizen, nomadic; 5%

The star in the line-up of this Cape Town contract brewery is a well-balanced quaffer, light in body with notes of biscuit, toffee, grapefruit and gooseberries

THE GUZZLER

Mad Giant, Johannesburg, Gauteng; 4.8%

Johannesburg's must-visit city-centre brewery boasts a solid core range, but this citrusy, dry-hopped pilsner steals the show.

LOXTON LAGER

Humanbrew, Johannesburg, Gauteng; 5.3%

With great whiffs of blackcurrant and mint and flavours to match, this is a singularly South African brew spiced with a secret blend of endemic herbs.

ICONIC BREWERY

DEVIL'S PEAK

Cape Town, Western Cape

Leading the way in the South African craft beer scene, Devil's Peak has legendary status among local beer aficionados. The exceptional **The King's Blockhouse IPA** (6%) is packed with grapefruit and lychee aromas, while the **Pale Ale** (4%) offers an approachable taste of hops. The superlative **Black IPA** (6%), with its pungent pine aroma, is usually only available at the Devil's Peak taproom, where you can also sample barrel-aged experimental brews, including the outstanding **Vannie Hout** (7.5%), a complex *Brettanomyces*-influenced *saison* with characteristic barnyard character.

MJÖLNIR IPA

Anvil Ale, Dullstroom, Mpumalanga; 6%

One of the country's most highly regarded IPAs, this packs a tropical-fruit punch, with the passion-fruit and peach backed up by a subtle but noticeable touch of toffee.

MR BROWNSTONE

Woodstock, Cape Town, Western Cape; 5.2%

The showstopper in this inner-city Cape Town brewery's much-lauded seasonal range is an almost chewy autumnal ale offering equal doses of chocolate, hazelnut and long-lasting hop bitterness.

PALE ALE

Striped Horse, nomadic; 5.2%

Contract brewed in the Winelands region and served at a seaside pub in Cape Town, toffee, breadiness and tangerine notes are served up in equal amounts in this refreshing amber brew.

SOWETO GOLD SUPERIOR LAGER

UBuntu Kraal, Soweto, Gauteng; 5.2%

Produced in one of the most culturally and historically important cities in South Africa, this amber-coloured lager is darker and sweeter than many of its peers, but still delivers a crisp, refreshing finish.

CAN'T-MISS BREWERIES

CAPE

Paarl, Western Cape

Best known for its German-style brews, this award-winning brewery also produces highly hopped ales plus seasonal and speciality beers. The go-to is the **Pilsner** (5.2%), beautifully balanced with biscuity aromas and a bitter, spicy finish, while of the various weissbiers, **Krystal Weiss** (5%) stands out for its banana-bread character and clean, crisp finish. In season, try the caramel-laden **Oktoberfest** (6.1%), or year round seek a coveted bottle of **Cape of Good Hops** (7.5%), a double IPA with heavy hits of gooseberry and passion-fruit.

JACK BLACK'S

Cape Town, Western Cape

After nine years of contract brewing, one of South Africa's largest and best-established brands has opened its own brewery. The flagship **Brewers Lager** (5%) is a quaffable and accessible all-malt brew, while the new **Keller Pils** (5%) offers complexity and superb balance. At the boozier end of the scale, **Skeleton Coast** (6.6%) is a more malt-forward IPA than most.

VALVE RIOT

Cape Town, Western Cape; 5.9%

Lashings of grapefruit, a mild hint of caramel and a long bitter finish are the hallmarks of this medium-bodied, golden-hued IPA showcasing South Africa's Southern Passion hop.

WEIZEN

Brauhaus am Damm, Rustenburg, North West; 4.5%

Orange-gold and topped with a crown of fluffy white foam, this is one of the country's top weissbiers, with a prominent banana aroma and background notes of spice and freshly baked bread.

BREWERIES TO WATCH

DRIFTER

Cape Town, Western Cape

Passionate owner Nick Bush brings a level of inspiring innovation to a core range that includes the excellent **Scallywag IPA** (6%) and the subtle, biscuity **Stranded Coconut** (4.5%), plus a series of experimental brews.

FRASER'S FOLLY

Bredasdorp, Western Cape

Owned by a boutique winery but brewer-led, making a light but big-tasting Anglo-pointing **Pale Ale** (3.7%) and **Stout** (5.4%), with new efforts in the pipeline, heralded by **Dark Continent Moer Koffie Condensed Milk Stout** (5%).

MOUNTAIN

Worcester, Western Cape

Brewery destination in an idyllic rural setting, already turning heads with off-style winners like Belgian *alt* **Cape Kraken** (4.8%), *tripel-hefeweizen* **Madala's Gold** (6.8%) and wheaty porter **Black or White** (5.2%), with more to come.

REST OF AFRICA

While the first rumblings of craft beer development have been felt in various parts of Africa, we have found little thus far that excites beyond the simple pleasure of discovering a moderately characterful summer ale or wheat beer among a sea of remarkably pedestrian light lagers. It is our hope and cautious belief that the beers below are merely the harbinger of much better and more exciting things to come.

ETHIOPIA

GARDEN BRÄU BLONDY

Beer Garden Inn, Addis Ababa; 4.5%

The country's older better-end brewery produces a reliable and fulsome, *Reinheitsgebot*-compliant, Hallertau-hopped, hazy light draught *helles* from handsome German coppers.

MOZAMBIQUE

LAURENTINA PRETA

Cervejas De Moçambique [AB InBev], Maputo; 5%

In a sea of pale lagers, this deep brown *dunkel*, with a dose of caramel, a note of chocolate and a palate-cleansing bitterness, stands out as Mozambique's most flavourful beer.

NAMIBIA

URBOCK

Namibian Breweries, Windhoek; 7%

Brewed just once a year, this rich wintry brew is brimming with treacle toffee, toasted bread, a touch of liquorice and just a hint of alcoholic warmth.

INDEX

CONTRIBUTOR BIOGRAPHIES

Christian Andersen is a journalist, communications consultant and beer blogger at durst.nu/. He also writes and reviews for various print media, serves as a member of the board for the Danish Beer Enthusiasts consumer group and is an instigator of the New Nordic Beer movement.

Max Bahnson was born in Argentina and moved to the Czech Republic in 2002. He blogs under the pen name of Pivní Filosof, "Beer Philosopher", and is the author of *Prague: A Pisshead's Pub Guide* and co-author with Alan McLeod of *The Unbearable Nonsense of Craft Beer*.

Jay R Brooks has been writing about beer for over 25 years and currently writes a syndicated newspaper column, "Brooks on Beer". His most recent book is *California Breweries North* . He is also president of the North American Guild of Beer Writers.

Phil Carmody and **Anna Shefl** sample, review, judge and enjoy beers, while also striving to advance the Baltic beer landscape through their consulting with breweries, restaurants and other businesses. They aim to encourage awareness of the developing landscape and appreciation of tradition.

Lucy Corne has written two books on South African beer and pens a popular blog documenting all things beer in southern Africa at brewmistress.co.za/. Lucy lives with her husband and son in Cape Town where she also helps to run the local home-brewing club.

John Duffy lives in Dublin and has been blogging as The Beer Nut since 2005. When not engaged in the Sisyphean task of keeping track of the modern Irish beer scene, he travels and writes about what he finds to drink there.

Per Forsgren is a Swedish beer enthusiast and ratebeer. com administrator who has been documenting beer on the web and in magazines since the early 1990s, both in his home country and during his worldwide travels now spanning more than 100 countries.

Jonathan Gharbi is the author of *Beer Guide to Vietnam* and has also written articles about beer for various magazines. He opened the first craft brewery in Burkina Faso (Brasserie Artisanale de Ouagadougou), but is now brewing in Morocco.

João Gonçalves is the owner of Portugal's leading craft beer site, Cerveja Artesanal Portuguesa (cervejaartesanalportuguesa.pt), and a contributor to Cerveja Depressão (cervejadepressao.wordpress.com), a humorous beer review blog. In his free time, he works as a Project Manager for a Portuguese Internet company.

Shachar Hertz is a UC Davis brewing graduate and owner of Beer & Beyond, a beer promotion company based in Israel. He is the author of two editions of *The Beer Brands in Israel* and a beer tour operator and guide.

Stan Hieronymus is a lifelong journalist who has been writing about beer since 1992. As his most recent book *Brewing Local: American-Grown Beer* suggests, he is

an advocate of terroir, and comments about it at www.appellationbeer.com/.

Matt Kirkegaard is one of Australia's most experienced beer writers and commentators. He is founder of leading online beer news and discussion site Australian Brews News, and in 2014 won the inaugural Beer Media trophy at the Australian International Beer Awards.

Rafał Kowalczyk and **Jan Lichota** are Polish beer judges. Rafał is a journalist and educator on beer who owns the Warsaw beer pub Jabeerwocky, while Jan is a beer lawyer, reporter and researcher who works in the tourism sector.

Maurizio Maestrelli is a professional journalist who has focused on beer, wine and spirits since 1997, and is author of *Birra and Thomas Hardy's Ale: the Story, the Legend*, as well as contributor to *1001 Beers You Must Try Before You Die* and *Baladin. La Birra Artigianale è Tutta Colpa di Teo*.

Mark Meli is senior writer for the *Japan Beer Times* and has written two books about Japanese craft beer. He lives in Kyoto, and is professor of ecocritical cultural studies at Kansai University in Osaka.

Neil Miller was the Brewers Guild of New Zealand Beer Writer of the Year 2014–15. His work has appeared in *Beer & Brewer*, *The Shout*, *Cuisine*, *New Zealand Liquor News*, *Sunday Star Times* and *Dominion Post*. He is also a regular on Radio New Zealand's The Panel.

Des de Moor is the author of The *CAMRA Guide to London's Best Beer, Pubs & Bars*, a contributor to *Beer Magazine*, *Beer Advocate* and *Time Out* among others, a respected international beer judge and a regular host of tutored tastings and brewery walks and tours.

Lisa Morrison began writing about beer professionally in 1997 and has authored or contributed to more than six books on beer. After two decades writing, speaking and teaching about beer, she is now co-owner of Belmont Station Bottle Shop & Taproom in Portland, Oregon.

Laurent Mousson is a Swiss beer activist and the former vice-chair of the European Beer Consumers Union (2008–11). He is also an international beer judge and active in beer education.

Alexander Petrochenkov has written seven books and many articles about beer, in so doing becoming Russia's most prolific beer writer. His latest book is *Крафтовое пиво*, translating to "Craft Beer".

Élisabeth Pierre is a French beer writer and the author of five books, including *Choisir et Acheter sa Bière en 7 Secondes*. She is also an international judge and founder of the Paris-based *L'Académie Bierissima*, offering beer training for brewing and hospitality professionals.

Daniel Rocamora and **Karen A Higgs** are Uruguayan beer and travel authorities. Daniel is probably the country's foremost beer expert and a frequent beer judge, while Karen is the author of *The Guru'Guay Guide to Montevideo* and creator of the English language Uruguay website guruguay.com/.

 Conrad Seidl, known as the Bierpapst, or "Beer Pope", is a beer writer based in Vienna, Austria. He has published several books on beer in German, including the annual *Conrad Seidls Bier Guide to Austria*, and has a website at www.bierpapst.eu/.

 Tim Skelton is the author of two beer books – *Beer in the Netherlands* and *Around Amsterdam in 80 Beers* and – and three editions of the *Bradt Travel Guide Luxembourg*. He is a regular judge at beer competitions.

 Espen Smith is a well-known Norwegian beer critic who regularly appears on television and talk radio, and writes for newspapers and magazines.

He also teaches classes on beer and brewing, guides frequent beer tours, has authored several books and consults on brewery development.

 Ricardo Solis is the Academic Director of the Instituto Cervezas de América in Santiago, Chile, and a professor on the Diplomado en Microcervecería course at the Universidad Católica de Valparaíso. He has more than 15 years of experience in the brewing industry.

 Péter Takács is a craft beer specialist in Hungary who, in various guises, supplies hops and exclusive grains mostly to craft brewers from Bratislava to Bucharest. He is a beer judge, a nomadic brewer, an advisor to aspiring brewers and an occasional beer writer.

 Joan Villar-i-Martí (aka "Birraire") is a Catalan writer, consultant and beer enthusiast. He writes mainly in specialized media and at his blog birraire.com, is co-author of *Guia de Cerveses de Catalunya* and part of the organization team of the Barcelona Beer Festival.